JANE FEATHER

— *Two Novels in One Volume* —

VICE

and

VIRTUE

JANE FEATHER

Two Novels in One Volume

VICE

and

VIRTUE

WINGS BOOKS

New York

Contents

VICE

Dedication

This one, *finally*, is for Jim. Always my inspiration. Always—well nearly always—the soul of patience. Always a rock of support and reassurance. Always my love.

Prologue

London—1750

I do not have such a piece at present, Your Grace."

"I didn't imagine you would, madam. But I assume you could procure one." Tarquin, third Duke of Redmayne, bent to inhale the fragrance of a rose in a deep bowl on the table at his side.

"Such specific requirements will not be simple to furnish," Mrs. Dennison mused from behind her painted fan.

A smile flickered over the duke's lean countenance. "You and Mr. Dennison will find the reward matches the effort, Elizabeth."

His hostess glanced over her fan and her eyes twinkled. "La, Duke, you know how I hate to discuss terms . . . so vulgar."

"Very vulgar," he agreed smoothly. "However, it must be the genuine article, madam. I have no interest in counterfeit maidenhead, however fresh the piece might appear."

Elizabeth Dennison looked wounded. "How could you suggest such a thing, Your Grace?"

The duke's smile broadened, but he shook his head slightly and drew a lapis lazuli snuffbox from the deep pocket of his full-skirted velvet coat. There was silence in the sunny parlor as he took a leisurely pinch, closed the box, and replaced it before dusting his nose with a lace-trimmed handkerchief.

"Is the piece to be for Your Grace's own use, may I ask?" the lady inquired a trifle hesitantly. One could never be certain with the Duke of Redmayne where he drew the line between useful inquiry and impertinence.

"You may assume when you go about the search that she will be for my exclusive use." The duke rose to his feet. "That way we can be certain she will meet the most exacting of standards."

"I trust you will find that all of our ladies meet the highest standards, sir." There was a note of reproof in her voice as Mistress Dennison rose in a rustle of silk. "My husband and I pride ourselves on the quality of our house." She pulled the bell rope.

"Had I believed otherwise, Elizabeth, I wouldn't have sought your help," the duke said gently, picking up his gloves and cane from the console table.

Mistress Dennison looked somewhat mollified. "I shall put inquiries in train immediately, Your Grace."

"Keep me informed of your progress. I give you good day, madam." Her visitor bowed courteously, but there was a glint in his hooded gray eyes that his hostess, sweeping him a low curtsy, found vaguely discomfiting. But it was a familiar sensation when doing business with the Duke of Redmayne, and she was not alone in feeling it.

She turned with an assumption of brisk assurance to the flunky who'd appeared in answer to the bell. "His Grace is leaving."

"Madam, your most obedient . . . ," the duke murmured with another bow. He followed the flunky from the room, into the hall. There was a hush over the house in the sunlit morning, the maids creeping about their business as if anxious not to disturb the sleepers above stairs—those whose business was conducted at night and who took their well-earned rest in the daylight.

The smile faded from Mistress Dennison's countenance as the door closed behind her visitor. The duke's commission would not be easy to fulfill. A piece still in possession of her maidenhood, who could be coerced into obeying the duke's dictates.

Virgins could be discovered easily enough . . . innocent country girls arriving friendless in the big city were ten a penny. But one who would have a reason to agree to the duke's dictates . . .

And not the dictates customary in this kind of contract, as the duke had been at pains to emphasize. He wanted no common whore, because he had a most uncommon use for her. He hadn't elaborated on that use.

Elizabeth Dennison shrugged her plump, creamy shoulders. She would put the situation to Richard. Her husband and business partner could be relied upon to come up with a plan of campaign. One didn't disoblige a client as wealthy and powerful as Tarquin, Duke of Redmayne.

Chapter 1

Juliana was suffocating. Her husband was making no attempt to protect her from the full force of his weight as he huffed and puffed, red-faced and bleary-eyed with wedding drink. She was perfectly resigned to this consummation and indeed was quite well-disposed toward Sir John, for all his advanced years and physical bulk, but it occurred to her that if she didn't alert him to her predicament in some way, she was going to expire beneath him.

Her nose was squashed against the mountainous chest and her throat was closing. She couldn't think clearly enough to work out what was happening to the rest of her body, but judging by John's oaths and struggles, matters were not proceeding properly. Black spots began to dance before her eyes, and her chest heaved in a desperate fight to draw air into her lungs. Panicked now, she flailed her arms to either side of her imprisoned body, and then her left hand closed over the smooth brass handle of the bed warmer.

With an instinctive desperation she raised the object and brought it down on her husband's shoulders. It was not a hard blow and was intended simply to bring him back to his senses, but it seemed to have the opposite effect.

Sir John's glazed eyes widened as he stared at the wall

behind her head, his panting mouth fell open; then, with a curious sigh like air escaping from a deflated balloon, he collapsed upon her.

If she thought he'd been heavy before, he was now a deadweight, and Juliana shoved and pushed, calling his name repeatedly, trying to wake him up.

If she'd been panicked before, she was now terrified. She tried to call out, but her voice was muffled by his body and lost in the thickly embroidered brocade bed curtains. There was no way anyone could hear her behind the firmly latched oak door. The household was asleep, and George had passed out after his third bottle of port on the couch in the library. Not that she could have endured being found here in this mortifying exposure by her loathsome stepson.

Juliana wriggled like an eel, her body slick with the sweat of effort; then, finally, she managed to draw up her knees and obtain sufficient leverage to free her legs. Digging her heels into the mattress, she heaved with her arms and shoulders, and John rolled sideways just enough for her to squiggle out before he flopped back again.

Slowly she stood up and gazed down at him, her hand over her mouth, her eyes wide with shock. She bent over him.

"John?" Tentatively, she touched his shoulder, shook him lightly. "John?"

There was no sound, and his face was buried in the pillows. She turned his head. His sightless eyes stared up at her.

"Sweet Jesus, have mercy!" Juliana whispered, stepping back from the corpse. She had killed her husband!

Dazed and incredulous, she stood by the bed, listening to the nighttime sounds of the house: the ticking clocks, the creaking floorboards, the wind rattling open casements. No sounds of human life.

Dear God, it was her cursed clumsiness again! Why, oh why did everything she ever did always come out wrong?

She had to waken someone. But what would they say? The round mark of the bed warmer stood out on the dead man's back. She must have hit him harder than she'd intended. But, of course, that was inevitable given her blunder-headed, accident-prone nature.

Sick with horror, she touched the bed warmer and found it still very hot. She'd struck and killed her husband with a burning object.

George would waste no time. He would listen to no reasonable explanations. He would accuse her publicly as he'd done privately that morning of gold digging. Of marrying a man old enough to be her grandfather just for his money. He'd accuse her of manipulating his father's besotted affections and then arranging his death so she'd be free and clear with all that had been allotted to her in the marriage settlements. Property that George believed was his and his alone.

It was petty treason for a woman to kill her husband. Just as it was for a servant to kill his master. If she was convicted, they would burn her at the stake.

Juliana backed farther away from the bed, pushing aside the bed curtains, rushing to the window, where she stood drawing deep gulps of the warm night air, enlivened by a faint sea breeze from the Solent. *They would burn her at the stake.*

She'd seen it happen once, outside Winchester jail. Mistress Goadsby had been convicted of killing her husband when he'd fallen down the stairs. She'd said he'd been drunk and had been beating her and he'd tripped and fallen. She'd stood in the dock with the bruises still on her face. But they'd tied her to the stake, hanged her, and set fire to her.

Juliana had been little more than a child at the time, but the image had haunted her over the years . . . the smell of burning flesh embedded in her nostrils. Nausea swamped her, and she ran back to the bed, dragging the chamber pot from beneath, vomiting violently.

Perhaps the magistrates would believe that John had died of natural causes in the midst of his exertions . . . but there was that mark on his back. He couldn't have put that there himself.

And George would see it. A stepmother convicted of murdering her husband couldn't inherit. The marriage settlements would be nullified, and George would have what he wanted.

Juliana didn't know how long she sat on the floor, hunched over the chamber pot, but gradually the sweat dried on her forehead and her mind cleared.

She had to leave. There was no one there to speak for her . . . to speak against the facts before their eyes. Her guardian had negotiated the marriage settlements, ensuring, of course, that he, too, benefited from the arrangements. He had then thankfully washed his hands of one who had been nothing but a troublesome charge from the first moment his orphaned infant niece had been delivered into his arms. There was no one else remotely interested in her.

She stood up, thrust the chamber pot back beneath the bed with her foot, and took stock. The stagecoach for London stopped at the Rose and Crown in Winchester at four o'clock in the morning. She could walk the ten miles to Winchester across the fields and be there in plenty of time. By the time the household awoke, or George emerged from his stupor, she would be far away.

They would pursue her, but she could lose herself easily in London. She just had to ensure she wouldn't draw attention to herself at the Rose and Crown.

Averting her eyes from the bed, Juliana went to the armoire, newly filled with her trousseau. But she'd secreted a pair of holland britches and a linen shirt. In this costume she'd escaped Forsett Towers on the frequent occasions when life had become more than usually unpleasant under the rule of her guardian's wife. No one had ever discovered the disguise, or the various places where she'd roamed. Of course, she'd paid the price on her return, but Lady Forsett's hazel switch had seemed but a small price to pay for those precious hours of freedom.

She dressed rapidly, pulling on stockings and boots, twisting her flame-red hair into a knot on top of her head, tucking telltale strands under a woolen cap pulled down low over her ears.

She needed money. Enough for her coach fare and a few nights' lodging until she could find work. But she wouldn't take anything that would be missed. Nothing that would brand her as a thief as well as a murderess.

Why she should concern herself about such a hair-splitting issue Juliana couldn't imagine, but her mind seemed to be working on its own, making decisions, discarding possibilities with all the efficiency of an automaton.

She took four sovereigns from the cache in the dresser drawer. She had watched John empty his pockets . . . hours ago, it seemed—after the revelers had finally left the bedroom door and taken their jovial obscenities out of the house, leaving the newlyweds to themselves.

John had been almost too drunk to stand upright. She could see him now, swaying as he poured the contents of his pocket into the drawer—his bloodshot blue eyes gleaming with excitement, his habitually red face now a deep crimson.

Tears suddenly clogged her throat as she slipped the still-unfamiliar wedding ring from her finger. John had always been kind to her in an avuncular way. She'd been more than willing to accept marriage to him as a way of escaping her guardian's house. More than willing until she realized she'd have to contend with George . . . malicious, jealous, lusting George. But it had been too late to back away then. She dropped the ring into the drawer with the remaining sovereigns. The gold circlet winked at her, its glow diffused through her tears.

Resolutely, Juliana closed the drawer and turned back to the cheval glass to check her reflection. Her disguise had never been intended to fool people close at hand, and as she examined herself, she realized that the linen shirt did nothing to disguise the rich swell of her bosom; and the curve of her hips was emphasized by the britches.

She took a heavy winter cloak from the armoire and swathed herself. It hid the bumps and the curves, but it was still far from satisfactory. However, the light would be bad at that hour of the morning, and with luck there'd be other passengers on the waybill, so she could make herself inconspicuous.

She tiptoed to the bedroom door, glancing at the closed bed curtains. She felt as if she should make some acknowledgment of the dead man. It seemed wrong to be running from his deathbed. And yet she could think of nothing else to do. For a minute she thought hard about the man whom she'd known for a bare three months. She remembered his kindnesses. And then she put him from her. John Ridge had been sixty-five years old. He'd had three wives. And he'd died quickly, painlessly . . . a death for which she had been responsible.

Juliana let herself out of the bedchamber and crept along the pitch-dark corridor, her fingers brushing the walls to guide her. At the head of the stairs she paused. The hall below was dark, but not as black as the corridor behind her. Faint moonlight filtered through the diamond panes of the mullioned windows.

Her eyes darted to the library door. It was firmly closed. She sped down the stairs, tiptoed to the door, and placed her ear against the oak. Her heart hammered in her chest, and she wondered why she was lingering, listening to the rumbling, drunken snores from within. But hearing them made her feel safer.

She turned to leave, and her foot caught in the fringe of the worn Elizabethan carpet. She went flying, grabbed at a table leg to save herself, and fell to her knees: a copper jug of hollyhocks overbalanced as the table rocked, and crashed to the stone-flagged floor.

She remained where she was on her knees, listening to the echo resound to the beamed ceiling and then slowly fade into the night. It had been a sound to wake the dead.

But nothing happened. No shouts, no running feet . . .

and most miraculously of all, no change in the stertorous breathing from the library.

Juliana picked herself up, swearing under her breath. It was her feet again. They were the bane of her life, too big and with a mind of their own.

She crept with exaggerated care toward the back regions of the house and let herself out of the kitchen door. Outside all was quiet. The house behind her slept. The house that should have been her home—her refuge from the erratic twists and turns of a life that had brought her little happiness thus far.

Juliana shrugged. Like a stray cat who had long ago learned to walk alone, she faced the haphazard future with uncomplaining resignation. As she crossed the kitchen yard, making for the orchard and the fields beyond, the church clock struck midnight.

Her seventeenth birthday was over. A day she'd begun as a bride and ended as a widow and a murderess.

"I give you good day, cousin," a voice slurred from the depths of an armchair as the Duke of Redmayne entered the library of his house on Albermarle Street.

"To what do I owe this pleasure, Lucien?" the duke inquired in bland tones, although a flicker of disgust crossed his face. "Escaping your creditors? Or are you simply paying me a courtesy visit?"

"Lud, such sarcasm, cousin." Lucien Courtney rose to his feet and surveyed with a mocking insouciance his cousin and the man who'd entered close behind him. "Well, well, and if it isn't our dear Reverend Courtney as well. What an embarrassment of relatives. How d'ye do, dear boy."

"Well enough," the other man responded easily. He was soberly dressed in gray, with a plain white neck cloth, in startling contrast to the duke's peacock-blue satin coat, with its gold frogged buttons and deep embroidered cuffs. But the physical resemblance to the duke was startling: the same aquiline nose and deep-set gray eyes, the same thin, well-shaped mouth, the same cleft chin. However, there the resemblance ended. Whereas Quentin Courtney regarded the world and its vagaries with the gentle and genuine sympathy of a devout man of the cloth, his half brother Tarquin, the Duke of Redmayne, saw his fellow man through the sharp and disillusioned eyes of the cynic.

"So what brings you to the fleshpots?" Lucien inquired with a sneer. "I thought you'd become an important official in some country bishop's diocese."

"Canon of Melchester Cathedral," Quentin said coolly. "I'm on my bishop's business with the Archbishop of Canterbury at the moment."

"Oh, aren't we rising far, fast, and holy," Lucien declared with a curled lip. Quentin ignored the statement.

"May I offer you some refreshment, Lucien?" Tarquin strolled to the decanters on the sideboard. "Oh, but I see you've already taken care of yourself," he added, noting the brandy goblet in the younger man's hand. "You don't think it's a little early in the morning for cognac?"

"Dear boy, I haven't been to bed as yet," Lucien said with a yawn. "Far as I'm concerned, this is a nightcap." He put down the glass and strolled to the door, somewhat unsteadily. "You don't object to putting me up for a few nights?"

"How should I?" returned Tarquin with a sardonically raised eyebrow.

"Fact is, my own house is under siege," Lucien declared, leaning against the door and fumbling in his pocket for his snuffbox. "Damned creditors and bailiffs bangin' at the door at all hours of the day and night. Man can't get a decent night's rest."

"And what are you going to sell to satisfy them this time?" the duke asked, pouring madeira for himself and his brother.

"Have to be Edgecombe," Lucien said, taking a pinch of snuff. He sighed with exaggerated heaviness. "Terrible thing. But I can't see what else to do . . . unless, of course, you could see your way to helpin' a relative out."

His pale-brown eyes, burning in their deep sockets like the last embers of a dying fire, suddenly sharpened, and he regarded his cousin with sly knowledge. He smiled as he saw the telltale muscle twitch in Tarquin's jaw as he fought to control his anger.

"Well," he said carelessly. "We'll discuss it later . . . when I've had some sleep. Dinner, perhaps?"

"Get out of here," Tarquin said, turning his back.

Lucien's chuckle hung in the air as the door closed behind him.

"There's going to be little enough left of Edgecombe for poor Godfrey to inherit," Quentin said, sipping his wine. "Since Lucien gained his majority a mere six months ago, he's run through a fortune that would keep most men in luxury for a lifetime."

"I'll not stand by and see him sell Edgecombe," Tarquin stated almost without expression. "And neither will I stand by and see what remnants are left pass into the hands of Lucien's pitiful cousin."

"I fail to see how you can stop it," Quentin said in some surprise. "I know poor Godfrey has no more wits than an infant, but he's still Lucien's legitimate heir."

"He would be if Lucien left no heir of his own," the duke pointed out, casually riffling through the pages of the *Gazette*.

"Well, we all know that's an impossibility," Quentin declared, stating what he had always believed to be an immutable fact. "And Lucien's free of your rein now; there's little you can do to control him."

"Aye, and he never ceases to taunt me with it," Tarquin responded. "But it'll be a rainy day in hell, my friend, when Lucien Courtney gets the better of me." He looked up and met his half brother's gaze.

Quentin felt a little shiver prickle his spine at this soft-spoken declaration. He knew Tarquin as no one else did. He knew the softer side of an apparently unbending nature;

he knew his half brother's vulnerabilities; he knew that the hard cynicism Tarquin presented to the world was a defense learned in his youth against those who would use the friendship of a future duke for their own ambitions.

Quentin also knew not to underestimate the Duke of Redmayne's ruthlessness in getting what he wanted. He asked simply "What are you going to do?"

Tarquin drained his glass. He smiled, but it was not a humorous smile. "It's time our little cousin took himself a wife and set up his nursery," he said. "That should settle the matter of an heir to Edgecombe."

Quentin stared at him as if he'd taken leave of his senses. "No one's going to marry Lucien, even if he was prepared to marry. He's riddled with the pox, and the only women who figure on his agenda of pleasure are whores from the stews prepared to play the lad."

"True. But how long do you think he has to live?" Tarquin inquired almost casually. "You only have to look at him. He's burned out with debauchery and the clap. I'd give him maybe six months . . . a year at the outside."

Quentin said nothing, but his gaze remained unwaveringly on his brother's countenance.

"He knows it, too," Tarquin continued. "He's living each day as if it's his last. He doesn't give a damn what happens to Edgecombe or the Courtney fortune. Why should he? But I intend to ensure that Edgecombe, at the very least, passes intact into competent hands."

Quentin looked horrified. "In the name of pity, Tarquin! You couldn't condemn a woman to share his bed, even if he'd take her into it. It would be a death sentence."

"Listen well, dear brother. It's perfectly simple."

Chapter 2

❧

By the time the stagecoach lumbered into the yard of the Bell in Wood Street, Cheapside, Juliana had almost forgotten there was a world outside the cramped interior and the company of her six fellow passengers. At five miles an hour, with an enforced stop at sunset because neither coachman nor passengers would travel the highways after dark, it had taken over twenty-four hours to accomplish the seventy miles between Winchester and London. Juliana, like the rest of the passengers, had sat up in the taproom of the coaching inn during the night stop. Despite the discomfort of the hard wooden settles, it was a welcome change from the bone-racking jolting of the iron wheels over the unpaved roads.

They set off again, just before dawn, and it was soon after seven in the morning when she alighted from the coach for the last time. She stood in the yard of the Bell, arching the small of her back against her hands in an effort to get the cricks out. The York coach had also just arrived and was disgorging its blinking, exhausted passengers. The June air was already warm, heavy with city smells, and she wrinkled her nose at the pervading odor of rotting garbage in the kennels, manure piled in the narrow cobbled lanes.

"Ye got a box up 'ere, lad?"

It took Juliana a moment to realize the coachman's question was addressed to her. She was still huddled in her cloak, her cap pulled down over her ears as it had been throughout the journey. She turned to the man sitting atop the coach, unlashing the passenger's baggage.

"No, nothing, thank you."

"Long ways to travel with not so much as a cloak bag," the man remarked curiously.

Juliana merely nodded and set off to the inn doorway. She felt as if she'd traveled not just a long way but into another world . . . another life. What it would bring her and what she would make of it were the only questions of any interest.

She entered the dark paneled taproom, where a scullery maid was slopping a bucket of water over the grubby flagstones. Juliana skipped over a dirty stream that threatened to swamp her feet, caught her foot on the edge of the bucket, and grabbed at the counter to save herself. Stable again, she nodded cheerfully to the girl.

"I give you good morning."

The girl sniffed and looked as if it was far from a good morning. She was scrawny and pale, her hair almost painfully scraped back from her forehead into a lank and greasy pigtail. "Ye want summat t'eat?"

"If you please," Juliana responded with undiluted cheerfulness. She perched on a high stool at the counter and looked around. The comparison with the country inns with which she was familiar was not favorable. Where she was used to fresh flowers and bunches of dried herbs, polished brass and waxed wood, this place was dark, dirty, and reeked of stale beer and the cesspit. And the people had a wary, hostile air.

The innkeeper loomed out of the dimness behind the counter. "What can I get ye?" The question was courteous enough, but his tone was surly and his eyes bloodshot.

"Eggs and toast and tea, if you please, sir. I've just come off the York stage." Juliana essayed a smile.

The man peered at her suspiciously in the gloom, and she drew the cloak tighter about her.

"I'll see yer coin first," he said.

Juliana reached into her pocket and drew out a shilling. She slapped it onto the counter and glared at him, her jade-green eyes suddenly ablaze.

The innkeeper drew back almost involuntarily from the heat of that anger. He palmed the coin, gave her another searching look, and snapped at the still-mopping scullery maid, "Ellie, get into the kitchen and bring the gentleman 'is eggs an' toast."

The maid dumped her mop into the bucket with a rough impatience that sent water slurping over the rim and, sighing heavily, marched behind the counter into the kitchen.

The innkeeper's pale, bloodshot eyes narrowed slyly. "A tankard of ale, young sir?"

"No, just tea, thank you."

His crafty glance ran over her swathed figure. "Tea'll maudle yer belly, lad. It's a drink fit only fer women. Didn't nobody teach ye to take ale with yer breakfast?"

Juliana accepted that her disguise was not convincing, but it had served its purpose thus far. She was certain no one had thought twice about her at the Rose and Crown in Winchester, and as far as the innkeeper was concerned, she'd just alighted from the York stage—almost as far from Winchester as it was possible to be this side of the Scottish border.

"I'm looking for lodging and work," she said casually, confirming his suspicions by default. "D'you know of anything around here?"

The man stroked his chin thoughtfully. "Well, now, I just might be able to think of summat. Let's see what ye've got under that cap."

Juliana shrugged and pulled off her cap. "I fail to see what my hair has to do with getting a job."

Ellie came back with the breakfast at this point and

gawped as the fiery mass, released from the confines of the cap, tumbled loose from its pins.

" 'Ere, what ye doin' dressed like a lad?" She thumped the plate in front of Juliana.

"It makes traveling easier," Juliana responded, dipping her toast into her egg. "And could I have my tea, please?"

"Oh, 'oity-toity, an't we?" Ellie said. "I'll bet yer no better than ye ought t' be."

" 'Old yer tongue and fetch the tea, girl," the innkeeper ordered, threatening her with the back of his hand.

Ellie ducked, sniffed, and ran off to the kitchen.

"So jest what's a lady doin', then, wanderin' the streets dressed like a lad?" he inquired with a careless air, polishing a dingy pewter tankard on his sleeve.

Juliana hungrily wiped up the last of her egg yolk with her toast and put down her fork. "I'm looking for work, as I told you."

"Ye speaks like a lady," he persisted. "Ladies don't look fer work 'ereabouts."

"Ladies down on their luck might." She poured tea from the pot Ellie had plumped down at her elbow, put the pot down again, and, as she moved her arm, caught the fold of her cloak on the spout. The pot rocked and clattered on the counter, but she managed to extricate her garment without too much spillage.

"Aye. I suppose they might," the innkeeper agreed, watching her struggles with the teapot.

"So do you know of anything?"

"Reckon I might. Just bide 'ere a while an' I'll see what I can do."

"Thank you." She smiled radiantly, and he blinked his little eyes, then stomped off into the nether regions, leaving Juliana alone with her tea.

In the kitchen he summoned a potboy, scrubbing greasy pans in a wooden tub beside the door. "Eh, you, lad. Take yerself to Russell Street in Covent Garden. Mr. Dennison's 'ouse. You tell Mistress Dennison that Josh Bute from the Bell might 'ave summat of interest. Got that?"

"Aye, sir, Mr. Bute," the boy said, tugging a forelock with a wet and greasy hand. "Right away, sir." He scampered off, and Mr. Bute stood for a minute rubbing his hands together. The Dennisons paid a handsome commission for a good piece, and there was something indefinable about the one sitting in his taproom that convinced the innkeeper he'd found a prime article for that very exacting couple.

Nodding to himself, he returned to the taproom. "I reckon I can do summat fer ye, miss," he said with a smile that he considered jovial but that reminded Juliana of a toothless, rabid dog.

"What kind of work?" she asked.

"Oh, good, clean work, miss," he assured her. "Jest as long as ye can please Mistress Dennison, ye'll be all set up."

"Is it live-in work?"

"Oh, aye, miss, that it is," he returned, drawing a tankard of ale for himself. "Genteel, live-in work. Jest the thing fer a young lady on 'er own. Mistress Dennison takes care of 'er girls." He wiped the froth off his mouth with the back of his hand and smiled his rabid smile.

Juliana frowned. It all seemed remarkably convenient, quick and easy. Too much so. Then she shrugged. She had nothing to lose by waiting to meet this Mistress Dennison, and if she *was* looking for a parlor maid or even a skivvy, then it would give her a start.

"Should I go to her?"

"Bless you, no. Mistress Dennison will come 'ere," he said, drawing another tankard of ale.

"Then I'll sit in the inglenook." Juliana yawned deeply. "I'll take a nap while I'm waiting."

"Right y'are," Mr. Bute said indifferently, but his eyes remained on her until she'd curled up on the wooden settle in the deep inglenook, her cheek pillowed on her hand. Her eyes closed almost immediately.

Mr. Bute sucked at his toothless gums with a slurp of satisfaction. She'd be no trouble until Mistress Dennison arrived. But he remained in the taproom, nevertheless, keeping a weather eye on the sleeping figure, until, two hours later, he heard the rattle of wheels in the stable yard and the sounds of bustle in the passageway outside.

He hastened from behind his counter and greeted his visitor with a deep bow.

"So what have you for me, Bute?" the lady demanded, tapping a high-heeled shoe of pink silk edged with silver lace. "It's devilish early in the morning for making calls, so I trust I'm not on a fool's errand."

"I trust not, madam," the innkeeper said with another bow, his nose almost brushing his knees. "The girl says she's off the York stage."

"Well, where is she?" Elizabeth plied her fan, her nose wrinkling slightly at the stale, unsavory air now embellished with the scent of boiling cabbage.

"In the taproom, madam." The innkeeper held open the door and the lady swished past, deftly twitching aside the hoop of her green satin skirts.

"In the inglenook," Mr. Bute said softly, pointing.

Mistress Dennison crossed the room, her step light, a speculative gleam in her eyes. She stood looking down at the sleeping figure wrapped in the cloak. Her assessing gaze took in the tumbled richness of the flame-red hair, the creamy pallor of her skin, the shape of the full, relaxed mouth, the dusting of freckles across the bridge of a strongly defined nose.

Not pretty, Mistress Dennison decided with an expert's eye. Too strongly featured for true prettiness. But her hair was magnificent. And there were many gentlemen who preferred something a little out of the ordinary. What in the world was she doing dressed in those clothes? What did she have to hide? Something, for sure. And if she should prove to be a maid . . .

Elizabeth's beautiful eyes narrowed abruptly. A virgin with something to hide . . .

She bent over Juliana and shook her shoulder. "My dear, it's time you woke up."

Juliana swam upward from the depths of a dreamless

sleep. She opened her eyes and blinked up at the face hovering over her. A lovely face: smiling red lips, kind blue eyes. It was not a face she knew, and for a moment she was completely disoriented.

The woman touched her shoulder again. "My dear, I am Mistress Dennison."

Memory rushed back. Juliana sat up on the settle, swinging her legs over the edge. Beside this radiant creature in rich satin, with a dainty lace cap perched atop dark-brown curls, she felt all grubby elbows and knees. She tucked her feet beneath the settle in the hope that they would stay out of mischief and hastily tried to push her hair back into its pins.

"Mine host seemed to think you might be looking for a parlor maid, ma'am," she began.

"My dear, forgive me, but you don't speak like one accustomed to service," Mistress Dennison said bluntly, taking a seat pushed forward by the eager Mr. Bute. "I understand you traveled on the York stage."

Juliana nodded, but Elizabeth's gaze sharpened. She was too well versed in the ways of the world to be fooled by an inexperienced liar. Besides, this girl had no hint of Yorkshire in her accent.

"Where is your home?"

Juliana pushed the last pin back into her hair. "Is it necessary for you to know that, ma'am?"

Elizabeth leaned over and placed her gloved hand over Juliana's. "Not if you don't wish to tell me, child. But your name and your age, perhaps?"

"Juliana Ri— Beresford," she corrected hastily. They would be looking for Juliana Ridge. "I am just past seventeen, ma'am."

The lady nodded. She hadn't missed the slip. "Well, why don't you come with me, my dear? You need rest and refreshment, and clothes." She rose in a satin rustle, smiling invitingly.

"But . . . but what work would you have me do,

madam?" Juliana was beginning to feel bewildered. Things were happening too fast.

"We'll discuss that when you've refreshed yourself, child." Mistress Dennison drew her to her feet. "My carriage is outside, and it's but a short ride to my house."

Juliana had a single sovereign left from her little hoard. It might buy her food and lodging of a sort for a day or two. But she was hopelessly inexperienced in this alarming city world, and to turn down the protection and hospitality of this charming, kind-eyed woman would be foolish. So she smiled her acceptance and followed her benefactress out of the inn and inside a light town carriage drawn by two dappled horses.

"Now, my dear," Mistress Dennison said confidingly, "why don't you tell me all about it? I can assure you I've heard every story imaginable, and there's little in the world that could surprise or shock me."

Juliana leaned her head against the pale-blue velvet cushions, her tired gaze swimming as she looked across at the gently smiling face. It occurred to her that the only other person who had ever smiled at her with such kindly interest had been Sir John Ridge. Tears welled in her eyes, and she blinked them away.

"My poor child, what has happened to you?" Elizabeth said, leaning over to take her hands. "You may trust me."

Why? But the question was a little niggle in the back of Juliana's mind. The temptation to take someone into her confidence, someone who knew the ways of the world, was overwhelming. If she didn't identify herself or where she came from, she could still keep the essentials of her secret. Still protect herself from the long reach of the law.

"It's a strange story, ma'am," she began.

If Your Grace would do me the inestimable honor of paying a visit to Russell Street this evening, I believe I might have something of interest to show you.

Your obedient servant,
Elizabeth Dennison

The Duke of Redmayne examined the missive, his expression quite impassive. Then he glanced up at the footman. "Is the messenger still here?"

"Yes, Your Grace. He was to wait for an answer."

Tarquin nodded and strolled to the secretaire, where he drew a sheet of vellum toward him, dipped a quill into the inkstand, and scrawled two lines. He sanded the sheet and folded it.

"Give this to the messenger, Roberts." He dropped it onto the silver salver held by the footman, who bowed himself out.

"So what was that about?" Quentin inquired, looking up from his book.

"I doubt you really want to know," the duke said with a half smile. "It concerns a matter that doesn't have your approval, my friend."

"Oh." Quentin's usually benign expression darkened. "Not that business with Lucien and a wife?"

"Precisely, dear boy. Precisely. Sherry?" Tarquin held up the decanter, one eyebrow raised inquiringly.

"Thank you." Quentin tossed his book aside and stood up. "You're really set on this diabolical scheme?"

"Most certainly." The duke handed his brother a glass. "And why should you call it diabolical, Quentin?" There was a gently mocking light in his eyes, an amused curve to his mouth.

"Because it is," Quentin said shortly. "How will you protect the girl from Lucien? Supposing he decides to exercise his marital rights?"

"Oh, you may safely leave that to me," Tarquin said.

"I don't like it." Quentin scowled into his glass.

"You've made that very clear." Smiling, Tarquin patted his brother's sober-suited shoulder. "But you don't care for most of my schemes."

"No, and I wish the devil I knew why I care for *you*,"

the other man said almost bitterly. "You're an ungodly man, Tarquin. Positively Mephistophelian."

Tarquin sat down, crossing one elegantly shod foot over the other. He frowned down at the sparkle of diamonds in the shoe buckles, musing, "I wonder if jeweled buckles aren't becoming a trifle outré. I noticed Stanhope wearing some very handsome plain silver ones at the levee the other morning. . . . But, then, I doubt that's a topic that interests you, either, Quentin."

"No, I can't say that it does." Quentin cast a cursory glance down at his own sturdy black leather shoes with their plain metal buckles. "And don't change the subject, Tarquin."

"I beg your pardon, I thought we'd reached an amiable conclusion." Tarquin sipped his sherry.

"Will you give up this scheme?"

"No, brother dear."

"Then there's nothing more to be said."

"Precisely. As I said, we have drawn the topic to an amiable conclusion." The duke stood up in one graceful movement, placing his glass on the table. "Don't fret, Quentin. It will only give you frown lines."

"And don't play the fop with me," Quentin declared with more passion than he usually showed. "I'm not fooled by your games, Tarquin."

His brother paused at the door, a slight smile on his lips. "No, thank God, you're not. Don't ever be so, if you love me, brother."

The door closed behind him and Quentin drained his glass. He'd known his half brother for thirty years. He remembered Tarquin's rage and disillusion as a boy of fifteen, betrayed because he wouldn't buy the friendship of his peers. He remembered the desperation when a year or two later the young man had discovered that the woman he loved with such fervor was interested only in what she could gain from being the mistress of the Duke of Redmayne.

Quentin knew how vitally important the family's heritage was to the third Duke of Redmayne. Tarquin had been brought up as the eldest son and heir to an old title and vast estates. He would uphold the family pride and honor to his dying day.

And Lucien was threatening that pride. For as long as he'd been Tarquin's ward, the duke had managed to keep control of the reins, but now he had no say in the way their cousin conducted his own life or managed his fortune and estates. Quentin understood all this, yet he still couldn't accept Tarquin's demonic scheme to save Edgecombe. Tarquin would come out the winner, of course, at whatever cost.

But surely there had to be another way. Quentin picked up his book again, seeking solace in Plutarch's *Parallel Lives*. He hoped the archbishop would take his time over the business that had brought Quentin to London. Someone needed to keep a steadying eye on events at Albermarle Street. Sometimes Tarquin would listen to Quentin and could be persuaded to modify his more far-reaching schemes. Quentin loved his half brother dearly. He had hero-worshiped him through their childhood. But he couldn't close his eyes to the darker side of Tarquin's nature.

"Ah, Your Grace, you are come." Elizabeth rose and curtsied as the duke was shown into her private salon.

"But of course, ma'am. With such incentive, how could I possibly stay away?" He withdrew an enameled snuffbox from his pocket and took a pinch. Mistress Dennison couldn't help but notice that the delicate gold and ivory of the snuffbox exactly matched His Grace's silk coat, waistcoat, and britches.

"Do you wish to see her now, Your Grace?"

"I am all eagerness, madam."

"Come this way, sir." Elizabeth led her guest out of the parlor. It was evening and the house was awake. Two young women in lace negligees sauntered casually down the corridor. They curtsied to the mistress of the house, who greeted them with a smile, before passing on.

A footman bearing a tray with champagne and two glasses and a platter of oysters knocked on a door at the end of the passage.

"The evening is starting early," the duke remarked.

"It often does, my lord," Elizabeth said complacently. "I understand His Royal Highness will be visiting us later."

"Alas, poor Fred," murmured the duke. The bumbling Frederick Louis, Prince of Wales, whose addiction to women was a society joke, was a regular visitor to the Dennisons' harem.

Elizabeth led him up a narrow flight of stairs at the rear of the corridor. It was a route unknown to the duke, and he raised an eyebrow as he followed the swaying, rich crimson hoop ahead of him.

"This is a private passage, Your Grace," Elizabeth explained as they turned down a narrow corridor. "You will understand its purpose in a minute."

She stopped outside a door at the end of the passage and softly opened it, standing aside to permit the duke entrance. He stepped past her into a narrow wardrobe, lit only by the candle in the sconce in the passage behind him.

"In the wall, Your Grace," Elizabeth whispered.

He looked and saw it immediately. Two round peepholes, at eye level and spaced for a pair of eyes.

Wondering if all Mistress Dennison's rooms provided opportunity for the voyeur, the duke stepped up to the peepholes. He looked into a candlelit chamber. He could see a dimity-hung poster bed, matching curtains billowing at an open window, a washstand with a flowered porcelain jug and ewer. It was a bedroom like many in this house.

But it contained a girl. She stood at the open window, idly brushing her hair. The candlelight caught the flames in the glowing tresses as she pulled the brush through with strong, rhythmic strokes. She wore a loose chamber robe that fell open as she turned back to the room.

He glimpsed firm, full breasts, a white belly, a hint of

tangled red hair below. Then she moved out of sight. He waited, his eyes focusing hard on the part of the room he could see. She came back into view. With a leisurely movement she threw off the chamber robe, tossing it over an ottoman at the foot of the bed.

The duke neither stirred nor made a sound. Behind him Elizabeth waited anxiously, hoping that he was seeing something worth seeing.

Tarquin looked steadily at the tall figure, noting the generous curve of hip, the fullness of her breasts that accentuated the slenderness of her torso, the tiny waist. He noted the whiteness of her skin against the startling flames of her hair. She moved toward the bed, and he noted the flare of her hips, the smooth roundness of her buttocks, the long sweep of thigh.

She raised one knee, resting it on the bed, then suddenly glanced over her shoulder. For a minute she appeared to be looking directly at him, her eyes meeting his. Those eyes were the color of jade, deep and glowing, wide-spaced beneath the uncompromisingly straight line of her dark brows. Her eyelashes, dark and as straight as her brows, swept down and up as she blinked tiredly. Then she yawned, covering her mouth with the back of her hand, and climbed into bed.

Leaning over, she blew out the candle.

The Duke of Redmayne moved out of the wardrobe, back into the light of the passage. He turned to face the expectant Mistress Dennison.

"Is she a maid?"

"I am certain of it, Your Grace."

"Can she be bought?"

"I believe so."

"Then let us talk terms, Elizabeth."

Chapter 3

❧ ❧

Juliana awoke to a bright dawn. Always an early riser, she came awake without intervening drowsiness and sat up immediately, gazing about the chamber. It was small but comfortable, well furnished, although not luxuriously so. The bed hangings and curtains were of starched dimity; simple hooked rugs were scattered on the waxed oak floor, cheerful cretonne cushions piled on the chaise longue.

It felt comfortingly familiar, similar to her bedchamber at Forsett Towers. But the sounds coming from the street outside bore no relation to the high cry of the peacocks strutting on the mansion's lawns or the clarion call of the roosters on the home farm.

She flung aside the bedcovers and stood up, stretching with a sigh of pleasure, then padded to the window. Drawing aside the curtains, she looked down into a narrow street crowded with wagons and drays, piled high with country produce. Raucous barrow boys pushed their way through the throng, heading for Covent Garden at the end of the street. Two disheveled young men in evening dress stumbled out of a tavern across the street and stood blinking in the daylight. A woman in a grubby red petticoat hitched up to show her calves, with torn, tawdry lace at her low neckline, sidled up to them, an insinuating smile on her face, and drew down the neck of her dress to bare her breasts.

One of the men grabbed her with a loud laugh and pressed his mouth against hers, holding her roughly by the head. Then he pushed her from him, still laughing, and the two men staggered toward the Strand. The whore picked herself up from the gutter, swearing and shaking her fist. Then she twitched the tawdry lace into position, shook out her skirts, and set off toward the market.

Fascinated, Juliana stared down at the scene below her window. Even Winchester on market day wasn't this lively.

Filled with the energy of curiosity and excitement, Juliana ran to the armoire. She took out the simple muslin gown and cotton shift that her benefactress had insisted on giving her when they'd arrived at the house the previous morning. Juliana had accepted the garments because of their very simplicity. The gown was the kind a well-looked-after serving maid might wear on Sundays.

She threw the shift over her head and stepped into the gown, hooking it up, fastening a muslin fichu discreetly at the neck. She thrust her bare feet into a pair of leather slippers, also provided by Mistress Dennison; splashed water from the ewer onto her face; brushed her hair, pinning it roughly in a knot on top of her head; and was out of the door and running down the wide staircase to the hall within ten minutes of waking.

The front door was open to the street, and a maid was on her hands and knees polishing the parquet. Juliana had seen little of the house the previous day. After changing her clothes she'd spent the rest of the time with Mistress Dennison in her private parlor. She'd dined there alone and retired early, too overwhelmed by the strangeness and excitements of the day following the fatigue of the journey to examine her position or her surroundings too closely.

Now, however, she was refreshed and clear-headed, and she looked around her with interest. Double doors stood open to the right of the hall, revealing a long, elegant salon. From what she could see, the furniture, apart from some deep, inviting sofas and plump ottomans, was all dainty gilt and elaborately carved wood, the carpet richly embroidered, the draperies and upholstery emerald-green velvet. The scent of tobacco and wine lingered in the air, fighting with the fragrance of fresh roses and potpourri from the bowls scattered on every surface.

Juliana could see a footman and a maid polishing the furniture in the salon, but apart from this activity the house seemed to lie under a curious hush. It was like a stage set, she thought. All ready and waiting for the players. The atmosphere wasn't like a private house at all, more like a hotel.

With a slightly puzzled frown she approached the maid polishing the floor. But before she could reach her, a voice said softly but with great authority, "And where d'ye think y'are off to, missie?"

She spun round, startled, not having heard footsteps behind her. A burly man in scarlet livery with a powdered wig, impressive gold braid and frogging on his coat, and a heavy gold watch chain slung across his broad chest surveyed her, hands on his hips.

"I was about to go for a walk," Juliana said, unconsciously tipping her chin, her expression challenging. "If it's any business of yours."

A strange little sound came from the maid still busily polishing on her hands and knees a few feet away. Juliana glanced quickly at her, but the girl's head was down, and she seemed to be putting even more effort into her work. Juliana looked back at the liveried butler, or so she assumed him to be.

He was surveying her with an air of incredulity. "It seems ye've a lot to learn about this 'ere establishment, missie," he declared. "And lesson number one: My name is Garston. *Mr.* Garston, to you, or just plain *sir*. And everything you do is my business."

Her eyes threw green fire at him. "My good man, the only person who's entitled to question my movements in this house is Mistress Dennison. Now, if you'll excuse me,

I'm going for a walk." She tried to step past him toward the door, but he moved his considerable bulk to block her way.

"Doors is closed, missie." He sounded amused rather than annoyed by her defiance.

"They are not!" she stated. "The door is wide-open to the street."

"Doors is closed to the ladies of the 'ouse, missie, until I says so," he said stolidly, folding his arms and regarding her with an amused smile.

What was this? Juliana stared up at him, for the moment nonplussed. As she tried to order her thoughts, a burst of laughter came from the open front door as two women entered the hall, followed by a footman. They were in evening dress, dominoes over their wide-hooped gowns, black loo masks over their eyes.

"Lud, but that was a night and a half," one of them pronounced, plying her fan vigorously. "Such a pair of swordsmen, I do declare, Lilly!"

The other woman went into a renewed peal of laughter and unfastened her mask. "That Lord Bingley, I dareswear, would have been all cut and thrust for another hour if I hadn't near swooned with exhaustion. . . . Oh, Mr. Garston, would you be so good as to send a salt bath to my room? I'm in sore need."

"Immediately, Miss Lilly." He bowed. "I gather you and Miss Emma 'ad a good night. Mr. and Mistress Dennison will be right 'appy to 'ear it."

"La, good enough, Mr. Garston." Miss Emma yawned. "But a tankard of milk punch won't come amiss."

"I'll order it straightway, miss. You go along up and leave it to me." Mr. Garston sounded positively avuncular now as he beamed at the two yawning young women.

Juliana was staring with unabashed curiosity. They were both very pretty, richly gowned, elaborately coiffed, but they were so thickly painted and powdered, it was hard to tell their ages. They were certainly young, but how young she couldn't decide.

"Lud, and who have we here?" Miss Lilly said, catching sight of Juliana behind the stolid figure of Mr. Garston. She regarded her with interest, taking in the simple gown and the roughly pinned hair. "A new servant?"

"I don't believe so, miss," Garston said with a meaningful nod. "But Mistress Dennison 'asn't made clear to me quite what 'er plans are fer the young lady."

"Oh?" Miss Emma examined Juliana with a raised eyebrow. Then she shrugged. "Well, I daresay we'll find out soon enough. Come, Lilly, I'm dead on my feet."

The two wafted up the stairs, chattering like magpies, leaving Juliana uneasy, annoyed, and exceedingly puzzled.

"Now, then, missie, you cut along to yer chamber," Mr. Garston said. "Ring the bell, there, and the maid'll come to ye. Anythin' ye wants, she can provide. I daresay Mistress Dennison will be seein' you when she rises."

"And what time's that?" Juliana debated whether she could duck past him and reach the door before he could catch her.

"Noontime," he said. "That's when she 'as visitors in 'er chamber, while she's dressing. But she'll not be ready fer ye much 'afore dinner." As if guessing her thoughts, he turned to the open door and banged it closed.

Juliana stood frowning. It seemed she was a prisoner. And what kind of woman was it who had visitors in her bedchamber while she was dressing for the day?

There didn't seem much she could do about the situation at present, so, thoughtfully, she returned upstairs to the peace of her own chamber to consider the situation. She couldn't be kept there against her will indefinitely, and Mistress Dennison had so far given no indication of wishing to do so.

The maid who answered the bell seemed tongue-tied, capable of little more than a curtsy and a murmured "Yes, miss" to all conversational sallies. She either couldn't or wouldn't answer direct questions about Mistress Dennison's establishment, and when she left, Juliana found her appetite for her breakfast tray had diminished considerably under her growing unease.

When a few minutes later she heard the key turn in the lock outside, she started from her chair, raced across the room to try the door, and found it locked. For ten minutes she banged on the door and called at the top of her voice. But she could hear nothing in the passage outside.

She ran to the window and gazed at the street three floors down. There were no handholds in the brickwork, no convenient wisteria or creepers. The windows on the floor below had small wrought-iron balconies, but Juliana couldn't imagine dropping safely onto one of them from the narrow sill outside her own chamber. She contemplated calling to the passersby in the street, but what could she say? That she was a prisoner? Who would take any notice? They'd assume she was an errant servant, locked in her garret for some peccadillo. No one would involve themselves in the domestic affairs of another householder.

Juliana flopped onto the chaise longue, nibbling at a fingernail, her brows drawn together in a fierce frown. It was her own fault for trusting a kind-seeming face. Just another piece of clumsiness, really. Tripping over her feet and stumbling headlong into something nasty. But there was nothing she could do until someone chose to explain matters to her and she fully understood the pickle she was in.

But the morning wore slowly onward, and it was early afternoon before the key turned again in the lock and the door opened to admit the little maid.

"Mistress is waitin' on ye in the small salon, miss." She curtsied. "If ye'd be pleased to come wi' me."

"It's about time," Juliana said, sweeping past the girl, who scurried after her, ducking ahead so she could precede her along the corridor, down a flight of stairs to a pair of double doors at the head of the main staircase.

The girl flung open the doors, announcing in shrill tones, "Miss is 'ere, madam."

A smiling Mistress Dennison rose from her chair. "My dear, I do apologize for the locked door," she said, coming forward with her hands outstretched to take Juliana's. "But after your little escapade this morning, I was so afraid you would run away before I'd had a chance to explain matters to you. Now, do say you forgive me." She grasped the girl's hands and smiled winningly.

Juliana could see no treachery in the wide blue eyes, could hear no devious undertone in the smooth and gentle voice. But she withdrew her hands firmly, although not discourteously, and said, "Madam, I find it hard to forgive something I don't understand. Had you asked me to remain within doors, of course I would have done so, after your kindness yesterday."

Elizabeth regarded her quizzically. "Would you?" Then she nodded. "Yes, perhaps you would have. Living in town makes one so suspicious, I'm afraid. One forgets the ingenuousness of the country girl."

She sat down on a velvet chaise longue and patted the seat beside her. "Do sit down, my dear. I have a proposition for you."

"A proposition?" Juliana sat down. "I am willing to work, madam, as I made clear yesterday. If you have work for me, then of course I shall be most grateful."

"Well, I don't know whether you would describe my proposition as work precisely," the lady said with a judicious little frown. "But I suppose it is work of a certain kind."

Juliana looked around the room. It was smaller and more intimate than the salon downstairs, its opulent, elegant furnishings seeming to invite the sensual pleasures of idleness.

"Madam, is this establishment a bawdy house?" She asked the question to which she'd already guessed the answer during her long hours of cogitation.

"Indeed not." Mistress Dennison drew herself up on the chaise, looking distinctly put out. "We have only the most select company in our salons, and our young ladies take their places in the best circles of society."

"I see," Juliana said aridly. "A high-class bawdy house."

Mistress Dennison abruptly lost some of her smiling

good humor. "Now, don't be foolish and missish, child. You have barely a penny to your name. You are being pursued for the murder of your husband. You are cast upon the town with neither friend nor fortune. I am offering you both friendship and the means to make your fortune."

"I am not interested in whoredom, madam." Juliana rose from the chaise. "If you will return my clothes, I will leave here as I came. I'm grateful for your hospitality and will willingly pay for it by working in your kitchens if you wish it."

"Don't be absurd!" Mistress Dennison seized Juliana's hands, examining the long fingers, the soft skin. "You've never done a day's manual work in your life, I'll lay any odds."

"I am perfectly ready to begin now." She pulled her hands free with an angry gesture. "I'm no milksop, Mistress Dennison. And I'm not in the least interested in harlotry. So if you'll excuse me—"

"Perhaps I can be a little more persuasive."

Juliana spun around at the soft drawl. A man stepped through a crimson velvet curtain at the end of the room, and she glimpsed a small chamber behind him. He wore riding britches and a deep-cuffed black coat edged with silver lace. A single diamond winked from the folds of his starched white stock.

He stood against the curtain, negligently taking a pinch of snuff. All the while his gray eyes rested on her face, and Juliana had the uncomfortable fancy that he was seeing into her soul, was seeing much more than she had ever revealed to anyone.

"Who are *you*?" she demanded, her voice sounding raw. She cleared her throat and took a step back toward the double doors behind her.

"Don't run away," the newcomer said gently. He dropped the silver snuffbox into his pocket. "There's no need to be alarmed, as Mistress Dennison will assure you."

"No, indeed not, my dear. This is His Grace the Duke

of Redmayne," Elizabeth said, placing an arresting hand on Juliana's arm. "He has a proposition to put to you."

"I have told you, I am not in the least interested in your propositions," Juliana declared, her voice shaking with anger. She flung Mistress Dennison's hand from her. "I no more care whether they come from a duke or a night-soil collector." She turned on her heel and made for the door, thus missing the startled look in His Grace's eyes.

Annoyance chased astonishment across the cool gray surface, to be banished by interest and a reluctant admiration. The duke, accustomed to fawning obsequiousness, was surprised that he found such cavalier dismissal of his rank somewhat amusing. But his reaction didn't sound in his voice.

"The penalty for murdering a husband is death at the stake, I believe."

Juliana stopped at the duke's low, considering drawl. Her hand on the door was suddenly slippery with sweat, and the blood pounded in her temples. Slowly she turned back to the room, and her great green eyes, living coals in her deathly pale complexion, fixed accusingly upon Mistress Dennison. "You broke my confidence."

"My dear, it's for the best," Elizabeth said. "You'll see what a wonderful opportunity this is, if you'll only listen to His Grace. I know a hundred girls who'd give their eyes for such an opportunity. A life of luxury, of—"

"Allow me to lay out the benefits and rewards, madam." The duke spoke with open amusement now, and the cleft in his chin deepened as his lips quirked in a tiny smile. "It seems the young lady requires a deal of persuasion."

"Persuasion . . . blackmail, you mean," Juliana snapped. "You would hold that over my head?"

"If I must, my dear, yes," the duke said in tones of the utmost reason. "But I trust you'll agree to accept my proposition simply because it's a solution to your problems, will not be too arduous for you, I believe, and will solve a major difficulty for myself."

Juliana turned the porcelain handle of the door. All she

had to do was push it, race across the hall and out into the street. But if she left the house in the clothes given her by Mistress Dennison, her erstwhile benefactress could set up a hue and cry and accuse her of theft. She wouldn't get far in those crowded streets once the cry went up. They'd hang her for theft. They'd burn her for petty treason.

"Elizabeth, would you leave us, please?" The duke's soft, courteous tones broke through the desperate maelstrom of Juliana's thoughts.

Her hand dropped from the doorknob. She was caught in the trap that she'd sprung herself with that foolish burst of confidence yesterday. There was nothing to be gained at this point by fighting the gin. Like a snared rabbit, she'd simply chew off her own foot.

She stepped away from the door as Elizabeth billowed across the room.

"Listen well to His Grace, my dear," Mistress Dennison instructed, patting Juliana's cheek. "And don't show him such a long face. Lud, child, you should be dancing for joy. When I think what's being offered—"

"Thank you, madam." There was a touch of frost in the duke's interruption, and a tinge of natural color augmented the rouge on Elizabeth's smooth cheek.

She curtsied to the duke, cast another look, half warning, half encouragement, at Juliana, and expertly swung her wide hoop sideways as she passed through the door.

"Close it."

Juliana found herself obeying the quiet instruction. Slowly she turned back to face the room. The Duke of Redmayne had moved to stand beside one of the balconied windows overlooking the street. A ray of sunlight caught an auburn glint in his hair, tied at his nape with a silver ribbon.

"Come here, child." A white, slender-fingered hand beckoned her.

"I am no child." Juliana remained where she was, her back to the door, her hands behind her, still clutching the doorknob as if it were a lifeline.

"Seventeen from the perspective of thirty-two has a certain youthfulness," he said, smiling suddenly. The smile transformed his face, set the gray eyes asparkle, softened the distinctive features, showed her a full set of even white teeth.

"What else do you know of me, sir?" she inquired, refusing to respond to that smile, refusing to move from her position.

"That you are called Juliana Beresford . . . although I expect that's a false name," he added musingly. "Is it?"

"If it is, you wouldn't expect me to tell you," she snapped.

"No. True enough," he conceded, reaching for the bell-pull over the chimney piece. "Do you care for ratafia?"

"No," Juliana responded bluntly, deciding it was time to take the initiative. "I detest it."

The duke chuckled. "Sherry, perhaps?"

"I drink only champagne," Juliana declared with a careless shrug, moving away from the door. She brushed at her skirt with an air of lofty dismissal, and her fingertips caught a delicate porcelain figurine on a side table, sending it toppling to the carpet.

"A plague on it!" she swore, dropping to her knees, momentarily forgetting all else but this familiar, potential disaster. "Pray God, I haven't broken it. . . . Ah, no, it seems intact . . . not a crack."

She held the figurine up to the light, her fingers tracing the surface. "I dareswear it's a monstrous expensive piece. I'd not have knocked it over otherwise." She set the figurine on the table again and stepped swiftly away from the danger zone.

The duke regarded these maneuvers with some astonishment. "Are you in the habit of destroying expensive articles?"

"It's my cursed clumsiness," Juliana explained with a sigh, watching the figurine warily to make sure it didn't decide to tumble again.

Any response her companion might have made was curtailed by the arrival of Mr. Garston in response to the bell.

"Champagne for the lady, Garston," the duke ordered blandly. "Claret for myself. The forty-three, if you have it."

"I believe so, Your Grace." Garston bowed himself out.

Juliana, annoyed that her clumsiness had distracted her at a moment when she'd felt she was regaining some measure of self-possession in this frightful situation, remained silent. The duke seemed perfectly content with that state of affairs. He strolled to a bookshelf and gave great attention to the gilded spines of the volumes it contained until Garston returned with the wine.

"Leave it with me, Garston." He waved the man away and deftly eased the cork from the neck of the champagne bottle. "I trust this will find favor, ma'am." He poured a glass and took it to Juliana, still standing motionless by the table.

Juliana had but once tasted champagne, and that on her wedding day. She was accustomed to small beer and the occasional glass of claret. But with the bravado of before, she took the glass and sipped, nodding her approval.

The duke poured a glass of claret for himself, then said gently, "If you would take a seat, ma'am, I might also do so."

It was such an unlooked-for courtesy in the circumstances that Juliana found herself sitting down without further thought. The duke bowed and took a chair opposite her sofa.

Tarquin took the scent of his wine and examined the still figure. She reminded him of a hart at bay, radiating a kind of desperate courage that nevertheless acknowledged the grim reality of its position. Her eyes met his scrutiny without blinking, the firm chin tilted, the wide, full mouth taut. There was something uncompromising about Juliana Beresford, from the tip of that flaming head of hair to the toes of her long feet. The image of her naked body rose unbidden in his mind. His eyes narrowed as his languid gaze slid over her, remembering the voluptuous quality of her nudity, the smooth white skin in startling contrast to the glowing hair.

"If you insist upon making this proposition, my lord duke, I wish you would do so." Juliana spoke suddenly, breaking the intensity of a silence that had been having the strangest effect upon her. Her skin was tingling all over, her nipples pricking against her laced bodice, and she had to fight against the urge to drop her eyes from that languid and yet curiously penetrating gray scrutiny.

"By all means," he said, taking a sip of his wine. "But I must first ask you a question. Are you still virgin?"

Juliana felt the color drain from her face. She stared at him in disbelief. "What business is that of yours?"

"It's very much my business," the duke said evenly. "Whether or not I make this proposition depends upon your answer."

"I will not answer such a question," Juliana declared from a realm of outrage beyond anger.

"My dear, you must. If you wish to spare yourself the inconvenience of examination," he said in the same level tones. "Mistress Dennison will discover the answer for herself, if you will not tell me."

Juliana shook her head, beyond words.

He rose from his chair and crossed the small space between them. Bending over her, he took her chin between finger and thumb and tilted her face to meet his steady gaze. "Juliana, you told Mistress Dennison that your husband died before your marriage was consummated. Is that the truth?"

"Why would I say it if it wasn't?" Somehow she still managed to sound unyielding, even as she yielded the answer because she knew she had no choice but to do so.

He held her chin for a long moment as she glared up at him, wishing she had a knife. She imagined plunging it into his chest as he stood so close to her she could smell his skin, and a faint hint of the dried lavender that had been strewn among his fresh-washed linen.

Then he released her with a little nod. "I believe you."

"Oh, you do me too much honor, sir," she said, her voice shaking with fury. Springing to her feet, she drove her fist into his belly with all the force she could muster.

He doubled over with a gasp of pain, but as she turned to run, he grabbed her and held on even as he fought for breath.

Juliana struggled to free her wrist from a grip like steel. She raised a leg to kick him, but he swung sideways so her foot met only his thigh.

"Be still!" he gasped through clenched teeth. "Hell and the devil, girl!" He jerked her wrist hard and finally she stopped fighting.

Slowly Tarquin straightened up as the pain receded and he could breathe again. "Hair as hot as the fires of hell goes with the devil's own temper, I suppose," he said, and to Juliana's astonishment his mouth quirked in a rueful smile, although he still held her wrist tightly. "I must bear that in mind in future."

"What do you want of me?" Juliana demanded. An overwhelming sense of helplessness began to eat away at her, challenging bravado; and even as she tried to fight it, she recognized the futility of the struggle.

"Quite simply, child, I wish you to marry my cousin, Viscount Edgecombe." He released her wrist as he said this and calmly straightened his coat and the disordered lace ruffles at his cuffs.

"You want me to do *what*?"

"I believe you heard me." He strolled away from her to refill his wineglass. "More champagne, perhaps?"

Juliana shook her head. She'd barely touched what was in her glass. "I don't understand."

The duke turned back to face her. He sipped his wine reflectively. "I need a wife for my cousin, Lucien. A wife who will bear a child, an heir to the Edgecombe estate and title.

"The present heir is, to put it kindly, somewhat slow-witted. Oh, he's a nice enough soul but could no more pull

Edgecombe out of the mire into which Lucien has plunged it than he could read a page of Livy. Lucien is dismembering Edgecombe. I intend to put a stop to that. And I intend to ensure that his heir is my ward."

He smiled, but it had none of the pleasant quality of his earlier smiles. "I shall thus have twenty-one years to put Edgecombe back together again . . . to repair the damage Lucien has done—as much as anything, I believe, to spite me."

"Why can't your cousin find his own wife?" she asked, staring incredulously.

"Well, I suspect he might find it difficult," the duke said, turning his signet ring on his finger with a considering air. "Lucien is not a pleasant man. No ordinary female of the right breeding would choose to wed him."

Juliana wondered if she was going mad. At the very least she had clearly stumbled among lunatics. Vicious, twisted lunatics.

"You . . . you want a *brood mare!*" she exclaimed. "You would blackmail me into yielding my body as a vehicle for your cousin's progeny, because no self-respecting woman would take on the job! You're . . . you're treating me like a bitch to be put to a stud."

Tarquin frowned. "Your choice of words is a trifle inelegant, my dear. I'm offering a marriage that comes with a title and what remains of a substantial fortune. My cousin doesn't have long to live, hence the urgency of the matter. However, I'm certain you'll be released from his admittedly undesirable company within a twelvemonth. I'll ensure, of course, that you're well looked after in your widowhood. And, of course, not a word of your unfortunate history will be passed on."

He sipped his wine. When she still gazed at him, dumbstruck, he continued: "Your secret will be buried with me and the Dennisons. No one will ever connect Lady Edgecombe with Juliana . . . whoever-you-were." His hand moved through the air in a careless gesture. "You will be safe, prosperous, and set up for life."

Juliana drained her champagne glass. Then she threw the glass into the fireplace. Her face was bloodless, her eyes jade stones, her voice low and bitter as aloes. "And to gain such safety . . . such rewards . . . I must simply bear the child of an undesirable invalid with one foot in the—"

"Ah, no, not precisely." The duke held up one hand, arresting her in midsentence. "You will not bear Lucien's child, my dear Juliana. You will bear mine."

Chapter 4

I cannot imagine how we can help you, Sir George." Sir
Brian Forsett offered his guest a chilly smile. "Juliana
ceased to be our responsibility as soon as she passed into
the legal control of her husband. Your father's unfortunate
death leaves his widow her own mistress, in the absence of
any instructions to the contrary in Sir John's will."

"And it leaves you, sir, holding her jointure in trust for
her," snapped Sir George Ridge. He was in his late twenties, a corpulent, red-faced man, with hands like ham
hocks. The son of his father, physically if not in character,
he was the despair of his tailors, who recognized that all
their skill and all their client's coin would never make an
elegant figure of him.

"That is so," Sir Brian said in his customarily austere
tones.

When he offered no expansion, his choleric guest began
to pace the library from window to desk, muttering to
himself, dabbing with his handkerchief at the rolls of sweating flesh oozing over his stock. "But it's iniquitous that it
should be so," he stated finally. "Your ward has murdered
my father. She runs away, and you still hold her jointure—a
substantial part of my inheritance, I tell you, sir—in trust
for her. I say again, sir, she is a murderess!"

"That, if I might say so, is a matter for the court," Sir Brian said, his nose twitching slightly with distaste. The warmth of the summer afternoon was having a malodorous effect on his visitor.

"I tell you again, sir, she is a murderess!" Sir George repeated, his nostrils flaring. "I saw the mark on my father's back. If she was not responsible for his death, why would she run away?"

Sir Brian shrugged his thin shoulders. "My dear sir, Juliana has always been a mystery. But until she is found, there is nothing we can do to alter the current situation."

"A murderess cannot inherit her victim's estate." Sir George slammed a fist on the desk, and his host drew back with a well-bred frown.

"Her children can, however," he reminded the angry young man. "She may be with child, sir. Her husband died in such circumstances as to imply that . . ." He paused, took a pinch of snuff, and concluded delicately, "As to imply that the marriage had been consummated."

His visitor stared in dismay. Such a thought had clearly never entered his mind. "It couldn't be." But his voice lacked conviction.

"Why not?" gently inquired his host. "You, after all, are proof that your father was not impotent. Of course, we may never know about Juliana. One would have to find her first."

"And if we don't find her, then it will take seven years to have her declared legally dead. Seven years when you will hold her jointure in trust and I will be unable to lay hands on half my land."

Sir Brian merely raised an eyebrow. He'd negotiated his ward's marriage settlement with the cold, calculated pleasure of a man who was never bested in a business deal. Bluff and kindly Sir John Ridge, heading into his dotage utterly infatuated with the sixteen-year-old Juliana, hadn't stood a chance against the needle wits of his acquisitive opponent. Juliana's benefit had been a mere sideline for Sir Brian in the general pleasures of running rings around the slow-witted and obsessed Ridge.

"Well, how are we to find her?" Sir George flung himself onto a sofa, scowling fiercely.

"I suggest we leave that to the constables," Sir Brian stated.

"And just how much do you think that lazy gaggle of poxed curs will bestir themselves?"

Sir Brian shrugged again. "If you have a better idea . . ."

"Oh, indeed I do!" Sir George sprang to his feet with an oath. "I'll go after the damned girl myself. And I'll bring her back to face the magistrates if it's the last thing I do."

"I commend your resolution, sir." Sir Brian rose and moved toward the door, gently encouraging his guest's departure. "Do, I beg you, keep me informed of your progress."

Sir George glared at him. There was only form politeness in Sir Brian Forsett's tone. The longer Juliana remained at large and in hiding, the longer Forsett would have to manage her jointure as he chose. It didn't take much imagination to understand that he would prove expert at diverting revenues from the trust into his own pocket.

"Oh, Sir George . . . pray accept my condolences. . . . Such a terrible tragedy." The crisp tones of Lady Amelia Forsett preceded the lady as she entered the library through the open terrace doors.

A tall woman of haughty demeanor, she sketched a curtsy. George, intimidated despite his anger, bowed low in return. Lady Forsett's clear pale-blue eyes assessed him and seemed to find him wanting. A chilly smile touched the corners of her mouth. "I trust I haven't interrupted your business with my husband."

"Not at all, my dear," Sir Brian reassured smoothly. "Sir George was just leaving." He pulled the bell rope.

Amelia curtsied again, and George, thus dismissed, found himself moving backward out of the library under the escort of a footman who seemed to have appeared out of thin air.

"What did that lumpen oaf want?" Amelia came straight to the point as the door closed behind their guest.

"As far as I can gather, he wishes to consign Juliana to the hangman with all dispatch, so that he can reclaim that part of his inheritance that formed her jointure."

"Dear me," murmured Lady Forsett. "What vulgar haste. His father is but three days in his own grave."

"The entire business is utterly distasteful," her husband said. "Of all the farcical—"

"Typical of Juliana," his wife interrupted, her thin lips pursing. "Such a clumsy, inconsiderate creature."

"Yes, but where *is* she?" Sir Brian interrupted with a familiar note of irritation. "Why would she run away? She couldn't possibly have been responsible for the man's death." He cast his wife an inquiring look. "Could she?"

"Who's to say?" Lady Forsett shook her head. "She's always been a wild and troublesome girl."

"With an immoderate temper," her husband put in, frowning. "But I find it hard to believe she could have deliberately—"

"Oh, not deliberately, no," Lady Forsett interrupted. "But you know how she's always doing the most inconvenient and inconsiderate things quite by accident. And if she flew off the handle . . ."

"Quite." Sir Brian chewed his lower lip, still frowning. "The whole business already bids fair to becoming the county scandal of the decade. If it comes to court, it will be hideous."

"Let us hope she isn't found," his wife said bluntly. "Then it will die down soon enough. If we don't search diligently for her, who else would bother?"

"George Ridge."

"Ahh . . . of course." Lady Forsett tidied up a tumbling pile of leather-bound volumes on a side table.

"But I doubt he has the wit to succeed," her husband said. "He's no brighter than his oaf of a father."

"Juliana, on the other hand—"

"Is as quick-witted as they come," Sir Brian finished for her with an arid smile. "If she doesn't wish to be found, I'll wager it'll take more than George Ridge to catch her."

George Ridge was still scowling as he rode out of the stable yard at Forsett Towers. His mount was a raw-boned gray, as ugly-tempered as his master, and he tossed his head violently, curling his lips back over the cruel curb bit. When his rider slashed his flank with his crop, the horse threw back his head with a high-pitched whinny, reared, and took off down the uneven gravel driveway as if pursued by Lucifer's pitchfork-carrying devils.

George had received even less satisfaction from the Forsetts than he'd expected. He cursed Sir Brian for an arrogant, nose-in-the-air meddler who hadn't the decency even to offer to assist in the search for his ungovernable, murdering, fugitive erstwhile ward.

Juliana. George pulled back on the reins as he turned the horse out of the gate and onto the lane. *Juliana.* Her image filled his internal vision in a hot, red surge of lust. He licked his lips. He'd lusted after her ever since he'd first seen her on the arm of his besotted, drooling father. His father's massive bulk had made her seem small as she walked beside him, but it couldn't disguise the voluptuous swell of her bosom beneath her demure bodice, the swing of her curving hips beneath the simple country gown that Lady Forsett insisted she wear.

Her hair had excited him as much as the hints of her body. A blazing, unruly mass of springing curls that seemed to promise an uninhibited and passionate nature. At first she'd been friendly, smiling at him, her green eyes warm, but then he'd made his mistake and yielded to the prompting of the lascivious dreams that swirled through his nights. He had attempted to kiss her, and she'd nearly scratched his eyes out. From then on her gaze had been cool and suspicious, her voice had lost its rich current of merriment, become distant and dismissive.

George's lust had not diminished, but anger and resentment had added a malevolent fuel. Now he saw his father's bride as the usurper. A twisting, manipulating bitch who had ensnared Sir John Ridge in his dotage with the promises of her youthful body. And in exchange for those promises she had been rewarded with the dower house in perpetuity, together with two thousand acres of prime land and all revenues accruing from its thick forests and tenant farms.

George had listened to his father's measured explanations for giving away George's inheritance. He had protested, but to no avail. Sir Brian Forsett had been adamant that these were the only terms on which he would agree to his ward's becoming Lady Ridge. And Sir John had been willing to agree to anything in order to have that sweet young body in his bed.

He'd had his wish, and it had killed him. George cut savagely at his horse's flanks. Juliana had disappeared, leaving her former guardian in possession of her jointure. And George was left with only half of his rightful inheritance.

But if he could find her, then her crime would disqualify her from her inheritance. Unless she was with child. If she pleaded her belly, they wouldn't sentence her to death. And her child would inherit the jointure. On the other hand, if she was to be married to Sir George Ridge—the grieving young widow wedded so appropriately to her late husband's son—then it wouldn't matter if she was with child or not. Everything would return to the Ridge family, and he, George, would have Juliana in his own bed.

Would she agree? He put spur to his horse, setting him at a high bramble hedge. The horse soared over, teeth bared in a yellow grimace, eyes rolling, and landed with a jolt on the far side.

George cursed the animal's clumsiness and jerked back on the curb rein. Juliana would agree because she would have no choice. In exchange he would swear that his father's death was accidental. No one would question George Ridge's interpretation of such an embarrassing incident. The story would be the joke of the county for months, and everyone would understand that a fat old man, drunk after his wedding, couldn't keep pace on his wedding night with a fresh filly of barely seventeen.

Juliana would agree. But first he had to find her.

He swung his mount to the right and headed for Winchester. She had to have left the area. And the only way to do that was by carriage or on horseback. No horses had been taken from the stables at Ridge Hall. But the stagecoaches departed from Winchester in the very early morning. He would inquire at the Rose and Crown, and he would post notices around the city just in case a wagoner or carter had taken up a lone woman in the middle of the night.

Juliana spent her next three days in the house on Russell Street in relative isolation, talking only to Bella, the maid who attended her and brought her meals. Her memory of the moments in the salon immediately after the duke's infamous proposition was vague. She had been devastated by outrage, rendered speechless; not trusting herself to remain in his company, she'd fled the room. No one had come after her, and no one had mentioned the matter to her again. Her chamber door was no longer locked, but on the one occasion she had ventured down to the hall, Mr. Garston had appeared out of nowhere and asked her in tones that brooked no argument to return to her chamber. She had been provided with everything she'd asked for: books, writing and drawing materials. But she was still unmistakably a prisoner in this topsy-turvy establishment that slept all day and awoke at night.

She would lie abed throughout the night listening to the strains of music from the salons, the bursts of feminine laughter, the sonorous male voices on the stairs, the chink of china and glass. Rich aromas from the kitchens wafted beneath her door, and she would entertain herself trying to identify the delicacies from which they emanated. Her own fare was the plain and plentiful food she assumed was served in the kitchens, but clearly the clients and the working ladies of the house dined very differently.

She would doze lightly throughout the night, usually falling deeply asleep at dawn as the door knocker finally ceased its banging and the sounds of merriment faded. As the sky lightened, she would hear voices in the corridor outside, soft and weary women's voices, the occasional chuckle, and once the sound of heart-wrenching weeping. The weeper had been comforted by a murmur of women, and then Mistress Dennison's voice had broken into the whisperings. Kindly but firm. Juliana had listened as she'd dispatched the women to their beds and taken the weeper away with her.

Apart from apprehension, which she fought to keep under control, Juliana's main complaint was boredom. She was accustomed to an active existence, and by the third day being penned in her chamber was becoming insupportable. She had asked no questions, made no demands for her freedom, stubborn pride insisting that she not give her captors the satisfaction of seeing her dismay. She would show them that she could wait them out, and when they saw she was adamant, then they would release her.

But on the early afternoon of the fourth day things changed. The little maid appeared in Juliana's chamber with her arms full of silk and lace.

"Y'are to dine downstairs, miss," she said, beaming over the gauzy, colorful armful. "And then be presented in the drawing room." She opened her arms, and her burdens toppled to the bed. "See what a beautiful gown Mistress Dennison 'as 'ad fashioned for ye." She shook out the folds of jade-green silk and held it up for Juliana's inspection.

"Take it away, Bella," Juliana instructed. Her heart was jumping in her breast, but she thought her voice sounded reassuringly curt and firm.

"Eh, miss, I can't do that." Bella stopped admiring the

gown in her hands and stared at Juliana. "Mistress Dennison 'ad it made up specially for ye. It wasn't ready till this morning, so ye've been kept up 'ere. But now y'are all set." She turned enthusiastically to the pile of material on the bed. "See . . . fresh linen, two petticoats, silk stockings, and look at these pretty slippers. Real silver buckles, I'll lay odds, miss! Mistress Dennison 'as only the best fer 'er girls." She held out a pair of dainty apple-green silk shoes with high heels.

Juliana took them in a kind of trance, measuring the heel with her finger. Her feet were unruly enough when they were flat on the ground; what they would get up to in these shoes didn't bear thinking of.

She dropped them onto the floor. "Would you inform Mistress Dennison that I have no intention of wearing these clothes or of being presented . . . or, indeed, of anything at all."

Bella looked aghast. "But, miss—"

"But nothing," Juliana said brusquely. "Now, deliver my message . . . and take these harlot's garments away with you." She gestured disdainfully to the bed.

"Oh, no, miss, I dursn't." Bella dropped a curtsy and scuttled from the room.

Juliana sat down on the window seat, ignored her pounding heart, folded her hands in her lap, and awaited developments.

They came with the arrival of both Dennisons within ten minutes. Elizabeth, resplendent in a gown of tangerine silk over a sky-blue petticoat, sailed into the room, followed by a tall gentleman clad in a suit of canary-yellow taffeta, his hair powdered and curled.

Juliana, reasoning that she had nothing to lose by showing courtesy, rose and curtsied, but her eyes were sharply assessing as they rested on her visitors. She had never met Richard Dennison but guessed his identity from Bella's descriptions.

"Now, what nonsense is this, child?" Elizabeth came straight to the point, sounding annoyed.

"I might ask the same of you, madam," Juliana said evenly. Her mind raced. Could they force her into prostitution? Could they have her raped and ruined, so she'd have nothing further to lose? Her skin was clammy, but her voice remained steady, and she kept her eyes firmly fixed on the Dennisons.

"There's no need for discourtesy, my dear." Richard Dennison's voice was deep and mild, but the tone was belied by his keenly penetrating eyes. He stepped up to the bed. "Do you find fault with the gown . . . or the linen?"

"They are the garments of a harlot, sir. I am not a harlot."

"Oh, for goodness' sake, girl!" exclaimed Elizabeth. "This gown is the dernier cri at court. Everything here is of the best quality and design."

"I thank you for your kindness, ma'am, but I will not take your charity."

"This is not *my* gift, child, but—" She stopped abruptly as her husband coughed behind his hand, his eyes darting a warning.

Juliana bit her lip. If the clothes were not the gift of the Dennisons, then there was only one explanation. "I beg you will inform His Grace, the Duke of Redmayne, that I have no need of *his* charity either."

"Why do you keep prating of charity, child?" demanded Richard. "You are being asked to perform a service in exchange for our hospitality and His Grace's generosity."

"A service I will *not* perform," she stated, astonished at how firm she sounded when her knees were quaking like a blancmange and her palms were slippery with sweat. "I am not a whore."

"As I understand it, His Grace is offering to make you a viscountess . . . a far cry from a whore," Mr. Dennison observed aridly.

"There is a buyer and a seller, sir. I see no difference."

"Obstinate ingrate," declared Mistress Dennison. "His

Grace insisted you should have time to reconsider his offer without persuasion, but—"

"Madam!" Juliana interrupted passionately. "I ask only to be allowed to leave this house unmolested. If you will return my original garments, I will go as I came and be no trouble to anyone. Why would you keep me here against my will?"

"Because it is our considered opinion, my girl, that you don't know what's good for you," Richard said. "How long do you think you'll last on the streets? You have no idea how to go on in London. You have no money, no friends, no protection of any sort. In this house you have been offered all that and more. In exchange we ask only that you put on those clothes and come downstairs to dinner."

Juliana felt the ground slipping beneath her feet as some of her assurance left her. Everything they said was true. She'd seen enough from her window to know that a sheltered life among county aristocracy had ill equipped her for the life of an indigent girl in London.

"Bella said I was to be presented in the drawing room," she said. "I believe I know what that means."

"I believe you do not," Richard said crisply. "No demands will be made of you except for your company. You will not be required to entertain, except perhaps to play a little music and converse as in any civilized drawing room."

"And the Duke of Redmayne . . . ?" she asked, hesitantly now.

Mr. Dennison shrugged easily. "My dear, the duke's business is not ours. It lies with you, and he will deal directly with you. Mistress Dennison and I ask only that you dine with the other members of this household and take tea in the drawing room."

"And if I refuse?"

A look of exasperation crossed Mr. Dennison's face, but he held up a hand as his wife seemed about to remonstrate. "I think you know better than to do so," he said. "You are in need of a safe haven, and you have one here. But it seems reasonable to ask that you obey the rules of the house."

Juliana turned away, defeated. The threat was clear enough. It wouldn't take the magistrates long to discover her true identity once they were told her story. The landlord of the Bell in Wood Street would remember that the Winchester coach had arrived at the same time as the York stage. Piecing together the rest would be easy for them.

"Come, my dear." Mistress Dennison's voice was soft and cajoling. She laid a gentle hand on Juliana's arm. "I'll ring for Bella and she'll help you to dress. The gown will set off your eyes and hair to perfection, I promise you."

"That is hardly an incentive in these circumstances, ma'am," Juliana said dryly, but she turned back to the room. "If you are determined to have my maidenhead, then it seems there's little I can do to prevent it."

"Don't be so untrusting," Elizabeth scolded, patting her arm. "My husband and I will force nothing upon you. Your business lies with the Duke of Redmayne, and you may negotiate with him however you please."

Juliana's eyes narrowed. "You would have me believe that you have no interest, financial or otherwise, in the duke's plans for me? Forgive me, ma'am, if I doubt that. A procuress expects to be paid, I'm sure."

"What a stubborn, ill-tempered chit it is, to be sure," Elizabeth declared to her husband. "I wish His Grace joy of her." She tossed her elaborately coiffed head in disgust and sailed from the room, followed by Richard.

Perhaps it was unwise to alienate those two on whom her present comfort and security depended, Juliana reflected with a rueful grimace. She went over to the bed and began to examine the garments. There was an apple-green quilted petticoat to pair with the jade-green gown, an underpetticoat and chemise of embroidered lawn, silk stockings and garters, a pair of ruffled engageantes to slip over her forearms, and those ridiculous shoes.

She sat on the bed and slipped one cotton-stockinged foot into a shoe. It fitted perfectly. Presumably they'd used her boots as a model. Her feet were so big, they couldn't have guessed the size with this accuracy. She extended her foot, examining the shoe with her head on one side. It did make her foot look uncharacteristically elegant. But could she walk on it? She slipped on the other shoe, then gingerly stood up. Equally gingerly, she took a step and swayed precariously. The shoes pinched now most dreadfully, squashing her toes and making her insteps ache.

"Oh, miss, aren't they pretty?" Bella cried from the door as she bustled in, bearing a jug of steaming hot water. "Would ye care for a bath afore dinner? I could 'ave a footman bring up a tub."

Juliana sat down again and kicked off the shoes. Her last bath had been on her wedding morning. Maybe it would be as well to prepare herself for whatever the evening was going to bring. Like a sacrificial virgin, she thought with an unlooked-for glimmer of amusement. Her sense of humor was frequently misplaced and had in the past involved her in as much trouble as her unruly feet. But in present circumstances, she reflected, it could hardly make things worse.

"Yes, please, Bella."

"I could make up an 'enna rinse fer your hair, if'n ye'd like it," Bella continued. "It'll give it a powerful shine. Miss Deborah uses it when she 'as an evening with Lord Bridgeworth. Not that 'er 'air's as pretty as your'n. Quite dull it is, next to your'n." She beamed as if she took special pride in Juliana's superiority in this field.

"I use vinegar at home," Juliana said.

"Oh, but 'enna's a powerful lot better fer yer color, miss."

In for a penny, in for a pound. "Very well. Whatever you think Bella."

Looking mightily pleased, Bella whisked herself out of the room, and Juliana returned her attention to the garments on the bed. It was true that they were in the first style of elegance. Lady Forsett had pored over the periodicals and patterns of London style and had all her clothes made up in Winchester to the latest specifications, although Juliana assumed that since the periodicals and patterns had been at least six months old by the time they'd reached Winchester, they were probably unmodish by court standards. Not that she'd expressed this opinion to her guardian's wife.

Lady Forsett had insisted that Juliana herself wear only the simplest country clothes suitable to a schoolgirl who had no business in the drawing room. She had softened a little over the wedding dress and trousseau, but Juliana had been well aware that the garments had deliberately been made up to outmoded patterns. Lady Forsett had said quite bluntly that Juliana would have no need of a truly fashionable wardrobe married to Sir John Ridge. He was a wealthy man, certainly, but not sufficiently refined to be received by the leaders of county society.

But that wardrobe had been left behind with her dead husband. Her britches and shirt had disappeared. The only clothes she had were those on her back and now these luscious, rippling, rustling silks and lawns. Juliana couldn't help but be seduced by the delicious image of herself dressed in such finery.

Bella returned with a footman and the boot boy, laboring with copper jugs of steaming water and a wooden hip bath. The footman and the lad bowed deferentially to Juliana as they left, and she began to feel that her position in the house had insidiously changed.

"Everyone's very excited, miss, that ye'll be joining the ladies tonight," Bella confided, pouring water into the tub. "Mr. Garston says as 'ow y'are already promised to a great patron. Everyone's very curious to meet ye."

It occurred to Juliana as she stripped off her clothes that while she had been kept in isolation above stairs, the entire household had been free to speculate on her position. Somehow she'd assumed that her lack of interest in them would be reciprocated. Not so, apparently.

She said nothing, however, stepping into the tub and lowering herself into the steaming water with a sigh of pleasure. She was unaccustomed to the services of a maid, Lady Forsett considering them unnecessary, but she soon discovered that Bella was as experienced as she was enthusiastic. In fifteen minutes Juliana was sitting on the ottoman while Bella vigorously dried her henna-rinsed hair.

"There y'are, miss, what did I tell you?" Bella held up a hand mirror as she took the towel from Juliana's head. "Glowin' like the sunrise."

Juliana ran her hands through the damp, springy curls until they stood out around her head like a sunburst. "But what are we to do with it now, Bella?" she inquired with a grin. "It's always been completely unmanageable after it's been washed."

"Mr. Dennison said as 'ow I was to leave it loose, miss. I'm to thread a velvet ribbon through it."

Juliana frowned. Mr. Dennison's voice, it seemed, penetrated into the intimate corners of his whores' bedchambers. She wouldn't have found Mistress Dennison's sartorial instructions offensive, she decided, but her husband's were quite a different matter. She would be obeying the orders of a pimp. But perhaps they were orders from the Duke of Redmayne, relayed through Mr. Dennison. If so, she had even less inclination to obey them.

"I shall pin it up myself," she declared, twitching the towel from Bella's slackened grip. She ignored the maid's protestations and roughly finished toweling the damp curls.

"Mr. Dennison was most particular, miss," Bella said, twisting her work-roughened hands in her apron.

"How I wear my hair is no business of his . . . or, indeed, anyone's." She tossed the towel to the floor and shook her head vigorously like a dog coming in from the rain. "There, now if I brush it carefully and use plenty of pins, I might be able to subdue it."

Bella, still looking very unhappy, handed her the new chemise and carefully unrolled the stockings. Juliana put them on and stepped into the underpetticoat. She glanced at herself in the cheval glass and decided that her wildly tangled ringlets resembled Medusa's snakes. Maybe she

should leave them just as they were—unbrushed and unpinned. It ought to be enough to cause even the Duke of
Redmayne to have second thoughts.

She glanced with distaste at the brocade stays Bella was
holding but turned her back so the maid could lace her.
She associated the restrictive garment with long, miserable
days when Lady Forsett had decreed she should be laced as
tightly as she could bear. It was supposed to have improved
both her bearing and her conduct, but it had only made
her more defiant.

She stood with her hands at her nipped-in waist, watching in the glass as Bella tied the tapes of the wide whalebone hoop. Juliana had never before worn anything but the
most modest frame. Now she took a step, watching the
hoop sway around her hips. It felt very cumbersome, and
the prospect of maneuvering herself on those impossibly
high heels struck her as laughable.

She stepped into the quilted overpetticoat, and Bella
dropped the jade-green gown over her head, hooking it at
the back. Juliana slipped the ruffled engageantes over her
hands, pushing them up to her elbows, where they met the
flounces sewn to the fitted sleeves of the gown. She slipped
her feet into the shoes and took a hesitant step.

Then she took another look at herself in the mirror. Her
eyes widened in astonishment. Apart from her disordered
hair, she didn't look in the least like herself. The stays
pushed up her breasts so that they swelled invitingly over
the décolletage of her gown, and the wide, swaying hoop
emphasized the smallness of her waist. The costume gave
her figure an air of enticing maturity that she found thoroughly disconcerting, although she was aware of a pleasurable prickle of excitement beneath the disquiet.

But did she look like a harlot? She put her head on one
side and considered the question. The answer was definitely
no. She looked like a woman of fashion. There was something indefinable about the gown that set it apart from
Lady Forsett's London imitations—a touch of elegance in
the fit or the style that could not be imitated.

"Oh, miss, ye look lovely," Bella said, darting around her, twitching at ruffles, adjusting the opening of the gown over the petticoat. "Now, if'n ye'd jest let me do yer 'air," she added wistfully, picking up a green velvet ribbon that exactly matched the gown.

"No, thank you, Bella. I'll do it myself." Juliana picked up the hairbrush from the dresser. She tugged it through the tangled curls until they fell in some semblance of order onto her shoulders, then twisted them into a knot on top of her head, thrusting pins into the flaming mass with reckless abandon. She felt like a hedgehog at the end, and wisps still escaped from the knot. She knew that within five minutes the whole thing would begin to tumble of its own volition and she'd be spending the evening adjusting pins in a desperate and finally futile attempt to keep it in place; but she stubbornly decided that she'd rather do that than obey the instructions of Richard Dennison or the duke.

"Will ye wear the ribbon as a collarette, miss?" Bella was still holding the velvet ribbon. "It would set off the neck of the gown."

Juliana acquiesced, and the maid looked somewhat happier as she pinned the ribbon around Juliana's throat. The deep green accentuated the whiteness of her skin, the slenderness of her neck, and drew the eye down to the swell of her breasts.

" 'Ere's yer fan, miss." Bella proffered a chicken-skin fan.

Juliana opened it and examined the delicate pattern of painted apple-green leaves. Someone had gone to a great deal of trouble to assemble this outfit.

"I'll show ye to the dining room, miss." Bella ran to the door, opening it wide. "Dinner's at four and it's almost five past."

Juliana snapped the fan closed and essayed a step. She realized immediately that her usual swinging stride from the hip was impossible with the hoop and the shoes. She was required to take mincing little steps, the hoop swinging gracefully around her. She could handle the little steps, she decided, so long as she didn't lose her balance and fall in a disorderly heap with her skirts thrown up around her head. Not that it would be the first time.

"I'm ready," she said grimly. "Lead on, Bella."

Chapter 5

Bella pranced ahead of Juliana, down the curving staircase to the front hall. Juliana proceeded much more slowly, one hand resting with apparent negligence on the banister, although in fact her fingers were curled over it as if it were a lifeline.

Mr. Garston came forward with a stately tread as she reached the bottom of the stairs. To her astonishment he bowed. " 'Ow nice to see you downstairs, miss. If ye'd care to follow me."

Her circumstances had definitely altered in the last hours. Juliana merely inclined her head and followed him to a pair of double doors at the rear of the hall. He flung them open and announced in ringing accents, "Miss Juliana."

"Ah, my dear, welcome." Elizabeth Dennison was all affability, as if the altercation in Juliana's bedchamber had never occurred. "Oh, yes, how very fetching that gown is. The color is perfect, isn't it, ladies?" She came toward her, extending her hands in welcome. "Let me present you to our little family."

Taking Juliana's hand warmly, she drew her forward to the oval table where ten young women stood at their chairs. She recognized Lilly and Emma from the encounter in the hall on her first day. Names and faces of the others blended with the speed of the introduction, but she managed to mark Deborah and take note of her hair. Bella was right that it didn't have the sparking vitality of her own. For some reason the recognition was satisfying. Juliana began to wonder what was happening to her. She rarely gave a passing thought to her appearance, and yet here she was, examining the other girls as if they were some sort of rivals. Rivals for what?

Lord of hell! She was beginning to think like a whore. It must be something to do with the atmosphere in the house.

She curtsied politely to each woman, receiving a similar salute in return, and she was aware that she was being assessed as shrewdly as she was assessing them.

"Sit down, my dears." Elizabeth waved a hand around the table. "Now we're all assembled, there's no need to stand on ceremony. Juliana, take your place beside Mr. Dennison."

The seat of honor? Juliana took the chair to Richard's right. He drew it out for her and bowed her into it as if she were indeed the guest of honor.

A footman moved around the table filling wineglasses. "Will you taste the partridge, Juliana?" Lilly inquired, deftly carving the breast of a bird on a platter before her.

Juliana noticed that most of the girls were occupied with one of the serving platters, filleting carp swimming in parsley butter, carving ducks, pigeons, and partridges.

"Are you skilled at carving, Juliana?" inquired Richard. "We consider it a necessary domestic art for a well-educated young lady of fashion."

For a whore? Juliana was tempted to ask, but she managed not to. It was not appropriate to insult her fellow diners even if she was engaged in a conflict with their keepers. "My guardian's wife also considered it necessary," she said neutrally. The fact that she could no more carve a bird elegantly than she could sew a straight seam was neither here nor there. She was well versed in the principles of both, just too ham-fisted to do either skillfully.

She took a sip of wine and listened to the conversation. The women in their rich gowns chattered like so many bright-plumaged birds. They all seemed to be in the greatest good humor, told jokes, discussed both their customers and the prospects of other women who'd left the house for secure establishments with some member of the nobility.

Juliana said nothing, and no one tried to draw her into the conversation, but she was aware of sidelong glances as they talked, as if they were assessing her reactions. She wondered whether this display of conviviality had been put on for her benefit . . . whether they'd been instructed to try to persuade her that they led charming, amusing lives under the Dennisons' roof and had only the brightest of futures to look forward to. If so, it was making not a dent in her prejudice and did nothing to relieve her suspicion and apprehension.

Richard Dennison also said little, leaving it up to his wife to direct the conversation. But Juliana felt his eyes were everywhere, and she noticed that some of the girls would hesitate in their speech if they felt him looking their way. Their whoremaster clearly exerted a powerful influence.

She could find no fault with the dinner, though. The first course was removed with a second course of plover's eggs, quail, savory tarts, Rhenish cream, a basket of pastries, and syllabub. Juliana quashed her apprehension for the time being and ate with considerable appetite, remembering how she had sat in her chamber trying to identify the various toothsome aromas wafting from the kitchens. Boiled beef and pudding, steak-and-kidney pie, stewed fish, were all very well for filling one's belly, but they did little to titillate the palate.

Eventually, Mistress Dennison rose to her feet. "Come, ladies, let us withdraw. Our friends will be arriving soon. Lilly, dear, you should touch up your rouge. Mary, there's a tiny smudge of sauce on your sleeve. Go to your maid and have it sponged off. There's nothing more off-putting to a gentleman than a slovenly appearance."

Involuntarily, Juliana's hands went to her hair, escaping from its pins as she'd known it would.

"Did Bella not tell you we wished you to leave your hair loose?" inquired Richard, still seated at the table as the ladies rose around him. He poured port into his glass and glanced up at Juliana.

"Yes, but I prefer it like this," she responded evenly. There was an almost imperceptible indrawing of breath in the room.

"You must learn to subdue your own preferences in such matters to those of the gentlemen, my dear," Elizabeth said gently. "It was a most specific request that you leave it loose this evening."

"No one's preferences have more weight than my own, madam," Juliana replied, her throat closing as her heart thundered in her ears. She would not submit to them without a fight.

To her astonishment Elizabeth merely smiled. "I dareswear that that will change quite soon. Come."

Juliana followed them out of the dining room and into the long salon she'd peeped into that first morning. It was candlelit with tall wax tapers, although the evening sun still shone through the windows. There were flowers on every surface, the scent of lavender and beeswax in the air. A long sideboard carried decanters, bottles, and glasses; there was both tea and coffee on the low table before the sofa, where Mistress Dennison immediately took her seat. The girls ranged themselves around her, took teacups, and sat down. An air of expectancy hung in the room.

Juliana refused tea and walked over to a window overlooking the street. Behind her the murmur of voices, the soft chuckles, filled the air. She heard Lilly and Mary return and Mistress Dennison approve of their adjustments. Someone began to play the harpsichord.

Along the street strolled two gentlemen coming toward the house. They swung their canes as they talked, and their sword hilts showed beneath their full-skirted velvet coats. When they reached the house, they turned up the steps. The front door knocker sounded. A whisper of tension rustled around the room. The girl on the harpsichord continued to play, the others shifted on their chairs, rearranged their skirts, opened fans, glanced casually toward the door as they waited to see who their first guests would be.

"Lord Bridgeworth and Sir Ambrose Belton," Mr. Garston announced.

Mistress Dennison rose and curtsied; the other women followed suit, except for Juliana, who drew back against the embroidered damask curtains. Deborah and a pale, fair girl she remembered as Rosamund fluttered toward the two gentlemen. Juliana recalled that Bella had said Lord Bridgeworth was Deborah's particular gentleman. Presumably Sir Ambrose and Rosamund made a similar pair.

The door knocker sounded again and a party of six gentlemen were announced. Juliana drew even farther back into the shadows, watching the scene as she nervously pushed loosening ringlets back into their pins. One of the new arrivals caught sight of her and bent to say something to Mistress Dennison. Juliana distinctly heard "His Grace of Redmayne" in amid Elizabeth's reply. Then Elizabeth turned with a smile and beckoned.

"Juliana, Viscount Amberstock wishes to be acquainted with you."

It seemed she had little choice. Juliana moved reluctantly from the semiconcealment of the curtains and crossed the room, taking tiny steps, feeling as insecure on the high heels as a baby who was just learning to walk.

"Redmayne's a lucky dog," the viscount boomed, taking her hand and raising it to his lips as he bowed with a lavish flourish. Juliana curtsied in silence, averting her eyes. "Good God, ma'am, is the wench too shy to speak?" the viscount exclaimed to his hostess.

"Far from it," Elizabeth replied calmly. "Juliana has a very ready tongue when it suits her."

"But it belongs to Redmayne, what?" The viscount

laughed merrily at this risqué sally. "Ah, well, the rest of us must pine." He dropped Juliana's hand. She curtsied demurely and returned to her place by the window.

"You will annoy Mistress Dennison if you remain apart in this way." Emma spoke softly as she drifted casually up to Juliana in a mist of pink spider gauze.

"I find that a matter of indifference."

"You won't if they become really angered with you," Emma said, frowning. "They look after us very well, but they expect cooperation. It's hardly unreasonable."

Juliana met Emma's frowning regard and read both curiosity and a desire to be helpful in her dark-brown eyes. "But I am here against my will," she explained. "I see no reason why I should cooperate. I wish simply to be allowed to leave."

"But, my dear, you don't know what you're saying!" Emma protested. "There are bawds and whoremasters out there who will take every farthing you earn in exchange for the right to ply your trade in a shack in the Piazza. They charge five shillings for a used gown and shawl, and they'll squeeze the last drop of blood from your veins for the wine and spirits that you must have for the customers. If you refuse, or can't pay, then they'll throw you into the Fleet or the Marshalsea and you'll never be released."

Juliana stared at her, both horrified and fascinated. "But I have no intention of becoming a whore," she said at last. "Not here, nor anywhere."

Emma's frown deepened. "But what else is there for any of us?" She gestured around the room. "We live in the lap of luxury. Our clients are noblemen, discriminating, considerate . . . for the most part," she added. "And if you play your cards right, you could find a keeper who'll treat you well and provide for your future."

"But I'm not here because I wish to be," Juliana tried again.

Emma shrugged. "Are any of us, dear? But we count our blessings. You should do the same, or you'll find yourself lying under the bushes in St. James's Park every night. Believe me, I know. . . . . Oh, here's Lord Farquar." With a little trill of delight—that may or may not have been feigned Emma hastened across the room toward an elderly man in a snuff-sprinkled scarlet coat.

Five minutes later Garston announced the Duke of Redmayne. Juliana's stomach dropped to her feet. She turned away from the room and stared out into the gathering dusk on Russell Street.

Tarquin stood in the doorway for a minute and took a leisurely pinch of snuff. His eyes roamed the room, rested on the averted figure in green by the window. Her hair blazed in a ray of the sinking sun. He couldn't see her face, but there was a rigidity to the sloping white shoulders. As he watched, a ringlet sprang loose from its pins and cascaded down the slender column of her neck. She remained immobile.

He strolled across the room to his hostess. "Elizabeth, charming as always." He bowed over her hand. "And the ladies . . . a garden of delights." He raised his quizzing glass and surveyed the attendant damsels, who curtsied as his gaze swept over them.

Elizabeth glanced pointedly over her shoulder to Juliana before raising an expressively questioning eyebrow. His Grace shook his head and sat down beside her on the sofa. "Leave her for the moment."

"She is as obstinate as ever, Your Grace," Elizabeth said in a low voice, passing him a cup of tea.

"But I see that you persuaded her to dress and come downstairs."

"With difficulty."

"Mmm." The duke sipped his tea. "You were obliged to coerce her?"

"To point out the realities of her situation, rather."

The duke nodded. "Well, I'm glad she's not stupid enough to ignore those realities."

"Oh, I don't believe Miss Juliana is in the least stupid," Mistress Dennison declared. "She has a tongue like a razor."

The duke smiled and laid his cup on the table. "If you'll excuse me, madam, I'll go and make my salutations." He rose and strolled across to the window.

Juliana felt his approach. Her spine prickled. A thick strand of hair worked its way loose from the knot and slid inexorably down her neck. Automatically her hands went to her head.

"Allow me." His voice at her shoulder was deep and dark, and although she'd been expecting him, she jumped visibly. "Did I startle you?" he inquired gently. "Curious . . . I could have sworn you knew I was here." His hands put hers aside and moved through her hair.

It took Juliana a moment to realize that he was removing the pins. "No!" she exclaimed, reaching for his hands. "I will not wear it loose."

"Your hair seems to have a different idea," he commented, capturing both her wrists in one hand. "It really seems to have a mind of its own, my dear Juliana." His free hand continued its work, and the fiery mass fell to her shoulders. "There, now, I find that infinitely more desirable."

"I am not in the least interested in what you find desirable, Your Grace." She tugged at her imprisoned wrists and they were immediately released.

"Oh, I hope to change that," he responded, smiling as his hands on her shoulders turned her to face him. "You look ready to thrust a dagger into my heart!"

"I would like to twist it like a corkscrew in your gut," she declared in a savage undertone. "I would carve my initials on your belly and watch you hanged, drawn, and quartered! And I would laugh at your agonies." She brushed her hands together with the air of a task well completed as she delivered the coup de grâce, her eyes sparking with triumph as if she really had disposed of him in such an utterly satisfying fashion.

Tarquin laughed. "What a fierce child you are, *mignonne*."

"*No child!*" she hissed, twitching herself out of his grasp.

"If you think I'm no more than an inexperienced simpleton to be twisted to your design like a straw, I tell you, sir, you quite mistake the matter!"

"I fear we're drawing attention to ourselves," he said. "Come, let us go somewhere private, and you may rail at me to your heart's content."

Juliana, aware that a curious hush had fallen over the room, glanced around. Eyes were swiftly averted and the buzz of conversation was immediately renewed.

"Come," he repeated, offering his arm.

"I will go nowhere with you."

"Come," he repeated, and a hint of flint lay beneath the smiling good humor in the deep-set gray eyes. As she still hesitated, he took her hand and tucked it into his arm, advising softly, "You have nothing to lose by behaving with good grace, my dear, and everything to gain."

Juliana could see no way out. All around her she saw men whose faces reflected the lascivious greed of those hungry for flesh. She could scream and create a scene, but she'd meet no sympathy or support from either the buyers or the sellers in this whorehouse masquerading as a softly lit, gracious salon. No one here would have any sympathy for a recalcitrant harlot.

Could she break free and run? But even supposing she could get past Garston and the burly footmen in the hall, where would she go? Dressed as she was, she could hardly lose herself in the narrow, twisting alleys around Covent Garden.

Her only chance was to appeal to the Duke of Redmayne's finer nature—Supposing he had one. Putting his back up wouldn't help.

In silence she allowed him to escort her from the salon. Covertly curious glances followed them. Richard Dennison was crossing the hall to the salon as they stepped through the double doors.

"Your Grace." He bowed low. His gaze flicked over Juliana, and he nodded as he noted her loosened hair. He smiled at her. "You will show His Grace all the hospitality of this house, Juliana."

"Were I a member of this household, sir, I should feel obliged to do so," Juliana retorted.

Richard's mouth tightened with annoyance. Tarquin chuckled, thinking he'd rarely met a creature with so much spirit. "I give you good evening, Dennison." He bore Juliana up the stairs and into the small parlor where she'd first met him.

Once inside, he released her arm, closed the door, and pulled the bell rope. "As I recall, you drink only champagne."

Juliana shook her head. That was a pretense that had little point now. "Not really."

"Ahh." He nodded. "You were attempting to put me in my place, I daresay."

"Is that possible?"

That made him laugh again. "No, my dear, I doubt it. What shall the footman bring for you?"

"Nothing, thank you."

"As you please." He asked the footman for claret, then stood behind an armchair, one long white hand resting on the back, his eyes on Juliana. She stood by the fireplace, staring down into the empty grate.

There was a quality to her that Tarquin found moving. A vulnerability that went hand in hand with the fierce determination to hold her own against all the odds. She was not in the least beautiful, he thought. She had an unruly, ungainly quirk that denied conventional beauty. But then he remembered her naked body, and his flesh stirred at the memory. No, not beautiful, but a man would have to be but half a man not to find her desirable. By the same token, she would be safe from Lucien. Her body was too voluptuous to appeal to him.

Suddenly she flung herself into a chair and kicked off her shoes with such vigor that one of them landed on a console table. The candlestick shook violently under the impact, and hot wax splashed onto the polished surface.

"A plague on the damnable things!" Juliana bent to massage her feet with a groan. "How could anyone wear such instruments of torture?"

"Most women manage without difficulty," he observed, much amused at this abrupt change of demeanor. Her hair obscured her expression as she bent over her feet, but he could imagine the disgusted curl of her lip, the flash of irritation in her eyes. Strange, he thought, that after only two meetings he could picture her reactions so accurately.

She looked up, shaking her hair away from her face, and he saw he'd been exactly right. "I don't give a damn what other women manage! I find them insupportable." She extended one foot, flexing it to stretch the cramped arch.

"Practice makes perfect," Tarquin said, taking the discarded shoe off the console table. He picked up the other one that had come to rest in the coal scuttle. He blew coal dust from the pale silk, murmuring, "What cavalier treatment for a fifty-guinea pair of shoes."

So he *had* paid for them. Juliana leaned back in her chair and said carelessly, "I'm sure they won't go to waste, Your Grace. There must be harlots aplenty eager to accept such gifts."

"That might be so," he agreed judiciously. "If women with feet this size were easy to find."

The return of the footman with the claret gave Juliana the opportunity to bite her tongue on an undignified retort. When the man had left, she was prepared to launch her appeal to the duke's finer feelings.

"My lord duke," she began, getting to her feet, standing very straight and still. "I must beg you to cease this persecution. I cannot do what you ask. It's preposterous . . . it's barbaric that you should demand such a thing of someone you know has no protection and no friends. There must be women who would be willing . . . eager, even . . . to enter such a contract. But I'm not of their number. Please, I beg you, let me leave this place unmolested."

Almost every woman Tarquin could think of in Juliana's situation would leap at what he was offering—wealth, posi-

tion, security. The girl was either a simpleton or *very* unusual. He kept his thoughts to himself, however,
remarking, "Somehow, I have the impression that pleading
is foreign to your nature, *mignonne.*" He took a sip of his
claret. "That little speech lacked a certain ring of conviction."

"Oh, be damned to you for a Judasly rogue!" Juliana
cried. "Base whoreson! Stinking gutter sweeping. If you
think you can bend me to your will, then I tell you, you
have never been more mistaken in your entire misbegotten
existence!"

She leaped across the space separating them, tripped over
the hem of her gown, grabbed at a chair to right herself,
and turned on him, shaking her hair out of her eyes, her
fingers curled into claws, her teeth bared, her eyes spitting
hatred.

Tarquin took a hasty step back. Abruptly he lost the
desire to laugh. Miss Juliana didn't take kindly to mockery.
"Very well." He held up his hands in a placating gesture. "I
ask your pardon for being so flippant. Sit down again, and
we'll begin anew."

Juliana stopped. A hectic flush mantled her usually
creamy cheeks, and her bosom rose and fell in a violent
rhythm as she struggled to control herself. "You are the son
of a gutter bitch," she said with low-voiced savagery.

Tarquin raised his eyebrows. Enough was enough. He
said nothing until her flush had died and her erratic breathing had slowed; then he asked coolly, "Have you finished
roundly abusing me?"

"There's no abuse I can inflict on you, my lord duke, to
equal that which you would inflict upon me," she said
bitterly.

"I have no intention of abusing you. Sit down before the
room disintegrates in your cyclone and take a glass of
claret."

The deliberately bored tone was deflating. Juliana sat
down and accepted the glass of wine he brought her. The
outburst had drained her, leaving her hovering on the

brink of hopelessness. "Why won't you find someone else?" she asked wearily.

Tarquin sat down opposite her. "Because, my dear, you are a perfect choice." He began to tick off on his fingers. "You have the necessary breeding to appear as Lucien's wife without causing raised eyebrows. And you have both the breeding and certain qualities that I believe will make you a good mother to my child. And, finally, you need what I am offering in exchange. Safety, a good position, financial security. And most of all, Juliana, independence."

"Independence?" She raised a disbelieving eyebrow. "And how does that square with being a brood mare?"

Tarquin stood up and went to refill his glass. The girl was not a simpleton, but he was beginning to wonder whether, unusual or no, she was worth the time and the trouble he was expending. There were other women, as she so rightly pointed out. Women who'd jump at what he was offering. He turned back and examined her in silence, reflectively sipping his claret.

She was sitting back again, her eyes closed, her hair living fire around her pale face. The deep cleft between her breasts drew his eye. There was something intriguing as well as unusual about her. Her defiant resistance was such a novel challenge, he found it irresistible. He wanted to know what made her so unexpected, so out of the common way. What soil had she grown in? Maybe he was being a fool, but his blood sang with the conviction that Miss Juliana was definitely worth the time and the trouble to persuade.

He put his glass down and came over to her. Bending, he took her hands and drew her to her feet. "Let me show you something."

Juliana opened her mouth in protest and then gasped as his mouth closed over hers. His hands were in her hair, holding her head steady, and his lips were firm and pliant on hers. His tongue ran over her mouth, darting into the corners in a warm, playful caress that for a moment took her breath away. She was enclosed in a red darkness, all her senses focused on her mouth, on the taste and feel of his. Her lips parted at the delicate pressure, and his tongue slid inside, moving sinuously, exploring her mouth, filling her mouth with sweetness, sending hot surges of confused longing from her head to her toes.

Slowly he drew back and smiled down into her startled face, his fingers still curled in her hair. "That was what I wanted to show you."

"You . . . you ravished me!"

Tarquin threw his head back and laughed. "Not so, *mignonne*. I made you a promise." He moved one hand to cup her cheek, his thumb stroking her reddened mouth.

Juliana stared up at him, and he read the confusion, the dismay, and the excitement in her eyes.

"I promised you that what happens between us will bring you only pleasure. Nothing will happen to you, Juliana, that you don't wholeheartedly agree to."

"Then let me go," she begged, recognizing with quiet desperation that if she was compelled to remain, then Tarquin, Duke of Redmayne, would defeat her. She had yielded to his kiss. She hadn't fought him. Sweet heaven, she'd opened her mouth for his tongue without a moment's hesitation.

"No, you must remain in this house—that I insist upon."

Slowly Juliana crossed the room and picked up her discarded shoes. Sitting down, she slipped her feet into them. She knew he would see it as a symbolic gesture of acceptance, but at the moment she was too dispirited for further fighting.

She rose as slowly and walked to the door. "I beg leave to bid you good night, my lord duke." She curtsied formally, her voice low and expressionless.

"You have leave," he responded with a smile. "We will begin anew tomorrow."

Chapter 6

❧❧

"Y ou want me to take a wife!" Lucien threw back his
head on a shout of derisive laughter that disintegrated
into a violent fit of coughing.

Tarquin waited impassively as his cousin fought for sobbing breaths, his chest rattling, a sheen of perspiration gathering on his pale, sallow complexion.

"By God, Tarquin, I do believe you've finally lost your
wits!" Lucien managed at last, falling back into his chair.
He was clearly exhausted, but he still grinned, a gleam of
malevolent interest in the dark, burning sockets of his eyes.

"I doubt that," the duke said calmly. He filled a glass
with cognac and handed it to his cousin.

Lucien drained it in one gulp and sighed. "That's better.
Eases the tightness." He patted his chest and extended his
glass. "Another, dear fellow, if you please."

Tarquin glanced at the clock on the mantel. It was ten in
the morning. Then he shrugged and refilled the viscount's
glass. "Are you able to listen to me now?"

"Oh, by all means . . . by all means," Lucien assured
him, still grinning. "Why else would I obey your summons
so promptly? Amuse me, dear boy. I'm in sore need of
entertainment."

Tarquin sat down and regarded his cousin in silence for a

minute. His expression was dispassionate, showing no sign of the deep disgust he felt for this wreck of a young man who had willfully cast away every advantage of birth, breeding, and fortune, pursuing a course of self-destruction and depravity that considered no indulgence or activity too vile.

Sometimes Tarquin wondered why Lucien had turned out as he had. Sometimes he wondered if he, as the boy's guardian, bore any responsibility. He'd tried to be an elder brother to Lucien, to provide an understanding and steadying influence in his life, but Lucien had always evaded him in some way. He'd always been dislikable, defeating even Quentin's determination to see the good in him.

"Your passion for little boys has become something of a family liability," he observed, withdrawing a Sevres snuffbox from his pocket. "That rather nasty business with the Dalton boy seems to have become common knowledge."

Lucien had ceased to look amused. His expression was sullen and wary. "It was all hushed up quite satisfactorily."

Tarquin shook his head. "Apparently not." He took a pinch of snuff and replaced the box before continuing. "If you wish to continue with your present lifestyle in London, you need to protect yourself from further whispers. A charge against you would inevitably mean your exile . . . unless, of course, you were prepared to hang for your preferences."

Lucien glowered. "You're making mountains out of molehills, cousin."

"Am I?" The duke raised an eyebrow. "Read this." He drew a broadsheet out of his waistcoat pocket and tossed it across. "That story on the front has been providing entertaining gossip in every coffeehouse in town. Remarkable likeness, I think. The artist has a fine eye for caricature."

Lucien read the story, his scowl deepening. The artist's caricature of himself was as lewd and suggestive as the scurrilous description of an incident in the Lady Chapel involving a nobleman and an altar boy at St. Paul's Cathedral.

"Who wrote this?" He hurled the sheet to the floor. "I'll have his ears pinned to the pillory."

"Certainly. If you want everyone to know who you are," the duke observed, bending to pick up the sheet. He shook his head, marveling, "It really is a remarkably good likeness. A stroke of genius."

Lucien tore savagely at his thumbnail with his teeth. "A plague on him! Just let me find out who he is, and I'll run him through."

"Not, I trust, in the back," Tarquin said, his voice mild but his eyes snapping contempt.

Lucien flushed a dark, mottled crimson. "That never happened."

"Of course not," Tarquin said in silken tones. "Never let it be said that an Edgecombe would put his sword into a man's back."

Lucien sprang to his feet. "Accuse me of that again, Redmayne, and I'll meet you at Barnes Common."

"No, I don't think so," Tarquin responded, his lip curling. "I've no intention of committing murder."

"You think you could—"

"Yes!" the duke interrupted, his voice now sharp and penetrating. "Yes, I would kill you, Lucien, with swords or pistols, and you know it. Now, stop sparring with me and sit down."

Lucien flung himself into the chair again and spat a piece of thumbnail onto the carpet.

"I lost interest long ago in trying to persuade you to choose another way of life," Tarquin said. "You are a vicious reprobate and a pederast, but I'll not have you bringing public dishonor on the family name. Which is what will happen if the parent of some other altar boy decides to bring charges against you. Take a wife and be discreet. The rumors and the scandals will die immediately." He tapped the broadsheet with a finger.

Lucien's eyes narrowed. "You're not foolin' me, Redmayne. You wouldn't give a damn if they hanged me, except for the blot on the family escutcheon." He smiled, looking very pleased with himself as if he'd just successfully performed a complex intellectual exercise.

"So?" Tarquin raised an eyebrow.

"So . . . why should I do what you want, cousin?"

"Because I'll make it worth your while."

A crafty gleam appeared now in Lucien's pale-brown eyes. "Oh, really? Do go on, dear boy."

"I'll take your creditors off your back," the duke said. "And I'll keep you in funds. In exchange you will marry a woman of my choosing, and you will both reside under this roof. That shouldn't trouble you, since Edgecombe House is in such disrepair at the present, and it will relieve you of the burden of maintaining a household."

"A woman of *your* choosing!" Lucien stared at him. "Why can't I choose my own?"

"Because no one remotely suitable would take you."

Lucien scowled again. "And just whom do you have in mind? Some ancient antidote, I suppose. A spinster who'll take anything."

"You flatter yourself," the duke said dryly. "No woman, however desperate, would willingly agree to be shackled to you, Edgecombe. The woman I have in mind will do my bidding. It is as simple as that. You don't need to concern yourself about her. You will have separate quarters and you will leave her strictly alone in private. In public, of course, you will be seen to have a young wife of good breeding. It should provide you with a satisfactory public facade."

Lucien stared at him. "Do your bidding! Gad, Tarquin, what kind of devil are you? What hold do you have over this woman to compel her in such a matter?"

"That's no concern of yours."

Lucien stood up and went to refill his glass at the sideboard. He tossed the contents down his throat and refilled the glass. "All my expenses . . . all my debts . . . ?" he queried.

"All of them."

"And you'll not be prating at me every minute?"

"I have no interest in your affairs."

"Well, well." He sipped his brandy. "I never thought to see the day the Duke of Redmayne begged *me* for a favor."

Tarquin's expression didn't alter.

"I have very expensive habits," Lucien mused. He glanced slyly at the duke, who again showed no reaction. "I've been known to drop ten thousand guineas at faro in an evening." Again no reaction. "Of course, you're rich as Croesus, we all know that. I daresay you can afford to support me. I wouldn't like to bankrupt you, cousin." He grinned.

"You won't."

"And this woman . . . ? When do I see her?"

"At the altar."

"Oh, that's going too far, Tarquin! You expect me to trot along to church like the veritable lamb to the slaughter without so much as a peek at the woman?"

"Yes."

"And what does she say about it? Doesn't she want to see her bridegroom?"

"It doesn't matter what she wants."

Lucien took a turn around the room. He hated it when his cousin offered him only these flat responses. It made him feel like a schoolboy. But then again . . . the thought of Tarquin's funding Lucien's lifestyle despite his unconcealed contempt and loathing brought a smile to the viscount's lips. Tarquin would squirm at every bank draft he signed, but he wouldn't go back on his word. And he had set no limits on Lucien's expenditure.

And to live here, in the lap of well-ordered luxury. His own house barely ran at all. He could rarely keep servants beyond a month. Something always happened to send them racing for the door without even asking for a character. But here he could indulge himself to his heart's content, live as wild and reckless as he pleased, all at his cousin's expense.

It was a delicious thought. In exchange he simply had to go through the motions of a marriage ceremony to some unknown woman. He'd never have to have anything to do with her. He had nothing to lose and everything to gain.

"Very well, dear boy, I daresay I could oblige you in this."

"You overwhelm me, Edgecombe." Tarquin rose to his feet. "Now, if you'll excuse me, I have another appointment."

"Go to it, dear fellow, go to it. I'll just sip a little more of this excellent cognac." He rubbed his hands. "You have such a magnificent cellar, I can hardly wait to sample it. . . . Oh, Quentin, my dear . . ." He turned at the opening of the door and greeted his cousin with a flourishing bow. "Guess what. I'm to take a wife . . . settle down and become respectable. What d'you think of that, eh?"

Quentin shot his half brother a look more in sorrow than in anger. "So you are proceeding with this, Tarquin."

"I am."

"And my wife and I will be taking up residence under Tarquin's roof," Lucien continued. "More suitable for the young lady . . . more comfortable. So you'll be seeing a lot of us, my dear Quentin."

Quentin sighed heavily. "How delightful."

"How un-Christian of you to sound so doubtful," scolded Lucien, upending the decanter into his glass. "Seems to be empty." He pulled the bell rope.

"Good day, Lucien." Abruptly Tarquin strode to the door. "Quentin, did you wish to see me?"

"No," his brother said. "It would only be a waste of breath."

"My poor brother!" Tarquin smiled and patted his shoulder. "Don't despair of me. This is not going to turn out as badly as you think."

"I wish I could believe that." Quentin turned to follow Tarquin from the library. Lucien's chuckle rang unpleasantly in his ears.

"Last Friday, you say?" Joshua Bute pulled his left ear, regarding his customer with a benign attention that belied his shrewd, cunning calculations.

"Friday or possibly Saturday," George Ridge said, raising his tankard to his lips and taking a deep, thirsty gulp of ale. "Off the Winchester coach."

"A young lady . . . unattended?" Joshua pulled harder at his ear. "Can't say I did see such a one, guv. A'course, the York stage comes in at the same time. Quite a bustle it is 'ereabouts."

George leaned heavily on the stained counter of the tap-room. Gold glinted between his thick fingers as he spun a guinea onto the countertop. "Maybe this might refresh your memory."

Joshua regarded the guinea thoughtfully. "Well, per'aps ye could describe the young person agin?"

"Red hair, green eyes," George repeated impatiently. "You couldn't mistake her hair. Like a forest fire, all flaming around her face. Pale face . . . very pale . . . deep-green eyes . . . tall for a woman."

"Ah." Joshua nodded thoughtfully. "I'll jest go an' ask in the kitchen. Mebbe one of the lads saw such a one in the yard, alightin' from the coach."

He trundled off into the kitchen, and George cursed under his breath. The Rose and Crown in Winchester had been no help. They couldn't remember who was on the waybill for either Friday or Saturday. The scullery maid thought she remembered a lad boarding on the Friday, but the information had been elicited after the outlay of several sixpences, and George couldn't be sure whether it was a true recollection. Anyway, a lad didn't fit the description of the voluptuous Juliana.

He loosened the top button of his waistcoat and fanned his face with his hand. A bluebottle buzzed over a round of runny Stilton on the counter. His only other companion was an elderly man in the inglenook, smoking a church-warden pipe, alternately spitting into the sawdust at his feet and blowing foam off the top of his ale.

The sounds of the city came in through the open door, together with the smells. George was no stranger to the farmyard, but the rank odor of decaying offal and excrement in the midday sun was enough to put a man off his dinner. A wagon rattled by on its iron wheels, and a barrow boy bellowed his wares. A woman screamed. There was the ugly sound of a violent blow on soft flesh. A dog barked shrilly. A child wailed.

George resisted the country boy's urge to cover his ears. The noise and the bustle made him nervous and irritable, but he was going to have to get used to it if he was to find Juliana. He was convinced she was in the city somewhere. It was the only logical place for her. There was nowhere for her to hide in the countryside, and she would never escape detection in Winchester or any of the smaller towns. Her story was by now on every tongue.

"Well, seems like y'are in luck, sir." Beaming, Joshua emerged from the kitchen.

"Well?" George couldn't keep the eagerness from his voice or countenance.

"Seems like one of the lads saw a young person summat like what ye described." Joshua's eyes were fixed on the guinea still lying on the counter. George pushed it across to him. The innkeeper pocketed it.

" 'E didn't rightly know which stage she come off, guv. But it could've been the Winchester coach."

"And where did she go?"

Joshua pulled his ear again. " 'E couldn't rightly say, Yer 'Onor. She disappeared outta the yard with all the other folk."

Dead end. Or was it? George frowned in the dim, dusty, stale-smelling taproom. At least he knew now that she was in London, and that she'd arrived in Cheapside. Someone would remember her. As far as he knew, she had no money. It appeared that she'd taken nothing from the house . . . a fact that mightily puzzled the constables and the magistrates. Why would a murderess not complete the crime with robbery? It made no sense.

"What was she wearing?"

Joshua's little eyes sharpened. "I dunno, guv. The lad

couldn't rightly say. It was early mornin'. Not much light. An' the yard was a mad'ouse at that time o' day. Always is."

George's frown increased. "Bring me a bottle of burgundy," he demanded suddenly. "And I presume you can furnish a mutton chop."

"Aye, guv. A fine mutton chop, some boiled potatoes, an' a few greens, if'n ye'd like." Joshua beamed. "An' there's a nice piece o' Stilton, too." He slapped at the bluebottle, squashing it with the palm of his hand. "I'll fetch up the burgundy."

He went off, and George walked over to the open door. It was hot and sultry, and he wiped his forehead with his handkerchief. He had to find lodgings and then a printer. Reaching into his inside pocket, he drew out a sheet of paper. He unfolded it and examined its message with a critical frown. It should do the trick. He would have twenty or so printed; then he could hire a couple of street urchins for a penny to post the bills around the area. A reward of five guineas should jog someone's memory.

" 'Ere y'are, sir. Me finest burgundy," Joshua announced. He drew the cork and poured two glasses. "Don't mind if I joins ye, guv? Yer 'ealth, sir." He raised his glass and drank. Everything was very satisfactory. He had a guinea in his pocket from this gent, and there'd be at least another coming from Mistress Dennison when his message reached her. In fact, he could probably count on two from that quarter. She was bound to be interested in this gentleman and his curiosity about her latest acquisition. Not to mention the fact that the girl hadn't come off the York stage, as she'd maintained, but from Winchester. It was all most intriguing. And bound to be lucrative.

Joshua refilled their glasses and beamed at his customer.

Chapter 7

Juliana, do you care to come for a walk with us?" Miss Deborah popped her head around Juliana's door. "Lucy and I are going to the milliner's. I have to match some rose-pink ribbon. Do come."

"I have the impression I'm not permitted to leave the house," Juliana said. It was noon on the day after her presentation in the drawing room, and she hadn't stirred from her chamber since parting from the Duke of Redmayne. The house had been quiet as usual throughout the morning, but in the last hour it had come to life, and Juliana had sat in her room waiting for something to happen.

"Oh, but Mistress Dennison told me to ask you," Deborah said in genuine surprise. "She said an airing would do you good."

"I see." Juliana rose. This was an unexpected turn of events. She had expected to be more, rather than less, confined after her conduct the previous evening. "How kind of her. Then let's go."

Deborah looked a little askance at Juliana's dress. She was back in the simple servant's muslin. "Should you perhaps change?"

Juliana shrugged. "That might be a little difficult, since I have nothing but what I'm wearing and the gown I wore last night."

Deborah was clearly nonplussed, but before she could say anything, Bella bobbed up beside her in the doorway. "Mistress sent me up with this gown, miss, fer yer walk. I'nt it pretty?" She held up a gown of bronze silk. "An' there's a shawl of Indian silk to go with it."

"Oh, how lovely." Deborah felt the gown with an expert touch. "The finest silk, Juliana." She sighed enviously. "His Grace must have spent a pretty penny. Bridgeworth is generous enough, of course, but I often have to remind him. And it's so uncomfortable to have to do that, don't you agree?" She looked inquiringly at Juliana, who was hard-pressed to find a response that wouldn't offend Deborah but that would express the truth.

"I haven't yet found myself in that position," she said vaguely, taking the gown from Bella. The silk flowed through her hands like water. She glanced toward the open window. The sun poured through. How long had it been since she'd been outside? Days and days. She was in London, and she'd seen nothing of it but the yard of the Bell in Cheapside, and the street beneath this window. If she had to take the duke's gown to leave her prison, then so be it.

"Help me, Bella."

Deborah perched on the end of the bed as Bella eagerly helped Juliana into the underpetticoat and hoop she'd worn the previous evening before dropping the bronze silk gown over her head. " 'Ow shall I do yer 'air, miss?"

"It's more subdued today," Juliana said, unable to hide the uplift of her spirits at the thought of being out in the sunshine. "If you pin it up securely, it should stay in place."

Bella did as asked, then arranged the shawl of delicate cream silk over Juliana's shoulders. She stepped back, nodding her approval. Juliana examined herself in the glass. The bronze was a clever complement to her own coloring. Again she reflected that someone knew exactly what would flatter her. Did the Duke of Redmayne make the decisions?

Or did he provide the money and leave the choice to Mistress Dennison?

Panic fluttered suddenly in her belly as a sense of helplessness washed over her. Every day the trap grew tighter. Every day she grew less confident of her own power to determine her destiny. Every day she grew insidiously more resigned.

A thrush trilling at the open window, the warmth of the sun on the back of her neck, sent the black wave into retreat. She was going out for a walk on a beautiful summer morning, and nothing should destroy her pleasure in such a prospect.

"Come, Deborah, let's go." She pranced through the door, thankful that no one had made objection to the comfortable leather slippers she still wore.

Lucy was waiting for them in the hall. "That's such a pretty gown," she said a little enviously as Juliana bounced exuberantly down the stairs. "Those pleats at the back are all the rage."

"Yes, and see the way the train falls," Deborah said. "It's the most elegant thing. I must ask Minnie to make up that bolt of purple tabby in the same style."

Juliana was too anxious to reach the door to pay any heed to this conversation. Mr. Garston opened it for her, with a bow and an indulgent smile. "Enjoy your walk, miss."

"Oh, I intend to," she said, stepping past him, lifting her face to the sun and closing her eyes with a sigh of pleasure.

"Ah, Miss Juliana. What perfect timing."

Her eyes snapped open at the suave tones of the Duke of Redmayne. He stood at the bottom of the front steps, one gloved hand resting on the wrought-iron banister, a quizzical gleam in his eye.

"Perfect timing for what?" She waited for her pleasure in the morning to dissipate, but it didn't. Instead there was the strangest fizz of excitement in her belly; her face warmed, and her lips prickled as if anticipating the touch of his mouth on hers.

"I was coming to take you out for a drive," he said. "And I find you quite ready for me."

"You're mistaken, sir. I'm engaged to these ladies." She gestured to Lucy and Deborah, who both swept the duke a curtsy, a salutation that Juliana had omitted.

"They will excuse you," Tarquin said.

"Yes, of course, Juliana," Deborah said hastily.

"But I have no wish to be excused."

"I give you good day, ladies. Enjoy your walk." Tarquin bowed to Deborah and Lucy and stood aside to let them pass him on the step. As Juliana made to follow them, he laid a hand on her arm. "You will much prefer to drive with me, Juliana."

Juliana's skin burned where he touched her, and the fizzing excitement spread through her body as if she had champagne in her veins. She looked up at him, bewildered agitation flaring in her eyes. Tarquin smiled, then lightly brushed her lips with his own.

"You're very rewarding to dress, *mignonne*. Not many women could wear such a color without looking sallow and drab."

"So you did choose it?"

"Most certainly. I've been much entertained in designing your wardrobe. I trust it will all meet with your approval when you see it."

Juliana looked wildly up and down the street as if hoping to see some escape route, some knight in shining armor galloping to her rescue. But she met only the indifferent glances of grooms, barrow boys, fishwives, hurrying about their business.

"Come, my horses are getting restless." The duke tucked Juliana's hand into his arm and firmly ushered her across the street to where a light, open phaeton stood, drawn by a pair of handsome chestnuts. A groom jumped from the driver's seat and placed a footstep for them.

Juliana hesitated. The duke's hands went to her waist, lifting her clear off her feet and into the carriage. "You seem remarkably dozy this morning," he observed, stepping lightly up behind her. "Perhaps you slept poorly." He sat down and took up the reins. "Grimes, you may go back to Albermarle Street."

The groom touched his forelock and set off at a loping pace down the street toward the Strand.

"Now, where would you like to go?" the duke inquired affably. "Is there something particular you'd like to see? Westminster, perhaps? The Houses of Parliament? Hyde Park? The lions in the Exchange?"

Juliana contemplated a sullen silence and then abandoned the idea. It would be cutting off her nose to spite her face. "All of them," she said promptly.

Tarquin nodded. "Your wish is my command, ma'am."

Juliana cut him a sharp sideways look. "I didn't think you were a liar, my lord duke."

He merely smiled. "We'll drive around Covent Garden first. You'll find it of some interest, I believe."

Juliana understood what he meant as soon as they turned the corner of Russell Street and she finally saw what was hidden from her window. The colonnaded Piazza was thronged with men and women of every class and occupation. Dandies lounged with painted whores on their arms; fashionably dressed women, accompanied by footmen, paraded the cobbles, inviting custom as obviously as their less fortunate sisters who leaned in the doorways of wooden shacks and coffeehouses, beckoning with grubby fingers, lifting ragged petticoats to display a knee or plump thigh. Barrow boys and journeymen carrying baskets of bread and pies on their heads threaded their way through the produce sellers shouting their wares.

Juliana stared in fascinated disgust at the prints displayed on a kiosk on the corner of Russell Street. The duke followed her eye and observed casually, "Obscenity sells well in the Garden. Obscenity and flesh," he added. "The two tend to go together." He gestured with his whip. "The hummums and the bagnios over there do a thriving trade in steam and sweat . . . and flesh, of course."

Juliana could think of nothing to say. She continued to

gaze around her, engrossed by the scene even as she was repelled by it.

"The Dennisons' young ladies do not frequent the Piazza. You're more likely to see them at court than here," the duke continued. Juliana stared at a couple standing against the wall of one of the bagnios. Then, abruptly, she averted her eyes, a crimson flush spreading over her cheeks.

"Yes, privacy is not a particularly valued commodity around here," her companion observed. "You could see the same in St. James's Park after dark . . . under every bush, against every tree."

Juliana remembered Emma's warning about lying under the bushes in St. James's Park. Her skin crawled. She wanted to ask him to take her out of this place, but she knew he had a reason for bringing her here, and she wouldn't give him the satisfaction of showing her dismay.

They turned onto Long Acre, and as they approached St. Martin-in-the-Fields, the duke slowed his horses. A ragged group of children were gathered around the church steps. Three elderly women walked among them, examining them, paying particular attention to the little girls. Some they dismissed with a wave; others they gestured to stand aside.

"What are they doing?" Juliana couldn't help asking the question.

"The children are for hire . . . some of them for sale," her companion told her nonchalantly. "The bawds are picking the ones that might appeal to their customers' particular fancies."

Juliana gripped her hands tightly in her lap and stared straight ahead.

"If they're hired, they'll get a decent meal and earn a few shillings," the duke continued in the same tone. "Of course, most of their earnings will go to whoever put them up for hire in the first place."

"How interesting, my lord duke." Juliana found her voice as she finally understood the point to this little tour of London's underbelly. Unless she was much mistaken, the Duke of Redmayne was showing her what life was like for the unprotected.

Tarquin turned the phaeton onto the Strand. He maintained a flow of informative chat as he drove her through St. James's Park and along Piccadilly, and Juliana was soon seduced by the other sights of London: the lavish shop fronts, the town carriages, the horsemen, the sedan chairs. Ladies carrying small dogs promenaded along the wide street, greeting acquaintances with shrill little cries of delight, exchanging curtsies and kisses. They were followed by powdered footmen in elaborate liveries and, in most cases, small liveried pages loaded with bandboxes and parcels.

Juliana began to relax. The streets in this part of London were cleaner, the cesspit stench not so powerful, the buildings tall and gracious, with glass windows glinting in the sunlight, shining brass door knockers, white honed steps. This was the London she'd imagined from the sheltered Hampshire countryside. Impressive and wealthy, and full of elegant people.

The duke drew up before a double-fronted mansion on Albermarle Street. The front door opened immediately, and the groom he'd sent home at Covent Garden came running down the steps. The duke descended and reached up a hand to Juliana.

"You will wish for some refreshment," he said pleasantly.

Juliana remained where she was. "What is this place?"

"My house. Be pleased to alight." The touch of flint she'd heard before laced the pleasant tones. Juliana glanced up the street, then down at the groom, who was staring impassively ahead. What choice did she have?

She gave the duke her hand and stepped out of the carriage. "Good girl," he said with an approving smile, and she wanted to kick him. Instead she twitched her hand out of his and marched up the steps to the open front door, leaving him to follow.

A footman bowed as she swept past him into a marble-tiled hall. Juliana forgot her anger and apprehension for a moment as she gazed around, taking in the delicate plaster molding on the high ceiling, the massive chandeliers, the dainty gilt furniture, the graceful sweep of the horseshoe staircase. Forsett Towers, where she'd grown up, was a substantial gentleman's residence, but this house was in a different class altogether.

"Bring refreshment to the morning room," the duke instructed over his shoulder, slipping an arm around Juliana's waist and sweeping her ahead of him toward the stairs. "Tea, lemonade, cakes for the lady. Sherry for myself."

"I imagine your servants are accustomed to your entertaining unchaperoned ladies," Juliana stated frigidly as she was borne up the stairs with such dexterity that her feet merely skimmed the ground.

"I have no idea whether they are or not," the duke responded. "They're paid to do my bidding, that's all that concerns me." He opened a door onto a small parlor, sunny and cheerful with yellow silk wallpaper and an Aubusson carpet. "I have it in mind that this should be your own private parlor. Do you think you would care for it?" A hand in the small of her back propelled her forward even as she wondered if she'd heard him aright.

"It's pleasant and quiet, overlooking the garden at the back," he continued, gesturing to the window. "If you wished to change the decor, then, of course, you must do whatever pleases you."

Juliana told herself that this was some dream . . . some ghastly, twisted nightmare that would all fall apart in a moment like a broken jigsaw puzzle. But he'd turned back to her and was smiling as he took her hands and drew her toward him. Her eyes fixed on his mouth, thin but so beautifully sculpted. There was amusement and understanding in the deep-set gray eyes, and something else—a flicker of desire that set her blood frothing again. And then she was lost in the warmth and scent of his skin as his mouth took hers, without hesitation, with assertion. And she was responding in the same way, without will or thought. His mouth still on hers, he ran a fingertip over the rich swell of her breasts above her décolletage. She moaned against his lips, and when his finger slid into the deep valley between her breasts, her stomach contracted violently with a wild hunger that she couldn't put words to. Instead she pressed herself against him, a deep, primitive triumph flowing through her as she felt his hardness rising against her belly.

A tap at the door broke the charmed circle, and Juliana jumped back with a little cry of alarm. She turned away, blushing, her hand covering her tingling lips, as the footman placed a tray on the sideboard and asked the duke if there was anything else he needed. Tarquin responded as coolly as if nothing untoward had happened in the last minutes. Juliana, vividly remembering the feel of his erection pushing so urgently against her couldn't believe he could sound so matter-of-fact. She was relatively hazy about male anatomy, but surely such a manifestation couldn't be comfortably ignored.

She jumped when his hand touched her shoulder. Spinning round, she saw that the room was now empty. Tarquin laughed at her startled expression. "*Mignonne,* you are delightful." He caressed her mouth with his forefinger. "I do believe we are going to enjoy ourselves."

"*No!*" she cried, finding her voice at last. "No. I won't let you do this to me." She flung herself away from him just as the door opened without ceremony.

"The footman said you were in here, Tarquin, I wanted . . . Oh, I do beg your pardon." Quentin's eyes ran over Juliana in one quick, all-encompassing assessment. "I didn't realize you had company," he said steadily. "Catlett should have told me."

"Allow me to present Miss Juliana Beresford, as she likes to be known." Tarquin took her hand, drawing her forward. "Juliana, this is my half brother, Lord Quentin Courtney. I'm sure you'll be getting to know him quite well."

Juliana was too flustered for a moment to do more than stare at the new arrival. Then she realized that he was bowing to her, and hastily she curtsied. "I give you good day, my lord."

Quentin surveyed her gravely, and she felt her blush deepen. She wondered if her lips were marked by the duke's kiss, if this man could detect something on her, something that would give away the shameless arousal that still pulsed in her belly. Was there an aura? A scent, perhaps? Unable to bear his gaze any longer, she turned away.

"Is it fair to the poor child to bring her here unchaperoned, Tarquin?" Quentin's voice was harshly reproving. "If she was seen on the street, her reputation will be compromised."

A flicker of hope sprang into Juliana's disordered mind. Perhaps in this mad world she had found a champion. "My lord, His Grace does not believe I have a reputation that could be compromised," she said in a low, plaintive voice. Slowly she turned and raised her eyes to the somber-suited man, noting the strong physical resemblance between the two men. "Are you perhaps a man of the cloth?" she asked, guessing from his dark, modestly cut coat and plain starched stock.

"I am, child." Quentin took a step toward her, but suddenly she flung herself to the floor at his feet, clasping his knees with a sob.

"Oh, sir, save me. Please, I beg you, don't let the duke have his wicked way with me." Ignoring the strange, strangled sound from the duke standing behind her, she burst into wrenching sobs.

"Oh, hush, child. Hush. Pray don't distress yourself so." Quentin bent to lift her to her feet. "Tarquin, this has got to stop! I won't permit this to go one step further." He stroked Juliana's bent head and handed her his handkerchief. "Dry your eyes, my dear. You have nothing to fear in this house."

Juliana took the handkerchief with a mumble and buried her face in the starched folds, every muscle strained to sense how the duke was reacting.

"Tarquin?" Quentin demanded. "You must let her go."

"Certainly."

Juliana's head shot up at this. She regretted it immediately when the duke caught her chin and turned her face toward him. "That was quite a performance, *mignonne*, I congratulate you. Real tears, too." He smudged the track of a tear on her cheek with his thumb. "Not many, but a respectable showing."

"Oh, you are loathsome!" she whispered, tugging her head free. "Let me go."

"But of course." He strode to the door and opened it. "You're free to go where you wish . . . except, of course, back to Russell Street. Mistress Dennison will have no incentive to continue to provide you with hospitality."

Juliana stared, uncomprehending. Was he really going to permit her to walk out of the house after everything that had been said?

"You may keep the clothes you have on your back, since the ones you arrived in appear to have been mislaid," he continued with an amiable smile that gave no hint of his inner uncertainty. Would she call his bluff? Or had he judged her correctly? Impulsive and yet far from irrational. Stubbornly defiant and yet clearheaded and intelligent.

Juliana looked down at her bronze silk gown, the fringe of the silk shawl. Where could she possibly go in such finery? She couldn't hire herself out as a servant dressed like this.

"Forgive me," he said gently, "but I grow weary holding the door for you."

Juliana walked past him, drawing her skirts aside. She marched down the stairs. The footman opened the door for her, and she stepped out into the street.

In the morning room Quentin turned on his half brother, rare anger snapping in his eyes. "How dare you treat her like that!"

"She's free to go. I won't keep her against her will. D'you care for sherry?"

"No," Quentin said shortly. "What's she to do now?"

"I really don't know." Tarquin poured himself a glass of

sherry. "She must have had a plan when she arrived in town. I imagine she'll put it into effect now."

Quentin went uneasily to the window, but it looked out over the back of the house, and he could see nothing of the street. "I'll go after her," he said. "Offer her money, at least. She's so young to be let loose on the city."

"My sentiments exactly, dear boy." Tarquin sipped his sherry, regarding his brother with narrowed eyes. "Far too young. And far too innocent."

"Gad, Tarquin, but you're a cold bastard," Quentin said as if he'd never spent three years in a seminary. "But if you'll do nothing for her, I will." He marched to the door just as it opened again.

Juliana stood there. Her eyes were on Tarquin. "Where am I to go?" she asked. "What am I to do?"

"Wherever and whatever you wish," he responded, but his voice had lost its hardness.

"You know what will happen to me. That's why you showed me all those things this morning, isn't it?" Her face was paler than ever, the dusting of freckles across the bridge of her nose standing out in harsh relief. Her eyes burned like green fire.

"My dear girl, you have no need to worry. I will give you some money and you can go home, back to your family." Quentin fumbled in his pockets.

Juliana shook her head. "Thank you, my lord. You are very kind, but you see I cannot go home, as the duke well knows. He also knows that I have no real choice but to do what His Grace demands."

Chapter 8

"Mistress Dennison asks that Your Grace would do 'er the honor of waitin' upon her." Mr. Garston bowed low, delivering this message as the Duke of Redmayne ushered Juliana into the hall at Russell Street half an hour later. "If you can spare the time, Your Grace."

"Certainly," Tarquin said. "I wish to speak with her anyway." He turned to Juliana. "Stay within doors. You'll be sent for shortly." He strode up the stairs without a backward glance.

"Looks like you and 'Is Grace 'ave come to some arrangement," Mr. Garston observed with a benign smile. "Lucky girl. A right proper gent is 'Is Grace. 'E'll see you right." He pinched her cheek. "Such a long face, missie. There's no call fer that. The other young ladies will be green with envy, you mark my words."

"Then I wish one of them would take my place," Juliana said wanly. She turned restlessly back to the front door, still open behind her.

"Now, now, missie. You 'eard what 'Is Grace said." Mr. Garston moved his large bulk with surprising speed to close the door. "Y'are to stay within doors till yer sent for."

Like a slave obeying her master, Juliana thought, still stunned by the magnitude of what she'd agreed to. She heard Emma's voice in the drawing room, followed by a giggle, and then a chorus of laughing voices.

They sounded so lighthearted. How could they accept this degrading servitude so cheerfully? Perhaps they could teach her a valuable lesson in resignation. Juliana went into the drawing room.

"Oh, Juliana, come and sit down." She was greeted with warmth and enthusiasm by the trio of women sitting heads together on the sofa, leafing through a pattern magazine. "You've been driving with the duke. Has he formalized his offer for you yet?"

"What do you mean . . . formalized?" Juliana perched on the arm of a chair.

"Oh, he has to make arrangements with the Dennisons. They draw up contracts if someone wants us exclusively," Rosamund explained. "Will you stay here, or will the duke set you up somewhere on your own? I don't think I'd like that myself, it would be so lonely." Her plump, pretty face beamed contentedly as she squeezed Emma's arm beside her.

"I am to marry the duke's cousin, Viscount Edgecombe," Juliana said flatly. She couldn't bring herself to tell them of the other half of the arrangement.

"Marriage!" gasped Emma. "Oh, my dear Juliana. How wonderful for you. You'll be set for life."

"So long as it's not a Fleet wedding," Lilly said darkly. "D'you remember Molly Petrie? She left Mother Needham's to marry Lord Liverton, only he took her to a marriage shop instead. And when he'd had enough of her, he threw her out with just the clothes on her back. And she ended up sleeping under the stalls in Covent Garden and taking anyone who'd give her a penny for gin."

"What's a Fleet wedding?" Juliana asked, curiosity finally penetrating her stunned trance.

"Oh, it's when they get an unfrocked preacher to perform the ceremony. There's marriage shops all around the Fleet," Lilly told her. "It's not a proper marriage, although sometimes the girl doesn't know it . . . like poor Molly."

"But that's dreadful!" Juliana exclaimed. "Wicked. It's evil to trick a woman like that."

Emma shrugged. "Of course it is. But men don't care. They do what they want. And there's not much any of us can do to stop 'em."

Juliana frowned fiercely, her straight brows almost meeting. "If you all got together and refused to be treated badly, then they'd have to change their behavior."

Lilly laughed indulgently. "My dear Juliana, don't be a simpleton. For every one of us who refused to give them what they wanted, there'd be half a dozen eager to take our place."

"It's not as if treating whores badly is a crime," Rosamund pointed out. "I mean, you couldn't go to a magistrate and lay a charge or anything."

"No, the magistrates are too busy persecuting us," Emma declared in disgust. "It's hard to earn any kind of a living if you're not in a respectable house. The others are always being raided, and the girls find themselves making a trip to Bridewell at the cart's arse."

Men and women whipped at the cart's tail through the streets of Winchester for vagrancy or disorderly behavior was a common enough sight, but Juliana had never expected to find herself in a world where such punishment was accepted as an occupational hazard. "I still think that if everyone protested, something would change."

"Brave talk, but you're new to the game, Juliana," Lilly said. "Wait for six months and see how brave you are then."

"If she's to be properly married to a viscount, she won't have to become accustomed," Rosamund pointed out. "But why is the duke procuring you for his cousin? It seems very peculiar."

"You'd best try to find out if this cousin wants anything special," Emma said. "Sometimes they have to have whores because respectable women won't do what they want. But he might want something bad . . . something hurtful. You want to be sure you know what you're getting into."

She couldn't tell these women that she was being black-mailed and that whatever the duke and his cousin wanted of her, she'd be obliged to provide. She couldn't tell them that all her brave protestations about making a stand and forcing a change in their conditions of service were so much posturing. She was as firmly caught as any one of them, with no more power to alter her destiny at this point than a pinned butterfly.

" 'Is Grace bids you join 'im and Mistress Dennison in the small salon, Miss Juliana," Mr. Garston spoke from the doorway.

Bids, not asks. Juliana rose. She had no choice but to do His Grace's bidding.

Outside the door to the small salon, she hesitated. She should knock. Then, with a little tilt of her chin, Juliana decided to make one small gesture. She threw open the door and stepped into the room.

"Oh, there you are, Juliana." Elizabeth looked startled.

"Not a surprise, madam, surely. I understood you had asked to see me."

Tarquin's lips twitched. Miss Juliana seemed to have re-covered her spirit. He stood up and came over to her. "Come and sit down, *mignonne*." Taking her hand, he brushed it with his lips, then deliberately and very lightly kissed her mouth.

It seemed a casual greeting, but Juliana understood it for what it was. A public statement of possession. A shiver ran up her spine, and she looked away.

"My dear, someone has been inquiring for you at the Bell," Mistress Dennison said. "Do you know who it could be?"

Juliana's blood ran cold. They had traced her to London. She shook her head.

"This gentleman seemed convinced you had come from Winchester, not York," the duke said gently. He raised an eyebrow as he met her gaze. "He described you rather accurately. But perhaps you have a twin somewhere."

"Don't play with me, my lord duke," Juliana said

fiercely. "I have no intention of denying that I got off the Winchester coach. What point would there be at this stage?"

"None whatsoever," he agreed, taking a seat opposite her. "So who would be searching for you . . . apart from the constables?"

"My guardian, Sir Brian Forsett, perhaps."

"I understand this was a young man," Elizabeth said. "Somewhat corpulent and a little . . . well, rustic, according to Mr. Bute."

"George," Juliana said flatly. "But why would he bother to find me? It's a case of good riddance, I would have thought. For everyone," she added almost in an undertone.

Tarquin's gaze sharpened, resting on her face. He watched the flicker of hurt in the green eyes, the momentary soft quiver of the full mouth. To his astonishment he wanted to take her in his arms and comfort her.

Only with one other woman had he had such an urge. Pamela Cartwright. How flattered he'd been when the beautiful Pamela had chosen him, a naive youth, over the sophisticated men-about-town, the wealthy roués, the powerful politicians, who clustered at her feet. And how long it had taken him to understand that she was interested only in his fortune. He'd bought every kiss, every caress, and convinced himself that she gave him love in return. He'd trusted her with his innermost feelings, had stripped himself bare for her, and she had trampled on his youthful passions, his burgeoning sensitivity.

But that was in the past, and he was no longer an idealistic young fool.

"Come, now," he said briskly. "You can't imagine that you can disappear off the face of the earth without some member of your family looking for you."

"I don't see why not," Juliana said. "My guardian and his wife were delighted to wash their hands of me. They'll be in no rush to find me, particularly when I'm supposed to be a murderess. They're more likely to disown me."

Her tone was matter-of-fact, but Tarquin saw the hurt

that still flickered in her eyes, still tremored slightly on her mouth, and he caught a glimpse of the lonely, unloved child she'd been.

"This George," Elizabeth prompted, bringing the duke sharply back to the issue at hand. "Is he a member of your family?"

"My husband's son," Juliana said. "Sir George, I suppose he is, now that John's dead. He probably wants to find me so he can get the marriage settlements back. He was furious at the conditions of my jointure."

"Ahh," said Tarquin. "Money. That's a powerful motivation. How clever is he, in your opinion?"

"Thick as a block," Juliana said. "But he's as vicious as a terrier when he gets an idea in his head. He won't let go."

"Well, I daresay we can put him off the scent," the duke declared. "As the wife of Viscount Edgecombe, you'll be beyond the reach of some country bumpkin."

"But not beyond the reach of the Duke of Redmayne," she flashed.

Tarquin regarded her wryly and in silence for a minute while she stared back at him, refusing to drop her eyes. Then he turned back to Elizabeth. "If you'd send for Mr. Copplethwaite, madam, we can complete the formalities. The sooner Juliana is established, the safer she will be."

"Established as what, might I ask?" To Juliana's annoyance her voice shook slightly. "Am I to be married by an unfrocked priest in a marriage shop?"

"Now, who could have put such an absurd and insulting idea in your head?" demanded Tarquin, genuinely startled.

"Such an ungrateful creature, she is," Elizabeth declared, glaring reproachfully at Juliana. "To be so ungracious when she's being offered such an opportunity."

"Oh, spare me your pious hypocrisies, madam!" Juliana leaped to her feet. "I am being compelled into prostitution, so pray let us call a spade a spade." She spun on her heel and stalked to the door. Unfortunately, the dramatic effect of her exit was somewhat diminished when her skirt caught in the door as she slammed it behind her and she was obliged to open it again to release herself.

The Duke of Redmayne took a leisurely pinch of snuff. "I foresee a somewhat turbulent few months," he observed. "But I expect I shall find it interesting, at the very least." He rose to his feet. "I'll return this evening. I don't wish Juliana to keep company with the other girls today, I'm inclined to think she's listened enough to their tales and gossip. She should keep to her chamber for the rest of the day. I would find her there alone when I come."

"And the lawyer, sir?" Elizabeth walked to the door with him.

"Instruct Copplethwaite to call upon me in Albermarle Street as soon as the contracts have been drawn up to your satisfaction," he said. "I will then procure a special license. The marriage should take place without delay. . . . Oh, and reassure the child about the marriage, will you? I won't have her believing I would play her false."

"I cannot imagine how she could have thought such a thing." Elizabeth curtsied at the door.

"Neither can I," he responded aridly. "Good day, ma'am." He bowed and strode down the stairs, leaving Elizabeth at the top, looking both thoughtful and annoyed, before she turned and made her way upstairs to Juliana's chamber.

Juliana had discarded her hoop and was struggling with the laces of her corset when Mistress Dennison entered. "You should summon Bella to help you," Elizabeth said.

"I am accustomed to looking after myself," Juliana responded, gyrating impatiently as she tugged at a recalcitrant knot. It came undone, and with a sigh of relief she pulled the garment from her, tossing it onto the bed. "Did you wish to speak with me, ma'am?"

"His Grace bids you remain in your chamber," Elizabeth said.

Juliana sat on the bed in her shift and underpetticoat. "Why?"

"His Grace was most distressed that you should have

heard tales of the marriage shops," Mistress Dennison said. "He prefers that you hear no more of such nonsense."

"Oh?" Juliana raised an eyebrow. "So it's nonsense, is it, ma'am? They were making it up?"

"No," Elizabeth responded. "It does happen, but girls who form contracts from this house are in no danger of such a deception. And His Grace of Redmayne is a man of honor."

"Pshaw!" Juliana declared disgustedly. "What he's proposing is hardly *honorable*, ma'am."

"Oh, I despair of you, girl." Elizabeth threw up her hands. "I won't argue with you further. Do I have your word that you'll remain in this room until His Grace returns? Or must I turn the key?"

"I'll not leave," Juliana said, falling back onto the bed and closing her eyes. "It makes no difference to me whether you lock me in or not. I'm a prisoner either way."

Elizabeth snorted and marched out, closing the door with a snap behind her.

As she lay on the bed, Juliana conjured up the image of the Duke of Redmayne. He was a powerful man, one clearly accustomed to getting his own way in everything. And he'd made it clear from the very beginning that he intended to have his own way in this.

She wondered how she would have reacted if he'd put the proposition to her in another way. If he'd *asked* her if she'd agree to it instead of threatening blackmail from the first moment.

If it had been put to her differently, she might have found the proposition almost enticing. If it had been suggested as a partnership that benefited them both, she might well have considered it. It could be no worse a fate than lying night after night beneath John Ridge, bearing his children. . . .

Unconsciously, she moved her hands over her body outlined beneath the thin shift. That strange effervescence was coursing through her again. A jubilant, exhilarated sense of anticipation. The Duke of Redmayne was an arrogant tyrant, but when he touched her, her body took off on some weird flight of fancy over which her mind had no control. She could enjoy that, if she decided to. She could enjoy the Duke of Redmayne, if she decided to. But she didn't have to let him know that.

A slow smile curved her mouth.

After Juliana's solitary dinner Bella came in, her habitual beam on her round face. "Mistress sent ye up a right pretty chamber robe, miss." She shook out the delicate cambric folds of a white lace-trimmed wrapper. "Shall you put it on?"

Juliana took the garment from her. It was an exquisite froth of lace and ruffles, embroidered with tiny cream daisies. Another of the duke's sartorial inspirations?

"It's for when the duke visits ye," Bella said, confirming this unspoken assumption. "I'm to 'elp you get ready for 'im."

"Now?" Despite her earlier resolutions, Juliana's blood began to speed and her heart banged against her ribs. It was too soon. She wasn't prepared.

" 'Is Grace will be along after tea," Bella said. "Mistress said as 'ow I was to show ye about perfume an' what kind of refreshments the gentlemen like." She put a small vial on the dresser. "We jest dabs this be'ind yer ears, and knees, an' between yer breasts. Some gentlemen care fer it in other places, too, but I daresay 'Is Grace will tell you what 'e wants. They usually does." She smiled and nodded reassuringly. "Miss Rosamund 'ad a gentleman once what liked it between 'er toes. He liked to suck 'em." Bella giggled. "She said it tickled summat chronic. But she couldn't laugh in case 'e got upset."

Bella matter-of-factly began to remove Juliana's shift and petticoat. Juliana was for the moment speechless as she absorbed the maid's informative chatter. She'd heard similar discussions about adorning a prize pig for auction at the summer fair.

"I wonder if'n we should put a little rouge on yer nipples," Bella mused. "I don't know as 'ow 'Is Grace would like it. Lots of 'em do." She poured hot water into the basin and dipped a washcloth in. "I'll jest wash ye a bit. Freshen ye up a bit. Very fussy Mistress Dennison is about cleanliness in this 'ouse. We don't 'ave no need of mercury treatments or Dr. Leakey's pills 'ere."

"What are they for?" Juliana was prompted out of her stunned silence by this.

"For the clap a'course," Bella said in surprise. "Don't ye know about the pox?"

"Not intimately," Juliana said aridly. "But I imagine it's an occupational hazard, like the cart's arse and Bridewell."

The sarcasm missed Bella completely as she plied the washcloth over Juliana's naked body. "Oh, our ladies don't worry about that, miss," she said. "This is a respectable 'ouse. Only the best customers and the freshest pieces. We don't dabble in the market. Don't get no raids 'ere."

"You relieve my mind." Juliana gave herself up to Bella's attentions. The girl clearly knew what she was about when it came to preparing a harlot for a customer. She patted Juliana dry, then dabbed perfume behind her ears, at her throat, on her wrists, and behind her knees.

"What about the rouge, then, miss?" Bella opened an alabaster pot and dipped a finger in. "Jest a touch." Her finger approached Juliana's breast.

Juliana jumped back. "No," she said, revolted. "There are some things I'll endure, but that's not one of them."

Bella looked disappointed, but she wiped her finger clean on the washcloth. "What about paintin' yer toenails? Lots of the gentlemen likes that."

"No," Juliana declared. "No paint, no powder, no rouge. Just pass me that robe."

Bella hastened to fetch the chamber robe and slipped it over Juliana's shoulders. It fell in soft folds to her bare feet, caressing her sweetly fragrant skin. Bella fastened the fringed embroidered girdle at her waist and adjusted the high ruffled neckline.

"Oh, that's so demure, miss," she said in awe. "Doesn't show nothin' of you at all. I wonder what 'Is Grace fancies, then? Some men like the girls to dress as schoolgirls . . . and that Lord Tartleton likes 'em dressed like a nun." She shook her head wisely. "None so strange as gentlemen."

Juliana examined herself in the mirror. *Demure* was certainly the word, and yet not quite. The material was so fine that her skin glowed pink beneath, and when she moved, the gown flowed over her, revealing the shapes and shadows of her body. It was a most seductive garment.

Lord of hell, she was beginning to think like a whore! She took several steps around the room, feeling the sensuous swish of the robe, inhaling her scent as her skin warmed the fragrance. A bud of excitement grew in her belly, little rivulets of fire darting into her loins.

"Yer 'air, miss." Bella flourished the hairbrush. "I'll brush it fer you."

Juliana sat down on the ottoman, her head drooping beneath Bella's strong, rhythmic strokes. Her hair crackled, springing out from beneath the brush with a life of its own. It seemed to fill the room with color. She watched in the mirror as the candle's glow caught each vibrant strand.

"Will I thread the ribbon through it?" Bella laid down the brush and took up an ivory silk ribbon. Juliana nodded. She hadn't the will to make small, pointless gestures of independence tonight. They could prepare her for the duke's bed however they thought best. She had enough to do with mental preparation.

She watched as Bella fastened the ribbon around her forehead so that her hair was caught and held at the top but poured out in a river of fire beneath, framing her face and cascading onto the white cambric of her robe. "I look like some virgin shepherdess," she murmured. For some reason the thought set her eyes alight with the excitement that was blooming in her belly.

"All innocent like," Bella agreed. "I expect that's what 'Is Grace fancies this evening."

"Do the gentlemen always make their preferences known beforehand?"

"Not always." Bella began to tidy up the dresser. "Sometimes the ladies 'ave to change all of a sudden like, if a gentleman 'as a change of fancy. I 'elps them, then. Me an' Minnie." She gathered up the basin, ewer, and washcloth. "I'll get rid of these, miss. Then I'll bring in the refreshments."

Juliana went to the window after the maid had bustled out. Dusk was falling, and the riotous sounds from the Piazza came clear on the still and sultry air. There was music, a fife and drums, rising above the general cacophony. In the street below a blind harpist sat on a box, plucking his strings mournfully in competition with a shoeblack who was hailing potential customers in a shrill singsong.

She was watching for the Duke of Redmayne. But even as she watched, she wondered if perhaps he was already in the house. The door knocker had been sounding for the last hour, and the customary evening buzz was in the air. Hurried footsteps, giggles, rushed whispers, came from outside her door as the girls returned to their chambers for some minor repair. She hadn't yet heard a male voice, but presumably they were still drinking tea and conversing in the drawing room as if this mansion on Russell Street was a conventional, fashionable household.

" 'Ere we are, then." Bella staggered in under the weight of a laden tray. She was followed by a flunky bearing a tray with bottles and glasses. He set the tray on a low table before the empty grate and studiously avoided looking at Juliana in her robe of seduction. Presumably that was a rule of the house, she thought. He turned and left, again without acknowledgment, and Bella began to lay out covered dishes on the table.

"Now, 'Is Grace is partial to the claret," she instructed. "It's the right year, Mr. Garston says, so we won't 'ave to worry about that. Now, there's lemonade for you. The girls don't usually drink when they 'ave a gentleman. But there's a wine glass if the duke wants ye to join 'im." She examined the table, tapping her finger against her teeth. "Now, there's lobster patties, an' a little salad of sparrow-grass. 'Is Grace is right partial to sparrowgrass, dressed with a little oil an' vinegar."

Juliana was not particularly fond of asparagus, and lobster brought her out in spots, but of course her own wishes were of no importance. There was also a bowl of strawberries and a basket of sweetmeats that in other circumstances might have enticed her; however, she was feeling too sick with nerves to contemplate eating anything.

"Now, is that everything?" Bella counted on her fingers as she inspected the room in minute detail. "There's fresh 'ot water in the jug on the washstand. Should I turn down the bed, or will ye do it, miss? It's 'ard to know what'd be best. Some gentlemen likes to feel that they're bein' seduced and don't want to come into the room and see it all ready, like. But others don't care to waste time."

"Leave it as it is," Juliana said, knowing that she could not sit and wait for the duke beside a turned-down bed.

"Right y'are then." Bella took one last look at Juliana, made a final adjustment to a ruffle at the sleeve of the white robe, then dropped a little curtsy. "If ye needs anythin', miss, jest pull the bell. I'll knock 'afore I comes in."

"Thank you, Bella." Juliana managed a smile.

"A'course I'll come to ye as soon as 'Is Grace leaves." The girl stood with her hand on the door. "Ye'll be wantin' a salt bath then, I daresay, bein' a maid an' all. An' I expect ye'll be glad of a mug of 'ot milk an' rum." With a quick smile she whisked herself out of the room, closing the door behind her.

Juliana stood in the middle of the chamber, arms crossed convulsively over her breasts. A salt bath! So matter-of-fact. How many virgins had Bella prepared for the loss of their maidenheads? And then it occurred to her that losing one's virginity in this knowledgeable, comforting, female-centered house was infinitely preferable to being bedded to Sir John Ridge, carried to the bridal chamber amid a chorus of obscene jokes from drunken male wedding guests who had abandoned her to her fate at the chamber door. She'd known very little about what was in store for her. Lady Forsett had not thought fit to prepare her husband's ward for her wedding night. She knew a little more now, but not much.

The door opened as she stood there. Her hands fell to her sides, sweat trickling down her rib cage. The Duke of Redmayne quietly closed the door behind him. He turned to Juliana. His gray gaze held hers for a minute in the charged silence, then drifted slowly down her body. He smiled and stepped lightly toward her.

Chapter 9

G ood," Tarquin said, taking her hands. "I'm glad to
see you're not using paint or rouge. I forgot to tell
Mistress Dennison that I don't care for it . . . or
at least," he added, "not on you." He stepped away from
her, still holding her hands, and scrutinized her appearance
again.

"You're very specific about your preferences, my lord
duke." Juliana's voice was low and flat as she tried to hide
the rush of heat that suffused her skin at his narrow-eyed
inspection.

"No more than most men," he said carelessly. "My preferences change from time to time, as I'm sure you'll discover."

"I trust I'll learn my duties quickly enough to please
you, my lord duke." She dropped her eyes, knowing that
they were blazing with impotent fury.

Tarquin caught her chin between finger and thumb and
obliged her to lift her face. He chuckled. "You look ready
to consign me to the fires of hell, *mignonne*."

"Unfortunately, I have no pitchfork," she snapped, unable to resist.

"Did I offend you? I beg your pardon," he said with
such an abrupt change of tone and manner that Juliana was

completely thrown off balance. And before she could recover herself, he had kissed her. A delicate, featherlike
brush of his lips on hers that brought goose bumps pricking
on her skin.

"I can be a little imperious on occasion," Tarquin said
gravely, caressing her cheek with a fingertip. "It's a consequence of my upbringing, I'm afraid. But I give you leave
to take me to task at the right moment."

"And when would that be?"

"Times such as this. When we're private and engaged
in . . . ." He raised a quizzical eyebrow. "In intimate conversation." He continued to stroke her cheek, and insensi-
bly she began to relax, the lines of her face softening, her
mouth parting, her eyes losing their fierceness.

When he felt the change in her, Tarquin released her
chin with a smile. He left her in the middle of the room
and went to pour himself a glass of wine. "Do you care for
claret, Juliana?"

"Yes, please." Maybe the members of the Dennisons'
seraglio *were* supposed to eschew alcohol during their
working hours, but Juliana felt the need of Dutch courage.
She took the glass he handed her and gulped down the
contents.

With a slight frown, Tarquin took the empty glass from
her and placed it on the table. "Are you frightened, *mignonne?*"

"No." But her hands were twisting themselves into impossible knots against the skirt of the robe.

He leaned back against the table, sipping his claret, his
eyes seeing right through the brave denial. "Tell me what
happened on your wedding night."

Juliana blinked. "You mean apart from nearly suffocating
and then hitting my husband with a hot warming pan and
killing him?"

"Yes, apart from that."

"Why do you wish to know?"

"I would like to understand certain things," he said.

"Did your husband touch you in the ways of love? Did he arouse you in any way?"

Juliana just shook her head. Sir John had simply fallen upon her on the bed.

"Were you naked?"

She nodded.

"So you know what a man's body feels like? You know what it looks like?" He was asking the questions with an almost clinical detachment.

"I know what it feels like to be almost suffocated," she declared. In truth she could remember little else of that dreadful half hour. John's body had been a great mass of sweating flesh pressing her into the bed, striving and struggling to do something that she knew he hadn't succeeded in doing.

Tarquin nodded. "Then let's assume that you know nothing at all." He set his glass down and hooked the ottoman toward him with one foot. Sitting down, he beckoned her.

Juliana approached tentatively.

The duke drew her between his knees and, with a leisurely movement, untied the girdle at her waist. The robe fell open, and he drew the sides farther apart so he could look upon her body. Juliana shivered. He put his hands on her. They were warm and hard and assured. She stood, his knees pressing against her thighs, her skin alternately hot and icy cold as his hands moved over her hips; his thumbs traced the sharp outline of her hipbones; his breath was warm on her belly. His hands spanned her waist, slipped up over her rib cage, gently cupped her breasts.

When he bent his head and took her nipple into his mouth, Juliana's body became a battleground of sensation, the urge to yield to the glorious liquid warmth seeping through her veins striving against a panicked instinct not to submit, because in doing so she would lose some part of her self.

Her eyes caught her reflection in the mirror. She gazed at her white body, the curve of her breasts and belly, framed in the delicate froth of her robe. The candlelight caught auburn glints in the bent head against the whiteness of her breast. And then his hands moved on her, slipped slowly over her belly. She watched, in a trance, as her eyes grew heavy and glowing, her skin flushed; her lips, moist and pink, parted on a swift breath as he touched her, opened her. It was as if she were watching some other woman, some other man; watching the woman dissolve with the exquisite pleasure that built deep in the pit of her stomach. She was watching, and yet it was she who was dissolving. From her own lips came the little sobbing cries of wonder. It was her own eyes that grew huge as they stared back at her, the irises black and glowing in the jade depths; then her mirror image was engulfed in the rushing climactic wave that filled every pore of her body, so that her eyes closed and her knees turned to honey.

Tarquin drew her down onto his lap as she fell against him. He held her lightly, stroking her hair. His loins were heavy with his own desire as she shifted on his knee and he inhaled the delicate fragrance of the perfume she wore mingled with the rich scents of her fulfillment.

"Come." He lifted her into his arms, reflecting a little wryly that one wouldn't want to carry this luscious body any great distance. He laid her on the bed and stood looking down at her. Her eyes were still dazed, her skin still flushed.

Juliana closed her eyes abruptly. How had it happened? How had she lost herself so completely?

"Open your eyes, Juliana."

She obeyed the soft command almost involuntarily. Tarquin removed his coat and began unbuttoning his waistcoat.

Juliana sat up. She gazed now with candid curiosity as he removed his clothes, every movement orderly and efficient. As he doffed each rich garment, he laid it over the chair. Her eyes widened as he took off the fine cambric shirt. But she had little time to become accustomed to his naked torso before he had pushed off his britches and drawers.

Juliana's breath caught in her throat as she stared at him, realizing helplessly that she was examining him as carefully as he'd scrutinized her when he had opened her robe.

Naked, the Duke of Redmayne was lean and sinewy, muscles rippling beneath taut, smooth skin. He was slim-hipped and broad-shouldered, a line of dark hair creeping over his belly to join the wiry tangle at the apex of his long thighs. Her gaze fixed upon his shaft of flesh, and she remembered feeling it pulsing against her belly when he'd kissed her in the morning room of his house on Albermarle Street.

"Well, ma'am?" He was smiling at the frank curiosity and excitement in her eyes. "Do I please you?"

She wanted him to turn around so she could see his back view, but she couldn't quite manage to ask. She nodded in silence.

As if he had read her mind, he slowly turned his back. Impulsively, Juliana leaned forward and touched his buttocks. The hard muscles tightened at her caress, and she rose to her knees, running a finger up from the cleft, flickering in the path of fine dark hair trailing up his spine. "You feel very different from me."

"Thank the merciful Lord," he said, turning back to her. Leaning over, he slipped his hands to her shoulders beneath the opened robe and pushed the garment from her. "Now, we meet on equal terms, *mignonne*." He twitched the robe from beneath her and tossed it to the floor before coming down onto the bed.

His hand passed over her in a leisurely caress that nevertheless insisted that she lie back. Juliana was both curious and excited. She felt no apprehension, and she'd lost all thought of what had brought them there. Instinctively, she reached to touch his erection, clasping the flesh in her hand as he leaned over her. The corded veins pulsed strongly against her palm, and her finger found the dampening tip. Tarquin murmured something, but Juliana knew that what she was doing was right. Her own excitement grew as she caressed him, feeling him flicker and harden against her hand. She looked up into his face and saw that he, too, was transported, as she had been. That he was lost in his own pleasure, as she'd seen herself in the mirror. Again instinctively, she increased the pressure of her caresses until abruptly Tarquin grasped her wrist and jerked it away from him.

"Enough," he said hoarsely.

"But why? I know you were enjoying it."

"You still have a few things to learn, *mignonne*." He laughed softly as his knee pressed her legs apart.

Juliana parted her thighs. Her hips lifted of their own accord as he slid into her moist, open body. For a moment the stretching fullness in her loins was almost unbearable. She stared wide-eyed into the steady gray eyes holding her gaze.

"Try to relax, Juliana. It'll ease in a minute." He drew back a fraction, then thrust deeply. Her body seemed to split apart, and she heard her own cry of pain. Then everything was smooth and even, and her body was responding to the strong, rhythmic thrusts of his flesh, and the tension that built now was of the most blissful kind. And when it exploded, Juliana dissolved yet again into a scatter of shooting stars.

His body rested heavily on hers, their sweat mingling. Juliana stroked his back as she floated down to earth and took possession of her self again. She could feel him still within her, growing smaller, and a wave of pleasure washed gently through her with the sense that he remained a part of her. Instinctively, she tightened her inner muscles around him and felt the flicker as his flesh responded.

Tarquin kissed the hollow of her throat. "Have patience," he said with a lazy chuckle. He disengaged slowly and rolled away from her. Juliana made a soft murmur of protest at the loss and followed him with her body, curling against him in blissful languor.

Tarquin pushed an arm beneath so her head rested on his shoulder. He caressed her breast, feeling her slide into a light sleep. He lay listening to her breathing, his own eyelids drooping in the candle glow. He hadn't expected such a passionate and trusting response. He'd expected to arouse her; he'd intended to make the loss of her maidenhead as painless as possible. He'd expected to enjoy her as much as he enjoyed most women. He had not expected to be moved by her. But her fresh innocence combined with that lusty, uninhibited passion stirred him. She had every reason to mistrust him, to hold herself back from him, and yet she'd ridden the wave of pleasure with a wonderful candor, giving herself to him and to sexual joy without reservation.

As he held her in his arms, he had the sense that he had found something to cherish. It was a strange, fanciful idea, and he wasn't sure where it had come from. Except that he'd given himself once with such joyful trust and he'd been betrayed. Juliana would not experience such betrayal at his hands.

Juliana stirred and awoke. She burrowed against him with a little murmur of pleasure. "How long was I asleep?"

"About five minutes." He stroked down her back and patted her bottom before extricating himself and sliding off the bed. "Wine, *mignonne*?"

"Yes, please." Juliana stretched and sat up. Blood smudged the long, creamy length of her thigh. She hopped off the bed with a little exclamation. "We should have pulled back the coverlet."

Tarquin turned from the table with a glass of wine. He smiled at her worried domestic frown as she examined the heavy damask for stains. He put down the glass and filled the basin on the washstand with warm water from the ewer. "Come, let me make you more comfortable," he invited, wringing out a washcloth.

Suddenly shy, Juliana approached him hesitantly. She reached to take the cloth from him, but he said, "Let me do it for you."

He gently nudged her thighs apart and Juliana submitted to his deft, intimate attentions, her awkwardness fading when she realized that he was enjoying what he was doing to her. That he was making of the simple cleansing a delicately arousing ritual.

Her eyes were heavy when he straightened and tossed the washcloth back into the basin. "That wasn't so bad, was it, now?" he teased, kissing her mouth.

"I feel most peculiar," Juliana confided matter-of-factly. "As if I've lost touch with the ground."

"Perhaps a little supper will bring you back to reality." Tarquin opened the armoire and drew out a man's velvet chamber robe. He shrugged into it and picked up Juliana's wrapper from the floor. "Put this on again for a little while."

Juliana took it. "A little while" seemed promising. Vaguely, she wondered how long his own robe had been hanging in her armoire. Equally vaguely, she wondered how he'd known it would be there. She took the glass of wine he handed her.

She shook her head when he offered lobster and asparagus but nibbled on a candied fruit, sipping her wine, watching him eat.

"I suppose we should make haste with the marriage ceremony," she said after a minute or two. "If I've conceived, it might be awkward to explain a premature infant."

Tarquin looked up from his supper with a quick frown. "There's no need to discuss that tonight, Juliana."

"But since it's the object of the exercise . . ." She didn't know why she was bringing it up now. It had immediately cast a pall over her rosy glow. But she couldn't seem to stop herself. "I beg your pardon, my lord duke." She sketched a curtsy. "It was very clumsy of me to bring it up. I daresay it's because I'm inexperienced in the art of pleasing men. When I've become more accustomed to life in a bawdy house, I'm certain I won't offend again."

The duke stared at her for a moment; then he chuckled. "What a provoking child you are," he said. "Have another sweetmeat." He passed her the basket.

Juliana hesitated; then, with a tiny shrug, she took a sugared almond and sat down on the chaise longue.

Tarquin's brief nod indicated approval, and he returned to his lobster. "As it happens, I believe we should proceed with the marriage ceremony with all speed," he observed, dabbing his mouth with his napkin. "In my waistcoat pocket you'll find something that might interest you."

Juliana went to the chair where his clothes still lay. She felt in the pocket of his waistcoat and drew out a piece of folded parchment. "What is it?"

"Take a look." He leaned back in his chair, sipping his wine, regarding her closely as she unfolded the paper.

"Oh? It's me!"

"That was the conclusion I came to."

Juliana stared at the poster. There was an artist's likeness of her . . . somewhat crude but accurate enough. The physical description, however, was minute and unmistakable, right down to the freckles on her nose. She glanced up at the mirror, comparing herself with the likeness and the description. Her hair and eyes were the giveaway.

"Where did you find this?"

"They're posted all over town." He selected an asparagus spear with his fingers and lifted it to his mouth.

Juliana read the description of her crime. *Wanted for the murder of her husband: Juliana Ridge of the village of Ashford in Hampshire. Substantial reward offered for any information, however small. Contact Sir George Ridge at the Gardener's Arms in Cheapside.*

"I wonder how much he's offering," she mused, initially more intrigued than alarmed by this evidence of George's pursuit.

The duke shook his head. "Whatever it is, you're not safe outside this house until you're beyond the reach of that country bumpkin. So once the contracts have been drawn up with Copplethwaite, I'll procure a special license. It should all be over by the end of the week."

"I see. And what will I think of your cousin?" Juliana still stood by the chair, still holding the poster.

"You'll undoubtedly dislike him heartily." He refilled his wineglass. "But you need have nothing to do with him in private. You will both lodge in my house in separate quarters. Lucien will leave you strictly alone."

"And once I've conceived, I imagine that will apply to you too, my lord duke?"

"That will depend on you," he snapped. He tossed his napkin to the table and stood up, not sure why her question disturbed him; it was, after all, a perfectly fair question. "It seems not impossible that I might set you up as my mistress after Lucien's death. It would be easy enough to arrange discreetly. My cousin's widow with a child in my wardship would have a natural claim upon my attention and protection."

"I see. A duke's established mistress. I'll be the envy of every courtesan in town, my lord."

"I'll bandy words with you no longer." He strode to his clothes on the chair.

"But can't you understand!" Juliana cried passionately. "Can't you try to understand what I feel?"

Tarquin paused in his dressing and turned to look at her flushed face framed in the flaming halo of her hair, the jade eyes expressing an almost desperate frustration. "I suppose I can," he said eventually. "If you can try to trust in me. I mean you no harm. Quite the opposite."

He dressed swiftly in the silence his words produced, then came over to her and kissed her. He kissed the corners of her mouth, the tip of her nose, and her brow. "There were a few moments this evening when you *didn't* wish to consign me to Lucifer's fires, weren't there?"

Juliana nodded. "Don't go," she said, suddenly sure of one thing she wanted.

"It's best if I do."

Juliana said nothing further, and he left her immediately. She took a sip of her neglected wine. Apparently she was not to have disagreeable arguments or unsettling opinions, or to ask provoking questions. Clearly His Grace of Redmayne didn't like that in a woman. In which case he'd picked the wrong woman for his schemes; she wasn't about to curb her own nature just to fit the duke's image of a suitable mistress.

Lord of hell! She was a mistress. A duke's mistress! The realization hit her for the first time. Abruptly she sat on the bed, aware of every inch of her sensitized skin, the vague soreness between her legs, the utterly pleasurable sense of having been used, filled, fulfilled. Did whores enjoy their work? Did they retire every morning filled with this wonderful, languid bodily joy? Somehow Juliana didn't think so. Did wives feel it? She knew with absolute certainty that the wife of John Ridge wouldn't have. If John hadn't died in the midst of his huffing and puffing, she would be his wedded, bedded wife, condemned never to know the glories that she'd just shared with the Duke of Redmayne.

So what did it all mean? That she should accept with a glad heart the hand fate had dealt her? Count her blessings and embrace the duke with cries of joy?

Oh, no! That was not the way it was going to be. She'd find a way to enjoy the benefits of this liaison while giving the duke a serious run for his money.

Juliana reached for the bellpull to summon Bella, her mind seething with energy, quite at odds with her body's languor.

Chapter 10

❧❦

Lawyer Copplethwaite was a small, round man whose waistcoat strained over an ample belly. He had a worried air and his wig was askew, revealing a polished bald pate that he scratched nervously.

"Mistress Ridge." He bowed as Juliana entered Mistress Dennison's parlor in response to a summons the following morning. His eyes darted around the room, looking everywhere but directly at her. In fact, he seemed thoroughly ill at ease. He appeared such an unlikely frequenter of a whorehouse that Juliana assumed his discomfort arose from his present surroundings.

She curtsied demurely to the lawyer, then to Elizabeth, who was seated on a sofa beneath the open window, a sheaf of papers in her lap.

"Good morning, *mignonne*." The duke, clad in a suit of dark-red silk edged with silver lace, moved away from the mantel and came over to her. Juliana hadn't been sure how she would greet him after the previous evening. They hadn't parted bad friends, but neither had they parted intimate lovers. Now she covertly examined his expression and saw both a glint of humor in his eyes, and very clear pleasure as he smiled at her.

On a mischievous impulse she curtsied low with an exaggerated air of humility. Tarquin took her hand and kissed it as he raised her. "I may be a duke, my dear, but I don't warrant the depth you would accord a royal prince," he instructed gravely. "Delighted though I am to see such a sweetly submissive salutation." The amusement in his eyes deepened, and she couldn't help a responding grin. She was going to have to get up very early in the morning to best the Duke of Redmayne in these little games.

"I trust you slept well," he said, drawing her farther into the room.

"I never have difficulty sleeping," she said meekly.

He merely raised an eyebrow and drew a chair forward. "Pray sit down. Mr. Copplethwaite is going to read that part of the contracts that concerns you."

The lawyer cleared his throat diffidently. "If I may, madam."

"Yes, of course." Elizabeth handed him the sheaf of papers. There was a moment's silence, disturbed only by the rustling of paper as the lawyer selected the relevant documents. Then he cleared his throat again and began to read.

There were a series of clauses, all very simple, all very much as had been explained to Juliana already. She listened attentively, and most particularly to the clause that concerned her possible failure to conceive within the lifetime of the present Viscount Edgecombe. The lawyer blushed a little as he read this and scratched his head so vigorously, his wig slipped sideways and was in danger of sliding right off its shiny surface.

Juliana tried to keep her own expression impassive as she listened. If she failed to conceive in the viscount's lifetime she would receive a reasonably generous pension on her husband's death. If she did give the duke the child he wanted, then she would receive a large stipend, and she and the child would be housed under the duke's roof until the child's majority. His Grace of Redmayne would be the child's sole guardian and the sole arbiter of his existence. His mother would have all the natural rights of motherhood and would be consulted on decisions concerning the child, but the duke's decision would always be final.

It was perfectly normal, of course. In law children belonged to their fathers, not to their mothers. Nevertheless, Juliana didn't like this cold laying out of her own lack of rights over the life of this putative infant.

"And if the child is female?"

"The same," the duke said. "There is no male entail on the estate. The title will go to Lucien's cousin, Godfrey, but there is nothing to prevent a daughter from inheriting the fortune and the property."

"And, of course, it's the property that concerns you?"

"Precisely."

Juliana nibbled her bottom lip, then turned to the lawyer. "Is that all, sir?"

"All that concerns you, Mistress Ridge."

"You can't tell me how much Mistress Dennison sold me for?" she inquired with an air of wide-eyed innocence. "I should dearly like to know how much I was worth."

The lawyer choked, loosened his collar, choked again. Elizabeth said reprovingly, "There's no need to embarrass Mr. Copplethwaite, Juliana."

"I should think he's accustomed to such questions by now," Juliana replied. "He must have drawn up enough such contracts in his time."

"Three thousand guineas," the duke said casually. "Quite a handsome sum, I think you'll agree." His eyes flickered across her face and then very deliberately over her body.

Juliana curtsied again. "I'm deeply flattered, my lord duke. I trust you won't be disappointed in your investment."

Tarquin smiled. "I think that most unlikely, *mignonne*."

"I don't imagine George is offering such a sum," Juliana mused. "It seems I must be more valuable to you, sir, than to my stepson. And, of course, I go only to the highest bidder."

His eyes flashed a warning. "Put up your sword, Juliana. I'm a more experienced fencer than you."

"If you'd care to sign the papers, Mistress Ridge . . . ?" The lawyer's tactful question broke the awkward moment.

"Whether I care to or not seems irrelevant, sir," Juliana stated acidly, getting to her feet. "Only His Grace's wishes are relevant here."

"Now, now, Juliana, there's no need for impertinence." Elizabeth rose in a swirl of pale silk and billowed across to the secretaire. "Come to the desk. Mr. Copplethwaite, would you bring the documents over here? Thank you. Now, the quill is nice and sharp." She handed Juliana a pen. "There is blue and black ink in the double standish. Whichever you prefer."

Mistress Dennison was clearly anxious to have the business over and done with, signed, sealed, and delivered. She hovered over Juliana, who very deliberately read through every clause before affixing her signature at the bottom of each page. What was she signing away? Her life? Her future? She was committing herself to a destiny laid down for her by these strangers into whose midst she'd dropped like manna from heaven.

A candle stood ready-lit to provide the wax for the seal. Lawyer Copplethwaite punctiliously dripped wax onto the bottom of the page, then impressed his own seal ring to witness her signature. "There, ma'am. I believe that's as right and tight as a document could be." Fussily, he aligned the edges of the sheets, an anxious frown beetling his brow. "If you're satisfied, Your Grace."

"Perfectly, I thank you. However, I have one final task for you, Copplethwaite."

"Yes, Your Grace." The man's worried frown grew more pronounced. "Anything, of course."

"I wish you to witness a marriage," the duke said as casually as if he were proposing a game of whist. "Between Mistress Ridge and Viscount Edgecombe. It's to take place at St. James's, Marylebone, in two hours. I could take you up in my carriage, if you wished."

"But you said the end of the week!" Juliana protested, shocked. "You said you would procure the license after the contracts had been signed, and it would be done at the end of the week."

"I was able to accelerate matters," he said. "I had thought it in your best interests . . . in the circumstances. Do you object?"

Juliana took a deep breath. "No, I have no objection. It makes little difference when it happens."

"I knew you were a sensible girl," Elizabeth approved briskly. "Let's go to your chamber and make you ready. His Grace has selected a most beautiful bridal gown."

She'd accepted his proposition a mere two days ago! But Juliana was becoming accustomed to the duke's ability to make things happen faster than it would seem possible.

It *was* a beautiful gown. A cream silk dress, opening over a white embroidered petticoat. For half an hour Bella fussed around her, tucking and adjusting at Elizabeth's sharp-eyed direction. She plaited Juliana's hair around her head in a severely restrained coronet before throwing a froth of gauzy lace over her head.

Juliana examined herself in the mirror through the shifting gossamer of the veil and thought of the wedding gown Lady Forsett had had made for her. Juliana had thought it pretty, but compared with this, it had been a dull and dowdy garment, ill fitting at the waist, with a barely existent hoop. The veil had been heavy, clipped to her hair with a hundred painfully tight pins.

She was to be married twice in ten days. The first ceremony had had its farcical elements, but this one was a charade to challenge reason. Juliana adjusted the veil, flicked at the lace ruffles at her elbows, and turned to the door. "Do you accompany me, ma'am? Or do I go alone?"

"Bella is to accompany you as far as the church, my dear. His Grace will be waiting there to give you away."

Juliana felt an almost irrepressible urge to burst into hysterical laughter at the solemnity of Mistress Dennison's voice. It wasn't as if the woman didn't know the truth about the sham marriage and the duke's intended role. And yet she could manage to sound completely convinced and convincing as she put forth this ludicrous version of the truth.

"It's so wonderful, miss," Bella breathed. "To see ye wed, all respectable, like."

"All respectable," Juliana murmured, opening the door. "Yes, of course."

She was unprepared, however, for the excited chorus of girls awaiting her in the hall. They fluttered around her, examining her gown, exclaiming at her good fortune with clearly genuine pleasure. They would take hope and encouragement from the luck of one of their number, Juliana reflected. Where one of them had good fortune, another could soon follow. She responded as warmly as she could, since the truth was not to be told, but was relieved when Mr. Dennison with great ceremony gave her his arm and ushered her outside, into a waiting hackney. Bella climbed in after her and busily straightened Juliana's skirts, making sure they were in no danger of catching in the door.

The church was in a small, quiet lane. Marylebone was almost in the country, and the air was cleaner, the sound of birdsong more easily heard. Bella jumped down from the coach first, and Juliana gathered up her skirts, praying that she would manage this maneuver without disaster. It would be typical of her luck to catch her heel on the footstep and tumble headfirst to the ground.

But the duke appeared in the open doorway. He was looking grave and held out his hand to assist her.

Juliana took the hand and managed to extricate herself and her skirts through the narrow aperture without mishap. "Where's your cousin?"

"Waiting at the altar." He straightened her veil with a deft twitch.

"Do I pass muster, my lord duke?" She couldn't manage to keep the sting from her voice, but he merely nodded.

"You look just as I expected." While she was still trying

to decide whether that was a compliment or not, he had tucked her hand into his arm. "Ready?"

As I'll ever be. Juliana lifted her head boldly and faced the open church door. Bella, with an air of great self-importance, bent to straighten the bride's skirts, then solemnly stood back and watched, dabbing a tear from her eye as the Duke of Redmayne and Juliana disappeared through the church doors to meet her bridegroom.

Lucien, standing at the altar with Quentin, looked impatiently toward the door, shuffling his feet on the cold stone. Lawyer Copplethwaite sat in the front pew, staring intently into the middle distance. The elderly priest flicked nervously through the pages of the prayer book as if looking for the right section.

"I can't think why you wouldn't officiate yourself," Lucien muttered. "Keep it in the family."

Quentin's face was carved in granite. "I'd not commit such sacrilege," he responded in a clipped whisper, wondering why he was there at all. Except that he had never been able to refuse his brother anything. And he felt a compulsion to stand by the girl. She was in need of a friend, however much Tarquin might swear that she would not be hurt . . . . would indeed only be better off by lending herself to his scheme.

He turned toward the door as the couple entered the dim nave, Juliana a shimmer of white against the duke's dark red.

"Tall, isn't she? Quite the Long Meg," Lucien observed in an undertone. "Hope she's not some hatchet-face into the bargain. Don't want to be the laughingstock of town."

Quentin's mouth tightened, and his fingers closed over the simple band of gold in his pocket. The bride and her escort reached the altar, and Quentin nudged Lucien to step forward. Juliana, still on the duke's arm, stepped up beside him. Quentin could detect no hesitation in her manner, but he could see nothing of her face beneath the veil.

Juliana peered through her veil at her bridegroom. Her

first impression was of a curiously shrunken figure, hunched and hollow-chested. She felt very tall and robust beside him. It gave her a comforting sense of advantage. She couldn't see his face too clearly, but his pallor struck her powerfully—the dead whiteness of a fish's underbelly. And his eyes were just sockets, deep-set, burning holes as he glanced incuriously at her when the priest began the service. A little prickle of apprehension lifted her scalp, and without volition she turned toward the duke on her other side. He placed his hand on hers as it rested on his arm and smiled reassuringly.

Juliana licked suddenly dry lips. How would she feel at this moment if she were marrying the Duke of Redmayne? Not apprehensive, certainly. It could surely be said that she knew all there was to know about him already.

She wasn't marrying him, but she was inextricably twining her life with his. He intended to be the father of her child. How much closer could two people get? Much closer than any counterfeit marriage could afford. The idea gave her courage, and she heard herself make her responses in a clear, firm voice.

Lord Quentin handed his cousin the ring. Only then did the duke remove the support of his arm from Juliana. She extended her hand. It was not quite steady, but not as shaky as it might have been. The viscount's fingers, however, trembled almost uncontrollably as he tried to slide the ring on her finger. He cursed savagely, muttering that it was deuced early in the day and he needed a drink to steady him. The undertone reached the priest, nervously nodding and smiling as he oversaw the ritual. He looked shocked and uttered a faint protest as the fumbling continued.

The duke moved swiftly. In the blink of an eye he had taken the ring from Lucien and slipped it onto the bride's finger. The priest, still clearly shocked, pronounced them man and wife in a quavering voice.

"Thank God that's over," Lucien declared as soon as the priest's voice had faded into the shadows. "Am I to be vouchsafed a look at this wife of mine?"

"Sir . . . I beg you . . . must you . . ." But Lucien ignored the stammering, violated priest and reached for Juliana's veil with his violently shaking hands. He threw it back and then surveyed her critically in the gloom.

"Better than I expected," he commented. "I need a drink. I bid you join me, madam wife, in a toast to this auspicious event." With a mocking bow he proffered his arm.

He was dressed impeccably and lavishly in emerald-and-gold brocade, but Juliana shuddered at the thought of touching him. Some infection seemed to emanate from him, from his caved-in chest and his thin shoulders, his burning eyes and ghastly green-white complexion. Like some graveyard maggot, she thought, feeling queasy. Some loathsome, crawling inhabitant of the tombs. He was supposed to be sick. But what could he have that would waste him so, would produce this waft of corruption, as if he were rotting from within?

Juliana's eyes darted in almost frantic appeal to Quentin, then up at the duke, as she hesitated. "I imagine we would all like some refreshment," Quentin said before Tarquin could move. "Come, my dear." He took her hand, tucked it under his arm, and Viscountess Edgecombe walked back down the aisle after her wedding on the arm of her husband's cousin. Her husband lounged after them, taking snuff, and Tarquin moved into the sacristy with the priest and Lawyer Copplethwaite, to settle the business side of the ceremony.

Outside Juliana breathed deeply of the sultry air and forced herself to look again at her husband. In the bright sunshine his color looked even worse. The greenish skin was stretched taut on his skull, showing every bone and hollow. He looked as old as Methuselah and as young as Juliana herself. Suddenly he doubled over with a violent coughing fit, his thin chest heaving, perspiration gathering on his brow. She gazed in sympathetic horror while he coughed as if he would vomit up his lungs.

"Can't we do something?" she said to Quentin, who was standing beside her, his face tight and furious.

"No," he said shortly. "He needs cognac."

"What is the matter with him?" she whispered. "The duke said he was ill . . . but what is it?"

"He didn't tell you?" Quentin's eyes flashed with anger, and he looked remarkably like his half brother.

"Didn't tell her what?" Tarquin's voice came from the church steps behind. He glanced at the still-convulsed Lucien, then came down the last step.

"The child does not know what ails her husband," Quentin said harshly. "For shame, Tarquin!"

"Juliana will have nothing to do with Lucien, so what does it matter to her what ails him?" Tarquin said, drawing out his snuffbox. "Your husband is riddled with the pox, *mignonne*. But I promise he will not lay so much as a finger upon you."

Juliana stared at the duke, speechless, as he took a leisurely pinch of snuff, dropped the box into his pocket again, and slapped Lucien hard on the back. "Come, Edgecombe. We'll put a glass of cognac down your gullet, and you'll be right as a trivet."

Lucien straightened, burying his streaming face in his handkerchief. "Odd's blood!" he rasped when he could catch his breath. "Thought I was never goin' to breathe again." He wiped his nose and mouth and thrust the handkerchief back into his pocket. Then he surveyed his wife with a distinct leer. "Sorry about that, m'dear. Not a particularly good first impression for a man to make on his bride, what?"

"No," Juliana said faintly. "Must we continue to stand on the street in this fashion?" She flicked at her bridal white with an expression of deep disgust. Of all the travesties, to be dressed up like this for such a diabolical mockery.

"My carriage is here." Tarquin took her arm, directing her across the street to where stood a light town chaise with the Redmayne arms emblazoned on the panels. "Quentin, do you accompany us back to Albermarle Street?"

His brother hesitated, still angry. But when Juliana looked at him in silent appeal, he gave a curt nod and crossed the street.

"You won't mind if I don't join you?" Lucien popped his head through the open carriage window. "Think I need to quench m'thirst without delay. Can't risk another fit. There's a tavern on the corner." He gestured with his hat.

"By all means," Tarquin said amiably.

"But I'll be there for the bridal feast . . . count on me for that." Laughing, Lucien went off, heading purposefully for the Lamb and Flag on the corner.

"*Bridal feast?*" Juliana glared at the two men sitting opposite her. "When will this mockery end, my lord duke?"

"Lucien's idea of a jest," Tarquin said. "I had planned no such thing. What I had planned was a visit to the play, followed by supper in the rotunda at Ranelagh. If that would please you, Juliana. D'you care to accompany us, Quentin?"

"If Juliana would permit me to join you," his brother said still coldly. "But maybe she would prefer to retire to her own quarters and weep."

"Oh, I don't believe Juliana is given to such melodrama," Tarquin responded. He was hoping his bracing words would keep her from losing courage. He knew instinctively that if she broke down now, it would be much more difficult for her later.

"And how would you know, sir?" Juliana was hunched into the corner, her baleful eyes never leaving the duke's face.

"An educated guess," he said. "Now, don't fall into a fit of the sullens, child. I'm suggesting an evening of pleasure. You'll not see Lucien—indeed, it's possible you won't see him until you have to make your society debut. Oh, I sent notices of the marriage to the *Morning Post* and the *Times,* so you can expect to receive bride visits within the week, I imagine."

"Without my husband's support, I suppose?"

"Oh, it's hardly Lucien's kind of thing. But Quentin and I will be there to lend our own support. Won't we, dear brother?"

"Of course." Quentin realized that whether he wished it or not, he was now deeply entangled in his brother's scheme. Juliana had embroiled him much more effectively than Tarquin. Juliana, who could be no match for Tarquin . . . no match for Lucien . . . would need all the friendship and protection he could provide. Her eyes were shadowed as they gazed out of the window, her mouth taut, her hands tightly knotted in her lap.

She was so young. So vulnerable. So innocent. Poor child. She could never have dreamed she'd find herself caught up in this twisted scheme of the Duke of Redmayne's. Tarquin had always preferred a devious route to his goals, and this was as cunning and artful as any route he'd ever taken. But how inexcusable that he should involve someone as unprotected and as inexperienced as Juliana.

He glanced sideways at the still figure of his brother beside him. Tarquin was leaning back against the squabs, arms folded, eyes half-closed. But Quentin knew they were resting intently on Juliana. Tarquin's mouth was slightly curved as if he found something amusing or pleasing. Startled, Quentin felt a curious softness emanating from his brother. He had always been able to read Tarquin's mood; it was a skill that arose from the years of closeness, from the years when he'd worshiped his half brother and tried to emulate him.

He no longer tried to emulate him . . . no longer chose to. Quentin had found his own path, and it was not his brother's. But the bond between them was as strong as ever. And now Quentin, to his astonishment, sensed a tenderness in Tarquin—a warmth, as he looked at Juliana, that belied the dispassionate cynicism of his manner.

Quentin returned his gaze to Juliana, so tense and still in her bridal white, the veil thrown back so that her hair blazed in the dimness of the carriage. If Tarquin was stirred by her in some way, then perhaps this would not turn out as badly as Quentin feared.

The chaise slowed and drew up. Juliana came out of her bitter, angry reverie. She looked out of the window and recognized the house on Albermarle Street. The house that was to be her home for the foreseeable future. And if she managed to give the duke the child he desired, then it would be her home for many, many years.

The footman opened the door. Tarquin jumped lightly to the ground, disdaining the footstep, and held out his hand to Juliana. "Welcome to your new home, Lady Edgecombe."

Juliana averted her face as she took his hand and stepped to the ground, Quentin following. Her anger burned hot and deep as the earth's core. How could he have wedded her to that defiled wreck of a man without telling her the truth? To his mind she was no more than an expensive acquisition with no rights to knowledge or opinion. He'd asked for her trust, but how could she ever trust in his word when he would keep such a thing from her?

But she would be revenged. Dear God, she would be revenged a hundredfold. The resolution carried her into the house with head held high, and her dignity didn't desert her even when she caught her heel on the doorstep and had to grab the bowing footman to stop herself from falling to her knees.

Quentin jumped forward to steady her with a hand under her elbow.

"Thank you," she said stiffly, moving away from both Quentin and the footman.

"Juliana has a tendency to topple and spill," Tarquin observed. "In certain circumstances she can produce the effect of a typhoon."

"How gallant of you, my lord duke," she snapped, roughly pulling the veil from her head and tossing it toward a rosewood pier table. It missed, falling to the marble floor in a shimmering cloud.

"Well, let's not brawl in front of the servants," Tarquin

said without heat. "Come with me and I'll show you your apartments." Cupping her elbow, he urged her toward the stairs.

Left behind, Quentin picked up the discarded veil, placed it carefully on the table, then made his way to the library and the sherry decanter.

Juliana and the duke reached the head of the horseshoe stairs.

"As I've already mentioned, I thought you might like to use the morning room as your own private parlor," the duke said with a determined cheerfulness, gesturing down the corridor to the door Juliana remembered on the first landing. "You'll be able to receive your own friends there in perfect privacy."

What friends? Juliana closed her lips firmly on the sardonic question. "Your bedchamber and boudoir are at the front of the house, on the second floor." He ushered her up the second flight of stairs to the right of the landing. "You'll need an abigail, and I've engaged a woman from my estate. A widow—her husband was one of my tenant farmers and died a few months ago. She's a good soul. Very respectable. I'm sure you'll deal well together."

He didn't say that he'd decided that Juliana needed a motherly soul to look after her, rather than one of the haughty females usually engaged as abigails to ladies of the fashionable world.

Juliana was still silent. He flung open a pair of double doors.

"Your bedchamber. The boudoir is through the door on the left." He gestured for her to precede him into a large, light chamber furnished in white and gold. The enormous tester bed was hung with gold damask, the coverlet of white embroidered cambric. The furniture was delicate, carved spindle legs and graceful curving arms and backs, the chaise longue and chairs upholstered in gold-and-white brocade. Bowls of yellow and white roses perfumed the air. Juliana's feet sank into the deep pile of the cream carpet patterned with gold flowers as she stepped into the room.

"Oh, what an elegant room!" Her bitter anger faded as she gazed around in delight. The involuntary comparison of this epitome of wealth and good taste with the ugly, heavy, scratched, dented, and faded furnishings in Sir John Ridge's house would not be quashed.

Tarquin smiled with pleasure, then wondered faintly why this chit of a girl's approval meant so much to him. Juliana had bounced over to the door of the boudoir, and he could hear her delighted exclamations as she explored the small, intimate room. "How pretty it is." She came back to the bedchamber, her eyes shining. "I never expected to find myself inhabiting such elegant surroundings," she confided.

"You will grace them, my dear," Tarquin said, an involuntary smile still on his lips at the sight of her ingenuous pleasure.

"Oh, I dareswear within ten minutes the entire chamber will look as if a typhoon hit it," she retorted.

Tarquin held out his hands to her. "Come, cry peace. I meant no offense. Actually, I find your . . . your haphazard locomotion very appealing."

Juliana regarded him incredulously. "I fail to see how anyone could find clumsiness appealing."

"There's something utterly alluring about you, Juliana. Whether you're on your head or your heels." His voice was suddenly a caress, his smile now richly sensual, issuing an irresistible invitation.

Juliana stepped toward him as the clear gray eyes drew her forward like the pull of gravity. He held her by the shoulders and looked down into her upturned face. "There are so many more enjoyable things for us to do, my sweet, than quarrel."

She wanted to tell him that he was a deceitful whoreson. She wanted to curse him, to bring down a plague on his house. But she simply stood, gazing up at him, losing herself in his eyes while she waited for his beautiful mouth to take hers. And when it did, she yielded with a tiny moan of sweet satisfaction, opening her lips for him, greedily pushing her own tongue deep into his mouth, inhaling the scent of his skin, running her hands through his hair, urgently pulling his face to hers as if she couldn't get enough of him.

He bore her backward to the bed, and she fell in a tumble of virginal white. His face hovered over hers, no longer smiling, expressive now of a deep, primitive hunger that set answering pangs deep in her belly. He was pushing up her skirts and petticoats, ignoring the awkward impediment of the hoop. His free hand loosened his britches, then slid beneath her bottom, lifting her on the shelf of his palm as he drove within her.

Juliana gasped at the suddenness of his penetration, but her body welcomed him with joy, her hips moving of their own accord, her buttock muscles tight against the warmth of his flat palm. He supported himself on one hand as he moved within her in short, hard thrusts. And her belly contracted with each thrust, the spiral tightening until a cry burst from her lips and waves of pleasure broke over her. His head was thrown back, his neck corded with effort, his eyes closed. Then he spoke her name in a curious wonder, and his seed gushed into her with each pulsing throb of his flesh, and when she thought she could bear no more, a surge of the most exquisite joy flooded every cell and pore of her body.

"Such enchantment," Tarquin murmured as he bent and kissed the damp swell of her breast rising above her décolletage.

Juliana lay sprawled beneath him, unable to move or speak until her racing heart slowed a little. With an effort she raised a hand and touched his face, then let it flop back again onto the coverlet. "I got lost somewhere," she murmured.

Tarquin slipped gently from her body. "It's a wonderful landscape to roam."

"Oh, yes," Juliana agreed, pushing feebly at her disordered skirts. "And one doesn't even need to get undressed for the journey," she added with an impish chuckle, suddenly invigorated. She sat up. "Where are my husband's apartments?"

"On the other side of the house, at the back." The duke stood up, refastening his britches, regarding her with a quizzical frown.

She slid off the bed, shaking down her skirts. "And where are *your* apartments, sir?"

"Next door to yours."

"How convenient," Juliana observed, beginning to unpin her loosening hair.

"Let me show you just how convenient." He turned to the armoire on the far side of the room. "Come, see."

Juliana, still pulling pins from her hair, followed curiously. He opened the door, and she gasped at the rich mass of silk, satin, and taffeta hanging there. "What's that?"

"I told you I've been busy with your wardrobe," he said. "But that's not what I wish to show you right now." He pushed the garments aside and stepped back so Juliana could see into the interior.

She saw a door at the back of the armoire.

"Open it," he said, enjoying her puzzlement.

Juliana did so. The narrow door swung open onto another bedchamber quite unlike her own. No dainty, feminine chamber, this one was all dark wood and tapestries, with solid oak furniture and highly polished floors.

"Oh," she said.

"Convenient, wouldn't you agree?" His eyes were alight with amusement.

"Very." Juliana stepped back, shaking her hair free of its plaited coronet. "Did you install it specially?"

He shook his head. "No, it was put in by the third duke, who, it was said, like to play little tricks on his duchess. He was not a pleasant man, by all accounts. But I imagine we can put it to better use."

"Yes." Juliana was beginning to feel dazed again. "Does everyone know of its existence . . . the viscount, for instance?"

"No. It's known to very few people. And I'll vouch for

it that Lucien is not one of them. He doesn't know this house well."

"Lord Quentin?"

"Yes, he knows, of course."

"Just as he knows everything about this scheme?" She ran her fingers through her hair, tugging at the tangles.

"Yes."

"And what does he think of it?"

"He completely disapproves," Tarquin stated flatly. "But he'll come round. He always does." He turned back to the armoire. "Shall we choose a gown suitable for Lady Edgecombe to wear to the play and a visit to Ranelagh?"

Why not? The man was an avalanche, rolling over all obstacles, unstoppable. And, although it confused her to realize it, for the moment she did not want him to stop.

Chapter 11

George Ridge emerged from the Cross Keys Bagnio in midafternoon feeling very much the man-about-town. He turned on his heel, enjoying the swish of his new full-skirted coat of puce brocade. His hand rested importantly on his sword hilt as he looked along Little Russell Street, debating whether to go into the Black Lion Chop-House for his dinner or return to the Gardeners' Arms to see if his posters had born fruit.

The ordinary table at the Gardener's Arms offered a reasonable meal, and the fellow diners tended to be hard drinkers with a taste for crude conversation and lewd jests. In general it suited George very well, but last night, when the ordinary table had been cleared of dinner and set up for gambling, he'd discovered that his fellow diners were deep gamesters. As the bottles of port circulated and the room grew hotter, George had grown louder and merrier and very incautious, peering with bleary bonhomie at the dice and throwing guineas across the table with an insouciance that later shocked him. He hadn't had the courage as yet to calculate his losses.

His father would have gone berserk if he'd known. But, then, Sir John had been an old prude, except in his taste for young women, and he'd been very careful with his wealth.

George had never been to London before his present visit. His father considered it a place for wastrels and idlers, inhabited by loose women and men ready to cut your throat for a groat.

George had enjoyed the loose women this afternoon in the bagnio. Three of them. Three very expensive women. His pockets were a deal lighter now than they had been when he'd left the Gardener's Arms that morning. But it had been worth every guinea. He supposed it was usual for London whores to drink champagne. Cider was all very well for a red-cheeked, wide-hipped country doxy in the barn or behind a haystack, but painted women in lawn shifts, with fresh linen on their beds, obviously had higher expectations.

But as a consequence he found himself guiltily aware that in twenty-four hours he'd probably spent enough to cover the farrier's bill for a twelvemonth. And if he returned to the Gardener's Arms, he would inevitably get drawn into the dicing later. A modest dinner at the Black Lion and a visit to the playhouse would definitely be the prudent course this evening. And since the Theatre Royal was but a couple of steps from the chophouse, he could be sure of arriving before the doors opened at five o'clock so he could get a decent seat in the pit.

He examined the silver lace on his new cocked hat with pride before carefully placing it on his head, ensuring that the pigeon's wings on his pigtail wig were not disarranged. He tapped the hilt of his sword with the heel of his hand and gazed around imperiously, as if about to issue a challenge. A shabby gentleman in a skewed bag wig hastily crossed to the other side of the street as he approached George with his belligerant stance. London was full of aggressive young men-about-town who thought it famous sport to torment vulnerable pedestrians.

George gave him a haughty stare, flicking a speck of snuff from his deep coat cuff. He didn't wear a sword in the country, but he'd realized immediately that in town it was the mark of a gentleman. He had purchased his present weapon from an armorer in Ebury Street, having been assured by that craftsman that it was not a mere decoration—that in the hands of a skilled swordsman, such as His Honor must be, it would be a most deadly weapon, and a powerful protection.

With a little nod of satisfaction George strolled toward the Black Lion. Having experienced the pleasures of London, he was determined that he would spend some weeks of every year in town—in the winter, of course, when the land needed less attention.

Juliana would make him a more than satisfactory consort. She'd grown up in a gentleman's establishment, educated in all the areas necessary for a lady. She knew how to behave in the best society . . . better than he, himself, George was obliged to admit. George was his father's son. The son of a blunt, poorly educated landowner, who was more interested in his crops and his woods, his sport, his dinner and the bottle, than in books or music, or polite conversation. But Juliana was a lady.

But where in the name of Lucifer was she? George's self-satisfaction and pleasure in the day suddenly evaporated. It was all very well making these happy plans, but they were castles in the air without the flesh-and-blood girl to make them real. He *had* to have her as his wife. He wanted her in his bed. He wanted to see the superiority and contempt chased from her eyes as she acknowledged him as her husband and master.

Juliana, with her eyes that could be as cold and green as the deepest ocean; Juliana, with her full mouth that could curl into a derisive smile that shriveled a man; Juliana, with that swirling forest fire of hair and the long limbs, and the full, proudly upstanding breasts.

He would have that Juliana, obedient and docile in his house and in his bed. Or he would see her burn at the stake.

George turned into the Black Lion and ordered a bottle of burgundy. He *would* find her, if he had to pay a hundred guineas to do so.

• • •

Juliana was in a very different frame of mind, Quentin thought as the three of them sat at dinner. On the two previous occasions he'd been in her company, she'd been clearly distressed, and this morning, bitterly angry into the bargain. But now her eyes were luminescent jewels, her pale skin had a glow that seemed to come from within. She was bright and bubbly, with ready laughter and a quick wit that showed an informed mind. She threw impish challenges at Tarquin, and occasionally a darting glance that always made the duke smile.

Quentin was neither a prude nor a stranger to women, despite his calling. It didn't take a genius to deduce that Lady Edgecombe had been enjoying some bedsport that afternoon. His brother's indulgent amusement and the unmistakable caress of his eyes when they rested on Juliana clearly indicated that however much at odds they might be in some things, the Duke of Redmayne and his cousin's bride were clearly well matched in the bedchamber.

Quentin supposed he should be disapproving. But he was not a hypocrite. He'd lent his countenance to Tarquin's abominable scheme—reluctantly, it was true, but he was still a part of it. If Juliana took pleasure in the duke's lovemaking, then it could be said that she was not really being coerced in this aspect, at least, of the arrangement.

Juliana wasn't sure whether her feeling of heady enjoyment in this dinner was a residue of the afternoon or had to do with the novel position in which she found herself. The only woman at the table, she was the focus of attention. At Forsett Towers, she'd been relegated to a cramped corner of the table, enjoined to be silent unless spoken to, and had thus endured interminable dinners, passing some of the most tedious hours of her life. At this table, whenever she opened her mouth to speak, both the duke and his brother paid her close and flattering attention.

"What is the play we're to see?" She reached for her

wineglass. A footman moved swiftly to catch the cascade of cutlery set in motion by her floating sleeve.

"Garrick as Macbeth," Tarquin replied with a twitch of amusement as she glared in mortification at the errant ruffles.

"There'll be a farce, too, no doubt," Quentin said. "And since Garrick appointed Thomas Arne as the musical director, one can be sure of lively entertainment during the musical interludes."

"I've never been to the play." Juliana held her sleeve clear of the table as she reached for a basket of pastries. "At home the mummers would come at Christmas, and occasionally during the fair, but there was never a real play."

"I trust you'll enjoy the experience." Tarquin was surprised at how enchanting he found her enthusiastic chatter and ready laughter. This was a Juliana he'd only fleetingly glimpsed hitherto. She also had a healthy appetite. Either no one had told her it was considered ladylike to modify one's enthusiasm for the table in public, or she had simply ignored the stricture. Probably the latter, he thought with an inner smile. Her conversation was both amusing and intelligent. Her guardians had clearly not neglected her education, however much they might have endeavored to stifle her personality.

"Have I a smut on my nose, my lord duke?" Juliana inquired, brushing her nose with a fingertip.

"I don't see one."

"You seemed to be looking at me with particular intensity," she said. "I made sure something was amiss with my appearance."

"Not that I can see." He pushed back his chair. "If you've finished, my dear, I suggest we adjourn to the drawing room for tea."

"Oh, yes." Juliana flushed and jumped to her feet, sending her chair skidding across the polished floor. "I should have thought, I beg your pardon. I'll leave you to your port."

"No need," Tarquin said, steadying the chair so she

could move easily around it. "Quentin and I are not overly fond of sitting long at the table. Isn't that so, brother?"

"Absolutely," Quentin agreed. "I see no reason why Juliana should sit in solitary state in the drawing room while we sozzle ourselves on port."

"Lucien, of course, would have a different view," Tarquin observed.

Juliana glanced quickly over her shoulder at him, but his expression was as dispassionate as his tone. What difference to the atmosphere would her husband's presence make? A significant one, she reckoned.

But she didn't allow such thoughts to interfere with her pleasure in the evening. She had fallen into this situation, and she might as well enjoy its benefits.

They drove to Covent Garden in the duke's town chaise, Juliana gazing out of the window, intrigued as London moved onto its nightly revels. It was the first time she'd been out in the evening since she had stepped off the coach at the Bell, and when they turned into Covent Garden, she saw it had a very different aspect from the daytime scene. The costermongers and barrow boys had gone, the produce stalls packed up for the day. The center of the Garden was now thronged with ladies accompanied by footmen, soliciting custom, and boys darting through the crowd crying the delights to be enjoyed in the specialized brothels masquerading as coffeehouses and chocolate shops.

Beneath the columns of the Piazza strolled fashionable people, quizzing the scene as they made their way to the Theatre Royal, whose doors stood open. It was now just before six o'clock, and the crowd at the doors was a seething mass of humanity, fighting and squabbling as they pushed their way inside to find a last-minute seat.

Juliana looked askance at the melee and wondered how she was to get through there with her wide hoop. She was bound to tear something in the process. "Doesn't the play begin at six?"

"It does." Tarquin handed her down to the cobbles before the theater.

"But if we have no seats—"

"We do, my dear," Quentin reassured with a smile. "Tarquin's footman arrived at the doors at four o'clock in plenty of time to secure us a box."

So that was how the privileged managed such things. Juliana raised an eyebrow and decided she liked being one of their number. She had the duke and Lord Quentin on either side of her as they approached the massed doorway. How it happened she couldn't tell, but a path materialized through the crowd and she was suddenly inside the theater, her gown in one piece, not even a ruffle torn, both shoes still on her feet, and her hoop behaving itself impeccably. She had a vague impression that her two escorts had touched a shoulder here and there, uttered a few words in low voices, edged an impeding body to one side. However it had been done, they were inside.

The orchestra was playing but could barely be heard above the buzz and chatter as people strolled between the seats, pausing to chat to friends or calling across heads to attract attention in other parts of the pit. Above the racket the cries of the orange sellers were pitched shrill and imperative.

"This way." Juliana was deftly ushered to a box overlooking the stage, where a footman in Redmayne livery stood bowing as they entered. Tarquin didn't release Juliana's elbow until she was seated at the front of the box. "Now, if you don't try to explore, you'll be safe and sound," he said, sitting beside her.

"I shan't go short of entertainment." Juliana leaned over the edge of the box. "If the play is half as absorbing as the crowd, I shall be very well satisfied. Why do they have those iron spikes along the stage?"

"To stop the audience jumping onto the stage." Tarquin smiled at her rapt expression. "You see the rather burly men behind? They're an added deterrent."

Juliana laughed. "I am so glad I came to London." Then she flushed, a shadow dimming the vibrancy of her expression. "Or I would be in different circumstances."

Quentin touched her shoulder in brief sympathy. Tarquin chose to ignore the comment. There was a moment of awkward silence; then the orchestra produced an imperative drumroll. The curtain went up, and David Garrick strode onto the stage to deliver the prologue to the evening's entertainment.

Juliana listened, entranced, as the play began. The audience continued to buzz and hum, carrying on their own gossipy conversations throughout, but Juliana was unaware of anything but the stage. It didn't occur to her as in the least strange that Macbeth should be played in contemporary costume, with Garrick in the title role dressed in the full regalia of a Hanoverian officer.

At the first interval she sat back with a little sigh of contentment. "How magical. It's quite different hearing the words from reading them, even aloud."

"I'm glad it pleases you, *mignonne*." Tarquin stood up. "If you'll excuse me for a minute, there's someone I must visit." He strolled off, and Juliana returned her attention to the crowd. An argument seemed to be turning nasty in the front row, and a man was threatening to draw his sword. Someone bellowed in jocular fashion and threw a handful of orange peel over the two opponents. There was laughter, and the moment of tension seemed to have dissipated.

Juliana glanced across the pit to the boxes opposite. She saw the duke directly opposite, standing behind the chair of a woman dressed in dark gray, almost black, with a white fichu at the neck and her hair tucked severely under a white cap. She was looking up at Tarquin as he spoke to her.

"Who's the duke talking to?"

Quentin didn't look up from his own perusal of the crowd. "Lady Lydia Melton, I imagine. His betrothed." There was something false in his studied, casual tone, but Juliana was too astonished by this intelligence to give it any thought.

"His betrothed?" She couldn't have kept the dismay from her voice even if she'd tried. "He's to be married?"

"Did he not tell you?" Still, Quentin neither looked at her nor at the object of the discussion.

"No . . . it seems there's a great deal he didn't tell me." All her pleasure in the evening vanished, and the bitter resentment of the morning returned.

"I daresay he thought his betrothal was irrelevant to you . . . to everyone," he added softly.

"Yes, irrelevant," she said acidly. "Why should it matter to me?"

"Well, it won't be happening for quite a while," Quentin told her, his voice flat. "The marriage was to have taken place two months ago, but Lydia's grandfather died and the entire family have put on black gloves. They'll be in mourning for the full two years."

"Then why's she at the play?" Juliana demanded tartly. "It seems hardly consistent with deep mourning."

"It *is* Macbeth," Quentin pointed out. "They'll leave before the farce."

"Seems very hypocritical to me." Juliana squinted across the playhouse, trying to get a better look at Lady Lydia Melton. It was difficult to form an impression in the flickering light of the flambeaux that lit the stage and the pit. "How old is she?"

"Twenty-eight."

"She's on the shelf," Juliana stated.

"I should refrain from passing judgment when you don't know the facts," Quentin said sharply. "Lydia and Tarquin have been betrothed from the cradle, but the death of Tarquin's mother three years ago postponed the marriage. And now Lydia's grandfather's demise has created another put-off."

"Oh. I didn't mean to sound catty." Juliana gave him a chastened smile. "I'm just taken aback."

Quentin's expression softened. "Yes, I can imagine you might be."

Juliana stared hard across the separating space and suddenly noticed that the lady was looking directly at her. It was clear that Juliana herself was under discussion when

Tarquin raised a hand in a gesture of acknowledgment and Lady Lydia bowed from the waist. Juliana responded in like manner. "I wonder what they're saying about me."

"I imagine Tarquin is explaining that you're Lucien's bride," Quentin observed. "The Meltons were bound to wonder what he and I were doing in a box at the theater with a strange lady."

"But won't they think it strange that the viscount isn't with us so soon after the wedding?"

"No," Quentin said without elaboration.

The orchestra began another alerting drumroll, and Tarquin disappeared from the Meltons' box. A few minutes later he appeared beside Juliana.

"You didn't tell me you were betrothed," she whispered accusingly as the second act began.

"It's hardly important," he returned. "Hush, now, and listen."

Juliana found it hard to concentrate on the rest of the play. She was wondering when Tarquin would have chosen to tell her about his fiancée. She was wondering what would happen to their arrangements when the new duchess took up residence. Presumably, the mistress and her child would be established in one wing of the house and the duchess and her children in another, and the duke would move between his two families as and when it pleased him.

Perhaps her present charming apartments rightfully belonged to the duke's wife. Surely with that proximity, not to mention the concealed connecting door, they must. So presumably she would have to move out of them when the new duchess took up residence.

Juliana opened and closed her fan with such violence that one of the dainty painted sticks snapped. Startled, both her escorts looked sideways.

The duke placed a restraining hand on hers, still roughly flicking the fan in her lap. She turned and glared at him with such fury, he could almost imagine being scorched by the flames in her eyes. There was one thing about Juliana, he reflected ruefully: One always knew where one stood with her. She was so full of passions of every kind that she was incapable of masking her emotions.

"If you wish to quarrel, let's do so later," he whispered. "Not in the middle of a crowded playhouse. Please, Juliana."

Juliana pointedly turned her eyes back to the stage, her mouth taut, her jaw set, her back as rigid as if a steel poker ran down her spine. Tarquin exchanged a glance with his brother, whose response was far from sympathetic.

The Melton party, as Quentin had predicted, left before the farce. They left so discreetly, Juliana didn't see them go. When she looked toward the box as the torches were lit again to illuminate the pit, she saw it was empty.

Tarquin leaned over the box and hailed an orange seller. She came up with a pert smile and tossed two oranges up to him. He caught them deftly, throwing down a sixpence. She grinned and curtsied, tucking the coin between her ripe breasts bubbling over the neck of her gown, which was kilted to show both calves and ankles. "Want to come and get it back, sir?" she called with a lascivious wink. "No 'ands allowed. An' if ye double it, there's no knowin' where it'll end up."

Tarquin laughingly refused the invitation. He took a small knife out of his waistcoat pocket and began to peel an orange. He broke off a segment and held it to Juliana's lips. "Open wide, my dear."

"I am not in the mood for teasing." She closed her lips firmly. But she took the orange segment in her fingers, rather than open her mouth for him to feed her, and offered a formally polite thank-you.

Tarquin gave her the remainder of the orange without further remark, peeled the other one, and shared it with Quentin, who was coming to the conclusion that Juliana was perhaps not quite the victim he'd believed her to be.

Her delight in the farce was so infectious that all previous tension dissipated. Tarquin and Quentin wouldn't normally have stayed for this low comedy that had the pits in hysterics, but Juliana was so entranced, found the bawdiest comments so hilarious, that they sat back and simply enjoyed her enjoyment.

As the curtain came down, she wiped tears of laughter from her eyes with a fingertip. "I haven't laughed so much since I saw Punch and Judy at the fair in Winchester."

George Ridge had also greatly enjoyed his evening, much preferring the farce to the long-winded, ponderous speeches of the tragedy, although he'd been quite impressed with the sword fights, which had seemed very realistic. And Lady Macbeth had dripped chicken blood, and the ghost of Banquo had been horridly gouged and smothered.

He made his way out of the pit, allowing the tide of humanity to carry him. At the door a crowd of gallants was gathered around a painted bawd and her collection of whores. They were bargaining for the women, with the sharp-eyed madam missing nothing as she auctioned off her girls. George hesitated, fancying a particular bold-eyed wench in a canary-yellow gown. Then the bawd shouted, "Ten guineas to the gentleman in the striped weskit," and shoved the girl forward into the arms of the man so described, who eagerly handed over ten guineas, which the bawd dropped into a leather satchel at her waist.

George decided he'd spent enough money on women for one day. He'd return to the Gardener's Arms and take his supper there, then maybe throw the dice a few times. He would set himself a strict limit so that he'd be in no danger of outrunning the carpenter.

He pushed his way out of the stuffy heat of the theater and drew a deep breath of the fresher air outside. He seemed to be getting accustomed to the stench of London, since it troubled him much less now. He was debating whether to take a sedan chair back to Cheapside, or save the fare and walk on such a fine night, when he saw her.

He stared, unable to believe his eyes, his heart jumping erratically. Juliana was on the other side of the street, facing him. She was talking animatedly to her two escorts, men whose dress made George immediately feel shabby and countrified. It didn't matter that he'd ordered his suit from a tailor on Bond Street. Compared to the two men with Juliana, he could have been wearing a laborer's smock and carrying a pitchfork.

And Juliana. He'd never seen her like this. In fact, if it weren't for her hair and the expression on her face and the voluptuous figure he'd lusted after for weeks, he would have thought his obsession had bested his senses. She was dressed as finely as any of the ladies he'd gawped at going into St. James's Palace or strolling in Hyde Park. Again, there was that indefinable air of fashion and quality about her clothes and the way she wore them that relegated George Ridge to the farmyard. He recognized that Lady Forsett would eat her heart out if she could see her erstwhile charge tricked out in such style. Such a wide hoop, and the most shockingly low neckline to her lavender silk gown.

He moved backward into the shadows so she wouldn't see him if she chanced to look across the street. Then he stood and continued to stare at the three of them. Who was she with? Had she turned whore? It was the only explanation he could think of—that somehow in the days since she'd arrived in London, alone and friendless, she'd managed to snag a rich and well-connected protector. Or maybe two. She was laughing and talking to her companions with an ease and informality that seemed to imply either long acquaintance or a degree of intimacy.

It was an explanation that made perfect sense to George. He licked his lips involuntarily, imagining how the life of a whore would change the haughty and inexperienced country girl he had known. But how would she respond to the prospect of returning to Hampshire as the wife of Sir George Ridge, when she'd dabbled in the playgrounds of fashionable London?

A chaise drew up on the other side of the street, obscuring them from his view. He darted out of the shadows in time to see one of the men hand Juliana into the carriage.

Both men followed her, and the door was closed. George stared at the ducal coronet emblazoned on the panels. He couldn't read the Latin motto or identify the arms, but he knew the carriage belonged to a duke. Juliana, it seemed, was flying high. Perhaps too high for a simple country landowner, however wealthy.

He pushed his way to a hackney that had come to a halt by a group of inebriated men, who were arguing about where they should continue their evening. George shoved roughly through them and into the hackney before they realized what was happening. "Follow the carriage ahead. The black-and-yellow one," George shouted at the jarvey, banging on the roof with his sword hilt.

The hackney started forward with a jolt, and its intended passengers turned and bellowed in startled fury. They made a halfhearted attempt to follow, one of them hanging on to the window straps for a few yards, cursing George for a sneak thief before falling off into the gutter.

George leaned anxiously out of the window, trying to keep the black-and-yellow carriage in sight as they bowled around a corner. The jarvey seemed to be enjoying the chase, took the corner on two wheels, and George was flung back against the cracked, stained leather squabs. He righted himself with a curse and leaned out of the window again.

" 'Ere y'are, guv. Ranelagh Gardens," the jarvey yelled down, coming to a halt before the wrought-iron gates. "Ye want me to go on in after 'em?"

"No, I'll go on foot." George jumped down, paid the jarvey, and hurried into the gardens, paying his half-a-crown entrance fee before making his way to the rotunda, where he guessed he would find them.

For the rest of the evening he dogged Juliana's footsteps, always careful to keep himself out of her line of sight. He watched her eat supper in one of the boxes in the rotunda, listening to the orchestra in the center. She was animated, but he could see no sign of a physical relationship with her two escorts. If she was there as their whore, he would have expected to see wandering fingers, a kiss or two, definitely flirtation; and yet, despite her elegant gown, the trio reminded him of a young girl being taken for a treat by two indulgent uncles.

Greatly puzzled, he followed them back out of the garden just as dawn was breaking. He set another hackney in pursuit of the yellow-and-black chaise, and when the ducal carriage stopped outside a house on Albermarle Street and its three passengers alighted, he instructed the jarvey to drive on past. He fixed the house in his memory as the three disappeared into its lighted hallway. Then he sat back and contemplated the evening's puzzles.

Juliana had entered the house with two men. It could only mean that she had joined the oldest profession in the world. And joined it high up the ladder. But she was still his father's murderess. A whore couldn't expect to duck such a charge, however powerful her protector.

He would find out what he could about the two men; then he would wait his moment. Then he would surprise her.

Chapter 12

"Good morning, my lady."

Juliana disentangled herself from the strands of a warm and fuzzy dream as bright sunlight poured over the bed. She blinked and hitched herself onto an elbow.

A small woman, round as a currant bun, with faded blue eyes and gray hair beneath a neat white cap, stood by the bed where she'd just pulled back the curtains to let in the daylight. She bobbed a curtsy.

"Good morning," said Juliana. "You must be . . ."

"Mistress Henley, m'lady. But the family call me Henny, so if ye'd care to do the same, we'll do very well together."

"Very well, Henny." Juliana sat up and gazed around the handsome bedchamber, memory of the evening returning. She blushed as her eye fell on the heap of carelessly discarded clothes by the window. The duke had insisted on playing lady's maid when they'd come back from Ranelagh and had shown little regard for the fine silks and delicate lawn of her undergarments. "I beg your pardon for leaving my clothes in such a mess," she said.

"Good heavens, my lady, what am I here for?" Henny responded cheerfully. "I'll have them picked up in no time while you take your morning chocolate." She turned to pick up a tray and placed it on Juliana's knees. Steam curled fragrantly from the spout of a silver chocolate pot.

Juliana's eyes widened at this unheard-of luxury. The routine at Forsett Towers had had her dressed and breakfasting by seven o'clock every morning. Lady Forsett had been a firm believer in the evils of the soft life on the young, and on winter mornings Juliana had had to crack the ice in the ewer before she could wash.

Carefully she poured the chocolate into the wide, shallow cup. The china was gold-rimmed and paper thin, alarmingly fragile. She leaned back against the pillows and took a cautious sip, then, emboldened, took a biscuit from the matching plate and dunked it into the chocolate. A soggy morsel splashed back into the cup when she carried the biscuit to her lips, and drops of chocolate splattered the coverlet.

"Is something the matter, my lady?" Henny, shaking out the folds of the lavender silk dress, turned at Juliana's mortified exclamation.

"I've spilled chocolate all over the bed," she said, biting her lip as she rubbed at the splashes. "I'm certain it'll stain."

"The laundress won't be defeated by a little chocolate." Henny bustled over to examine the damage. "Dearie me, it's hardly anything."

"It looks like a lot to me," Juliana said disgustedly. "Perhaps I'd better drink it sitting in a chair." She handed the tray to Henny and jumped out of bed.

"I give you good day, madam wife."

Juliana whirled to the door that had opened without warning. Lucien came into the room. He was fully dressed but looking very disheveled, as if he'd slept in his clothes. He carried a glass of cognac and regarded his wife with a satirical gleam in his bloodshot, hollowed eyes.

"My lord." She took a hasty step backward, catching the hem of her nightgown under her heel.

"Lud, but you seem surprised to see me, my lady. I made sure it was customary for a husband to visit his bride on the morning after their wedding night." He sipped brandy, his eyes mocking her over the rim of his glass. But there was more than mockery in his gaze. There was a touch of repulsion as he examined the shape of her body beneath the fine lawn of her nightgown.

Juliana decided abruptly to return to bed. "You startled me, my lord," she said with as much dignity as she could muster. She climbed back into bed, pulling the covers up to her neck. "Henny, I'll take my chocolate again."

The woman gave her the tray back and curtsied to the viscount. "Should I leave, my lord?"

"No," Juliana said swiftly. "No, there's no need for you to go."

Lucien merely smiled and shrugged. He lounged over to the bed and perched on the end. "So you passed a pleasant evening, I trust." He took a gulp of cognac.

It seemed best to play this straight . . . behave as if it were a perfectly ordinary conversation with a man who had every right to be where he was. "Yes, thank you, sir. We went to the play and after to Ranelagh." She dunked another biscuit into her cup with what she hoped was an air of insouciance and successfully conveyed it, intact, to her mouth.

"Insipid entertainment!" Lucien's lip curled. "If you really wished to see the town, madam, you should put yourself in my hands."

"I doubt His Grace would approve of such a scheme," she responded, leaning back against the pillows, her eyes suddenly narrowed.

Lucien gave a shout of laughter that disintegrated into another of his violent coughing spasms. He doubled over on the bed, the emaciated body racked as his chest convulsed and he grabbed for air.

"There, there, my lord. Take it easy, now." Henny took the cognac from his hands and stood waiting until the spasms diminished. "Drink it down, sir." She handed it back with the air of one who knew the remedy. Presumably, as an old family retainer, she knew their skeletons.

Lucien drained the glass in one gulp and sighed with relief. "Forgive me, m'dear. An unpleasant habit for a bridegroom." He grinned, and Juliana noticed for the first time that he was missing four of his front teeth. It was hard to pinpoint his age, but even at her most generous estimate, he was too young to be losing teeth to decay.

"Now, what was it you said that made me laugh . . . ? Oh, yes . . . Tarquin most certainly wouldn't look kindly on my acting as your guide to London life." He chuckled, but carefully this time.

Juliana nodded thoughtfully. It was not difficult to imagine the Duke of Redmayne gnashing his teeth in such a case. Not difficult . . . indeed, positively delicious . . . an utterly delectable prospect . . .

"Good morning, Lady Edgecombe. . . . Ah, Lucien. I see you're paying your bride a morning visit." The Duke of Redmayne materialized from her thoughts. Juliana, startled, turned to the doorway. Tarquin, in a brocade chamber robe, lounged against the doorjamb, but his indolent air was belied by the harsh light in his eyes.

For some reason no one in this household thought it appropriate to knock upon her door, Juliana reflected. "I give you good day, Your Grace." She took another sip of chocolate, trying to appear as if she were perfectly accustomed to entertaining gentlemen in bed in her nightgown. Of course, it was a perfectly appropriate venue for both husbands and lovers, and she had one of each. A bubble of laughter threatened. Hastily she put down her cup and pushed the tray to safety on the far edge of the bed.

"You seem mighty free with my lady's bedchamber, Tarquin," Lucien sneered. "Should I play the outraged husband, I wonder?"

"Don't be a fool." Tarquin looked merely bored by his cousin's barb as he strolled into the room. "I suppose you haven't been to bed as yet?"

"You suppose right, dear boy." Lucien held his empty glass to the light. "Dear me, empty again. I swear the glass must have a leak. D'you still keep a decanter in your room, Redmayne?"

"Go to your own chamber, Lucien," Tarquin instructed in the same bored tone. "Your man is waiting for you, and I'm certain you'll find everything necessary for your comfort."

Lucien yawned profoundly and stood up. "Well, perhaps you're right. Desolated to bring this enchanting little chat to a close, my dear bride."

"I consider it merely postponed, sir."

Tarquin's air of indolent boredom vanished. "I beg your pardon, Juliana?"

Juliana's smile was all innocence. "I merely said I look forward to continuing the discussion with my husband, sir. Is something wrong?"

Tarquin looked so dumbfounded, she was hard-pressed to keep a straight face.

"Can't keep a wife from her lawful husband, y'know, Tarquin," Lucien stated, fumbling with his snuffbox. He had no idea why Juliana should be intent on needling the duke, but he was more than willing to join in the mischief.

Tarquin walked to the door and opened it. "Good day, Lucien."

Lucien looked hurt. "Throwing me out of my own wife's bedchamber, cousin? Seems I have the right to throw *you* out, not the other way round."

"Get out." The duke's voice was very soft, but the pulse in his temple was throbbing and his nostrils were pinched and white.

Lucien glanced toward Juliana, who, having decided prudently to withdraw from the confrontation, avoided eye contact. She didn't care for the look of the Duke of Redmayne at the moment and was not prepared to provoke him further by obviously aligning herself with the viscount. At least not until she'd formulated a coherent plan.

Lucien shrugged and made for the door, knowing that without an ally he couldn't hold his ground. He wasn't too sure what the issue was anyway, but, surprisingly, it seemed that young Juliana was not a completely compliant participant in the duke's schemes. He offered his cousin a mocking bow as he went past him into the corridor.

"Lady Edgecombe will ring when she needs you, Henny," the duke said curtly, still holding the door.

The abigail bobbed a curtsy, picked up Juliana's neglected chocolate tray, and bustled out.

"Now, just what was all that about?" The duke came over to the bed.

"All what?" Juliana's smile was as innocent as ever. "My husband came to visit me. We were talking."

"I see." Tarquin's eyes searched hers. "Are you throwing down the glove, Juliana?"

"Why ever should I do such a thing?"

"I don't know. But if you are, I should warn you that I will pick it up."

"There would be little point in throwing it, my lord, if you did not. . . . Not," she added sweetly, "that I am, of course."

Tarquin stood frowning at her. She was radiating mischief, vibrating with a current of energy that seemed to make her hair crackle. But he couldn't begin to think what pleasure or point there might be for her in cultivating Lucien, unless it was to annoy Tarquin himself. Deciding not to encourage her by pursuing the subject further, he changed the topic with an amiable smile. "I forgot to tell you last night that you'll probably receive a bridal visit this morning from Lady Lydia Melton and her mother."

"Oh? Your betrothed is very kind," she said distantly.

"It's hardly kindess to pay a duty visit to her fiancé's newly acquired relative, who also happens to be living under his roof."

"No, I suppose not," Juliana mused. "Is she aware, I wonder, that this newly acquired relative is also installed in the duchess's apartments?"

"Don't be absurd."

Juliana plaited the coverlet with busy fingers. "I presume I'll be moved elsewhere once your marriage is celebrated

. . . or will this arrangement be terminated when I conceive your child?"

"You seem determined to quarrel with me this morning," Tarquin observed. "I woke up half an hour ago feeling as if I'd been touched by magic." His voice deepened, his eyes glowed, and his mouth curved in a smile of rich sensual pleasure. "The memory of you was on my skin, running in my blood."

Leaning over her, he planted his hands on the pillow on either side of her head. Juliana couldn't tear her eyes from his, so close to her now, compelling her response. His breath was warm on her cheek, his mouth poised above hers . . . poised for an eternity until, with a little moan of defeat, she grasped his face with her hands and pulled his mouth to hers. She kissed him hungrily, pushing her tongue into his mouth, tasting him, drawing his own special scent into her lungs. He kept himself still for her exploration, leaving her with the initiative, until, breathless, she released his face and moved her mouth from his.

"A much more pleasing greeting," Tarquin said, smiling. "Are you always bad-tempered in the morning? Or did you not get enough sleep last night?"

"My questions were perfectly reasonable," Juliana replied, but her voice was low and sweet, her mouth soft, her eyes aglow.

He sat down on the bed beside her. "Maybe I should have mentioned before that I was to be married, but I really didn't think it important. No matter what our arrangements are my dear, I must be married at some point. And no matter what I might prefer," he added a trifle ruefully, "I have a family duty."

"Would you rather not marry Lady Lydia?" Juliana forgot her own concerns in this much more intriguing question.

"It's a marriage of convenience," he explained evenly. "In my position one does not wed for anything else. For amusement, passion—love, even—one keeps a mistress. Surely that doesn't come as a surprise?"

"No, I suppose not. Do you have other mistresses? Someone . . . someone you love, perhaps?" Her fingers were busier than ever with the counterpane, and she couldn't look up at him.

All expression died out of Tarquin's eyes; his face became blank, featureless. "Love, my dear, is a luxury a man in my position must learn to do without."

She looked up now, startled at the bitterness she sensed beneath his flat tone. "Why must you learn to do without it?"

"What an inquisitive child you are." He looked at her for a moment in silence as she gazed back at him with frank curiosity. "If a man has power and wealth, he can never really trust the sincerity of those around him. Perhaps it takes a certain amount of trust to be able to love," he said simply.

"How wretched!" Juliana reached a hand to touch his as it rested on the bed. "Have people pretended to love you, then, but all they wanted was what you could give them?"

He looked down at her hand curled over his. Such an instinctive and generous gesture of comfort, he thought, gently sliding his hand out from under hers. "When I was young and foolish," he said lightly. "But I learned my lesson."

"At least people pretended to like you," Juliana said thoughtfully. "No one even *pretended* to like me. I don't know which would be worse."

"Of course people liked you," he protested, shocked despite his own cynicism at this matter-of-fact statement from one so young and appealing.

Juliana shook her head. "No," she stated. "I wasn't what anyone wanted, except Sir John, of course. I do think he genuinely liked me . . . or perhaps it was only lust. George said he was a perverted old man who lusted after schoolgirls."

Tarquin leaned over and caught her chin on the tip of his finger, lifting it to meet his steady gaze. "*I* like you, Juliana."

Her eyes gazed into his, searching for evidence of the kindly lie beneath the surface. She couldn't see it; in fact, his eyes were suddenly unreadable, glittering with a strange intensity that made her uncomfortable. She blundered onto a new tack, shattering the mesmerizing focus like a sheet of crystal under a fork of lightning.

"So when Lady Lydia becomes your duchess, where had you intended to put me?"

Tarquin dropped her chin, the strange mood broken. "I hadn't intended to *put* you anywhere. Of course, if you produce an heir to Edgecombe, you will move to your own suite of apartments, both in this house and at Redmayne Abbey. Where you choose to be will be entirely up to you. If you wish to leave this house and set up your own establishment, then you may do so; the child, however, will remain here."

"And if I do not have a child?"

"I thought we had discussed this with Copplethwaite," he said, impatiently now.

"The question of your marriage was not raised."

With an air of forbearance, he began to enumerate points on his fingers. "After my marriage . . . after your husband's death . . . whether or not you have a child, you will be free to take up residence at Edgecombe Court as the viscount's widow. However, the child, if there is one, will remain under my roof. If there is no child, the arrangement is perfectly simple. If there is, and you choose to live elsewhere, you will have generous access to the child. I thought that had all been made clear."

"I daresay I'm a trifle slow-witted, Your Grace."

"And the moon is made of cheese."

Juliana fought a silent battle to keep her bitter resentment hidden. All her instincts rebelled against this cold, rational disposition of maternal rights. Supposing she and the duke fell out irrevocably, had some dreadful quarrel that couldn't be papered over? How was she to continue under his roof in such circumstances? And how could she possibly move out and leave her own child behind?

But of course, for the Duke of Redmayne, both she and the child were possessions. Women were bought and sold at all levels of society. Starving men sold their wives in the marketplace for bread. Royal princesses were shipped to foreign courts like so much cattle, to breed and thus cement alliances, to join lands and armies and treasure chests. She'd known all this since she'd been aware of a world outside the nursery. But how hard it was to see herself that way.

Tarquin was regarding her with a quizzical frown. When she remained quiet, he gently changed the subject: "Do you have plans for today?"

The question startled her. She'd been ruled by others all her life—ruled and confined in the house on Russell Street. It hadn't occurred to her that freedom to do what she pleased and go wherever she fancied would be one of the rewards for this oblique slavery.

"I hadn't thought."

"Do you ride?"

"Why, yes. In winter in Hampshire it was the only way to travel when the roads were mired."

"Would you like a riding horse?"

"But where is there to ride?"

"Hyde Park for the sedate variety. But Richmond provides more excitement." Her delighted surprise at this turn of the conversation sent a dart of pleasure through him. How easy she was to please. And also to hurt, he reminded himself, but he quickly suppressed that thought. "If you wish, I'll procure you a horse from Tattersalls this morning."

"Oh, may I come too?" She threw aside the covers and leaped energetically to her feet, her nightgown flowing around her.

"I'm afraid not. Ladies do not frequent Tattersalls." His eyes fixed on the swell of her breasts, their dark crowns pressing against the thin bodice. "But you may trust me with the commission," he said slowly. "Take off your nightgown."

Juliana touched her tongue to her lips. "Someone might come in."

"Take it off." His voice was almost curt, but she didn't mistake the rasp of passion.

She unfastened the laces at her throat and drew the gown slowly up her body, sensing that he would enjoy a gradual unveiling. When she threw it aside and stood naked, his eyes devoured her, roaming hungrily over her body, but he made no attempt to reach for her.

"Turn around."

She did so slowly, facing the bed, feeling her skin warm and flushed with his scrutiny as if it were his hands, not his eyes, that were caressing her.

Tarquin unfastened his robe with one swift pull at the girdle and came up behind her. His hands slid around her waist, cupping the fullness of her breasts, and she could feel his turgid flesh pressing against her buttocks. Then his hands moved over her belly, traced the curve of her hips, stroked the cheeks of her buttocks.

Juliana caught her breath at the insinuating touch of his fingers sliding down the cleft of her bottom and between her thighs, opening the moist, heated furrow of her body. Lust flooded her loins, tightened her belly, sent the blood rushing through her veins. She moved against his fingers, her own hands sliding behind to caress his erect shaft until she could feel his breath swift and hot against the nape of her neck.

"Put your palms flat on the bed."

Juliana obeyed the soft, urgent command, aware of nothing now but his body against hers and her own aching core begging for the touch that would bring the cataclysm. His hands ran hard down her bent back, tracing the curve of her spine, then gripped her buttocks as he drove into her. It felt different—wildly, wonderfully different—his hard belly slapping against her buttocks with each powerful, rhythmic thrust that drove his flesh deeper and deeper inside her. She could hear her own little sobbing cries; her head dropped onto the rumpled sheets, her spine dipped. Her mouth was dry, the swirling void grew ever closer . . . the moment when her body would slip loose from its moorings. His fingers bit deep into the flesh of her hips and his name was on her lips, each syllable an assertion and a declaration of his pleasure.

Juliana fell slowly, as slowly as a feather drifting downward on a spring breeze. The void came up to meet her, and she was lost in its swirling sensate wonder. She toppled forward onto the bed and Tarquin came with her, his body pressed to her back, his hands now around her waist, holding her tightly as his own climax tore him asunder. His face was buried in the tangled flame-red hair on her neck, and his breath was hot and damp on her skin. The void receded and the tension left her limbs inch by inch, and her body took his weight as his strength washed from him with the receding wave of his own joy.

It was a long while before Tarquin eased himself upright onto his feet. He drew his robe together again and reached down to stroke Juliana's back. "*Mignonne*, come back."

"I can't. I'm lost," she mumbled into the coverlet. "That felt so different."

He bent over her and rolled her onto her back. He stroked her face with a fingertip, and his eyes were dark with the residue of passion and something that looked remarkably like puzzlement. "I don't know what you are," he said simply. He kissed her and then, quietly, he left her.

Juliana sat up slowly. Her body thrummed. At the moment she didn't know what she was either. A bride, a mistress . . . a whore? A woman, a girl? A person or a possession?

And if she no longer knew herself, she knew the duke even less.

Chapter 13

It was noon when Juliana left her apartments, dressed for the day in a wide-hooped yellow silk gown opened over a green-sprigged white petticoat. She felt very much the fashionable lady appearing at such a disgracefully late hour and dressed in such style. Lady Forsett, a firm believer in domestic industry, would have disapproved mightily. Ladies of the house didn't put off their aprons and dress for the day's leisure until just before dinner.

The thought made her chuckle and she gave a little skip, recollecting her position when she caught the eye of a curt-sying maidservant who was clearly trying to stifle her grin. "Good day to you," Juliana said with a lofty nod.

"My lady," the girl murmured, respectfully holding her curtsy until Lady Edgecombe had passed her.

Juliana paused at the head of the stairs, wondering where to go. She had seen the mansion's public rooms yesterday and was a little daunted at the prospect of sailing down the horseshoe stairs and into the library or the drawing room. Strictly speaking, she was only a guest in the house, although her position was somewhat ambivalent, whichever way one looked at it. Then she remembered that she had her own private parlor.

She opened the door onto the little morning room, half-afraid she would find it changed, or occupied, but it was empty and just as she remembered. She closed the door behind her and thought about her next move. A cup of coffee would be nice. Presumably she had the right to order what she pleased while she was there. She pulled the bell rope by the hearth and sat down on the chaise longue beneath the window, arranging her skirts tastefully.

The knock at the door came so quickly, it was hard to imagine the footman who entered at her call could have come from the kitchen regions so speedily. But he appeared immaculate and unhurried in his powdered wig and dark livery as he bowed. "You rang, my lady."

"Yes, I'd like some coffee, please." She smiled, but his impassive expression didn't crack.

"Immediately, madam. Will that be all?"

"Oh, perhaps some bread and butter," she said. Dinner wouldn't be until three, and the morning's activities had given her an appetite.

The footman bowed himself out, and she sat in state on the chaise, wondering what she was to do with herself until dinnertime. There were some periodicals and broadsheets on a pier table beneath a gilt mirror on the far wall, and she had just risen to go and examine them when there was another light tap on her door. "Pray enter."

"Good morning, Juliana." Lord Quentin bowed in the doorway, then came in, smiling, to take her hand and raise it to his lips. "I came to inquire after you. Is there anything I can do for you . . . anything you would like?"

"Employment," Juliana said with a rueful chuckle. "I'm all dressed and ready to see and be seen, but I have nowhere to go and nothing to do."

Quentin laughed. "In a day or two you'll have calls to return, and I understand Tarquin is procuring you a riding horse. But until then you may walk in the park, if you'll accept my escort. Or you could visit a circulating library and the shops. There's a sedan chair at your disposal, as well as the chaise. But if you prefer to walk, then a footman will accompany you."

"Oh," Juliana said faintly, somewhat taken aback by such a variety of options. "And I suppose I may make use of the duke's library also?"

"Of course," Quentin responded. "Anything in this house is at your disposal."

"Did His Grace say so?"

Quentin smiled. "No, but my brother is openhanded to a fault. We all live on his bounty to some extent, and I've never known him to withhold anything, even from Lucien."

Juliana could believe in the duke's generosity. It was one thing about him that she felt was not prompted by self-interest. She had a flash of empathy for him, thinking how painful it must be for him to sense when his generosity was abused.

"Do you live here, my lord?"

"Only when I'm visiting London. My house is in the cathedral close in Melchester, in Hertfordshire, where I'm a canon."

Juliana absorbed this with a thoughtful nod. Canons were very important in the church hierarchy. She changed the course of the subject. "Why does my husband live here? Doesn't he have a house of his own?"

The footman appeared with the coffee, and Quentin waited to answer her. Juliana saw that there were two cups on the tray. Obviously, the servants made it their business to know where their masters were in the house.

"It was part of the arrangement Tarquin insisted upon," Quentin told her after the footman had left. He took a cup from her with a nod of thanks. "For your benefit. Obviously, you would be expected to reside under the same roof as your husband. Lucien's own establishment is uncomfortable, to put it mildly. He's besieged by creditors. And, besides, Tarquin can keep an eye on him if he stays here."

"Ensure he doesn't molest me?" Juliana raised an eyebrow.

Quentin flushed darkly. "If I believed that Tarquin

would not protect you, ma'am, I would not be a party to this business."

"Would you have a choice?" she inquired softly. "Your brother is very . . . very persuasive."

Quentin's flush deepened. "Yes, he is. But I like to believe that he could not *persuade* me to do something against my conscience."

"And this manipulative scheme is *not*?" Juliana sounded frankly incredulous as she took a piece of bread and butter from the plate. She regretted the question when she saw how distressed Quentin was. She bore him no grudge— indeed, sensed that he would stand her friend and champion without hesitation if she asked it of him.

"How can I say it isn't?" he said wretchedly. "It's an abominable design . . . and yet it will solve so many embarrassments and difficulties for the family."

"And the family interest, of course, is supreme?"

"For the most part," he said simply. "I'm a Courtney before I'm anything else. It's the same for Tarquin. But I *do* believe he will ensure that you don't suffer from this . . . and . . ." He paused uncomfortably. "Forgive me, but it does seem to me that you could benefit from this scheme if you don't find Tarquin himself distasteful."

Juliana was too honest to lie. She set down her cup, aware that her cheeks were warm. "No," she said. "It's all very confusing. I hate him sometimes and yet at others . . ." She shrugged helplessly.

Quentin nodded gravely and put down his own cup. Taking her hands in a tight clasp, he said earnestly, "You must understand that you may count on me, Juliana, in any instance. I have some influence over my brother, although it may seem as if no one could have."

His gray eyes were steady and sincere resting on her face, and she smiled gratefully, feeling immeasurably comforted. It was the first real statement of friendship she'd ever been given.

Another knock at the door interrupted the moment of tense silence, and the butler appeared. "Lady Melton and

Lady Lydia, madam," he announced. "I took the liberty of showing them into the drawing room."

"Thank you, Catlett," Quentin replied swiftly. "Lady Edgecombe will be down directly. . . . Don't worry," he said to Juliana with a quick smile as the butler departed. "I'll lend you my company for the ordeal."

"Will it be one?" Juliana examined her reflection in the mirror and patted her hair with a nervous hand.

"Not at all. Lydia has the sweetest nature in the world, and Lady Melton is not too much of a gorgon."

"The duke seems not inclined to marry Lady Lydia," Juliana said, licking her fingertip and smoothing her eyebrow. "He said it was a marriage of convenience." She caught sight of Quentin's expression in the mirror behind her, and her heart jumped at the bleak frustration, stark in his eyes. Then he'd turned aside and opened the door, holding it for her. Vividly now, she remembered his studied indifference at the theater, an indifference that she'd been convinced had masked a deep tension.

But this was not the moment for examining the puzzle. Juliana tucked it away for future reflection and prepared for her first social encounter as Lady Edgecombe. It was only as she was crossing the hall to the drawing room that she realized she had no story to explain her marriage to the viscount. Who was she? Where had she come from? Had the duke said anything to the Meltons at the play? If so, what?

Panicked, she stopped dead in the middle of the hall, seizing Quentin's black silk sleeve. "Who am I?" she whispered.

He frowned, puzzled; then his brow cleared. "A distant cousin of the Courtneys from York. Didn't Tarquin tell you . . . but, no, of course he didn't." He shook his head.

"I could cut his tongue out!" Juliana whispered furiously. "He is the most inconsiderate, insufferable, dastardly—"

"My dear Juliana." The duke's soft voice came from the

stairs behind her. "Could you be referring to me?" His eyes twinkled.

She whirled on him and caught her heel in the hem of her gown. There was a nasty ripping sound. "Oh, hell and the devil!" she exclaimed. "Look what you've made me do!"

"Go and ask Henny to pin it up for you," Tarquin said calmly. "Quentin and I will entertain your guests until you're ready."

Juliana gathered up her skirts and cast him what she hoped was a look of utter disdain. But he pinched her nose lightly as she swept past him to the stairs, and she stuck out her tongue with lamentable lack of dignity. Their chuckles followed her upstairs.

When she entered the drawing room twenty minutes later, Tarquin came forward immediately. "Lady Edge-combe, pray allow me to make you known to Lady Melton and Lady Lydia Melton." He took her hand, drawing her into the room.

The two ladies, seated side by side on a sofa, bowed from the waist as Juliana curtsied. They were both dressed in black, Lady Melton also wearing a black dormeuse cap that completely covered her coiffure. Her daughter wore a more modest head covering of dark gray. But the overall impression was distinctly melancholy.

"I am honored, ma'am," Juliana murmured. "Pray accept my condolences on your loss."

Lady Melton smiled fleetingly. "Lady Edgecombe, I understand you only recently arrived from York."

Juliana nodded and took the fragile gilt chair Tarquin pushed forward. Lady Lydia smiled but said little throughout the interview, leaving the talking to her mother. Juliana was far more interested in the daughter than the mother, noting a sweet but not particularly expressive face, a pair of soft blue eyes, a somewhat retiring disposition. The duke was formally polite with both ladies—distant, it seemed to Juliana, unlike his brother, who was warm and attentive. She noticed that most of Lady Lydia's shy smiles were directed at Lord Quentin.

The visit lasted fifteen minutes, and Juliana was gratefully aware that she was being steered through it by the Duke of Redmayne. He answered most questions for her, but in such a way that it appeared she was answering for herself. He delicately introduced neutral, superficial topics of conversation that took them down obstacle-free avenues of purely social discourse and touched on subjects that he knew would be familiar to Juliana. When the ladies took their leave, Juliana was confident enough to think she might be able to manage the next one on her own.

Quentin and the duke escorted the ladies to their carriage. Juliana watched from the drawing-room window. It was Quentin who handed Lady Lydia into the carriage, while Tarquin did the honors for her mother—which was odd, Juliana thought. Lydia smiled at Quentin as she settled back on the seat, and he solicitously adjusted the folds of her train at her feet.

And then, with blinding impact, it struck Juliana that if she was asked who was affianced to whom, she would guess Quentin and Lady Lydia were to make a match of it. It would explain Quentin's strangeness at the theater, and it would certainly account for that fierce, bleak look she'd surprised on his face when she'd carelessly repeated what Tarquin had said about his impending marriage. It seemed she had put her foot in it with her usual clumsiness.

As she watched, Quentin walked off down the street after the carriage, and the duke turned back to the house. She heard his voice in the hall and waited for him to come back to her, but he didn't. She'd expected a word of approval . . . a moment's conversation about the visit . . . something, at least. Crossly, she went into the hall.

"Where's His Grace, Catlett?"

"In the library, I believe, my lady."

She turned down the corridor to the library at the back of the house. She knocked and marched in.

Tarquin looked up from his newspaper with an air of surprise.

"Did I conduct myself appropriately, my lord duke?" she said with an ironic curtsy.

Tarquin laid down his newspaper and leaned back in his chair. "I have offended you again, I fear. Tell me what I've done wrong so that I can correct my faults."

This assumption of chastened humility was so absurd, Juliana burst into a peal of laughter. "I fear you're a lost cause, my lord duke."

Before the conversation could go further, the butler appeared in the open door behind her.

"Visitors for Lady Edgecombe. I've shown them to your private parlor, madam."

Juliana turned, startled. "Visitors. Who?"

"Three young ladies, madam. Miss Emma, Miss Lilly, and Miss Rosamund. I thought they would be more comfortable in your parlor." Not a flicker of an expression crossed his face.

Had Catlett guessed the ladies from Russell Street were of a different order from Lady Melton and her daughter? Or had he assumed she would entertain her own friends in her own parlor?

"Excuse me, Your Grace." With a smile and curtsy she left him and hurried upstairs to her own private room.

Tarquin raised an eyebrow to the empty room and shrugged. The only woman he'd ever lived with until now had been his mother. Apparently he had something to learn in his dealings with the gentler sex—and it seemed that Juliana Courtney, Viscountess Edgecombe, was going to provide the education. Absently, he wondered why the prospect wasn't more irritating.

Juliana hurried up to her parlor, vaguely surprised at how eager she was to see her friends from Russell Street. She hadn't had much time to get to know them, but living under one roof with them even briefly had fostered the kind of easy camaraderie that came out of shared laughter as well as shared anxieties.

"Juliana, this is the most elegant parlor," Rosamund declared as Juliana came in.

"Lud, but the whole mansion is in the first style of elegance." Lilly floated across the room to embrace Juliana. "You are the luckiest creature. And just look at your gown! So pretty. And real silver buckles on your shoes, I'll be bound." The eye of the expert took in every detail of Juliana's costume.

"I swear I'll die of envy," Emma lamented, fanning herself. "Unless, of course, there is some unpleasantness here." Her eyes sharpened as she looked at Juliana over her fan. "You must have to pay for all this in some way."

"Yes, tell us all about it." Rosamund linked arms with Juliana and pulled her down onto the sofa beside her. "You can say anything you wish to us."

Juliana was tempted to confide the whole as they sat around her radiating both complicit sympathy and alert curiosity. But an instant's reflection canceled the dangerous impulse. She must learn to keep her own secrets better than she had done so far. If she hadn't yielded to weakness in the first instance and told Mistress Dennison her story, she wouldn't be in this tangle now.

"There's nothing to tell," she said. "It is exactly as you see it. I was wed to Viscount Edgecombe yesterday, and he and I both reside under the Duke of Redmayne's roof."

"So the duke didn't buy you for himself?" Emma pressed, leaning forward to get a closer view of Juliana's face.

"In a manner of speaking he did," Juliana said cautiously.

"So both he and the viscount are your lovers." Lilly smoothed her silk gloves over her fingers, her hazel eyes sharply assessing.

"Not exactly."

"La, Juliana, don't be so mysterious!" Emma cried. "Everyone wants to know how you managed such a piece of amazing good fortune. There's nothing strange about being

shared . . . particularly when you're provided for with
settlements. You are, of course?"

"Yes." Juliana decided that it would be simpler to let
them believe that she was shared by the duke and his young
cousin. It wasn't a total fabrication, anyway. "I'm well provided for, and I suppose you could say that I belong to both
the duke and the viscount." She rose and pulled the bell
rope. "Will you take ratafia, or sherry . . . or champagne?" she added with wicked inspiration. "Do you care
for champagne?"

"La, how wonderful," Lilly declared. "You can order
such things for yourself in this house?"

"Anything I please," Juliana said with a hint of bravado
as the butler arrived in answer to the summons. "Catlett,
bring us champagne, if you please."

"My lady." Catlett bowed and left without so much as a
flicker of an eyelid.

"See," Juliana said with a grin. "I have the right to
command anything I wish."

"How enviable," Rosamund sighed. "When I think of
poor Lucy Tibbet . . ." A cloud of gloom settled over
Juliana's three visitors, imparting a cynical, world-weary air
to the previously bright and youthful countenances.

"Lucy Tibbet?" she prompted.

"She worked in one of Haddock's millinery shops,"
Emma said, her usually sweet voice sharp as vinegar. "Keep
away from Mother Haddock if you value your life, Juliana."

"She's every bit as bad as Richard Haddock,"
Rosamund said. "We all thought when he died, his wife
would be easier to work for. But Elizabeth is as mean and
cruel as Richard ever was."

Catlett's arrival with the champagne produced a melancholy silence broken only by the pop of the cork and the
fizz of the straw-colored liquid in the glasses. Catlett passed
them around and bowed himself out.

"What's wrong with a millinery shop?" Juliana sipped
champagne, wrinkling her nose as the bubbles tickled her
palate.

"It's a whorehouse, dear," Lilly said with a somewhat pitying air. "They all are in Covent Garden . . . so are the chocolate houses and coffeehouses. It's just a different name to satisfy the local constables. We can't call them whorehouses, although everyone knows that's what they are."

The others chuckled at Juliana's quaint ignorance. "The Haddocks rent out shops and shacks in the Piazza . . . usually for three guineas a week. They pay the rates and expect a share of the profits."

"Not that there ever are any profits," Lilly said. "Lucy spent ten pounds last week on rent and linen and glasses that she had to buy from Mother Haddock, and she had only sixpence for herself at the end of the week."

"She'd given Richard a promissory note before he died for forty pounds," Rosamund continued with the explanation. "He'd bailed her out of debtors' prison once, and she was supposed to pay him back every week. But she can't do that out of sixpence, so Mother Haddock called in the debt and had her thrown into the Marshalsea."

"We're having a collection for her," Lilly said. "We all try to help out if we can."

"You never know when it might be you," Rosamund added glumly.

"Some of the bawds will make an interest-free loan if they like one of the girls who's in trouble," Lilly said. "But Lucy made a lot of enemies when she was doing well for herself, and now she's down on her luck, none of the bawds will lift a finger."

"And the jailers at the Marshalsea are really cruel." Emma shuddered. "They torment the prisoners and won't give them food or coal or candles if they can't pay the most outrageous sums. And Lucy doesn't have a penny to her name."

"But how much does she need?" Juliana's mind raced. She'd seen enough in her few days in London to find Lucy's plight appalling but believable. After all, the duke had gone to great pains to show her how easy it was for an unprotected girl to slip into the sewer. And once in, there was no way out.

"She needs the forty pounds to free herself from Mother Haddock," Rosamund replied. "The girls at Russell Street have put together ten pounds, and we hope the other houses will contribute too."

"Wait here." Juliana sprang to her feet, spilling champagne down her bodice. She brushed at the drops impatiently. "I'll be back in a moment." She put down her glass and whisked herself from the parlor.

Tarquin was crossing the hall on his way to the front door when she came racing down the stairs, holding her skirts well clear of her feet.

"My lord duke, I need to speak with you, it's most urgent."

He regarded her impetuous progress with a faint smile. Her eyes glowed with a zealot's fire, and her tone was vehement. "I'm at your service, my dear," he said. "Will it take long? Should I instruct the groom to return my horse to the mews?"

Juliana paused on the bottom step. "I don't believe it should take long . . . but then again it might," she said with a judicious frown. "It rather depends on your attitude, sir."

"Ahh." He nodded. "Well, let's assume that my attitude will be accommodating." He turned back to the library. "Catlett, tell Toby to walk my horse. I'll be out shortly."

Juliana followed him into the library, closing the door behind her. It seemed simpler to come straight to the point. "Am I to have an allowance, sir?"

Tarquin perched on the arm of a sofa. "I hadn't given it any thought, but, of course, you must have pin money."

"How much?" she asked bluntly.

"Well, let's see . . ." He pulled on his right earlobe with a considering frown. "You already have an adequate wardrobe, I believe?" He raised an inquiring eyebrow.

"Yes, of course," Juliana said, trying to restrain her impatience. "But there are—"

"Other things," he interrupted. "I do quite understand that. If you were to take your place at court, of course, two hundred pounds a year would be barely sufficient for personal necessities, but since that's not going to happen, I would have thought—"

"Who said it wasn't going to happen?" demanded Juliana, momentarily deflected from her original purpose.

Tarquin looked perplexed. "I thought it was understood. Surely you don't wish to enter society?"

"I might," she said. "I don't see why I shouldn't have the option."

Tarquin's perplexity deepened. He'd had a very clear idea in his head of how Juliana would conduct herself under his roof, and joining the exclusive court circles had not been part of it. He remembered how she'd seemed to encourage Lucien's company that morning—another contingency he hadn't considered. Was it just mischief on her part? Or was she going to be more trouble than he'd bargained for?

"Let's leave that issue for the moment," he said. "I suggest we settle on fifty pounds a quarter at this stage. I'll instruct my bankers accordingly." He stood up and moved toward the door.

"Well, could I have forty pounds now, please?" Juliana stood between him and the door, unconsciously squaring her shoulders. She had never been given money of her own and had never dared ask for it before. But she reasoned that since she was now a viscountess, she was entitled to make some demands.

"Whatever do you want such a sum for?"

"Do I have to tell you how I spend my pin money?"

He shook his head. "No, I suppose not. Are you in some difficulties?"

"No." She shook her head vehemently. "But I have need of forty pounds . . . well, thirty I suppose would do . . . but I need it immediately."

"Very well." Still clearly puzzled, Tarquin went to the desk and opened the top drawer. He drew out a strongbox, unlocked it, and selected three twenty-pound notes. "Here you are, *mignonne*."

"That's sixty pounds," she said, taking the notes.

"You may have need of a little extra," he pointed out. "Will you give me your word you're in no difficulties?"

"Yes, of course, how should I be?" she said, tucking the notes into her bosom. "Thank you very much. I'm very much obliged to you, my lord duke." Spinning on her heel, she half ran from the library, again holding her skirts clear of her feet.

Tarquin stood frowning for a minute. Did that urgent request have anything to do with her visitors from Russell Street? It seemed likely. Highly likely, and he wasn't at all sure that he approved of Juliana's subsidizing Elizabeth Dennison's harlots. But she did have the right to some money of her own, and he didn't have the right to dictate how she should spend it. He found he'd lost interest in his ride and stood in fiercely frowning silence in the middle of the room.

"There, that's forty pounds." Juliana placed two of the bills on the table in her parlor before the astounded eyes of her friends. "So you won't need to spend your own money for Lucy's bail. Shall we go at once?"

"But . . . but is this your own money, Juliana?" Even the down-to-earth Lilly was astonished.

"In a manner of speaking," she said airily. "The duke gave it to me as part of my allowance. I wasn't sure whether I was to have one or not, but Lord Quentin said His Grace was generous to a fault, so I thought I'd put it to the test. And there you are." She indicated the riches on the table with a grandiose flourish, rather spoiling the effect by adding, "It isn't as if he can't afford it, after all."

"Well, I for one won't question such good fortune," Lilly said, tucking the notes into her beaded silk muff. "And I know Lucy won't."

"Then let's go at once." Juliana energetically strode to the door. "Do you know how to get there? Can we walk?

Or should I order the carriage?" she added with another grand gesture.

"We can't go ourselves," Rosamund protested, shocked.

"But you have a footman downstairs."

"It's still no place for ladies," Emma explained. "The jailers are horrid and rude, and they'll ask for all sorts of extras before they'll release Lucy. Mr. Garston will go for us. They won't intimidate him."

"They won't intimidate *me*," Juliana declared. "Come, let's go. We'll hail a hackney, as there's not a moment to lose. Heaven only knows what miseries Lucy's enduring."

This consideration overrode further objections, although her companions were still rather dubious as they followed her down the stairs, where they collected the Dennisons' footman, Juliana told Catlett that she expected to be back for dinner, and they stepped out into the warm afternoon.

Chapter 14

"Where are you off to, Lady Edgecombe?" Quentin was coming up the front steps as they emerged from the house. He bowed courteously to her companions.

"To the Marshalsea," Juliana said cheerfully. "To bail someone out."

"To the Marshalsea?" Quentin stared at her. "Don't be absurd, child."

"The footman will accompany us," she said, gesturing to the flunky behind her.

"The footman may accompany your friends, but Lady Edgecombe does not go to a debtors' prison," Quentin stated.

"Truly it would be best to ask Mr. Garston to go for us, Juliana," Emma put in, laying a tentative hand on Juliana's arm.

"Tarquin would flay me alive if I permitted it," Quentin declared.

Juliana regarded him steadily. "I understood I was free to go where I please."

"Not to the Marshalsea."

"Not even if you accompanied me?"

"Juliana, I have not the slightest desire to visit a debtors' prison."

"But you're a man of the cloth. Surely you have a duty to help your fellow man in need? And this *is* an errand of mercy." Her voice was all sweet reason, her smile cajoling, but Quentin was aware of a powerful determination behind the ingenuous facade.

"Why not follow your friend's suggestion and ask this Mr. Garston to go for you?"

"But that will take time. And that poor girl shouldn't languish in that place a minute more than necessary. I heard that the jailers torture the inmates for money, when of course they can't have any funds, because if they did, they wouldn't be there in the first place." Her eyes sparked with indignation and her cheeks were pale with anger, all pretense of ingenuous cajoling vanished. "You have a duty, Lord Quentin, to help those in trouble. Don't you?"

"Yes, I like to think so," Quentin said dryly. He was uncomfortably reminded that as a canon of Melchester Cathedral, he hadn't spent much time tending a flock. He was beginning to wonder why he'd ever felt Juliana needed protection and guidance. At this moment she hardly seemed like anyone's victim.

"We have the money," Juliana continued. "All forty pounds of Lucy's debt. And if the jailers demand more, I shall tell them to go hang," she added with a flashing eye. "If we allow them to get away with extortion, they'll do it to everyone."

"I'm sure you will keep them in line," Quentin murmured. "I pity the man who tries to stand in your path."

"Oh, you sound just like the duke," Juliana said. "So toplofty. But I tell you straight, my lord, you won't persuade me out of this."

"You are right that I am obliged to help those in trouble." His mouth took a sardonic quirk that made him look even more like his half brother. "I am also obliged to keep people *out* of trouble. And I assure you, my dear Juliana, you will be up to your neck in hot water if Tarquin discovers you've been roaming around a debtors' prison."

Juliana was standing on the top step, half facing the open front door. Out of the corner of her eye she caught sight of Lucien crossing the hall toward the drawing room. "If my husband doesn't object, I fail to see why the duke should," she said with a flash of inspiration. "I do beg your pardon for teasing you, Lord Quentin. Of course you mustn't trouble yourself over this for another minute."

She gave him a radiant smile and turned to the three young women. "I'll be back in an instant. Wait here for me." She hurried into the house, leaving Quentin staring uneasily after her, unsure whether he'd heard her aright.

"Oh, dear," Emma said. "Do you think Juliana is perhaps a little impetuous?"

"I fear that 'a little' is something of an understatement, ma'am," Quentin said. "Surely she's not intending to enlist Edgecombe's support?"

"I believe so, my lord," Rosamund said, her brown eyes wide and solemn in her round face.

"Excuse me." Quentin bowed briefly and strode into the house in search of Tarquin, leaving the women still on the steps.

Juliana had followed Lucien into the drawing room and closed the door behind her. "My lord, I need your leave to go on an errand," she stated straightaway.

"Good God! What's this?" Lucien exclaimed. "*You* are asking *me* for permission?"

"Indeed, my lord." Juliana curtsied. "You are my husband, are you not?"

Lucien gave a crack of laughter. "That's a fine fabrication, my dear. But I daresay it has its uses."

"Precisely," she said. "And since you are my husband, yours is the only leave I need to run my errand."

Lucien's harsh laugh rasped again. "Well, I'll be damned, m'dear. You're setting yourself up in opposition to Tarquin, are you? Brave girl!" He flipped open an enameled snuffbox and took a liberal pinch, his eyes like dead coals in his grayish pallor.

"I'm not precisely in opposition to His Grace," Juliana said judiciously, "since I haven't consulted him on the matter—indeed, I don't consider it his business. But I *am* consulting *you*, sir, and I would like your leave."

"To do what?" he inquired curiously.

Juliana sighed. "To go to the Marshalsea with bail for a friend of my friends."

"What friends?"

"Girls from the house where I was living before I came here," she said a touch impatiently, hoping that the duke wouldn't suddenly appear, summoned by Lord Quentin.

Lucien sneezed violently, burying his face in a handkerchief. It was a few minutes before he emerged, a hectic flush on his cheeks, his eyes streaming. "Gad, girl! Don't tell me Tarquin took you out of a whorehouse!" He chuckled, thumping his chest with the heel of one hand as his breath wheezed painfully. "That's rich. My holier-than-thou cousin finding me a wife from a whorehouse to save a family scandal. What price family honor, eh!"

Juliana regarded him with ill-concealed distaste. "You may believe what you please, my lord. But I am not and never have been a whore."

Lucien raised a mock-placatory hand. "Don't eat me, m'dear. It doesn't matter to me what you were . . . or, indeed, what you *are*. You could have serviced an entire regiment before dinner, for all that I care."

Juliana felt her temper rise. Her lip curled and her eyes threw poisoned daggers at him. Firmly she told herself that Viscount Edgecombe was not worth her anger. "Will you give me leave to go to the Marshalsea, my lord?" she demanded impatiently.

"Oh, you may have leave to do anything you wish if it'll irritate Tarquin, my lady." He chuckled and wheezed. "By all means visit the debtors' prison. By all means choose your friends from the whorehouses of Covent Garden. By all means do a little business of that sort on the side, if it appeals to you. You have my unconditional leave to indulge in any form of debauchery, to wallow in the stews every night. Just don't ask me for money. I don't have two brass farthings to rub together."

Juliana paled and her freckles stood out on the bridge of her nose. "Rest assured, I will ask you for nothing further, my lord." She dropped an icy curtsy. "If you'll excuse me, my friends await me."

"Just a minute." He raised an arresting hand, impervious to her anger. "Perhaps I'll accompany you on this errand. Lend a touch of respectability . . ." He grinned, the skin stretched tight on his skull. "If your husband bears you company, Tarquin will have to gnash his teeth in silence."

Juliana wasn't happy at the prospect of enduring her husband's company. On the other hand, the idea of thwarting the duke had an irresistible appeal. He did, after all, have it coming.

"Very well," Juliana murmured.

"Well, let's be about this business." He sounded relatively robust at the prospect of sowing mischief and moved to the door with almost a spring in his step. Juliana followed, her eyes agleam now with her own mischief.

Just as they reached the front door, Quentin and the duke emerged from the library.

"Juliana!" Tarquin's voice was sharp. "Where do you think you're going?"

She turned and curtsied. "For a drive with my husband, my lord duke. I trust you have no objections."

The duke's mouth tightened and an ominous muscle twitched in his cheek. "Lucien, you're not encouraging this outrageous scheme."

"My wife has asked for my permission to help a friend, and I've offered her my company in support, dear boy." Lucien couldn't hide his glee. "Wouldn't do for Lady Edgecombe to go alone to the Marshalsea . . . but in my company there can be no objection."

"Don't be absurd," the duke snapped. "Juliana, go upstairs to your parlor. I'll come to you directly."

Juliana frowned at this curt order. "Forgive me, my lord duke, but my husband has commanded my presence. I do believe that his commands must take precedence over yours." She curtsied again and whisked herself out of the house before Tarquin could gather his wits to react.

Lucien grinned, offered his cousin a mock bow, and followed his wife.

"Insolent baggage!" Tarquin exclaimed. "Who the hell does she think she is?"

"Viscountess Edgecombe, apparently," his brother said, unable to hide a wry smile. It wasn't often that Tarquin was routed.

The duke stared at him in fulminating silence; then he spun on his heel and strode back to the library. He left the door ajar, so after a moment's hesitation Quentin followed him.

"If that child thinks she can use Lucien to provoke me, she'd better think again," the duke said, his mouth a thin, straight line, his eyes cold and hard as agate. "What could she possibly hope to gain by such a thing?"

"Revenge," Quentin suggested, perching on the wide windowsill. "She's a lady of some spirit."

"She's a minx!" The duke paced the room with long, angry strides.

"They won't come to any harm," Quentin soothed. "Lucien will—"

"That drunken degenerate is only interested in putting one over on me," Tarquin interrupted. "He's not concerned about Juliana in the least."

"Well, no one need know about it," Quentin said.

"No one need know that Viscountess Edgecombe in the company of three whores went to the rescue of a pauper harlot in the Marshalsea!" Tarquin exclaimed. "Goddammit, Quentin! They may not recognize Juliana, but they will certainly recognize Lucien."

"Not if they take a closed carriage," Quentin suggested lamely.

A dismissive wave showed what Tarquin thought of this

possibility. He resumed his pacing, an angry frown knotting his brow. Lucien would cause whatever evil he could. Juliana was only a country innocent, and she had no idea what she was dealing with. Somehow he would have to put a stop to her foolish alliance with Lucien.

George Ridge climbed up from the basement steps of the house opposite the duke's mansion on Albermarle Street and stood watching the group of four women and a man followed by a footman stroll down the street. He stood with his feet apart, adjusting his waistcoat with a complacent tug, his right hand resting on his sword hilt. He'd been watching the house on Albermarle Street since midmorning, and nothing he'd seen made any sense. Last night he'd assumed that Juliana had been bought for the night by the two men who'd taken her into the house. But now it seemed as if she lived there. His first thought was that it was a whorehouse and the men were visiting her there. But two ladies, evidently irreproachable in their somber clothes, had arrived in a carriage with an earl's arms on the panels. Then the two men he'd seen the previous night had escorted them back to the carriage with all due ceremony and courtesy. Then the three young women, accompanied by a footman, had arrived. Some altercation had occurred, he was convinced, between Juliana and one of the two men who seemed to live in the house, and now there she was in the company of yet another man, prancing down the street with the other women.

None of it made any sense. Juliana's dress was fine as fivepence and didn't look in the least whorish, but there was an air about her present companions that he would swear labeled them as Impures. High Impures, certainly, but definitely not fit companions for a young lady of Juliana's birth and breeding. And what of the man whose arm she held? Unsavory-looking creature, George thought, although the view from his hiding place was partially obscured by the iron railings. Something very rum was going on, and the sooner he got to the bottom of it, the sooner he'd be able to decide on his next move.

He stood for a few more minutes until the party reached the end of the street; then he strolled off toward the mews at the back of the house. Someone there would tell him to whom the house belonged. It would be a start.

"Don't you think we should get a hackney, sir?" Juliana inquired as they emerged onto the crowded thoroughfare of Piccadilly.

"Oh, all in good time . . . all in good time," Lucien responded easily. "I've a mind to show myself to the world in such charming company. It's a rare sight for me to be surrounded by a bevy of the doves of Venus. We're bound to meet up with some of my friends . . . an acquaintance or two. Introduce you, m'dear wife . . . and of course your friends . . . your previous fellow laborers." He chuckled.

Juliana's lips thinned. She wasn't prepared to sacrifice her reputation just to annoy the duke. Lucien was taking matters too far.

A hackney carriage trundled along Piccadilly toward them, and with swift resolution she hailed it. "Forgive me, my lord, but I don't believe we have the time for social dalliance." She tugged on the handle of the carriage door as it came to a stop beside them. "I think we can all fit in, if you don't mind sitting on the box, sir." She offered him a placating smile and was taken aback by the flash of sullen anger in the ashy coals of his eyes.

"I say we walk along Piccadilly, madam."

Juliana's smile remained unwavering as her three friends were handed into the coach by the footman. "Indeed, my lord, but we cannot spare the time. Poor Lucy could even now be dying of starvation in that place. We don't have a minute to lose." She turned to follow her companions into the hackney. Seating herself, she leaned out of the still-open door.

"If you don't wish to sit on the box, my lord, perhaps you could follow us in a separate hackney."

Lucien glowered at her. Juliana coaxed, "Please come, my lord. If I go alone, His Grace will feel he has cause to be vexed with me. But as you so rightly said, if you come, he'll have to bite his tongue."

It worked. The viscount, still glowering, climbed onto the box beside the jarvey. "The Marshalsea," he growled. The jarvey cracked his whip and the hackney moved off, the footman leaping onto the step behind, hanging on to the leather strap.

"Why are you so set on this, Juliana?" Lilly fanned herself in the warm interior, her languid air belied by the sharpness of her gaze. "I warrant it has to do with more than Lucy's plight."

"Perhaps it has," Juliana said with a serene smile. "But Lucy's situation is the first consideration."

Rosamund was sitting in silence in a corner, the muslin collar of her short cloak drawn up around her ears as if she were hiding from something. When she spoke, her voice was husky and awkward. "Forgive me, Juliana, I don't wish to pry. But . . . but that is your husband who's accompanying us?"

"Yes, for my sins," Juliana replied with a shudder. Once out of the viscount's presence she couldn't hide her repulsion.

"He's a sick man," Rosamund said hesitantly. "I don't know if—"

"He's poxed," Lilly stated flatly. "There's no need to beat about the bush, Rosamund, we all know the signs. Have you been in his bed, Juliana?"

Juliana shook her head. "No, and I shall not. It's not part of the arrangement."

"Well, that's a relief!" Emma sighed and relaxed. "I didn't know what to say . . . how to warn you."

"There's no need. I've had fair warning," Juliana responded, looking out of the window to conceal her expression from her companions. "And I'm in no danger . . . at least not of that sort," she couldn't help adding in a low voice.

"It's to be hoped we don't catch something in the Marshalsea," Rosamund muttered. "There's jail fever and all sorts of things in that place. Just breathing the air can infect you."

"Then you may stay in the hackney," Juliana said. "The viscount and I will go inside and procure Lucy's release."

"I'm certainly coming in," Lilly said stoutly. "You don't know Lucy. She won't know to trust you."

"No, she's had so much ill luck," Emma agreed with a sigh. "She won't know whom to trust."

The carriage came to a rattling halt on the uneven cobbles in front of a fearsome high-walled building. Great iron gates stood open to the street, and ragged creatures shuffled through them, exuding a desperate kind of defeat.

"Who are they?" Juliana gazed out of the door as the footman opened it.

"Debtors," Lilly said, stepping down to the road ahead of her.

"But they aren't incarcerated."

"No, they're paroled from dawn to dusk so they can beg—or work, if they can find something," Emma explained, following Juliana to the cobbles. "And they have visitors, who bring them food, if they're lucky. There are whole families in there. Babies, small children, old men and women."

Lucien clambered off the box, the maneuver clearly costing him some effort. He stood for a minute wheezing, leaning against the carriage, sweat standing out on his pallid brow. "I must be mad to agree to such a ridiculous scheme," he muttered, mopping his forehead with his handkerchief. "You go about your business, madam wife. I'm going to settle my chest in that tavern over yonder." He gestured to a ramshackle building with a crooked door frame and loose shutters. Its identifying sign was unreadable and hung by a single nail over the door. "Come to me in the taproom when you're finished with your errand of mercy."

Juliana silently resolved to send the footman through that unsavory-looking door, but she curtsied meekly to her husband, eyes lowered to the mud-encrusted cobbles.

Lucien ignored the salutation and hurried off, the smell of cognac drawing him like a dog to a bone.

"Oh, dear, I thought the viscount was going to negotiate for us," Rosamund said, dismayed.

"We have no need of Edgecombe for the moment." Juliana gathered up her skirts and set off toward the gate, watching her feet warily as she picked her way through the festering kennel in the middle of the street, praying she wouldn't catch her high heel on an uneven cobble.

The gatekeeper stared blearily at them as they stopped at his hut. His little eyes were red-rimmed and unfocused, and he smelled most powerfully of gin. He took a swig from the stone jar on his lap before deigning to answer Juliana's question.

"Lucy Tibbet?" He wiped his mouth with the back of his hand. "Tibbet, eh? Now, who'd 'ave put 'er in 'ere?"

"Mistress Haddock," Lilly said.

"Oh, that bawd!" The gatekeeper threw back his head and guffawed, sending a foul miasma into the steamy summer air. "Lucifer, but she's an 'ard one, she is. Worse than that 'ubby of 'ers. That Richard. Lor' bless me, but 'e was worth a bob or two, weren't 'e?"

"If by that you mean he took every penny his girls earned, I'd agree with you," Lilly said acerbically. She was clearly made of sterner stuff than Rosamund and Emma, who were hanging back, holding their skirts well clear of the matted straw and rotting vegetables littering the cobbles.

"You one of 'em, missie?" The gatekeeper leered. "Mebbe we could come to some arrangement, like."

"And maybe you could tell us where to find Mistress Tibbet," Juliana said, stepping forward. The gatekeeper drew back involuntarily from the tongues of jade fire in her eyes, the taut line of her mouth, the tall, erect figure. This lady looked as if she were unaccustomed to meeting with opposition, and she held herself with an assurance that whores generally lacked.

"Well, now, mebbe I could, my lady . . . fer a consideration," he said, pulling his whiskery chin.

"I have forty pounds here to pay her debt," Juliana said crisply. "In addition I will give you a guinea, my good man, if you make things easy for us. Otherwise, we shall manage without you."

"Oho . . . hoity-toity, aren't we!" The gatekeeper lumbered to his feet. "Now you listen 'ere, my fine lady. The name's Mr. Cogg to you, an' I'll thankee to show a little respect."

"And I'll thank you to mind your manners," Juliana said. "Are you interested in earning a guinea or not?"

"Ten guineas it'll be to secure 'er release." His eyes narrowed slyly.

"Forty guineas to pay off her debt, and one guinea for your good self," Juliana said. "Otherwise, I shall visit the nearest magistrate and arrange for Mistress Tibbet's release with him. And you, Cogg, will get nothing."

The gatekeeper looked astounded. He was unaccustomed to such authoritative young women at his gates. In general, those who came to liberate friends and relatives were almost as indigent as the prisoner. They addressed Mr. Cogg as *sir*, with averted eyes, and crept around, keeping to the shadows. They were not comfortable with magistrates, and in general, a threatening word or two was sufficient to ensure a substantial handout for the gatekeeper.

Lilly had stepped up to Juliana's shoulder, and she, too, glared at the gatekeeper. Emma and Rosamund, emboldened by their friends' stand, also gazed fixedly at Mr. Cogg.

After a minute the gatekeeper snorted and held out his hand. "Give it 'ere, then."

Juliana shook her head. "Not until you've taken us to Mistress Tibbet."

"I'll see the color of yer money, first, my lady." He drew

himself upright, but even standing tall, his eyes were only on a level with Juliana's. She regarded him as contemptuously as an amazon facing a pygmy.

"I'm going to find a magistrate." She turned on her heel, praying the bluff would work. It could take hours to find a magistrate and hours to secure Lucy's release by that route. And Juliana always hated to alter her plans. Having once set her heart and mind on walking out of this place with Lucy, she was loath to give up.

" 'Old on, 'old on," the gatekeeper grumbled. He knew that if a magistrate ordered the prisoner's release, he'd see not a penny for himself. A golden guinea was better than nothing. He took another swig from his stone bottle and came out of his little hut, blowing his nose on a red spotted handkerchief. "This a-way."

They followed him across a yard, thronged with people. Two small boys darted between the legs of the crowd and cannoned into the gatekeeper, whose hands moved seamlessly, clouting them both around the ears even as he continued to walk. The boys fell to the ground, wailing and rubbing their ears. A woman screamed at them and came running over, waving a rolling pin. The children scrambled to their feet and disappeared so quickly, it was almost as if they'd never been there.

The gatekeeper went through another gate into an internal courtyard, as busy as the other. There were cooking fires there, and women scrubbing clothes at rain butts. The stick-thin bodies were clad in rags, the children half-naked, for the most part. The scene reminded Juliana of the gypsy encampments in the New Forest during her childhood.

But inside the building things were very different. Here there was sickness and despair. Rail-thin, hunched figures sat on the filthy stone stairs, their eyes blank, as the gatekeeper, followed by Juliana and her companions, puffed his way upward. Juliana glimpsed rooms off the landings— rooms without furniture, with unglazed windows and straw on the floor. And in the straw lay huddled bodies, crumpled like pieces of discarded paper. The air reeked of death and desolation. These people were dying there. These were the folk for whom there was no salvation. Who had no one in the world with money either to procure their release or to ensure them at least sufficient bread to keep body and soul together.

Her three companions were silent, looking neither to right nor left, avoiding the sight of the horrors that hovered on the edges of their own lives. The horrors that inevitably came to the old and infirm of Covent Garden if they weren't clever or lucky enough to provide for the uncertain future.

"She's in 'ere." Mr. Cogg stopped at an open doorway at the top of the last staircase. He was breathing heavily, sweat running down his face. "Lucy Tibbet!" he bellowed into the dimly lit attic room. "Lucy Tibbet . . . show a leg there."

A faint groan came from the far wall, and Lilly pushed past him and almost ran into the room, her pink skirts swinging gracefully. The others followed, blue and palest green, bending together over a shape on the straw. They looked like summer butterflies in a dungeon, Juliana thought as she crossed the room to join them, her nose wrinkling at the powerful stench emanating from a tin bucket in the corner.

Lucy lay in the straw, her eyes half-closed. She was filthy, her hair matted, shoeless and clad only in a torn chemise. The hectic flush of fever was on her thin cheeks, and a clawlike hand fluttered in Lilly's palm.

"Sweet heaven, what have they done to you?" Emma cried, dropping to her knees on the dirty straw. "Where are your clothes?"

"Jailer took them," Lucy croaked. "To pay for bread and water. Until there was nothing left . . ." She turned her head on the straw, two tears trickling from behind her closed eyelids. "They took my good shift and gave me this one in its place. I suppose I should be thankful they didn't leave me naked."

"Oh, how wicked!" Rosamund's tears fell onto the straw.

"We've come to take you out of here," Juliana said, seeking in brisk action to mask her own appalled distress. "Rosamund, if you lend Lucy your cloak, it will protect her a little until we can get her into the hackney."

Rosamund eagerly unclasped her cloak. Lilly lifted Lucy from the straw and draped the soft silk garment around her shoulders. The contrast between the shimmering silk and the girl's filthy, matted hair, thin cheeks, and torn shift was shocking.

"Can you walk?" Juliana half lifted Lucy to her feet and held her as she swayed dizzily.

"My head's spinning." Lucy's voice was weak and shaky. "I haven't stood up for days."

"You'll feel stronger in a minute," Emma said, stroking Lucy's emaciated arm. "I could drive a knife into Mother Haddock!" she added ferociously. "We didn't know you were in here until a few days ago. The bawd told her girls to keep quiet about it if they didn't want to find themselves joining you."

"There has to be a way to get even," Lilly muttered, staring around the attic as if taking it in for the first time. "She intended you should die in this hole."

"We'll think about getting even later." Juliana slipped a supporting arm around Lucy's waist. "Lilly, you take her other arm."

The gatekeeper was still in the doorway, watching the scene with scant interest. His little eyes focused sharply, however, when he saw Lucy on her feet. "Eh, you don't leave 'ere until I gets me money."

Lilly, at a nod from Juliana, withdrew the two crisp notes from her muff. "This is the sum of her debt." Mr. Cogg stretched out a hand for them, but she held on to the notes.

"However did you—"

"Hush, dear, don't talk until we're safely outside," Rosamund said, patting Lucy's hand. "We'll explain everything then."

"Give it 'ere, then." Mr. Cogg snapped his fingers.

"It has to be paid to Mistress Haddock," Juliana said. "I'm not giving it to you until you give me a receipt for it."

Mr. Cogg shot her a look of intense dislike. "Fer such a young thing, you knows yer way around," he grumbled, turning back to the stairs. "Where was you brung up, then? In a moneylender's?"

It was intended to be a deep insult, but Juliana merely laughed, thinking that Sir Brian Forsett's example when it came to money dealings could as well have been set in a moneylender's.

She wrote out the receipt herself and stood over Mr. Cogg as he put his mark to it. Then she laid the forty pounds on the rickety table in his hut. "I have only a twenty-pound note. Does anyone have a guinea to give to this kind gentleman?"

Rosamund produced the required coin and they left the Marshalsea, Lucy hobbling on her bare feet between Juliana and Lilly. The footman and the hackney carriage were waiting where they'd left them; of Lucien there was no sign.

"Fetch Viscount Edgecombe from the tavern, if you please," Juliana instructed the servant, who was staring with unabashed curiosity at the pathetic scarecrow they were lifting into the hackney.

Lucy sank onto the cracked leather squabs with a groan. "Are you hungry, dear?" Emma inquired tenderly, sitting beside her and chafing her hands.

"I don't feel it anymore," Lucy told her, her voice still low and weak. "It was painful for the first week, but now I feel nothing."

"Where are we to take her?" Lilly sat opposite, a frown drawing her plucked eyebrows together. "We can't take her back to Mother Haddock."

"What about Mistress Dennison?" Juliana was looking out of the window, watching for her husband.

"No," Rosamund said. "She's already said she won't help Lucy."

"Lucy refused a wealthy patron that Mistress Dennison presented to her," Emma explained.

"He was a filthy pervert," Lucy said with more strength than she'd shown hitherto. "And I didn't need him or his money then."

"She was in the keeping of Lord Amhurst," Lilly said. "Mistress Dennison had arranged the contract and thought Lucy owed her a favor. It was only for one night, apparently."

"One night with that piece of gutter filth!" Lucy fell back, exhausted, and closed her eyes.

"Anyway, that's why Mistress Dennison won't help her," Rosamund stated.

"She can come back with me," Juliana declared with rather more confidence than she felt. The duke was not going to be best pleased with her as it was. Asking him to house the indigent Lucy in her present condition was a favor no one would blame him for refusing even in his most charitable frame of mind.

"Well, that's settled." Lilly sounded relieved as she set the seal on Juliana's offer. "And while you're getting better, Lucy, we'll try to persuade Mistress Dennison to take you in when you're ready to work again."

"She's quite good-hearted, really," Emma put in. "In fact they both are if you keep on the right side of them."

A discussion began on the likelihood of the Dennisons' relenting, but Juliana continued to peer out of the window toward the tavern. The footman finally reemerged and trotted back to the hackney. He was alone.

"Beggin' your pardon, m'lady, but his lordship says as how he's not ready to leave just yet and you should go on without him."

"Damn," Juliana muttered. The viscount was not a reliable partner in crime. Without him at her side things would go harder for her when they got back to Albermarle Street, and she wouldn't be able to refer Tarquin's complaints to her husband, as she'd intended doing. She debated going in after Lucien herself, then decided against it. If he was far gone in cognac, she'd achieve only her own discomfort.

"Very well. Tell the jarvey to return to Albermarle Street," she instructed, withdrawing her head from the window. Lucy was huddled between Lilly and Rosamund, a tiny, frail figure in her thin shift against the butterfly richness of the other women. She didn't look more than twenty. What kind of life had she led so far that she could have been condemned so young to such a hideous death?

Chapter 15

The carriage drew up on Albermarle Street and Juliana alighted, reaching up to help Lucy as her friends half lifted her down.

"Should we come in with you?"

Juliana, after a moment's reflection, shook her head. "No, I think I'd better do this alone, Emma. It could be a little awkward. I can manage to get Lucy up the steps without help."

"If you're sure," Rosamund said, trying to conceal her relief but not quite succeeding.

"You would be better employed persuading the Dennisons to shelter Lucy when she's recovered her strength," Juliana said, supporting Lucy with a strong arm at her waist. "I'll come to Russell Street tomorrow and tell you how she is. Also," she added with an intent frown, "I have an idea that I want to talk over with you all. And the other girls, too, if they'd be interested."

"Interested in what?" Lilly leaned forward, her eyes sharp.

"I can't explain here. I have to think it through myself first, anyway." She smiled and raised a hand in farewell. "Until tomorrow."

There was a chorus of good-byes as she supported Lucy

up the steps to the front door. Catlett opened it before she could knock, and for once his impassive expression cracked when he saw her companion. Juliana couldn't blame him. Lucy was a dreadful sight. Rosamund's incongruous, delicate, muslin-frilled cloak only accentuated her half-naked condition. However, Juliana merely nodded to Catlett as she helped the girl into a chair in the hall.

Lucy fell back, her face whiter than milk, her eyes closed, her heart racing with the effort of getting from the carriage to the chair. Juliana stood looking at her, for the moment nonplussed. What orders should she give? There must be spare bedchambers in the house, but did she have the right to dispose of one without the duke's leave? Probably not, she decided, but there didn't really seem to be much option.

"Catlett, would you ask the housekeeper to show me to——"

"What in the devil's name is going on here?"

Juliana spun round at the duke's voice. So he hadn't recovered his good humor in her absence—not that she'd expected that he would have. She glimpsed Quentin behind him, overshadowed by his brother, not so much by height as by Tarquin's sheer presence.

She cleared her throat and began, "My lord duke, this is the woman we brought from the Marshalsea, and——"

"Catlett, you may leave." The duke interrupted her with this curt order to the servant, who was staring at the pale, crumpled figure of Lucy, as fascinated as if she were a two-headed woman at the fair.

"Now you may continue," Tarquin said as Catlett melted away into the shadows behind the stairs.

Juliana took a deep breath. "If you please, sir——"

Lucy moaned faintly, and Quentin, with a muttered exclamation, pushed past his brother and bent over her.

Juliana tried again. "She's been starved," she said, her voice stronger as she thought of Lucy's plight. "Tortured with starvation and left to die in that filthy place. She needs to be looked after, and I said she could come here."

"Indeed, Tarquin, the girl has been shockingly mistreated." Quentin straightened, his expression stricken. "We should send for the physician as soon as she's put to bed."

The duke looked over at Lucy and his expression softened for a minute, but when he turned his eyes back to Juliana, they cooled again. "For the time being you may take her upstairs and hand her over to Henny. She will know what to do for her. But then I would like to speak with you in my book room."

Juliana stepped back from him and dropped a curtsy. "Thank you, my lord duke. I am yours to command." She lowered her eyes in feigned submission and thus missed the spark of reluctant amusement that flared in his eyes. When she looked up, it was extinguished. He gave her a curt nod and stalked off to his book room.

"Come, Juliana, I'll help you get the poor girl upstairs. She's barely conscious." Quentin lifted Lucy into his arms, seeming unaware of her filthy clothes and hair pressed to his immaculate white shirt and gray silk coat. He carried her to the stairs, Juliana following.

"I'll put her in the yellow bedchamber," Quentin said almost to himself, turning right at the head of the stairs. "Then we'll ring for Henny."

He laid Lucy on the bed and drew the coverlet over her with all the tenderness of a skilled nurse. Juliana rang for Henny and then sat on the edge of the bed beside Lucy. "How *dare* they?" she said with soft ferocity. "Look at her! And that place was full of skeletons . . . little children. . . . Oh, it's disgusting!"

"I wish it were possible to change such things," Quentin said uncomfortably.

"But *you* could!" Juliana sprang to her feet, her eyes flashing with a zealot's enthusiasm. "You and people like you. You're powerful and rich. You could make things happen. You *know* you could."

Quentin was saved from a reply by the arrival of Henny,

who took charge with smooth efficiency, showing no apparent surprise at the condition of her patient.

"Come, let's leave Henny to tend her." Quentin drew Juliana toward the door. "And you must go to Tarquin."

Juliana grimaced. "He seems very vexed."

"You could say that." A smile touched his mouth. "But if you play your cards right, he won't remain so. Believe it or not, he's really a very fair man. He was easygoing as a boy . . . except in the face of injustice or deliberate provocation." Quentin's smile broadened as he recollected certain incidents of their shared boyhood. "At those times we all learned to keep out of his way."

"I don't seem to be able to stay out of his way," she said with a helpless shrug. "If I'd been able to do that, I wouldn't be living here now."

Tarquin had been trying to recapture a sense of control over events. He couldn't understand how a chit of a girl could have such a profoundly disturbing effect on the smooth running of his life. But ever since he'd seen her through the peephole, naked in the candlelight, she'd exerted some power over him . . . a power that had intensified as he'd introduced her to the ways of passion. He was moved by her. He no longer knew what to expect—from her, from himself. It was not a pleasant sensation; indeed, he found it almost frightening.

When Juliana tapped at the door, he flung himself into the chair behind the massive mahogany desk and picked up a sheaf of papers. "Enter." He didn't look up from the documents as the door opened.

Juliana stood in the doorway, waiting for him to acknowledge her. Instead he said, still without looking up, "Close the door."

Juliana did so and stepped into the room. Her chin went up. If he was intending to humiliate her by this insulting treatment, he would find it didn't work. Without invitation she sat down casually on a chair, her wide skirts flowing gracefully around her, and picked up a copy of the *Morning Post* from a side table.

Tarquin glanced up, and that same glimmer of reluctant laughter sprang to his eyes as he surveyed the red head bent over the newspaper, the graceful curve of her neck, the absolute resistance radiating from the still figure. Viscountess Edgecombe wasn't yielding an inch.

He put the papers aside and said, "Let's not beat around the bush, *mignonne*. As I understand it, you intend to form an alliance with Lucien. Is that correct?"

Juliana's eyebrows lifted. "I don't know what you mean, sir. The viscount is my husband. I am absolutely allied with him in the eyes of the Church and the law."

Tarquin's lips thinned. "I tell you straight, Juliana, that I will not tolerate it. Also, as of now, you will have nothing further to do with Mistress Dennison's girls. They will not visit you here, and you will not visit them. You mustn't be tainted with the whorehouse."

"But am I not already tainted? What am I but your whore, bought under contract to a bawd?"

"You are my mistress, Juliana. That doesn't make you a whore."

"Oh, come now, my lord duke," she said scornfully. "You bought me for three thousand pounds, as I recall. Or was it guineas? I'm flattered that I should be worth so much to you, but I suppose the breeding aspect to this arrangement makes me more valuable. I may be naive, but I *do* know that men don't buy their mistresses. They buy whores."

"I think you've said all there is to say on that subject," the duke said coldly. "Repeatedly, I might add. I will now repeat myself. You will have no further contact with the girls on Russell Street. Henny will take care of that unfortunate creature upstairs until she's well enough to leave, at which point I'll give her a sum of money that will enable her to establish herself without a protector."

Quentin had said the duke was generous to a fault. It seemed he hadn't exaggerated, and this liberal benevolence toward a girl he didn't know from Eve rather took the edge off Juliana's hostility. However, since it didn't suit her plans to be cut off from Russell Street, the battle must continue.

"You're very kind, sir," she said formally. "I'm certain Lucy will be suitably grateful."

"For God's sake, girl, I'm not asking for gratitude," he snapped. "Only for your obedience."

"As I'm aware, I owe obedience only to my husband, sir."

"You owe obedience to the man who provides for you," he declared, standing up in one fluid movement. Juliana had to force herself to stand her ground as she found herself looking up at him.

He leaned forward, his flat palms resting on the desk. "You have already played into Lucien's hands by encouraging him to embarrass me. God only knows who saw you this morning. Who knew where you were going. Whom he will tell. He paraded you through the streets of fashionable London with a trio of High Impures, and he played you for a fool, you silly child. These naive schemes of retaliation will hurt you a damn sight more than they'll hurt me."

Juliana paled. It hurt her that he believed Lucien had made a fool of her. Surely, she deserved more credit than that. "Your cousin's conduct doesn't appear to have affected your standing in society so far, sir," she said with icy calm. "I fail to see why his wife should alter the situation." She curtsied again. "I beg leave to leave you, sir."

Tarquin came out from behind the desk. He took her chin and brought her upright. "Don't do this, Juliana," he said quietly. "Please."

She looked up at him, read the sincerity in his eyes and the harsh planes of his face. She recognized that he was offering her an opening to back down without loss of face, but her anger and resentment ran too deep and too hot to be swept away so easily.

"My lord, you reap what you sow."

For a long moment their eyes held, and she read a confusion of emotion in his. There was anger, puzzlement, resignation, regret. And beneath it all a torch of desire.

"So be it," he said slowly. "But bear in mind that *you* also reap what you sow." He bent his head to take her mouth with his. It was a kiss of war, and her blood rose to meet the power and the passion, the bewildering knowledge that she could fight tooth and nail yet respond with desperate hunger to the touch and the feel, the scent, the taste, the glorious rhythms, of his body.

When he released her, his gaze still held hers, taking in the full red richness of her lips, the delicate flush of desire against the creamy pallor of her cheeks, the deep jade depths of her eyes, the flame of her hair. He could feel her arousal pulsing like an aura, and he knew she was as aroused by the declaration of war as she was by passion.

"You have leave to leave me," he said.

Juliana curtsied and left, closing the door gently behind her. She passed an unfamiliar footman as she walked down the corridor toward the hall. "Do you know if Viscount Edgecombe has returned to the house?"

"I don't believe so, my lady."

He kept his eyes fixed on the middle distance beyond her head, and it occurred to Juliana that, with the exception of Henny, the servants in this house had been trained to avoid eye contact with their employers.

"Would you inform me when he does return?" she asked pleasantly. "I shall be in my parlor."

The footman bowed and she went on her way, her mind whirling as she tried to organize her thoughts. She couldn't free her mind from the bubbling volcano of her body. The duke had started something with that kiss that wouldn't be soon extinguished. She wondered if he'd known it . . . if it was the same for him. She guessed grimly that he knew what he'd done to her, and that unlike her, he was able to control his own responses.

Upstairs in the yellow bedchamber she found Lucy propped up on pillows, with Henny feeding her gruel. "Oh, you look so much better," she said, approaching the bed. Lucy's hair was clean, although dull and straggly, and her thin face was no longer grime encrusted. She wore a white nightgown that clearly swamped her, but her dark eyes had regained some life.

She turned her head toward Juliana and smiled weakly. "I don't know who you are. Or where I am. But I owe you my life."

Juliana shook her head briskly. She'd done no more than any compassionate human being would have done, and gratitude struck her as both unnecessary and embarrassing. "My name's Juliana," she said, sitting on the edge of the bed. "And you're in the house of the Duke of Redmayne. I'm married to his cousin, Viscount Edgecombe."

Lucy looked even more bewildered. She shook her head as Henny offered her another spoonful of gruel. "I don't think I could eat any more."

"Aye, I daresay your belly's not used to being full," Henny said cheerfully, removing the bowl. "I'll leave you with her Ladyship. Just ring the bell if you want me." She indicated the rope hanging beside the bed and bustled out.

"How do you know Lilly and the others?" Lucy asked, lying back against the pillows.

"Ah, there hangs a tale," Juliana said with a grin. "But you look as if you need to sleep, so I'll tell you later, when you're stronger."

Lucy's eyes were closing and she did not protest. Juliana drew the curtains around the bed and tiptoed from the room. She went to her own parlor and stood at the window, looking out over the garden, her brow knitted in thought. Tarquin could prevent Lucy's friends from visiting her in his house, but she couldn't see how he could prevent her from visiting Russell Street if she had her husband's permission to do so. It sounded as if he thought he could, but how would he do so?

By compelling Lucien to withhold his permission, of course. He could do that by withdrawing his financial support. So she had to get to Lucien before the duke did. She had to find a way to persuade him to stand against Tarquin, whatever pressure was brought to bear. It ought to be possible. Lucien didn't strike her as particularly clever. Vindictive, spiteful, degenerate, but not needle-witted. She should be able to run rings around him if she came up with the right motivation.

Quentin walked into the garden below her and strolled down a flagstone path. He carried a pair of secateurs and stopped beside a bush of yellow roses. He cut half a dozen and then added another six white ones from the neighboring bush. Juliana watched him arrange them artistically into a bouquet, a little smile on his face. It was astonishing how different he was from his half brother. In fact, it was astounding how vastly different the three Courtney men were from each other. Lucien was utterly vile. She believed that Tarquin, beneath the domineering surface, was essentially decent. She was not afraid she would come to harm under his protection. But he lacked his brother's sensitivity and gentleness.

Quentin came back into the house with his bouquet of roses, and she wondered who they were for. Lady Lydia, perhaps?

The thought popped into her head. Something had given her the impression that that would be a match made in heaven. And from what she'd seen, she guessed it was a match they both yearned for. Or at least *would* yearn for if they thought it could ever be a possibility. But the Duke of Redmayne stood between them. And the duke had little interest in taking Lady Lydia to wife—he was merely satisfying an obligation. Maybe she could change that. People often didn't know how to get out of their own tangles. Witness herself, she thought wryly.

There was a tap at her door, and Lord Quentin came in at her response. He carried the roses, and for a minute she thought they were for her. But he said with a quick smile, "I thought your friend might take comfort from some flowers. They have such a lovely scent and they're so fresh and alive. I don't wish to burst in upon her unannounced, so I wondered if you would accompany me to her chamber."

"Yes, of course." Juliana sprang to her feet. Her hoop swung in a wide arc as she hastened eagerly to the door. A small round table rocked under the impact of the hoop. She paused to steady the table automatically before resuming her swift progress. "She was feeling sleepy when I left her, but it would be lovely to open one's eyes on a bowl of roses. Aren't they beautiful?"

Quentin smiled as she buried her nose in their fragrance. "You have only to give order for the servants to cut some for your own apartments."

Juliana looked up quickly, afraid that he might have read her mind earlier. "Oh, I would pick them myself," she said. "But someone has already put roses in my bedchamber and boudoir." She accompanied him down the corridor to Lucy's chamber, wishing she had the art of small talk to cover her moment of awkwardness.

She opened Lucy's door quietly and tiptoed in, peeping behind the bed curtains. Lucy opened her eyes and offered a tired smile.

"Lord Quentin has brought you some roses." Juliana stood aside so that Quentin could approach the sickbed. "I'll ring for a maid to put them in water." She reached for the bellpull, then stepped back in case Quentin wished to talk to Lucy alone. He might intend to have a pastoral conversation. But Quentin's voice was cheerful, and more avuncular than clerical, as he asked Lucy how she did and laid the roses on the bedside table.

"The maid will look after these. I don't wish to disturb your rest."

"Thank you, sir." Lucy's smile brightened considerably. "I don't know what I've done to deserve such kindness."

"You don't have to deserve it," Juliana stated with a touch of indignation. "When someone's been so ill treated, they're entitled to all the compassion and care that decent people can offer. Isn't that so, Lord Quentin?"

"Indeed," he agreed, even as he wondered why he

found her passionate declaration such a novel concept. As a man of the cloth, he should have been expounding the principle himself, but somehow it hadn't crossed his mind until now. The poor were a fact of life. Cruelty and indifference were everywhere in their lives. If he'd thought of their plight at all, he'd simply considered it to be one of the inevitable evils of their world. The rich man in his castle, the poor man at his gate. Juliana was opening his eyes on a new landscape.

Lucy looked incredulous, and he was glad he hadn't shown his own surprise at Juliana's revolutionary doctrine. "I'll leave you to your rest," he said. "But should you ever wish to talk to me, please send for me." He bowed and eased out of the room.

"What would I talk to him about?" Lucy inquired, struggling up on the pillows. "I wouldn't dare to send for him."

"He's a clergyman," Juliana informed her, sitting on the edge of the bed. "So if you wanted to talk on churchy matters, then, of course, he'd be available."

"Oh, I see." Lucy looked less bewildered. "Tell me your story, Juliana. I feel much stronger now."

Juliana told her as much as the other girls knew, breaking off when a maid entered to put the roses in water. Henny came in a few minutes later with a hot posset for the invalid. Juliana left to dress for dinner.

In her bedchamber she examined herself in the cheval mirror, frowning at her untidy appearance. Her morning's activities in the Marshalsea had wreaked havoc with her earlier elegance. It was disconcerting to think that she'd had her confrontation with the duke looking like a grubby schoolgirl. That hadn't prevented him from kissing her, however. She knew she hadn't mistaken the desire in his eyes, and surely he couldn't have feigned the passion of that kiss. Perhaps he found scruffy gypsies arousing. Bella at Russell Street had described in her worldly way some of the strange fancies of the men who visited there. Nuns and schoolgirls . . . who was to say the duke was any different?

Henny bustled in at that point, and she put the interesting question aside, submitting to the deft, quick hands of the abigail, who plaited her hair and arranged the unruly curls that wouldn't submit to the pins into artful ringlets framing her face. She didn't ask Juliana's opinion about her gown but chose a sacque gown of violet tabby opened over a dark-green petticoat. She arranged a muslin fichu at the neck, adjusted the lace ruffles at her elbows, twitched the skirt straight over the hoops, handed her a fan and her long silk gloves, and shooed her downstairs like a farmer's wife with her chickens. But Juliana found this treatment wonderfully comforting. She had not the slightest inclination to argue with the woman or play the mistress to her servant.

"Ah, well met, my lady. Shall we go down together?" Lucien emerged from his bedchamber as she passed. His voice was slightly slurred, his eyes unfocused, his gait a trifle unsteady. The reek of cognac hung around him. "Don't in general dine at m'cousin's table. Dull work, except that the wine's good and his chef is a marvel. But thought I'd honor my bride, eh?" He chuckled in a restrained fashion so that it brought forth no more than a wheeze. "Take my arm, m'dear."

Juliana took the scarlet-taffeta arm. It was utterly unimpeachable for her to go into dinner on her husband's arm. But how it would plague the Duke of Redmayne! She smiled up at Lucien. "After dinner, my lord, perhaps I could speak with you in private."

"Only if you promise not to bore me."

"Oh, I can assure you, sir, I shall not bore you." Her eyes, almost on a level with his, met and held his suddenly sharp gaze as he looked across at her. Then he smiled, a spiteful smile.

"In that case, my lady, I shall be honored to give you a moment of my time." He stood aside with a bow to allow her to precede him into the drawing room.

Chapter 16

George Ridge sat staring into his turtle soup with the air of a man who has undergone a deep shock. Around him the noise and revelry in the Shakespeare's Head tavern rose to a raucous level as the customers washed down the tavern's famous turtle soup with bumpers of claret. A group of Posture Molls was performing in the middle of the room, but George barely noticed their lewdly provocative positions as they exposed the most intimate parts of their bodies to the patrons. Posture Molls operated on a look-but-don't-touch principle, arousing the spectators to wild heights but refusing to make good the promises of their performance.

It was a lucrative business and ran less risk of the pox than more conventional whoredom. But George was unmoved. He believed in getting his money's worth and considered this form of entertainment to be a snare and a delusion. When the girls crawled around to pick up the coins showered upon them by the overexcited audience, he turned his back in a pointed gesture of dismissal. One of the women approached him, her petticoat lifted to her waist. She pushed her pelvis in his face and reached to stroke his hair. He slapped her hand away and cursed her, half rising from his chair in a threatening movement.

"Stinking whoreson," the woman said, her lip curling. "You look but you don't pay. A plague on you." She spat contemptuously into the sawdust at his feet and stalked off, still holding her shift to her waist as she went in search of a more appreciative member of the audience.

George took up his tankard of punch and drained it, reaching forward to the bowl in the middle of the table and ladling the fragrant contents into the pewter tankard. He gulped down half of it and returned to his turtle soup.

Juliana was married to a viscount! He dropped his spoon into the pewter bowl with a clatter as for the first time this fact really penetrated his brain. He hadn't been able to credit it at first, when the groom in the stables had told him nonchalantly that he was in the employ of the Duke of Redmayne. George had offered a description of the two men he'd seen with Juliana, and the groom had identified them as the duke and his brother, Lord Quentin. A description of the sickly-looking gentleman who'd gone off with the women that morning brought forth a contemptuous curl of the lip and the information that it must have been Viscount Edgecombe, His Grace's cousin. And then the startling words: "Just married yesterday. Brought 'is wife back 'ere . . . poor creature!"

Wife! It wasn't possible, but the groom had absolutely identified Lady Edgecombe as a lady with unmistakably striking hair and a taller than usual figure. There could be no possible doubt.

George picked up his spoon again. No sense wasting an expensive delicacy. He scraped the bowl with his spoon, then wiped it out with a hunk of bread. Then he sat back and glared at the grimy wall. Behind him there were bursts of laughter and applause. He sneaked a look over his shoulder and then hastily turned his eyes away. Two women were apparently coupling on a table. George found it deeply offensive. Such depravity didn't go on in Winchester, or even in the stews of Portsmouth, where you could find a sailor and his whore making the beast with two backs on every park bench.

He would have left the Shakespeare's Head at this point, except that he'd ordered a goose to follow the soup, thinking that a good dinner might quell the roiling turmoil in his belly. If Juliana was truly married to a viscount, then she couldn't marry George Ridge. Unless it had been a Fleet marriage. The thought gave him some hope, so he was able to face the platter of roast goose swimming in its own grease with more enthusiasm than he might otherwise have shown.

He chewed with solemn gusto, tearing the bird apart with his fingers, spearing potatoes on the point of his knife, heedless of the grease running down his chin, as he drank liberally of the bottle of claret that the landlord had thumped down at his elbow. He was now oblivious of the riotous goings-on behind him. A Fleet marriage seemed more and more likely. How could Juliana in such a few days be truly married to a duke's cousin? George didn't know much about the highest echelons of the aristocracy, but he was pretty certain they didn't marry on a whim. And they didn't marry women with no name, even if they were gently bred, as Juliana certainly was. So it must be some whoredom arrangement. Presumably she'd been tricked by an illegal ceremony. It made perfect sense, since George had had difficulty imagining Juliana's seeking her bread by selling her body.

Feeling immeasurably more cheerful, he wiped his chin with his sleeve and called for a bottle of port and a dish of lampreys. Juliana would have to be grateful for the prospect of rescue once she understood the falsity of her present position. He, of course, would have to be very magnanimous. Not many men would wed a harlot. He would be sure to point this out to Juliana. That and the promise to remove all suspicions of her involvement in his father's death should produce abject submission to his every fancy.

He grinned wolfishly and stuck his fork into the dish of eellike fish, scooping them into his mouth without pause until the dish was empty; then he launched an attack on a steamed pudding studded with currants.

Two hours later, overcome by sleepiness, but having first ensured that he was sitting firmly upon his money pouch, he allowed his head to fall upon the table and was soon snoring loudly amid the debris of his dinner. No one took the slightest notice of him.

Viscount Edgecombe took a gulp of cognac and gave a crack of amusement as he stared at his wife in her parlor after dinner. "By all means, I'll show you the town, m'dear." He hiccuped once and chortled again. "I can show you some sights. Gad, yes." He drained his glass and laughed again.

Juliana said steadily, "His Grace will not care for it."

"Oh, no, that's for sure." Lucien blearily tried to focus his eyes, producing only a squint. "He'll forbid it, of course." He frowned. "Could make himself a nuisance, you know."

"But you're not under his control, are you, sir?" She opened her eyes wide. "I can't imagine your submitting to the orders of anyone."

"Oh, ordinarily, I wouldn't," he agreed, refilling his glass from the decanter. "But I'll tell you straight: Tarquin holds the purse strings. Very generous, he is, but I'd not care to risk his closing the purse on me. I can't tell you how expensive it is to live these days."

"Why does he finance you?" She waited for a coughing fit to subside as he choked on the cognac.

"Why, m'dear, in exchange for agreeing to this sham marriage," he told her with a final wheeze.

"Then surely you could say that if he doesn't continue, you'll repudiate me as your wife," suggested Juliana, idly smoothing the damask on the sofa where she sat.

Lucien stared at her. "Gad, but you're a devious creature. Why's it so important to have at Tarquin?"

Juliana shrugged. Lucien presumably didn't know the full details of her contract with the duke. "I object to being manipulated in this way."

A sly look crept into Lucien's hollowed eyes. "Ah," he said. "Tarquin said you would do his bidding. Have something on you, does he?"

"Merely that I am friendless and without protection," she said calmly. "And therefore dependent upon him."

"So why would you want to put his back up?" The sly look hadn't left his eyes. "Not in your interests, I would have said."

"I have a legal contract that he can't renege upon," Juliana replied with a cool smile. "It was drawn up by a lawyer and witnessed by Mistress Dennison. He is obliged to provide for me whatever happens."

Lucien produced his skeletal grin at this. "Out of the goodness of my heart, m'dear, I'll tell you you'll have to get up very early in the morning to put one over on Tarquin."

"That may be so," Juliana said with a touch of impatience. "But I wish to go to Covent Garden. I wish to see what it's like there, how the people live, particularly the women. Your cousin wouldn't take me to the places I wish to visit, but you can. Since you spend your time there, anyway, as I understand it, taking me along shouldn't inconvenience you in any way."

"Well, I daresay it won't. But it'll inconvenience Tarquin." He took more cognac and surveyed her costume critically. "Of course, society women do frequent the bagnios. Poor Fred always has some courtier's lady in tow."

"Poor Fred?"

"Prince of Wales. Everyone calls him Poor Fred—poor devil can never get anything right, leads a dog's life. His father loathes him. Humiliates him in public at every opportunity. Wouldn't change places with him for all the crowns in Europe."

"So there wouldn't be anything really objectionable about my coming with you?"

He choked again on his cognac. "Nothing objectionable! Little simpleton!" he exclaimed. "It ain't respectable, m'dear girl. But not everyone in society is as high starched as my estimable cousins." He set his glass down with a snap. "It'll be worth it, just to see Tarquin's face. We'll do it, and if he threatens to cut me off, I'll threaten him back."

"I knew you had spirit," Juliana declared warmly, hiding her revulsion under a surge of triumph. "Shall we go at once?"

"If you like." Lucien surveyed her again with a critical frown. "Don't suppose you've a pair of britches, have you?"

"Britches?" Juliana looked astonished. "I *did* have, but—"

"No matter," he said, brusquely interrupting her. "You've too many curves to be appealing. No way you could look like a lad, however hard you tried."

For a moment Juliana could think of nothing to say. She remembered the look of repulsion in his eyes when he'd seen her in her nightgown. Finally she asked slowly, "You like your women to dress up as lads, sir?"

He grimaced. "I prefer the lads themselves, my dear. But if it must be a woman, then I've a fancy for the skinny kind, who can put on a pair of britches and play the part."

Dear God, what else was she going to learn about her husband? She'd heard of men who liked men, but it was a capital crime, and in the bucolic peace of Hampshire such preferences carried the touch of the devil.

"What a little innocent you are," Lucien mocked, guessing her thoughts. "It'll be a pleasure to rid you of some of that ignorance. I'll introduce you to the more unusual amusements to be had in the Garden. And who knows, maybe you'll take to them yourself. Fetch a cloak."

Juliana had a moment of misgiving. What was she getting herself into? She was putting herself in the hands of this vile, pox-ridden degenerate . . . but, no, she wasn't. She had money of her own and could return home at any time without his escort. And she *did* want to see for herself what happened to the women who earned their living in the streets of Covent Garden.

"I'll only be a moment." She went to the door. "Will you await me here?"

"My pleasure," he said with a bow. "So long as the decanter's full." He strolled to the table to refill his glass.

Juliana took a dark hooded cloak from her wardrobe and clasped it at her throat. She wore no jewelry because she had none, except for the slim gold band on her wedding finger, and the richness of her gown was concealed by the cloak. It made her feel a little easier about this expedition, almost as if she were going incognito.

She hastened back to her parlor, where Lucien was slumped on the sofa, sunk in reverie, twirling the amber contents of his glass. He looked up as she came in, and it seemed to take a minute for recognition to enter his dull eyes. "Oh, there you are." He stood somewhat unsteadily, and Juliana noticed that his speech had become more slurred in the few minutes she'd been absent.

"Are you sure you're well enough to go out?"

"Don't be a fool!" He threw back his head and in one movement poured the remaining liquid in his glass down his throat. "I'm fit as a flea. And I've no intention of spending the evening in this mausoleum." He weaved his way toward her where she stood in the doorway and rudely pushed past her.

Frowning, she followed him out of the house and into a passing hackney.

Five minutes later Tarquin emerged from the drawing room. He had decided to go to White's Chocolate House on St. James's Street for an evening's political discussion and a game of faro. Taking his cloak and gloves from the footman, he told him to leave the front door in the charge of the night watchman since he expected to be back late. He then went forth into the balmy evening. It didn't occur to him to ask where Juliana might be. He assumed she was in her parlor, or sitting with the invalid in the yellow bedchamber.

Juliana, swathed in her cloak, sat back in a corner of the hackney, watching the scene through the window as the vehicle stopped and started through streets as thronged as if it were midmorning. The main thoroughfares were lit with oil lamps, but when they turned onto a side street, the only light came from a link boy's lantern as he escorted a pair of gentlemen, who walked with their hands on their sword hilts.

Covent Garden was as lively as it had been the previous evening. The theater doors were already closed, the play having begun, but the hackney took them to the steps of St. Paul's Church and halted. Juliana alighted, drawing her cloak tightly around her. Lucien followed somewhat unsteadily and tossed a coin up to the jarvey, who, judging by his scowl, considered it less than adequate payment.

A noisy crowd was gathered before the steps of the church; a man played a fife barely heard above the ribald yells and drunken curses as the throng swayed and surged.

"What's going on over there?"

Lucien shrugged. "How should I know? Go and look."

Juliana made her way to the outskirts of the crowd, standing on tiptoe to see over the heads.

"Push your way to the front," Lucien said at her shoulder. "Politeness won't get you anywhere in this place." He began to shove his way through the throng, and Juliana followed, trying to keep at his heels before the path closed behind him. She remembered how Tarquin and Quentin had cleared a way through the crowd at the theater; but they'd done it almost by magic, never raising their voices or appearing to push at all. Lucien cursed vilely, using his thin body like a battering ram, and he received as many curses as he threw out. Somehow they reached the front of the crowd.

A man in rough laborer's clothes stood on the steps, beside him a woman in a coarse linen smock and apron, her hair hidden beneath a kerchief. Her hands were bound and she had a rope halter around her neck. She kept her eyes on the ground, her shoulders hunched as if she could make herself invisible. The crowd roared with approval when the man caught her chin and forced her to look up.

"So what am I bid?" he called loudly above the noise. "She's good about the 'ouse. Sound in wind and limb . . . good, strong legs and wide 'ips." He touched the parts in question and the woman shivered and tried to draw back. But the man grabbed the loose end of the halter and jerked her forward again.

Lucien laughed with the crowd. Juliana, horror-struck, glanced up at him and saw such naked, malevolent enjoyment on his face that she felt nauseated. "What's going on?"

"A wife-selling. Isn't it obvious?" Lucien didn't take his eyes off the scene on the steps as the husband enumerated the wretched woman's various good points.

Suddenly a voice bellowed above the crowd. "Ye've 'ad yer fun, Dick Begg. Now, let's be done with this." A brawny man pushed his way to the steps and jumped up beside the couple. The woman flushed deepest crimson and tried to turn aside, but her husband jerked again on the halter he still held, and she was able only to avert her head.

"Ten pound," the newcomer declared. "An' ye leave 'er alone from now on."

"Done," the husband announced. Both men spat on their palms and clapped them together to seal the bargain. The second man counted ten coins into the other's hand while the crowd roared its approval again; then he took the end of the halter and led the now weeping woman away from the crowd, toward the rear of the church.

Dick Begg pocketed his coins. "Good riddance to bad rubbish," he stated, grinning. "Niver did get on wi' the bitch anyways."

"How disgusting!" Juliana muttered. She'd heard of such auctions but had never seen one before. The crowd was dispersing now that the entertainment was over, until a fight started up between two burly costermongers. They were going at each other with bare fists, and swiftly a cheering, catcalling circle formed around them.

It was Lucien's turn to look disgusted. "Animals," he

said with a curling lip. He strode away toward the Green Man tavern, not troubling to wait for Juliana.

She followed him into the low-ceilinged taproom, her eyes immediately beginning to water with the tobacco smoke that hung in a thick blue haze in the air.

"Blue ruin!" Lucien bellowed at a passing potboy as he pulled out a bench at a long table and sat down. The bench was as filthy as the stained encrusted planking of the table. Juliana brushed ineffectually at the grime and then sat down with an internal shrug. Her cloak was dark and would keep most of it off her gown.

"Not too nice in your tastes, I trust," Lucien said with a sneer.

"Not overly," Juliana responded evenly. "But this place is a pig sty."

"Don't let mine host hear you saying that." Lucien chuckled. "Very proud of his establishment is Tom King." He slapped a sixpence on the table when the potboy appeared with a stone jar and two tankards. "Fill 'em up."

The lad did so, wiping the drips from the table with his finger, which he then licked. His hands were as filthy as his apron, and his hair hung in lank, greasy locks to his shoulders. He took the sixpence and vanished into the crowd as someone else yelled for him. He didn't arrive quickly enough, apparently, because he was greeted with a mighty clout that sent him reeling against the wall.

Juliana gazed at the scene in horrified fascination, blinking her watering eyes. When Lucien pushed a tankard toward her with the brisk injunction "Drink," she carried it to her lips and absently took a large gulp.

Her throat was on fire, her belly burning as if with hot coals. She doubled over the table, choking, her eyes streaming.

"Gad, what a milksop you are!" Lucien thumped her back with his flat palm, using considerable force. "Can't stomach a drop of gin!" But she could hear his malicious amusement as he continued to pound her back. Presumably, she was reacting exactly as he'd intended.

"Leave me alone!" she said furiously, straightening and shaking off his hand. "Why didn't you warn me?"

"And spoil my fun?" He clicked his tongue reprovingly.

Juliana set her lips and pushed the tankard as far from her as she could. She wanted a glass of milk to take away the taste, but the thought of asking for such a thing in this place was clearly absurd.

"Gad, it's Edgecombe!" A voice called from the mists of smoke. "Hey, dear fellow, what brings you here? Heard you'd become leg-shackled."

Three men weaved their way through the room toward them, each carrying a tankard. Their wigs were askew, their faces flushed with drink, their gait distinctly unsteady. They were young, in their early twenties, but the dissipation behind the raddled complexions and bloodshot, hollowed eyes had vanquished all the bloom of youth.

Lucien raised a hand in greeting. "Come and meet my lady wife, gentlemen." He rose from the bench and bowed with mock formality as he indicated Juliana. "Lady Edgecombe, m'dear fellows. Madam wife, pray make your curtsy to Captain Frank Carson, the Honorable Bertrand Peters, and the dearest fellow of them all, Freddie Binkton." He flung his arm around the last named and hugged him before kissing him soundly.

Juliana stood up and curtsied, feeling ridiculous in these surroundings, but not knowing how else to behave. The three men laughed heartily and bowed, but she sensed a hostile curiosity in all their expressions as they scrutinized her in the dim light.

"So why the devil did ye take a wife, Lucien?" Captain Frank demanded, having completed his examination of Juliana. "Thought you was sworn to bachelorhood."

"Oh, family pressure, m'dear." Lucien winked and took another swig of his tankard. "My cousin thought it would avoid scandal."

They all went into renewed laughter at this, and Juliana sat down again. There was something indefinably horrible about the group. They made her skin crawl, and she could feel their covert glances even though they appeared now to ignore her, all of them absorbed in some scandalous tale of the captain's. She glanced toward the door, where an elegant lady stood, a footman at her back, deep in conversation with a rotund gentleman in an old-fashioned curly wig.

As Juliana watched, the elderly gentleman counted out five coins into the lady's hands. She passed them to the footman, who pocketed them; then she tucked her arm into the gentleman's, and they entered the tavern and went up a rickety pair of stairs at the rear of the taproom. The footman leaned against the doorjamb, idly picking his teeth, watching the passersby.

The woman had looked too prosperous to be soliciting on the streets, Juliana reflected. And certainly too well dressed to be taking her clients to a back room in this noisome place. She must remember to ask Lilly to explain it.

"Lud, madam, you're not drinking?" the Honorable Bertrand declared in mock horror. "Lucien, Lucien, you neglect the dear lady shamefully."

Lucien grinned. "Tried her on blue ruin, but it didn't seem to suit her. What else can I offer you, my dear? Ale, perhaps? Port?"

"Milk punch, if you please, sir," Juliana said, her nerves prickling as she realized they wanted to make sport of her in some way. She glanced around, but there would be no help available in this riotous assembly. A couple were rolling around on the floor, the woman's legs in the air, her skirts tumbled about her head, exposing her body to the waist. Juliana felt sick. She pushed back the bench and stood up.

"If you'll excuse me, my lord, I find I have the headache. I'll take a hackney outside."

"Oh, but I don't excuse you," Lucien slurred, grabbing her hand and pulling her back beside him. "You owe obedience to your husband, madam, and your husband bids you keep him company and drink your milk punch."

Juliana thought she could probably break Lucien's hold without too much difficulty, but the eyes of the others were fixed upon her with a sinister intensity, waiting to see what she would do. She couldn't break free from them all if they tried to hold her. No one in this place would come to her aid. And she would be utterly humiliated. And Lucien would relish every minute of it. It was what he'd enjoyed about the wife-selling. The woman's total degradation had made him lick his lips like a hyena salivating over a rotting carcass.

She sat down again with a calm smile. "As you please, my lord."

Lucien looked a trifle disappointed; then he clapped his hands and bellowed for the potboy to bring milk punch. Juliana sat still, trying to maintain her calm smile and an air of nonchalant interest in her surroundings. The woman on the floor was on her hands and knees now, the man behind her, striking her flanks with his open palms as he mimicked the act of copulation to the roaring acclamation of his audience, who raised their tankards in a series of cheering toasts. The woman was laughing as much as anyone, throwing her head back and thrusting backward as if to meet him with orgasmic enjoyment.

Juliana kept the disgust from her face. She noticed that Lucien seemed to have no interest in the scene, although his friends were participating in the general uproar, thumping their tankards on the table and yelling encouragement.

"Does she get paid for that?" she inquired casually.

Lucien looked startled at the question. His blurry eyes searched her face suspiciously. She gave him a bland smile as if nothing about this place could possibly disturb her.

"I daresay," he said, shrugging. "It's not my idea of entertainment." He pushed back the bench and stood up. "Come."

"Where are we going?"

"To show you a few of the other entertainments available in this salubrious neighborhood. You did ask me to introduce you to London society . . . and your wish is ever my command, my dear ma'am." He bowed ironically.

Juliana curtsied in the same vein and took his arm, determined not to give him the satisfaction of seeing her dismay.

"Oh, must we go?" lamented the captain, getting unsteadily to his feet.

"Oh, yes. Wherever Lucien and his wife go, we go, too," Bertrand said, draining his tankard. "Wouldn't wish 'em to want for company on this bridal evening." He took Juliana's other arm, and she found herself ushered to the door and out into the Piazza.

"Where to now?" Freddie asked, looking around with an assumption of alert interest.

"Hummums," answered Lucien. "Show m'lady wife here what goes on in the steam rooms."

"I don't think a steam room would be a good idea," Juliana demurred. "Won't it ruin my gown?"

"Gad, no, ma'am!" laughed the captain. "They'll take all your clothes from you and give you a towel. Very friendly place, the hummums."

Juliana was not going to the hummums, however friendly. She walked in the midst of her escort, awaiting her moment to break free. They had reached the corner of the Little Piazza, and she paused at the kiosk selling the obscene prints that she'd seen with the duke. "What do you think of these, gentlemen?" she asked with a smile.

Distracted, they peered into the kiosk. Juliana slipped her arms free and turned swiftly. Too swiftly. Her foot slipped on a patch of nameless slime on the cobbles, and she grabbed at the nearest object to save herself. Captain Frank proved a reliable support, although he laughed heartily at her predicament. When she was stable again, her heart was beating violently against her ribs, the captain was holding her too tightly for comfort, and she could see no escape from the hummums.

"I've a mind for a cockfight," announced Bertrand, slipping an arm through Lucien's. "What d'ye think, Lucien? It's been a while since we had a wager on the birds."

"By the devil's grace, so it has." Lucien was immediately diverted. "Madam wife, here, will enjoy it, I'll be bound." He gave Juliana his skeletal grin, and his eyes were filled with spiteful glee. "What d'ye say? The Royal Cockpit or the hummums, m'dear?"

At least in the cockpit she could keep her clothes on. And surely she could endure the cruelty if she kept her eyes closed. "The cockpit, if you please, sir." She managed another insouciant smile and achieved a certain satisfaction in seeing that her carefree response had disconcerted her husband.

"Let's to it, then!" Bertrand hailed a hackney. "After you, Lady Edgecombe."

She found herself hustled into the dark interior, the others piling in after her with much laughter. But there was an edge to their merriment that filled her with trepidation.

"The Royal Cockpit, jarvey." Lucien leaned out of the window to shout their direction. The jarvey cracked his whip, and the horses clopped off toward St. James's Park.

Chapter 17

It was three o'clock in the morning when Tarquin returned home. He nodded at the night porter, who let him in, and headed for the stairs. The man shot the bolts again and returned to his cubbyhole beneath the stairs.

The duke strode into his own apartments, shrugging off his gold brocade coat. His sleepy valet jumped up from his chair by the empty fireplace and tried to stifle a yawn.

"Good evening, Your Grace." He hastened to take the coat from his employer, shaking it out before hanging it in the armoire. "I trust you had a pleasant evening."

"Pleasant enough, thank you." Tarquin glanced toward the armoire with its concealed door, wondering if Juliana was awake. Presumably she'd retired hours ago. His valet tenderly helped him out of his clothes and handed him a chamber robe. The duke sat at his dresser, filing his nails, while the man moved around the room, putting away the clothes, drawing back the bed curtains, turning down the bed.

"Will that be all, Your Grace?"

The duke nodded and dismissed him to his bed. Then he stepped through the door in the wardrobe and softly entered the next-door chamber. The bed was unslept in.

Henny snored softly on the chaise longue. Of Juliana there was no sign.

"Where the devil—"

"Oh, lordy me, sir!" Henny jumped to her feet at the sound of his voice. Her faded blue eyes were filmed with sleep. "You did give me a start." She patted her chest with a rapid fluttering hand.

"Where's Juliana?" His voice was sharp, abrupt.

"Why, I don't know, Your Grace. I understand she went out with Lord Edgecombe. They haven't returned as yet. But His Lordship is never one to seek his bed before dawn," she added, smoothing down her apron and tucking an escaping strand of gray hair back under her cap.

Tarquin's initial reaction was fury, mingled immediately with apprehension. Juliana could have no idea where and how Lucien took his pleasures. She was far too innocent of the urban world even to imagine such things. It was that very innocence that he'd believed would make her a compliant tool in his scheme. And now it was the same innocence combined with that defiant spirit that was leading her into the horrors of Lucien's world. Perhaps he'd erred in his choice. Perhaps he should have involved a woman who knew her way around the world, who would have entered a business contract with her eyes open. But such a woman would not have been virgin. And a whore could not be the mother of the heir to Edgecombe.

But he'd made his choice and was stuck with the consequences. He'd assumed he'd be able to put a stop to her mischief with Lucien, but he hadn't expected her to move so fast. He would learn the lesson well.

"Is everything all right, Your Grace?" Henny sounded troubled, a deep frown drawing her sparse eyebrows together, as she examined the duke's livid countenance. "If I did wrong—"

"My good woman, of course you didn't," he interrupted brusquely. "Lady Edgecombe is not in your charge. Take yourself to bed now. She won't need you tonight."

Henny looked a little doubtful, but she curtsied and left

the chamber. Tarquin stood for a minute, tapping his fingernails on a tabletop, his mouth grim.

He turned on his heel and went back to his own chamber, where he threw off the chamber robe and dressed swiftly in plain buckskin britches, boots, and a dark coat. The sword at his waist was no toy, and his cane was a swordstick. He strode downstairs again, and the puzzled night porter hurried to open the front door.

"Do you know what time Lord and Lady Edgecombe left?"

"No, Your Grace. I understood from Catlett that they left quite early, before Your Grace."

The duke cursed his own stupidity. Why hadn't he thought to check on her before he went out? He'd completely underestimated her, assuming her defiance to be no more than that of a thwarted schoolroom miss.

He left the house and called to a link boy, standing in a doorway opposite, his oil lamp extinguished at his feet. The lad shook himself awake and came running across the street. "Where ye goin', m'lord?"

"Covent Garden." It would be Lucien's first and probably last stop of the evening.

The lad busily trimmed the wick of his lantern before striking flint on tinder. The yellow glow threw a welcoming patch of illumination as the lad hurried along beside the duke, trotting to keep up with Tarquin's swift, impatient stride.

Juliana gulped the fresh air of St. James's Park, trying to get the stench of blood out of her nostrils. She couldn't rid her mind of the images, however. Even though she'd kept her eyes shut much of the time, the torn and mangled birds lying inert in the sawdust ring, surrounded by blood-soaked feathers like so many bloody rags, tormented her inner vision. She could still hear the deafening uproar as the wild betting had grown increasingly frenzied with each new pair of cocks, armed with silver spurs, being set down in the pit. Open mouths screaming encouragement and curses, drink-suffused eyes filled with greedy cruelty, the astonishing determination of the birds, fighting to the death even when clearly mortally wounded, were indelibly printed on her mind, and for the first time in her life she'd been afraid she would swoon.

Somehow she'd held on, aware of Lucien's quick glances at her deathly pallor, her closed eyes. She would not give him the satisfaction of breaking down at this hideous sight. His eyes, sunk in their dark sockets, grew more spiteful as the ghastly business progressed. Vaguely, she was aware that he was losing money hand over fist. Bertrand had cheerfully handed over a fistful of coins when Lucien turned out his empty pockets with a vile oath. But it wasn't until the fourth pair of birds had been tearing each other apart for forty-five minutes, blood and feathers spattering the audience on the lower ring of seats, that Lucien stood up from the matted bench and announced that he'd had enough of this insipidity.

Juliana had staggered out of the circular room, into the warm night. She wanted to crawl behind a bush and vomit her heart out. But she would not give her loathsome husband the pleasure.

"Well, my dear, I trust you're enjoying your introduction to London entertainments." Lucien took snuff, regarding her with a sardonic smile.

"It's certainly an education, my lord," she responded, both surprised and thankful that her voice was clear and steady.

Lucien frowned, glowering at her in the flickering light of the flambeaux illuminating the path from the cockpit to the gate. The woman was proving a disappointment. He'd expected her to break before now.

"Gad, man, but I've a thirst on me to equal a parched camel's," Frank Carson declared, loosening his already crumpled cravat. "Let's to the Shakespeare's Head. I've a mind for some dicing."

"Aye, good thought," Freddie approved, wiping his perspiring forehead with a lace-edged handkerchief. "You comin', Edgecombe?"

"Indeed," the viscount said. "The night's but barely begun. Come, madam wife." He grabbed Juliana's elbow and dragged her beside him down the path and onto the street. "Hackney! Hey, fellow. You there, idle bastard!" He waved belligerently at the driver of a cab, smoking peacefully in the stand of hackneys touting for customers emerging from the Royal Cockpit.

The jarvey cracked his whip and directed his weary horse across the street. "Where to, guv?"

"Shakespeare's Head." Lucien clambered up, leaving Juliana to follow. Her petticoat was grimy from the filthy matting in the cockpit, her dainty slippers soiled with something unidentifiable but disgusting. She drew her cloak tighter around her, despite the warmth of the night, and huddled into the shadowy corner as the others rowdily entered the vehicle.

She was extremely weary, and growing increasingly frightened. There was a frenzy to her husband's behavior, an alarming glitter in his burning eyes. His color was, if anything, worse than usual, and his breath rasped in his chest. She knew instinctively that he intended to make game of her in some way. Foolishly, she had attempted to ally herself with him in opposition to the duke. Foolishly she had thought she'd found the perfect motive for Edgecombe's cooperation. Foolishly she'd thought she could use him for her own ends. But Lucien was not cooperating with her. He was using her for his own amusement. And he wasn't finished yet.

There was nothing she could do, outnumbered as she was, but watch and wait and try to escape. Maybe they would become so involved in the gambling, so besotted with drink, that she could slip away without their noticing. Maybe a visit to the outhouse at the tavern would give her an opportunity.

Covent Garden was still thronged, but the crowd's inebriation had reached a new peak. Voices were loud and slurred, raised in anger and curses as often as in laughter. Men and women swayed over the cobbles, clutching stone jugs of gin, and Juliana watched a woman tumble in a drunken heap into the kennel, spilling the drink all over her. The man she was with fell on her with a roar, throwing her skirts up over her head to chanting encouragement from passersby.

Juliana averted her eyes. She had no idea whether the woman was a willing participant in what was going on, or merely insensible. She didn't seem to be struggling. Someone screamed from one of the shacks under the Piazza, a loud squeal like a stuck pig. Juliana shuddered, her scalp crawling. A woman came flying out of the building, wearing only a thin shift. A man raced after her, wielding a stick. His face was suffused with fury, the woman's pale with terror. Juliana waited for someone to intervene, but no one took any notice as the woman weaved and ducked through the crowd, trying to escape the ever-swinging stick.

"Filthy whore—up to her tricks again," Bertrand said, grinning. "The trollops think they can get away with murder."

"So what's she done?" Juliana demanded, her eyes snapping in the flickering orange light from flambeaux and oil lamps.

Bertrand shrugged. "How should I know?"

"Cheated, most like," Frank said. "It's what they all do. Cheat their customers, cheat their whoremasters, cheat their bawds. They all need a spell in Bridewell now and again. Shakes 'em up."

Juliana swallowed her rage. It would only amuse them. There had to be a way to improve the conditions under which these women sold themselves. She understood that it was the only living available to them . . . understood it now from bitter experience. But surely they need not be so vulnerable to the merciless greed of those who exploited them.

She found herself being ushered with a determined arm

toward a tavern, where the door stood open to the square and raucous, drunken voices poured forth with the lamplight on a thick haze of pipe smoke.

A bare-breasted woman swayed over to them with a tray laden with brimming tankards of ale. "What can I do fer ye, m'lords?" She winked and touched her tongue to her lips in a darting, suggestive fashion.

"Ale, wench!" Bertrand announced, slapping her backside with unnecessary vigor so that the tray shook in her hand and the ale spilled over. "Clumsy slut," he said with an offhand shrug, pulling out a bench from under one of the long tables.

Juliana sat down with the rest. She was parched, and ale was a welcome prospect. On the other side of the room, through the harsh babble of clamoring voices, she could hear the bets being called amid oaths and exclamations as the dice were rolled. There was a sharp edge of acrimony to the hubbub, a warring note that made the hairs on her nape prickle in anticipation of the violence that bubbled just beneath the surface of the apparent excitable jocularity.

A tankard of ale was thumped in front of her. The resulting spill dripped into her lap, but she'd long given up worrying about her clothes on this horrendous evening. If a soiled petticoat and a beer stain on her gown were the worst that would happen, she'd count herself fortunate. She drank deeply and gratefully.

After a few minutes, when it seemed that her companions were absorbed in wagering on the possible dimensions of a spreading ale spill, she rose to her feet, trying to slide unobtrusively away.

Lucien's hand shot out and grasped her wrist. She looked down at the thin white fingers and was distantly surprised at how strong they were. The blood fled from her skin beneath the grip. "Where are you off to, madam wife?" he demanded, his tone acerbic, his words slurred.

"The outhouse," she responded calmly. "You're hurting me."

He laughed and released her wrist. "It's out the back, past the kitchen. Don't be long now."

Juliana made her way through the room. She was accosted at almost every step by drunken revelers and dice players, but she avoided eye contact and shook the grasping hands from her arm with a disdainful air.

The privy was in an enclosed backyard, and Juliana could see no escape route. She wrestled with her skirts in the foul darkness, her head aching with the noise and the smoke, and her bone-deep weariness. How was she to get away? Lucien would delight in thwarting any attempt, and his friends would cheerfully lend their physical support. It wasn't worth risking the humiliation of defeat and Lucien's malevolent amusement.

She paused for a moment in the inn doorway before reentering the taproom. Lucien was watching the door, waiting for her reappearance. He beckoned imperatively and rose unsteadily to his feet as she approached. "We're going to play," he announced, taking her elbow. "You shall stand at my shoulder, madam wife, and smile on the dice."

Juliana could see no option, so she forced a smile of cheerful compliance and accompanied them to the dice table. They were greeted with rather morose stares, and room was somewhat unwillingly made for them at the table. Juliana yawned, swaying with exhaustion as the excitement grew with each throw of the dice. Lucien's voice grew increasingly slurred. A hectic flush stood out against his greenish pallor, and his eyes burned with a febrile glitter as the level in the brandy bottle he now held went steadily down.

He won initially and, thus encouraged, began to bet ever more immoderately. And as he grew more excited, so his losses mounted. He'd lost all his own money at the cockpit and now ran through Bertrand's loan, threw down his watch, a ring, and his snuffbox before resorting to IOUs, tossing them onto the table with reckless abandon. It was clear to Juliana through her sleepiness that his fellow players were not happy with these scrawled scraps of paper, and finally one of them declared disgustedly, "If you can't play with goods or money, man, I'll not throw again. I've no use for promises."

"Aye, what good's a piece of paper when a man wants to buy ale?" The chorus swelled and the faces pressed closer to the table, glaring at Lucien.

"Devil take you all," he swore. "My IOUs are as good as gold, I'll have you know. Underwritten by His Grace, the Duke of Redmayne. Present them at his house on Albermarle Street in the morning, and he'll pay you with interest."

"Who wants to wait till mornin'?" There was a rumble around the table, and one man half rose from his seat. He had massive fists, like sledgehammers, and a wandering eye that lent added menace to his drunken squint. "Pay up, *my lord*," he said with sneering emphasis, "or I'll 'ave the coat off yer back."

Lucien fumbled for his sword but not before Captain Frank Carson had hurled back his chair and leaped to his feet, his sword in his hand. "You dare to insult the honor of a gentleman!" he bellowed, his eyes rolling back in his head as he struggled to focus them. "Have at you, sir!" He lunged across the table. The burly man sidestepped with surprising agility, and the candlelight flickered on the blade of a cutlass. A woman screamed and the crowd in the taproom drew closer, some standing on their chairs to get a better view.

Juliana was now wide-awake. Her eyes flew to the door, tantalizingly open. But eager spectators pressed close behind them, and she was pinned to the table's edge. The mood in the room was ugly. Lucien and his friends, with drawn swords, faced a veritable army of knife-wielding rogues. The dice lay abandoned in the middle of the table, and the rowdy clamor died as a moment of expectant silence fell.

It was Freddie Binkton who broke the menacing tension. They were hopelessly outnumbered, their retreat cut

off by the spectators. "Let's not be hasty, now," he said
with a nervous titter. "Lucien, dear fellow, you must have
something about you to raise a bit of blunt. We can all
contribute something." He patted his pockets as if he could
conjure coins from their depths.

"I'd put in my watch," Bertrand said, adding dolefully,
"but I wagered it on that damn red cock . . . had no
more spirit than a mewling lamb. Gave up without a fight
. . . lost my watch . . . worth all of fifty guinea . . .
lost it for a paltry ten-pound wager." His voice trailed off
with his wandering attention, the sword in his hand drooping.

As if acceding to the truce, the ruffianly group lowered
their knives, relaxed their aggressive stance, and glared at
Lucien, waiting for his response.

Lucien looked around, his mouth tight, a pulse throbbing in his temples, the same febrile flush on his face, as
garish as a clown's paint. Juliana, standing so close to him,
could feel the savage fury emanating from his skin,
mingling with the sour smell of fear and sweat. His gaze fell
on her, and she shrank back, instinctively trying to merge
with the people around her. Something flared suddenly in
the pale-brown eyes, and he smiled slowly with a ghastly
menace.

"Oh, I believe I've something to sell," he said, barely
moving his lips.

"No!" Juliana whispered, her hand at her throat as she
understood what he intended. "No, you cannot!"

"Oh, but I believe I can, madam wife," he said airily.
"Wives are their husbands' chattel. You are mine, and I
may dispose of you how I please. You should be glad to be
of service, my dear." His hand shot out and gripped her
wrist again in that painful vise. "Someone bring me a
length of rope. We should do this properly."

"Come now, Lucien, it isn't right," Frank mumbled,
half-apologetically. He looked uneasily at Juliana, who simply stared back at him, unseeing in her horror.

"Don't be such a ninny," Lucien said with a petulant

scowl. "It's not for you to say what's right or not when it comes to my wife. Ah, rope." He took the rope handed him by a grinning ostler and looped it into a halter. "Here, madam. Bend your head."

"No!" Juliana pulled back from him, terrified as much by the evil embodied in the grinning death's-head countenance as by his intention. Someone grabbed her arms and pulled them behind her so she was forced to stand still. Lucien, still with that venomous grin, roughly pulled the halter over her head. Hands tugged and pulled at her, shoving her up onto the table. She fought them, her rage now superseding her terror. She kicked and scratched, barking her shins on the edge of the table as she was pushed and pulled and dragged upward. But despite her struggles, they got her onto the table, and Lucien seized the end of the halter.

Juliana, blinded by her wild rage, kicked at him, catching him beneath the chin with the sole of her shoe. He went reeling backward, dropping the rope. She made to jump from the table, but two men grabbed her ankles, holding her still as Lucien came up again, his eyes narrowed, one hand to his chin.

"Bitch," he said softly. "You'll pay for that."

She would have kicked him again if they hadn't been holding her ankles so tightly. She swayed dizzily on her perch, nausea rising in her throat, a cold sweat breaking out on her back. How had she walked into this nightmare? She'd known Lucien was vile, but not even in her darkest imaginings could she have suspected him capable of such viciousness. But the duke had known. He had always known what his cousin was capable of. He'd known but it hadn't stopped him from using her . . . from exposing her to this evil.

Lucien was calling in a drunken singsong, "So what am I bid for this fine piece, gentlemen? Shall we start at twenty guineas?"

A chorus of responses filled the air. Juliana looked down and saw little red eyes peering greedily up at her, stripping her naked, violating her with their lascivious grins. She couldn't move, her ankles were circled so tightly, and Lucien was pulling on the rope so that it cut into the back of her neck.

George Ridge awoke from his postprandial sleep as the shouts around him grew even more raucous. He raised his head, blinking, for a moment disoriented. He remembered where he was when he saw that he'd been sleeping in the midst of the detritus of his dinner. He belched loudly and lifted the bottle of port to his lips. There was a swallow left, and he smacked his lips, set the bottle down, and turned to call for another.

His eyes fell on the scene at the far side of the room. At first he couldn't make out what was going on, the noise was so loud, the crowd so thick. They were wagering on something, and there was a frenzied edge to the bidding that struck him forcefully. He blinked, shaking his head to rid his brain of muzziness. Then he blinked again and sat up.

Juliana was standing on the table. It couldn't be anyone else. Not with that tumbling forest fire of hair, those jade-green eyes flashing with such desperate fury, that tall, voluptuous figure.

But what in the devil's name was going on here? He pushed back his chair and stood up slowly, trying to isolate the words from the general hubbub. He heard someone call, "A hundred guineas. Come, gentlemen. My wife is worth at least that."

Wife! He approached the outskirts of the crowd. The bidding was getting livelier. A hundred and fifty, two hundred. Juliana stood like a stone. The man holding the rope, the man calling himself her husband, worked the crowd to renewed frenzy as he began to point out Juliana's attractions.

George's mouth was dry. He swallowed, trying to produce some saliva. The situation was unbelievable, and yet it was real. He pushed through the crowd, cleared his throat. "Five hundred guineas!" His voice sounded cracked and feeble, and at first no one seemed to hear him. He tried again, shouting. "I bid five hundred guineas for her."

Juliana heard George's voice, penetrating the trance into which she'd retreated from the unbearable humiliation, the waves of terror sucking at her. *Don't look at him. Don't react.* The instruction screamed in her brain even through her daze. She mustn't acknowledge him. If she refused to know him, then he couldn't prove her identity. She was still Viscountess Edgecombe. She was still under the protection of the Duke of Redmayne. Dear God, was she?

"Five hundred guineas," Lucien said, turning to George with another of his savage grins. "Why, sir, that's a jump bid if ever I heard one. But she's a prime article, and you've a fine eye."

George didn't seem to hear him. He was staring at Juliana, willing her to look at him. But she was a graven image, her eyes fixed straight ahead. He reached to touch her ankle, and she didn't move.

"Any advance on five hundred for my dear wife, or shall this gentleman have her?" Lucien called out merrily. "He's got a bargain, I'm telling you."

"There are times, Edgecombe, when you surprise even me with the depths of your depravity." The cool voice cut through the raucous merriment as the Duke of Redmayne crossed the room from the door, where he'd been standing unnoticed for the last few minutes.

The nightmare had such a grip upon her that for a moment Juliana didn't react. Then the clear tones of salvation pierced her trance. Slowly she turned on her perch, George forgotten in the flood of incredulous relief. He'd come for her.

"Tarquin . . ." It was more plea than statement, as if she still didn't dare to believe that he was there.

"I'm here," he affirmed. His voice was a caress, the soft reassurance balm to her agonized soul. His gray gaze encompassed her, all-seeing; then he turned on Lucien.

Lucien shrank back against the table as his cousin's livid eyes blazed at him. A muscle twitched in the duke's cheek, but he said nothing, merely tapped one clenched fist into the palm of his other hand. Then, very slowly, he brought up the fist and—almost gently, it seemed—touched Lucien on the edge of his chin. The viscount fell back into the crowd without a sound.

A murmur passed through the throng as the duke's eyes ran slowly around them. Suddenly a wicked blade flickered in his hand at the end of the swordstick. He still said nothing, but the crowd fell back, and the two men holding Juliana's ankles stepped away from the table.

George Ridge cleared his throat. He didn't know what was going on here, but he could see his prize slipping away from him. The newcomer spun round at the sound, and George flinched from the piercing stare, as cold and lethal as an arrowhead. He dropped his gaze in involuntary submission to this unknown but infinitely more powerful force.

Tarquin turned back to Juliana. He reached up and lifted her to the ground. He removed the halter and threw it into the crowd.

His eyes were still those he'd turned upon Lucien, cold and deadly, but he touched her hair, brushing a strand from her forehead. His long fingers moved fleetingly over the curve of her cheek. "Are you hurt?"

She shook her head. Her voice was barely a whisper, but she managed to say frankly, "Only my pride."

Surprise glimmered in his eyes, softening the implacable steadiness of his gaze. Any other woman would have broken down in tears and hysteria. But Juliana was unique. "Can you walk?"

Her knees were quivering uncontrollably, but there was something in his appraising scrutiny that gave her strength to say "Of course," even as she clutched his arm for support. Somehow she put one foot in front of the other as the crowd fell back. Then they were outside. Dawn was breaking, and a curious quiet had fallen over the Piazza and the square. A few bodies lay sleeping under the colonnades, a pair of slatternly women leaned in a doorway, drinking ale between yawns. A shout and a crash came from Tom King's coffeehouse as a man flew through the door to land in the gutter, where he lay in a heap, clutching a stone jar of gin.

The duke raised a finger and a hackney appeared as if by magic. Tarquin gave Juliana a boost into the interior with an unceremonious hand under her backside and followed almost in the same movement, pulling the door shut with a slam.

For the first time in hours Juliana was no longer terrified. The gloomy, musty interior of the carriage was a haven, private and utterly protected. Faint gray light came through the window aperture, showing her the duke's countenance as he sat opposite, regarding her in reflective silence.

"What are you thinking?" Her voice sounded shrunken, as if the events of the night had leached all strength from it.

"Many things," he replied, running his fingertips over his lips. "That you are the most perverse, stubborn, willful wench it's ever been my misfortune to have dealings with. . . . No, let me finish answering the question." He held up an arresting hand as Juliana's mouth opened indignantly. "That Lucien's evil tonight surpassed even my expectations; and most of all, that I should never have let you set eyes on him."

"So you're sorry you devised this demonic scheme?"

"No, I didn't say that. But I deeply regret involving you."

"Why?"

Tarquin didn't immediately reply. It was on the tip of his tongue to say simply that she wasn't cut out for the role, not sufficiently compliant. It was how he believed he would have responded just a few short hours ago. But something had happened to him when he'd seen her on that table, exposed to the sweating, lusting, depraved gaze of London's vicious underworld. When he'd seen her freshness, her simplicity, her ingenuous candor mentally fingered by that vile mob, he'd known a rage greater than any he could remember. And to his discomfort and confusion that rage was directed at himself as much as at Lucien.

"Why?" Juliana repeated. "Am I not sufficiently biddable, my lord duke?" As her terror receded, her bitterness grew. On one level Tarquin was as guilty of that hideous violation as Lucien had been. "I'm sorry to have put you to such inconvenience this evening." She tore angrily at a loose cuticle on her thumb, stripping the skin away with her teeth.

Tarquin leaned over and took her hand from her mouth. He clasped the abused thumb in his warm palm and regarded her gravely in the growing light. "I'm willing to accept a hefty share of the blame for this night's doings, Juliana, but you, too, bear some responsibility. You chose to cultivate Edgecombe to be avenged upon me. Will you deny it?"

Honesty forced her to shake her head. "But what else would you expect me to do?"

The exasperated question brought a low, reluctant chuckle to his lips. "Oh, I expected you to be good and obedient and allow me to know what's best for you. Foolish of me, wasn't it?"

"Very." Juliana tried to extricate her hand, but his fingers closed more firmly around hers.

"I will ensure that Lucien doesn't come near you ever again. Do I have your assurance that you won't seek him out?"

"I learn from my mistakes, sir," she said with acid dignity.

"I shall endeavor to learn from mine," he said wryly, releasing her hand as the carriage came to a halt on Albermarle Street. "And maybe we can look forward to a harmonious future."

Maybe, Juliana thought, but without too much optimism. She'd finished with Lucien, but after tonight she was more than ever determined to help the women of Covent Garden.

Her head swam suddenly as she stepped to the pavement.

Her knees buckled under an invincible wash of fatigue, and she reached blindly for support. Tarquin caught her against him, holding her strongly.

"Easy now, *mignonne*." His voice steadied her, and she leaned into the warmth and strength of his hold.

"I'm all wobbly," she mumbled apologetically into his coat. "I don't know why."

He laughed softly. "Well, I do. Come on, let's get you to bed." He lowered his shoulder against her belly and tipped her over. "Forgive the indignity, sweetheart, but it's the easiest way to accomplish the task."

Juliana barely heard him. She was almost asleep already, her body limp and unresisting as he carried her inside.

Chapter 18

❦

Tarquin awoke to filtered sunlight behind the bed curtains. The covers had been thrown back, and his naked body stirred deliciously as he felt the moist, fluttering caresses over his loins. Juliana's skin was warm against his, her hair flowing over his belly, her breath rustling on his inner thighs. Her fingers were as busy as her mouth, and he closed his eyes on a wave of delight, yielding to pleasure. His hand moved over her curved body, caressing the small of her back, smoothing over her bottom, tiptoeing over her thighs. He felt her skin quiver beneath his fingers and smiled.

He'd helped her undress and tumbled her into bed in the clear light of a rosy dawn, and by the time he'd thrown off his own clothes and prepared to join her, she'd been sleeping like an exhausted child, her cheek pillowed on her hand. He'd slipped in beside her, wondering why he chose to share her bed only to sleep when his own waited next door. He made it an invariable practice never to spend an entire night with his mistresses, but there had been something so appealing about Juliana. The deep, even breathing, the dark crescent of her eyelashes against the pale cheeks, the dusting of freckles across the bridge of her nose, the turn of her bare shoulder against the pillow, the vibrant cascade of her hair escaping from her lace-trimmed night-cap. Unable to resist, he'd slid in beside her, and she'd stirred and nuzzled against him like a small animal in search of warmth and comfort.

He'd fallen asleep smiling and awoken with the same smile. Now he smacked her bottom lightly. "*Mignonne,* come up."

Juliana raised her head and turned on her belly to look up at him. "Why?" She pushed her hair away from her face and gave him a quizzical smile.

"Because you are about to unman me," he replied.

Juliana reversed herself neatly and stretched her body over his, her mouth nuzzling the hollow of his throat, her loins moving sinuously over his. "Better?" she mumbled against his pulse.

With a lazy twist of his hips he entered her as she lay above him. He watched the surprise dawn in her eyes, to be followed immediately by a wondering pleasure. "This is different."

He nodded. "If you kneel up, you'll find it's even more so."

Juliana pushed herself onto her knees. She gasped at the changed sensation and slowly circled her body around the hard, impaling shaft. She touched his erect nipples with a feathery fingertip, searching his face for his response, chuckling when he groaned with pleasure.

"Does it feel good when I do this, sir?" She rose on her knees, then slowly sank down again, arching her back as she grasped her ankles with her hands. His flesh pressed against her body's sheath, and she suddenly lost interest in Tarquin's reaction as a wave of glorious sensation broke over her. She cried out, her body arched like a bow, the near unbearable tension building in ever tightening circles.

Tarquin lay still, knowing she needed no help from him to reach this peak. He watched her through half-closed eyes, reveling in the innocent candor of her joy. And when she cried out again, he grasped her hips and held her tightly as she rocked on his thighs with each succeeding wave of her climax.

"But what happened to you?" she gasped when she could finally speak, tears of joy glistening in her eyes. "Did I leave you behind?"

"Not for long," he promised softly. The exquisitely sensitized core of her body lay open for his touch, and he played delicately upon her as Juliana moved herself over and around him, her tongue caught between her teeth as she concentrated on her lover's pleasure, her own ever present but taking secondary importance. But when he drove upward with another almost leisurely twist, she was surprised yet again by the rushing, heated flood of ecstasy that dissolved muscle and sinew like butter in the sun.

He gripped her hips, his fingers biting deep into the rich curves, holding her as if she were his only anchor to reality in the storm-tossed sea of sensual bliss. And when it was over and he became aware of the lines and contours of his body on the mattress, of the dust motes in the ray of sun creeping through the curtains, he drew her down to lie along his length, his hand stroking over her damp back, his flesh diminishing slowly within her.

What was it about this woman that she could so transport him? Make him forget everything but the glories of their joining? What was it that made him want to protect her, to make her happy? He was thirty-two, affianced from childhood to a perfect match—a woman who would be his wife but who would not object to his mistresses. A woman who knew the rules of their society. A woman he *wanted* to marry. So why, then, did the prospect suddenly seem drab? When he thought of the well-ordered years ahead, he felt dull and depressed. But why? He and Lydia were two grown people who knew what each expected of the other. His marriage would follow the rules of all successful relationships. He gave people what they expected from his money, position, and influence, and he made sure he received what he was due in his turn.

It had always worked before, but it wasn't working with

Juliana. He was convinced that another woman in her position would have jumped at the chance of a title and a comfortable settlement for life. But not Juliana. She wasn't interested in what he had to offer; she seemed to want something more. She wanted something from *him*. Something far deeper than mere material offerings. And the thought stirred him, filled him with a restless excitement, was the source of this sudden impatience with his carefully laid-out future.

And holding this long, luscious body, feeling her jade gaze on his face, fiery tendrils of hair tickling his nose, he understood deep at his core that he lacked something fundamental to his happiness. He held it in his arms, but he couldn't grasp it and make it his. He didn't know how to. It was embodied in Juliana's unusual, tempestuous, forthright spirit, and he didn't know how to capture it. He didn't understand Juliana's rules.

He pulled himself up sharply. Juliana was a novelty, he told himself as she slept the brief sleep of satiation on his breast. He was confusing his fascination with her novelty with something deeper and unnameable. She was young and fresh. Her spirit amused him, her passion touched him. Her courage and resolution moved him. With luck she would be the mother of his child. In the best of all possible worlds she would remain his mistress as she mothered his child. There was no place—no need—for deeper, unnameable emotions.

Juliana stirred and opened her eyes. She kissed his neck sleepily. "I forgot to mention that George Ridge was in the tavern last night."

His hand stilled on her back. "Good God! What in heaven's name made you forget such a thing?"

"There was so much else to worry about," she said, sitting up, brushing hair out of her eyes. "And then I got so wobbly, and everything else went out of my head."

"I suppose it's understandable." He reached lazily for one full breast, cupping it in his palm, a fingertip circling the nipple. "Did he see you?"

"He could hardly miss me when I was standing on the table with a rope around my neck." She drew back from his caressing hand with a shiver, saying abruptly, "I don't seem to feel like being touched."

Tarquin dropped his hand immediately, his expression suddenly drawn with anger. "Lucien will pay in full measure for what he did to you," he promised savagely. "When he comes back to the house, he will pay." He stood up abruptly and strode to the window, staring out into the bright morning.

Juliana looked at his rigid, averted back and shivered slightly at the powerful anger she sensed. She wasn't to know how much of it was directed at himself. "I'll get over it," she said. "It was only a passing moment just then." She sat hunched on the bed, her arms crossed protectively over her breasts. "It all came back . . . the cockfight, and the wife-selling before, and the gin—"

"Gin?" he exclaimed, swinging back to the room, diverted from his bitter self-reproach. "Lucien permitted you to drink gin?"

"He forced it on me. I didn't know what it was." Her eyes flashed with her ever-ready temper.

Tarquin silently added it to the score he would settle with his cousin and said calmly, "Let's return to George Ridge. He recognized you?"

Juliana nodded, accepting the change of subject as an apology of some kind. "Enough to bid five hundred pounds for me."

Tarquin frowned. He stood beside the bed, his hands on his hips, his air as self-possessed as if he was fully dressed instead of starkly, and most beautifully, naked. "What did you do?"

"Nothing," she said somewhat absently, now thoroughly distracted by the sight of him, her eyes dwelling on the spare frame, the play of muscle, the lean, sinewy length of thigh. His sex was quiescent, but as her eyes lingered on the soft flesh, it flickered and rose beneath the intent gaze as if responding to an unspoken wish.

Tarquin appeared unaware. "What do you mean, you did nothing? You must have responded in some way."

Juliana reached forward to touch him, her tongue peeping from between her lips, a little frown of concentration on her brow.

Tarquin stepped back, observing with a smile, "I think I'd better don a chamber robe if we're to have a sensible discussion here." He turned to pick up his robe from the chaise longue. Juliana's gaze feasted on his lean back, the cluster of dark hair in the small of his back, and the dark trail that led downward to vanish in the cleft between the taut buttocks. Her fingers itched to slide between his thighs, and in another moment she would have sprung from the bed, but he slung the robe around his shoulders, thrusting his arms into the sleeves, and turned back to the bed, tying the girdle firmly at his waist.

Juliana couldn't hide her disappointment. Tarquin chuckled. "I'm flattered, *mignonne*. You certainly know how to compliment a man."

"It wasn't flattery," she denied with a sigh, wriggling beneath the covers again.

"Now, answer my question. What do you mean by 'nothing'?"

"It seemed sensible to behave as if I didn't know who he was," she explained. "I couldn't think too clearly, but I thought that if I refused to acknowledge him, then he would find it harder to identify me. If I deny that I'm Juliana Ridge, it's only his word against mine."

"Mmmm." Tarquin pulled at his chin. "That was quick thinking. But in the long term your guardians could identify you."

"But I could still deny it. And you could vouch for my identity as a whole other person. Who would challenge the Duke of Redmayne?"

Juliana showed a touching faith in the ability of the aristocracy to circumvent the law. But while Tarquin might be able to use his rank and influence to intimidate George Ridge and possibly the Forsetts, rank and influence would do little good before the bar. "It would be best if Ridge didn't see you again," he stated after a moment of frowning thought. "Keep to the house for the time being, unless you're with me . . . or possibly Quentin."

Juliana's face dropped. She couldn't do that and meet with her friends on Russell Street. "I'm not afraid of George," she protested. "I can't agree to be a prisoner just because that idiot George is hanging around. He's such a blockhead, he couldn't find his way out of a cloak bag. It was different when I was friendless and had no protection, but how could I be at risk when I have the mighty protection of His Grace of Redmayne?" She gave him a sweet smile, pulling the sheet up to her chin. "You are surely a match for a country lout, my lord duke."

"And that's exactly why you're not to go out without me or Quentin as escort." He bent over and kissed her lightly. "Do the sensible thing for once and oblige me in this." His gray gaze was calm, his voice quite without threat, but Juliana knew she'd been given fair warning.

After Tarquin left her, Juliana leaped from bed, rang for Henny, and began to plan for the day. She would take every precaution. She would travel only in a closed carriage, and she wouldn't show her face on the streets, at least not unless it was absolutely necessary.

Lucy was sleeping when she visited her on her way down to breakfast. Even in sleep the girl was beginning to look better already. It was as if her spirit had reentered her body and she was once more taking a grip on the world.

Juliana tiptoed out without waking her and went down to the breakfast parlor, where she found Quentin at breakfast. He looked up and cast a swift, almost involuntary, glance over her that made her immediately pleased with her gown of pale-green muslin over a pink petticoat. Henny had worked her usual magic with her hair, making a virtue of the unruly ringlets, arranging them artfully at her ears.

Quentin rose to his feet, bowing with a smile. "The

house has taken on a quite different air, my dear, since you came to join us. May I carve you some ham?"

"Thank you." Juliana took the chair pulled out for her by an attentive footman. She frowned slightly, wondering what he meant by "a different air." When people said things of that nature to her, they were usually scolding, but Lord Quentin had no such manner about him. "Is it a pleasanter air, sir?" she asked tentatively.

Quentin laughed. "Oh, most definitely. The house feels altogether lighter and merrier."

Juliana smiled broadly. "I hope His Grace agrees with you."

"Agrees with what?" Tarquin entered the room, taking a chair at the head of the table. He cast an eye over the *Gazette* beside his plate.

"Lord Quentin was so kind as to say that I've made the house merrier." Juliana took a piece of bread and butter, confiding cheerfully, "I'm not accustomed to being told such things. Mostly people say I make life uncomfortable for them."

The duke pursed his mouth consideringly. "Perhaps it amounts to the same thing for some people."

"How ungallant, my lord duke!"

"I suppose some people might actually enjoy chasing all over town after you at three o'clock in the morning."

"Oh! How could you speak of that now!" she exclaimed, her eyes flashing with indignation. "That is *most* unchivalrous!"

Tarquin smiled faintly. "My dear, as you said to me so aptly once, you reap what you sow." But to Juliana's relief he turned to Quentin with a change of subject. "No word on when you must leave us?"

"No, the archbishop seems perfectly content to keep me kicking my heels in London while he ponders my bishop's request."

"Well, I shall be loath to see you leave," the duke said civilly. "So I hope the pondering continues for a while longer."

Juliana soon excused herself and left the brothers to their breakfast. It seemed sensible to wait until the duke had gone about his morning's business before making her own move, so she lurked in the upstairs hallway, listening to the comings and goings in the hall below, waiting for the duke's departure.

He left shortly before noon, having first called for his horse. Juliana ran to her bedchamber and watched from the window as he rode up the street on a powerful piebald hunter. That left only Quentin. She hurried down the stairs and asked Catlett to call her a chair.

"My lady, surely you would prefer to take His Grace's conveyance?" Catlett said disapprovingly.

Juliana remembered that Quentin had told her the duke's own chair was at her disposal. If she used it, she would be under the protection of Tarquin's own men. She could always say she assumed that was as good as having his own escort, if he challenged her on her return.

"Yes, thank you, Catlett," she said with a sweet smile. "I wasn't sure whether His Grace was using the chair himself."

Somewhat mollified, Catlett bowed and sent the boot boy round to the mews for the sedan chair. The bearers brought the chair into the hall, where Catlett assisted Juliana inside; then he instructed the bearers to "Look alive, there. And be careful of 'Er Ladyship. No jolting." Leaning into the chair, he inquired, "Where shall I tell them to take you, m'lady?"

"Bond Street," Juliana said off the top of her head. She'd redirect the chairmen when they were outside.

They trotted off with her up Albermarle Street, oblivious of the man standing in a doorway opposite. They didn't notice him as he set off after them, almost at a jog in his haste not to lose them, sweat breaking out profusely on his forehead with his exertion, his waistcoat straining across his belly, his habitually red face turning a mottled dark crimson.

Juliana waited until they'd turned the corner onto Piccadilly. Then she tapped on the roof with her fan. "I've changed my mind. Carry me to Russell Street, if you please," she said haughtily.

The chairman looked a little surprised. Covent Garden addresses were not for the likes of Lady Edgecombe. But he shouted the change to his companion carrying the rear poles, and they set off in the new direction.

George hailed a sedan chair and fitted his ungainly bulk inside. "Follow that chair. The one with the coronet."

The chairmen hoisted the poles onto their muscular shoulders, taking the strain of their passenger's weight with a grimace. Then they set off after the chair emblazoned with the ducal coronet, their pace considerably slower than their quarry's.

Juliana alighted at the door of the Dennisons' house. She smoothed down her skirts and glanced up at the house that had once been her prison. First a refuge, then a prison. She could see her own third-floor window, where she'd lain in bed at night listening to the occupants of the house at work. What would have happened to her if the innkeeper hadn't sent for Elizabeth Dennison? She would never have known Tarquin, Duke of Redmayne, that was for sure. Her hand drifted to her belly. Did she even now carry his seed?

Briskly dismissing the thought, she said to the chairmen, "You had best wait for me here."

The lead chairman tipped his hat and adjusted the pads on his shoulders where the poles had rested. His companion ran up the steps to hammer on the knocker. Juliana followed him with the same haughty air of before, silently challenging them to question what she could be doing in such a place.

Mr. Garston opened the door and looked for a moment completely startled. Then he bowed as he'd never bowed to Juliana Ridge. "Pray step within, m'lady."

Juliana did so. "I've come to see Miss Lilly and the others." She tapped her closed fan in her palm and looked pointedly around the hall, as if finding its furnishings wanting in some way. To her secret delight Mr. Garston seemed a little intimidated, a little unsure of how to treat her. It was small revenge for their first meeting, and the subsequent occasions when he'd barred the door to her.

"Would ye care to wait in the salon, m'lady?" He moved with stately step to the room she remembered so vividly, flinging open the double doors.

The salon had been cleaned and polished, but the smell of wine and tobacco, and the girls' perfume, still lingered from the previous evening, despite the wide-open windows. It was a decadent combination of odors. Juliana wandered to the window and stared out at the scene in the street outside. Sunshine did much to mute the grimness: the one-legged child, hobbling on a crutch, thrusting his upturned cap at passersby with a whining, singsong plea for a penny; the woman asleep or unconscious in the gutter, a bottle clutched to her breast. Two gentlemen emerged from Thomas Davies's bookshop opposite, at Number 8. They had the air of learned men, with their flowing wigs and rusty black frock coats. Both carried leather-bound volumes, and they were talking earnestly. They stepped over the woman without so much as looking down and brushed past the crippled child, ignoring his pathetic pleas as he followed them down the street. Pleas that turned rapidly into curses when it became clear they were not going to put a penny in his cap.

As the child hopped, muttering, back to his position in the shadow of the bookshop doorway, Juliana frowned in puzzlement. There was something not quite right about him. She stared, leaning out of the window into the narrow street. Then she saw it. The child's leg was bent up at the knee and fastened with twine around his thigh. He was not one-legged at all. But he must be in the most awful discomfort, she thought, compassion instantly chasing away the moment of distaste at the fraud. Presumably he had a beggars' master, who had hit upon this cheat. Perhaps he was fortunate he hadn't been mutilated permanently.

Shuddering, she turned from the window as the door opened on a babble of excited voices.

"How is Lucy, Juliana?" Rosamund, her pretty face grave with concern, was the first into the room. The others followed in a gay flutter of filmy wrappers and lace-edged caps. They were still in dishabille, as Juliana remembered from her own days in the house. They wouldn't dress formally until just before dinner.

"She was sleeping when I left. But I think she's recovering quickly. Henny is looking after her." Juliana perched on the arm of a brocade sofa. "His Grace will not permit her to have visitors, because she needs to rest," she explained tactfully. "So I'll have to act as your messenger."

Fortunately no one questioned this polite fabrication, and Lilly launched into a description of the Dennisons' reaction to Lucy's plight and the request that they consider taking her in when she was well enough to work again.

"Mistress Dennison was pleased to say that since Lucy appeared to have His Grace's favor, then they would consider it," Emma said, sitting on the sofa and patting Juliana's arm confidingly.

"What a difference it makes to have an influential patron," sighed Rosamund, shaking her curls vigorously.

"Actually, I don't think it has much to do with the duke," Lilly declared acerbically. "It's just that Mistress Dennison would be delighted to thwart Mother Haddock."

There was a chuckle at this; then Lilly said, "So what was this plan you had, Juliana?"

"Ah." She opened and closed her fan restlessly. "Well, I thought that if we all banded together, we could look after each other. Protect each other so that what happened to Lucy couldn't happen again."

"How?" asked one of the girls with a mop of dark-brown curls and a sharp chin.

"If everyone in the various houses agreed to contribute a small sum every week from their earnings, we could have a rescue fund. We could pay debts like Lucy's . . . bail people out of debtors' prison."

The circle of faces looked at her in dubious silence.

Then someone said, "That might be all right for us . . . and for girls in some of the better houses, but for most of them, they don't earn enough to keep body and soul together after they've paid their whoremasters for the drink and the candles, and coal, and a gown, and linen. Molly Higgins told me she spent over five pounds last week because she had to have wax candles for her clients and new ribbons for her nightcap because she can't look shabby if she's to attract the right kind of customers. And the five pounds didn't include the present she had to give to madam to keep her sweet."

"But if they didn't have to buy all those things from their masters, then they would be better off," Juliana pointed out.

"But those are the terms on which they rent the places where they do business," Emma pointed out with an air of patience, as if explaining self-evident truths to an infant.

"But if they all refused to accept those terms, and if we managed to collect enough money to lend them for those necessary supplies, then they wouldn't be dependent on the whoremasters and bawds."

"It seems to me that you're talking of a vast deal of money," a dark girl said, nibbling a fingernail.

"Money's the key to everything," Rosamund replied gloomily. "I don't see how we can do it, Juliana."

"It's not money so much as solidarity," Juliana persisted. "If everyone agrees to put in what they can, you'd be surprised how it will mount up. But everyone has to take part. Everyone has to agree to stand by each other. If we do that, then we can stand up to the bawds and whoremasters."

There was another doubtful silence, and Juliana realized she had her work cut out. These women were so accustomed to a life of exploitation and powerlessness that they couldn't grasp the idea of taking their lives back. She opened her reticule and drew out her remaining twenty-pound note.

"I'll start the fund with this." She put the note on the table in front of her.

"But, Juliana, why should you contribute?" Lilly asked. "You're not one of us. In fact, you never have been."

"Oh, but I am," she said firmly. "My position is a little different, a little more secure, but I'm still in a situation I didn't choose, because I was alone and friendless and vulnerable. I was as much exploited as any one of you. And I'm as much dependent on the goodwill of a man who wouldn't call himself my whoremaster, but in essence that's exactly what he is."

Juliana glanced involuntarily toward the window as she said this, suddenly afraid that she might see the Duke of Redmayne standing there. If he heard himself described in such terms, his reaction didn't bear thinking about. But, then, he wasn't a man to appreciate the unvarnished truth when applied to his own actions.

"We should discuss it with the girls in the other houses," Lilly said. "If no one else wants to take part, then it won't work. We couldn't do it all ourselves."

"No," Juliana agreed. "It must be a real sisterhood."

"Sisterhood," mused Rosamund. "I like that word. I like what it means. Will you come with us to talk to the others, Juliana? You sound so convincing . . . so certain. And it was your idea."

Juliana nodded. "But not today." She didn't explain that she thought she'd been out of the house long enough. An extended absence would inevitably come to the duke's notice, but a short airing in his own chair would probably draw no more than a sigh and a raised eyebrow in their present state of accord.

"It would be best if we could gather everyone together," Emma said. "We should send round a message with a meeting place and a time."

"Where should we meet?" All eyes turned to Lilly, who seemed to have the role of natural leader.

"The Bedford Head," she said promptly. "We'll ask Mistress Mitchell if she'll lend us the back room one forenoon. She won't be busy then."

Juliana had seen the Bedford Head during her nightmare

with Lucien. It was a tavern in the center of Covent Garden—not a place she was eager to revisit. However, needs must when the devil drives, and the Garden was bound to be less wild in the morning.

A footman entered with tea and cakes and the message that Mistress Dennison requested Lady Edgecombe's company in her parlor when she'd completed her visit with the young ladies.

"A request, not a demand," Juliana mused with a wicked grin. "That's a novelty."

A chorus of laughter greeted this, and the mood lost its solemnity. The conversation became as light and fizzy as champagne, with much laughter and fluttering of fans. Juliana had once wondered if their gaiety was genuine, not merely a performance to hide their real feelings, but she'd soon become convinced that it was perfectly real. They allowed little to upset them. Presumably because if they stopped too often to reflect and look around, they'd never laugh again.

She'd never enjoyed female company before. Her friends in Hampshire had been restricted by Lady Forsett to the vicar's solemn daughters, both of whom had regarded Juliana as if she were some dangerous species of the animal kingdom, shying away from her whenever they were alone in her company. Of course, she had developed the reputation as a hoyden when she'd fallen from the great oak at the entrance to Forsett Towers and broken her arm. It had been a youthful indiscretion, but one that had blackened her among the ladies of the county. The cheerful and undemanding camaraderie of the women on Russell Street was therefore a delightful new experience.

Outside George Ridge was engaged in idle conversation with the duke's chairmen. Initially they'd regarded the large young man, sweating in his lavishly trimmed coat of scarlet velvet, with contempt and suspicion. But it didn't take them long to figure out that he was the classic pig's ear struggling to make a silk purse of himself. Their manner became more open, although none the less slyly derisive.

"So what kind of a house is this?" George gestured to the front door with his cane.

" 'Ore'ouse, like as not." The chairman spat onto the cobbles and resumed picking his teeth. "An 'igh-class one, mind ye."

"The lady didn't look like a whore," George remarked casually, feeling for his snuffbox.

"What? Lady Edgecombe?" The second chairman guffawed. "Proper little lady she is . . . or so that maid of 'er's says. 'Is Grace keeps a wary eye on 'er. Told Mistress 'Enny she needed a bit o' motherin'. 'E didn't want no 'ighfalutin abigail attendin' to 'er."

"That so?" The first chairman looked interested. "A'course, Mistress 'Enny's yer brother's mother-in-law, so I daresay she'd tell ye these things."

"Aye," the other agreed with a complacent nod. "Tells me most everythin'. Except," he added with a frown, "what's goin' on wi' that girl what 'Er Ladyship brought to the 'ouse yesterday. Mr. Catlett said as 'ow 'Is Lordship weren't best pleased about it. But Lord Quentin, 'e told 'im 'e 'ad a duty . . . or summat like that." He spat again, hunching his shoulders against a momentary sharp breeze coming around the street corner. "Blessed if I can get a thing outta 'Enny, though. Mouth's tighter than a trap."

"So what's Lady Edgecombe doing visiting a whorehouse?" George wondered aloud. Both chairmen looked at him suspiciously.

"What's it to you?" There was a belligerence to the question, and George thought that perhaps he'd got as much out of them as he was going to.

He shrugged. "Nothing, really. It's just that I thought I saw her in the Shakespeare's Head last even. With a group of men. Perhaps her husband . . . ?"

Both men spat in unison. "The viscount's no 'usband fer anyone. Can't think what persuaded 'im to take that poor young thing to wife. A dog's life, 'e'll lead 'er."

"But 'Is Grace is keepin' an eye out," his companion reminded him. "Eh, man, the affairs of the quality is no concern of ours. Couldn't understand 'em in a million years."

"Aye, that's a fact."

They both fell into a ruminative silence, and George finally offered a brief farewell and walked away. The mystery was growing ever deeper. Was Juliana really married to the viscount, who'd tried to sell her last night? Or was she embroiled in some whore's masquerade? The latter seemed the most likely, since it was impossible to imagine the real Viscountess Edgecombe taking part in that business in the tavern. A man of the viscount's breeding would never expose his wife to such ghastly humiliation. Whores were paid to participate in such playacting. But if the duke's servants believed she was truly wedded to the viscount, then something very deep was afoot. The woman, Mistress Henny, an old family retainer who'd been assigned to look after Juliana, was a very convincing detail in the narrative. But why would Juliana be part of such a deception?

Money, of course. She had left her husband's home without a penny, hadn't even taken her clothes. Somehow she'd fallen under the duke's influence, and he was requiring her to earn her keep by playing this part. He'd come to her rescue last night, so he must be deeply involved. But did he know that the strumpet he was employing was wanted for murder? Perhaps someone should tell him.

George turned into a tavern under the Piazza and called for ale. Perhaps he should confront Juliana before exposing her to her protector. Maybe she would be so intimidated by seeing him and understanding how much power he now held over her, that she would capitulate without a murmur. So long as she wasn't legally married, then nothing stood in the way of his own possession. She hadn't appeared to recognize him last night, but she'd been in great distress then and probably unaware of anything around her. He would ensure that next time she looked him full in the face and acknowledged his power.

George drained his tankard and called for a bottle of burgundy. He was beginning to feel that he would soon steer a path through this muddle and emerge triumphant. All he had to do now was to waylay Juliana when she was alone and with no easy exit. He would easily convince her to see which side her bread was buttered.

The burgundy arrived, but after a few sips he stood up and walked restlessly to the tavern door. The thought of Juliana drew him like a lodestone. His feet carried him almost without volition back to Russell Street, where he took up a stand on the steps of the bookshop, apparently minding his own business.

Juliana found Mistress Dennison friendly and hospitable. She bade her sit down and pressed a glass of sherry on her, then sat down herself and said with crisp matter-of-factness, "Do you know yet whether you've conceived?"

Juliana nearly choked on her sherry before she reminded herself that in this household there were no taboo intimate subjects when it came to female matters.

"It's too early to tell, ma'am," she responded with creditable aplomb.

Mistress Dennison nodded sagely. "You do, of course, know the signs?"

"I believe so, ma'am. But anything you wish to impart, I should be glad to hear."

Mistress Forster had broken her silence on all such matters only once, to tell Juliana that if she missed her monthly terms, she could assume she had conceived. Juliana suspected that there was more to the business than that bald fact, so she was grateful for Elizabeth's interest.

Elizabeth poured herself another glass of sherry and began to describe the symptoms of conception and the method of calculating the date of an expected birth. Juliana listened, fascinated. Mistress Dennison minced no words, called a spade a spade, and left no possibility for misunderstanding.

"There, child. I trust you understand these things now."

"Oh, yes, completely, ma'am." Juliana rose to take her leave. "I'm very thankful for the enlightenment."

"Well, my dear, you must always remember that even when a girl leaves here for such a splendid establishment as yours, she is still one of my girls. Any questions you may have, you will find the answers here. And when the time comes, I shall gladly assist at the birth. We are a close family, you understand." She smiled warmly at Juliana.

"I trust you'll see your way to opening your family to Lucy Tibbet, ma'am." Juliana dropped a demure curtsy. "His Grace has been kind enough to say that he'll give her a sum of money when she leaves his house so she'll be able to set herself up, but she will need friends. As we all do," she added.

Mistress Dennison looked a trifle vexed at being pressed on this matter, but she said a little stiffly, "His Grace is all condescension as always, Juliana. Lucy is very fortunate. Perhaps more than she deserves. But it's to be hoped she's learned a valuable lesson and will be a little more obedient in future."

Juliana dropped her eyes to hide the tongues of fire. "I'm sure you will do what you think best, ma'am."

"Yes, indeed, child. I always do." Elizabeth inclined her head graciously. "And I daresay, if Lucy is truly penitent, then Mr. Dennison and I will see our way to assisting her."

"Ma'am." Juliana curtsied again and turned to leave the room before her unruly tongue betrayed her. In her haste she tripped over a tiny spindle-legged table and sent the dainty collection of objets d'art it supported flying to the four corners of the room. "Oh, I do beg your pardon." She bent to pick up the nearest object, and her hoop swung wildly and knocked over an alabaster candlestick on a low table.

"Never mind, my dear." Elizabeth rose rather hastily to her feet and reached for the bellpull. "A servant will see to it. Just leave everything as it is."

Juliana backed cautiously from the room, her high color due not to embarrassment but to hidden anger.

She made her way down the stairs. The women had all retired to their chambers to dress for the day's work. A maid bustled across the hall with a vase of fresh flowers for the salon. Juliana glimpsed a footman refilling the decanters on the pier table. In a couple of hours the clients would begin to arrive.

Mr. Garston bowed her ceremoniously out of the door, clicking his fingers imperiously to the idling chairmen. "Look sharp, there. 'Er Ladyship's ready fer ye."

The chairmen snarled at Garston but jumped to attention as Juliana came down the steps. As she turned to step into the chair, she saw George watching her from the steps of the bookshop at Number 8. He offered her a clumsy bow, his lips twisting in a humorless grin. Juliana frowned as if in puzzlement. She spoke in carrying tones.

"Chairman, that man over there is staring at me in the most particular way. I find it offensive."

The first chairman touched his forelock. "Ye want me to wipe the grin off 'is face, m'lady?"

"No," Juliana said hastily. "That won't be necessary. Just carry me back to Albermarle Street."

George cursed her for an arrogant strumpet. How dare she look through him as if he were no more than a slug beneath her feet? What did she think she was playing at? But now that he'd found her, now that he knew that she went out alone, he could plan his campaign. Next time she left Albermarle Street alone, he would take her. He'd bring her to a proper respect for her late husband's heir. He returned to his burgundy with renewed thirst.

Chapter 19

The duke had not returned when Juliana got back to the house. One less confrontation to worry about, she thought cheerfully. The longer she could keep him in ignorance of her excursions to Russell Street, the simpler life would be. George was a damnable nuisance, though. If he was going to dog her footsteps at every turn, she was going to have to tell Tarquin, which would mean admitting her own journeyings. For some reason she had absolute faith in the duke's ability to dispose of George Ridge in some appropriate fashion . . . and she also had a grim foreboding that he'd be able to put a stop to her own activities if he chose. But that was a bridge to be crossed later.

She sat down at the secretaire in her parlor and drew a sheet of paper toward her. Dipping the quill into the standish, she began to set out a list of items the Sisterhood's fund would have to cover if it was to do any good. They could support only their contributing members, she decided, although that would leave out many of the most vulnerable women of the streets. The ones who sold themselves for a pint of gin against the tavern wall, or rolled in the gutter with whoever would have them for a groat. But one had to start great enterprises with small steps.

A footman interrupted her calculations with the message that His Grace was at the front door and wished her to join him. Puzzled, she followed the footman downstairs. The front door stood open, and as she approached, she heard Tarquin talking with Quentin.

"Ah, there you are, *mignonne*," he called as she appeared on the top step. "Come and tell me if you like her."

Juliana caught up her skirts and half tumbled down the stairs in her eagerness. Tarquin was standing beside a roan mare with an elegant head and aristocratic lines.

"Oh, how pretty she is." She stroked the velvety nose. "May I ride her?"

"She's yours."

"Mine?" Juliana stared, wide-eyed. She had never had her own mount, having to make do with whatever animal no one else wished to ride in Sir Brian's stables—doddery old riding horses for the most part, ready to be put out to pasture. "But why would you give me such a wonderful present?" A glint of suspicion appeared in her gaze, and she stepped almost unconsciously away from the horse.

"I promised to procure you a mount," he said smoothly. "Did you forget?" He could almost see the suspicions galloping through her mind, chasing each other across her mobile countenance. She was wondering what he wanted in exchange.

"No, I haven't forgotten," she said cautiously. "But why such a magnificent animal? I've done nothing to deserve her, have I?"

"Oh, I don't know," he said solemnly. "I can think of certain things, *mignonne*, that have given me limitless pleasure." His eyes were filled with a seductive smile, making clear his meaning, and Juliana felt her cheeks warm. She glanced sideways at Quentin, who appeared to be taking an inordinate interest in a privet hedge.

Juliana nibbled her bottom lip; then she shrugged and stepped up to the mare again. She decided not to spoil her pleasure in the gift by worrying about whether there were strings attached. If there were, she would ignore them. She took the mare's head between her hands and blew gently into her nostrils. "Greetings."

Once again Tarquin was entranced by her ingenuous delight. Her pleasure in his gift filled him with a deep satisfaction that had nothing to do with his intention to keep her so happy and busy that she had neither the time nor the inclination to cause him further trouble.

Quentin smiled with his brother. You couldn't find two women more different from one another than Lydia Melton and Juliana Courtney, he reflected. The one so quiet and composed, with the pale gravity of a cameo. The other a turbulent, wildfire creature, ruled by passion. The comparison struck him to the heart with the familiar shaft of pain that came whenever he thought of Lydia. Of how impossibly unfair it was that Tarquin should have her and not truly want her, and he should be left on the outside, watching, his heart wrung with love and loss. But he must bow his head to God's will. Railing against the Almighty's plans was no proper behavior for a man of the cloth.

"What will you name her?" he asked abruptly.

Juliana patted the silken curve of the animal's neck. "Boadicea."

"Now, why that, in heaven's name?" Tarquin's eyebrows shot into his scalp.

"Because she was a strong, powerful woman who did what she believed in." Juliana's smile was mischievous, but her jade eyes were shadowed. "An example for us all, sir."

Tarquin smiled with resigned amusement and gestured toward the man holding the horses.

"This is Ted, Juliana. He's your groom, and he'll accompany you wherever you go."

Juliana looked startled. The man wore a leather jerkin and britches instead of livery. He had a broken nose, and his face had the misshapen appearance of one that had been in contact with a variety of hard objects over the years. He was very tall and very broad, but Juliana had the impression that his bulk was not fat, but muscle. His hands were huge, with hairy knuckles and splayed fingers.

He offered her a morose nod of the head, not a smile
cracking his expression, not a glint of humor or pleasure in
his eyes.

"Everywhere?" she queried.

"Everywhere," Tarquin repeated, the smile gone from
his eyes.

"But I have no need of a bodyguard," Juliana protested,
horrified at the implications of such a restriction.

"Oh, but you do," Tarquin declared. "Since I can't rely
upon you to take sensible precautions, someone must take
them for you." He reached out a hand and lightly caught
her chin in his palm. "No Ted, no horse, Juliana."

It appeared he knew of her expedition. Juliana sighed.
"How did you find out? I didn't think you'd come back."

"Not much goes on under my roof without my knowledge." He continued to hold her chin, his expression
grave. "Do you accept the condition, Juliana?"

Juliana looked again at the morose Ted. Was he to be spy
as well as protector? Presumably so. How was she to manage the projected visit to the Bedford Head in his dour
company? Well, she'd get around him somehow. She returned her attention to Boadicea, saying by way of answer,
"I should like to ride her immediately."

"It wants but ten minutes to dinner," Quentin said,
amused.

"After dinner you may ride her in the park during the
promenade, with Ted's escort," Tarquin suggested, hiding
his relief at her capitulation. "Everyone will be wondering
who you are. You'll create quite a stir."

Juliana laughed at this, not displeased with the idea. "I'd
better tidy myself before dinner." She dropped a mischievous curtsy to the brothers and ran back inside.

Quentin chuckled, linking his arm in his brother's as
they returned inside. "If she needs protection, Ted's as
good a man as any for the task."

Tarquin nodded. "The best." They both smiled, each
with his own boyhood memories of the taciturn, uncompromising gamekeeper, who'd taught them to ride, to

tickle trout, to snare rabbits and track deer. Ted Rougley was utterly devoted to the Courtney family, with the exception of Lucien, and his loyalty was unwavering. Tarquin would never give him an order, but if he made a request, Ted would carry it out to the letter. Juliana would find it hard to take a step unguarded.

"I understand Juliana needs to be kept away from that stepson of hers, but what of Lucien?" Quentin asked as they entered the dining room.

Tarquin's nostrils flared, his mouth becoming almost invisible. "He hasn't returned to the house as yet. I'll deal with him when he does."

Quentin nodded and dropped the subject as Juliana came into the room.

"So," Juliana said conversationally, helping herself to a spoonful of mushroom ragout. "I'm to receive no visitors and go abroad only escorted by that morose-looking bodyguard. Is that the way it's to be?"

"My dear, you may have all the visitors you wish—"

"Except my friends," she interrupted Tarquin.

"Except Mistress Dennison's girls," he finished without heat.

"I suspect I am going to be bored to tears," she stated, sounding remarkably cheerful at the prospect.

"Heaven preserve us!" the duke declared, throwing up his hands in mock horror. "The combination of you and boredom, my dear Juliana, doesn't bear thinking of. But you will meet plenty of people. There will be those who come to pay a bridal visit. You may go to Vauxhall and Ranelagh, the play, the opera. You will be introduced to people there, and I daresay you'll be invited to soirees and card parties and routs."

"Well, that's a relief," Juliana said as cheerfully as before, popping a roast potato into her mouth.

Tarquin smiled to himself. Quentin sipped his wine, reflecting that there was a rare softness, an indulgence, in Tarquin's eyes when they rested on the girl, even when they were sparring.

Juliana left them when the port decanter appeared, saying she wished to get ready for her ride, and the brothers sat over their port in companionable silence, each with his own thoughts.

Twenty minutes later Juliana's head peeked around the door. "May I come in again, or is it inconvenient?" she asked delicately. Chamber pots were kept in the sideboard for the convenience of gentlemen sitting long over their port, and she knew better than to burst in unannounced.

"Come in by all means," Tarquin invited, leaning back in his chair, legs stretched out and ankles crossed. Quentin saw the warm, amused look spring into his eyes again.

"I thought since you must have chosen my riding dress, you'd like to see what it looked like." Juliana stepped into the room. "It's very beautiful." She couldn't disguise her complacence as she presented herself expectantly for their admiration. "Don't you think the velvet on the collar and cuffs is a clever touch?" She craned her neck to examine her reflection in the glass of the fireplace. "It does such nice things for my eyes and skin." With a critical frown she adjusted the angle of her black, gold-edged hat. "I've never had such an elegant hat, either."

Tarquin smiled involuntarily. He'd amused himself giving orders for this wardrobe, but his enjoyment was tripled with Juliana's clear pleasure and the fact that his eye had been accurate. The green cloth coat and skirt with a cream silk waistcoat and dark-green velvet trimmings accentuated the lustrous jade of her eyes and her vivid hair. The nipped waist of the jacket and graceful sweep of the skirt made the most of the rich lines of her body.

She swept them both a curtsy, then rose and twirled exuberantly. The train of her full skirt swirled and wrapped itself around the leg of a table. With a muttered curse she extricated herself before any damage could be done.

"You look enchanting," Quentin declared. "Tarquin has always had a good eye when it comes to women's clothes."

"Do you spend this amount of time and trouble, not to

mention money, on all your mistresses' wardrobes?" Juliana tweaked at her snowy linen cravat, smoothing a fold.

Quentin turned aside to hide his grin as Tarquin stared in disbelief at the insouciant Juliana. "Do I what?"

"Oh, was that indiscreet of me?" She smiled sunnily. "I didn't mean to be. I was only interested. It's unusual, I believe, for men to take such an interest in women's clothes."

"Let's drop the subject, shall we?" The duke sat up straight, his brows coming together in a fierce frown.

"Oh, very well." She shrugged. "But how many do you have?"

"How many what?" he demanded before he could stop himself.

"Mistresses."

Tarquin's face darkened, his indulgent equanimity destroyed. Quentin hastily intervened, pushing back his chair and getting to his feet. "Juliana, my dear, I think you had better go for your ride. I'll escort you to the mews and see you mounted." He had swept her from the room before she could say anything else devastating, and before Tarquin could give voice to his bubbling wrath.

"Not exactly the soul of tact, are you?" Quentin observed in the stable yard.

"Did you think it an indelicate question?" Juliana asked airily, stepping up to the mounting block. "I thought it perfectly reasonable." She settled into the saddle, her skirts decorously arranged, and shot Quentin a mischievous grin that he couldn't help but return.

"You're incorrigible, Juliana."

Ted mounted a sturdy cob and examined Juliana critically. "The roan's fresh, ma'am. Think ye can 'andle her wi'out a curb?"

"Of course." Juliana nudged the mare's flanks, and Boadicea plunged forward toward the street. Juliana, unmoved, pulled back on the reins and brought the animal to a stop.

Ted grunted. "Seat's all right," he commented with a nod at Quentin. "Daresay she'll do."

Quentin raised a hand in farewell as the horses walked sedately out of the yard; then he went back into the house to fetch his hat and cane. It was a beautiful afternoon, and a stroll in Hyde Park was a pleasing prospect.

Juliana threw out a few conversational gambits to her escort but received only monosyllabic responses. Soon she gave up and settled down to enjoy her ride in private. She was so intent on managing Boadicea and displaying herself to advantage that she didn't see George slip out of a doorway as they clopped down Albermarle Street. She didn't notice him following at a steady pace and a safe distance; she was far too busy looking around, assessing the reactions of fellow travelers to her passing. It was gratifying to receive curious and admiring glances when at home she was accustomed to drawing not so much as a second look.

Ted, however, was aware of their follower. He took his charge on a roundabout route to the park, down side streets and through alleys, always at a pace that wouldn't outstrip a determined pursuer. The man dogged them every step of the way.

George was filled with an impotent rage. He'd been waiting for her to emerge for hours, imagining how he would go up to her, how he would scoop her up from the street, bundle her away. But she was still way beyond his reach, accompanied by that ugly-looking customer who gave the unmistakable impression of a man who would know how to handle himself in a fight.

George was in the grip of an obsession. He'd lost all interest in the fleshly pleasures of London; his dreams both waking and sleeping were filled with Juliana and the corrosive fear that even though he was so close to her, yet he might still be too far. He had followed her back to Albermarle Street from Russell Street and taken up his usual stand on the basement steps opposite. He'd watched with greedy, predatory eyes when she'd appeared on the steps with the two men and the roan mare. He couldn't hear what they said, but it was clear they were discussing something pleasing. He watched her go into the house, and his gut twisted at the bitter reflection that the men behaved toward her with a consideration more suited to a respectable wife than to a harlot.

And now she was riding through London, dressed in the very peak of fashion, on a well-bred and very expensive lady's horse, in the company of a groom. He had to get his hands on her. Force her to acknowledge him. His hands curled into fists at the thought of how she'd looked straight through him. It had been with such conviction that he could almost have believed that he was mistaken—that this pampered creature of fashion was not Juliana Ridge, the neglected and unsophisticated country girl, his father's murderess and the legal owner of a substantial portion of George Ridge's inheritance.

But he knew from the way his loins were afire and his blood ran swift whenever he was in her vicinity that he was not mistaken. This was Juliana. *His* Juliana.

His quarry turned into Hyde Park, and he dodged behind a tree as they reined in the horses and seemed to be having a discussion about which direction to take. He could achieve nothing by continuing to follow them. He couldn't haul her from her horse . . . not here . . . not now. They would return to Albermarle Street eventually, and he'd do better to scout around there while he waited, but he couldn't bring himself to turn his back on Juliana. His eyes drew him forward onto the tan strip of sand running beside the pathway, where they put their horses to the trot and then to a canter, too fast now for him to keep them in sight.

He could sit and wait for them to come full circle, or he could go back to his post. His belly squalled, reminding him that he'd been so intent on his vigil, he'd had no dinner. He decided to return to the Gardener's Arms and drown his frustrations. He would return to watch and await his opportunity in the morning. It was the sensible decision, but he still had to force himself to walk away.

Juliana settled comfortably into the roan's rhythm. The mare had an easy gait and seemed to be enjoying the exercise as much as her rider. The dour Ted kept pace on his cob.

They were on their second circuit when she saw Quentin on the path ahead, walking toward them with a lady dressed in black taffeta. Juliana recognized Lady Lydia despite the heavy black veil concealing her face. She drew rein as she came up with them. "I give you good day, Lady Lydia. Lord Quentin."

For a moment she read dismay in Quentin's eyes, and she was convinced her interruption was unwelcome; then his customary serene smile returned. "Dismount and walk with us awhile." He reached up a hand to help her down. "Ted will take Boadicea."

"Boadicea? What an unusual name for such a pretty lady," Lydia said in her soft voice, responding to Juliana's curtsy with her own, but not lifting her veil.

"She's pretty," Juliana agreed, "but I believe she has a mind of her own." She handed the reins to Ted and took Quentin's other arm, turning with them on the path. "How fortuitous that we should all meet like this. I didn't realize you were going to be in the park, too, Lord Quentin."

"It was a sudden impulse," he responded. "Such a beautiful afternoon."

"Yes, quite lovely," Lydia agreed. "I couldn't bear to be inside another minute. We are still in strict mourning, of course, but there can be no objection to my taking a walk when I'm veiled."

"No, of course not," Quentin said warmly.

"Are you enjoying London, Lady Edgecombe?"

"Oh, immensely, Lady Lydia. It's all so very new to me. Hampshire is such a backwater."

Quentin kicked her ankle at the same instant she realized her mistake.

"Hampshire?" Lydia put up her veil to look at her in surprise. "I thought your family came from York, in the north."

"Oh, yes," Juliana said airily. "I was forgetting. I used to visit relatives in Hampshire and liked it much better than York. So I always think of it as home."

"I see." Lydia's veil fell again. "I didn't know there were any Courtneys in Hampshire."

"My cousin's family," Juliana offered. "A very distant cousin."

"How curious that you should be closer to a distant cousin's relatives than to your own," Lydia mused, puzzled.

"Lady Edgecombe has some unusual views on the world," Quentin said flatly. "I'm sure you must wish to continue your ride, Juliana. It must be dull work walking when a new mount awaits you."

Juliana wasn't sure whether he was getting rid of her for his sake or hers, but she took her cue, signaling to Ted, who rode a little way behind them, leading Boadicea.

Lydia put up her veil again to bid her farewell. "I do hope we'll be like sisters," she said, kissing Juliana's cheek. "It will be so pleasant to have another woman in the house."

Juliana murmured something and returned the kiss. She glanced again at Quentin. His face was almost ugly, and she knew he was thinking, as was she, of Tarquin's setting up two families under his roof. Installing the woman Quentin loved as the mother of one of them.

Juliana was no longer in any doubt that Quentin loved Lydia Melton, and she suspected his love was reciprocated. Tarquin had admitted that he did not love Lydia, yet he was her betrothed. There must be a way to sort out this tangle. Quentin was not quite such a magnificent catch as his brother, but he was still the younger son of a duke, wealthy in his own right, and clearly destined for great things in the Church. He would be an excellent match for Lydia—once her engagement to Tarquin could be broken off.

But that would leave Tarquin without a wife. Without a mother for his legitimate heirs.

A problem for another day. She remounted with Ted's assistance, waved a cheerful farewell to Quentin and his lady, and trotted off. "Have you known the Courtney family for long, Ted?"

"Aye."

"Forever?"

"Aye."

"Since His Grace was a boy?"

"Since 'e was nobbut a babby."

That was a long sentence, Juliana thought. Maybe it was a promising sign. "Have you known Lady Lydia and her family for long?"

"Aye."

"Always?"

"Aye."

"So they've known the Courtneys for always?"

"Aye. Melton land marches with Courtney land."

"Ah," Juliana said. That explained a lot, including a marriage of convenience. Ted might well prove a useful source of information if she picked her questions correctly. However, his lips were now firmly closed, and she guessed he'd imparted as much as he was going to for the present.

She dismounted at the front door and Ted took the horses to the mews. Juliana made her way upstairs. As she turned toward her own apartments, she came face-to-face with Lucien. Her heart missed a beat. Tarquin had said she'd never have to face her vile husband again. He'd said he would deal with him. So where was he?

"Well, well, if it isn't my not so little wife." Lucien blocked her passage. The slurring of drink couldn't disguise the malice in his voice, and his eyes in their deep, dark sockets burned with hatred. His chin was blue-bruised. "You left in such a hurry last night, my dear. I gather the entertainment didn't please you."

"Let me pass, please." She kept her voice even, although every millimeter of skin prickled, her muscles tightened with repulsion, and the hot coals of rage glowered in her belly.

"You weren't so anxious to be rid of me yesterday," he declared, gripping her wrist in the way that sent a wave of remembered fear racing through her blood. He twisted her wrist and she gave a cry of pain, her fingers loosening on the riding crop she held. He wrenched it from her slackened grasp.

"What an unbiddable wife you've become, my dear." Catching a clump of her hair that was escaping from her hat brim, he gave it a vicious tug as he pulled her closer to him. "I promised you would pay for that kick last night. It seems you're getting quite above yourself for a Russell Street harlot. I think I must teach you proper respect."

Out of the corner of her eye Juliana caught the flash of movement as he raised the whip. Then she screamed, with shock as much as pain, as it descended across her shoulders in a burning stripe.

Lucien's eyes glittered with a savage pleasure at her cry. He raised his arm again, at the same time pulling brutally on her hair as if he would tear it from her scalp. But he'd underestimated his victim. It was one thing to take Juliana by surprise, quite another to face her when she'd had a chance to gather her forces. She had learned over the years to control the worst of her temper, but she made no effort to quench it now.

Lucien found he had one of the Furies in his hands. He clung on to her hair, but she seemed oblivious of the pain. The whip fell to the ground as her knee came up with lethal accuracy. His eyes watered, he gasped with pain. Before he could protect himself, she kicked his shins and was going for his eyes with her fingers curled into claws. Instinctively, he covered his face with his hands.

"You filthy bastard . . . son of a gutter-born bitch!" she hissed, driving her knee into his belly. He doubled over on an anguished spasm and was racked with a violent coughing fit that seemed to pull his guts up from his belly. Juliana grabbed up the whip, raised her arm to bring it down across his back.

"Jesus, Mary, and Joseph!" Tarquin's voice pierced the scarlet circle of her blind rage. He had hold of her upraised wrist and was forcing her arm down. "What in the name of damnation is going on here?"

Juliana struggled to regain control. Her bosom was heaving, her cheeks deathly pale, her eyes on fire, seeing nothing but the loathsome, squirming shape of the man who had dared to raise his hand to her. "Gutter sweeping," she said, her voice trembling with fury. "Slubberdegullion whoreson. May you rot in your grave, you green, slimy maggot!"

Tarquin removed the whip from her hand. "Take a deep breath, *mignonne*."

"Where were you?" she demanded, her voice shaking. "You said I would never have to see him again. You *promised* you would keep him away from me." She touched her sore scalp and winced as the movement creased the stripe across her back.

"I didn't know until just now that he'd returned," Tarquin said. "I wouldn't have let him near you if I had. Believe me, Juliana." She was shivering violently and he laid a hand on her arm, his expression tight with anger and remorse. "Go to your apartments now and leave this with me. Henny will attend to your hurts. I'll come to you shortly."

"He hit me with that damned whip," Juliana said, catching her breath on an angry sob.

"He'll pay for it," Tarquin said grimly. Fleetingly, he touched her cheek. "Now, do as you're bid."

Juliana cast one last, scornful look at the still convulsed Lucien and trailed away, all the bounce gone from her step.

Tarquin said with soft savagery, "I want you out of my house within the hour, Edgecombe."

Lucien looked up, struggling for breath. His eyes were bloodshot, filled with pain, but his tongue was still pure venom. "Well, well," he drawled. "Reneging on an agreement, my dear cousin! Shame on you. The shining example of honor and duty has feet of clay, after all."

A pulse flicked in Tarquin's temple, but he spoke without emotion. "I was a fool to have thought it possible to have an honorable agreement with you. I consider the contract null and void. Now, get out of my house."

"Giving up on me at last, Tarquin?" Lucien pushed himself up until he was sagging against the wall. His deep-sunk eyes glittered suddenly. "You promised me once you would never give up on me. You said that you would always stand by me even when no one else would. You said blood was thicker than water. Do you remember that?" His voice had a whine to it, but his eyes still glittered with a strange triumph.

Tarquin stared down at him, pity and contempt in his gaze. "Yes, I remember," he said. "You were a twelve-year-old liar and a thief, and in my godforsaken naïveté I thought maybe it wasn't your fault. That you needed to be accepted by the family in order to become one of us—"

"You never accepted me in the family," Lucien interrupted, wiping his mouth with the back of his hand. "You and Quentin despised me from the first moment you laid eyes on me."

"That's not true," Tarquin said steadfastly. "We gave you every benefit of the doubt, knowing the disadvantages of your upbringing."

"Disadvantages!" Lucien sneered, the blue bruises standing out against his greenish pallor. "A demented father and a mother who never left her bed."

"We did what we could," Tarquin said, still steadily. But as always, even as he asserted this, he wondered if it was true. It was certainly true that he and Quentin had despised their scrawny, deceitful, cunning cousin, but they had both tried to hide their contempt when Lucien had come to live among them, and then, when Tarquin had become his guardian, they had both tried to exert a benign influence on the twisted character. Tried and most signally failed.

For a moment he met his cousin's eyes, and the truth of their relationship lay bare and barren for both of them. Then he said with cold deliberation, "Get out of my house, Edgecombe, and stay out of my sight. I wash my hands of you from this moment."

Lucien's mouth twisted in a sly smile. "And how will that look? Husband and wife living apart after a few days of marital bliss?"

"I don't give a damn how it will look. I don't want you breathing the same air as Juliana." Tarquin turned contemptuously.

"I'll repudiate her," Lucien wheezed. "I'll divorce her for a harlot."

Tarquin turned back very slowly. "You aren't good enough to clean her boots," he said with soft emphasis. "And I warn you now, Edgecombe, you say one word against Juliana, in public or in private, and I will send you to your premature grave, even faster than you can do yourself." His eyes scorched this truth into his cousin's ghastly countenance. Then he swung on his heel and stalked away.

"You'll regret this, Redmayne. Believe me, you'll regret it." But the promise was barely whispered and the duke didn't hear. Lucien stared after him with fear and loathing. Then he dragged himself down the passage to his own apartments, soothing his mortified soul with the promise of revenge.

Chapter 20

Lucien emerged at twilight from Mistress Jenkins's Elysium in Covent Garden. He bore the well-satisfied air of a man who has relieved both mind and body. Jenkins's flogging house was a highly satisfactory outlet for anger and frustration. The Posture Molls knew exactly how to accommodate a man, whichever side of the birch he chose to be, and he had given free rein to his need to punish someone for the humiliation of his debacle with his wife and Tarquin's subsequent edict.

His eyes carried a brutal glint, and his mouth had a cruel twist to it as he strolled up Russell Street and into the square. But it didn't take long for the reality of his situation to return. He'd been thrown out of his cousin's house, cut off from that bottomless and ever-open purse. And he had a cursed woman to blame for it.

He entered the Shakespeare's Head, ignored the greetings of acquaintances, and sat down in morose silence at a corner table, isolated from the company. He was well into his second tankard of blue ruin when he became aware of a pair of eyes fixed intently upon him from a table in the window. Lucien glared across the smoke-hazed taproom; then his bleary gaze focused. He recognized the overweight man looking as if he was dressed up to ape his betters, squashed into the clothes of a fashionable man-about-town, his highly colored face already suffused with drink. As Lucien returned the stare, the man wiped a sheen of grease from his chin with his sleeve and pushed back his chair.

He made his ponderous and unsteady way through the crowded tables and arrived in Lucien's corner. "Beggin' your pardon, my lord, but I happened to be here last even when you were selling your wife," George began, as intimidated by the death's-head stare and the man's sickly, greenish pallor as he was by the depthless malice in the sunken eyes.

"I remember," Lucien said grudgingly. "Five hundred pounds you offered for her. Fancied her, did you?"

"Is she truly your wife, sir?" George couldn't disguise the urgency of his question, and Lucien's eyes sharpened.

He buried his nose in his tankard before saying, "What's it to you, may I ask?"

George started to pull back a chair, but the viscount's expression forbade it. He remained standing awkwardly. "I believe I know her," he said.

"Oh, I should think you and half London knew her," Lucien responded with a shrug. "She came from a whorehouse, after all."

"I thought so." George's flush deepened with excitement. "She's not truly your wife, then. A Fleet marriage, perhaps?"

"No such luck." Lucien laughed unpleasantly. "I assure you she's Lady Edgecombe all right and tight. My cursed cousin made sure of that. A plague on him!" He took up his tankard again.

George was nonplussed. His disappointment at hearing that Juliana was legally wed was so great that for a moment he could think of nothing to say. He'd convinced himself that she couldn't possibly be what she seemed, and now all his plans came crashing around his ears like the proverbial house of cards.

"So why are you so interested in the whore?" Lucien demanded.

George licked his dry lips. "She murdered my father."

"Oh, did she now?" Lucien sat up, his eyes suddenly alive. "Well, that doesn't surprise me. She half killed me this afternoon. If I had my way, I'd put a scold's bridle on her, strap her in the ducking chair, and drown her!"

George nodded, his little eyes glittering. "She's a murderess. I won't rest until I see her burn."

"Take a seat, dear fellow." Lucien gestured to the chair and bellowed at a potboy, "A bottle of burgundy here, you idle lout!" He leaned back in his chair and surveyed George thoughtfully. "It seems we have a desire in common. Tell me all about my dear wife's sordid history."

George leaned forward, dropping his voice confidentially. Lucien listened to the tale, his expression unmoving, drinking his way steadily through the bottle, for the most part forgetting to refill the other man's glass. He had no difficulty reading the lust behind Ridge's desire for vengeance, and he knew it could be put to good use. The man was a country-bred oaf, with no subtlety. But when the twin devils of lust and vengeance drove a man, he could be an invincible enemy under proper direction. A most valuable tool.

If Lucien could expose Juliana, could see her quivering in the dock to receive the death sentence, Tarquin's disgrace would be almost as devastating as the girl's. His damnable pride would crumble in the dust. He'd be the jesting stock of London.

George finished the story and drained his glass. "I thought I would tell the duke first," he said, looking mournfully at the empty bottle. "Expose Juliana to him and see what he says."

Lucien shook his head. "Depend upon it, he knows it all."

George pointedly picked up the empty bottle and up-ended it into his glass. "How can you be sure?"

"Because he as good as told me." Lucien finally beckoned the potboy for another bottle. "Told me the harlot would do his bidding. Thought then he must have something on her. Something to hold over her." His voice was becoming increasingly slurred, but the spite in his eyes grew more pronounced.

"If I laid a charge against her," George said eagerly, "if I did that, she'd have to answer it, even if she denied that she was who she was. But if I could get her guardians to identify her as well as myself, well, surely that should convince the magistrates."

Lucien looked doubtful. "Problem is, Tarquin's up to every trick. A man has to be sharp as a needle and slippery as an eel to put one over on him."

"But even the duke couldn't withstand the testimony of Juliana's guardians. She lived with them from the time she was four years old. If they swear and I swear to her identity, surely that would be enough."

"It might. So long as Tarquin didn't get wind of it first." Lucien stared into his glass, swirling the rich red contents. "It might be easier to work on the whore herself."

"Kidnap her, you mean." George's eyes glittered. "I've been thinkin' along those lines myself. I'd soon get a confession out of her."

George stared into the middle distance. Only when he had Juliana in his hands would he be able to satisfy this all-consuming hunger. Then he would be at peace, able to reclaim his rightful inheritance. He was no longer interested in having her to wife. But he knew he would get no rest until he'd indulged this craving that gnawed at his vitals like Prometheus's vultures.

Lucien's mouth moved in a derisive, flickering smile. He could read the man's thoughts as if they were spelled out. Slobbering, incontinent bumpkin . . . couldn't wait to possess that repellently voluptuous body. "I think we should attempt the legitimate route first," he said solemnly, enjoying the clear disappointment in his companion's fallen face. "Lay a charge against her with the support of her guardians. If that doesn't work, then . . ." He shrugged. "We'll see."

George traced a dark, rusty stain in the table's planking

with a splayed fingertip. Red wine or blood, it could be either in this place. The realization entered his befuddled brain that if Juliana was in prison, guards could be bribed. He could have her to himself for as long as it would take. Either plan would give him the opportunity he craved.

He looked up and nodded. "I'll go back to Hampshire in the morning. Lay the matter before the Forsetts. Where will I find you, my lord?"

Lucien scowled, remembering anew that he was now condemned to lodge under his own besieged and uncomfortable roof. "My house is on Mount Street, but here's as good a place as any other. Leave a message with Gideon." He gestured with his head toward the man filling pitchers of ale at the bar counter before taking up his glass again, partially turning his shoulder to George in a gesture that the other man correctly interpreted as dismissal.

George pushed back his chair and stood up. He hesitated over words of farewell. It seemed too inconclusive simply to walk away, but there was no encouragement from the viscount. "I bid you good night, sir," he said finally, receiving not so much as a grunt of acknowledgment. He walked away, intending to return to his previous bench, but he was filled with a restless energy, a surge of elation at the thought that he was no longer alone in his quest. He went outside instead. A slatternly young woman approached him with a near toothless smile.

"Half a guinea, honorable sir?" She thrust her bosom at him, her black eyes snapping.

"Five shillings," he returned.

She shrugged, took his hand, and led him off to the bulks beneath the market holders' stalls. For five shillings, it wasn't worth taking him to her room on King Street, where she'd have to pay for candles and probably change the linen.

"The Bedford Head on Wednesday forenoon."
The word flew around the houses of Covent Garden,

dropping in the ears of languid women gathered in parlors in the morning's dishabille, idly comparing notes of their previous night's labors, sipping coffee, discussing fashions in the latest periodicals. The word was brought by women from Mistress Dennison's establishment. It was whispered to heads bent in an attentive circle and received with hushed curiosity. The words *sisterhood* and *solidarity* were spoken on tongues stumbling over the unfamiliar concepts. And the Russell Street women went on to the next house, leaving the seed to germinate, with Lucy's former plight as fertilizer.

Mistress Mitchell of the Bedford Head had listened to Lilly's explanation that a group of Covent Garden cyprians wished to have a small party to celebrate a birthday. She was asked to provide refreshments, and Lilly didn't bat an eyelid at Mistress Mitchell's exorbitant price for such simple fare as coffee, chocolate, and sweet biscuits. She tripped out of the Bedford Head with a cheerful smile, leaving Mistress Mitchell in frowning thought.

Why would the women wish to rent private space for a party when any one of them could have entertained the others under her own bawd's roof? There wasn't a High Impure in the Garden whose abbess would refuse permission for such an event.

Mistress Mitchell went on her own rounds, consulting her fellow abbesses. None could come up with an explanation. It was decided that Mistress Mitchell would position herself at the peephole to the back room on Wednesday forenoon. With the aid of a glass against the wall, she would be able to hear the women's conversation.

While she was sitting with Lucy, Juliana received a message from Lilly that the meeting was arranged for Wednesday forenoon. Lucy was sufficiently strong now to leave her bed and was ensconced on the chaise longue beneath the window. Juliana read the note, which contained a variety of messages for Lucy from Russell Street, and then handed it to her companion.

Lucy looked up from the letter. "What is this meeting, Juliana?"

Juliana explained. "It's time we did something," she finished with her usual vehemence. "These people make their living out of us, why should they get away with treating us as badly as they please?"

Lucy looked puzzled. "But not you, Juliana. You're not involved at all. Who's making their living out of you?"

"The duke paid Mistress Dennison three thousand guineas for me," Juliana responded succinctly. "I was bought and sold like a slave, simply because I had no protection, no money of my own, no friends, and nowhere to turn. If the Sisterhood had existed then, I would have had somewhere to go. A few guineas would have made all the difference. And think what it would have done for you."

Lucy leaned back, the letter lying open in her lap. "I don't think you understand the power of the whoremasters and bawds, Juliana."

"I understand it as well as I wish to," Juliana retorted. "And I know that it's that defeatist attitude, Lucy, that gives them the power that they have." She turned at a knock on the door, calling "Come in" before recollecting that it was Lucy's bedchamber not her own.

Tarquin entered the room. Lucy, who'd seen her host only the once when she'd been brought into the house, struggled to stand up.

"Don't disturb yourself," Tarquin said, coming over to the chaise longue. "I wished to find out how you were feeling."

"Oh, much better, Your Grace," Lucy stammered, flushing as she adjusted her wrapper. "I . . . I'm sure I'll be able to leave in the morning if—"

"There's no need for that." He bent to pick up the letter that had fluttered to the floor from Lucy's lap. "You're very welcome under my roof until Henny considers you fit to leave." He handed her back the letter, and Juliana couldn't tell whether he'd seen the contents or not. He hadn't seemed to glance at it, but one could never tell with Tarquin. His eyes were everywhere even when he seemed at his most unconcerned.

He took a pinch of snuff and glanced around the room. "I trust you're quite comfortable, ma'am."

Lucy's flush deepened at both the question and the courtesy title. "Oh, yes, indeed, Your Grace. I can't express my gratitude enough for your kindness. I'm sure I don't deserve such—"

"Of course you do!" Juliana interrupted fiercely. "You are as deserving of kindness and consideration as any other human being. Isn't that so, my lord duke?" Her eyes hurled the challenge at him.

"Oh, Juliana, you mustn't say such things," Lucy protested faintly. "Indeed, I don't wish to be a nuisance."

"You aren't being. Is she, sir?"

Tarquin shook his head with a wry quirk of amusement but refused to be drawn. He pushed himself off the windowsill and tipped her chin, lightly kissing her mouth. "When you've completed your visit with Lucy, come and see me in my book room."

Juliana, thrown off course by the kiss, glanced at Lucy, who was studiously rereading her letter. Lucy, of course, wouldn't think twice about a gentleman's playful dalliance with his mistress.

"I wish you a speedy recovery, ma'am." Tarquin bowed to the flustered Lucy and left them.

"Oh, he's so kind," breathed Lucy.

"It seems so," Juliana said, ruffled. "And yet I don't believe he ever does anything that doesn't suit him. I don't believe he would ever really put himself out for someone. He's kind only when it doesn't inconvenience him. But he would as easily leave someone bleeding by the roadside if his direction took him elsewhere or he didn't have the time to help."

Even as she spoke, she remembered how he'd come to her rescue when Lucien was tormenting her and how overpoweringly grateful she'd been to see him. Lucien was now banned from the house because he'd hurt her. Family quarrels were incredibly inconvenient, and yet the duke had sacrificed his peace to champion Juliana. Of course, he'd exposed her to the dangers of Lucien in the first place, so strictly speaking it was his responsibility to repair the damage.

Lucy was looking reproachful but understanding, and Juliana remembered that she had yet to explain Tarquin's generous offer to set the girl on her feet again. It was certainly kind of him but would hardly inconvenience him. He had so much wealth, he wouldn't notice such a sum. Quentin had said his brother was generous to a fault, but was it true generosity when one could give without the slightest sacrifice to oneself?

However, she was obliged to listen to Lucy's astonished gratitude, singing the duke's praises to the heavens when she heard of her good fortune.

Tarquin was seated at his desk, rewriting a speech his secretary had written for him to give to the House of Lords that evening. His secretary was a worthy soul, but somewhat dull, and the duke was convinced the speech would send its presenter to sleep halfway through it, let alone his audience. Not that his peers would pay much attention to the most exciting debate. They'd be snoring off a large and bibulous dinner, for the most part.

He looked up as Juliana came in on her knock. She curtsied demurely. "You wished to see me, my lord duke?"

He pushed back his chair and beckoned to her. When she came to him, he took her hands in his, turning them palm up. To her astonishment he raised them to his lips and kissed her palms. "How are your bruises, *mignonne?*"

"My shoulders are still sore, despite Henny's arnica," she responded, her voice strangely thick. His breath rustled warmly over her hands, which he now held clasped together against his mouth. He kissed each pointed knuckle in turn, his tongue darting snakelike between her bent fingers, each moist, swift, unexpected stroke lifting the fine hairs on her nape, her skin prickling with excitement.

"Have you forgiven me for not getting to Lucien in time?" The wicked little caresses continued, his lips now nuzzling the backs of her hands, his teeth playfully grazing the skin.

Juliana was losing her grip on reality. She barely heard his words. Her feet shifted on the Persian carpet, and she gazed down at the top of his bent head, distractedly noticing how his hair waved thickly back from his broad forehead. How could she say she hadn't forgiven him for anything when one loving touch could turn her body to molten lava?

He looked up, folding her hands securely in his. His eyes were smiling but his tone was grave. "There is so much to enjoy, *mignonne.* Can we take a pleasanter path from here on?"

Juliana could find no words. Her body said one thing, her mind another. How could she possibly forget that she was still captive to his plan? She was still to bear his child, to give it up to his sole control, to live a life of deceit, emotionally dependent on the duke's continuing favor. She looked down at him, her eyes bewildered but her tongue silent.

After a long minute Tarquin released her hands. There was regret in his eyes, but he said in an equally normal tone, "I think it's time for you to return Lady Melton's visit. One mustn't be backward in the courtesies."

"No," Juliana agreed, eagerly grasping this ordinary topic as a lifeline through the labyrinth of her confusion. "Should I go alone?"

"No, I'll take you up in my phaeton." He examined her appearance with a critical air. "I don't care for the breast knot on that gown. It spoils the line of the bodice."

Juliana looked down at the little posy of silk orchids sown to the low neck of her gown. "I thought them pretty."

"So they are, but not on you. They're too frilly . . . fussy." He waved a hand in an impatient gesture. "Your bosom needs no decoration."

"Oh," said Juliana.

"Change your gown now, and tell Henny to remove the flowers before you wear it again."

"As you command, my lord duke." Juliana swept him a low curtsy. "Do you have any other instructions regarding my costume, sir?"

"Not for the moment," he replied, ignoring her sardonic tone. "Except that I have yet to see you in the blue-sprigged muslin. It opens over a dark-blue petticoat, as I recall. There's a lace fichu that will be sufficiently modest for paying a visit to a house in mourning."

Juliana confined her response to another exaggeratedly submissive curtsy. Tarquin's eyes glowed with amusement. "You may have half an hour." He sat down at his desk again, picking up his quill in pointed dismissal.

Juliana stalked upstairs to change into the required gown. It was such a wonderful relief to be simply annoyed with him again. Her emotions were so much clearer when she was responding to his dictatorial manner than when he confused her with softness and the spellbinding invitation of his caresses.

He was awaiting her in the hall when she came down just within the half hour, carrying her gloves and fan. She paused on the bottom step, tilting her head to one side inquiringly as she invited his inspection.

Tarquin solemnly ran his eyes from the top of her head to the toe of her kid slippers. Then he described a circle with his forefinger. Juliana stepped to the hall and slowly turned around.

"Yes, much better," he pronounced. "Let us go. The phaeton is at the door."

He handed her up and took his seat beside her. "It won't be necessary to spend more than fifteen minutes with Lady Melton. If she's unavailable, you may leave your card."

"But I don't have a card."

"Yes, you do." He reached into his breast pocket and handed her a crisp white card on which, in an elegant hand, was inscribed, "Viscountess, Lady Edgecombe." "My secretary took the task upon himself. He has a good hand, I'm sure you'll agree."

"Better than mine," Juliana responded, turning the card between her fingers. It seemed to give her a sense of permanence, as if she could really begin to see herself as Lady Edgecombe. As if nothing could now dislodge her from this extraordinary peak.

At the Melton residence Tarquin handed the reins to his groom, who leaped from the back ledge to take them, and stepped to the street. Juliana gathered her skirts around her and prepared to alight, holding prudently on to the side of the carriage as she gingerly put her foot on the top step.

"I think it might be safer all round if I lift you down," Tarquin said, observing these wise precautions. Taking her around the waist, he swung her to the ground and remained holding her waist until he was certain she was firmly lodged on her two feet.

His hands at her waist were hard and warm, and he held her for a fraction longer than strictly necessary. Juliana felt the old confusion rushing back, but then he was ushering her up the steps through the door held by a bowing footman, and into the hall. He handed the footman his card and gestured to Juliana that she should do the same. The footman bowed them into the salon.

Once more in possession of her senses, Juliana looked around with interest. The furnishings were old-fashioned and heavy, for the most part draped in dark holland covers. The curtains were pulled halfway over the long windows, plunging the room into gloom.

"Lady Melton observes the most strict mourning," Tarquin answered her unspoken question. He took a pinch of snuff and leaned against the mantel, his eyes, suddenly inscrutable, resting on Juliana.

"Lucy received a letter from her friends this morning?"

Juliana jumped, guilt flying flags in her cheeks. Had he

read the note in its entirety? He couldn't have had time, surely. But if he had, he would know of the projected meeting on Wednesday forenoon. And he would know she was intending to be there. "Do you object?" She took refuge in challenge, hoping annoyance would explain her sudden flush.

"Not at all. Should I?" He continued to regard her in that unreadable fashion.

"I can't imagine why you would. But since you won't permit her friends to visit her in person, I wasn't sure whether a sullied piece of paper could be allowed through your door."

Tarquin's response died at birth with the return of the footman. Her Ladyship and Lady Lydia would be happy to receive them in the family's parlor.

The family parlor was not much less gloomy than the salon, despite its air of being lived in. The curtains and chair covers were dark and heavy, the pictures all carried a black border, and there were no flowers in the vases.

Lady Melton held out her hand to Juliana with a gracious nod and greeted the duke with a complacent smile. Lydia rose and gave Juliana her hand with a warm smile before offering her reverence to the duke with downcast eyes. He drew her to her feet with a pleasant word of greeting, raising her hand to his lips.

Quentin, who had been seated beside Lydia on the sofa, stood up to greet Juliana with a brotherly kiss on the cheek.

"Quentin, I was unaware you intended to call upon Lady Melton this morning," Tarquin said.

Juliana was immediately aware of a slight stiffening from Lady Lydia beside her, but Quentin said easily that he had been passing the door and thought he would discuss a sermon with Lady Melton, but he was about to take his leave. He bowed to Her Ladyship before kissing Lydia's hand. "I must remember to bring the book of gardens to show you, Lydia, next time I'm passing. The fourteenth-century herb garden is most interesting."

"Thank you, Lord Quentin. I look forward to it." She

left her hand in his for a moment, then very slowly withdrew it, her fingers lightly brushing his as she did so.

Juliana glanced at Tarquin. He appeared to notice nothing, devoting his attention to his hostess. Juliana quirked an eyebrow at this, remembering her old nursemaid's frequent mutter that there's none so blind as those who won't see. But, of course, it wouldn't occur to the Duke of Redmayne that something as frivolous and inconvenient as misplaced love could upset his plans.

"Do sit by me, Juliana," Lydia invited with her soft smile, patting the sofa beside her before picking up her embroidery frame. Juliana took the seat and settled down to observe, maintaining an easy conversation with Lydia with half her mind. The duke remained beside Lady Melton, deep in some discussion. He'd barely exchanged two words with his betrothed, beyond the courtesies, and Lydia showed no sign of feeling neglected. Presumably a marriage of convenience didn't require close attention between the partners.

The arrival of two other somewhat formidable ladies prevented Juliana's making any further observations of the betrothed couple. She was introduced, questioned as to her husband's whereabouts.

"You reside under His Grace's roof at present, I understand," declared the dowager Duchess of Mowbray.

"My husband's house is in need of repair," Juliana replied. "His Grace has kindly offered his hospitality until it's ready to receive us."

"I see. So Edgecombe's residing at Albermarle Street also, Redmayne?"

"My cousin is occupied with the renovations to his house," Tarquin said smoothly. "He finds it more convenient to live there while he supervises the work."

Juliana swallowed a laugh at this astonishing fabrication. Surely no one who knew Lucien would believe it. She glanced covertly around the room, gauging their reactions.

"What's that you say?" demanded the dowager's companion, Lady Briscow, leaning forward and cupping her ear.

The dowager took a speaking trumpet from the lady's hand and bellowed, "Redmayne says Edgecombe is livin' in his own house. The gal's sheltered under Redmayne's roof."

Lady Briscow seemed to take a minute to absorb this, while the boomed words echoed around the room. "Ah," she pronounced finally. "Well, I daresay that's for the best." She turned to examine Juliana. "Very young, isn't she?"

"I am past seventeen, ma'am." Juliana decided it was time to speak up for herself.

"Too young for Edgecombe," declared the lady loudly. "Besides, I thought he didn't care for women."

"Now, Cornelia, that's not a fit subject in front of the young ladies," the duchess protested.

"What's that you say? Thought the man only liked little boys."

"Cornelia!" pleaded the duchess through the ear trumpet. "That's not for the ears of the young ladies."

"Pshaw!" declared Lady Briscow. "Innocence isn't going to do the gal much good with that husband of hers."

"We must take our leave, Lady Melton." Tarquin rose to his feet, his expression as bland as if he'd heard nothing of the preceding exchange. Juliana jumped up hastily, too hastily, and a dish of tea resting on the chair arm crashed to the floor. Dregs of tea splattered on the carpet, and the delicate cup rolled against a chair leg and shattered.

She bent to pick up the pieces with a mortified exclamation. Lydia dropped to her knees beside her. "Oh, pray don't worry, Lady Edgecombe." She gathered up the shards swiftly, her cheeks on fire. The conversation had amused Juliana, but Lydia was deeply shocked. But, then, she was probably as innocent as Juliana had been on her wedding night with John Ridge. Juliana could no longer imagine such naïveté, and yet it was only a few short weeks since she'd been a country virgin with no prospect of ever venturing farther afield than Winchester or Portsmouth.

She stood up, apologizing profusely for her clumsiness, though her diversion had relieved everyone but Lady Briscow, who clearly needed no relief.

Lady Melton said hastily, "It was so easy to do, Lady Edgecombe. Such a stupid place to put the dish. I can't think why the footman would have placed it there."

Juliana attempted to excuse the footman and blame herself, but Tarquin said coolly, "Come, my dear Lady Edgecombe. No harm's done, and you're making a great matter out of a very little one." He swept her with him out of the parlor.

"I wish I weren't so damnably clumsy," Juliana lamented, once more ensconced in the phaeton. "It's so embarrassing."

"Well, on this occasion your clumsiness did everyone a good turn," the duke said wryly. "Cornelia Briscow has the crudest tongue in town."

"But is my husband's . . . uh . . . predilection . . . generally known, then?"

"Of course. He's caused enough scandal in his time to ruin a dozen families. But it's not generally the subject for polite conversation."

"Nor a subject to be mentioned before his bride gets to the altar," she said tartly.

Tarquin glanced sideways at her. "I couldn't imagine what possible good it would do you to know."

He sounded so infuriatingly certain of himself. Did he never question his actions, or their consequences? But he had shown remorse for the whole debacle with Lucien, she reminded herself, so there was nothing to be gained by continuing to pluck that crow.

"Lord Quentin seems to find Lady Lydia's company agreeable," she observed casually after a minute.

"So do most people," the duke said, sounding a trifle surprised at this conversational turn.

"Yes, of course," Juliana agreed. "She's a most charming lady. Very kind, I believe."

"She's certainly that."

"Very pretty, too. I think men find pale fairness most appealing."

"Now, what would you know about it?" Tarquin looked at her again with an amused smile.

"Well, I can't see how they wouldn't. Lord Quentin certainly seems to find Lady Lydia very attractive."

"She's a very old friend," he said with a slight frown. "Quentin has known Lydia from early childhood."

"I wonder when he'll get married," Juliana mused. "Canons do get married, don't they?"

"Certainly. Bishops too." He turned his horses into the mews behind his house. "Quentin will find himself the perfect bishop's wife, one who will grace the bishop's palace and set a fine example to the wives of his clergy, and they'll have a quiverful of children."

He tossed the reins to a groom and jumped to the cobbles. "Come."

Juliana took his proffered hand and jumped down beside him, her hoop swinging around her. She stood frowning at a rain barrel, where a water beetle was scudding across the murky surface.

"Hey, penny for your thoughts?" Tarquin tilted her chin.

She shook her head dismissively. She wasn't about to tell him that she was trying to think of a way to sow a little seed in his stubborn brain. "I was thinking perhaps Lucy might like an airing in the barouche."

"By all means," he said. "But you will take Ted as escort."

Juliana grimaced but made no demur. She dropped him a tiny curtsy and went into the house through the back door.

Tarquin gazed after her. She hadn't been thinking about Lucy at all. Something much more complicated had been going on behind those great green eyes.

He found himself wishing that he could know her thoughts, wishing that he could slide behind her eyes into the private world of Juliana herself. She gave so much of herself, but there was always a little that was kept back. He would like to know her as well as she knew herself . . . maybe even better than she knew herself. And with that urge came another: That she should know and understand him as no one else had ever done.

He shook his head as if to dispel these extraordinary fancies. Romantic nonsense that had no place in his scheme of things. He'd never been troubled by such sentimental notions before. Maybe he had a touch of fever. He passed a hand across his brow, but it felt quite cool. With another irritated head shake he followed Juliana into the house.

Chapter 21

"Here's that horrible man again." Lady Forsett turned from the drawing-room window, her aquiline nose twitching with disdain.

"What horrible man, my dear?" Sir Brian looked up from his newspaper.

"John Ridge's son. Such an uncouth oaf. What can he possibly want now?"

"I would imagine it has something to do with Juliana," her husband observed calmly. Amelia had conveniently forgotten all about their erstwhile ward. He couldn't remember hearing her refer to the girl once since her disappearance.

Lady Amelia's nose twitched again, as if it had located a particularly unpleasant odor. "The child has never been anything but trouble," she declared. "It would be just like her to plague us with that vulgar man."

"I doubt Juliana would be encouraging George Ridge to pester us," Sir Brian pointed out mildly. "Knowing Juliana, I would imagine she would be wishing her stepson to the devil."

"Really, Sir Brian, must you use such language in my company?" Lady Forsett opened and closed her fan with reproving clicks.

"I do beg your pardon, my dear. . . . Ah, Dawkins, show the gentleman in." The footman, who'd arrived to announce the visitor, looked surprised at having his errand anticipated.

"Not in my drawing room," Amelia protested. "He's bound to have manure on his boots. Show him into the morning room."

The footman bowed and removed himself. "I daresay you don't wish to meet Ridge," Sir Brian said, rising reluctantly from his chair. "I'll see him alone."

"Indeed, sir, but I wish to hear what he's come about," his wife declared firmly. "If he has news of Juliana, then I want to hear it." She sailed to the door in a starched rustle of taffeta. "You don't suppose he could have found her, do you, sir?" Her pale eyes reflected only dismay at the prospect.

"I trust not, my dear. The man couldn't find an oak tree if it stood in his path. I daresay he's come to demand Juliana's jointure or some such bluster." Sir Brian followed his lady to the morning room.

George was standing ill at ease in the middle of the small room. He was very conscious of his London finery and tugged at his scarlet-and-green-striped waistcoat as the door opened to admit his hosts. He bowed with what he hoped was a London flourish, determined that these supercilious folk would acknowledge the town bronze he'd acquired in the last week.

"Sir George." Sir Brian sketched a bow in return. Lady Forsett merely inclined her head, disdaining to offer a curtsy. George visibly bristled. She was looking at him as if he'd come to call reeking of the farmyard with straw in his hair.

"Sir Brian . . . madam," he began portentously, "I am come with news that in happier circumstances would bring you comfort, but, alas, in prevailing circumstances I fear it can only bring you the utmost distress." He waited for a response, and waited in vain. His hosts merely regarded him with an air of scant interest. He licked his dry lips and involuntarily loosened his stiffly starched cravat. He was parched, and no mention had been made of refreshment . . . not even a glass of wine.

"Juliana," he tried again. "It concerns Juliana."

"I rather assumed so," Sir Brian said politely. "You seem a little warm, Sir George. I daresay you had a hot ride."

"Devilish hot . . . oh, beggin' your pardon, ma'am." He flushed and fumbled for his handkerchief to wipe his brow.

"Maybe you'd like a glass of lemonade," Amelia said distantly, reaching for the bell rope.

George cast Sir Brian an anguished look, and his host took pity on him. "I daresay the man would prefer a tankard of ale on such a hot afternoon." He gave order to the footman who had appeared in answer to the summons, then turned back to George. "Am I to assume you've found Juliana, Sir George?"

"Oh, yes, yes, indeed, sir." George stepped forward eagerly. Sir Brian stepped back. "But I found her in the most distressing circumstances."

"She is in want?" Lady Forsett asked coldly.

"No . . . no, I don't believe so, ma'am. But the truth is . . . well the truth is . . . not something for the lady's ears, sir." He turned with a significant nod to Sir Brian.

"I can assure you my ears aren't so nice," Amelia said. "Do, I pray you, get to the point."

George took a deep breath and rushed headlong into his tale. His audience gave him all their attention, interrupting him only to press upon him a foaming tankard of ale. Lady Forsett took a seat on a delicate gilt chair and remained motionless, her hands clasped on her fan in her lap. Sir Brian tapped his mouth with a forefinger but other than that showed no emotion.

When George had reached the conclusion of his narrative and was thirstily drinking his ale, Sir Brian said, "Let me just clarify this, Sir George. You're saying that Juliana is now Viscountess Edgecombe, lodged under the roof of the Duke of Redmayne?"

"Yes, sir." George nodded vigorously, wiping a mustache of foam from his upper lip with the back of his hand.

"Legally married?"

"Apparently so."

"Then surely she's to be congratulated."

George looked confused. "She's turned whore, sir. I thought I explained that."

"But she's respectably wed to a member of the peerage?" Sir Brian offered a puzzled frown. "I fail to see how the two states can coexist."

George began to feel the ground slipping from beneath his feet. "She denies who she is," he said. "She ignores me . . . looks straight through me."

"I would never have credited her with so much sense," Amelia murmured.

"Madam, she murdered her husband . . . my father." George slammed his empty tankard onto a table.

"Not so hot, sir . . . not so hot," Sir Brian advised. "There's no need for a show of temper."

"But I will have her brought to justice, I tell you."

"By all means, you must do what seems best to you," Sir Brian said calmly. "I wouldn't stand in your way, my dear sir."

George looked nonplussed. "But if she refuses to acknowledge her identity, and she has the duke's protection, then it will be difficult for me to challenge her masquerade, and I must do that if I'm to lay charges against her. I need you to verify my identification," he explained earnestly, as if his audience might have failed to grasp the obvious point.

Sir Brian's eyebrows disappeared into his scalp. "My good sir, you cannot be suggesting I journey to London. I detest the place."

"But how else are you to see her?" George stumbled.

"I have no intention of seeing her. If, indeed, she is so established, I would be doing her a grave disservice."

"You won't have her brought to justice?" George's eyes popped.

"I find it difficult to believe that Juliana was responsible for your father's death," Sir Brian said consideringly. "It was, of course, a most unfortunate occurrence, but I can't believe Juliana should be punished for it."

"I will see her burned at the stake, sir." George strode to the door. "With or without your assistance."

"That is, of course, your prerogative," Sir Brian said.

George turned at the door, his face crimson with rage and frustration. "And I will have my inheritance back, Sir Brian. Don't think I don't know why it suits you to let her go unchallenged."

Sir Brian raised an eyebrow. "My dear sir, I do protest. You'll be accusing me of ensuring her disappearance next."

George went out, the door crashing shut behind him.

"Dear me, what a dreadful fellow," Sir Brian declared in a bored tone.

Lady Forsett's fan snapped beneath her fingers. "If he has found Juliana and it is as he says, then we cannot acknowledge her. Apart from the scandal over Sir John's death, her present situation is disgraceful. She may be married, but it's certain she took the whore's way to the viscount's bed, and you may be sure there's something most irregular about the connection."

"I doubt Juliana wishes to be acknowledged by us," her husband observed with an arid smile. "I suggest we wish her the best of luck and wash our hands of the whole business."

"But what if that oaf manages to bring her before the magistrates on such a charge?"

"Why, then, my dear, we simply repudiate her. She's been out of our hands since her wedding day. We have no obligation either to help her or to hinder her, as I see it."

"But if she is discovered, then either way you will lose control of her jointure."

Sir Brian shrugged. "So be it. But you may be sure that while I have it, I am making the most of it, my dear. The trust is turning a handsome profit at present. And, besides," he added with another humorless smile, "she may well be carrying a child. In which case her jointure will remain in my hands if she's found guilty of her husband's death. Her first husband's death," he amended. "She really has been remarkably busy. I must commend her industry. But, then, she always did have a surplus of energy."

Amelia dismissed this pleasantry with an irritated wave. "The jointure will remain in your control only if the child can be proved to be Sir John's."

"How would they prove otherwise?"

"It would be a matter of dates," Amelia pointed out. "The child must be born within nine months of Sir John's death."

"Quite so," her husband agreed tranquilly. "Let us see what happens, shall we? If she is found and brought to justice, then we will simply wash our hands of her very publicly. But I trust that won't happen. I really don't wish Juliana injury, do you, my dear?"

Amelia considered this with a frown. "No," she pronounced finally. "I don't believe I do. She was always a dreadful nuisance, but so long as she doesn't cause us any further inconvenience, she may marry a duke if she pleases, or go to the devil with my blessing."

Her husband nodded. "Benign neglect is in everyone's best interests, ma'am. Except, of course, Sir George's."

"Juliana will be a match for that fool," pronounced Lady Forsett.

"And if she's not, then we shall rethink our position." Sir Brian strolled to the door. "I'll be in my book room until dinner."

His wife curtsied and rang the bell rope to tell the servants to air the morning room. The man's pomade had been overpowering, almost worse than the stale sweat it was designed to mask.

Mistress Mitchell crouched closer to the wall, the upturned tumbler pressed to her ear. She could hardly believe what she was hearing. The ungrateful hussies were complaining of their usage, of the terms of their employment, were exchanging stories of mistreatment, and now were proposing to set up against their protectors. They were talking of buying their own supplies of candles, wine, coal. Of having a joint fund to support them in need so they wouldn't have to go into debt to their abbesses or whoremasters. It was unheard of. It was rebellion. And it was all coming from that sweet-tongued serpent that Elizabeth Dennison had placed with the Duke of Redmayne. She'd clearly got above herself since her removal to His Grace's establishment. Didn't she know she owed Mistress Dennison gratitude on her knees? But if she thought she could lead the others astray, then Miss Juliana, or whatever she called herself, was in for a nasty surprise. Indeed, they all were.

Mistress Mitchell forced herself to continue listening, resisting the urge to run immediately to her fellow bawds with the news of this traitorous meeting. She was glad of her restraint when she heard them plan to meet again. There was some discussion as to time and venue, its being agreed that they shouldn't use the same place twice, in case they aroused suspicion. Mistress Mitchell snorted derisively at this. Whatever precautions they took, how could they possibly expect to carry off such a heinous scheme of treachery under the very noses of those who managed them?

She pressed closer to the wall as the murmur of voices grew more indistinct. Then she heard Mother Cocksedge mentioned. She smiled grimly. A most unpleasant surprise could be arranged if they met in Cocksedge's house.

From the scrape of chair on floor, the rustle of skirts, the increased volume of their voices, it sounded as if they were preparing to break up the party, so she took her considerable bulk down the back stairs with creditable speed and was hovering in the taproom as they came tripping down in a chattering group.

"Had a good party, dearies?"

"Yes, thank you, Mistress Mitchell." Deborah dropped a polite curtsy.

"And whose birthday was it?"

There was an infinitesimal silence; then Lilly said firmly, "Mine, ma'am. And I have to thank you kindly for your hospitality."

"Not at all, dearie, not all." The woman smiled and nodded, busily polishing a brass candlestick on her apron. "Anytime, my dears."

Juliana was the last down the stairs. She stood for a moment, listening to this exchange, wondering what it was about the woman that made her uneasy. There was something false about her kindly jollity, something artificial in her smile. Then she realized that the smile came nowhere near the woman's sharp black eyes—that those eyes were shifting and darting around the room, looking everywhere but directly at the group of women.

"Come, Juliana. Will you walk with us to Russell Street?" Lilly turned to her, and Juliana shook herself free of unease. It had been a most heartening meeting. Her proposals had been greeted with more enthusiasm than doubt, although there were some skeptics in the group— those who couldn't believe a whore could exist without the protecting and exploiting arm of a master.

She went outside with the others, nodding farewell to Mistress Mitchell, whose smile revealed blackened stumps in a flaccid mouth. The bawd was of a different order from Mistress Dennison, Juliana reflected. The social hierarchy in this underworld was as rigidly defined as it was in her own world.

She walked arm in arm with Lilly toward Russell Street, glancing over her shoulder, half expecting to see the imperturbable Ted on her heels. She'd managed to evade him with the simple expedient of leaving the house by the back stairs and telling no one. She would face the inevitable fireworks on her return. She didn't have to admit where she'd been. The duke had not mentioned Lucy's letter again, so she assumed he hadn't read the relevant paragraph.

She turned back to Lilly, who was excitedly describing her surprise at how enthusiastic everyone had been at the meeting. Suddenly Juliana jerked her head sideways again. Immediately she cursed herself for the reflex action. George was standing on the corner of Russell Street, gazing at her. He'd seen her turn. He would have seen the startled flash of recognition in her eyes, however rapidly it was suppressed.

She couldn't risk taking a chair now on her own. It would be all too easy for George to follow, to force himself upon her. Now she would have given anything for the sight of the imperturbable Ted. She was aware of George following them down the street. He was making no attempt to hide his pursuit; indeed, his step was almost jaunty. It was almost as if he was mocking her, challenging her to evade him.

When they reached the house, she accompanied the others inside, managing not to look behind her, although the skin on her back prickled. "Is there a back way out of the house?"

"Why?" Lilly looked at her in puzzlement.

Juliana frowned, wondering whether she could take them into her confidence. She settled for half the story. "There's a man following me. I don't wish to speak with him."

"Juliana, who is he?" They all pressed closer, eyes shining with curiosity.

"A man from the past," Juliana said mysteriously. "An odious creature who's been pestering me for days."

"Like that dreadful Captain Waters," Rosamund said. "He followed Lilly around for months. Even after Mr. Garston had warned him off."

"Lud, he was a vile nuisance." Lilly fanned herself vigorously as if she would waft away the memory. "He never paid his bill or brought presents, or even left me a little something for myself. It's no wonder Mr. Dennison barred him from the house."

"But he still came around making sheep's eyes at you." Emma chuckled. "Offered to wed you, didn't he?"

"La! I'd not throw myself away on a wet-handed pauper," Lilly declared with disgust. "I know my worth, let me tell you."

All interest in Juliana's pursuer had been forgotten in this reminiscence, and when she asked again for a way out of the back, Rosamund without further question directed her to a door through the kitchens that opened onto a narrow alley piled with kitchen refuse.

George couldn't believe his luck. Juliana was in the whorehouse again. This time she hadn't been conveyed in the duke's chair and there were no stalwart ducal employees to protect her. There was no sign, either, of the ugly-looking customer who had been accompanying her hitherto. The field was clear. He'd tried the legitimate path with his appeal to the Forsetts. Now he would do what he really wanted to do. He would take her off the street. And he would keep her until he'd had enough of her. Then he would give her up to the magistrates. He didn't need the help of that drunkard Edgecombe. This he could do alone.

But she'd seen him. He'd seen the flash of recognition in her eyes. She wouldn't walk into his arms. Pleased with his cunning, George retraced his steps, looking for the back of the house. Juliana was an artful bitch. She would attempt to give him the slip, and there was only one way she could do that.

Juliana stepped into the narrow alley and looked around, conscious of the door to safety at her back. A mangy dog sniffed at the refuse in the kennel, but there was no other movement in the alley. She slipped into the open and hastened toward Charles Street, a square of light at the end of the gloomy, noisome cobbled corridor. She emerged into the busy street and looked around for a chair or a passing hackney.

Then it happened. One minute she was standing in the sunshine, the next enveloped in a dense, suffocating blackness. She had heard nothing, seen nothing. Now her limbs were caught up in thick folds of material. A hand was pressed hard against her face stifling her cries. She was lifted, twisted, bundled, thrust through a narrow aperture, banging her covered head on the edge of something. Arms like iron bands clutched her, holding her still and steady. A whip cracked, and she realized she was in a coach of some kind. The vehicle lurched forward and the arms around her tightened. She struggled and kicked, but the hand pressed the wadded material against her mouth and nose until black spots danced in front of her eyes and her lungs screamed for air. She fell still and immediately the suffocating pressure was eased. She was accustomed to thinking of herself as big-boned and ungainly, strong enough to break most holds, but she couldn't fight against suffocation.

She forced herself to keep still. The blanket swaddling her smelled strongly of horse. As her mind cleared, she realized that she was in George's hands. Her captor was a big man, like George, and she could feel his flabbiness, feel the excess flesh rolling over his frame as he held her against him. A shudder of revulsion ripped through her. What was he going to do with her? But she knew the answer to that perfectly well. In her mind's eye she saw George in his cups, his little eyes lusting, his loose lips wet and hungry. She could almost feel his great hands on her body, pulling the clothes from her, falling onto her as she lay pinned beneath him, his fetid breath suffocating. . . .

Panic flooded her and she began to struggle again, her legs flailing desperately against the confining folds of her skirts and the enfolding blanket. Again the wadded material pressed against her nose. Again she fought for breath . . . and then suddenly the vehicle lurched to a halt. There were confused shouts, bumps. A violent thud that set the coach rocking as if someone had jumped into the vehicle. The pressure was abruptly lifted. Her lungs gulped at the hot, stale air trapped in the musty folds of the blanket.

George was bellowing, still clutching at her but not as securely as before. She renewed her struggles to free herself from the blanket. She had no idea what was going on around her, but whatever it was, it gave her a slim chance to escape.

George's arms suddenly went slack, and she tumbled off his knee and onto the floor of the carriage. She rolled over onto her hands and knees and heaved herself upright, throwing off the blanket, emerging pink, breathless, and sweaty . . . to find George slumped unconscious against the squabs of the hackney and Ted, his hand still in a fist, regarding her with undisguised irritation.

"I've better things to do than chasin' all over town looking for you," he stated before throwing open the door and calling up to the box. "Hey . . . jarvey. 'Elp me get rid of this bloke."

The jarvey appeared in the open door. He gazed dispassionately at the unconscious George. "Who'll be payin' me fare, then?"

Ted didn't answer. He grabbed George by the shoulders and hauled him off the bench. " 'Ere, take his legs."

The jarvey obliged. A small crowd had gathered around them, but no one seemed concerned as the two men swung George out of the carriage and propped him up against the wall of a tavern.

"Right," Ted said, brushing off his hands. "Albermarle Street, now, jarvey."

"So ye'll be payin' the bloke's fare as well as your'n?" the jarvey asked suspiciously.

"Ye'll be paid," Ted said impatiently, swinging himself into the vehicle with surprising agility for such a big man. It occurred to Juliana that the thump she'd heard must have been Ted's surprise entrance into the hackney.

"Right y'are." The driver, whistling cheerfully, mounted his box. "Go anywhere, do anything, that's Joe Hogg fer ye. Jest as long as I gets me fare. All in a day's work to me."

Juliana kicked the smelly horse blanket under the seat. Presumably the obliging jarvey had lent it to George. After what she'd seen in the streets of London since her arrival in the city, she was not surprised that George had been able to abduct her without interference.

Ted slumped in a corner, regarding her in morose silence.

"How did you know where to look for me?" Juliana asked tentatively.

" 'Is Grace 'ad an inklin'."

So he had read the letter. But why hadn't he said anything . . . done anything to prevent her giving Ted the slip? But perhaps she hadn't given Ted the slip. "Have you been following me all morning?"

Ted grunted an affirmative.

"So I was never really in any danger from George," Juliana mused, relief giving way to anger. Ted had deliberately let her walk into George's ambush.

Ted made no response. The carriage drew up at Albermarle Street, and Juliana jumped to the ground after Ted. Leaving him haggling with the jarvey, she stalked up the steps and into the house.

"Where's His Grace, Catlett?"

"Here." The duke spoke from the library door before Catlett could answer. His gray eyes were cold as a winter sky, his mouth tight. "Let us go to your bedchamber, Lady Edgecombe." He gestured that she should precede him up the stairs.

Juliana hesitated, then acquiesced, reasoning that she couldn't give full rein to her own outrage in front of the butler. The duke might consider he had a grievance, but she had one as well.

She marched up the stairs and threw open the door of her bedchamber, swinging round to face him as he entered behind her. He slammed the door and, before she could open her mouth, took her by the shoulders and shook her. "Just look at you, Juliana. You look as if you've been dragged through a hedge backward. You're a disgraceful sight." He propelled her toward the cheval glass. "Take a look at yourself! Anyone would think you'd been rolling in a ditch with a farmhand!"

Juliana was so taken aback by this seemingly irrelevant attack that she couldn't speak for a minute. She stared at her image in the glass. Her hair was tumbling loose around her shoulders, bits of fluff and what looked like straw clinging to the curls. Her gown was covered in dust and woolen fibers and what were clearly horse hairs. Her face was smudged with dirt.

She found her voice. "What do you expect me to look like after I've been manhandled by that oaf, rolled in a stinking horse blanket, and half suffocated? And whose fault is it, I should like to know? *You* let me walk into his trap." Her voice shook with renewed anger. "You're an unmitigated whoreson!" She rubbed the side of her hand over her mouth, trying to rid her tongue and lips of still-clinging threads of blanket hair.

"So George is responsible for your state! Dear God, you are an incorrigible chit!" Tarquin exclaimed. "He does what he's been threatening to do for weeks because you almost invite him to, and then you dare blame me for your reckless stupidity."

"Yes, I do," she cried. "Ted was following me all morning. You read Lucy's letter and you knew where I was going, and you told Ted to let George abduct me."

"Oh, now wait a minute!" His hands closed hard over her shoulders again. "Hold your tongue and listen to me. You deliberately exposed yourself to a danger that you knew was out there. You deliberately chose to evade the protection I had provided for you. You did the same with Lucien, and though I'm willing to accept some share of the blame there, I will not shoulder any responsibility for this morning! Do you hear me?" He shook her in vigorous emphasis.

"Maybe I did underestimate George, but you aided and abetted him," Juliana stated, aware, to her fury, that tears were starting in her eyes. "You're a treacherous cur!" She sniffed and dashed a hand across her eyes. "Of all the heartless, vile, despicable things to do. You let me walk into George's trap. You let me be frightened and manhandled. You let me think I was in danger when I wasn't."

"I don't know what you're talking about," he said impatiently. "I had no idea George was on the scene this morning. I knew only that you were planning some expedition with Dennison's girls. I didn't tell you I knew because I rather hoped that your better judgment would prevail. When it didn't, I sent Ted after you. I never tell Ted how to do his job. His instructions were to see that no harm came to you and to bring you back, when I intended to make my feelings known to you in no uncertain terms. How he accomplished his task was his business."

Juliana swallowed, her anger doused as effectively as a fire with a bucket of water. "You didn't tell him to let me be kidnapped?"

"No, of course I didn't. But he obviously thought you needed a lesson. Ted doesn't take kindly to people attempting to get the better of him."

"Oh." Rather forlornly, Juliana wiped her nose with the back of her hand.

Tarquin released his grip on her shoulders, pulled a handkerchief out of his pocket, and briskly wiped her nose and her eyes. "Weeping won't improve your appearance."

"I'm only crying because I'm angry," she said. "Or at least I was. But I still don't see how you can say my actions have nothing to do with you. If you hadn't forbidden me to see my friends, then I wouldn't have had to try to go alone. You have the right to forbid them under your roof, but you don't have the right to prevent me from visiting them under theirs."

"We have a contract," he stated flatly. "And one of its clauses is that you behave in a manner befitting Viscountess Edgecombe. Consorting with whores is not appropriate behavior. Wandering the streets looking like a haystack is not appropriate behavior. Therefore, you will not do it."

Juliana turned away from her image in the glass. It lent too much weight to the duke's argument. She would not back down on her right to choose her friends. But nothing would be served by saying so at this point. "You speak of a contract, my lord duke. Can it be a true contract when one side was blackmailed into signing it?"

"You signed it in exchange for my protection, for the security and comfort of my home, for the assurance that you would never be in want. That's a strange kind of blackmail to my mind." His voice was icy.

"And if I hadn't signed it, you would have betrayed me," she threw at him bitterly.

"Did I ever say that?"

Her mouth opened in astonishment. "No, but . . . but you implied it."

He shrugged. "How you choose to interpret my words is not my responsibility."

"How could you say that?" She stared at him in disbelief. "Of all the treacherous, slippery *snakes!* Oh, go away and leave me alone!" She turned away again with an angry gesture, trying to control her tears.

Tarquin regarded her averted back in frowning silence, running his fingertips reflectively over his lips. He would never have betrayed her to the law, but there was no way Juliana could have known that. He *had,* however, rescued her from a miserable life on the streets and probably a premature, wretched death. The fact that he'd done so for his own ends didn't change that truth. Why wouldn't she just accept the situation? He couldn't understand what she had to object to in her present life. She enjoyed the passion they shared. She was safe from Lucien. She was provided for for the rest of her life. So why did she take such pleasure in defying him? She was the most perverse creature he'd ever had dealings with. If he'd known she would cause him so much trouble when he'd watched her through Mistress Dennison's peephole, he would have looked elsewhere for the tool to control Lucien.

"Go away!" Juliana repeated crossly. "You've made your point. There's no need to gloat."

Gloat! He almost laughed aloud. If anyone should be gloating, it was Juliana. Turning on his heel, he left her to her angry tears.

Chapter 22

I daresay you've known Lady Lydia all your life," Juliana remarked to Lord Quentin several mornings later, when he returned to her parlor after escorting her visitors to their carriages.

"What makes you say that?" He walked to the window overlooking the garden and stood looking out so she could see nothing of his face.

"Oh, just that you seem very easy together. Like very old friends." She refilled their coffee cups with an air of nonchalance.

In the last few days Lady Lydia had been a frequent visitor to Lady Edgecombe. Somehow her visits coincided with Lord Quentin's seemingly casual presence in Juliana's parlor. Lady Lydia never came alone; she always had some friend or acquaintance of her mother's in tow, a lady anxious to pay a courtesy visit to the new bride. But it was clear to Juliana, at least, that these chaperons were merely a blind. Behind their presence, Lady Lydia and Lord Quentin could talk and smile, brush hands in a fleeting gesture, sit side by side on a sofa, their heads bent together over a book of illustrations.

"We are old friends." Quentin turned from the window

to take his refilled cup, that same bleak look haunting his eyes.

"But you feel more for each other than friendship." Juliana found herself taking the bull by the horns without conscious thought. Her impulses were always getting the better of her, but maybe in this case it might prove helpful.

Quentin said nothing for a minute. He drank his coffee, then said, "Is it that obvious?"

"To me."

"I am trying so hard to control it, Juliana." Quentin's voice was low and anguished, reflecting the misery in his eyes. "But I can't bear the idea of her marrying Tarquin. Of her marrying anyone but me." He began to pace the room from window to door, the words bubbling forth as if Juliana had unplugged a well. "I should go back to Melchester at once. Put myself beyond temptation. But I can't do it."

"Have you finished your business with the archbishop?"

Quentin shook his head. "If only I had, I wouldn't have an excuse to stay . . . to betray Tarquin every minute I'm in Lydia's company."

"You're too harsh with yourself," Juliana said practically. "You're not betraying the duke by sitting with Lydia—"

"I lust after her!" he interrupted in anguish. "God help me, Juliana, but I lust after another man's wife."

"She's not his wife yet," Juliana pointed out.

"Don't split hairs." He sat down, dropping his head in his hands. "It's mortal sin. I know it and yet I can't stop myself."

"But she feels the same way about you."

Quentin raised his head. His face was haggard. "She has said so. God forgive me, but I asked her. I forced her to acknowledge her own sin." He dropped his head in his hands again with a soft groan.

Juliana tucked an errant ringlet behind her ear. All this talk of sin, she supposed, was only to be expected from a man of the cloth, but since it was impossible to believe that Quentin had carried his devotion to Lydia as far as consummation, he did seem to be going overboard with the self-flagellation.

"Why don't you ask the duke to release her?" It seemed a simple enough solution.

Quentin gave a short, bitter laugh. "Sometimes I forget how unworldly you are. Lydia's family would never countenance a match with me. Not when their daughter is destined to be a duchess. Our world doesn't work that way, my dear."

Juliana refused to be satisfied with this. "But Lydia surely is not so mercenary?"

"Lydia! Sweet heaven, no! Lydia is an angel!"

"Yes, of course she is. But if she doesn't care about becoming a duchess, surely she can persuade her parents that she loves someone else."

Quentin shook his head, almost amused by this naive pragmaticism. "Lord and Lady Melton would never give up such an advantageous match for their daughter."

"But supposing the duke offered to release Lydia?" she suggested. "Perhaps he would do it for your sake. If he understood how you feel—and how Lydia feels."

"My dear girl, it would be the same as jilting her. Tarquin would never do that to her . . . or her family. Besides," he added with a rueful sigh, "I could never ask Tarquin to make such a sacrifice. He wants this match. He's done so much for me over the years, I couldn't bring myself to ruin his life."

"Oh, pshaw!" Juliana exclaimed in disgust. "You wouldn't be ruining his life. He'd soon get over it. It isn't as if he's in love with her. And as far as jilting Lydia is concerned, a private rearrangement is no concern of anyone's. It'll be a nine days' wonder at worst."

Quentin wondered if she was right, and for a moment hope flickered. Then it died as swiftly as it had arisen.

"Lydia has been educated to be Tarquin's wife. She will bring him Melton land to augment his own. She knows her duty and she knows what to expect. She will be a good wife and mother to his children, and she'll expect no more than courtesy and consideration in return. She won't think about other women in his life, because she knows that all women of her social status do not marry for love. She knows that she must expect her husband to seek his pleasure outside the marriage bed." The bitterness was back in his voice now. "Tarquin has no truck with sentimentality, Juliana. And love comes into that category."

"I suppose so." Her fingers plucked restlessly at an overblown rose in a bowl beside her chair. The petals showered down. She and Tarquin had had no private talk since their last confrontation. He had been polite and distant, but he hadn't come to her bed. She wondered if he was waiting for an invitation. She had told him to leave her alone, after all.

"Don't you think he could change, Quentin?" She pinched a rose petal between her fingers, not raising her eyes as she asked the question.

"He already has a little," Quentin said thoughtfully. "I think you've had a softening effect on him."

Juliana looked up with a quick flush. "Do you think so?"

"Mmmm. But then you, my dear, are a most unusual young woman." He rose to his feet and took her hand, raising it to his lips. "Unusual, and most perceptive. I didn't mean to burden you with my troubles."

Juliana's flush deepened with pleasure. "You didn't burden me with anything, sir. I'm honored with your confidence."

He smiled again and bent to kiss her cheek. "You have, at least, enabled me to see clearly again. If it's so obvious to you what Lydia and I feel, then it may become obvious to Tarquin also. I don't want that to happen."

"So what will you do?"

"Write to my bishop and ask to return before my mission is completed."

It was a sad—indeed, rather pathetic—solution, Juliana thought, but she merely nodded as if in agreement, and he left her.

She leaned back against the chair and closed her eyes for

a moment. Her hand drifted over her belly. Had she conceived? It was five weeks since her last monthly terms. She
felt no different, none of the signs so painstakingly pointed
out by Mistress Dennison. And yet she had this strange,
deep knowledge inside her body that something different
was going on. She couldn't put words to it, but it was a
definite conviction known in her blood if not in her brain.

She would wait until she was sure, of course, before
telling the duke. In their present state of estrangement he'd
probably be delighted that there was no further need for
their lovemaking. She ought to be pleased herself, but Juliana was too honest to pretend that the thought brought her
anything but a hollow pain. She hated the present coldness,
but some stubborn streak kept her from making the first
move. It was up to the duke to heal the breach if he wanted
to.

" 'E's lodgin' at the Gardener's Arms, in Cheapside, Yer
Grace." Ted took a thirsty gulp of ale. Tracking George
Ridge across London had been hot and thirsty work.

The duke was perched on the edge of the desk in his
book room, a glass of claret in hand, his canary silk coat
and britches a startling contrast to his companion's rough
leathern britches and homespun jerkin. Yet it would be
clear to anyone walking into the room that there was a
definite equality in the relationship between the Duke of
Redmayne and the stalwart Ted Rougley.

"Has he recovered from your little intervention?"

Ted grinned. "Aye, 'e's large as life an' twice as ugly."
He drained his tankard and smacked his lips.

Tarquin nodded, gesturing to the pitcher that stood on
the silver tray at the far end of the desk. Ted helped himself
with a grunt of thanks.

"An' there's summat else ye should know, Yer Grace."
Ted's tone was faintly musing, yet carried a note of some
import. Seeing he had the duke's full attention, he contin-

ued. " 'Cordin' to the missis at the Gardener's, 'e's bin
'avin' a visitor. Regular like."

"Oh?" Tarquin's eyebrows crawled into his scalp.

"Right sickly-lookin' gent, the missis said. Gave 'er the
creeps 'e did. All green an' white, with eyes like the dead."

"She has a colorful turn of phrase," Tarquin observed,
sipping his claret. "Are we to assume that Lucien and
George have set up an unholy alliance?"

He took out his snuffbox and stood for a minute tapping
a manicured fingernail against the enamel. He was remembering that George had been in the Shakespeare's Head the
night Lucien had put Juliana on the block. Juliana said he'd
made a bid on her. It was possible that these two, both
bearing grudges against Juliana, and in Lucien's case overwhelmingly against his cousin, should have formed the
devil's partnership.

Ted didn't answer what he knew had been a rhetorical
question, merely regarded his employer stolidly over his
tankard.

"Let's deal with George first," Tarquin said. "We'll pay a
little visit to the Gardener's Arms later tonight . . . when
the oaf should have returned from his amusements in the
Garden. Bring a horsewhip. We must be sure to emphasize
my point."

"Right y'are, Yer Grace." Ted deposited his empty tankard on the tray, bowed with a jerk of his head, and left.

The duke frowned into space, twirling the delicate stem
of his glass between finger and thumb. He'd been intending to put a stop to George's antics as soon as Ted had
tracked him down after the attempted abduction, but if
Ridge had joined forces with Lucien, then the situation
was much more menacing. Lucien was unpredictable and
could be quite subtle in his malevolence. Ridge, as he'd
already demonstrated, would rely on brute force. They
made a formidable combination.

He stood up suddenly, impelled by a force he'd been
fighting for the last couple of days. He wanted Juliana. This
estrangement tore at his vitals. It was becoming almost im-

possible to keep up the cool, distant facade. Every day he looked at her across the dinner table, at the fierce vibrancy of her hair, the luster of her eyes, the rich curves of her body. And he held himself away from her. It was torture, a wrenching on the rack. And Juliana, damn her, was giving as good as she got. Her stare was as cool as his, her voice as flat, her conversation never transcending the banality of small talk between strangers. He wanted to throttle her as much as he wanted to assuage his aching longing on her willing, eagerly responsive body.

Never had he felt like this before. As if every carefully woven strand of his personality was tangled, his life a jumbled jigsaw. And all because a seventeen-year-old chit didn't know what was good for her. What else did she want of him, for God's sake?

With a muttered oath he flung himself out of the book room and took the stairs two at a time. He entered Juliana's parlor without knocking, shut the door behind him, then stood leaning against it, regarding her in brooding silence.

Juliana had been writing a note to Lilly. At midnight they were all due to meet at Mother Cocksedge's establishment. Juliana had planned the evening very carefully. She was going to the opera in a party assembled by one of Lady Melton's acquaintances. It would be easy enough to slip away before supper. She could plead a headache, insist on returning alone in a hackney, and instead have herself driven to Covent Garden. In the unlikely event that the duke returned from his own entertainment before her, he would assume the party was sitting late over supper.

She was explaining in her letter to Lilly that she would arrive at Cocksedge's just after midnight when Tarquin burst in. She felt herself flush. Instinctively she thrust the sheet of vellum to the back of the secretaire.

"My . . . my lord. This is a surprise," she managed to say, trying for the cold tone she'd perfected recently.

"I miss you, dammit!" he stated, pushing himself away from the door. "Goddamn you, Juliana. I can't go on like this. I don't know what you've done to me." He pulled her up from her chair. He held her face between both hands and kissed her with a deep urgency. His hands moved upward, pulling the pins from her hair, his fingers roughly running through it as he loosened it; all the while his tongue hungrily probed her mouth.

Juliana was so taken aback that for a minute she didn't respond; then a wild, almost primitive, triumph flashed through her veins. She had this power over him. A woman's power. A power she was positive he had never acknowledged before. Now she clung to him, at last after days of deprivation able to give expression to the unquenchable well of passion that bubbled at her core. Her tongue fenced with his, her body reached against him, rubbing, pressing, moving with sinuous temptation, and she felt him hard and urgent against her belly.

Tarquin bore her backward to the sofa, and she fell in a tangle of skirts to sink onto the shiny taffeta. He didn't release her mouth, merely pushed up her skirts to her waist, released his own aching stem, and drove deep into her body. Her legs curled around his back, and her body moved with all the urgency of a passion that had many causes but only one outlet. Anger, hurt, mistrust, desire, all consumed in the flames.

He drew her legs onto his shoulders, his palms running up the firm calves, over the smooth flesh of her thighs above her garters, cupping her buttocks. His eyes were closed as he held her in his hands, and his flesh was plunging deep into the dark, velvet depths of her body. As the little ripples of her approaching climax tantalized his flesh, he opened his eyes and looked down at her. Her own eyes were wide-open, glowing with joy, not a sign of misgiving or withholding beneath the jade surface. She was giving herself to him as if there had never been a word of doubt between them, and he knew, in that moment, that the giving was a true expression of her soul.

And in the same instant he understood what she wanted from him. A gift that came without reservations. The gift of himself. He had beneath him, her body encompassing his as he possessed hers, the possibility of a love for all time. A partner of his heart and soul.

Juliana reached up and touched his face, a look of wonder now in her eyes. He looked transformed. Her breath caught in her throat as she read the message in the intensity of his gaze. This was no longer a man who couldn't believe in the reality of love.

Chapter 23

George Ridge threw the dice. They rolled across the square of table cleared of debris and came to a halt in a puddle of ale. A six and a one. He spat disgustedly on the sawdust at his feet and tipped the bottle of port against his mouth, taking a deep draft. His guineas were scooped up with a gleeful grin by his fellow player, who spat twice in his hand, tossed the dice from palm to palm, murmured a blasphemous prayer, and rolled them. A groan went up from the crowd around the table as they saw the numbers. The one-eyed sea captain had had the luck of the devil all evening.

George pushed back his chair. He'd continued playing long past his limit and had the sinking feeling that his losses were probably greater than he realized. His brain was too addled by ale and port to function well enough for accurate calculation, but in the cold, aching light of day he'd be forced to face reality.

As he struggled unsteadily to his feet, a hand descended on his shoulder and a voice spoke quietly into his ear. It was a voice as cold as a winter sea, and it sent shivers down his spine as if he were about to plunge into such waters.

"Going somewhere, Ridge?"

George turned under the hand on his shoulder and

found himself looking up into a pair of expressionless gray eyes in a lean and elegant countenance. The thin mouth was curved in the faintest smile, but it was a smile as cold and pitiless as the voice. He recognized the man immediately. His eyes darted around the room, looking for support, but no one was paying attention. Their bleary gazes were focused on the play.

"I think we'll find it more convenient to have our little discussion in the stable yard," said the Duke of Redmayne. He removed his hand from George's shoulder. Suddenly George found himself in the grip of a pair of fists that fastened on his elbows from behind as tenaciously as the tentacles of an octopus.

"This a-way, boyo," an encouraging voice said in his ear. George's feet skimmed the ground as he was propelled through the crowded taproom and out into the yard behind the inn.

The night was hot. Two ostlers, sitting on upturned water butts smoking pipes and chatting in desultory fashion, glanced up, at first with scant interest, at the three men who'd entered the yard. Their eyes widened as they took in the curious group. A gentleman in black, gold-embroidered silk looking as if he'd just walked out of the Palace of St. James's; a second gentleman, bulky and red-faced, in a suit of crimson taffeta and a yellow-striped waistcoat; a third man in the rough leather britches and jerkin of a laborer. The second gentleman was beginning to protest, trying to free himself from the grip of the laborer. The elegant gentleman leaned casually against a low stone wall. He carried a long horsewhip that snaked around his silver-buckled shoes of red leather.

"Take your hands off me!" George blustered thickly, finally managing to get a look at the man holding him. He had but a confused recollection of the disruption in the hackney before he'd lost consciousness, but there was something horribly familiar about his captor. He struggled with renewed violence.

"I just want a word or two," the duke said carelessly, snapping the whip along the ground.

George's eyes darted wildly downward. There was something menacingly purposeful about the thin leather lash flickering and dancing across the cobbles. Ted adjusted his grip almost casually, but his victim immediately recognized that he was held even more firmly than before.

"Listen to 'Is Grace, I should," Ted advised. "Listen well, boyo."

Tarquin subjected George Ridge to a dispassionate scrutiny before saying, "Perhaps you would care to explain why you issued such a pressing invitation to Lady Edgecombe. I understand from her that she was not at all inclined to enter your hackney."

Ted shifted his booted feet on the cobbles and gazed about him incuriously, but his grip tightened yet again, pulling George's arms behind his back.

George licked suddenly dry lips. "You have a murderess under your roof, Your Grace. The murderer of my father, Juliana Ridge's late husband." He tried to sound commanding with this denunciation, full of self-confidence and righteous indignation, but his voice emerged stifled and uncoordinated.

"And just, pray, who is this Juliana Ridge?" the duke inquired in a bored tone, withdrawing his snuffbox from the deep-cuffed pocket of his coat. He flipped the lid and took a leisurely pinch while George struggled to make sense of this. Viscount Edgecombe had been convinced the duke knew all Juliana's skeletons.

He took a deep breath. "The woman living in your house. The woman who calls herself Viscountess Edgecombe. She was married to my father, Sir John Ridge of the village of Ashford, in the county of Hampshire." He paused, regarding the duke anxiously. His Grace's expression hadn't changed; he looked merely politely bored.

George continued somewhat desperately, "I daresay, Your Grace, when you found her in the whorehouse you knew nothing of her history . . . but . . ." His voice faded under the duke's now blazing gaze.

"You appear to have lost your wits, sir," the duke said softly, coiling the whip into his hand. "You would not otherwise insult the name of a woman wedded to my cousin, living under my roof and my protection. Would you?"

The last question was rapped out, and the duke took a step toward George, who couldn't move with the man at his back holding his arms in a vise.

"My lord duke," he said, clear desperation now in voice and eyes. "I do assure you I know her for what she is. She has hoodwinked you and she must be brought to justice. Her husband intends to repudiate her as soon as she's brought before the magistrate and—"

"I think I've heard enough," the duke interrupted. He didn't appear to raise his voice, but the two ostlers sat up attentively.

The duke pushed the shiny wooden handle of the whip beneath George's chin, almost gently, except that its recipient could feel the bruising pressure. "The lady living under my roof is a distant cousin of mine from York. You would do well to check your facts before you slander your betters."

The gray eyes pierced George's blurred gaze like an icicle through snow. But George knew the duke was deliberately lying. The man knew the truth about Juliana. But in the face of that bold statement, the derisive glare that challenged him to dispute it, George was dumbstruck.

The duke waited for a long moment, holding George's befuddled gaze, before saying almost carelessly, "Do not let me ever see your face within half a mile of Lady Edgecombe again." He removed the whip, tossed it to Ted, who caught it neatly with one hand.

The duke gazed silently at George for what seemed to the disbelieving Ridge to be an eternity of cold intent; then he nodded briefly to Ted, turned on his heel, and walked out of the yard.

"Well, now, boyo," Ted said genially. "Let's us come to an understanding, shall us?" He raised his whip arm. George stared, horror-struck, as the lash circled through the air. Then he bellowed like a maddened bull as he finally understood what was to happen to him.

Juliana found it impossible to concentrate on the opera, as much because her mind was on the meeting in Covent Garden as because everyone around her was chattering as if the singers on stage were not giving their hearts and souls to the first performance of Pergolesi's new work.

The Italian Opera House in the Haymarket was brilliantly lit throughout the performance with chandeliers and flaming torches along the stage. King George II was in the royal box with Queen Caroline, and Juliana found them more interesting than the incomprehensible Italian coming from the stage. It was probably as close as she would ever get to Their Majesties.

George II was an unimpressive-looking man, florid of face, an untidy white wig standing up around his bullet-shaped head. He had a most disagreeable expression, glaring around at his companions, bellowing critical comments to his aides throughout the performance in his heavily accented broken English that rose easily above the general hubbub.

After the first interval Juliana judged it time to wilt a little. She began to ply her fan with increasing fervor, every now and again sighing a little, passing her hand over her brow.

"Is something the matter, Juliana?" The eldest Bowen daughter, Lady Sarah Fordham, leaned forward anxiously. "Are you unwell?"

"The headache," Juliana said with a wan smile. "I get them on occasion. They come on very suddenly."

"Poor dear." Sarah was instantly sympathetic. She turned to her mother beside her. "Lady Edgecombe is unwell, Mama. She has a severe headache."

"Try this, my dear." Lady Bowen handed over her smelling salts. Juliana received them with another wan smile. She sniffed delicately; her eyes promptly streamed, and she gasped at the powerful burning in her nostrils. Leaning back, she closed her eyes with a sigh of misery and plied her fan with no more strength than an invalid. She'd had to revise her original plan to leave the opera and go to Covent Garden in a hired hackney. Tarquin had insisted she take his own coachman for the evening so she wouldn't be dependent upon Lady Bowen for transport. He'd meant it considerately, but it was a damnable nuisance. Now she would have to get rid of John Coachman.

"I do fear I shall swoon, ma'am," she murmured. "If I could but take the air for a few minutes . . ."

"Cedric shall escort you." Lady Bowen snapped her fingers at Lord Cedric, a willowy, effete young gentleman who happened to enjoy the opera—not that he had much opportunity to do so in the noisy clamor of his mother's box. "Take Lady Edgecombe for some air, Cedric."

Reluctantly, the young man abandoned the soprano-and-tenor duet that he'd been straining to hear. Bowing, he offered his arm to Juliana, who staggered to her feet with another little moan, pressing her hand to her forehead.

Outside, on the steps of the opera house, she breathed the sultry air and sighed pathetically. "I really think I must go home, sir," she said in a weak voice. "If you could make my excuses to your mama and summon my coachman, I need not keep you from the music another minute."

"No trouble, ma'am . . . no trouble at all," he stammered, but without the true ring of conviction. Leaving Juliana on the top step, he ran down to the street and sent an urchin to summon the Duke of Redmayne's carriage. It appeared within five minutes. Juliana was installed within, the coachman instructed to return with all speed to Albermarle Street, and Cedric Bowen hastened back to his music.

Juliana banged on the roof of the carriage as it was about

to turn right onto Pall Mall. The coachman drew rein and leaned down from his box.

"Take me instead to Covent Garden," Lady Edgecombe instructed in her most imperious tones. "I left my fan in a coffeehouse there this morning. I would see if it's still there."

The coachman had no reason to disobey Her Ladyship's orders. He withdrew to the box, turned his horses, and drove to Covent Garden. Juliana tried to control her apprehension, which was mixed with a curious excitement, as if she were embarking on a great adventure. She was hoping that some of the street women would come to the meeting as well as the more highly placed courtesans. It would be convenient for them to take an hour off work and slip into Cocksedge's tavern, where Juliana hoped to convince them that a simple investment of trust and solidarity could make an enormous difference to their working conditions. A few of the High Impures would be unable to leave their establishments to attend, but there were plenty who could find an excuse for visiting clients outside the house, and Lilly had decided to plead sickness early in the evening in order to make her escape from Russell Street.

But Juliana knew that with or without her friends' support, the success of this embryonic plan depended upon her powers of persuasion and her own energy and commitment. She had to make them see her own vision, and see how to make it reality.

She banged on the roof again when they reached St. Paul's Church. "Wait here for me," she instructed, swinging open the carriage door and stepping to the cobbles, managing to avoid a pile of rotting, slimy cabbage leaves just waiting to catch the foot of the unwary. Gathering her skirts in her hands, she picked her way through the market refuse toward Mother Cocksedge's establishment. The church clock struck midnight.

Noise spilled through the open door of the chocolate house run by Mother Cocksedge. Drunken voices, raucous laughter, the shrill skirl of a pipe.

Juliana stepped through the door and blinked, her eyes slowly adapting to the gloom. The sights were becoming familiar. The whores swayed drunkenly in various stages of undress, either touting for custom or satisfying the demands of a customer. Two dogs fought over a scrap of offal in the center of the room amid a loudly wagering circle of young gentlemen, dressed in the finery of courtiers; their cravats were loose, their wigs in disarray, their stockings twisted. Women crowded around them, touching, stroking, petting, receiving kisses and occasional rowdy slaps in exchange, as the young bloods drank from tankards of blue ruin and shouted obscenities to the rafters.

Juliana felt immediately exposed. This was not like slipping upstairs to Mistress Mitchell's back room. But she knew that the women they were hoping to gather tonight would be more comfortable in this place than in a more exclusive and expensive establishment. She pushed her way through to the back of the taproom, her tall figure and flaming hair attracting immediate attention.

"Hey, where're you off to, my beauty?" A young man grabbed her arm and grinned vapidly at her. "Haven't seen you in these parts before."

"Let me go," Juliana said coldly, shaking her arm free.

"Oho! Hoity-toity madam," another young man bellowed, his eyes small and red in a round, almost childlike, face. "Give us a kiss, m'dear, and we'll let you pass." He lurched toward her, leering.

Juliana gave him a push, and he tumbled backward against the table amid shrieks of laughter. Before he could recoup, Juliana had pushed through to the rear of the room.

"Juliana!" Lilly's fierce whisper reached her as she paused, wondering where to go and whom to ask. The young woman beckoned from a doorway. "Quickly. They don't know we're in here, but if they find out, they'll start such a ruckus." She pulled Juliana into the room, slamming the door behind her. " 'Tis the very devil, but there's no key to the door. And the young bloods are always the

worst. They'll start a melee at the drop of a hat, and before
we know it, we'll be in the middle of a riot."

"I can believe it," Juliana said grimly, shaking out the
folds of her gown, which had become crushed as she'd
fought her way through the room. "Nasty little beasts."

"Our bread and butter," a woman said from the table,
raising a tankard of ale to her lips. "But not for the likes of
you, my lady." She smiled sardonically. "It's all very well to
be full of grand plans when it's not yer livelihood at stake."

"Now, Tina, don't be so sharp. Let the girl say what she
'as in mind." An older woman in a tawdry yellow dress
gave Juliana a much nicer smile. "Come on in, dearie. Take
no notice of Tina, she's sour because 'er gentleman jest
passed out on 'er an' she couldn't get a penny outta him."

Juliana looked around the room, recognizing amid the
substantial group some faces from the earlier meeting.
Women sat at the table, lounged on the broad windowsill,
perched on the settles on either side of the hearth. They
were all drinking, even the Russell Street women, and for
the most part those unknown to Juliana looked skeptically
at her when she introduced herself.

"Well, let's 'ear what ye've to say," Tina said, still belligerently. "We ain't got all night. Some of us 'ave a livin' to
earn."

Juliana decided that attempting to justify her own position would be pointless. Let them believe what they would
of her. She had more important matters to concentrate on.
The street women were harried and thin-faced, their
clothes shabby finery that she guessed had been on other
backs before. Beside them, the girls from Russell Street and
similar houses looked pampered and affluent, but they all
shared something: A wariness, a darting mistrust in their
eyes, an air of resignation to the vagaries of fate, as if what
security they had today could be gone tomorrow and there
was nothing they could do about it. Beside them, the safety
and permanence of her own situation must look like
heaven. And these were not the poorest of the women out
there. There were women and young girls, little more than

children, lying against the bulks, winter and summer, with whoever could give them a crust of bread or a sip of gin.

She began to explain her idea, slowly and simply, but soon the images of what she'd seen, the knowledge of what lives these women led, the deep knowledge that she had escaped it by a hairbreadth, took over, and her voice grew passionate, her eyes flashing with conviction.

"It's not inevitable that we should be obliged to live as the bawds and whoremasters dictate. It's not inevitable that we should see our earnings disappear into the pockets of greedy masters. It's not inevitable that we should live in fear of prison for the slightest offense, for the smallest word out of turn. None of this is inevitable if we support each other." She had instinctively used "we" throughout. If she didn't identify with the women, she would seem like a preacher, distant on a pulpit. And, besides, she *did* identify with them, even if her situation was vastly different.

She paused for breath and Lilly jumped in, her eyes misty with tears. "We have to have a fund, as Juliana says. We each put into it whatever we can afford—"

"Afford!" exclaimed Tina, coughing into a handkerchief. "That's rich, that is. It's all right fer you what've got a decent 'ouse an' all found. But fer us . . . there's nowt twixt us an' the devil but a sixpence now an' agin if we're lucky."

"But that's my point," Juliana said eagerly. "Listen, if you didn't have to pay all those expenses, you would be able to contribute to the Sisterhood's fund. Those of us who have the most will put in the most—that's only fair. And the rest contribute what they can. But we'll find our own suppliers for coal and light and food and wine. If we can guarantee a certain amount of business, I'm sure we'll find some merchants willing to do business with us. Willing to give us credit to get started."

"Lord luv us, darlin', but who's goin' to give us credit?" wheezed a woman on the settle, laughing at the absurdity of such a prospect.

"They'll give Viscountess Edgecombe credit," Juliana said stubbornly.

A thoughtful silence fell at this. Juliana waited, her blood on fire with her passionate need to persuade them that they *could* take control of their lives. It had to be possible.

"Ye'd be willin' to put yer name out, then?" Tina looked at her with a sudden degree of respect.

"Yes." She nodded in vigorous emphasis. "I will put my own money in every week, just like everyone else, and I will undertake to find the merchants willing to do business with us."

"But, Juliana, they aren't going to be doing business with *you*," Deborah pointed out. "You have no need to buy supplies to conduct your own business."

Juliana shrugged. "I don't see that that makes any difference."

"Well, if ye don't, then us'll thankee kindly fer yer assistance," Tina stated. "That so, ladies?"

"Aye." There was a chorus of hesitant agreement, and Juliana was about to expand on her plan when the piercing squeal of a whistle drowned her words. There was a crash, a bellow, shrieks, more whistles from the room beyond. The young bloods were calling in their high-pitched excitement, furniture crashed to the floor, the sound of blows.

"Oh, dear God, it's a riot," Emma said, her face as white as a sheet. "It's the beadles."

The women were surging to the back of the room, looking for another door. Someone flung up the casement sash and they hurled themselves at the opening. Juliana just stood there in astonishment, wondering what the panic was all about. The disturbance was all in the room next door. If they stayed quiet, no one would come in. They'd done nothing. They were doing nothing to disturb the peace.

Suddenly a voice bellowed from the open window, "No ye don't, woman. Y'are not gettin' away from me. All right, my pretties, settle down now. Mr. Justice Fielding is awaitin' on ye."

Deborah gave a low moan of despair. Juliana stared at the

glowering face of the beadle in the window, his rod of office raised threateningly. Behind him, two others were wrestling with one of the women who'd managed to get through the window. Then the door flew open. She had a glimpse of the room behind, the scene of chaos, the mass of grinning or scowling faces lost in a frenzied orgy of destruction. Then she saw Mistress Mitchell standing with another woman in a print gown and mob cap. They were both talking to a constable as his fellows surged into the room where the women were now huddling, swinging their batons to left and right, grabbing the women, herding them toward the door.

Juliana was caught up with the rest. She lashed out with a fist and a foot and had the satisfaction of feeling them meet their mark, but it did her little good. She was hustled out, pushed and shoved by the officious and none too gentle constables. And as she looked over her shoulder, Mistress Mitchell smiled with cold triumph.

They had been betrayed, and it was clear by whom. The whoremasters of Covent Garden wouldn't see their nymphs escape the yoke without a fight.

Chapter 24

The duke's coachman was sitting on an ale bench outside a tavern under the colonnades of the Piazza, pleasantly awaiting the return of his passenger. He could see the carriage and the urchin who held the horses, but he could see little else beyond the sea of bodies eddying around the square. He heard the ruckus from Cocksedge's as just another exploding bubble in the general cacophonous stew and called for another tankard of ale.

"Beadles is raidin' some 'ouse," a shabby bawd observed from the bench beside him. "Daresay some of them varmints from up town are causin' trouble. Breakin' 'eads no doubt, drunk as lords . . . a'course, most of 'em is lords." She cackled and drained her tankard. "Not that that Sir John'll do much more 'an turn a blind eye to *their* goings-on. It's the women who'll suffer, as usual."

She stared into her empty tankard for a minute, then gathered herself to her feet with a sigh. "That ale does go through a body summat chronic." She staggered into the road, raising an imperative hand to a flyter, who stood with his pail and telltale voluminous cloak a few yards away. He trotted over to her, and she gave him a penny. The flyter set his bucket on the cobbles and then spread his cloak as a screen for the woman, who disappeared into its folds to relieve herself in relative privacy.

John Coachman paid scant interest to a sight that could be seen on every street corner in the city. He eyed his carriage in case the disturbance should show signs of coming this way. There were the sounds of running feet, more yelling and cursing, mostly female. With a grunt he hauled himself to his feet and clambered onto the box of the coach to see over the heads to the turmoil across the square.

He could make out little, except a group of constables herding a crowd of women toward Bow Street, presumably to bring them before Sir John Fielding, the local magistrate. Around the beadles and their prisoners surged a crowd of raging women, throwing rotten fruit at the constables, cursing them with fluent vigor. The constables ducked the missiles, ignored the curses, and moved their prisoners along with the encouragement of their rods. The young men from Cocksedge's roared and swayed in a drunken circle before suddenly affected by a common impulse; like lemmings, they turned in a body and reentered Cocksedge's. The sound of breaking glass and smashing furniture was added to the general tumult, Mother Cocksedge's vituperations and desperate pleas rising above it all.

John Coachman began to feel a little uneasy. Where in all this chaos was Lady Edgecombe? Presumably he should have accompanied her on her errand, but she hadn't really given him the opportunity to offer. A little shiver of apprehension ran down his spine at the thought of the duke's possible reaction to this dereliction of duty.

He stood on his box and gazed intently over the throng. The party of women and beadles was reaching the corner of Russell Street. He caught a glimpse of a flaming red head in the midst, and his heart jumped. Then he sat down again with a thump. Lady Edgecombe couldn't possibly be in the company of a group of arrested whores. Presumably she was waiting for the tumult to die down before she came back to the carriage. He couldn't leave the horses to go and look for her, even if he knew where in this inferno she had gone. If she came back to find him not there, they would be worse off than they already were. He yawned, sleepy from the ale he'd been imbibing freely, and settled down on the box, arms folded, to await Lady Edgecombe's return.

Juliana was continuing to struggle and protest as she was borne out of Covent Garden toward Bow Street. She could see only Lilly and Rosamund of the Russell Street girls and hoped that the others had escaped. The beadles couldn't possibly arrest the entire roomful of women, and it seemed to her that they were somewhat selective in the ones they harried along the street. She noticed that several women at the outskirts of the group were permitted to duck away from their captors and disappear into the dark mouths of alleys as they passed. But there was no possibility of such a move for herself. She had a beadle all to herself, gripping her elbow as he half pulled her along.

Rosamund was weeping; Lilly, on the other hand, cursed at her captors with all the vigor of a Billingsgate fishwife. Her face was tight and set, but Juliana didn't think she was going to break down. "Where are they taking us?" she asked.

"Fielding's," Lilly said shortly through compressed lips. "And then Bridewell, I expect."

Juliana gulped. "Bridewell? But what for?"

"It's a house of correction for debauched females," Lilly told her with the same curtness. "Surely you're not so naive you don't know that."

"Yes, of course I know it. But we weren't doing anything." Juliana tried to keep her temper, knowing that Lilly's impatience was fueled by apprehension.

"We were in the middle of a riot. That's all it takes."

Juliana chewed her lip. "Mistress Mitchell was there, together with some grimy-looking creature I assume was Mother Cocksedge."

"I saw her."

"D'you think she put the beadles on to us?"

"Of course." Lilly turned to look at Juliana and her fear

was now clear in her eyes. "We tried to tell you that it's impossible to escape the rule of the bawds," she said bleakly. "I was a fool to be carried away by your eloquence, Juliana. There was a moment this evening when I thought it might happen. We would buy our own necessities, look after each other in illness or ill luck, thumb our noses at the bastards." She shook her head in angry impatience. "Fools . . . we were all fools."

Juliana said no more. Nothing she could say at this moment would improve the situation, and she needed to concentrate on her own plight. She couldn't admit her identity to the magistrates—neither of her identities. She had to keep the Courtney name out of her own disgrace. The duke, for all his deviousness, didn't deserve to have his cousin's wife publicly hauled off to Bridewell.

Hauled off? Or carted? Her blood ran cold, and a clammy sweat broke out on her hands and forehead. Would they drive them to Bridewell at the cart's tail? Was she about to be whipped through the streets of London?

A wave of nausea rose in her throat. She knew it was part of the customary punishment for bawds. But they weren't bawds. They were the slaves of bawds. Surely that would be a lesser offense in the stern eyes of Sir John Fielding.

They reached a tall house on Bow Street, and one of the constables banged on the door with his staff. A sleepy footman answered it. "We've harlots to be brought before Sir John," the constable announced with solemnity. "Creating a fracas . . . debauching . . . soliciting . . . inciting to riot."

The footman looked over his head to the surrounded women. He grinned lasciviously as he noted their disordered dress. Even the well-dressed women had suffered in the arrest and now tried to hold together torn bodices and ripped sleeves. "I'll waken Sir John," he said, stepping back to open the door fully. "If ye takes 'em into the front parlor where Sir John does 'is business, I'll fetch 'im fer ye."

The constables herded their little flock into the house and into a large paneled room on the left of the hall. It was sparsely furnished, with a massive table and a large chair behind it, rather giving the impression of a throne. The women were pushed into a semicircle around the table while another yawning footman lit the candles and oil lamps, throwing a gloomy light over the bare room.

Then silence fell, as deep as a crypt—not so much as the rustle of a skirt, the scrape of a foot on the bare floor. It was as if the women were afraid to speak or to move, afraid that it might worsen their condition. The beadles kept quiet, as if awed by their surroundings. Only Juliana looked around, taking in details of the molding on the ceiling, the embossed paneling, the waxed oak floorboards. She was as scared as the rest of them, but it didn't show on her countenance as she tried to think of a way out of this dismal situation.

After an eternal fifteen minutes the double doors opened and a voice intoned, "Pray stand for 'Is Honor, Sir John Fielding."

As if they had any choice, Juliana thought with a brave attempt at humor, unable to ignore the shiver that ran through her companions.

Sir John Fielding, in a loose brocade chamber robe over his britches and shirt, his hastily donned wig slightly askew, took his seat behind the table. He surveyed the women with a steady, reproving stare.

"Charges?"

"Disorderly be'avior, Sir John," the head beadle spoke ponderously. "Inciting to riot . . . debauchery . . . damage to property."

"Who brings the charges?"

"Mother Cocksedge and Mistress Mitchell, Yer 'Onor."

"Are they here?"

"Awaitin' yer summons, sir." The beadle tapped his staff on the floor and twitched his nose with an air of great self-importance.

"Then summon them."

Juliana turned her head toward the door. The two women bustled in. Mistress Mitchell looked like a respectable housewife in her print dress and mob cap; Mother Cocksedge had thrown her apron over her head and appeared much affected by something, her shoulders heaving, great sobs emerging from beneath the apron.

"Cease yer blubbin', woman, an' tell 'Is Lordship yer complaint," instructed one of the constables.

"Oh, I'm ruint, Yer 'Onor, quite ruint," came from beneath the apron. "It's all thanks to those evil girls . . . them what encouraged the young gennelmen to break up my 'ouse. Flaunted theirselves at 'em, got 'em all excited like, then wouldn't deliver. An' them three . . ." With a dramatic gesture Mother Cocksedge flung aside her apron and pointed at Juliana, Lilly, and Rosamund. "Them three, what ought to know better, they was encouragin' the others, poor souls what don't 'ave 'alf the advantages, to use my establishment fer *h*immoral purposes."

Juliana gasped. "Why, you old—"

"Silence!" The justice glared at Juliana. "Open your mouth once more, woman, and you'll be carted from St. Paul's Church to Drury Lane and back again."

Juliana shut her mouth, seething as she was forced to listen to the two women spin their tales. Mistress Mitchell was all hurt feelings and good nature taken advantage of as she explained that she'd allowed some girls to use her best parlor for a birthday party, but instead they'd been preparing to create a riot at Mother Cocksedge's oh-so-respectable chocolate house. They had a grievance against Mother Cocksedge and intended to be avenged upon her by causing her house to be wrecked by a group of angry young bloods.

They were evil, fallen women with no morals, set on their wicked ways, put in Mother Cocksedge, once more retreating beneath her apron. "But me an' Mistress Mitchell, 'ere, Yer 'Onor, we don't think as 'ow they should all be punished as much as them what lead 'em into evil. Them three from Russell Street."

Mistress Mitchell bristled and agreed with a dignified nod.

Sir John Fielding regarded the two complainants with an expression of distaste. He was as aware as anyone of the true nature of their trade. But they were not on this occasion brought before him, and their complaint was legitimate enough. His head swung slowly around the semicircle of defendants, and his gaze rested on the three chief malefactors.

Lilly and Rosamund immediately dropped their eyes, but the bold-eyed redhead met his accusatory glare head-on, her green eyes throwing a challenge at him.

"Name?" he demanded.

"Juliana Beresford." She spoke clearly and offered neither curtsy nor salutation.

Lilly and Rosamund, on the other hand, both curtsied low and murmured their names when asked, with an "If it please Your Honor."

"Do you have anything to say to these charges?" He gestured to Juliana.

"Only that they're barefaced lies," she replied calmly.

"You were not gathered in this woman's chocolate house?" The justice's eyebrows rose in a bushy white arc.

"Yes, we were, but—"

"You weren't gathered behind a closed door?" he interrupted.

"Yes, but—"

He thumped his fist on the table, silencing her again. "That's all I wish to know. It is against the law for people to gather together for the purposes of incitement to violence and riot. I sentence you and your two companions to three months in the Tothill Bridewell. Those whom you have corrupted are free on payment of a five-shilling fine."

With that he pushed back his chair and rose to his feet, yawning prodigiously. "I sat overlate last even, and then to be dragged from my bed in the small hours to deal with a trio of hotheaded troublemaking harlots is more than a man can abide," he remarked loudly to a somber-suited man who had stood behind him throughout the trial and who now accompanied him from the room.

"Ye'll be showin' a little more respect to yer betters after three months beatin' 'emp," Mother Cocksedge declared, coming up to the three young women with a leer in her little pink eyes. "I doubt Mistress Dennison and 'er man 'll be ready to take ye back afterward. We don't like trouble-makers in the Garden, and don't ye ferget it, missie." She jabbed a finger at Juliana's chest. Juliana would have retali-ated if she hadn't been held so tightly by a constable. The urge to spit in the woman's face was almost overpowering, but somehow she resisted it and looked away from the hateful, triumphant grin.

"Rosamund cannot survive Bridewell," Lilly whispered to Juliana. "I can, and you can. But Rosamund is fragile. She'll not last on her feet for more than a week."

"She won't have to," Juliana declared with a confidence she didn't feel. They were binding her hands in front of her with coarse rope, and with each twist and knot she was secured in the chains of powerlessness.

Lilly gave her a scornful look as if to say "Face reality" and endured her own bonds with tight lips. Rosamund continued to weep softly as she was similarly bound. The other women had been hustled from the room and could be heard across the hall, declaring penitence and gratitude as the two bawds paid their fines. They'd just been given a lesson on which side their bread was buttered, and it would be a rainy day in hell before they would contemplate stand-ing up for themselves again.

"Come along, then, me pretties." A beadle grinned at them and chucked Rosamund beneath the chin. "Ye'll spoil them lovely eyes with yer tears, missie. Save 'em for the Bridewell, I should." A hearty laugh greeted this sally, and Juliana, Lilly, and Rosamund were half pushed, half dragged out of the house to an open cart waiting outside.

Juliana waited in sick dread for them to fasten her bound hands to a rope behind the cart and pull her bodice to her waist. But they were shoved upward into the cart, and her relief was so great that for the first time since this ordeal had begun, she thought she might faint. She put an arm around Rosamund and took Lilly's hand in a fierce grip as they stood in the benchless vehicle, swaying and lurching over the cobbles.

Dawn was breaking, and the city streets were filling with costermongers, night-soil collectors, barrow boys, servants of all kinds hurrying to the market. The nighttime din had died down in Covent Garden, replaced with the coarse cries of the market people, the rattle of wheels and the clop of horses. As the cart bearing the three bound women was drawn through the streets, people jeered and threw clods of mud and pieces of rotten fruit; small boys ran along beside the cart, chanting obscene songs.

Juliana thought of being burned at the stake. She imagined being tied to the stake in front of a jeering crowd. She thought of the noose around her neck, mercifully squeezing consciousness from her body before they lit the faggots. She lived that nightmare and thus defeated the ghastly reality of the humiliating journey.

John Coachman had fallen asleep on the driver's box. He'd intended to nod off for a minute or two, but when he awoke, it was almost full light. He leaped from the carriage with an oath, still thick with sleep but his heart pounding with fear. Abandoning his horses, he plunged across the Garden, dodging the market folk as they put up their stalls. He'd seen Lady Edgecombe disappear in this direction, but where had she gone then? He stood wildly looking around as if he would see her sitting at her ease under the Piazza. But he knew that something was very wrong. And he'd slept through it. The duke would have his hide and throw him without a character into the street to starve.

"Lost summat, mate?" a friendly carter inquired, pausing with his laden basket of cabbages delicately balanced on his head.

John Coachman looked bewildered. "My lady," he stammered. "I've lost my lady."

The carter chuckled. "Covent Garden's the place fer

losin' a lady friend, mate. But there's plenty 'ere where that one came from."

The coachman didn't attempt to explain something that he didn't understand himself. His great fear was that Lady Edgecombe had been abducted, a fine lady in this den of iniquity. It wouldn't be the first time. And it must have happened at least an hour ago. She could be anywhere in the city's maze of mean, narrow streets and dark, dank courts.

"D'ye 'ear of the business last night at Cocksedge's?" the carter asked, reaching in his pocket for his clay pipe, his basket immobile on his head despite his movements. He struck flint on tinder and lit the pungent tobacco.

The coachman hardly heard him. He was still gazing frantically around, trying to think of his next course of action.

"A group of them 'igh-class nymphs was taken up by the beadles at Cocksedge's," the informative carter rattled on between leisurely puffs. "Incitin' a riot, or so the old bawd says. Got summat agin 'em, I'll bet. She's got the evil eye, that one, make no mistake."

Slowly the words sank in. John remembered the scene he'd witnessed earlier. The flame-red hair stuck in his memory. "What's that you say?"

The carter repeated himself cheerfully. "Took 'em to Fielding's, so I 'eard, but . . ." He stared after the coachman, who was now racing back to his carriage and the stamping, restless horses.

John Coachman clambered onto the box, cracked his whip with a loud bellow of encouragement, and the horses broke almost immediately into a canter, the coach swaying and lumbering behind. They sideswiped a stall and the owner raced after them, yelling curses. A child was snatched just in time from beneath the pounding hooves by an irate woman. A mangy dog dived between the wheels of the carriage and miraculously emerged unscathed on the other side.

Outside the magistrate's house on Bow Street, the

coachman pulled up his sweating horses and with trembling hands descended to the street and ran up the steps to bang the knocker. The footman who answered was lofty and unhelpful until he saw the ducal coronet on the panels of the carriage. Then he was all affability. Yes, there had been a group of whores brought before Sir John an hour or so ago. Three of them sentenced to Tothill Bridewell, the others let off with a fine that their bawds had paid. And, yes, one of the women sent to Tothill had been a tall green-eyed redhead. He vaguely remembered that she'd been wearing a dark-green gown.

John Coachman thanked the man and retreated to his carriage. His world seemed to have run amuck. Lady Edgecombe taken up for a whore; hauled off to Tothill Bridewell. It made no sense. And yet there was no other explanation for Her Ladyship's inexplicable disappearance.

He turned his horses toward Albermarle Street, his mind reeling. It was backstairs gossip that there was something smoky about the way Lady Edgecombe had come to the house. The whole marriage with the viscount reeked to the heavens. And she was installed in the chamber next to the duke, her bridegroom now gone from the house.

He knew well, however, that the conclusions he drew would avail him nothing when facing the duke's wrath. It was with sinking heart that he drove into the mews, handed the horses over to a groom, and entered the house by the back door.

The house was in its customary quiet but efficient early-morning bustle, waxing, polishing, brushing, dusting. The kitchen was filled with the rich aromas of bacon and black pudding, the boot boy and scullery maid carrying steaming salvers into the servants' hall. The coachman knew he would have to confide in Catlett if he was to speak with the duke. And he knew that he must speak with His Grace before many minutes had passed.

He approached the august figure of Catlett, seated at the head of the long table sampling his ale and examining with a critical eye the offerings laid before him by the boot boy.

The lad's mouth watered as he watched the dishes move down the table. He and the scullery maid would have to wait until everyone had eaten before they'd be allowed to rummage for scraps to break their own fasts.

"Eh, John Coachman, and 'ow be you this fine mornin'?" Catlett asked genially, spearing a chunk of black pudding with the end of his knife.

"I'd like a word in private, if ye please, Mr. Catlett." The coachman turned his hat between his hands, his eyes filled with anxiety.

"What? In the middle of me breakfast?"

"It's very urgent, Mr. Catlett. Concerns 'Er Ladyship and 'Is Grace."

Catlett irritably pushed back his chair. "Best come into me pantry, then. You, lad. Put me plate on the 'ob to keep 'ot. I'll dust yer jacket fer ye if 'tis a mite less 'ot than 'tis now."

Wiping his mouth with a napkin, he led the way to his pantry. "So what is it?"

He listened, his eyes widening, as the coachman told him of the night's happening and the total absence of Lady Edgecombe.

"Taken up fer a whore?" Catlett shook his head in incredulity. " 'Ow could that be?"

"Dunno. Accident, I daresay. She went to fetch a fan, got caught up in the riot." John snapped his fingers.

"Sir John wouldn't send Lady Edgecombe to Tothill Bridewell," Catlett declared. "So she must not 'ave told 'im 'oo she is."

"Aye. But why?"

"Not fer us to ask," Catlett pronounced. "But 'Is Grace must be told at once. Ye'd best come wi' me to 'is chamber. 'E's only been back fer a couple of hours."

The coachman followed Catlett into the front of the house and up the stairs. A parlor maid, waxing the banister, gave him a curious look, then dropped her eyes immediately as Catlett clipped her around the ear. "You got nuthin' better to do, my girl, than gawp at yer betters?"

"Yes, sir . . . Mr. Catlett . . . no, sir," she mumbled.

Outside the duke's bedchamber Catlett said, "Wait 'ere." He pushed open the door and entered the darkened chamber. The bed curtains were drawn around the bed. He twitched them aside and coughed portentously.

The duke seemed to be deeply asleep, an arm flung above his head, his face in repose curiously youthful, his mouth relaxed, almost smiling.

Catlett coughed again and, when that produced no response, went to draw back the window curtains, flooding the room with light.

"What the devil . . . ?" Tarquin opened his eyes.

"I beg your pardon, Your Grace, but it's a matter of some urgency." Catlett moved smoothly back to the bed, his practiced working accents crisp and well modulated.

Tarquin struggled up onto an elbow and blinked at the man. "Why are you waking me, Catlett, and not my valet?"

Catlett coughed. "I thought, Your Grace, that you'd prefer as few people as possible to be a party to the situation."

Tarquin sat up, instantly awake. His eyes flew to the armoire and its concealed door. *Juliana.* She hadn't returned when he'd come in earlier, but he hadn't thought twice about it. She was with his own coachman, escorted by the formidable and ultrarespectable Lady Bowen.

"Tell me."

"John Coachman's waiting outside, Your Grace. It's probably best if he tells it in his own words." Catlett bowed.

"Fetch him."

Visibly trembling, the coachman approached the duke's bed. He was still twisting his hat between his hands, his cheeks flushed as he stammered through his recital. The duke listened without a crack in his impassivity, his eyes flat, his mouth thin.

When the coachman had finished his tale and stood miserably pulling at his hat brim, eyes lowered, the duke flung aside the bedclothes and stood up. "I'll deal with you later," he said grimly. "Get out of my sight."

The coachman scuttled off. Catlett moved to pull the bell rope. "You'll be wanting your valet, Your Grace."

"No." Tarquin waved him away. "I'm perfectly capable of dressing myself. Have my phaeton brought round immediately." He threw off his nightshirt and pulled a pair of buckskin britches from the armoire.

Catlett left with a bow, and Tarquin flung on his clothes, his mind racing. He could think of no rational explanation for Juliana's predicament. But, then, Juliana didn't need logical reasons for getting herself into trouble, he thought grimly. He knew that George Ridge couldn't have been involved, since he'd been occupied elsewhere. It was the kind of vengeance that would appeal to Lucien, certainly, but he hadn't the patience to orchestrate such a sophisticated plan. He was a man who acted on vicious impulse. But what in the name of all that was good had taken Juliana, against his express orders and her own past experiences, to Covent Garden at the height of the night's debauchery?

Simple mischief? Pure deviltry? Another demonstration of her refusal to yield to his authority? Somehow he didn't think it was that simple. Juliana wasn't childish . . . hotheaded, certainly; but she was also surprisingly mature for her years—a product presumably of her loveless childhood. She was probably involved in another misguided mission like the one that had taken her to the Marshalsea. For some reason the women of Russell Street held a dangerous fascination for her.

He ought to leave her in Bridwell for a few days, he thought wrathfully, thrusting a thick billfold into the pocket of his britches. She'd soon learn just how dangerous a fascination it was.

But he knew it was fear more than anger that spoke. The purity of his anger was muddled with a piercing dread. He couldn't endure the idea of Juliana's being hurt or frightened. It was as if some part of himself was suffering and he couldn't detach himself from the pain.

It was inexplicable, and a damnable nuisance. He strode out of his chamber, slamming the door behind him, and headed at a run for the stairs.

"Good morning, Tarquin. Where are you off to at the peep of day?" Quentin's voice hailed him from the library as he crossed the hall. Quentin, always an early riser, looked fresh and serene.

"Juliana has contrived to get herself sent to Bridewell," he told Quentin tersely. "Against my better judgment I'm about to spring her loose before she endures too much punishment in that hellhole."

Quentin stared in disbelief. "But how for mercy's sake did—"

"I've no idea," Tarquin interrupted. "The temperamental chit is a loose cannon. And, by God, I'm going to keep her on a leash in future!"

"I'll accompany you." Quentin dropped the prayer book he'd been carrying onto a side table.

"There's no need. I can handle Juliana without assistance."

"I'm sure you can." Quentin followed him out into the bright morning. "Nevertheless, you might need a supporting cast. You don't know what you're going to find."

Tarquin shot him a bleak look, and their eyes held for a minute. They both knew that Quentin's remark was not lightly made. Then the duke climbed with an agile spring into the waiting phaeton, followed by his brother.

Quentin felt Tarquin deliberately relax as he took up the reins. He glanced up at his profile and saw that all emotion was wiped clear from his countenance. He was not fooled by this apparently calm exterior. He'd been convinced for some time now that the careless affection Tarquin showed for his *mignonne* masked a much deeper feeling.

Tarquin whipped up his horses. It was the only indication of his urgency as he fought to subdue the images of what Juliana could be going through at this moment. She was so intractable, so bold and challenging, that it wouldn't be long before she would provoke the jailers to break her spirit. They had crude but sure methods of doing so.

Chapter 25

Juliana stumbled forward under a vigorous shove from her escort, through a doorway and into a long, narrow, filthy room. An iron-barred door clanged behind her. A minute or two earlier the cart had drawn up in a stinking courtyard, surrounded by a high wall. The three women had been hauled down to the cobbles by two men wielding rods, and driven like cattle into the low building. Rosamund had tripped over an uneven flagstone and, unable to help herself with her bound hands, had fallen to her knees. One of the jailers had promptly brought his rod down on her shoulders, cursing her vilely. Sobbing piteously, she'd managed to stand up again and totter forward.

Now the three women stood with their bound hands facing a sea of hostile, predatory eyes as the women in the dimly lit room stared at them, hungrily taking in the quality of their clothes. The walls were of bare brick, glistening and slimy with oozing damp; the air was dank and foul; the only light came from a minute window high up in the far wall under the roof timbers. Far too high to reach from the ground, and far too small to admit even a climbing boy.

The women, for the most part clad only in ragged underpetticoats, coarse stockings, and clogs, stood in front of rows of massive tree stumps beating hanks of hemp with heavy wooden mallets. Juliana saw with dread that several of them wore leg irons, shackling them to the stumps. The dull, rhythmic pounding bounced off the stone walls. A woman with a slit nose cackled as Rosamund gave a low moan and swayed.

"First time 'ere, is it, dearies?" She dropped her mallet and came over to them. Her hands were flayed and bleeding from the hemp. Juliana wondered what crime had merited the slit nose, even as she drew back from the unequivocal malice in the woman's eyes. The woman reached for Rosamund's muslin fichu. "Fancy gewgaws ye've got. Fetch quite a pretty penny, they will."

"Leave her alone," Juliana snapped.

The woman's eyes narrowed dangerously, and she tore the fichu from Rosamund's quivering neck. "I'll 'ave 'er clothes, and your'n, too, missie. Soon as the day's work's done. An' if ye don't watch yer tongue, we'll strip ye nekkid. We knows 'ow to tame a proud spirit in 'ere. Innit so, girls?"

There was a chorus of agreement, and the eyes seemed to move closer, although the women remained at their posts. Juliana involuntarily turned to the jailer as if seeking protection.

The man merely laughed. "Don't go upsettin' Maggie. She'll scratch yer eyes out soon as look at ye. An' 'er word goes in 'ere. What 'appens in 'ere, when y'are locked up fer the night, is none of me business." He moved in front of them and sliced their bonds with his knife. "Get to work now. Them three stumps over there." He gestured to three unoccupied work sites, the massive mallets resting atop.

Maggie followed them over and stood, hands on hips, as the jailer pulled three thick hanks of hemp from a basket on the wall and threw them onto the stumps. The woman reached over and took Rosamund's shrinking hand. "This'll not last long," she observed, turning the small white hand over in her grime-encrusted, blood-streaked palm. "I give ye an hour, an' yer 'ands'll be bleedin' so 'ard ye won't be able to bear to touch the mallet." She cackled, and a ripple of mirth ran around the room from the others, who had taken a rest from their labors to watch the induction.

The jailer grinned. "Them what won't work goes in the pillory."

Rosamund was dazed with fright and was weeping so hard now, she couldn't take anything in, but Juliana and Lilly both looked to where the man's finger was pointing. A wall pillory, the holes high enough to keep the victim on her toes and to put an intolerable strain on her shoulders. Above it inscribed the legend: *Better to work than stand thus.*

Juliana picked up the mallet and brought it down on the hemp with an almighty swing. The weight of the mallet astounded her, and any effect of the blow on the hemp was invisible. The stuff had to be pounded until the core fibers split and could be separated from the thick fibrous covering. After three blows her wrists ached, the skin of her palms was beginning to rub, and the hemp showed no more than a slight flattening. She glanced at Rosamund, who was tapping feebly through her tears and making no impression at all on her hank. Lilly, tight-lipped, white-faced, was swinging her mallet above her shoulder and bringing it down with resolute violence. In a short while she'd be exhausted, Juliana thought apprehensively. If she was exhausted, she wouldn't be able to continue.

She glanced again at Rosamund's hemp, then swiftly picked up her own partially split hank and swapped it with Rosamund's barely touched one. Lilly gave her a quick approving nod, whispering, "Between us we should be able to keep her going."

"Eh, stop yer jabberin' over there." The jailer came toward them swinging his rod. "There's no time fer talkin'. Ye'll 'ave six of 'em ready by noontime, or ye'll find yerself at the whippin' post."

A chilling desperation took a hold on Juliana. She could see no way out. There was no one to appeal to. They were imprisoned in this fetid hole so far from civilization that they could have dropped off the face of the earth for all the contact they would have with the outside world. But surely someone would be wondering where she was. The coachman would be looking for her. Someone would discover what had happened.

But why would they do anything to help her? What right had she to expect help? The duke would be thinking that it served her right. To obtain her release, he'd have to acknowledge his connection with a convicted whore in a house of correction. She couldn't imagine why anyone, let alone the Duke of Redmayne, would wish to do that.

Except, of course, to protect his investment. Furiously, she swung the mallet, ignoring the pain in her hands, ignoring the drops of blood that began to fall on the stump and made the handle of the mallet slippery. She welcomed the anger because it defeated the dreadful, numbing desperation that she knew instinctively was her greatest enemy.

She and Lilly must do their own six hanks and share Lilly's if they were to keep her from the pillory—or worse, the whipping post. In this hellhole, inhabited by the dregs of humanity, the weak would go to the wall. Juliana knew that she would be able to stand up to the jailer, and to the vile Maggie, as long as she kept her strength and diverted the deadening sense of helplessness. Lilly, too, would be difficult to break. But Rosamund stood not a chance. Her spirit was already broken, and to watch her complete disintegration would provide merry sport for the degraded wretches who surrounded them.

Sir John Fielding regarded his visitors in polite astonishment. "Lady Edgecombe among the whores I sent to Tothill Bridewell? My dear sir, surely you must be mistaken."

"I don't believe so," Tarquin said, his mouth so thin and tight it was barely visible. "Red hair, green eyes. Tall."

"Aye, I marked her well. A bold-eyed wench," the magistrate opined, stroking his chin. "Now you mention it, she did seem rather out of the common way for strumpets. But why wouldn't she identify herself? How could she get caught up—"

"Forgive me for interrupting." Quentin stepped forward. "I believe it must have had something to do with Juliana's interest in the lives of the street women." He coughed discreetly. "She was much exercised over young Lucy's plight, if you recall, Tarquin. Insisted upon bringing her out of the Marshalsea. I believe it would be in character for her to . . . to extend her field of operations, if you will."

Tarquin nodded tersely. "It would certainly be in character."

"What's that you mean to say, your lordship?" Sir John looked puzzled. "Don't quite catch your meaning. What interest could a lady have in a whore's life?"

"The inequities of their position, I believe, troubles Lady Edgecombe most powerfully," Quentin explained gravely.

"Well, I'll be damned. Out to reform them, is she?" Sir John took up a dish of coffee and guzzled it with relish.

"Probably not reformation, Sir John," Quentin said, sipping his own coffee. "Juliana is of a practical turn of mind."

"Not when it comes to self-preservation," Tarquin stated grimly.

"Well, if she's been meddling in the profits of the likes of Mitchell and Cocksedge, it's no wonder she aroused the wrath of the demons," Sir John observed. "Devil take it, sir, but His Lordship should keep a tighter rein on his wife."

"Oh, believe me, Sir John, from now on the tightest rein and the heaviest curb," Tarquin promised, setting aside his coffee dish and standing up with an abrupt movement. "If you'll provide me with an order for her release, sir, we'll be about our business."

"Aye, Your Grace. Aye, indeed." The magistrate summoned his somber-suited secretary, who'd been listening with wagging ears to the conference. "Write it up, Hanson. Immediate release of Lady Edgecombe."

"I believe Her Ladyship called herself Juliana Beresford, sir," the secretary reminded. "It's down as that in the register of committal."

"I daresay she thought her real identity might prove an embarrassment for you," Quentin murmured to his brother.

"Juliana is always such a paragon of consideration," Tarquin retorted.

They waited, the duke in visible impatience, for the secretary's laborious penning of the order. Tarquin almost snatched it from the man, thrusting it into his coat pocket, throwing a curt thank-you over his shoulder to Sir John as he strode from the room, Quentin on his heels.

"How long has she been in there, d'ye reckon, Quentin?" Tarquin's voice was taut, his face a mask as he whipped up his horses, setting them at a racing pace through the rapidly crowding streets.

Quentin glanced at his fob watch. It was nine o'clock. "They were at Fielding's just before dawn. Reached Bridewell maybe two hours later."

"Seven o'clock, then. Two hours." A note of relief crept into his voice. It would take a lot longer than that to break Juliana. "Has she talked to you about this obsession she has with the whores?" He kept out of his voice his annoyance that she had not confided in him—an annoyance that was directed more at himself than at Juliana. He hadn't questioned exactly what she'd been doing in Covent Garden on her last excursion, which had led to George's attempted abduction. He'd assumed she'd been simply meeting her friends for her own entertainment. Now it seemed there may have been more to it.

"A little. Usually when we've been sitting with Lucy. Juliana's own experiences, I believe, have made her particularly sensitive to the women's plight. Exploitation, as she calls it."

"Death and damnation!" Tarquin overtook a lumbering dray on the narrow street, so close he shaved the varnish on

the phaeton. "Exploitation! Who the hell has exploited
her?"

"You have."

Tarquin's expression blackened, and his eyes took on the
flat glitter of anger. But he said nothing, and Quentin prudently held his own peace.

The forbidding building of the Tothill Bridewell loomed
before them. Tarquin drew his horses to a halt before the
massive iron gate. The postern gate swung open and an ill-
kempt guard stepped through. He took in the equipage and
the haughty impatience of the driver. He tugged his forelock in a halfhearted gesture. "Sure ye 'aven't come to the
wrong place, good sirs?"

Tarquin jumped from the phaeton. "Take the reins," he
instructed, thrusting them into the astonished guard's
hands. "Where will I find the keeper of this place?"

"Eh, Yer 'Onor, at 'is breakfast, I don't doubt." The
guard looked in alarm at the two pawing horses that had
become his charge. "In 'is 'ouse," he added helpfully.

"And where might that be?" Quentin asked swiftly,
sensing Tarquin was within an inch of throttling the guard.

" 'Cross the yard, on the left. 'Ouse that stands alone."

"Thank you." Quentin fished out a sovereign. "For your
trouble. There'll be another when we return." Then he set
off after Tarquin, who had already disappeared through the
postern gate.

The yard was surrounded by high walls. A whipping post
stood prominently in the middle, stocks and a pillory beside it. To one side a massive treadmill turned, groaning
with each revolution. A team of women, petticoats kilted
to their knees, feet bare, wearily trod its circumference, a
jailer with a long-lashed whip exhorting them to greater
effort as he paced around them.

One quick glance told both men that Juliana had not
been harnessed to that barbarous toil. Tarquin banged on
the door of a squat cottage standing apart from the long,
narrow, low-pitched building that housed the Bridewell.

"All right . . . all right . . . I'm a-comin'." The

door opened and a woman poked her head out. She would once have been pretty, smooth-cheeked, with merry blue eyes and golden hair. But her face now was pitted with smallpox, her eyes shadowed with spite and the barren acceptance of a barren existence, her gray-streaked hair hanging in lank ringlets to her scrawny shoulders. Her eyes widened as she took in the visitors.

"I wish to have speech with the keeper of this place," Tarquin stated brusquely. "Fetch him, my good woman."

" 'E's at 'is breakfast, my lord." She bobbed a curtsy. "But if'n ye'd care to step this way." She gestured behind her into a dingy, smelly passageway.

Tarquin took the invitation, Quentin on his heels. The passage gave onto a square room, reeking of stale fried onions and boiling cods' heads. A man in a filthy waistcoat, collar unbuttoned, sleeves rolled up, was scooping boiled tripe into his mouth with the blade of his knife.

He looked up as the door opened. "Agnes, I told you I weren't to be disturbed. . . ." Then his voice faded as he saw his visitors. A sly look came into his eyes. He wiped his dripping chin with the back of his hand and said in a fawning tone, "Well, what can Jeremiah Bloggs do fer ye, good sirs?"

Tarquin could see he was already calculating how much of a bribe he could squeeze out of whatever this situation was. Keepers of the prisons earned no salary, but they were free to extort and "fee" both prisoners and their visitors for anything they could come up with.

"I have an order for the release of a woman brought in here by mistake this morning," he said, laying the document on a corner of the dirt-encrusted table. "If you'd be so good as to have her fetched."

The sly look intensified. Bloggs stroked a loose-flapping lower lip with a thumb tip. "Well, it ain't quite that easy, 'onored sir."

"Of course it is," snapped the duke. "This document states that the prisoner Juliana Beresford is to be released immediately. Without let or hindrance. If you have difficulty performing your duties, my good man, I shall ensure that you are replaced by someone who does not."

The sly look became a malevolent glare. "I don't know where she might be 'eld, Yer 'Onor," he whined. "There's a dozen or so wards, includin' the lunatic ones. Per'aps ye'd like to look fer 'er yerselves. Might be quicker, like."

"Certainly. But you are accompanying us."

Muttering under his breath, the keeper abandoned his tripe, drained his mug of blue ruin, picked up a massive ring of keys, and stomped ahead of them out to the court.

The stench of excreta overwhelmed them the minute the door was opened onto the building. Quentin choked. Tarquin pulled out his handkerchief and held it to his nose, his expression even grimmer than before. The keeper was unaffected by the reek. He maneuvered his large bulk down the passage, stopping at each barred ward, unlocking the door and gesturing sullenly that they should look in.

Thin, dull-eyed women looked back at them without pausing in the rhythmic pounding of their mallets. Rats rustled through the filthy straw at their feet; their jailers sat taking their ease on stools against the walls, occasionally swinging their rods when they judged someone was slacking.

Quentin couldn't keep the horror from his face. He had always known these places existed and, indeed, had assumed that houses of correction were necessary for the smooth running of society. But in the face of this unutterable reeking misery, he began to question his assumptions. He glanced at his brother. Tarquin's countenance was utterly impassive—a sure sign of turmoil within.

At the sixth ward they stopped outside an iron-bound door. Mr. Bloggs inserted the key. "If she ain't in 'ere, sirs, I can't think where she'd be. Less'n she be lunatic already; or they've put 'er on the treadmill. Which it's to be 'oped they 'aven't. Seein' as 'ow it's all a mistake, like." He grunted with what could almost have been a chuckle at the thought of an innocent suffering from such an error.

"Can't think what Sir John could be a-doin', makin' such a mistake." He swung the door open and stood aside.

Juliana was lost in the rhythm of the mallet. She allowed her eyes to see only the hemp in front of her. As the fibers began to separate, a grim satisfaction filled her. She thought of nothing more than the disintegration of the hemp. The pounding was in her ears, in her blood, the condition of her hands a distant agony that she knew instinctively she mustn't focus upon. Beside her Lilly pounded away. Without exchanging a glance they flipped Rosamund's pathetic work from one stump to another. But despite their efforts Rosamund's hands were bleeding and mangled within the first hour, as Maggie had gleefully foreseen, and her tears mingled with the blood dripping onto the hemp.

There had to be a way out of this nightmare. But Juliana's brain was deadened by the numbing, repetitive noise and the creeping dullness of fatigue. She'd had no sleep for twenty-four hours, and this work would presumably continue until nightfall. It wasn't possible to think, to do anything, but force her body through the motions and watch the hemp.

At the moment the door opened, Rosamund cried out. The mallet dropped, bouncing on the tree stump. She stared with fixed intensity at her hands, her eyes widening in horror. She raised her eyes to gaze wildly around the room, as if coming to a realization of her surroundings for the first time; then, with another cry of despair, she crumpled to the filthy straw.

Juliana dropped to her knees, Lilly beside her. They ignored the commotion at the door. Lilly lifted Rosamund's head, laying it in her lap. Juliana wanted to chafe her hands but didn't dare to touch them. Her own stung unmercifully now that her concentration had been broken, but she stroked Rosamund's deathly white cheek.

"Fetch some hartshorn and water, man!" She threw the instruction over her shoulder in the direction of where she'd last seen the jailer.

Maggie cackled. "'Arts'orn and water. And would m'lady like 'er smellin' salts, then? Or a burned feather, per'aps?"

Juliana was on her feet in one bound. She turned on the grinning woman, her eyes spitting rage, her bloody hands raised. Maggie took a step backward as the flaming-haired Fury advanced on her.

"Juliana! Don't make matters worse than they are."

She whirled toward the door as the quiet voice crashed through her crimson rage. His voice was quiet but his eyes were hot as lava, and there was a white shade around his taut mouth, a muscle twitching in his cheek. Juliana saw only anger—no indication of his agonies of the last hour, not a hint of the glorious rush of relief as he saw her unbroken and not seriously harmed.

"What are *you* doing here?" She couldn't believe the petulant words even as they emerged from her lips. She wanted to rush to his arms, to be folded in the power of his body, secure in the knowledge of his protection. She wanted to be soothed and cuddled, to hear the soft words of love on his lips. She'd chosen to believe that if he came for her, it would be because it suited his purposes, not because he wished to. But as he stood there, such fearsome rage in every taut muscle, she felt a deeper disappointment than she'd ever known.

Her eyes flew to Quentin standing behind the duke, his expression a rictus of horror. Quentin would understand what had brought her to this. He would see, where his brother didn't, her weakness and her unimaginable relief that the ordeal was over.

"I might ask the same of you," the duke replied, coming toward her.

He took her hands, his own warm and strong, and turned them over. His rage knew no bounds at what he saw, and it was all he could do to keep himself from cradling the torn, bruised flesh, soothing the hurts with the balm of his kisses. But this was not the time. She was safe, and he had to get her out of this filthy place of terror before he did anything else.

"Come," he said, his voice curt with anxiety. He turned to the door.

Juliana snatched her hands from his grasp, their pain as nothing compared to the surge of angry disbelief. Did he really expect her to walk out with him, abandoning her friends?

"I'll not leave here without Lilly and Rosamund." She picked up her mallet again. "They're here because of me. They have no more business being here than I do. Those spawn of a gutter bitch betrayed us, and I'll not leave my friends in this hell. I neither need nor want your intervention." She raised the mallet with both bloody hands and brought it down again, fighting with every muscle the screaming agony of her torn flesh.

Tarquin swung back to her with an incredulous *"What?"* Quentin suppressed a smile at the sight of his unflappable brother so completely confounded.

Juliana ignored the question, and Tarquin, frowning fiercely, looked at the pathetic, crumpled body of the girl on the floor, the white-faced desperation of the other girl, and he suddenly felt ashamed.

It was not an emotion to which he was accustomed. Impatiently, he snatched the mallet from Juliana, throwing it to the floor. "Quentin, take her out of here while I arrange about the others." He seized her in his arms and spun her across to his brother, who caught her against him.

"I'm not leaving without them!" Juliana's protest was muffled against Quentin's black waistcoat.

"Juliana, for once in your short life do as you're bid," Tarquin declared dangerously.

"Come," Quentin murmured. "Tarquin will negotiate their release."

Juliana looked from one brother to the other and saw only truth and confidence in their eyes. "Rosamund will need to be carried," she said matter-of-factly. "We must find a litter for her."

"You may leave that with me. Now, get out of this foul air. There's no knowing what infection lurks in it. . . . Bloggs, a word with you." He jerked his head at the keeper, whose eyes now glittered. Unless he'd misunderstood, he was about to receive a substantial bribe. He oiled his way over to the duke, who'd withdrawn to the far corner of the ward.

Juliana allowed Quentin to draw her away. When they reached the sunshine of the courtyard, she took the air in great gulps. "Did you know such places existed, Quentin?"

"Yes," he said shortly. "But I'd never been inside one before." The horror of what he'd seen still lingered in his eyes. He drew her toward the postern gate, anxious to leave the last vestiges of this hell behind.

"I won't be defeated," she said with low-voiced determination, stepping out into the street beside him. "I won't let those evil women get the better of me."

"In God's name, Juliana! You can't possibly take on the world of vice all on your own." He took the horses from the relieved guard, handing him another coin.

"I won't do it alone," she said fiercely. "People like you will help me. People like you with the power to challenge the exploitation and the misery. Then things would change."

Touched by her fervency, Quentin was unwilling to spoil her dreams with his own cynicism.

"Here's Tarquin," he said with relief. The duke, carrying Rosamund in his arms, Lilly a pace or two behind, appeared at the gate, Jeremiah Bloggs at his side, a beatific smile on his face as he counted again the wad of notes that had bought the women's release. The duke hadn't even haggled over the terms, just peeled off the bills with an expression of disgust and contempt that ran off the keeper like water on a greased hide.

Juliana hurried over to them. "We must get Rosamund to the physician . . . but no, Henny will be able to look after her as well as any physician. They can't go back to the

Dennisons' until we discover whether Mistress Dennison had anything to do with the plot."

Once again Juliana was turning his house into a rescue mission and convalescent home for ill-used strumpets. Tarquin surprised himself with a wry grin. He lifted Rosamund into the phaeton and refrained from comment. He had one interest, and only one. He intended to have Juliana stripped, scrubbed, and in bed without a moment's delay.

Quentin climbed up and took Rosamund on his lap, cradling her tightly. Lilly, silent, white-faced, and shivering violently in the aftermath of this sudden escape from hell, took her seat beside him.

"There's not enough room for me," Juliana said. "I'll take a hackney. . . . Oh, but I don't have any money. My lord duke, could you . . . ?"

"No, I could not!" he snapped. "If you think I'm going to let you out of my sight again, you are vastly mistaken, my child." He half lifted her onto the step, put a hand under her backside with his customary familiarity, and shoved her upward. "You'll have to squash up."

"I would, but the hoop's in the way." Juliana struggled to sit down on the inch of bench available between Lilly and the driver's seat.

"Then take it off."

"Here?" She looked askance at the open street.

"Yes, here," he affirmed flatly. "Get down again." He reached up and pulled her to the ground. "Turn around and lift up your skirts."

After an instant's hesitation Juliana obeyed with a shrug. After everything else that had happened, being divested of her hoop before the gaze of curious passersby seemed little more than a minor inconvenience. She noticed, however, that Quentin discreetly averted his eyes when she raised her skirts, revealing the frothy if now grimy folds of her underpetticoat.

Tarquin deftly untied the tapes at her waist and freed the

whalebone panniers. He tossed them from him into the side of the street and once again boosted Juliana into the phaeton, climbing up beside her.

She gathered the soft folds of her gown and petticoats about her and made herself as small as possible. Tarquin's thigh pressed hard against hers as he occupied the remaining space on the bench and gave his horses the office to start. Juliana touched Lilly's hand, as much for her own comfort as to offer it. Lilly gave her a wan smile, and they both looked at Rosamund, held tightly in Lord Quentin's arms. Her eyes were open, staring sightlessly up at the sky from her deathly pale countenance. She appeared to be in a state of shock, immobile and unaware of her surroundings.

Rosamund was not cut out for the hand life had dealt her, Juliana thought. Lilly could manage to live it without loss of self. Indeed, she often enjoyed it. Most of the girls on Russell Street could take pleasure in their lot. They found plenty to laugh about; they shared a close camaraderie. They were not in want, and there was always the possibility of a grand and secure future if luck looked in their direction. But there was also the possibility of a Bridewell. Of a Marshalsea. Of spreading their legs beneath the bulks at Covent Garden for half a loaf of bread. But they chose not to brood about the consequences of ill luck, and who could blame them?

Grimly, Juliana acknowledged that alone she couldn't work miracles. She glanced sideways at the duke's unyielding countenance. He would make a powerful advocate if he could be persuaded to wield his influence. But that was a forlorn hope.

Unless . . . Her bruised hand touched her belly. Soon she must tell Tarquin of the child she carried. Presumably he'd be delighted. Maybe he'd be so delighted that he'd be open to suggestion. Willing to exert himself in someone else's interests for once. But then again, maybe he'd simply become even more protective of her, even more anxious that she should not be sullied by contact with Covent Garden life. Maybe he'd just keep her even more closely confined, to protect his unborn child. She and that child were his investment, after all. And he was a man who looked after his investments.

Chapter 26

George Ridge stepped out of the sedan chair, wincing as the skin on his back creased with the movement. He glowered up at the cracked stone facade of Viscount Edgecombe's town house on Mount Street. The building had a seedy, run-down air, the brass on the door unpolished, the windows dingy, the paintwork scuffed. Despite the early hour a small group of men, whom George immediately recognized from both dress and manner as bailiffs, were gathered lounging against the iron railings at the bottom of the steps leading to the front door. As George approached the steps, their air of weary waiting dissipated, and they straightened, eyes suddenly alert.

"Ye 'ave business with 'Is Lordship, sir?" one of them inquired, picking his teeth with a dirty fingernail.

"What's it to you?" George pushed past him, scowling.

"Jest that if Yer 'Onor's goin' to get that door open, y'are a sight cleverer than we are," the man said scornfully. " 'Oled up in there, tighter than a chicken's arse."

George ignored him and hammered on the knocker. There was no response. He stepped back, looking up at the unyielding facade, and glimpsed a face in an upstairs window, peering through the grime. He hammered again and this time, after a few minutes, heard the scraping of bolts.

His companions heard it too and surged up the steps. The door opened a crack. A disembodied hand grabbed George's sleeve and dragged him through the aperture. The door crashed shut on a bailiff's foot. There was a roar of outrage from outside, then violent banging on the knocker, setting a dusty porcelain figurine on a table shivering on its pedestal.

"Viscount's upstairs." The body belonging to the hand was skinny, the narrow face weasellike, with a pair of very long incisors that jutted beyond the thin lips. The man jerked his head toward the stairs. "First door on the left." Then he slithered away into the shadows beyond the staircase.

George, his scowl deepening, stomped up the stairs, which were thick with dust. His eyes were red with drink and burned with a rage so fearsome it was almost inhuman. George Ridge was a goaded bull, only one thought and one aim in view. Vengeance on the man who had ordered him thrashed like a serf. A vengeance he would obtain through Juliana. The Duke of Redmayne had made it painfully clear that Juliana's health, reputation, and general well-being were vitally important to him. Juliana would burn at the stake in Winchester marketplace. And before she did, her stepson would possess her . . . would bring her arrogant contempt to the dust. He would see her humbled, he would see her protector powerless to protect. And with her conviction he would regain his own inheritance.

He pushed open the door at the left of the staircase. It creaked on unoiled hinges, revealing a sparsely furnished apartment, its air of neglect failing to mask its handsome proportions and the elaborate moldings on the ceiling.

Lucien was slumped in a sagging elbow chair by a grate filled with last winter's ashes. A cognac bottle was at his feet, another, empty, lying on the threadbare carpet. A glass dangled from his fingers.

He jerked upright as George entered. "Dick, you bastard, I told you I . . . oh." He surveyed his visitor with

an air of sardonic inquiry. "To what do I owe this pleasure?"

"You're going to help me," George stated. He bent to
pick up the cognac bottle, raised it to his lips, and drank
deeply.

Lucien's eyes sharpened. Something very interesting had
occurred. Sir George had lost his air of bumbling, overawed
ineptitude.

"Help yourself, dear boy," Lucien invited, his languid
tone belied by the arrested look in his eyes. "There's more
where that came from. At least I trust there is."

"Thankee." George drank again, his throat working as
the fiery liquid burned down his gullet to add fuel to the
fire that raged in his belly.

"So how can I be of assistance?" Lucien took back the
bottle and tilted it to his own mouth. "Damnation, it's
empty! Ring the bell for Dick, dear fellow." He gestured
to the frayed bell rope beside the door.

George pulled on it, half expecting it to come away in
his hand, but faintly, from the bowels of the silent house,
came the jangle of the bell.

"I am going to take Juliana," he said, pacing the room,
each movement generating a painful stab, reminding him
with hideous clarity of his humiliation at the hands of the
duke's groom. "And this time I'll not be stopped."

"Oh?" Lucien sat up, the gleam of malevolent curiosity
in his eye intensifying.

"I intend to abduct her tomorrow," George said, almost
in a monotone, as if he were reciting a well-learned lesson.
"I will have a closed carriage ready, and we'll take her
immediately to Winchester. The Forsetts will be compelled
to identify her if the magistrates demand it. And there are
plenty of other folk in the neighborhood who'll recognize
her. She won't have that *devil* to run to, and once she's
locked up in Winchester jail, there'll be nothing he can do
to save her."

Lucien tugged his right earlobe. "Something happen to

rouse you, dear boy . . . Ah, Dick. Bring up another bottle of that gut-rotting brandy."

"Not sure there is any," the surly manservant muttered.

"Then go and buy some!"

"Wi' what, m'lord?" he demanded with a mock bow.

"Here." George dug a note from his pocket and handed it to him.

"Ah, good man!" Lucien approved. "Get going, then, you lazy varlet. I'm dry as a witch's tit."

Dick sniffed, pocketed the note, and disappeared.

"Impudent bugger," Lucien observed. "Only stays around because I haven't paid him in six months and he knows if he leaves before I'm dead, he won't see a penny. So," he continued with another sharp glance, "why the urgency about this abduction?"

George was not about to reveal to his malicious partner what the duke had done to him. He shrugged, controlled a wince, and said, "I've an estate to get back to. I can't hang around here much longer. But I need your help."

Lucien nodded. "And what incentive are you offering, dear boy?"

George looked startled. He'd assumed that Lucien's own desire for vengeance would be sufficient incentive. "You'll have her in your hands," he said. "You can have her first . . . for as long as you like."

He was astounded at the look of repulsion that crossed the viscount's expression.

"I want to be rid of her, man. Not *have* her," Lucien pointed out disgustedly. "I thought you understood that. You lay charges against her. I can repudiate her. Tarquin is helpless and mortified. The girl is destroyed. But I ask again, what incentives are you offering for my assistance?" His eyes narrowed.

George's puzzlement deepened. "Isn't that enough?"

Lucien chortled merrily. "Good God, no, man. I'll have a thousand guineas off you. I think that would be a reasonable remuneration. Depending, of course, on what you have in mind." He leaned back, crossing his legs with a casual grin.

George struggled with himself for barely a moment. He could lay hands on a thousand guineas, although it went against the grain to throw it down before this loathsome, grinning reptile. But he needed the viscount's help.

"I need you to help me get her out of the house," he said. "We have to go in there and winkle her out."

"Good God!" Lucien stared at him, for the first time startled out of his indolent and cynical amusement. "And just how do you propose doing that?"

"At dead of night. We go into her room. We overpower her while she's sleeping and we carry her out of there." George spoke with the flat, assertive confidence of a committed man. "You'll know where her room is. And you'll know how to get undetected into the house."

"What makes you think I can perform such miracles?" Lucien inquired with a lifted eyebrow.

"I know you can," George responded stubbornly. "You lived in the house. You probably have a key."

Lucien resumed the gentle tugging of his earlobe. He *did* have a key to the side door, as it happened. He'd had one copied several years earlier when he'd still been a lad. Tarquin had been an exasperatingly strict and watchful guardian, and Lucien had had frequent resort to subterfuge to evade both the duke's rules and his guard.

"Perhaps I do," he conceded after a minute. "Getting in might not be too difficult, but getting out again, with that red-haired virago screeching and fighting, is a different matter."

"She won't make any noise," George asserted in the same tone.

"Oh?" Lucien inclined his head inquiringly.

"I'll make sure of it."

Lucien examined his expression for a minute, then slowly nodded. "I believe you will. I almost feel sorry for my lady wife. I wonder what could have happened to arouse such vicious urgency in your breast, dear fellow."

He waited, but no explanation was forthcoming. Ridge's reticence increased his curiosity a hundredfold, but he was prepared to bide his time. "There's one other small difficulty," he continued in a musing tone. "My estimable cousin has the chamber next door to our quarry. I daresay he finds the proximity convenient."

"You know for a fact that Juliana is his mistress?" George's voice was thick. He knew it, but he wanted it confirmed.

"Why else would my cousin take such an interest in the wench?" Lucien shrugged. "I've never known him to take a woman under his roof before, either. I suspect he'll be most disconcerted to lose her." He grinned. "I think I can contrive to lure my cousin from the house tomorrow. It would be best if he was elsewhere while we're abducting his doxy. . . . Ah, at last . . . Dick with the cup that cheers. We will drink a toast to this enterprise. Set it down there, man. No need to pour it. I've strength enough for that."

George took the smudged glass handed to him by his host. He drank, his eyes for the moment turned inward on his vengeance. He was a man in the grip of madness. The Duke of Redmayne had unleashed demons when he'd set out to subdue Sir George Ridge.

The duke reined in his horses outside the house on Albermarle Street. Ted appeared as if by a wizard's conjuring, running down the steps lightly for such a big man. He'd heard the coachman's story, as had the rest of the household, and now glared at Juliana, as if personally insulted by her grim adventure.

"Take the horses, Ted." Tarquin sprang down, reaching up a hand to assist Juliana, then Lilly. He took Rosamund from Quentin so that his brother could alight unencumbered, then handed the still-limp figure back to Quentin and strode ahead of the party into the house.

"Catlett, summon the housekeeper and have these two

young women escorted to a bedchamber. Send a maid to attend them. And ask Henny to come to Lady Edgecombe's apartment immediately."

"Oh, no!" Juliana exclaimed. "No . . . I have no need of Henny. She must look to Rosamund. Truly I can look after myself, but Rosamund has need of expert care."

He took her hands, turning them palm up. "You can do nothing for yourself with your hands in this condition. If you won't have Henny, then *I* will attend to you."

"There's no need for you to trouble yourself, sir." Her voice was stiff. "I have no need of a nurse."

Impatience flared in his eyes. He drew a sharp breath and said, "You will have either Henny or myself to attend to you. Take your pick."

"You, then," she replied dully, seeing no option. Rosamund needed all Henny's skills.

"Very well." He nodded briefly, then turned back to Catlett. "I want a bath, hot water, salve, bandages, and lye soap taken up to Lady Edgecombe's apartment immediately. . . . Quentin, you'll see the other two installed?"

"Of course."

"Come, Juliana." The duke took her wrist in a firm encircling grip and set foot on the stairs. Juliana followed him up willy-nilly.

Her bedchamber was filled with sunlight; the bowls of roses were replenished daily, and the air was heavy with their scent. The sight of the bed with its crisp, lavender-fragrant sheets, the downy invitation of the feather bed and plump pillows, drew her toward it as the nightmare images of Bridewell became smudged by the familiar comforts of home.

Home. This was home? It felt like home. Her own place. The duke's voice broke into her train of thought.

"Bed will have to wait, Juliana. There's no knowing what you might have picked up in that filthy hole. Vermin, infection . . ."

"Vermin?" Her hands flew to her tangled hair, her eyes widening in disgust. That was why he'd ordered lye.

"Stand still. I don't want to touch your clothes any more than I must, so I'm going to cut them off you." He went to the dresser for the pair of scissors Henny kept to make minor repairs or adjustments to Juliana's wardrobe.

Juliana stood rigid, shuddering with disgust. She remembered the woman Maggie touching her dress, tearing Rosamund's fichu, her gnarled, filthy, bleeding hands sullying as they clawed and fondled. A wave of nausea rose violent and abrupt in her throat. With an inarticulate mutter she pushed Tarquin aside as he approached with the scissors, and dived for the commode.

Tarquin put down the scissors and went over to her. His hand was warm on her neck, soothing as he rubbed her back. Distantly he realized that if anyone had told him a few weeks ago that he wouldn't think twice about ministering to a vomiting woman, he'd have laughed. But that was before Juliana had swept into his life.

"I beg your pardon," she gasped as the spasms ceased. "I don't know what came over me." She envied Rosamund Henny's calm, attentive presence. Vomiting in front of a man, even one's lover—especially one's lover—was a wretched mortification, and she cringed at the thought of what he must be thinking. But his hand on her back just then had been ineffably comforting.

"There's no need for pardon," Tarquin said gently, dampening a washcloth with water from the ewer. He wiped her mouth and brow, attentively matter-of-fact, and when she searched his face, she could see no inkling of his earlier rage. There was a rather puzzled frown in his eyes, but his mouth was relaxed. He tossed aside the cloth, picked up the scissors, and swiftly cut the laces of her bodice.

She was naked in a very few minutes, his hands moving with deft efficiency, cutting away her petticoats, her chemise, slicing through her garters. She rolled down her stockings herself, tossing them onto the heap of discarded clothing. Then she stood, awkward and uncertain, wishing for Henny, not knowing where to put her hands, wanting absurdly to cover herself with her hands, as if she'd never shared glorious intimacies with this man; as if he hadn't touched and probed every inch of her skin, every orifice of her body; as if his tongue hadn't tasted her essence; as if his hard, pursuing flesh hadn't taken and possessed her fragility; as if she hadn't, in yielding the ultimate secrets of her body, possessed his.

His gaze was not in the least desirous; in fact, he seemed to be going out of his way to be matter-of-fact about the whole business. But that made things all the more confusing. How she wanted Henny. A woman; a nursemaid. Someone whose attentions would be straightforward and uncomplicated, and she could receive them in the same way.

A bang at the door yanked her out of her reverie. She looked in panic at Tarquin, who merely handed her a wrapper and gestured toward the shadows of the bed curtains at the head of the bed. Juliana retreated, drawing the folds of the muslin wrapper tightly around her, listening as two footmen labored with a porcelain hip bath, copper jugs of steaming water; a maid followed with bandages, salve, the pungent lye soap, a heap of thick towels.

No one spoke. No one glanced toward Juliana's retreat. The duke remained perched on the windowsill, arms folded, watching the preparations. Then the entourage withdrew, the door was closed. Juliana stepped forward.

"I'll bandage your hands first." He poured hot water into the basin on the dresser.

"How can I wash myself with bandaged hands?" Juliana objected.

"You aren't going to, *mignonne*. I am doing the washing." A flickering smile played over his mouth, reminding her vividly of the last time they'd made love, when he'd looked down at her, looked into her very soul, with so much wonder and warmth. Where had his anger gone? Juliana was plunged anew into the chaos of bewilderment. What *was* he feeling?

He gestured to the dresser stool. "Sit down and give me

your hands." As deft and gentle as an expert nurse, he bathed the raw strips of flesh, smoothed on salve, then wrapped around bandages, tearing the material at the ends to make a knot. He was as surprised as Juliana at this new-found skill, and his smile deepened with an unlooked for pleasure and satisfaction.

Juliana nibbled her bottom lip. "Were you concerned for me when you heard where I was?" The question was tenta-tive, and it was only as she asked it that she realized she hadn't intended to.

"Sit in the tub," he responded. "Keep your hands well clear of the water."

"But were you?" she persisted, one foot raised to step into the hip bath. Suddenly the question was more impor-tant than any she'd ever asked.

"I wouldn't leave my worst enemy in such a place," he said flippantly. "Are you going to sit down of your own accord?"

Juliana hastily slipped into the water. It was not a satis-factory answer. She stared down at the water.

Tarquin caught her chin, bringing her face up. "I have never been more concerned in my life," he stated flatly, both expression and tone now devoid of flippancy. "You frightened the living daylights out of me, Juliana. And if you ever scare me like that again, I can safely promise that you will rue the day you were born."

Releasing her chin, he poured hot water over her hair. Juliana snuffled, impatiently pushing aside the drenched mass of curls so she could see his face again. That same luminous glow was in his eyes despite the conviction of his threat. And for some reason she found the threat as pleasing as the glow. Satisfied, she bent her head beneath his strong fingers.

Juliana grimaced at the smell of the lye as he rubbed it vigorously into her tangled hair. It reminded her of sheep dip. It was even worse when he scrubbed her body with the washcloth, leaving not an inch of skin untouched. He was not rough, but very thorough, and when he soaped her breasts, she had to force herself not to flinch at their new tenderness.

Tarquin noticed the almost imperceptible wince. He wondered how long it would be before she told him of her pregnancy. Presumably it didn't occur to her that he might have guessed for himself. There was something touchingly naive about the idea that she didn't realize he was as attuned to her bodily cycles as she was. He smiled to himself but gave no indication of his thoughts; she would tell him in her own good time.

"I think you're clean," he announced finally. "No vermin that I could find. It's to be hoped you weren't in there long enough to catch an infection either. Step out." He picked up a large towel.

Juliana stood still while he dried her as gently as if she were a china doll, attending to the most intimate parts of her body with a careful thoroughness that again was deliberately matter-of-fact. Finally he dropped her nightgown over her head.

"Now you may get into bed and tell me precisely what flight of fancy led to this latest debacle."

"Flight of fancy! Is that what you call it?" Juliana, fatigue and confusion momentarily forgotten, glared, her damp hair flying about her face. "I try to help those women see a way to gain some power over their lives, and you call it a flight of fancy!" The contempt in her eyes scorched him. "There's a world of slaves out there . . . slaves whose bodies you enjoy, of course, so it's in your interests to keep them enslaved."

She turned aside with a little gesture of defeat and climbed into bed. "You have no compassion, no soul, my lord duke. Just like the rest of your breed. If you would speak out . . . you and Lord Quentin, and others like you . . . then people would listen. If you insisted on fair treatment for the women whose bodies you use, then it would happen." She dragged the covers over her and thumped onto her side, facing away from him.

Tarquin stared at the curve of her body beneath the coverlet. Absently, he raked a hand through his hair in an uncharacteristic gesture of bewilderment. No one had ever spoken to him, looked at him, with such furious derision before. And instead of reacting with anger, he felt only dismay. A seventeen-year-old chit accused him of utter callousness in his way of life, his view of the world, and he was standing there wondering if she was right.

She was driving him to the edge of madness. When she wasn't terrifying him with her crusading adventures, she was unraveling every neat thread in the tapestry of his life, forcing him to look and see things that had never troubled him before. More than a few of those revelations concerned himself, and they were not comfortable.

He took a step toward the bed, then, with a bewildered shake of his head, left the chamber, softly closing the door behind him.

As the door closed, Juliana rolled onto her back. She gazed up at the flowered tester, her eyes fixed unseeing on a strand of ivy. She closed her lids on the tears that spilled over, telling herself she was crying only because she was fatigued. Because of reaction to what she'd endured.

Chapter 27

"Mercy me, but I don't know what the world's coming to when you young things can get yourselves into this state." Henny shook her head as she untied the bandages on Juliana's ruined hands the following morning.

"How is Rosamund?" Juliana was feeling limp, filled with a deep and most unusual languor. She'd slept all day and all night and now couldn't seem to drag herself fully awake. Rain drummed against the windowpane, and her chamber was candlelit, which didn't help matters.

"She'll do. Had a nasty shock, but she's recoverin' nicely. That Mistress Dennison came and took them both home."

"Already?" Juliana winced as a strand of bandage stuck to an open cut. "Why didn't someone tell me?"

"You were sleeping, and His Grace gave order that you weren't to be disturbed until you rang." Henny dipped a cloth into a bowl of warm water. "When y'are dressed, he'd like to see you in the library. If you feel up to it, that is." She bathed Juliana's palms and patted them dry before applying fresh salve.

Juliana closed her heavy eyes, wondering if she could have unknowingly swallowed a sleeping draft. She could remember nothing after Tarquin had left her in yesterday's morning sunshine. Who had informed Mistress Dennison that Lilly and Rosamund were here? Did she bear them a grudge? It would seem not, if they were received back into the fold so quickly. Tarquin would have the answers.

Depression slopped over her as she remembered how he'd left her in anger, without saying a word to her bitter accusations. She'd most effectively doused whatever warmth he'd been feeling toward her. She didn't regret what she'd said, she'd meant every word of it, but now it seemed mean-spirited to have attacked him on the heels of his ministrations.

"I think ye'd be best off back in bed, dearie," Henny clucked, deftly retying the bandages. "I'll let His Grace know that y'are not ready to go downstairs."

"No . . . no, of course I am." Juliana forced her eyes open. She couldn't avoid seeing him for long, and, besides, she wanted answers to her questions. "I'll wash my face and drink some coffee, and then I'll be wide-awake. It's because it's raining and so close in here."

Henny tutted but made no further demur, and half an hour later Juliana surveyed herself dispiritedly in the cheval glass. Her hair was particularly unruly this morning, startlingly vivid against her face, which was even paler than usual. Her eyes seemed very large, dark shadows beneath them that she decided gave her a rather interesting look. Mysterious and haunted. The whimsical notion made her feel slightly more cheerful. Anyone less mysterious and haunted than her own ungainly, big-footed, clumsy self would be hard to find. But the pale-lavender muslin and her white-bandaged hands did give her a more delicate air than usual.

"Off you go, then. But don't stay down too long. You'll need to rest before dinner."

"You're so kind to me," Juliana said. "No one ever took care of me before or worried about me." Impulsively, she gave Henny a kiss that made the woman smile with pleasure as she shooed her away with a "Get along with you, now, m'lady."

Juliana didn't at first see Tarquin's visitor as she entered the library, her questions tumbling from her lips even before she was through the door. "Was Mistress Dennison angry with Lilly and Rosamund, sir? How did she know they were here? Are you sure she won't be unkind to them?"

"No. I told her. Yes," Tarquin replied, rising from his chair. "Take a deep breath, *mignonne*, and make your curtsy to Mr. Bonnell Thornton."

Juliana took a deep breath. To her amazement she saw that the duke was smiling, and the same warm light was still in his eyes. There was no sign of the chill she'd been expecting.

"Juliana?" he prompted, gesturing to his companion, when she didn't immediately move forward.

"I beg your pardon, sir. I didn't see you at first." Juliana recollected herself and curtsied to the tall, lean gentleman in an astonishing pink satin suit.

"I am delighted to make your acquaintance, ma'am." The gentleman bowed. "His Grace has told me all about your misadventures and their cause."

Juliana looked inquiringly toward Tarquin, unsure how to take this. He handed her a broadsheet. "Read this, and you may begin to understand that you're not the only champion of the cause, Juliana."

She had not come across the *Drury Lane Journal* before. Its subtitle, *Have at Ye* became clear as soon as she began to read. It was a scurrilous, gossipy journal, full of innuendo and supposedly truthful accounts of scandalous exploits among the members of London's fashionable and political world. It was also wickedly amusing. But Juliana was puzzled as to what Tarquin had meant. She skimmed through reviews and critiques of plays and operas and then looked up. "It's very amusing, sir, but I don't see . . . ."

"In the center you'll find an article by one Roxanna Termagant," Mr. Thornton pointed out.

She went back and found the column. Her lips parted on a soundless O. Miss Termagant had given a precise descrip-

tion of the so-called riot at Cocksedge's, directly accusing
both Mitchell and Cocksedge of orchestrating the riot and
the subsequent raid in order to achieve the arrest of four
women—one of whom was no whore but the wife of a
viscount. The account was followed by an impassioned cas-
tigation of the authorities, who'd allowed themselves to
serve the devious purposes of the bawds and had imprisoned innocent women who'd merely been gathering for a
peaceful discussion on how to improve their working and
living conditions.

"Who is this lady?"

Mr. Thornton bowed with a flourish. "You see her before you, ma'am." He grinned mischievously.

Maybe it explained the pink satin. However, she was still
confused. "My lord duke told you all of this?"

"It's not an unusual story, my lady. Any attempt by the
women to demand basic rights of their so-called employers
is always defeated. However"—he took the paper from her,
tapping it against the palm of his hand—"we can make life
uncomfortable for them with public ridicule and public
outrage. Unfortunately, it's difficult for me to find out
about all the horrors that go on. I didn't know about the
case of Miss Lucy Tibbet, for instance. So I have a proposition for you, Lady Edgecombe."

Juliana perched on the arm of the sofa. She glanced at
Tarquin, who was leaning back in his chair, his fingers
steepled against his mouth, his eyes resting on her face.
"Not all members of our society close our eyes to injustice,
mignonne. Mr. Thornton has a powerful voice in Covent
Garden. I believe his methods are more effective than inciting harlots to rebellion and landing yourself in Bridewell."

"So you . . . you want to help too?" she asked with a
doubtful frown. It seemed impossible to believe, but what
else could he mean?

"Let's just say you've opened my eyes," he said wryly.

Juliana was so taken aback, she wasn't aware for a moment that Mr. Thornton had begun to talk again. He
coughed pointedly to attract her attention and continued.

"As I was saying, Lady Edgecombe, I understand you have friends in the Garden. Women who are in a position to know what goes on. If you can encourage them to confide in you, then I will have the material to make war."

"Act as a spy, you mean?"

"An informant," Tarquin said.

"I will also hold whatever funds you're able to collect," Mr. Thornton went on, "and take responsibility for disbursing them to those women in need. Their employers may quarrel with my apparent philanthropy, but they'll have no excuse to be avenged upon the women, so no one need fear reprisals." Mr. Thornton nodded his head decisively.

"I prefer to be *doing* things," Juliana said. "Just telling tales seems a little pathetic."

"But when you *do* things, Juliana, you fall head over heels into trouble," the duke pointed out. Bonnell Thornton chuckled, and Juliana flushed but didn't attempt to deny the truth.

"Your fault, *mignonne,* lies in overestimating your abilities to change the world," continued Tarquin. "You can't do it without assistance."

"That's what I said yesterday."

"And as you see, I took it to heart."

"Yes," she agreed slowly. It was still hard to believe her words could have had such an effect. She turned back to Bonnell Thornton. "Well, if you think this will work, Mr. Thornton, then of course I'll help however I can."

"Good. You will see that we can make a difference little by little. . . . Well, I'll take my leave now. Your Grace . . ." He bowed to the duke, who rose politely and escorted him to the door. Juliana curtsied as the visitor took her bandaged hand gently and lightly kissed her fingertips. "Good day, Lady Edgecombe. I look forward to our association."

Tarquin closed the door after him, then turned back to Juliana. "I know you think it poor work, my dear, but believe me, it's the best you can do."

Juliana was not too sure about that. She could think of many ways in which she could become more actively involved in Mr. Bonnell Thornton's activities. But it would not be politic to mention them at this point. "I can't do Mr. Thornton's work without visiting my friends," she pointed out.

"No," he agreed, strolling to the sideboard to pour himself a glass of sherry. "But you won't forget to take Ted with you, will you?"

Juliana shook her head. "Why have you changed your mind?"

He set down the decanter and came across to her. Cupping her face between his hands, he brushed her eyelids with his lips. "You work the strangest magic, *mignonne*. I believe if you put your mind to it, you could melt a heart of marble." He ran his thumb over her mouth, his smile rueful. "I can't say I enjoy being the target of your reforming zeal." He kissed her as she was still searching for a response. "Go back upstairs now. You look exhausted."

She was suddenly feeling both queasy and overwhelmingly sleepy. Her brain couldn't get around his words. Were they really a declaration of some kind? A promise of some kind? She tried to find a response, but there was something in his eyes that told her he didn't want her to say anything. His hands on her shoulders were turning her toward the door. "Go to Henny, Juliana." And she went without a word.

She lay back on the chaise longue beneath the bedroom window while Henny took off her shoes and unlaced her bodice. Her hand drifted to her belly. This child would know only a guardian and an uncle. He would never know a father. All the loving tenderness in the world couldn't soften that fact. And once Tarquin knew she was carrying his child, it would no longer be exclusively hers, even in her womb. How long could she keep it to herself?

•   •   •

"Henny says Juliana can't seem to wake up today." Quentin sounded worried as he stood before the library fire, lit against the damp chill of the rainy day. "Could she have suffered more than we saw?"

"I don't believe so." Tarquin sipped his port. "I believe there's something else behind it."

"What?" Quentin reached for his own glass on the mantel.

Tarquin yawned. "It's for Juliana to say. I daresay she'll tell me in her own good time." He stretched his legs to the fire. "There are times when an evening at home is most delightful."

"Particularly listening to that." Quentin gestured to the window where the rain drummed monotonously. "It's a foul night to be abroad."

"Yes, and the thought that my troublesome *mignonne* is tucked up safely in her bed is very comforting." Tarquin yawned again.

Quentin looked into his glass. "Will you hide this liaison from Lydia when she's your wife?" His voice was stiff, his eyes strained.

Tarquin looked up, the sleepy indolence vanishing from his eyes. "What do you mean, Quentin?"

"What do you think I mean?" Quentin jumped to his feet. The agony of his frustration was suddenly no longer bearable. "You will have both Juliana and Lydia under your roof. Will you conceal your true relationship with Juliana from Lydia?"

Tarquin stared at him in astonishment. Quentin's face was pale, his lips bloodless.

"I cannot endure it, Tarquin! I cannot endure that you would treat Lydia in such fashion. I *love* her, God help me. And I will not stand by and watch you ruin both our lives." His hands twisted themselves into impossible knots, his gray eyes burning holes in his white face.

"You . . . you and Lydia!" Tarquin stuttered. "You and Lydia?"

"Yes."

"Lydia . . . Lydia knows how you feel?" He still couldn't seem to grasp this.

"Yes."

"And . . . and does she return your feelings?"

Quentin nodded.

"Dear God!" Tarquin ran a hand through his hair. "You and Lydia love each other? I know you've always had a special regard for her, but . . ."

"Sometimes, Tarquin, you are so damned blind you can't see the nose on your face!" Quentin declared, feeling suddenly purged, as if a great load had been taken from him. "It took Juliana five minutes to see—"

"Juliana!" Now he remembered her hints. "Jesus, Mary, and Joseph," he muttered.

"I will not stand by and see you insult Lydia by keeping your mistress under the same roof," Quentin reiterated, his voice now strong.

Tarquin said nothing, merely stared into the fire. He was realizing that he couldn't imagine insulting Juliana in such fashion either. What in the devil's name was happening to him?

"Do you hear me, Tarquin?"

He looked up and shook his head with a half laugh of disbelieving resignation. "Oh, yes, I hear you, brother. As clearly as I hear myself."

Quentin waited for more, but his brother turned back to the fire, twisting his port glass between his fingers. It was as if he'd put up a wall around himself. The silence lengthened and finally Quentin left the room, closing the door softly behind him. Nothing had been resolved, but he'd made his statement. The truth was in the open, and instead of feeling bad about it, he felt only an overpowering relief.

Tarquin remained immobile for a long time. Eventually he rose and refilled his port glass. His eye fell on the miniature of Lydia Melton on the mantel. Grave, composed, dignified. The perfect wife for a bishop.

Suddenly he laughed aloud. How very simple it all was if one looked at the world through Juliana's eyes.

He was still chuckling to himself when there was a knock at the door and Catlett entered with a note on a silver salver. "I beg your pardon, Your Grace, but a messenger has just brought this. He says it's of the utmost urgency."

Tarquin frowned, taking the wafer-sealed paper. He read the ill-penned, ill-spelled contents, his expression darkening. "Damn that degenerate, profligate fool!" He scrunched the note and hurled it into the fire. "Have my carriage brought around."

"You're going out, Your Grace?" Catlett's eyes darted to the rain-blackened window.

"You may assume so from my order," the duke said acidly. "Tell my man to bring my cloak and cane."

Damn Lucien! Lying sick unto death in a sponging house. The note had come from the owner of the house, presumably at Lucien's urging. A debt of five hundred pounds to be cleared to obtain his release. Until then he was lying in the cold and the damp, coughing his heart out, without medicines, food, or blankets.

Tarquin didn't question the situation. It was not the first time it had happened in the last five years. It didn't occur to him either to abandon Lucien to his fate, despite casting him from his door with such finality. He knew just as Lucien had known that in extremis Tarquin would always come to his aid. However vile and despicable Lucien had become, Tarquin couldn't free himself from the chains of responsibility.

He opened the strongbox in his book room and took out five hundred pounds. It was a minute part of Lucien's overall debt, so presumably he'd been caught by one of his minor creditors. A tailor or a hatter, probably.

His valet brought him a heavy caped cloak and his swordstick. Tarquin turned up the deep collar, thrust his hands into his gloves, and went out into the driving rain. The coachman shivered on his box.

"Ludgate Hill." Tarquin didn't glance at him as he gave the order and climbed into the coach.

The coachman cracked his whip. He was new to the duke's service and far too anxious to make a good impression to complain about turning out in the middle of such a foul night.

After the coach disappeared into the sheeting rain, George and Lucien emerged from the basement steps opposite. "Hell and the devil," grumbled Lucien, water pouring from the brim of his hat. "Why this night of all nights? It hasn't rained in a month."

George dived across the street, head down against the wall of water. He was unaware of the rain, the hot blood of vengeance warming him to his core. He was so close now. He darted around the side of the house into the alley that led to the mews and stopped, leaning against the wall, panting.

Lucien appeared beside him, a drenched wraith in comparison with his companion's bulk. "You'll owe me another five hundred for this," he said, coughing into his sleeve.

George merely gestured impatiently to the door set into the wall of the house. "Will the servants be up?"

"Not at this hour . . . unless Catlett's still roaming." Lucien hawked into the street. "The night watchman will be in his cubbyhole under the stairs, but we'll not be going anywhere near the front of the house."

"What of this Catlett?"

"He'll be in his pantry if he's not abed. I know the routine." Lucien fitted the key into the lock, and the door swung open without so much as a creak. "Well-maintained household we have here," he observed sardonically, stepping into a narrow foyer. "Now, keep your mouth shut and be light on your feet."

He opened another door, revealing a set of stairs set into the wall. It was pitch-dark, no candles in the sconces, but Lucien went up with the sure-footed tread of one who could find his way in the dark. George fumbled behind him, trying not to breathe, conscious of his rasping excitement, of a heaviness in his loins that hitherto he had associated only with carnal congress.

Lucien opened another door at the head of the stairs and peered around. The corridor was dimly lit with sconces at wide intervals along the wall. There was not a sound. He slipped into the corridor, George looming behind him, the man's shadow huge on the wall ahead.

The house was as quiet as the grave when they reached Juliana's door. Lucien stepped back, pressing himself against the wall. "She's in there. You find your own way out. I'll fetch a hackney and bring it to the street corner."

George nodded, his eyes glittering in the waxy, sweating face, his lips wet. He put a hand on the latch as Lucien flitted away to safety. The viscount had no desire to get any closer to this abduction.

George pushed the door, and it opened soundlessly. The room was in darkness, except for the faint glow of embers in the fireplace. The bed curtains were not drawn around the bed, and he had a clear view of the sleeping figure. For a minute he watched her. Watched the way the sheet lifted over her bosom with each even breath. The way her hair spread out in a rich pool against the white lawn of the pillow. He frowned at her bandaged hands, then shrugged. She wouldn't be needing them for what he had in mind.

He bent over her, his hands large, heavy, the fingers strong as any laborer's. Those fingers went around Juliana's throat and squeezed.

Her eyes shot open, filled with sleep and terror; her bandaged hands scrabbled at the fingers pressing her throat. She opened her mouth to scream, but not a sound came out. She was drowning, suffocating, and her befuddled brain didn't know whether this was real or nightmare. The face hanging over her, so intent, so closed in on its purpose, was familiar, and yet it wasn't. It was a mask . . . a mask of hideous menace . . . a mask from a nightmare. Surely only a nightmare. Please, dear God, only a nightmare. But she couldn't breathe. She struggled to wake up.

Her eyes were popping in their sockets. Her chest was col-
lapsing. A black wave rolled over her.

George released his hold as she sank limply into the pillows, her eyelids drooping over her terrorized eyes. The
marks of his fingers were shadows in the darkness on the
white of her throat. He placed his hand over her mouth.
She was still breathing, but light and shallow. He took a
thick scarf from his pocket and tied it around her mouth,
knotting it at the back of her head. Then he pulled back
the bedclothes and looked at her unconscious form, every
curve and hollow outlined beneath the thin lawn shift.

He dragged his eyes from her, conscious of the passing of
every minute, and opened the armoire. He pulled out a
thick cloak and rummaged through the dresser drawers,
finding a pair of silk stockings.

Bending over her, he bound her ankles together with
one stocking, pulled her arms in front of her, and tied her
wrists with the other; then he swaddled her still form in the
cloak, bringing the hood over her head. Her breathing was
still shallow, but it was regular. He maneuvered her over his
shoulder, took one last look around, then made for the
door. His excitement was such that it was difficult to move
slowly and cautiously along the deserted corridor. At any
moment he expected a door to open, to be accosted with a
shout of outrage. But he reached the door to the internal
staircase without mishap.

He slipped into the darkness, closing the door behind
him. The house was pitch-black and there was no Lucien
to guide him. He waited, his heart hammering, his hands
wet, until he was steady enough to step down the steep,
narrow flight, an arm encircling his burden. He could feel
the shape of her, could smell her hair and skin, could feel
her breath warm on his neck.

At the foot of the stairs he stepped into the narrow
lobby. The side door was slightly ajar, and his heart leaped.
He was a second away from success. He stepped through
the door and into the alley.

A shrill whistle made him jump. But it was Lucien,

beckoning from the end of the alley. George set off at a lumbering run, Juliana's head bumping against his back. A hackney stood in the street, Lucien already inside, shivering with cold and wet.

"Goddammit, but I'll get an ague with this night's work," he complained as George tipped Juliana off his shoulder onto the bench and clambered up after her. "So you got her." He examined his wife's unconscious body with an air of mild curiosity. "What did you do to her? She's not dead, is she?"

George loosened the cloak, tipped back the hood. Juliana's head fell back against the stained leather squabs. Lucien raised his eyebrows at the gag, then leaned over and lightly touched the bruises on her throat, observing casually, "Dear me, quite rough weren't you, dear boy?"

"I wasn't taking any chances," George replied, sitting beside Lucien, where he could see his victim as she lolled against the cushions with each jolt of the iron wheels over the cobbles. He smiled and stroked his chin.

Lucien's teeth chattered, and he fumbled for the flask of cognac in his pocket. With a shudder he put the neck to his mouth and tipped the contents down his throat. "Dear God, but I'm cold." He drank again, desperate to warm the icy void in his belly. His hands and feet were numb, his fingers blue-white, as if his blood had stopped flowing. He cursed again as his chest heaved and he was convulsed with a violent spasm of coughing.

George had never seen anyone cough with such violence. Lucien grabbed for a handkerchief and held it over his mouth. George saw the white cloth darken with blood. Instinctively, he moved a little away from him along the bench, fearing some contamination. He reached into his pocket for a small vial of smelling salts.

Lucien continued to cough, his hollow eyes bloodstreaked with the strain. But he watched through the paroxysms as his companion uncorked the vial, leaned forward, and pushed it beneath Juliana's nose.

"What d'you want to wake her for?" Lucien croaked.

"Wait until we get there, you fool. You don't want her making any trouble."

"She won't," George said sullenly, but he sat back again, replacing the vial in his pocket. He wanted to be there when she came to. He wanted to see her eyes open. He wanted to see her realize what had happened to her. He wanted to see her eyes fall upon him and know that she was powerless as she felt the bonds at her wrists and ankles, the gag in her mouth. But he would wait. He turned his head to look out at the black night, and he missed the moment when Juliana's eyes fluttered, opened, then closed again.

Her throat hurt. It was agony to swallow. She couldn't move. She couldn't open her mouth. The faint stinging tang of smelling salts was in her nose. She kept her eyes shut. What had happened? The memory of the terrifying nightmare flooded back. The hands at her throat. George's face, swollen and greasy and triumphant.

No nightmare.

She kept still, trying to work out why she couldn't move; her befuddled brain took what seemed an eternity to conclude that she was gagged and bound.

"We're coming up to the Bell now."

Lucien's voice. Dear God, she had both of them to contend with. A cold sweat broke out on her back. How could they possibly have spirited her away from the house without someone's knowing? Where was Tarquin? Why hadn't he been there? Tears pricked behind her eyes, and she tried to swallow them. Her throat was agony, but she couldn't bear the idea of tears seeping down her face, into the gag, and she unable to move her hands to wipe them away.

The hackney rattled to a halt. There were noises. Running feet, shouting voices. Light shone on her closed eyelids as she was hauled up and out of the chaise, still swaddled tightly in the cloak. George hoisted her over his shoulder again. She risked opening her eyes and saw that they were in the familiar yard of the Bell of Cheapside. A postchaise stood at the door, horses in the traces, ostlers sheltering from the rain under the eaves of the inn.

She was carried across. George thrust her into the interior of the chaise and slammed the door. "The lady's sick," he told the ostlers. "Sleeping, so don't disturb her. We'll be back in a minute." To Lucien he said, "Let's get a bite of supper. I'm wet as a drowned hen, and parched as the desert."

Lucien glanced at the closed door of the chaise, then shrugged and followed George into the taproom. "What happens if someone looks in?"

"No one's business but mine," George growled into a cognac bottle. "Besides, she's not going to make a sound. She can't move. Who's to look inside?"

It wasn't his business, Lucien reflected, shivering with that bone-deep cold. He'd not been responsible for the abduction. He drank thirstily of the brandy but waved away the meat pie and bread and cheese that George was eating with greedy gusto. He felt ill and knew from experience that the ice in his marrow presaged one of his serious bouts of fever. Perhaps he should take a room there and sweat it out.

But he wanted his thousand guineas, and he wasn't prepared to leave George until he had them firmly in his hand. He understood the man couldn't lay hands on such a sum until he got home; therefore, Lucien would accompany him home. Besides, it might be amusing to see how his wife reacted when she recovered her senses.

Juliana lay in the chaise just as she'd been thrust, half on and half off the seat. She thought she could maneuver herself fully onto the bench, but if she did that, they would know she had moved. Instinctively, she knew that she must maintain her unconsciousness until they reached wherever they were going. At some point they would have to untie her. She was acutely uncomfortable, every muscle twisted and crying out for relief. She tried to take her mind off her discomfort, wondering what the time was. How close to dawn. What time had she been abducted? And where, for pity's sake, were they taking her?

George needed her dead or convicted of murder in order

to reclaim her jointure. So which of the two did he have in mind? Neither alternative appealed.

They came back. She could smell cognac as they breathed heavily into the cramped space, thumping down on the bench opposite. Lucien's cough rasped, hacked. She kept her eyes tightly closed when hands moved beneath her legs and lifted her fully onto the seat. She was grateful for the small mercy. A whip cracked, the chaise rattled over the cobbles. Where in the name of pity were they taking her?

Tarquin stood in the rain, staring in disbelief at the ruined building on Ludgate Hill. It was burned out . . . had been for months. A roofless, blackened shell. He knew he had the address right. There was no sponging house here.

Lucien had tricked him. Had wanted him out of the house.

He spun on his heel. "Home!" he snapped to the drenched coachman. "And be quick about it." He leaped into the chaise, slamming the door shut as the horses plunged forward under the zealous coachman's whip.

His mind was in a ferment. Whatever reason Lucien had had for luring him away must have to do with Juliana. But what? It was so unlike the impulsively vicious Lucien to plan.

He was out of the carriage almost before it had halted. "Stay here. I may need you again."

The coachman nodded miserably and pulled his hat brim farther down.

The night porter opened the door at the duke's vigorous banging. "Who's been here in my absence?" the duke snapped.

The man looked alarmed, defensive, as if he were being accused of something. "No one, Your Grace. I've been sittin' 'ere all alone. Not a soul 'as come in or out, I'll swear to it."

Tarquin didn't respond but raced up the stairs two at a

time. He flung open Juliana's door, knowing what he would find and yet praying that he was mistaken.

He stared at the empty bed. There were no signs of a struggle. The armoire door was ajar, the dresser drawers opened, their contents tumbled. He pulled the bell rope again and again until feet came running along the corridor. Catlett pulling on his livery, Henny bleary-eyed, Quentin in his nightshirt, eyes filled with alarm.

"Lady Edgecombe is not in the house," the duke rasped. "Henny, find out what's missing from her clothes. Catlett, ask the servants if they heard anything . . . saw anything unusual in the last two hours."

Quentin stared stupidly at the empty bed. "Where would she go on a night like this?"

"Nowhere of her own volition," Tarquin said bleakly. "Lucien has a hand in this, but how in God's name did he manage to spirit her out of here? She's stronger than he is. And even if he managed to overpower her, he couldn't possibly carry her down the stairs."

"Why would he?"

"Why does Lucien ever plot mischief? . . . Well?" he demanded of Henny, who'd finished her examination of the armoire and dresser.

"Just a heavy cloak, Your Grace, and a pair of stockings," she said. "Can't see nothin' else missing."

"No shoes?"

Henny shook her head. "Seems like she's gone in nothin' but her shift, sir."

"*George*," said Tarquin softly, almost to himself. "*George Ridge.*" He'd miscalculated, grossly misread the man's character. Instead of intimidating him, he'd succeeded in rousing the devil. Lucien would have provided the means to get to her, George the brute force to remove her.

"What are you saying?" asked Quentin, still too shocked to absorb the situation.

"George and Lucien, the devil's partnership," Tarquin said bitterly. "God, I've been a fool." He turned as Catlett hurried in, his livery now neat, his wig straight. "Well? Anything?"

"No, Your Grace. The household's been abed since before you left. I was up myself for a short while, in my pantry, but I retired soon after your departure."

Tarquin nodded, tapping his lips with his fingertips as he thought. They all watched him, hanging on every nuance of his expression. "We have to guess," he said finally. "And God help us all if I guess wrong. Henny, pack up a cloak bag for Lady Edgecombe. Basic necessities . . . her riding habit, boots. You'll know what she needs. Catlett, tell the coachman to bring around my phaeton with the grays harnessed tandem. Quentin, do you accompany me?"

"Of course. I'll dress." Quentin didn't ask where they were going; he would know soon enough. A night drive in an open phaeton in the pouring rain was not a particularly appealing prospect, but speed was obviously of the essence, and the light vehicle would make much better time than a coach.

Chapter 28

They changed horses three times before dawn. Juliana didn't move, even when a strand of hair tickled her nose and she was sure she was going to sneeze. Lucien coughed and shivered and was generally silent, taking frequent pulls from a cognac flask. George stared fixedly at the bundled figure on the opposite bench.

A gray dawn broke, the sky weeping a thin drizzle. They rattled into the yard of the Red Lion at Winchester, the horses drooping. The coachman had driven them hard, a substantial bonus resting on achieving the seventy miles to Winchester in seven hours. Twice the speed of a stage-coach. George stuck his head through the window.

"Change the horses. We'll not stop for more than that."

"Flask is empty," Lucien muttered through clenched teeth. "Get it filled." He leaned to open the door and was seized with another paroxysm, doubling over, the reddening handkerchief pressed to his mouth.

"Here, give it to me." Impatiently, George snatched the flask from his limp grasp. He left the carriage and hurried across the yard to the taproom. "Fill this, and give me three extra bottles." At the rate Lucien was drinking, he reckoned that three bottles should last for the rest of the day.

He returned to the chaise, returned to his watch on

Juliana. He couldn't understand why she hadn't regained consciousness. She was breathing. Her face was deathly white, it was true, but her complexion was always milky pale against the vivid flame of her hair. He leaned over her, touched her cheek. Her skin was reassuringly warm.

Juliana knew that she couldn't keep up the pretense for much longer. Her muscles screamed for relief, and worst of all, she had a pressing need for the privy. How she would express the need with the gag in her mouth she didn't know, but if they didn't stop soon, she was going to have to make some effort to communicate. She'd been given no clues to their destination during the changes, but she guessed from the length of the journey, and from what she knew of George, that he was taking her back to his house. To the scene of the crime. Was he going to haul her before the magistrates immediately? Or did he have a more devious plan? The chaise jolted violently in a pothole, and her discomfort magnified. She closed her mind to it, forcing herself to remember, room by room, the physical plan of the house. To envisage the windows, the doors, the outbuildings, the lane that ran behind the stables.

The chaise turned up the drive to the Ridges' squat redbrick house and came to a halt before the front door. George jumped down, reached in for Juliana, and dragged her out feet first. Her head bumped on the floor, and she opened her eyes.

"Ah, my sleeping beauty, that woke you," he said with satisfaction, toppling her forward over his shoulder again. "We're going to amuse each other, I believe." He carried her up to the door. It opened as he reached it. An elderly housekeeper curtsied, her eyes startled.

"Eh, Sir George, we wasn't expectin' ye."

He merely grunted and pushed past her. Lucien followed, hunched over the deep, deep chill in his body, teeth chattering, limbs trembling.

"See to my guest, Dolly," George ordered as he strode to the stairs. "The man needs fire, hot water, bed."

"Cognac," Lucien declared feebly, raising the flask to his lips.

The woman stared at him in horror. She knew when she looked upon the dying. "This a-way sir." She took his arm, but he shook off her hand with a curse.

"Just bring me cognac and hot water, woman." He stumbled into a room to the side of the hall, handkerchief pressed to his mouth as the bloody phlegm was dredged from his lungs.

Juliana, listening to this, felt a smidgeon of hope. Lucien was clearly too ill to be capable of serious violence. That left only George. But trussed up as she was, George was quite enough to deal with.

George kicked open a door at the head of the stairs and threw Juliana down onto the bed. "Remember this room, my dear? Your wedding chamber." He pulled the cloak loose, flinging her onto her belly as he dragged it away from her.

Juliana was conscious of her shift riding up on her thighs, the air cool on the backs of her legs. With a jerk she twisted onto her back, trying to push down her shift with her bound and bandaged hands.

George chuckled and twitched it up again. "I like it just the way it was."

She moved her hands to her mouth, trying to pluck at the gag, her eyes signaling frantically. At this point she had only one thing on her mind.

"Want to say something?" He smiled. "You'll be doing a lot of talking soon, my dear stepmother. You'll be giving me a full confession of murder. You'll write it out for me, and then we'll visit the magistrates, and you'll be able to tell them all about it, too."

Juliana heaved her legs over the side of the bed and kicked her feet backward under the bed, trying to locate the chamber pot. George looked puzzled for a minute; then he smiled again.

"Ah, I understand. Allow me to help you." Bending, he pulled the pot out and pushed it with his foot into the middle of the chamber. "There," he said solicitously. "I trust you can manage. I'll be back when I've breakfasted."

Juliana's eyes spat green fire. But at least he'd left her to struggle alone. And her hands were tied in front rather than behind. There was always something to be thankful for, she thought wryly, standing up and hopping across to the chamber pot.

She managed somehow, and with little shuffles also managed to push the pot back beneath the bed; then she hopped over to the windowsill and took stock. The gag was so tight in her mouth, she couldn't work it loose with her fingers and, with her wrists tied, couldn't get at the knot behind her head. The strips of silk stocking were tight, and she couldn't slip her bandaged hands free.

Her eyes roamed around the room, saw Sir John's razor strop hanging on the wall by the washstand. Where there was a strop, there was usually a razor. She hopped to the washstand. The straight blade lay beside the ewer and basin, waiting for Sir John, as it had every morning of his adult life. No one had touched the room since his death.

Gingerly, she picked up the blade with her fingertips and tried to balance it on its edge, the cutting blade uppermost. She slid her hands forward until the silk at her wrists was directly over the blade, then sawed the material against the edge. It was blunt, in need of the strop, but she was too impatient now to attempt to sharpen it. It fell over. Carefully, she rebalanced it, holding it steady with the tension of the silk. Began again. Little by little the thin, strong silk began to fray. Twice the blade fell over when the tension of the silk lessened. Patiently, she replaced it, her heart thudding, ears strained to catch the sound of a footstep outside, the creak of a floorboard. Her throat hurt so badly, she wasn't sure she would be able to talk even if she weren't gagged. Then the material parted, the razor clattered to the washstand.

Juliana shook out her wrists, cramps running up her arms, clawing her fingers. Then she struggled with the gag and freed her mouth. Wool stuck to her tongue and her lips, reminding her vividly of Ted's ruthless lesson in the dangers of the London streets. Sleeping in one's bed seemed to be as hazardous as anything else, she thought, slashing the razor through the bonds at her ankles.

She was free. Her hurts were forgotten under a rush of exhilaration. She had heard George turn the key in the lock of the door as he'd left. She ran to the window. It was a long drop to the soft earth of a flower bed beneath. But the ivy was strong. Or looked it, at least. Whether it would bear her weight remained to be seen. There was no other option.

She pushed up the casement. The wind blew cold and wet, pressing her thin shift against her body, but she ignored it. Twisting sideways, she dropped from the window-sill, gripping the edge with her fingers, ignoring the pain in her torn palms. Her feet scrabbled for purchase in the ivy. Found a toehold of brick. Heart in her mouth, she let go of the sill with one hand, moved it down to clutch at the creeper. It held. She brought the other hand down, and now her entire weight was supported by the ivy and the toehold. Hand over hand she inched downward, feeling the creeper pull away from the wall. But each time she managed to move her hands and feet to another site before the vine gave way.

She was concentrating so hard on her hazardous climb, she didn't hear the pounding feet in the room above. But she heard George's wild bellow. Looked up, saw his face suffused with rage, staring down at her. She let go and dropped the last ten feet to the soil. She landed awkwardly, twisting her ankle. For a fateful minute or two she sat in the soil, gasping with pain. Then she heard George's bellow again, knew he was running downstairs, would appear out of the kitchen door. She was up and running through the drizzle, ignoring the pain of her ankle, making for the driveway around the house. Instinctively seeking somewhere out in the open, where there might be other eyes to witness.

She could hear George behind her now, hear his heavy,

panting breath, imagined she could almost feel it on the
back of her neck. In ordinary circumstances she could have
outstripped him easily. But she was barefoot and the gravel
was sharp. Her ankle turned with each step, bringing tears
to her eyes. She rounded the side of the house. The gravel
drive stretched ahead to the lane. If she could make it to
the lane, maybe there'd be a carter passing, a farm laborer
. . . someone . . . anyone.

George ate up the distance between them. His breath
raged in his heaving chest, his great belly jounced, his massive hands were in fists, but he was gaining on her. She was
slowing, her feet troubling her. He reached out, seized the
hem of her shift, hauled her backward as she fought,
kicked, scratched, hair swinging wildly.

Somehow she wrenched herself free, hearing the thin
material of her shift rip as she hurled herself forward,
toward the gate to the lane . . . so close . . . three more
steps . . .

George's breath was on the back of her neck, his hands
reaching for her. The sound of iron wheels on the lane,
jouncing over the rough pebbled surface . . . With the
last gasp of breath Juliana leaped into the lane, in front of a
hay wagon.

The driver pulled back on the reins, staring in disbelief at
the frantic figure in the path of his shire horses.

"Please . . ." Juliana struggled for sufficient breath to
speak. "Please . . . help me . . . I—"

She got no further. George had seized her from behind,
clamping his hand over her mouth, twisting her hair
around his other hand, holding her head still. His voice was
calm, sensible. Not his voice at all as he explained to the
astounded farm laborer that she was deranged, was kept
confined for her own safety. That she'd escaped from her
chamber by attacking the servant who'd brought her food.
That she was violent and dangerous.

The laborer looked at the half-naked, wild-haired, frantic figure struggling in the hands of a man who was clearly
in full possession of his senses, who spoke so rationally,

with such assurance. The girl gazed at him with desperate, almost feral, eyes, and he shuddered, muttering a prayer, averting his eyes from the danger of a lunatic's stare. He shook the reins urgently as George pulled the madwoman aside, and drove off, urging the horses to greater speed.

Juliana bit deep into George's palm. He bellowed and slammed his flat palm against the side of her head, dazing her. Then he hoisted her over his shoulder before the ringing in her ears had subsided and carried her back to the house.

Lucien stumbled out of the drawing room, glass in hand, as the front door shivered behind George's kick. "Good God," he slurred. "Now what?"

"Thought she could escape . . . tricky bitch," George declared. He pushed past Lucien into the drawing room and threw Juliana into a chair.

She lay still, slumped into the cushioned depths, her head numb with shock and the stinging pain of the blow. For the moment she was defeated.

George poured himself a measure of cognac, downed it, and poured another. "The sooner she's locked up in Winchester jail, the better." He drained the second glass. "Let's go."

"Go where?" Lucien lounged against the door frame. His eyes burned with fever, tremors racked his body, and he clutched the cognac glass as if it were his only connection with life.

"To the Forsetts," George said, throwing his glass down. "They'll identify this whore before a magistrate, and you'll identify her as your wife and say how and when she became so. They'll arraign her and lock her up. And then . . ." He wiped his mouth slowly, lasciviously, with the back of his hand. "And then . . . my dear stepmother . . . I shall pay you some visits in your cell."

Juliana still said nothing. She was drained of physical strength and knew she couldn't get away from George again. Not here . . . not now. Maybe the Forsetts would offer her protection. But she knew that was a fond hope.

They wouldn't want to be touched by any scandal created by the ward they'd thoroughly disliked and resented. They'd repudiate her as soon as look at her.

"Come, Edgecombe," George said brusquely. "We'll ride. I'll take the whore up with me."

Lucien shook his head, opened his mouth to speak, and was promptly engulfed in a coughing spasm worse than any Juliana had witnessed. When he could speak, he gasped, "Can't possibly, dear boy. Couldn't sit a horse like this. Stay here . . . rest a bit . . . you go about your business." He gulped at the cognac.

"Oh, no," George said with soft fervor. "You're coming, Edgecombe. I need you. You won't see a penny of that money until you've done what I need you to do."

Lucien stared at him, the realization in his eyes that he couldn't withstand this man . . . this oaf whom he'd despised and thought he was using for his own revenge. Lucien wasn't using Ridge, Lucien was being used, and George now carried himself with all the cold, calculating assertion of a man possessed.

George took a menacing step toward him, his great hands bunched into fists. Lucien shrank back, all the strength of his own malice dissolved in the face of this threat, leaving him as weak and timid as any coward facing a bully.

"All right," he croaked, pressing the bloodstained kerchief to his mouth. "All right, I'll come."

George nodded brusquely and turned back to Juliana's slumped figure. She'd closed her eyes as the easiest way to absent herself from what was happening. He hauled her to her feet and grasped her chin, his other hand again twisting in her hair. "You don't want to be hurt, do you, my dear?"

She shook her head, still keeping her eyes closed.

"Then you'll do as I bid you, won't you?"

She nodded, then felt his mouth on hers, hard, bruising, vile, pressing her lips against her teeth. He forced his tongue into her mouth so she could taste the stale sourness of his brandy breath. She gagged and went suddenly limp.

George drew back and looked down into the white, closed face. He was holding her up by her hair as she sagged against him. He smiled. "Not quite so full of yourself now, Lady Edgecombe?" he taunted. "And when you've spent a week or so in a jail cell . . ." He chuckled and spun her to face the door. "Let's go."

In the hall he paused to pull a heavy riding cloak from a hook on the wall and swathed Juliana in its thick and musty folds. She walked as if in a trance as he pushed her ahead of him out of the house and to the stables, Lucien stumbling behind. The wind still blew cold and damp from the sea, and Juliana was pathetically grateful for the cloak, even though she knew it had been provided not to lessen her miseries but to avoid drawing attention to her. Lucien shivered and shook, and it seemed he had no strength left even to cough.

A groom brought two horses from the stables, saddled them, looking curiously at the trio but knowing better than to say anything in front of his master. He assisted Lucien to mount. Lucien slumped in the saddle like a sack of potatoes, feebly grasping the reins, his head drooping.

George lifted Juliana onto his horse and mounted behind her, holding her securely against him as he gathered up the reins. Juliana tried to hold herself away from the hot, sweaty, triumphant maleness of his body, but he jerked her closer and she yielded before he did anything worse.

They trotted out of the yard and took the road to Forsett Towers.

Tarquin drew up in the yard of the Rose and Crown in Winchester. Quentin stepped out of the phaeton, stretching his cramped, chilled limbs in the damp morning air. "Where to now?"

Tarquin turned from giving the ostler instructions to change the horses. "I'm not certain. Let's break our fast and make some inquiries."

Quentin followed him into the inn. In a few minutes

they were ensconced in a private parlor, a maid setting light to the kindling in the hearth.

"A drop of porter for the cold, my lord?" the innkeeper suggested, casting a critical eye around the wainscoted room, checking for tarnished copper, smudged window-panes, a smear of dust.

"If you please." Tarquin peeled off his gloves. "And cof-fee, sirloin, and eggs." He strode to the window, peering down into the street. "Where is the nearest magistrate?"

"On Castle Street, my lord."

"Send a lad to me. I need someone to run an errand." The landlord bowed himself out.

"So?" Quentin leaned over the new flame, rubbing his hands. Rain dripped off his sodden cloak.

"So we discover if Ridge took her straightway to the magistrate," Tarquin said succinctly, discarding his own dripping cloak. "Ah, thank you." He nodded at the girl who placed two pewter tankards of porter on the table.

"Ye be wantin' an errand run, sir?" A cheerful voice spoke from the doorway, where stood a rosy-cheeked lad in a leather apron, spiky hair resisting the discipline of water and brush.

Tarquin gave him brisk instructions. He was to go to the magistrate and discover if a woman had been brought be-fore him in the last few hours.

"And if not?" Quentin took a grateful draft of porter.

"Then we assume he took her to his own house."

"And if not?" Quentin tossed his own cloak onto a set-tle, where it steamed gently in the fire's heat.

"Forsett Towers." Tarquin drank from his own tankard. His voice was flat. "If I'm wrong, then . . . I don't know." He shrugged, but the careless gesture did nothing to conceal his bone-deep anxiety.

Breakfast arrived and they ate in silence, each distracted with his own thoughts. The lad returned. The magistrate had not yet left his bed and had spent an undisturbed night.

Tarquin nodded, gave him a coin, and summoned the landlord. "D'ye know the Ridge estate?"

"Aye, sir. Ten miles south as the crow flies." The man gave precise directions. "Big stone gateposts . . . crumblin' like, m'lord. Ye can't miss it."

"Ready, Quentin?"

"On your heels, brother." Quentin put down his tankard and followed Tarquin downstairs and out into the yard. The incessant drizzle had stopped, and there was the faintest lightning in the sky. Tarquin paid their shot as fresh horses were harnessed to the phaeton.

They turned through the crumbling stone gateposts just as a feeble ray of sun poked through the clouds. The horses splashed through puddles along the driveway where Juliana had run with such desperation an hour earlier.

The housekeeper answered the furious tolling of the bell, her expression startled, her gray hair escaping from beneath her cap. She curtsied, her eyes like those of a scared rabbit. The morning had brought too many alarums and excursions into her normally peaceful routine.

"Sir George . . . is he at home?"

Dolly gazed up at the splendid figure in the caped driving cloak. His voice was cold and haughty, but his eyes were colder and carried a fearful menace.

"No, sir . . . no. . . . 'E left . . . . a short while ago. 'E and 'is visitors."

"Visitors?" Tarquin raised an inquiring eyebrow.

"Yes . . . yes, indeed, sir. A gentleman . . . mortal sick 'e was. Coughin' fit to raise the dead . . . an' a girl . . . a young woman . . . sick, too. Sir George carried 'er upstairs. Then they all left." Her scared eyes flitted sideways, found Quentin's reassuring gaze. She seemed to take courage, and her fingers loosed her apron where they'd been anxiously pleating and tucking.

"Do you know where they went?" Quentin asked gently.

She shook her head. "No, sir. But they went on 'orseback. The three of 'em on two. So they can't 'ave gone far."

"What road do we take to Forsett Towers?" Tarquin's

voice still betrayed none of his agitation. He knew now that he was within a hand's grasp of Juliana, and his rage was cold and deadly. George and Lucien would have had to hurt her to compel her thus far. And they would pay. He drowned the images of what they might have done to her in the icy certainty of their punishment.

Lucien fell just as they turned onto the gravel driveway leading to the gray stone mansion of Forsett Towers. He had been barely conscious throughout the ride, slumped over the horse's neck, the reins loose in his fingers. Every few minutes his body would be convulsed with violent spasms as he shivered and coughed into the now scarlet handkerchief. When his horse stumbled into a pothole on the drive, Lucien slipped sideways. The horse, startled, broke into a sudden trot, and his rider tumbled off the saddle.

Juliana watched in horror as the confused horse quickened his pace and Lucien, still with one foot in the stirrup, was bumped along the gravel. He was making no attempt to free his foot, just dangled inert until George managed to seize the animal's bridle and pull him to a halt.

George dismounted, hauling Juliana down with him. Still maintaining a tight grip on her wrist, he released Lucien's foot and then stared down at the still figure on the ground. Lucien had struck his head on something sharp, and blood pulsed from a gash on his forehead. His eyes were closed and he was barely breathing.

"Damn him to hell!" George declared, the calm, controlled facade cracking for the first time since he'd caught Juliana on the lane. He dragged Juliana back to his horse and pushed her up into the saddle, mounting behind her again.

"You can't just leave him." Juliana at last found her voice again. She wished Lucien to the devil, but the thought of abandoning him unconscious and bleeding was appalling.

"He's no good to me in that condition." George picked

up the reins of Lucien's horse, roughly kicked his own mount's flanks, and started off again to the house, leading the riderless animal.

Juliana twisted round to look at the figure still lying on the drive. "We should carry him into the house."

"Someone else can do it. Now, hold your tongue!" He pulled on her hair in vicious emphasis, and she fell silent again. She'd always known George was a brute and an oaf, but she hadn't understood quite how brutal he was.

At the house George sprang down, dragging Juliana with him. He held her by the hair and the nape of the neck, shoving her up the steps to the front door, where he banged the knocker as if to sound the last trump. A footman opened it, looking both outraged and alarmed at such an uncivilized summons. He stared at Juliana as if he couldn't believe his eyes. "Why, Miss Juliana . . ."

George pushed past him, thrusting Juliana ahead of him. "Where's your master?"

"In the library . . . but . . ."

George ignored him, pushing Juliana toward the library door. Before he reached it, however, it opened. Sir Brian looked at them with an expression of acute distaste.

"I see you found her." His voice expressed only annoyance.

"Yes . . . and I'll see her burn outside Winchester jail," George stated, shoving Juliana into the library. He held her by the neck and glared in triumph at Sir Brian. "And you, sir, and your lady wife will identify her before a magistrate this very day."

"Goodness me, whatever's going on?" Amelia's irritated tones came from the door. "Juliana, whatever are you doing here?"

"Nothing of my own volition, ma'am," Juliana said, recovering some of her spirit in these drearily familiar surroundings. "There's a badly injured man on the driveway. Would you send some men to carry him in?"

Amelia looked between the sweaty, glowering, triumphant George and his pale prisoner. "You were never anything but trouble," she declared. "First you bring this clod into my house . . . and now you want me to take in some accident victim. Who is he?"

"My husband, ma'am. Viscount Edgecombe." Juliana began to feel a bubble of hysterical laughter welling in her chest. It was extraordinary that they should continue to behave toward her with the same exasperation of her childhood. She was about to be arraigned on murder charges. She was half-naked, battered and bruised, in the clutches of a vicious brute, her husband was lying near death in a puddle on their driveway, and they were both blaming her for disturbing their peace, as if she'd brought mud into the house, or broken a precious dish.

Amelia sighed and turned back to the hovering footman. "Dawkins, take some men and see about it, will you?"

"Yes, my lady."

"And send someone to the nearest magistrate," George demanded belligerently. "Tell him it's a matter of murder and he should come here immediately."

Dawkins looked askance at his master. Sir Brian said shortly, "You may ignore that instruction, Dawkins. If Sir George wishes to find a magistrate, he may go in search of one himself . . . and take his prisoner with him," he added coldly.

"You would obstruct justice, sir?" George's sweaty face flushed crimson. "I tell you straight, sir, I'll lay charges against you of impeding the process—"

"Oh, hold your tongue, man," Amelia interrupted acidly. "Do you think we wish to listen to your puffing and blowing? If you have a grudge against Juliana, then you may do what you wish, but don't expect us to assist you."

Juliana was somewhat surprised. True, they weren't taking her part, but neither were they taking George's.

"A grudge!" George exclaimed. "Is that how you would describe the willful murder of my father . . . her husband. Petty treason is what it is, and I tell you—"

"You will tell us nothing," Sir Brian snapped. He turned

to his erstwhile ward and asked calmly, "Juliana, did you by any chance murder your husband?"

"No."

"That's rather what we assumed. It was just another unfortunate piece of clumsiness, I daresay."

"It was certainly very clumsy of you to run away," Amelia scolded. "I can't think what could have possessed—"

"Put him down on that settle . . . careful now. Send someone for the physician."

The crisp tones of the Duke of Redmayne came from the open doorway to the hall. Amelia stopped in midsentence. George inhaled sharply. Juliana wrenched her head around, ignoring the savage tug on her captured hair. Her heart thudded so loudly, it was impossible that only she could hear it. She stared at the door.

Chapter 29

"I give you good morning, ma'am. Sir Brian." The duke stepped into the library. "Accept my apologies for this disturbance. I wouldn't have had it happen for the world."

"And who might you be, sir?"

"Redmayne," Tarquin said with a courteous bow. "Lady Edgecombe is in my charge during her husband's indisposition. May I introduce my brother, Lord Quentin Courtney?" He gestured to Quentin, who stood behind him. Quentin bowed in his turn and murmured a pleasant greeting.

Juliana wondered whether anyone was going to notice her as she stood silent, still held captive by her hair. The scene resembled a stage farce with this exchange of polite greetings in the stuffy formality of the library.

Then Tarquin came over to her. "Take your hands off her," he said quietly.

George recovered himself. "Don't you give me orders, Redmayne. She's my prisoner, and I'm accusing her before a magistrate of petty treason."

Tarquin shook his head. "No," he said consideringly. "No, you are not going to do any such thing. *Take your hands off her!*"

George's hands fell to his sides. He could no more have withstood the soft-voiced ferocity of the order than he could have changed the direction of the wind.

"It wasn't my fault this time," Juliana croaked through her bruised throat. "I didn't get myself into this trouble, it came and found me. I was perfectly innocently asleep in my bed—"

"I am aware," the duke interrupted, taking her hands. "Are you hurt?"

"Only my throat, and I twisted my ankle," she rasped, wishing that he would take her in his arms, wishing that he wouldn't look at her with those strangely dispassionate eyes.

Tarquin saw the bruises on her throat, and livid fire chased the dispassion from his gaze. He touched her throat. "He did this to you?"

Juliana nodded, her skin alive beneath the gentle brushing of his fingers. Surely he would take her in his arms now. But he didn't. He turned back to George, his expression once more unreadable.

"Step outside. I don't want your blood on Lady Forsett's carpet." The same cold, invincible tone. The gray eyes were as pitiless and implacable as the Last Judgment. He paid no further attention to Juliana, every fiber of his being concentrated on the annihilation of George Ridge. A wicked blade suddenly flickered at the end of the cane he held in his hand. "Step outside, sir." The blade pushed between George's fat thighs.

George could feel the sensation in his groin. His knees went to water. The pitiless eyes held him, mocking his terror. He stumbled toward the door. Quentin stood aside. Tarquin followed him out, the tip of the sword still menacing George's quivering manhood.

"Lucien?" Juliana shook her head in an effort to dispel the trancelike sensation. "Is he all right, Quentin?"

Quentin didn't answer. He crossed to her in two long strides, taking her hands in his strong grip. "My poor child," he said. "What you must have suffered."

"Not that much." She smiled a wan smile. "I'm so glad to see you."

"Did you imagine Tarquin wouldn't come for you?" Quentin sounded almost reproachful.

"Your husband is dying in my hall," Amelia announced before Juliana could respond. "I really do think it most inconsiderate of you, Juliana, to bring these people down upon us."

"I hardly think Juliana is to blame, ma'am," Quentin said. "If you'll excuse me, I'll go back to my cousin and await the physician."

Juliana followed him out to where Lucien lay on the settle, his body strangely limp, his complexion waxen. Clotted blood formed over the gash on his forehead, and blood flecked his blue lips. He didn't seem to be breathing. Juliana placed her hand lightly over his mouth and felt the faint stirring of air. "He's still alive." She kept her hand there, filled now with a perverse pity for the man who had tormented her. She glanced up and read the same emotion in Quentin's eyes.

Outside George was pinned against the stable wall with a piece of wood across his throat. He didn't know how it had happened, but one minute he'd been on his feet and the next felled with a blow to the back of his neck. He'd been hauled upright and slammed against the stable wall. The duke pressed the wood tighter. "Not a pleasant feeling, I believe," he said coolly. He dropped the wood and once again pushed his unsheathed swordstick between George's pudgy thighs. George's eyes rolled.

"Listen to me very carefully now, my friend. You are going to tell the nearest magistrate that Juliana could not have been responsible for your father's death. You will say that your father was old, had a weak heart, had been drinking heavily. You will say that you have no doubt at all that he died from excitement and overexertion, leaving his child bride blameless but alone and terrified."

George's eyes rolled again. He tried to shake his head, tried to speak, but managed only a grunt that changed to a

squeak as the sword pressed upward and he could feel the
blade, razor sharp against his shriveled softness.

"Let me tell you why you will do this, you dolt." Tarquin paused, glancing over his shoulder at a groom who'd
sauntered into the yard and now stood staring at the tableau. The duke dismissed him from his mind and turned
back to Sir George.

"If you say anything else, I will lay against you charges of
assault with intent to murder Lady Edgecombe. I will lay
charges of stalking, of abduction, of breaking into my
house, of thievery. I will have witnesses to your every action. I will say that you are obsessed with Lady Edgecombe,
that you believe she is your father's widow. I will prove
beyond a shadow of a doubt that Lady Edgecombe is *not* Sir
John Ridge's widow. I will say that you bear me a grudge
because I had you thrashed for trying to break into my
house. Believe me, I can do these things. Whom do you
think a magistrate is going to believe? The Duke of
Redmayne, or an ignorant dolt of a country squire?"

George stared into the cold gray eyes. He knew he had
lost. He had no defense against the charges. He knew the
duke would produce witnesses who would swear blind to
his guilt. He knew he would be bumbling and inarticulate
and the duke and his lawyers would run rings around him.
They would discount anything a convicted felon said
against Viscountess Edgecombe, the Duke of Redmayne's
cousin by marriage. They would hang him . . . transport
him if he was lucky.

"Of course, if my words aren't sufficiently persuasive,
there are other ways," the duke mused. The sword moved
upward. George's gut loosened; he opened his mouth on a
bellow of fear, but no sound came out. "It is really very
tempting," Tarquin murmured. "Emasculation seems such
an apt punishment, don't you think?" George felt the
sword nick his inner thigh. He couldn't believe it might
happen, and yet he could believe anything of this avenging
devil with his ice-cold eyes. The sword nicked his other

thigh, and George groaned with terror, bitter bile filling his mouth. He retched helplessly.

Tarquin stepped away from him with a disgusted curl of his lip. "You are a fool," he said contemptuously. "Oh, you might have succeeded in intimidating Juliana if she hadn't been under my wing. She's still an innocent . . . a child in many ways. But when you crossed swords with me, my friend, you made the biggest mistake of your bumbling oafish life. If you ever come within ten miles of Juliana again, I will unman you. I suggest you believe it." He turned on his heel and left George sagging against the wall, vomiting up his breakfast.

In the hall Juliana and Quentin still stood beside Lucien. Of Sir Brian and his wife there was no sign. Tarquin came over to the settle. Juliana still had her hand over Lucien's mouth, but she didn't know why anymore. She looked up at Tarquin. "He's dying."

"He's been dying for a long time," Tarquin replied. "What happened to him?"

Juliana started to explain, then stopped as Lucien's eyes fluttered open. He stared up at them, and she shrank back from the naked malice in the rapidly glazing eyes. "God rot the lot of you!" Lucien declared. His head dropped to one side, his eyes staring sightlessly at the wall.

Juliana stepped backward, suddenly conscious of an invisible thread connecting Tarquin and Quentin. As she slipped into the library, Tarquin bent over and closed Lucien's eyes. Quentin laid his hands on his breast. They stood in silence, looking down at the dead man.

"He's dead," Juliana said flatly as she entered the library.

"Who? Your husband or that oaf Ridge?" Sir Brian asked, sounding only mildly curious.

"Edgecombe."

"Well, I never knew the man, but if he was anything like that crude ox, the world's well rid of him," declared Lady Forsett. "But I consider it in the very worst of taste to die in a stranger's hall."

"No one could ever accuse Edgecombe of having taste,

ma'am," Tarquin said ironically from the door. "But I do apologize once again for the inconvenience. It was most thoughtless of him to sully your house in such fashion."

"Well, I daresay it was not exactly your fault," Sir Brian allowed. "It was that clod Ridge who brought him here, as I understand. Or was it Juliana?"

"I didn't bring anyone here," Juliana said wearily. "I was dragged here against my will. I can assure you I would never knowingly have troubled you."

"Well, since you're now a widow again, what's to become of you?"

"After a suitable period of mourning, Juliana will become my wife."

The duke's cool statement produced a stunned silence. Sir Brian blinked; Amelia stared at Juliana as if she couldn't believe such a thing of the ugly duckling. Juliana and Quentin merely stared at the duke.

"But . . . but Lydia . . . ," Quentin finally stammered.

"She will be eloping with you, my dear." Tarquin leaned against the mantel, an enigmatic smile on his face. He was clearly enjoying the effect he was having. "It seems the only workable solution. You and Lydia will elope. I will of course be the gentleman. Suitably upset at being jilted, but very noble about relinquishing my betrothed to the man of her heart. Lord and Lady Melton will have no choice but to put a good face on it. It's hardly a bad match, dear boy."

"But . . . but an elopement! I'll be drummed out of the Church." Quentin still gaped in disbelief at this impossible scenario.

"Nonsense," Tarquin said briskly. "People will know only that a private marriage took place with the blessing of Lydia's parents. It had to be quiet because of the bereavement. I will give my blessing graciously. Your bishop will welcome your most excellent wife, and everything will be smooth as silk."

The astonishing words fell into Quentin's brain like diamonds, sharp-edged and shining with clarity. It sounded so easy. He looked at Juliana, saw the glow on her pale cheeks, the light in her eyes. He looked at Tarquin, who was smiling softly to himself, his eyes resting on Juliana. And it became clear to Quentin that it was the only possible step for any of them to take.

"You wish to marry me?" Juliana found her voice at last. She still clutched the old cloak around her shoulders.

"So it would seem."

"I have always been astonished at your energy, Juliana, but three husbands in one year is industry beyond belief," Sir Brian remarked dryly.

"But you do seem to have done remarkably well for yourself," Amelia observed. "I would never have believed you could make a duchess."

"She will make an exemplary duchess, ma'am," Quentin said with one of his rare flashes of anger. "Juliana is a very special person."

Amelia looked surprised. "Do you think so, indeed? We always found her a great trial."

"How very unfortunate and how very blind, Lady Forsett." Tarquin stepped toward Juliana and took her hands. "Those of us who know her find her only a source of delight."

Juliana flushed and her fingers fluttered in his palm. "Really?"

"Really." He bent and kissed her lightly.

"There's something I should tell you."

"There's no need." His hand moved to her belly, rested there.

"You guessed?"

"Yes, my dear. It was not difficult." He laughed at her chagrined expression. "I have known that you're my heart and soul for many weeks now, *mignonne*. There are no secrets you can keep from me."

"There are no secrets that I would wish to keep," she affirmed, lost in his gaze, in the overwhelming wonder following so hard on the heels of despair, unaware of Quentin's discreetly ushering their hosts out of the room. Unaware of anything now but the sweetness of his mouth on hers, the sudden fire as his body moved against hers. The absolute knowledge of love.

VIRTUE

Prologue

The quill scratched on the parchment. A log spat in the grate. The guttering tallow candle flared as a needle of night wind pierced the ill-fitting shutters.

The man at the table paused in his writing. He dipped his nib in the inkstand and looked around the dim, shabby apartment. The paneled walls were cracked and inlaid with years of grime, the floor sticky beneath his booted feet. He huddled into his cloak and glanced toward the fire. It was low in the grate, and he bent to pick up a log from the basket. Then he let it fall back again. It was an extravagance he didn't need. Not now . . . not in a very few minutes.

He turned back to his writing, and the scratching of the quill was the only sound. Then he reached for the sander and dusted the epistle. Without reading what he had written, he folded the paper with scrupulous care and neatness, dropped a thick blob of candlewax on the folds, and pressed his signet ring into the seal. He sat for a minute, gazing fixedly at the initials imprinted in the wax: G·D. Then he wrote again on the front of the sealed paper.

He rose from the table and propped the paper on the mantelpiece against a tarnished candlestick. There was an inch of brandy in the bottle on the table. He poured it into a glass and tossed it back, savoring the rough burn on his tongue, the warmth as it slid down his throat. It was a rough and ready brew for a man who had once known only the finest cognac, and yet it comforted.

He went to the door and opened it softly. The passage outside was dark and quiet. Soft-footed, he crept along the corridor and paused outside the two facing doors at the end. They were securely shut. Gently he turned the knob of the right-hand door. The door swung open and he stood in the opening, looking across the darkness to the shape of the bed and the mound beneath the covers. His lips moved soundlessly as if in benediction, then he closed the door with the same gentleness and repeated the exercise in the other doorway.

He returned to the candlelit apartment, closed the door, and went back to the table. He opened a drawer and drew out the silver-mounted pistol. He spun the chamber. There was one bullet. But he needed no more.

The single shot shattered the silence of the night. The letter on the mantelpiece bore the legend: Sebastian and Judith: My dearest children. When you read this, you will at last understand.

1

What the devil was she doing? Marcus Devlin, the most honorable Marquis of Carrington, absently exchanged his empty champagne glass for a full one as a flunkey passed him. He pushed his shoulders off the wall, straightening to his full height, the better to see across the crowded room to the macao table. She was up to something. Every prickling hair on the nape of his neck told him so.

She was standing behind Charlie's chair, her fan moving in slow sweeps across the lower part of her face. She leaned forward to whisper something in Charlie's ear, and the rich swell of her breasts, the deep shadow of the cleft between them, was uninhibitedly revealed in the décolletage of her evening gown. Charlie looked up at her and smiled, the soft, infatuated smile of puppy love.

It wasn't surprising his young cousin had fallen head over heels for Miss Judith Davenport, the marquis reflected. There was hardly a man in Brussels who wasn't stirred by her: a creature of opposites, vibrant, ebullient, sharply intelligent—a woman who in some indefinable fashion challenged a man, put him on his mettle one minute, and yet the next was as appealing as a kitten; a man wanted to pick her up and cuddle her, protect her from the storm . . .

Romantic nonsense! The marquis castigated himself severely for sounding like his cousin and half the young soldiers proudly sporting their regimentals in the salons of Brussels as the world waited for Napoleon to make his move. He'd been watching Judith Davenport weaving her spells for several weeks now, convinced she was an artful minx with a very clear agenda of her own. But for the life of him, he couldn't discover what it was.

His eyes rested on the young man sitting opposite Charlie. Sebastian Davenport held the bank. As beautiful as his sister in his own way, he sprawled in his chair, both clothing and posture radiating a studied carelessness. He was laughing across the table, lightly ruffling the cards in his hands. The mood at the table was lighthearted. It was a mood that always accompanied the Davenports. Presumably one reason why they were so popular . . . and then the marquis saw it.

It was the movement of her fan. There was a pattern to the slow sweeping motion. Sometimes the movement speeded, sometimes it paused, once or twice she snapped the fan closed, then almost immediately began a more vigorous wafting of the delicately painted half moon. There was renewed laughter at the table, and with a lazy sweep of his rake, Sebastian Davenport scooped toward him the pile of vowels and rouleaux in the center of the table.

The marquis walked across the room. As he reached the table, Charlie looked up with a rueful grin. "It's not my night, Marcus."

"It rarely is," Carrington said, taking snuff. "Be careful you don't find yourself in debt." Charlie heard the warning in the advice, for all that his cousin's voice was affably casual. A slight flush tinged the young man's cheekbones and he dropped his eyes to his cards again. Marcus was his guardian and tended to be unsympathetic when Charlie's gaming debts outran his quarterly allowance.

"Do you care to play, Lord Carrington?" Judith Davenport's soft voice spoke at the marquis's shoulder and he turned to look at her. She was smiling, her golden brown eyes luminous, framed in the thickest, curliest eyelashes he had ever seen. However, ten years spent avoiding the frequently blatant blandishments of maidens on the lookout for a rich husband had inured him to the cajolery of a pair of fine eyes.

"No. I suspect it wouldn't be my night either, Miss Davenport. May I escort you to the supper room? It must grow tedious, watching my cousin losing hand over fist." He offered a small bow and took her elbow without waiting for a response.

Judith stiffened, feeling the pressure of his hand cupping her bare arm. There was a hardness in his eyes that matched the firmness of his grip, and her scalp contracted as unease shivered across her skin. "On the contrary, my lord, I find the play most entertaining." She gave her arm a covert, experimental tug. His fingers gripped warmly and yet more firmly.

"But I insist, Miss Davenport. You will enjoy a glass of negus."

He had very black eyes and they carried a most unpleasant glitter, as insistent as his tone and words, both of which were drawing a degree of puzzled attention. Judith could see no discreet, graceful escape route. She laughed lightly. "You have convinced me, sir. But I prefer burnt champagne to negus."

"Easily arranged." He drew her arm through his and laid his free hand over hers, resting on his black silk sleeve. Judith felt manacled.

They walked through the card room in a silence that was as uncomfortable as it was pregnant. Had he guessed what was going on? Had he seen anything? How could she have given herself away? Or was it something Sebastian had done, said, looked . . . ? The questions and speculations raced through Judith's brain. She was barely acquainted with Marcus Devlin. He was too sophisticated, too hardheaded to be of use to herself and Sebastian, but she had the distinct sense that he would be an opponent to be reckoned with.

The supper room lay beyond the ballroom, but instead of guiding his companion around the waltzing couples and the ranks of seated chaperones against the wall, Marcus turned aside toward the long French windows opening onto a flagged terrace. A breeze stirred the heavy velvet curtains over an open door.

"I was under the impression we were going to have supper." Judith stopped abruptly.

"No, we're going to take a stroll in the night air," her escort informed her with a bland smile. "Do put one foot in front of the other, my dear ma'am, otherwise our progress might become a little uneven." An unmistakable jerk on her arm drew her forward with a stumble, and Judith rapidly adjusted her gait to match the leisured, purposeful stroll of her companion.

"I don't care for the night air," she hissed through her teeth, keeping a smile on her face. "It's very bad for the constitution and frequently results in the ague or rheumatism."

"Only for those in their dotage," he said, lifting thick black eyebrows. "I would have said you were not a day above twenty-two. Unless you're very skilled with powder and paint?"

He'd pinpointed her age exactly and the sense of being dismayingly out of her depth was intensified. "I'm not quite such an accomplished actress, my lord," she said coldly.

"Are you not?" He held the curtain aside for her and she found herself out on the terrace, lit by flambeaux set in sconces at intervals along the low parapet fronting the sweep of green lawn. "I would have sworn you were as accomplished as any on Drury Lane." The statement was accompanied by a penetrating stare.

Judith rallied her forces and responded to the comment as if it were a humorous compliment. "You're too kind, sir. I confess I've long envied the talent of Mrs. Siddons."

"Oh, you underestimate yourself," he said softly. They had reached the parapet and he stopped under the light of a torch. "You are playing some very pretty theatricals, Miss Davenport, you and your brother."

Judith drew herself up to her full height. It wasn't a particularly impressive move when compared with her escort's breadth and stature, but it gave her an illusion of hauteur. "I don't know what you're talking about, my lord. It seems you've obliged me to accompany you in order to insult me with vague innuendos."

"No, there's nothing vague about my accusations," he said. "However insulting they may be. I am assuming my cousin's card play will improve in your absence."

"What are you implying?" The color ebbed in her cheeks, then flooded back in a hot and revealing wave.

Hastily she employed her fan in an effort to conceal her agitation.

The marquis caught her wrist and deftly twisted the fan from her hand. "You're most expert with a fan, madam."

"I beg your pardon?" She tried again for a lofty incomprehension, but with increasing lack of conviction.

"Don't continue this charade, Miss Davenport. It benefits neither of us. You and your brother may fleece as many fools as you can find as far as I'm concerned, but you'll leave my cousin alone."

"You talk in riddles," she said. There was no way he could prove anything; no public accusations he could bring, she told herself. But when they went to London . . . supposing he put the word around . . . ?

She needed time to think. With a dismissive shrug, she turned from him, as if intending to return to the ballroom.

"Then allow me to solve the riddle for you." He caught her arm. "We'll walk a little away from the light. You will not wish others to hear what I have to say."

"There is nothing you could say that could be of the remotest interest to me, Lord Carrington. Now, if you'll excuse me . . ."

His derisory laugh crackled in the soft June air. "Don't cross swords with me, Judith Davenport. I'm more than a match for a card-sharping hussy. You may live upon your wits, ma'am, but I can assure you I've been using mine rather longer than you've been using yours."

Judith abruptly dropped a clearly useless pretense. It would only increase his antagonism and thus the danger. She said evenly, "You can prove nothing."

"I'm not interested in proving anything," he replied. "I've said, you may make gulls of as many of these empty-headed idiots as you wish. But you'll leave my family alone." He took her elbow and began to walk down the shallow flight of steps onto the lawn. Twin oak trees threw giant moonshadow at the edge of the grass. In the dim obscurity, the marquis stopped. "So, Miss Davenport, I want your word that you will put an end to Charlie's infatuation."

Judith shrugged. "It's hardly my fault if he fancies himself in love with me."

"Oh, but it most certainly is your fault. Do you think I haven't watched you?" He leaned against the trunk of the oak, folding his arms, his eyes on the pale glimmer of her face, the golden glow of her eyes. "You are a masterly coquette, madam. And I would have you turn your liquid eyes and undeniable arts upon some other young fool."

"Whom your cousin chooses to love is surely his business," she said. "I fail to see how it could have anything to do with you, my lord."

"It has everything to do with me when my ward's embroiled with a fortune-hunting, unprincipled baggage with no—"

Her palm cracked against his cheek, bringing a sudden dreadful silence in which the strains of music drifted incongruously from the house.

Judith spun away from him with a little sob, pressing her hands to her lips, as if struggling with her tears in an excess of wounded pride and sensibility. Marcus Devlin had to be disarmed, somehow, and if honesty wouldn't do it, then she'd have to take another tack. She couldn't run the risk that he would spread his accusations around the London clubs when the Davenports made their entry into London Society. On the spur of the moment, she could think only to offer him the picture of deeply affronted innocence and hope to create if not compassion then some willingness to make amends with his future silence.

"You know nothing of me," she said in stifled tones. "You can know nothing of what we endure . . . of how we are in this situation. . . . I have never knowingly injured anyone, let alone your cousin . . ." Her voice died on a gulping sob.

She was certainly a consummate actress, Marcus reflected, for some reason not deceived for one minute by this masterly display. He stroked his stinging cheek, feeling the raised imprint of her fingers. There had been more conviction there, but such a violent exhibition of outraged virtue seemed hardly consonant with the disreputable woman he believed her to be. Ignoring the bravely stifled sobs, he observed dispassionately, "You've a deal of power in your arm for one so slight."

That was not the response she'd hoped for. Raising her head, she spoke with a brave, aloof dignity. "You owe me an apology, Lord Carrington."

"I rather think the boot is on the other foot." He continued to rub his cheek, regarding her with a penetrating scrutiny that did nothing to reassure her.

It seemed most sensible to escape the close confines of the shadows and an increasingly unstable confrontation that was not following her direction. Judith shrugged faintly. "You are no gentleman, my lord." She turned to go back to the house.

"Oh, no, you're not running off like that," the marquis said. "Not just yet. We haven't concluded our discussion, Miss Davenport." He caught her arm and for a second they stood immobile, Judith still turned toward the house, her captor still leaning against the tree. "That was a singularly violent assault, madam, in response to—"

"To an unmitigated insult, sir!" she interrupted,

hoping she didn't sound as back-to-the-wall as she was beginning to feel.

"But one not without justification," he pointed out. "You have admitted by default that you and your brother are . . . how shall we say . . . are expert gamesters, with somewhat unorthodox methods of play."

"I would like to return to the house." Even to Judith's ear, it was a pathetic plea rather than a determined statement of intent.

"In a minute. For such an accomplished flirt, you're playing the maiden of outraged virtue most convincingly, but I've a mind to taste a little more of you than the sting of your palm." He pulled her toward him like a fisherman drawing in his line and she came as reluctantly as any hooked fish. "It seems only right that you should soothe the hurt you caused." Cupping her chin with his free hand, he tilted her face. The black eyes were no longer hard and Judith could read a spark of laughter in their depths . . . laughter, and a most dangerous glimmer that set her nerve endings tingling. Desperately she sought for something that would douse both his laughter and that hazardous glimmer.

"You would have me kiss it better, sir, like a child's scraped knee?" She offered an indulgent smile and saw with satisfaction that she had surprised him, and surprise afforded advantage. Swiftly she stood on tiptoe and kissed his cheek. "There, that'll make it better." After twisting out of his abruptly slackened hold, she danced backward out of the shadows into the relative light of the garden. "I bid you good night, Lord Carrington." And she was gone, flitting under the moonlight, her body lissome as a hazel wand under the fluid silk of her topaz gown.

Marcus stared after her through the gloom. How the hell had such a disreputable baggage managed to win that encounter? He ought to be more than a match for a slip of a girl. He was annoyed; he was amused; but more than anything he was challenged by her. If she wouldn't be warned away from Charlie, then he'd have to find some more potent inducement.

Judith returned to the card room, but only to make her farewells, pleading a headache. Charlie was all solicitude, begging to escort her home, but Sebastian was on his feet immediately.

"No need for that, Fenwick. I'll take m'sister home." He yawned himself. "In truth, I'll not be sorry to keep early hours myself tonight. It's been a hard week." He grinned engagingly around the table.

"A demmed lucky one for you, Davenport," one of the players said with a sigh, pushing across an IOU.

"Oh, I've the luck of the devil," Sebastian said cheerfully, pocketing the vowel. "It runs in the family, doesn't it, Judith?"

Her smile was somewhat abstracted. "So they say."

Sebastian's eyes sharpened and his gaze flickered to the door of the card room, to where the Marquis of Carrington stood, taking snuff. "You look a little wan, m'dear," Sebastian said, taking his sister's arm.

"I don't feel quite the thing," she agreed. "Oh, thank you, Charlie." She smiled warmly as the young man arranged her shawl around her shoulders.

"Perhaps you won't feel like riding tomorrow," Charlie said, unable to hide the disappointment in his voice. "Shall I call upon you—"

"No, indeed not. My aunt detests callers," she broke in, touching his hand fleetingly as if in consolation. "But I shall be perfectly well tomorrow. I'll meet you in the park, as we arranged."

Brother and sister made their way out of the card room. Marcus bowed as they reached the door. "I bid you good night, Miss Davenport . . . Davenport."

"Good night, my lord." She swept past him, then, on an impulse she didn't quite understand, murmured over her shoulder, "I am riding with your cousin in the morning."

"Oh, I fully understand that you've thrown down the glove," he said, as softly as she. "But you have not yet tasted my mettle, ma'am. Take heed." He bowed again in formal farewell and turned away before she could reply.

Judith bit her lip, aware of a strange mingling of apprehension and excitement unlike anything she'd felt before, and she knew it was as dangerous as it was uncomfortable.

"What's amiss, Ju?" Sebastian spoke as soon as they were out of the mansion and on the cobbled street.

"I'll tell you when we get home." She climbed into the shabby carriage that awaited them on the corner, sitting back against the cracked leather squabs, a frown drawing her arched brows together, her teeth closing over her lower lip.

Sebastian knew that expression. It usually meant that his sister's eccentric principles were aroused. She wouldn't say anything until she was ready, so he was content to sit back and wait for her to tell him what was absorbing her.

The carriage drew up outside a narrow house on a darkened lane in a part of town that had definitely seen better days. Brother and sister alighted and Sebastian paid the driver for the evening's work. Judith was already unlocking the front door, and they stepped into a narrow passage, lit by a single tallow candle in a sconce on the stairway wall.

"One of these days someone's going to notice how

we never give anyone our direction," Sebastian observed, following his sister up the stairs. "The tale of the irritable aunt won't hold good forever."

"We won't be in Brussels for much longer," Judith said. "Napoleon's bound to make his move soon and then the army will be gone. There'll be no point in our remaining in an empty city." She pushed open a door at the head of the stairs onto a square parlor.

The room was dark and dingy, the furniture shabby, the carpet threadbare, and the gloomy light of tallow candles did nothing to improve matters. She tossed her India shawl on a broken-backed couch and sank into a chair, a deep frown corrugating her brow.

"How much did we make tonight?"

"Two thousand," he said. "It would have been more, but after you'd gone off with Carrington, I lost the next hand by miscounting an ace." He shook his head in self-disgust. "It's always the way; I grow careless if I rely on you for too many hands."

"Mmm." Judith kicked off her shoes and began to massage one foot. "But we need to practice now and again to keep our hands in. In fact, I think we must spend some serious time perfecting the moves because I must have made a mistake, although I can't think how. But the Most Honorable Marquis of Carrington is wise to us."

Sebastian whistled. "Hell and the devil. So now what?"

"I don't know exactly." Judith was still frowning as she switched feet, pulling on her toes with an absent vigor. "He said he'd not call foul on us, but he issued a most direct command that I cure Charlie of his infatuation."

"Well, that's easily done. You've never had any difficulty disentangling yourself from an overzealous suitor."

"No, but why should I? I have no intention of hurting Charlie. In fact, a little sophisticated dalliance will do wonders for him, and if he loses a few thousand at cards, it's not as if he can't afford it. Apart from those few minutes tonight, the only unfair odds he's faced are in your native talent. He plays because he chooses to, and I fail to see why Carrington should be allowed to meddle."

Sebastian regarded his sister warily. It was definitely a case of offended principles. "He is his guardian," he pointed out. "And we're a disreputable pair, Ju. You shouldn't take it too much to heart if someone realizes that and behaves accordingly."

"Oh, nonsense!" she said. "We're no more disreputable than anyone else. It's just that we're not hypocrites. We have to put a roof over our heads and bread on the table, and we do it in the only way we know."

Sebastian went to the sideboard and poured cognac into two goblets. "You could always go for a governess." He handed her one of the goblets, chuckling at her horrified expression. "I can just see you imparting the finer points of watercolors and the rudiments of Italian to frilly little girls in a schoolroom."

Judith began to laugh. "Not at all. I would teach them to play piquet and backgammon for large stakes; to flutter their eyelashes and offer amusing little sallies to gentlemen who might be induced to play; to know when it's time to move on; to find the cheapest lodgings and servants; to slip away in the night to avoid the bailiff; to create a wardrobe out of thin air. In short, I would teach them all the elements for a successful masquerade. Just as I was taught."

The laughter had left her voice half way through the speech and Sebastian took her hand. "We'll be avenged, Ju."

"For Father," she said, lifting her head and taking a sip of her cognac. "Yes, we'll be avenged for him."

Silently Sebastian joined her in the toast, and for a moment they both stared into the empty grate, remembering. Remembering and reaffirming their vow. Then Judith put the glass on a side table and stood. "I'm going to bed." She kissed his cheek and the gesture reminded her of something that brought a glitter of determination to her eyes. "I'm in the mood to play with fire, Sebastian."

"Carrington?"

She nodded. "The gentleman needs to be disarmed. He said he wouldn't cry foul on us, but supposing he decided to alert people in London to beware of playing with you? If I can intrigue him . . . engage him in a flirtation . . . he'll be less likely to concern himself with what you do at the tables."

Sebastian regarded his sister dubiously. "Are you a match for him?"

Was she? For a minute she felt again the press of his fingers on her skin, saw again the sharp shrewdness in the black eyes, the unconciliatory slash of his mouth, the prominent jaw. But of course she was a match for any town beau. She knew things, had seen and done things, that had honed her wits to a keenness he would not be expecting.

"Of course," she declared confidently. "And there'll be great satisfaction, I can tell you, in seeing him succumb as easily as his cousin did. It'll teach him to be so high-handed."

Sebastian looked even more dubious. "I don't like it when you mix motives like that. We're so close to catching up with Gracemere, Judith. Don't risk anything."

"I won't, I promise. I'm just going to show the most honorable marquis that I don't take kindly to insults."

"But if you arouse his curiosity, he's going to want to know who we are and where we come from."

She shrugged. "So what? The usual fiction will satisfy him. We're the children of an eccentric English gentleman of respectable though obscure lineage, recently deceased, who, after the death of his wife at a tragically early age, chose to travel the Continent for the rest of his life with us in tow."

"Instead of the truth," Sebastian said. "That we're the children of a disgraced Yorkshire squire, disinherited by his family, driven out of England by scandal and his wife's subsequent suicide, forced to change his name and earn his bread at the gaming tables of the Continent." The story rolled glibly off his tongue, but Judith knew her brother and could hear his pain; it was her own, too.

"And he taught his children all he knew, so that from a horribly precocious age they were his enablers and assistants," she finished for him.

Sebastian shook his head. "Too harsh a truth for the delicate sensibilities of the Quality to handle, my dear."

"Just so." Judith nodded with a return to briskness. "Don't worry, Sebastian. Carrington won't get so much as a sniff at the real story. I'll invent some playful reason for that piece of dubious card play this evening. Mischief rather than need, I think. And if he doesn't catch us at it again and I manage to charm him a bit, I'm sure he won't mention it again."

"I've not yet met the man you can't entangle when you put your mind to it," Sebastian agreed, chuckling. "Just watching you at work is an everlasting delight."

"Wait until I turn my charms on Gracemere," his sister said, blowing him a kiss. "That'll be a treat, I promise you."

She went into her bedroom next door—a room as dingy as the parlor and none too clean. The landlord's serving maid was less than thorough at her tasks, but the Davenports had been living in such lodgings for as long as they could remember and were accustomed to seeing only what they chose to see.

Undressed, she climbed into bed and lay looking up at the faded canopy. Gracemere was in London. They would need maybe twenty thousand pounds in ready money to set themselves up in London in a reasonably fashionable part of town. There would be servants to pay, some form of carriage and horses, even if they were only hired. They would both need large and elaborate wardrobes and at least an illusion of a generous income. The gaming would take care of their everyday expenses once they were established, but they would have to tread a fine line. High-stakes gaming was an accepted activity in Society, for women as well as men, but one must never give the impression that it mattered whether one won or lost.

They would operate their double act only in the final stages of the plan, when it was time to administer the coup de grace. It was too dangerous and powerful a tool to be used except in extremity.

George Davenport had never known of the double act. He had taught his children to rely on wits and skill at the tables, but there had been times of dire necessity . . . those days, sometimes weeks, when he had retreated into the dark world of his soul and there had been no money for food or fuel or even lodging. Then Judith and her brother had learned to fend for themselves.

Tonight they had been practicing, as they did now and again, but somehow she had slipped up and been discovered.

Marcus Devlin, Marquis of Carrington.

Bernard Melville, third Earl of Gracemere.

Her strategem with the one must advance her plans for the other. Sebastian was right about the dangers of mixed motives. She must concentrate only on the need to disarm the marquis in order to guarantee his silence. And any personal satisfaction she might garner from his submission would be a purely private and secondary pleasure. Nothing must be permitted to jeopardize the grand design . . . the driving force behind the life she and Sebastian presently led.

2

"My dear Bernard, how will I endure two whole months without you?" Agnes Barret sighed and stretched out a bare leg, examining the supple curve of calf, the delicate turn of ankle with a complacent smile. She pinched her thigh several times between finger and thumb; the flesh was as firm as a girl's.

"Your husband's entitled to a honeymoon, my dear." The Earl of Gracemere watched his lady with a knowing smile laced with desire. Agnes's vanity was one of her few weaknesses—her only weakness, in fact, and she was undoubtedly entitled to it. At forty-three she was more beautiful than she'd been at twenty, he thought. Her hair was still as lustrously auburn as ever, her tawny eyes as luminous, her skin as soft and translucent, her figure as lithe and elegant. In truth, there wasn't a woman to touch her, and Bernard Melville had known many women. But always there had been Agnes. She was woven into the fabric of his life as he was woven into hers.

"Oh, Thomas!" Agnes dismissed the inconvenient bridegroom with a languid wave of one white hand. "He's suffering from another attack of gout, would you believe? He can't bear anyone to come within six feet of his left foot, which should rather cut down on the customary activities of a honeymoon." She picked up a glass of wine from the bedside table and sipped, glancing at the earl over the rim.

"Is that a cause for complaint?" Bernard inquired. "I was under the impression that you were dreading the duties of the conjugal bedchamber with an elderly husband."

"Well, so I am, but one must have something to do to while away two months of rustication," Agnes returned, a shade tartly. "I assume *you* will find solace for your empty bed somewhere in Yorkshire . . . a village girl, or a milkmaid, or some such."

"Jealous, Agnes?" He smiled and took up his own glass. He walked to the window, looking down at the sluggishly flowing River Thames below. A horse-drawn barge inched along the south bank of the river. One of London's many church bells pealed on the hot June air.

"Hardly. I don't consider country wenches as rivals."

"My dear one, you have no equal anywhere, so you cannot possibly fear a rival." He took a sip of wine and bent over her, holding the wine in his mouth as he brought his lips to hers. Her mouth opened beneath his and the wine slid over his tongue to fill her mouth with a warm sweetness. His hands went to her breasts in a leisurely caress and she fell back on the bed beneath him.

The evening sun had set, turning the river below

their window to a dull, gunmetal gray, before they spoke again.

"I don't know how soon I'll be able to ask Thomas for a sum sufficient to quieten your creditors." Agnes shifted and the bedropes creaked. "It's a little awkward to demand a substantial sum from one's bridegroom as one leaves the altar."

"That's why I'm going into Yorkshire," Bernard said, letting his hand rest on her turned flank. "I can escape my creditors for the summer, while you, my love, work upon the gouty but so wealthy Sir Thomas."

Agnes chuckled. "I have my appealing story well prepared . . . an indigent second cousin, I believe, suffering from rheumatism and living in a drafty garret."

"I trust you won't be required to produce this relative," Bernard remarked with a responding chuckle. "I don't know how good a master of disguise I would prove."

"You are as much a master of deception as I, my dear," Agnes said.

"Which is why we suit each other so remarkably well," Bernard agreed.

"And always have done." Agnes's mouth curved in a smile of reminiscence. "Even as children . . . how old were we, the first time?"

Bernard turned his head to look at the face beside him on the pillow. "Old enough . . . although some might say we were a trifle precocious." He moved his hand lazily to palm the delicate curve of her cheek. "We were born to please each other, my love." Hitching himself on one elbow, he brought his mouth to hers, exerting a bruising almost suffocating pressure as his palm tightened around her face and he held her flat and still with his weight. When finally he released her mouth, there was an almost feral glitter of excitement in her tawny eyes. She touched her bruised and swollen lips with a caressing finger.

Bernard laughed and lay down beside her again. "However," he said as if that moment of edging violence had not occurred, "I shall look around me for a fat pigeon to pluck at the beginning of the Season. I don't wish to be totally dependent upon your husband's unwitting charity."

"No, it would be as well not. It's a pity Thomas is no gamester." Agnes sighed. "That was such a perfect game we once played."

"But, as you say, Thomas Barret is no George Devereux," Gracemere agreed, reaching indolently for his wineglass. "I wonder what happened to that husband of yours."

"It's to be hoped he's dead," Agnes said, taking the glass from him. "Otherwise I am a bigamist, my dear." She sipped, her eyes gleaming with amusement.

"Who's to know but you and I?" Her companion laughed with the same amusement. "Alice Devereux, the wife of George Devereux, has been dead and buried these last twenty years as far as the world's concerned . . . dead of grief at her husband's dishonor." He chuckled richly.

"Not that the world saw anything of her, either before or during her marriage," Agnes put in with remembered bitterness. "Having married his country innocent, George was interested only in keeping her pregnant and secluded in the Yorkshire wilds."

"But with the death of reclusive Alice in a remote convent in the French Alps, the sociable Agnes was born," Gracemere pointed out.

"Yes, a far preferable identity," Agnes agreed with some satisfaction. "I enjoyed making my society debut as the wealthy young widow of an elderly Italian count.

Society is so much more indulgent toward women of independent means, particularly if they have a slightly mysterious past." She smiled lazily. "I wouldn't be an ingenue again for all the youthful beauty in the world. Do you ever miss Alice, Bernard?"

He shook his head. "No, Agnes is so much more exciting, my love. Alice was a young girl, while Agnes was born into womanhood . . . and women have much more to offer a man of my tastes."

"Sophisticated, and perhaps a little *outré*," Agnes murmured, again touching her bruised mouth. "But to return to the question of money . . ."

"I still have George's Yorkshire estate," Bernard said.

"But it yields little now."

"No, it's a sad fact that property needs to be maintained if it's to continue to support one," he agreed, sighing. "And maintenance requires funds . . . and, sadly, funds I do not have."

"Not for such mundane concerns as estate maintenance," Agnes stated without criticism.

"True enough, there are always more important . . . or, rather, more enticing ways of spending money." He swung himself off the bed. "On which subject . . ." He crossed to the dressing table. Agnes sat up, watching him, greedily drinking in his nakedness even though his body was as familiar to her as her own.

"On which subject," he repeated, opening a drawer. "I have a wedding present for you, my love." He came back to the bed and tossed a silk pouch into her lap, laughing as she seized it with eager fingers. "You were always rapacious, my adorable Agnes."

"We're well suited," she returned swiftly, casting him a glinting smile as she drew from the pouch a diamond collar. "Oh, Bernard, it's beautiful."

"Isn't it?" he agreed. "I trust you'll be able to persuade your husband to reimburse me at some point."

Agnes went into a peal of laughter. "You are a complete hand, Bernard. My lover buys me a wedding present that my husband will be required to pay for. I do love you."

"I thought you'd appreciate the finer points of the jest," he said, kneeling on the bed. "Let me fasten it for you. Diamonds and nakedness are a combination I've never been able to resist."

"I don't see your cousin this evening, Charlie." Judith slipped her arm through her escort's as they strolled through the crowded salon. She glanced around, as she had been doing all evening, wondering despite herself why the Marquis of Carrington had chosen not to honor the Bridges' soiree.

"Marcus isn't much of a one for balls and such frippery things," Charlie said. "He's very bookish." His tone made this sound like some fatal ailment. "Military history," he elucidated. "He reads histories in Greek and Latin and writes about old battles. I can't understand why anyone should still be interested in who won some battle way back in classical times, can you?"

Judith smiled. "Perhaps I can. It would be interesting to work out how and why a battle turned out as it did, and to make comparisons with present-day warfare."

"That's exactly what Marcus says!" Charlie exclaimed. "He's forever closeted with Wellington and Blücher and the like, discussing Napoleon and what he might decide to do on the basis of what he's done in the past. I can't see why that should be as useful as going out and getting on with the fighting, but everyone seems to think it is."

"Battles aren't won without strategy and tactics," Judith pointed out. "And only careful strategy can minimize casualties." She reflected that perhaps nineteen-year-olds on the eve of battle, drunk on dreams of heroism and glory, probably wouldn't take this particular point.

"Well, I can't wait to have a crack at Boney," Charlie declared, looking a trifle disappointed at his goddess's lack of enthusiasm for the blood and guts of warfare.

"I'm certain you'll have your chance soon enough," Judith said. "As I understand it, Wellington's only waiting for Napoleon to make his approach and then he'll attack before he's properly in position."

"But I don't understand why we can't just go out and meet him. He's already left Paris," Charlie complained in an undertone, glancing around to make sure none of his fellow officers in their brilliant regimentals could overhear a possibly disloyal comment. "Why do we have to wait for him to come close?"

"I imagine it would be rather cumbersome to move 214,000 men at this stage in order to intercept him," Judith said. "They're strung out from Mons to Brussels, and Charleroi to Liege, as I understand it."

"You sound just like Marcus," Charlie observed again. "It seems very poor-spirited to me."

Judith laughed and took the opportunity to return the conversation to its original topic, one that interested her rather more. "So your cousin doesn't care for balls and assemblies. It's perhaps fortunate he doesn't have a wife in that case." She said it casually, with another light laugh.

"Oh, Marcus is not overfond of ladies' company in the general run of things."

"Why not?"

Charlie frowned. "I think it may have something to

do with an old engagement. But I don't fully understand the reasons. He has women . . . other sorts of women . . . I mean . . ." He stammered to a halt, his face fiery in the candlelight.

"I know exactly what you mean," she said, patting his arm. "There's no reason to be embarrassed with me, Charlie."

"But I shouldn't have mentioned such a thing in front of a lady," he said, still blushing. "Only I feel so comfortable with you . . ."

"Like an older sister," Judith said, smiling.

"Oh, no . . . no, of course not . . . how could I . . ." Again he fell silent and Judith could almost hear the recognition of what she'd said falling into place like the tumblers of a lock. She chuckled to herself. Charlie was well on the way to curing himself of his infatuation without the heavy-handed intervention of an overanxious guardian. Not that she was about to inform the most honorable marquis of that fact. . . . Not that he was around to be informed, anyway.

Marcus put in an appearance as the clock struck midnight. He could see no sign of his ward or Miss Davenport, although the world seemed gathered in the Bridges' salons. After greeting his hostess he strolled into the card room. The faro table was crowded, the atmosphere lively and good humored. Sebastian Davenport was a steady winner. The marquis stood watching the table intently. There was nothing amiss with the way the man was playing. He certainly had luck on his side, but there was something else. Some innate ability to make judgments on the odds. He examined Sebastian's face. It was quite impassive while he was making his bet, then the minute he'd declared, tossing his rouleaux onto the table, he was as relaxed and lighthearted as ever. A true gamester, Marcus thought. It took a combination of brains and nerve, and Sebastian Davenport had both. Marcus didn't think his sister lacked those qualities either, although he hadn't yet observed her play.

Unprincipled adventurers, the pair of them, he decided. But he could see no reason at this point to expose them. Only the greedy and the foolish fell victim to hardened gamesters, and they got what they deserved. He would take steps to protect Charlie himself.

"Davenport . . . a game of piquet?"

The suggestion surprised Sebastian. He looked up at the marquis, remembering Judith's encounter the previous evening. But the suggestion was seemingly innocuous and piquet was Sebastian's game. "Why, certainly," he said cheerfully. "A hundred guineas a point?"

Marcus swallowed this without a blink. "Whatever you say."

Sebastian settled with the faro table and rose. The marquis was waiting for him at a small card table in a relatively quiet corner of the room. He indicated a fresh deck of cards on the table as he took his place. "Do you care to break them, Davenport?"

Sebastian shrugged and pushed them across to the marquis. "You do the honors, my lord."

"As you wish." The cards were shuffled and dealt and a silence fell between the two men. Sebastian had a full glass of claret at his elbow but Marcus noticed that although he seemed to raise it to his lips frequently, the level barely went down. A most serious gamester. And an expert card player. Marcus, who was no mean player himself, recognized that he was outclassed after the third hand. He relaxed, resigned to his losses, and began to enjoy playing with a master.

"Well, my lord, this is a pleasant surprise." Judith's dulcet tones came from behind him and she offered him her most ravishing smile. "I have been sadly disappointed at your absence."

"Stand behind your brother," he snapped, quite impervious to this coquettry.

"I beg your pardon?" She frowned in puzzlement.

"Stand behind your brother, where I can see you."

Comprehension dawned. She stared at him in dismay, all pretense at flirtation vanishing under the sting of such an unwarranted assumption. "But I wouldn't—"

"Wouldn't you?" he interrupted, without looking up from his cards; it was a damnably difficult discard he had to make. "Nevertheless, I prefer not to take the risk. Now move."

She stepped sideways, struggling for composure, seeking support from her brother. "Sebastian . . . ?"

Sebastian gave a rueful chuckle. "He caught you at it, Ju. I can't call him out for you. Not in the circumstances."

"No, I don't think you can," Marcus agreed, discarding a ten of spades. "Not that you need any help from your sister." He watched with resignation as his opponent picked up the discard. "You'll not even spare me the Rubicon, I fear."

Sebastian totted up the points. "I'm afraid not, Carrington. I make it ninety-seven."

"What were the stakes?" Judith demanded, this issue taking immediate precedence over hurt feelings.

Marcus began to laugh. "What an incorrigibly unprincipled pair you are."

"Not really," Sebastian said. "Ju, at least, has some very strong principles . . . it's just that they tend to be eccentric. Her view of ethics doesn't always coincide with the common view."

"I don't find that in the least difficult to believe," Marcus said.

"That's true of you, too, Sebastian," Judith pointed out. "You should understand, my lord, that we obey our own rules." Maybe a different form of flirtation would work with this intransigent marquis. If he preferred challenge to coquettry, she could offer him that.

Disappointingly, Marcus shook his head. "That's provocation for another day, ma'am. . . . I'll settle up with you in the morning, Davenport." He scrawled an IOU on the pad at his elbow and pushed it over. "Fill in the sum. What have you done with my cousin, Miss Davenport?"

"He's gone off with Viscount Chancet and his friends. They had an engagement. And he is feeling very much in charity with me, my lord."

Marcus stood up. "Mmmm. Somehow that doesn't surprise me. However, don't rest on your laurels, my dear." He pinched her cheek. "As I told you yesterday, you haven't yet tasted my mettle."

"He's damned familiar with you," Sebastian observed as the marquis walked off.

"Yes, and I could cut his throat," Judith declared. "I'm trying to flirt with him and he treats me like a tiresome child in the schoolroom. I think he believes that now he knows what we are, he can be as familiar as he pleases."

Sebastian frowned. "That's perhaps understandable. Just so long as he keeps his knowledge to himself."

Judith sighed. "I don't seem to be doing too well with my present strategy to ensure that he does."

"You were confident enough yesterday," her brother reminded her, gathering up the cards. "And you've never failed yet."

"True." Judith nodded resolutely to herself. "There has to be some way to persuade him to take me seriously. I suspect quarreling with him is the answer."

Sebastian laughed. "Well, you're the fire-eater of the family, Ju."

"Yes, and I intend to put it to good use." A tiny smile flickered over her mouth. She was unable to deny the prickle of excitement at the prospect of joining in a battle of wits and wills with the most honorable marquis.

3

"*G*ood morning, Charlie." Marcus greeted his cousin the next morning. Charlie was already at the breakfast table facing a platter of sirloin and mumbled an answering greeting through a mouthful of beef.

"How much did you lose at the tables the other night?" Marcus inquired casually, pouring himself coffee. "When you were playing macao at Davenport's table." He regarded the chafing dishes on the sideboard with an appraising eye.

Charlie swallowed his mouthful and took a gulp of ale. "Not much."

"And how much is not much?" Marcus helped himself to a dish of deviled kidneys.

"Seven hundred guineas," his cousin said with an air of defiance. "I don't consider that beyond my means."

"No," Marcus agreed affably enough. "So long as one doesn't do it every night. Do you play often at his table?"

"That was the first time, I believe." Charlie frowned. "Why do you ask?"

Marcus didn't reply, but continued with his own questions. "Did his sister suggest you play at her brother's table?"

"I don't remember. It's not the kind of thing a fellow does remember." Charlie stared at his cousin in puzzlement and some apprehension. In his experience, Marcus rarely asked pointless questions, and it seemed this series might well be leading up to a stricture on gaming . . . familiar but nevertheless mortifying.

But Marcus merely shrugged and opened the newspaper. "No, I suppose it's not. . . . By the by . . ." He folded back the paper and spoke with his eyes on the page. "Don't you think Judith Davenport's a little too rich for your blood?"

Charlie flushed. "What are you trying to say?"

"Nothing much," Marcus replied, glancing briefly over the newspaper. "She's an attractive woman and a practiced flirt."

"She's . . . she's a wonderful woman," Charlie exclaimed, pushing back his chair, his flush deepening. "You cannot insult her!"

"Now don't fly into the boughs, Charlie. I doubt she'd deny the description herself." Marcus reached for the mustard.

"Of course she's not a flirt." Charlie glared at his cousin over the stiffly starched folds of his linen cravat.

Marcus sighed. "Well, we won't argue terms, but she's too much for a nineteen-year-old to handle, Charlie. She's no schoolroom chit."

"I don't find schoolroom chits in the least appealing," his cousin announced.

"Well, at your age, you should." He looked across the table and said, not unkindly, "Judith Davenport is a sophisticated woman of the world. She plays a deep game and you're way out of your depth. She eats greenhorns for supper, my dear boy. People are already beginning to talk. You don't want to be the laughingstock of Brussels."

"I think it's most unchivalrous, if not downright dishonorable, of you to insult her when she's not here to defend herself," Charlie declared with passion. "And I take leave to tell you—"

"Please don't," Marcus interrupted, waving a dismissive hand. "It's too early in the morning to hear the impassioned rambles of a besotted youth." He forked kidneys into his mouth. "If you want to make a cake of yourself, then you may do so, but do it when I'm not around."

Charlie huffed in speechless indignation, his face burning, then he stormed out of the breakfast parlor.

Marcus winced as the door slammed shut. He wondered if he'd chosen the wrong tactic in this instance. In the past, a cutting comment, a decisively adverse opinion, had been sufficient to bring Charlie back on the right track when he'd been about to stray into some youthful indiscretion. But then Charlie was no longer a schoolboy, and maybe the tactics appropriate for schoolboys wouldn't work with the tender pride of a young man in the throes of first love.

He'd have to try some other approach. His fork paused halfway to his mouth as the approach presented itself, neat and most enticing. What better way to remove Charlie from dangerous proximity to Miss Davenport than to take his place? At present, Marcus had no mistress living under his protection. He had brought his last *affaire* to an expensive close without regret, before coming to Brussels. Supposing he made Judith Davenport an offer she couldn't refuse? It would most effectively remove her from Charlie's orbit. And just as effectively, it would cure Charlie of his infatuation, when he saw her for what she was. And for himself . . .

Dear God in heaven. Images of rioting sensuality suddenly filled his head as he found himself mentally stripping her of the elegant gowns, the delicate undergarments, the silken stockings, revealing the lissome slenderness, the supple limbs, the white fineness of her skin. Would she be a passionate lover or passive . . . no, definitely not passive . . . wild and tumbling, with the eager words of hungry need, the tumultuous cries of fulfillment unchecked upon her lips. Impossible to believe she could be otherwise.

Marcus shook his head clear of the images. If they alone could arouse him, what would the reality do? The proposition took concrete shape. Yes, he would make Miss Judith Davenport an offer she couldn't possibly refuse: one beyond the wildest dreams of a woman who earned her bread at the gaming tables.

An hour later, in buckskin britches and a morning coat of olive-green superfine, his top boots catching the sunlight like a polished diamond, his lordship set out in search of Miss Davenport. There was a powerful tension in the Brussels' air, knots of people gathered on street corners, talking and gesticulating excitedly. He discovered the reason in the regimental mess.

"It looks like Boney's going to attack," Peter Wellby told him as he joined the circle of Wellington's staff and advisors deep in an almost frenzied discussion. "He issued a *Proclamation à l'armee* yesterday, and it's just come into our hands." He handed Marcus a document.

"He's reminding his men that it's the anniversary of the battles of Marengo and Friedland. If they've succeeded in deciding the fate of the world twice before on this day, then they'll do it a third time."

Marcus read it. "Mmm. Napoleon's usual style," he commented. "An appeal to past glories to drum up spirit and patriotism."

"But it usually works," Colonel, Lord Francis Tallent observed a touch glumly. "We've been sitting on our backsides waiting to catch him off guard, and the bastard takes the initiative right out from under our noses. We're prepared to attack, not defend."

Marcus nodded. "It would have been worth remembering that Napoleon has never waited to be attacked. His strategy has always been based on a vast and overwhelming offensive."

There was a moment of uncomfortable silence. Marcus Devlin had been vociferous in this view for the last week, but his had been a lone voice crying in the wilderness. "We did receive a report from our agents that he was taking up the defensive on the Charleroi road," Peter said eventually.

"Agents can be fed mistaken information." Marcus's wry observation generated another silence.

"Marcus, I'm glad to see you, man." Arthur Wellesley, Duke of Wellington, came out of a next-door office, a chart in his hand. "You seem to have had the right idea. Now, look at this. He can attack at Ligny, Quatre Bras, or Nivelles. Do you have an opinion?" He laid the chart on a table, jabbing at the three crossroads with a stubby forefinger.

Marcus examined the chart. "Ligny," he said definitely. "It's the weakest point in our line. There's a hole where Blücher's forces and ours don't meet."

"Blücher's ordered men up from Namur to reinforce

his troops at Ligny," the duke said. "We'll concentrate our army on the front from Brussels to Nivelles."

"Supposing the French swing round to the north toward Quatre Bras," Marcus pointed out, tracing the line with a fingertip. "He'll separate the two forces and force us to fight on two fronts."

Wellington frowned, stroking his chin. "Can you join me in conference this afternoon?" He rolled up the chart.

"At your service, Duke." Marcus bowed.

His own plans ought to seem less urgent in the face of the present emergency, but for some reason they weren't. He would see Judith tonight, of course, at the Duchess of Richmond's ball, but he was in a fever of impatience, almost as if he were still a green youth pursuing the object of hot and flagrant fantasy. Reasoning that he could be of little use until the afternoon's conference, he decided to continue his search.

He ran her to earth at the lodgings of one of Wellington's aides-de-camp. It seemed as if half Brussels were gathered there, chattering and exclaiming over the news that, incredibly, Napoleon had taken Wellington by surprise and was even now preparing for an attack on the city.

"But the duke has all well in hand," a bewhiskered colonel reassured a twittering, panicked lady in an Angoulême bonnet. "He'll concentrate his troops on the Nivelles road to meet any attack on the city."

"I'm sure there's nothing to concern us, dear ma'am," came the dulcet tones of Miss Davenport. She was standing by the window and a shaft of sunlight ignited the rich copper hair braided in a demure coronet around her head. She was in flowing muslins, a wisp of lace doing duty as a hat, and Carrington regarded her for a minute in appreciative silence. There was something wonderfully tantalizing about the contrast between her demurely elegant dress and the wicked gleam in the gold-brown eyes as she surveyed the room and its alarmed inhabitants with the faintest tinge of derision. A jolt of anticipatory excitement surprised him. He didn't think he'd felt such powerful lust since his youth.

He crossed the room toward her. "Your sangfroid is estimable, ma'am. Don't you feel the slightest tremor at the thought of the ogre?"

"Not in the least, sir." Idly she twirled her closed parasol on the floor. "I trust you've recovered from your losses last night. They were rather heavy, I believe."

"Are you referring to my losses to your brother, or to his sister, ma'am?" His eyes narrowed as he flipped open his snuff box and took a delicate pinch.

"I was not aware of any winnings, sir." She looked up at him through her eyelashes. "Only of the need to keep up my point."

"I'm hoping to persuade you to lower that point." He replaced the enameled snuff box in the deep pocket of his coat. "I have a proposal to make, Miss Davenport. May I call upon you this afternoon?"

"Unfortunately, my aunt, who lives with us, is indisposed and visitors quite put her out of curl. The sound of the door knocker is enough to throw her into strong hysterics," she said with a bland smile.

"What a masterly fibber you are, Miss Davenport," he observed amiably. "I won't ask why you see a need to keep your direction a close secret."

"How gentlemanly of you, Lord Carrington."

"Yes, isn't it? But perhaps I could induce you to call upon me."

"Now, that, my lord, is not a gentlemanly suggestion."

"I was, of course, assuming your aunt would escort you as chaperone," he murmured.

An appreciative twinkle appeared in her eyes. This was much more amusing than an ordinary flirtation. Marcus Devlin was certainly an entertaining opponent when it came to challenges. "I'm afraid she doesn't go out of doors, either."

"How very inconvenient . . . or do I mean convenient?"

"I don't know what you could mean, Lord Carrington."

"Well, what's to be done? I wish to have private speech with you; how is it to be contrived?"

"You seemed remarkably expert at abduction the other evening," Judith heard herself say, astonished at the recklessness of her response.

He bowed, and his black eyes glittered. "If that's how you'd like to proceed, I am always happy to oblige. Make your farewells, we're going in search of privacy."

"You would find it difficult to abduct me from this room, I think, sir." She gestured to the crowd.

"Do you care to make a wager, ma'am?"

She caught her lower lip between her teeth, putting her head on one side as she considered the question. This was infinitely more entertaining than simple flirtation. "Twenty guineas?"

"We have a wager, Miss Davenport." The next instant, he had swept her off her feet and bundled her into his arms. It was so startling, she was momentarily speechless. And then he was pushing through the crowd with his burden. "Miss Davenport is feeling faint. I fear the news of Napoleon's advent has quite overset her."

"Oh, goodness me, and it's no wonder," the bewhiskered colonel said. "We must protect the delicate sensibilities of ladies from such news."

"Just so, Naseby," Marcus agreed. "I'm going to take her into the air. It's very close in here." People fell back, clucking solicitously, clearing his path to the door. Judith, recovered from her surprise, still found it impossible to say anything that wouldn't make the situation even more farcical, and was obliged to close her eyes tight and remain still as he carried her out of the house and into the street.

There he set his seething burden on her feet, dusted off his hands with great satisfaction, and said, "You owe me twenty guineas, Miss Davenport."

"That was shameless!" she exclaimed. "And to say I was swooning with fear of Napoleon was . . . was . . . was . . . Oh, I can't think of the right words."

"Dastardly," he supplied helpfully. "Despicable, shabby . . ."

"Unsporting," she snapped. "Adding insult to injury."

"But irresistible, you must admit."

"I admit nothing." She smoothed down her skirts and adjusted a pin in the diminutive lacy cap, before putting up her parasol. "I don't have twenty guineas with me, my lord. But I will send it around to your house this afternoon."

"That will be quite convenient." He bowed. "However, I'm more interested at the moment in finding somewhere private. We'll walk in the park, I think." He drew her arm through his.

"I don't care to walk in the park." Petulance seemed to have replaced mature challenge.

"Would you prefer me to escort you home?" he offered with prompt courtesy.

"You know I would not."

"Then it must be the park."

And that seemed to be that. Short of turning and

running, which would be ridiculously undignified, there seemed no alternative but to do as he said. She'd husband her resources for the time being.

They passed through the iron gates at the entrance to the park and Lord Carrington directed their steps unerringly to a small copse.

Judith hesitated as they moved into the cool, green seclusion. Something didn't feel right. "Can't we have this discussion in the open, my lord?"

"No, because I can't be walking around when I say what I wish to say, and if we were to stand still in the middle of the path it would look very odd." Releasing her arm, he sat down on a stone bench encircling the trunk of a pine tree and patted the space beside him.

Judith was unsure whether it was invitation or command, but it didn't seem to matter. She sat down, curiosity now getting the better of unease.

"I'll come straight to the point," he said.

"Do."

He ignored the sardonic interjection. "A house and servants in Half Moon Street; a barouche and pair, or laundelet, if you prefer; a riding horse; and a quarterly allowance of two thousand pounds."

"Good God," Judith said. "Whatever are you saying?" She turned to look up at him, her eyes wide. "I think you are run mad."

"It seems reasonable," he said. "Such an allowance should be more than enough to keep you in style . . . of course, there'll be presents. You'll not find me ungenerous, my dear."

"Sweet heaven." The color had drained from her cheeks. "Could you be utterly precise about what you're offering me, my lord?"

It struck him she was being unusually obtuse. "A carte blanche," he elucidated. "And I will make provision for your future should we . . . should we tire of one another." He smiled. "There now, what could be fairer than that?"

Judith rose from the bench. Turning her back on him, she walked a few paces away. Her game of intrigue had suddenly got out of hand. It was one thing to engage a man in a pointful flirtation, quite another to be his paid whore. *How dared he make such a proposition . . . make such assumptions about her?*

Marcus watched her fumble in her reticule and thought perhaps she was looking for her handkerchief. Such an offer would be sufficient to bring tears to the eyes of the most grasping female.

"I don't have anyone to defend my honor, Lord Carrington, so I must do it for myself." She turned. In her hand was a small, silver-mounted pistol, and it was pointed in the most workmanlike fashion at his heart. "You have insulted me beyond bearing. Davenports are not whores. Even highly paid whores."

Carrington was vaguely aware that his jaw had dropped and his mouth was hanging open as he stared in shocked amazement, his eyes riveted to the small, deadly muzzle pointing at his chest. "Don't be ridiculous," he said, swallowing hard. "Put the gun away, Judith, before you do something stupid."

"I am an excellent shot, I should tell you," she said. "I'm not about to do anything stupid. Indeed, I consider putting a bullet in you, my lord, to be one of my more sensible notions."

"God in heaven," he whispered, trying to order the turmoil raging in his brain. For some reason, he had the unshakable conviction that Judith Davenport was more than capable of pulling the trigger. "I intended no insult," he tried. "Not to you or to your family. The manner in which you and your brother live led me to assume you wouldn't be averse to an unconventional but nevertheless convenient source of income. You don't live like a woman of virtue, ma'am, however skillful you are at the masquerade. You and your brother lead a raffish, hand-to-mouth existence in the shadows of the gaming tables. Can you deny that?"

Judith didn't attempt to do so. "That doesn't justify offering me such a dishonorable proposal. My circumstances are not of my own making. You can know nothing of them."

Marcus swallowed again. His mouth was very dry. He wondered if he could cross the space between them before she pulled the trigger. He couldn't. He watched, mesmerized, as she squinted down the barrel, extending her hand with the pistol straight in front of her. The sharp report and the flash of fire from the barrel were simultaneous. The smell of cordite hung in the muggy air. He waited for the pain, but there was nothing. He followed the direction of her eyes, between his feet. The bullet had dug a neat hole in the ground, directly in the middle of the space between his boots. It was no accident.

"I decided you weren't worth hanging for," Judith said coldly. She dropped the pistol in her reticule. "I'll send the twenty guineas to your house as soon as I return to my lodgings."

Marcus cleared his throat. "In the circumstances, I am prepared to forgo the wager."

"I always pay my debts of honor," she said. "Or did you think that I was without honor in that respect also?"

He waved his hands in hasty retraction. "It was only a suggestion. One quite without merit, I realize."

Judith glared at him for a minute, then she turned and marched away through the trees.

Marcus let out his breath on a slow exhalation, running his hands through his hair. He had assumed she received such proposals often enough. She lived by her wits, it was only to be expected that she might use her body, too. But what had her brother said? Something about his sister's eccentric principles. Presumably, he'd just been given a lesson in them.

Sweet heaven, what an exciting partner in passion such a woman would make. Perversely, he found he had not the slightest intention of giving up his pursuit.

"Good God, what's happened to send you into such a temper, Ju?" Sebastian looked up from the chess board as his sister banged fuming through the door of their living room.

"I don't think I have ever been angrier," she said, drawing her gloves off her trembling hands. "Lord Carrington has just had the . . . the unmitigated gall to offer me a carte blanche." She tossed her gloves onto the sofa and pulled the pins loose from her hat.

Sebastian whistled. "What did you say?"

"I shot him." She pulled the pistol from her reticule and hurled it onto the sofa.

Her brother reached over and picked up the weapon. The smell of cordite was acrid on the muzzle. He spun the chamber. It was empty. "Well, you certainly shot something," he observed. "But somehow I doubt it was the marquis. You've the devil of a temper, but I don't see you as a murderess."

Judith bit her lip. Sebastian could always bring her down to earth. "I shot between his feet," she said. "But I frightened him, Sebastian. He really thought for a minute he was about to meet his maker." She chuckled suddenly, relishing the memory. "Pour me a glass of sherry, love. It's been a most trying morning, one way or another."

Sebastian filled two sherry glasses from the decanter on the sideboard. "What were the terms of the carte blanche?" he asked with a bland look. "Just as a matter of interest, of course."

When she told him, he whistled once more. "If it weren't for Gracemere, it might have done very well for both of us."

"You would sell your own sister?" she exclaimed.

"Oh, only to the highest bidder," he assured her solemnly.

Judith threw a cushion at him, then bent to examine the chess problem positioned on the board. Chess was a way of sharpening their wits, particularly before an evening's gaming.

"Of course, if anyone suspects for one second that we're not what we seem when we get to London, we'll never be able to move in Gracemere's circles," Sebastian said, serious now. He sipped his sherry. "You've inadvertently given Carrington the wrong impression. I think, m'dear, that it may be time to cultivate higher necklines and a pious air."

"And what will you cultivate, brother?" She regarded him over the lip of her glass.

"Oh, I shall be a most serious student of foreign parts," he declared. "I shall have traveled extensively and be most amazingly knowledgeable, and most amazingly boring, as I prose on and on about the flora and fauna of exotic places."

Judith chuckled, imagining her good-humored, insouciant sibling in such a guise. "You'd have to forsake striped waistcoats and starched cravats, and play whist for penny points."

"Well, that I don't think I could manage," he said.

"Not if we're to have enough to pay our expenses." He came to look at the chess board with her. "Can you see it? White to move and mate in three. I've been looking at it for half an hour and can't get beyond queening the pawn. But then it's stalemate."

Judith frowned, considering. What if the pawn knighted, instead? She ran through the consequences in her head. "Let's try pawn to queen seven."

Sebastian moved the pieces, following the logic now on his own, bringing the problem to solution. "Clever girl," he said, toppling the black king with a fingertip. "You've always been able to see farther than I can."

"At chess, but you're better at piquet."

Sebastian shrugged, but offered no disclaimer. "Shall we have nuncheon?" He gestured to the table.

Judith wrinkled her nose at the dull and insubstantial repast laid out by their landlady. "Bread and cheese again."

"But we're dining with the Gardeners," he reminded her, cutting into the loaf. "And supper at the Duchess of Richmond's ball should be more than palatable."

"And I daresay the Most Honorable Marquis of Carrington will be present." Judith sat down and dug a knife into the wedge of cheese. "I don't seem to have done too well at disarming him, do I?" She frowned. "Threatening to shoot a man isn't very flirtatious." She took the cheese off the knife with her fingers and absently popped it into her mouth. "Oh." She was suddenly reminded. "I have to settle a debt of honor. I owe Carrington twenty guineas."

4

$\mathcal{I}$t hardly seemed possible that Napoleon and his army were gathered a stone's throw from the city, Judith thought, as she and Sebastian joined the receiving line that night, slowly progressing up the wide shallow staircase, to be announced to the Duchess of Richmond standing at the head.

There were more men in uniform than in civilian evening dress. The women glittered under the brilliant chandeliers—a swarm of jeweled butterflies in gowns every shade of the rainbow. But something lurked beneath the gaiety—a feverishness to the conversations, a slightly shrill pitch to the laughter, the distracted darting of eyes around the room, on the watch for a sign, a hint of new information. The world contained in the Duchess of Richmond's salons this hot June night was in waiting.

The Marquis of Carrington was speaking with the Duke of Wellington and General Karl von Clausewitz across the salon from the double entrance doors as Judith and Sebastian entered the room. Judith glanced sideways into the massive gilt-framed mirror on the wall, checking her reflection. She was abruptly annoyed with herself. After this morning's debacle, Carrington was unlikely to approach her, and why did she want him to? The man had offered her the most offensive insult imaginable. She turned to her brother. "Dance with me, Sebastian."

"If you wish." He looked at her quizzically. "But since when have you been dependent on your brother for a partner?"

"My card is filled from the third cotillion," she said, taking his arm. "I refused partners until then because I didn't think I'd want to dance immediately. But I find that I do."

Sebastian said nothing, merely clasped her waist lightly and whirled her into the dance.

They were a strikingly handsome couple, Carrington reflected, watching them, his mind wandering from the discussion of the need for latitudinal support for the Prussians behind the Sambre. Copper-haired and with those fine golden-brown eyes, flecked with green, they could almost be twins. There must be barely a year between them. Judith's chin was slightly more rounded than her brother's, but they both had straight, well-proportioned noses and generous mouths, slanting cheekbones and firm jawlines. An elegant pair of disreputable adventurers. Who were they? And where the devil had they sprung from?

Would she refuse to dance with him after the morning's fiasco? A man's pride could take only so many defeats at the hands of an impudent, though admittedly clever, baggage.

After excusing himself from his companions, he moved around the dance floor until the Davenports were abreast of him. Then he weaved his way deftly between dancing couples and lightly tapped Sebastian's shoulder. It was a most unorthodox procedure, but sometimes a man must be creative.

"Will you yield your sister, Davenport? It seems a crying shame that you should keep her to yourself when you have the advantage of her company at all other times."

Sebastian grinned. "Well, as to that, Carrington, it's for Judith to say."

"Ma'am?" Carrington bowed with a self-mocking gallantry. His eyes smiled, both colluding and conciliatory.

Judith glanced around, well aware of the notice the byplay was attracting. Marcus Devlin had rather cleverly cornered her.

"I suppose a woman must grow accustomed to being passed from hand to hand like a parcel," she said, gracefully moving out of Sebastian's encircling arm and turning into her new partner's hold.

"Baggages are usually handled in such fashion," Marcus murmured, savoring the feel of her. She was light and compact . . . and as sleek and dangerous as a lynx.

Judith drew a sharp breath. "I suppose, after this morning, I must expect such an insult from you, sir."

"Is that the best you can do?" His eyebrows lifted quizzically. "You disappoint me, Judith."

"Unfortunately, I don't have my pistol with me," she returned. "I trust you've recovered your equilibrium, sir."

"It took awhile," he admitted. "I've never had dealings with a lynx before, you see."

"A lynx?" She was betrayed into looking up at him.

His black eyes laughed down at her, rich with enjoyment.

"Yes, my lynx, exactly so."

A tinge of pink appeared on her high cheekbones. It seemed sensible to ignore such a statement. "You received the payment of my debt of honor, I trust, sir."

"I did indeed. I am grateful for the improvement in my financial state."

She caught her lip between her teeth and resolutely fixed her gaze in the middle distance over his shoulder. But it was impossible, and finally she chuckled and he felt the tension leave her body.

"Am I forgiven?" he asked, suddenly serious.

"For what, my lord?"

"I'm not playing games now, Judith. I have begged your pardon for this morning. I should like to know if my apology is accepted."

"It would be ungenerous of me to refuse to do so, my lord."

"And you are not, of course, ungenerous."

She met his eye then. "No, I am not. It's not the Davenport way. Any more than it's our way to be dishonorable."

"Card sharping is honorable then?" It was not a playful question and she bit her lip again, but not this time to hide her laughter.

"I can't explain about that."

"No, I should imagine it's very difficult to explain."

"We don't make a habit of it," she said stiffly.

"I'm relieved to hear it."

"When we win at the tables, we win on skill and experience," she said. "What you saw . . . or thought you saw—"

"I saw it."

"We were merely practicing for a couple of hands. The money involved was insignificant."

"You'll forgive me if I remain unconvinced of the scrupulous purity of your play."

Judith was silent. There seemed nothing more to say.

When he spoke again, the hard edge had left his voice. "I might, however, be induced to understand why you were obliged to learn such dubious arts."

Her chin went up and for the first time he saw the shadows in the lynx eyes. "Would you, my lord?" she said coldly. "That's really too kind of you. But I hope you won't consider me discourteous if I tell you my business is my own. Your understanding is a matter of complete indifference to me."

Marcus drew breath in sharp anger. His hand tightened around hers, crushing the slender fingers. Then the dance ended and she had pulled free of him. Fighting his anger, he watched her walk off the floor, her gown of ivory spider gauze over deep cream satin setting off the rich burnished copper hair falling in delicate ringlets to her shoulders. He wondered whether the topaz necklace and earrings were paste. If they were, they were remarkably good copies. But then he couldn't fault the skill with which the Davenports conducted their masquerade.

Who the devil were they? And why did she arouse in him this savage hunger?

He shook his head impatiently and stalked off the dance floor. An image of Martha drifted into his head: soft, brown-haired, doe-eyed Martha, who wouldn't say boo to a goose. Gentle, simple Martha . . . the perfect prey. A lamb on the one hand and an untamed lynx on the other. There must be a middle course.

Judith retreated to the retiring room. She was more shaken than she cared to admit by the intimacy of Carrington's questions. They trespassed on the darkness, the darkness that only Sebastian could ever truly know and understand, because he shared it. She confided only in her brother. It was the way it had to be. Their secrets and their griefs and their plans were their own. They knew no other way of living.

She bent to the mirror, adjusting a pin in her hair. The room was filled with chattering women, making repairs to dress or countenance. The talk was all of what they would do when the battle was joined.

"I'm not staying here to be raped by a horde of Frenchmen," one lady declaimed, fanning herself vigorously as she sat on a velvet stool in front of a mirror.

"Oh, dear countess, how could you imagine such a thing happening?" squeaked a dim, brown mouse of a woman, dropping a comb to the floor. "The duke would never leave us to the mercies of the ogre."

"Once our own men have left the city, those Frenchies will be here, you mark my words," the countess said with an almost salacious dread as she brushed a haresfoot across her rouged cheeks.

"Well, they do have to defeat our own armies first," Judith pointed out demurely. "One mustn't presume disaster too quickly."

"Indeed not," the stout wife of a colonel put in. "You're quite right, Miss Davenport. Our men need our support, not whining snivels. Of course they'll defeat Boney."

"Of course," Judith agreed. "No purpose is served by panic."

Thus chastised, the countess and the brown mouse fell into an injured silence.

"There'll be a run on horses once the battle's joined," another woman remarked calmly. "Alfred's hidden away our carriage horses in a stable outside the city. Once he's left for the front, he's instructed me to leave the city. Just in case," she added, with a smile at Judith and the colonel's wife. "Sensible people make provision for every eventuality."

"You wouldn't find me leaving Colonel Douglas in the heat of battle," Colonel Douglas's wife declared, disappearing behind the commode screen, her voice rising above the stiff rustlings of her taffeta skirts. "It's the duty of a soldier's wife to wait behind the lines and the heartbreak of a soldier's wife to wait in fear. I've been at the colonel's side through every battle on the Peninsula and I'm not running shy now . . . damned Frenchies or not. I'd like to see them try their tricks with me."

Judith chuckled, her composure restored, and left the retiring room. As she was making her way back to the ballroom she ran into Charlie.

"I saw you dancing with Marcus," he said accusingly. "You said you wouldn't agree to dance until the third cotillion."

"I wasn't intending to," she replied with a reassuring smile. "But my brother persuaded me to waltz and your cousin cut in on us."

"Marcus can be rather high-handed," Charlie said, slightly mollified. "Though I've noticed that women seem to like that sort of thing."

"My dear Charlie," she said with asperity. "We're not all accepting of the yoke."

Charlie looked startled at such a novel thought. His tentative laugh was unconvincing. "You're always funning."

"Oh, make no mistake, Charlie, I was not funning." She tapped his arm lightly with her fan. "You haven't known many women yet, but that'll change."

"You think me a mere greenhorn." Disconsolately he remembered his cousin's words over the breakfast table.

Judith smiled to herself and made haste to bolster his

wounded self-esteem. "No, of course I don't. But a soldier has little time for dalliance."

"Yes, that's certainly so." Charlie brightened. "We have other things on our minds. The duke is wonderfully calm, don't you think? He says he's made his dispositions and is perfectly certain of how things will develop."

Judith glanced thoughtfully across the room to where Wellington was laughing with a group of his officers in the midst of an admiring circle of ladies. He had a glass of champagne in his hand and certainly didn't appear a man whose mortal enemy was drawing up battle lines a few miles away. Was he a fool or a genius? The latter, it was to be hoped. Otherwise Brussels could become rather uncomfortable.

"Miss Davenport, have you been introduced to the Duke of Wellington?"

The Marquis of Carrington's voice at her shoulder startled Judith into a betraying flush. "No," she said, fanning herself vigorously. "Must you creep up on me like that?"

Marcus glanced around the crowded salon and raised his eyebrows. "Creep up on you in this crowd? Come now, Miss Davenport, I didn't intend anything so theatrical." He drew her arm through his. "Allow me to introduce you to the duke. He flirts outrageously with all pretty women, but he appreciates a nimble wit as well as a pretty face."

Judith allowed herself to be swept off. The introduction was a great honor, and perhaps Carrington intended it as a peace offering of some sort. It would be churlish to reject it. Her escort cleared a path for them through the crowd with a touch on a shoulder, a soft excuse, an occasional bow, until they reached the corner where the duke was holding court.

"May I introduce Miss Davenport, Duke." Marcus drew Judith forward.

"Delighted, ma'am." The duke bowed over her hand, his eyes twinkling appreciatively over his prominent nose. "Quite charming . . . I have been watching you all evening and wondering how to effect an introduction. Fortunately, my friend Carrington tells me he has the great good fortune to be a friend of yours."

So it wasn't a peace offering at all. She'd been commandeered—if not procured—for the great man's entertainment.

"It's the barest acquaintanceship, sir," Judith said, smiling brilliantly at the duke over her fan. "But I'm honored his lordship considered it sufficient to bring me to you. I stand in his debt."

"No, no, ma'am, it's I who stand in his debt," the duke said expansively. "A glass of champagne now. And we shall have a good talk." Linking his arm in hers, he drew her out of the circle, gesturing with his free hand to a servant bearing a tray of glasses.

Barest acquaintanceship indeed! The insolent baggage had made him out to be a coxcomb who fancied an intimacy that didn't exist. Torn between amusement and annoyance, Marcus watched her walk off on the duke's arm.

It was almost three o'clock in the morning when the Duchess of Richmond's grand ball disintegrated into a confusion of panicked civilians and galvanized officers. An equerry had entered the ballroom and stood for a minute with his gaze raking the glittering throng in search of the commander-in-chief. Then he hurried through the crowd to where the duke was sitting on a window seat beside Judith.

Wellington was delighted with his companion, who

was not in the least prudish and quite prepared to flirt as openly and outrageously as he was.

"I do enjoy women of the world, my dear," he said, patting her hand. "None of these die-away airs and touch-me-nots about you, Miss Davenport."

"Shame on you, Duke." Judith laughingly chided without moving her hand from his. "You'll ruin my reputation."

"Not so, ma'am. Your reputation's safe enough with me."

Judith put her head on one side and gave him an arch smile. "More's the pity."

Wellington roared with laughter. He was still laughing when the equerry reached him.

"Duke?"

"What is it, man?" he demanded testily.

"Dispatches, sir." The equerry looked around the room. "In private, my lord."

Wellington stood up immediately. "Excuse me, Miss Davenport." He was suddenly a different man, his face as somber as if it had never known laughter.

Judith rose with quick understanding, holding out her hand. "I'll leave you to your business, Duke."

He took her hand and kissed it, then strode off, beckoning to members of his staff as he made his way to a small room off the ballroom. "Ask Lord Carrington to join us," he said to an aide.

Marcus entered the salon a few minutes later, closing the double doors behind him. "Quatre Bras?" he said immediately.

"You were damned right, Marcus. Boney's left has swung round to the north. The Prince of Orange has him checked at Quatre Bras, but Napoleon's preparing to open the attack."

"And with his right, simultaneously attack the Prussians at Ligny," Marcus said.

"Ligny to the east and Quatre Bras to the west," Wellington agreed, bending over a chart. "Sound general quarters. We'll make our stand at Quatre Bras."

Outside the small salon, the ballroom buzzed. The musicians continued to play, but dancers were few as knots of people gathered in corners and the officers discreetly melted away. Judith was searching for Sebastian when Charlie approached her, his expression radiating excitement.

"Judith, I must go and join my regiment."

"What's happened?"

"General quarters has been sounded and we're to march to Quatre Bras."

He couldn't conceal his eagerness and Judith felt a great surge of affection for him, followed by apprehension. So many young men all so ready to find a bloody death on the battlefield.

"My first battle," he said.

"Yes, and you will be brave as a lion," she said, smiling with a great effort. "Come, I'll see you off."

She walked with him downstairs. Men in uniform milled around the hall. Orders were hastily and quietly given. Groups of soldiers took their leave, trying to appear as if nothing out of the ordinary had happened as they went through the great doors standing open to the stone steps outside. Once outside, however, discretion went to the four winds and they were off and running, calling for carriages, yelling orders and information.

Judith reached up and kissed Charlie lightly on the corner of his mouth. "Be safe."

"Oh, yes, of course I shall." He was impatient to be off, his eyes chasing around the hall. "Oh, there's Larson. He's in my company."

"Off you go, then." She gave him a friendly little push. He gave her a rueful, slightly guilty smile, then ducked his head and kissed her with a jerky bob.

"I do think you're wonderful, Judith."

"Of course you do," she said. "Be off with you. You have more important things on your mind now than dalliance."

"Yes, yes I have. That's quite true."

She waggled her fingers at him as he backed away into the crowd. He grinned suddenly, blew her a kiss, and then turned and plunged into the melee, calling for his friend.

Feeling stricken, Judith turned and went back up the stairs. Sebastian was looking for her. He held her cloak, his own already around his shoulders. "Judith, I must take you home."

She glanced around at the emptying salons. "Yes, there seems little point remaining. Although maybe we might hear some more news."

"There'll be no more news to be had here." Her brother draped the gold taffeta cloak around her shoulders. "Wellington and Clausewitz have left with their entourages. They're to set out for Quatre Bras within the half hour." He urged her down the stairs with an impatient hand under her elbow.

"What's your hurry, Sebastian?"

"Oh, come on, Ju." He looked anxiously around. "I don't want to miss anything."

"Miss what?"

"The battle," he said, again propelling her down the stairs.

"You're going?" But she knew the answer. It would be impossible for Sebastian to kick his heels in Brussels while the fate of Europe was being decided such a short distance away.

He gave her the same rueful, slightly guilty smile she had received from Charlie. "I'd give my eye teeth to have a crack at Boney myself, Ju. Since I can't do that, I must at least *be* there."

She made no attempt to dissuade him. If their lives had been different—had been as they should have been —her brother's birthright would have included a pair of colors in the Scots Greys, the regiment that had seen the service of generations of Devereux. It must be torment for him to be forced to stand on the sidelines while his peers in their brilliant regimentals plunged into the fray.

But soon it would be put right. Soon Sebastian would reclaim his birthright. She linked her arm through his and squeezed it tightly. He returned the squeeze absentmindedly and she knew that for once his thoughts were a great distance away from her own.

5

At their lodgings, Judith waited in the sitting room while Sebastian changed out of his evening dress and into buckskins and riding boots.

"Where are you going to find a horse?"

"Steven Wainwright has offered to mount me on his spare nag." He checked through his pockets, counting the bills in his billfold. "You'll be all right, Ju?"

She wasn't sure whether it was statement or question. "Of course. We'll meet here when it's all over."

He bent to kiss her. "I hate to leave you . . . but . . ."

"Oh, go!" she said. "Don't give me a second thought. But just be careful. We have things to do and we can't risk a stray bullet."

"I know. Do you doubt me?" The excitement faded

in his eyes to be replaced by the shadowed intensity so often to be found in his sister's.

She shook her head. "Never."

Judith listened to his booted feet on the stairs and the slam of the front door. She went to the window overlooking the narrow lane and watched as he strode, almost at a run, toward the center of town.

It was four o'clock in the morning and the city was as alive as if it were midday. Bells were ringing; people leaned out of windows in their nightcaps, shouting across the narrow lanes. She could hear the roar of the crowds in the streets a short distance away, a roar edged with hysteria. The citizens of Brussels were terrified.

Judith had no intention of missing the drama herself, although she couldn't have told Sebastian that. It would have ruined his own adventure. Swiftly she changed out of her ball dress into a dark-blue riding habit of serviceable broadcloth and drew on her York tan gloves. She unlocked the wooden chest under her bed, put away the paste jewelry she had been wearing, and took a wad of bank notes from the supply, tucking them away in the deep pocket of her coat. Into the other pocket went her pistol, cleaned and primed.

She let herself out of the house, locking the door behind her, then hesitated, wondering which direction to take. She needed transport, but she suspected that tonight horses couldn't be acquired for love or money. The inhabitants of Brussels would be holding onto their horseflesh in preparation for flight.

Following a hunch, she turned into an alley that would lead her even farther away from the fashionable part of town, into the poorer commercial areas. The people here would see less need to run from the ogre.

Raucous shouts, singing, and laughter came from a tavern at the end of the lane, yellow light spilling from the open door onto the mired cobbles. Some people were not intimidated by the prospect of battle on their doorstep. A farmer's cart stood in the shadows and her heart leaped exultantly. Between the shafts, a thin horse hung a weary head.

Judith crept up to the cart, patting the nag's hollowed neck. The cart was empty so presumably its owner had sold his produce that evening and, judging from the noise within the tavern, was probably drinking up his profits. With luck he wouldn't surface for hours and she could return the horse before he'd missed it. She unhitched the bridle from the post. Cautiously she backed the horse and cart away from the tavern. Then she sprang onto the driver's seat, shook the reins gently, and clicked her tongue. With a heavy sigh, the horse pulled away down the lane.

As soon as she emerged from the poorer sections, Judith realized the panic in the city was full blown. Houses stood open as their residents ran back and forth with possessions, filling carriages and dog carts. Men and women hurried through the streets, and everywhere was heard the cry for horses.

As she drove down a narrow cobbled lane, two men came out of the shadows, seizing her nag by the bridle, close to the bit. The horse came to an immediate stop with a snort indicative of relief. "All right, miss, we're requisitioning your horse," one of the men said. He wore the baize apron of a servant, but the man accompanying him was a stout, florid gentleman in satin waistcoat and knee britches. He stood breathing heavily, hanging onto the bridle for dear life.

"On whose authority?" Judith demanded, her hand moving to her pocket, closing over the pistol.

"Never you mind on whose authority," the stout gentleman wheezed. "I need that horse."

"Well, so do I," Judith pointed out. "Let go of the bridle, if you please, sir."

The man in the baize apron came round to the side of the cart, his expression menacing. In his hand, he held a club. "Now, don't make trouble for yourself, miss. You step down from there nice and quick, and no one's going to get hurt."

"I hate to disillusion you, but someone is most definitely going to get hurt." Judith drew the pistol from her pocket, leveling it at the man with the club. "Step away from the cart, and you, sir, release the horse."

The stout man dropped the bridle on a wheezing gasp, but his servant was made of sterner stuff. "She won't use it, sir. Never met a woman yet who could stand to hear the sound of a gun, let alone fire one."

"Well, let me introduce you to a new experience, my good man." For the second time that day, Judith fired her pistol. The bullet whistled so close to the servant's ear, he could feel the breeze. With a foul oath, he jumped back. The startled horse leaped forward at the same moment and Judith snapped the reins in further encouragement. The ancient nag fairly galloped down the cobbles, the cart swinging and bouncing on its iron wheels behind him.

Judith laughed with pure exhilaration, then she noticed that her hands were gripping the reins so tightly they were numb. She hadn't been conscious of fear during the confrontation, but now her heart began to pound. She drew back on the reins as they left the cobbled alley behind them and took several deep breaths until she felt calmer.

She turned down the broad, tree-lined thoroughfare that would take her to the Quatre Bras road.

Lord Carrington was standing outside a tall town house, observing the antics of his fellow man with both astonishment and amusement. He was in riding dress, tapping his whip against his boots, as he waited for his horse to be brought round from the mews. He had no difficulty recognizing the driver of the cart turning onto the street. She was hatless and the tumbling copper ringlets were unmistakable in the moonlight.

Where the devil was she going? Without conscious purpose, as she came abreast of him, he moved to intercept her. He swung himself upward with an agile twist, and landed on the seat beside her. "Whither away, Miss Davenport? I find it hard to believe you're running."

Judith blinked at him, bemused by this abrupt, unexpected manifestation. "No, of course I'm not, but Sebastian has gone to view the battle and I'm not to be left behind to cool my heels while the men have all the excitement. What are you doing in my cart?"

"Hitching a ride," he said shortly. "What the hell do you think you're doing, going to Quatre Bras?"

"What's it to you, Lord Carrington, where I go?"

He didn't trouble to answer that question. "You're an irresponsible madcap, Miss Davenport," he roundly informed her. "What was your brother about to leave you to brew such mischief alone?"

"I am perfectly able to have a care for myself, my lord, as I rather think you're aware." She glared at him in the gray light of the false dawn.

"Against one unarmed man, maybe. But facing a rabble of looting, rapine soldiery in the aftermath of battle? Permit me to doubt it, ma'am."

"I've just protected myself and my horse most satisfactorily against two armed men," she retorted.

"Pray accept my congratulations," he said caustically. "However, I am not in the least impressed by your powers of self-defense, or your foolhardy courage."

"This is no business of yours!"

"On the contrary, you seem to be becoming my business with dismaying speed." He stretched his long legs in front of him, settling down with every appearance of permanence. "I've a mind to further our *bare* acquaintance." He cast her a sharp look and she had the grace to blush. "I should have expected a hornet's response from you to something kindly meant," he said, rubbing in salt.

Judith took a deep breath. "Maybe I seemed ungracious, but I don't much like being procured."

"Being what!" he exclaimed. "Well, of all the . . ." His shoulders began to shake. "What an eccentric vocabulary you have, lynx. Or perhaps it's just the product of an overactive imagination."

"I don't like being laughed at, either," Judith said crossly.

"Well, you shouldn't be so absurdly insulting."

Judith gave up a battle in which she seemed to be severely handicapped. The road for the moment was deserted, a pale glimmering ribbon ahead of them, the trees and hedgerows slowly taking shape as the night faded. The sky was a deep blue, the North Star a brilliant pinprick, and she had the sensation that they were alone together at the edge of the universe . . . alone and waiting for something to which she could attach no name. She had a slight sinking feeling in her belly and her skin seemed to have a life of its own. The tautly muscled thigh beside her suddenly touched hers on the narrow seat and her whole body jolted with a current of unidentifiable energy.

Marcus felt the jolt deep in his own body, the energy emanating from her, joining with his own. He increased the pressure of his thigh against hers. A recklessness had entered his soul. He wanted this woman as he didn't remember wanting any other, and he didn't care what he had to do to possess her. If he could take advantage of the strange magic of this dawn journey, the apprehension and excitement and drama of events shaping the present moment, then he would. He felt the tension building in the body so close to his and kept silent for a long while, letting her grow accustomed to arousal. When he spoke, it was with a cheerful nonchalance, quite at odds with the brooding tension of the previous silence.

"How did you manage to come by this dog-eared conveyance?" he inquired, watching her hands on the reins.

Judith stared out between the horse's ears, the ordinary question offering a breathing space. After a minute she replied calmly, "Oh, I found it outside a tavern. The owner is probably so far under the hatches by now, he won't notice its absence for hours."

Marcus sat up straight. "Are you telling me you *stole* it?"

"No, I just borrowed it," she said with an airy wave of a hand. "I'll put it back when I've finished with it."

"You are an incorrigible, unscrupulous, card-sharping, horse-thieving hussy!" Marcus declared, truly shocked. "By God, someone had better take you in hand, before you do some serious damage and find yourself at the end of the hangman's rope."

He jerked the reins from her grasp and guided the horse over to the side of the road, in the shadow of a bramble hedge. The horse dropped his head and began to crop at the grassy verge.

"What are you doing?" Judith demanded.

"I don't know yet." He turned on the bench, catching her shoulders, and the minute he touched her that jolting current surged between them. Judith looked into his eyes, glittering with purpose, and she shivered, feeling the heat in her belly slowly turning bone and sinew to molten lava.

"You weave the strangest magic, Judith," he said, his voice a husky murmur, his eyes holding hers. "You confuse me so much I don't know whether I want to beat you or make love to you . . . but I have to possess you one way or the other."

Judith shook her head dumbly. She seemed to have forgotten how to speak. She knew only that she wanted his hands on her; rough or gentle, it was immaterial.

Marcus groaned in defeat and pulled her against him, his mouth coming down on hers with a crushing violence akin to punishment. Judith responded unhesitatingly to the bruising pressure, her lips parting for the determined thrust of his tongue. Her hands found their way around his neck, her fingers raking through the thick, dark hair. Deep within her was a warm, throbbing core of excitement and wanting that seemed to spread in waves through her body. She had never felt anything like it before and she yielded to the hot, red sensation, reaching against him as if she would be a part of him as his hands moved over her, outlining her body, learning its contours.

Slowly Marcus released her mouth for as long as it took him to readjust his hold so that he could pull her sideways onto his thighs. "I need a little more of you," he said softly, finding her mouth again. Her head rested against his shoulder, her mouth below his now more vulnerable and accessible to the deepening exploration of his tongue. His hands found her breasts, molding the soft swell beneath her jacket, and she felt in some way opened to him. She stirred on his lap, her thighs parting without volition as the deep red heat within her threatened to consume reason and reality.

"Dear God, but there's a passion in you, my lynx." He raised his head, gazing down into the bemused but desirous golden eyes.

"It must be the champagne," Judith murmured, reaching for his head again, bringing it back to her.

Marcus pulled back, laughter sparking in his gaze, rippling in his voice, lust's flame abruptly reduced to a smolder. "Did I hear you aright? You attribute such a passionate response simply to an excess of champagne?"

"I think it must contribute," she said, grinning up at him. But the mischief couldn't hide the banked fires in her eyes, the deeply sensual curve of her mouth.

"Wretch," he said softly. "I don't know what you deserve for interrupting me like that." His hand moved again to her breast, fingers deftly unhooking the frogged buttons of her jacket. Judith quivered, the moment of levity past. The tiny buttons on her lawn shirt flew apart and his fingers were on her skin, warm, firm, knowing. She raised one hand to caress his head, her body arching upward into his hand with the swelling urgency of her wanting.

"I have never felt like this," she whispered on a tiny gasp of excitement.

"That's much better," he murmured. "We'll have no more nonsense about the uninhibiting effects of champagne." He smiled at her, a glinting smile of male satisfaction. Holding her gaze, he dropped one hand to her knee, hitching up her skirt inch by inch. The warm breath of a summer's night brushed her bared legs as the skirt reached her thighs. His palm cupped her knees and slid upward beyond her stocking tops, over the satin softness of her inner thighs.

"If you knew how often I've dreamed of this," Marcus said, still smiling, still watching her face, as his fingers crept upward on an intimate, tantalizing invasion. "While you've been treating me to the sharpest edge of your razor tongue, I've been tormented with visions of your body, with fantasies of how your body would respond to mine."

Judith made no response, but her tongue touched her lips, her eyes narrowing as she drifted in sensation, the rapid rise and fall of her bosom the only indication of her mounting excitement.

Abruptly the self-enclosed world of arousal was shattered by the sound of voices, the tramp of feet, a harsh clarion call of a bugle. The horse between the shafts started and plunged forward into the hedge. Judith fell off Marcus's knee with a thump and a yowl of indignant surprise. Marcus, swearing, grabbed up the reins he had negligently let fall and hauled back on them, dragging the terrified horse out of the hedge.

"Hell and the devil!" Judith expostulated, clambering back onto the bench.

"Nicely put," Marcus approved, looking over his shoulder. "We appear to find ourselves in the midst of a regiment on the way to battle."

"Well, it's most inconvenient of them," grumbled Judith, smoothing down her skirt.

Marcus shot her a sideways glance, radiating amusement. It seemed they must take a brief respite from passion.

"Tell me," he said with deceptive innocence. "Why would you consider my proposal this morning to be without honor, whereas a scrambling tangle in a hedgerow like a milkmaid and her swain on May Day is perfectly acceptable?"

Judith combed her fingers through her disordered curls. "Is that a serious question, my lord?"

"Most certainly."

"You haven't offered to pay for my services on this occasion. Surely you can see the difference between a whore and a lover."

Marcus inhaled sharply and then slowly exhaled, steadying himself. Eccentric principles were at work again. But he didn't care on what terms they conducted their liaison, only in its fact.

"And you are willing to be my lover?" he asked quietly. "I want you, Judith, with the most powerful hunger. If you say so, I'll get down here and leave you to continue your journey, and I will never interfere in your life again. Otherwise . . ." There was no need to complete the sentence.

"I don't want you to leave," she said, meeting his eye with clear candor.

"And you know what that means?"

"I know what that means."

Relief swamped him. It was a pleasure to deal with a woman who was plain speaking and unvirtuous. He'd never had a taste for ingenuous, virginal misses, and found sophistication and honesty infinitely more arousing.

He glared impatiently at the ranks of men marching along the road. How the hell long was the column?

Judith shifted on the bench. "Where are we going?" The die was cast, and yet she was suddenly apprehensive.

"There's an inn up ahead," he said. "If I remember the road aright. . . . Thank God, I think the column's passed."

He drove the cart back onto the road and resumed the journey toward Quatre Bras. Full dawn was breaking. Red streaks slashed the sky, finally permeating the gray with a deep rosy glow.

"How beautiful," Judith said. "I've always loved traveling in the dawn."

He glanced sideways at her. "It's an unusual time of day for travel."

She shrugged. "Perhaps. For other people."

Marcus said nothing. He didn't want her to expand on that . . . not now . . . not at a moment when he wanted her to forget the constraints of the past, to be driven only by the urgent desire that he knew matched his own. She was an adventuress, wicked and unfettered, and right now he wanted her just as she was.

A thatched-roof building loomed ahead in the gray light, a creaking sign swinging in the dawn breeze.

"Journey's end," he said quietly.

Or journey's beginning, Judith thought. Her head swirled with an intoxicating brew: equal parts excitement, apprehension, anticipation. She didn't question her actions or her motives. She was accustomed to following instinct, but even if she hadn't been, she knew she was in the grip of a compulsion that must be satisfied. She wanted the man beside her, his body on hers, within hers. She wanted to feel his skin, to touch every part of his body, to know his body as she knew her own. It was a primitive bodily hunger, and at this moment she was as red in tooth and claw as any lynx in the jungle.

6

The whitewashed bedroom beneath the eaves was sparsely furnished but clean. A rush mat covered the uneven planking, faded muslin curtains blew at the open dormer window, matching the tester of the poster bed. Judith walked across to the window, noticing distantly that her hands were shaking as she drew off her gloves. She looked out unseeing over the kitchen garden and the panorama of fields beyond. Behind her Marcus patiently dismissed Madame Berthold, the innkeeper's wife, whose anxious descriptions of the room's amenities were interspersed with dread predictions on the possible outcome of the coming battle.

Finally Madame was induced to leave and Marcus leaned against the closed door, regarding Judith's turned back, allowing the silence to fill the room, the anticipation to build again. He tossed his whip onto a chair and slowly drew off his own gloves. Judith didn't move.

Marcus came up behind her. He lifted the massed copper curls from her neck and laid his lips softly on her warm nape. A shudder went through her and he felt again that jolting surge of energy that met and matched his own. His lips moved to the soft vulnerable spot behind her ear, his breath whispering over her skin.

"My beautiful lynx, I want to see you naked." He drew her backward into the room, turning her to face him, taking her chin between thumb and forefinger. Judith read the brilliant sensual sheen in his eyes, as vibrant with longing as his words, and she felt herself slipping into some half world where the only reality was contained within the powerful surges of her responses. Her need and her hunger were his. She whispered that she wanted his nakedness as he wanted hers, and she ran her flat palm over his cheek, lightly tracing his mouth with her little finger. His hand came up to grasp her wrist, holding her hand steady, and he sucked her probing finger into his mouth, delicately nibbling the tip.

It was an exquisite sensation. The nerve endings in the tip of her finger seemed to be connected to other parts of her body. Her tongue ran over her own lips and her eyes glowed up at him, the sensual currents as frank and clear as his own.

"Sweet heaven, but I want you, Judith." His loins were on fire with wanting. "I have to look at you." He lifted her, feeling again her light, tensile muscularity. A true golden-eyed lynx.

He carried her to the bed and sat her on the edge, dropping to his knees to pull off her boots. He rose and drew her to her feet again. "I'll find it easier to undress you standing up," he said with a smile, kissing the corner of her mouth.

"I could do it more quickly," Judith offered.

Marcus shook his head, taking a handful of her hair in each fist, holding her face steady as he kissed her mouth. Her breasts pressed against his chest and she moaned softly beneath his lips. With a sharply in-drawn breath, he released her head. His fingers, swift and deft, moved to her jacket. The buttons flew undone and he pushed the garment off her shoulders with rough haste, before turning his attention to the buttons of her lawn shirt.

The soft mounds of her breasts, the nipples hard and erect with desire, disappeared into his warm palms. Judith closed her eyes on a deep shudder of pleasure as his fingertips teased the taut crowns. He ran his hands down the narrow rib cage, feeling the shape of her, the smoothness of her skin, the delineation of her ribs, until he spanned her waist. He took a step backward and looked at her, bared to the waist for his hungry gaze, her hair lustrous against the whiteness of her skin, her breasts moving gently with her swift breath.

She smiled, a deep, self-absorbed smile, her eyes hooded as she ran her own hands over her bared breasts in offering. "Take your skirt off," he rasped.

She unfastened the hooks at the back of her skirt, sliding her hands into the loosened waistband, easing the garment over her hips, until it slithered to her ankles. She stood in front of him, clad only in her thin cambric petticoat. Putting his hands on her hips, he turned her. Judith shivered at his touch, at the warm imprint of his hands through the thin material. He ran a flat finger down her spine, feeling her skin ripple. Holding her shoulders, he bent his head and his tongue followed the path of his finger, a hot, moist stroke that brought a low moan to Judith's lips. She tried to keep still, but her feet shifted restlessly on the wooden floor.

The button at the waist of her petticoat came un-done and the garment slipped to her ankles. Marcus ran his hands in a lingering caress over the curve of her hips, the firm rise of her buttocks, the supple slenderness of her thighs. Then, with his hands on her hips, he turned her around to face him.

Again stepping backward, he took in her body, from the tip of the burnished head to the toes of her still-stockinged feet. Lacy garters banded her thighs, just above the knee, and he decided he would leave them there. There was something rather wonderfully wicked about them, something that went with the essential Judith he thought he was beginning to know.

"So beautiful," he said. "As beautiful as in my wildest imaginings."

Judith stepped toward him, reaching her arms around his neck, pressing her nakedness against the slight roughness of his coat, feeling the smooth leather of his britches against her thighs. Her head fell back, offering him the porcelain column of her throat, her hair cascad-ing in a burnished river over her shoulders, her loins pressed hard against him in a gesture as eloquent as any words of arousal.

"Dear God, Judith," he whispered, cupping her but-tocks and lifting her against him. "Dear God, lynx. What are you doing to me?" He took a step to the bed and let her fall onto the coverlet. He stood looking down at her for a second, then began to throw off his own clothes.

Judith watched. She gazed with a predator's lustful greed as the powerful, athletic body was revealed. When he shrugged out of his shirt, she dwelled on the broad chest, lightly dusted with dark curls, the narrow waist, and then stared with uninhibited curiosity as he unfas-tened his belt and pushed off his britches; a concave belly, slim hips, long muscular legs, the hard, erect evi-

dence of his arousal . . . . He turned to throw his
britches on the chair, revealing taut-muscled buttocks,
and she drew in a sharp breath, her body stirring on the
coverlet.

He came down to the bed, stretching himself beside
her, kissing the soft pulse at the base of her throat as he
caressed her belly, tickled a fingertip in her navel, inhaling the scents of her body. He touched the line of her
body, from below her ear to her hip, feeling the tender
curves, the deep indentations, and she moaned beneath
his hand, whispering his name. His mouth moved to her
breasts, his teeth lightly grazing her nipples, and Judith
was awash in sensation, the liquid fullness in her loins a
near unendurable urgency. Shifting her body, she felt his
hardness against her thigh and reached down to take the
turgid, ridged flesh in her hand, feeling the blood pulsing
strongly against her palm. It was a curious and wonderful
sensation as she curled her fingers around him, enclosing
him in a warm grip.

Marcus groaned softly under the knowing caress, and
his tongue trailed a moist and fiery path over her belly.
She opened her thighs in sudden demand, still caressing
his flesh, her fingers now conveying an acute urgency in
their tips.

"Such impatience," he whispered, slipping a hand
beneath her, his fingers closing like pincers over the firm,
sweet flesh of her buttocks. "Slow down, sweetheart." He
pinched just hard enough to pierce the self-enclosed
trance of her need and her eyes opened, focusing fully on
the face hanging over her. "You'll have me over the edge
in a minute," he said, smiling. "And that would be a
great pity for both of us."

She nodded in fierce understanding, clenching the
cheek of her captured backside against his fingers.

Marcus moved his hand, flipping her onto her stomach. And now his lips were cool, his breath warm, erasing the marks of his fingers on the imprisoned flesh. His hand slid between her thighs, delicately probing, opening the soft swollen petals, feeling her warm readiness. She opened to his touch, moving her body backward against his hand, her little whimpers of pleasure filling the room.

"Turn over now," he said softly, moving his hand, kissing the nape of her neck. "I want to look into your eyes when I'm a part of you."

She rolled onto her back and gazed up at him through half-closed eyes. "I cannot describe how I feel." It seemed to both of them the first time she'd spoken in an eternity, and her voice sounded to Judith rusty and thick from disuse.

Marcus kissed her again, his pleasure in her pleasure glowing in his eyes as he eased himself between her legs with a low sibilant murmur of fulfillment. She felt the press of his manhood against the cleft of her body and instinctively tightened against him. Surprise skimmed his eyes, and then he touched her again with his hand, and her body surged against him, her legs lifting to receive him as he pressed within her, her heels gripping his buttocks with a wild urgency. Too late he became aware of her tightness, of the thin membrane momentarily barring his entrance. And then he was deep within her, his body a part of hers, and the tears glittered in her eyes, but her lips were parted on an exultant little cry and she was moving with his rhythm and the full force of Napoleon's Imperial Guard couldn't have stopped either of them then.

A look of astonishment appeared in her eyes, her head fell back, her throat arching, and her legs curled around his waist, pulling him into the cleft of her body. With a supreme effort of will, he held himself still, glorying in her velvet warmth as her climax surged around him. He wanted to stay forever on the precipice, reveling in the feel of her, the grip of her body around him, but the deep spiraling urgency could not be controlled. With a sharp stab of loss, he forced himself to withdraw from the tight sheath in which she held him, gathering her against him as his own climax throbbed.

"Sweet heaven." Judith gasped. "What a wondrous thing."

Marcus fell back on the bed beside her, his eyes tightly closed, and for a long minute he didn't say anything. Then finally he asked in a curiously flat voice, "Why didn't you tell me?"

"Tell you what?"

He rolled over, propping himself on an elbow. "That you were a virgin." His gaze fell on the bright blood smearing her thighs as she lay sprawled in wanton abandonment beside him. "Why the hell didn't you tell me?" he demanded, his eyes hard as the shared glory of that union was abruptly tarnished by a wash of guilt and confusion.

"Did you think I wasn't?" she asked.

"How could I think you were? You behaved like an experienced woman. How could I possibly have imagined you to be still virtuous?"

"Does it matter?" Judith sat up, unease puncturing her euphoria.

"Of course it matters." He fell back on the pillows again. "I don't make a habit of deflowering virgins."

"But we only did what we both wanted." She was genuinely puzzled. "Nothing happened that wasn't supposed to happen."

He looked at her closely. "No," he said slowly. "Perhaps that's true. Nothing happened that wasn't supposed to happen."

There was an edge to the flat statement that was as

confusing to Judith as it was dismaying. She slid off the
bed and went to the dresser, pouring water from the ewer
into the basin. "You sound angry. I don't seem to understand why." She squeezed a cloth in water and sponged
her thighs. "How have I upset you?"

Marcus stared up at the flowered canopy, trying to
sort out the raging confusion in his brain. Perhaps he was
wronging her. Why would she have contrived such a
happening? And surely not even the most consummate
actress could have faked her passion, her need, her fulfillment?

"Come to bed," he said. "It's well past dawn and we
need to sleep."

"But won't you explain?" She came across to the
bed, her eyes huge with tiredness and a distress that he
would swear was genuine. With a wash of remorse, he
reached up and drew her down beside him.

"*Tristesse de l'amour,*" he said gently. "Forgive me. It
happens sometimes, and you did take me by surprise. I
feel a little guilty, but it'll fade after a few hours' sleep.
Close your eyes now." He closed her eyelids with his
fingertips, stroking her cheek until he felt her relax
against him, yielding anxiety to the soft billows of exhaustion.

Judith breathed deeply of the sweat tang of his skin
and the lingering perfume of their loving as she slipped
into unconsciousness. The whole business was so new to
her it was no wonder it had some puzzling aspects.

She awoke to a rumbling, booming roar. For a moment she lay, disoriented, aware of the contours of an
unfamiliar bed, staring up at the muslin canopy. Then
memory rushed back and she sat bolt upright. "Whatever is that noise?"

"Guns." Marcus was standing at the window. He

had on his britches and was in the act of putting on his shirt. "The battle has been joined."

"What time is it?"

"Four o'clock." He turned to the bed. Judith was an artless yet bewitchingly wanton sight, sitting up, her hair tumbling around her shoulders, the sheet tangled around her thighs. He remembered the abandonment of her responses, the wild and glorious honesty of her desire. Honest . . . except that she hadn't told him of her innocence, had left him to discover it when it was too late for control or caution. But perhaps that was part of the openness of her response; she genuinely hadn't given it a second thought in the blind world of arousal. She was an adventuress, after all. He allowed doubt and confusion to fade and enjoyed the sight of her as she blinked and shook her head in some bemusement, struggling to come back to the bright world of daytime reality.

"We've slept the day away," she said finally.

"So it would seem." He crossed the room and bent to kiss her. "How do you feel?"

Judith took stock. "A little sore," she said, after due consideration.

He winced and said wryly, "I did ask, I suppose. There's hot water in the ewer. But how do you feel in yourself?" His voice was serious, telling her he wanted an equally serious answer.

"Wonderful," she declared. "Virginity is a much overprized condition." She smiled up at him. "Why were you worried about it last night? There's no need to feel guilty; you weren't responsible."

Marcus frowned. "Of course I was responsible." He caught a tangled ringlet and twisted it around his finger. "Things happened very fast . . . perhaps too fast."

"Oh, I don't know," she said, putting her head on

one side. "I rather thought it was a very leisurely business."

Marcus gave up trying to persuade her to feel badly about something she clearly didn't regret in the least. Any regrets he might have would fade soon enough. It was done now, and there was nothing to hinder the progress of this liaison. Indeed, if it wasn't for the sound of cannon and the knowledge of what that meant, not to mention his own very empty belly, he'd be back in bed with her in a trice.

He laughed and pulled the sheet away from her legs. "Get up! Shameless wanton! I'm going belowstairs in search of an extremely delayed luncheon."

"Good, because I am starving. Are we going on to Quatre Bras, then?"

He was, but he had no intention of taking Judith into the theater of war. However, that tussle could wait on a full stomach. "As soon as possible. I'll be needed at Wellington's headquarters. I should have arrived there last night, but I daresay I'll think of some excuse other than the truth: that I was delayed by delight." He chuckled and drew the heavy, gold signet ring from his finger. "You had better wear this while you're here, for appearance's sake. Madame Berthold is sure to notice such an absence."

"Yes, of course. I hadn't thought," she said, slipping the ring on her finger. "It's a bit big, but I can hold it on." She poured water from the ewer into the basin.

Marcus stood transfixed by the door, watching the matter-of-fact manner in which she sponged her body. His loins stirred anew and, with a muttered oath, he fled the webs of enchantment and went down to the taproom that served as parlor and dining room.

"Oh, there you are, my lord. I was just explaining to these officers that we had a benighted gentleman and his wife as guests." Madame Berthold, the innkeeper's wife, looked up from the keg of ale from which she was drawing foaming tankards. She looked frightened. "The battle has begun, my lord. All day we've been waiting for the sound of the guns, only it didn't start till but an hour or two past. Boney's been delaying his attack, these gentlemen say."

"Carrington, good God, man, what brings you here?"

Marcus silently swore every oath he knew as he recognized the Dragoon officer and his two companions, lounging against the bar counter. "I'm on my way to Wellington's headquarters, Francis." He stepped into the room, nodding at the other men. "Whitby, George. Good day."

Colonel, Lord Francis Tallent, looked at his old friend with a suddenly arrested expression. "Wife?"

"We all have our secrets, Francis," Marcus said casually. His friends would draw the correct conclusion and discreetly drop the subject. A man's amorous adventures were his own concern. He turned to the innkeeper's wife. "Could you have a nuncheon taken abovestairs, madame?"

"And would your good lady like a dish of tea with that, sir, or perhaps a glass of sherry?" The woman bobbed a curtsy, looking helpful.

"Oh, there's no need to wait upon me. I can perfectly well be served in the taproom. I'm so hungry, I could eat a horse."

Judith Davenport swept smiling into the room. She was still putting up her hair as she walked, blind fingers twisting the ringlets into a knot, pushing in securing pins. She wore no jacket and her lawn blouse was carelessly opened at the neck, her breasts lifted by her upraised arms. "Marcus, I was thinking . . ." Her voice died as she took in the room's other inhabitants, all of whom had turned the color of beetroot. Her hands dropped to her sides.

Had she heard the voices? How could she not have heard them as she came down the stairs? The world spun on its axis as Marcus faced what had happened and its immutable consequence. He'd once found a poacher caught in the steel jaws of a man trap. His sick horror at the man's plight was what he now felt for himself as the vicious jaws of his own trap clamped. He had no choice . . . no choice whatsoever. Adventuress she may be, but he'd taken her virginity and knew she was no whore . . . not unless he made her one.

"You know my wife, of course, Francis," he said. He crossed to the door and took her hand, drawing her into the room. "My dear, are you also acquainted with Viscount Whitby and George Bannister?"

"We have met, I believe," Judith replied distractedly, her head spinning as she took in the disaster. These men were all prominent members of London Society. The story of this encounter would be on everyone's lips and she'd never be able to enter the hallowed portals of the ton . . . and neither would her brother. And her father would go unavenged. Marcus's fabrication was her only protection at the moment, and she had to go along with it until she could think things through clearly.

"Devil take it, Marcus, but you're a dark horse!" Francis exclaimed. "Secrets, eh? Pray accept my congratulations, Lady Carrington."

"Yes, indeed. This calls for a bottle," Bannister announced. "My good woman, champagne."

"Well, I don't know as we've got any, sir," the flustered woman said, "I'll go and ask Berthold." She hastened out of the room and a short silence fell. The puzzlement of the other men was evident, although they were trying politely to disguise it.

"So, you're taking Lady Carrington to Quatre Bras?" Whitby said, raising his tankard of ale to his lips.

"In the manner of a honeymoon," Marcus agreed without blinking. "A little unusual, but then the times are not exactly accommodating." His smile was a trifle twisted.

"Quite so," Lord Francis said.

"What news of the battle?" Marcus changed the subject abruptly.

"As expected, he's attacking Blücher at Ligny and Wellington at Quatre Bras."

"Why did he wait so long to attack? He's left himself but five hours until sunset."

"According to our agents, he didn't make his usual early-morning reconnaissance and thought he was only facing Blücher's one corp at Ligny. He didn't realize Ziethen's forces had come up in support, so he didn't see any need to hurry," Francis replied.

"But despite the delay, we're being mangled on both fronts," Whitby said somberly. "Wellington's taking very heavy losses at Quatre Bras and we've orders to call up reinforcements at Nivelles."

"Here's a nuncheon, my lord, and a bottle of Berthold's best claret." The innkeeper's wife came in with a heavily laden tray. "I hope it'll do. We've no champagne, sir."

"It will do very well," Carrington reassured. He drew out a chair at the table. "Judith, come and sit down. Gentlemen, will you join us?"

"Thank you, no, Carrington. Beg you'll excuse us, ma'am." Whitby bowed formally. "Fact is, had nuncheon some time ago."

"It is rather late in the day," Judith managed to say.

She took the chair Marcus held for her, casting him a quick glance as she did so. His expression was impassive, his eyes unreadable.

"May I carve you some ham?" he asked with a distant courtesy.

"Thank you, sir." A pink tinge touched her cheekbones.

"A morsel of chicken also?"

"Please." She dropped her eyes to the tablecloth, feeling as if she had committed some dreadful crime for which retribution waited in the wings.

Wretched, she concentrated on her food and left the conversation to the men. The steady booming of the guns continued until the sound was abruptly overtaken by a swelling roar from outside. The roar gradually separated itself into shouts, screams, and pounding feet.

Lord Francis ran to the inn doorway, followed by the others. A torrent of humanity, some on horseback, some in gigs and dog carts, but most on foot, poured down the lane toward Brussels. Women carried babies, small children clinging to their skirts, stumbling on the hard mud-ridged road; the men were armed with whatever they had been able to grab in their haste: staves, knives, a blunderbuss.

"What the devil?" Marcus exclaimed.

"Looks like a rout," Whitby said. "Wellington must be retreating."

"Napoleon's not beaten him so far," Marcus said. "I can't believe he'll do it this time."

"Oh, sirs, they say the army is retreating!" Berthold, the innkeeper, came running in from the road, where he had been chasing after information among the fleeing crowd. "Wellington's falling back on Brussels. The Prussians are retreating to Wavre."

"Hell and damnation!" George Bannister grabbed up his hat. "We'd best be about our business."

"Berthold!" Marcus bellowed as the innkeeper ran for the door again. "Have my nag put to the cart." He strode to the stairs leading to the bedchamber and took them two at a time. Judith stood in the now-empty taproom, listening to the roar of humanity outside. Then she ran up the stairs after Marcus.

He was shrugging into his coat, checking the contents of his pockets. He glanced up as she came in and said curtly, "I'm going to Quatre Bras. You'll stay here. I'll pay our shot when I come back for you."

"You seem to be forgetting that *I* was going to Quatre Bras, too," she said, swallowing the lump that seemed to be blocking her throat. With what was happening at the moment, it was hardly feasible for them to discuss the personal mess they were in, but the coldness of his voice was surely unwarranted. And she couldn't believe he intended simply to take off and leave her stranded, cooling her heels in a lonely inn, not knowing anything of what was happening.

"Well, you're not going now," he said in clipped accents. "It's too dangerous with that horde out there, and you'll only be in the way."

Judith lost her temper. It was a relief to do so since it banished her feeling of helplessness and concealed for the time being the apprehension that something very hurtful lurked around the next corner of her relationship with Marcus Devlin.

"That's *my* horse and *my* cart," she said with furious emphasis. "And I'll have you know, Lord Carrington, that I go where I please. You have no right to dictate to me." She snatched up her jacket and gloves. "If you wish to hitch another ride in my cart, then you're welcome to do so. Otherwise, I suggest you find your own transport."

Before he could respond, she had turned and run from the room. With a muttered oath, Marcus grabbed up his whip and sprang after her. He reached the stableyard on her heels. Judith leaped onto the driver's seat of the cart, standing ready as ordered, and snapped the reins. Marcus grabbed the bridle at the bit and held the horse still.

"You're behaving like a spoiled child," he said. "A battlefield is no place for a woman. Now get down at once."

"No," Judith snapped. "You really are the most arrogant, high-handed despot! I told you, I go where I please and you don't have any right of command."

"At this moment, I'm exercising a husband's authority," he declared. "A battlefield is no place for a woman and most definitely not for my wife. Now, do as you're told."

For a moment Judith was speechless. "I am not your wife," she managed to get out finally.

"To all intents and purposes you are now. And as soon as I can find a damned priest, you will be in the eyes of the church."

It was too much for a saint to bear. "I wouldn't marry you if you were the last man on earth!" she cried.

"As far as you're concerned, my dear Judith, that's exactly what I am," he announced aridly. "The first and last man you will know, in the fullest sense of that word."

White-faced, Judith stood up in the cart and whipped at the horse with the reins. The animal plunged forward with a snort, catching Marcus off guard. He stumbled, still holding the bit as the horse lunged. He regained his balance just in time and released the bit before he was dragged forward by the now caracoling animal. He grabbed the side of the cart and sprang upward, seizing the reins from her. The horse shot off as if a bee were lodged beneath his tail.

"Monsieur . . . monsieur . . ." came the outraged screams of the innkeeper's wife behind them.

Judith looked over her shoulder. Madame Berthold was pounding up the road in their wake, waving a skillet at them, her apron flapping into her face. Her cap flew off into the ditch but her charge continued regardless.

"I think you forgot to pay your shot," Judith said on a strangled gasp, an almost hysterical laughter suddenly taking the place of her rage.

"Damnation!" Marcus hauled back on the reins, and the near-demented horse reared to a snorting halt. He turned to look at Judith, who was now doubled over, weeping with laughter. His lip quivered and his shoulders began to shake at the absurdity of the scene. He glanced over his shoulder to where Madame Berthold still pounded, panting, toward them.

"One of these days, I really will wallop you," he commented to the gasping Judith, as he reached into his pocket for his billfold. "You nearly had me taken up for a thief." Leaning down to the red-faced, indignant Madame Berthold, he gave her his most charming smile and poured forth a flood of apologies, blaming the urgency of the moment for his forgetfulness.

Madame was appeased with a handful of sovereigns that more than compensated for her hospitality, and stood breathless and perspiring in the road as Marcus started the cart again.

"Now, where were we?" he said.

Judith had finally stopped laughing and leaned back against the rough wooden seat back. "On the road to Quatre Bras. Where we're *both* going against the traffic."

"So it would seem. We'll find a priest there."

"There must be some other way," she said, biting her lip. But she couldn't think of one that wouldn't ruin everything. How could Sebastian ever forgive her for destroying months and months of planning in the willful pursuit of passion?

"I took your maidenhead and we were discovered in a situation that would ruin you. In such a circumstance, there is no honorable alternative." He stated the facts bluntly, without inflection.

"But have you forgotten, my lord, that I am a card-sharping, horse-thieving, disreputable hussy, living on the fringes of Society, in the shadow of the gaming tables?" Her voice thickened and she swallowed crossly.

"No, I haven't forgotten. I'll just have to wean you away from your undesirable pursuits."

"And if I am not to be weaned, my lord?"

He shrugged. "It's not a matter for jest, Judith. As my wife, you will have responsibilities to my name and my honor. You'll accept those responsibilities as your part of the bargain."

Bargain? Judith turned away from him, trying to sort out the maelstrom raging in her head. Marriage to the Marquis of Carrington would work beautifully for both herself and Sebastian. Installed as the Marchioness of Carrington, she would have immediate and natural access to the circles frequented by Gracemere, as would Sebastian as the marquis's brother-in-law. Their position in Society would be assured and their present funds would be more than ample to set Sebastian up as a bachelor in London. He would need fashionable rooms instead of a house; one servant instead of a houseful. Their accumulated money would go much farther. It would mean they could begin to enact their revenge so much sooner than they'd anticipated. And when it was over,

Sebastian would be established in his own right. This card had been dealt to her hand; only a fool would refuse out of scruple to play it.

But Marcus mustn't know anything of that. There was a lifetime of secrets he couldn't know. So how could she fulfill her side of this bargain?

"I know nothing of you," she said aloud. "Why have you never married?"

There was silence. Marcus stared across the past and contemplated the truth . . . and the half-truth that had become the truth. Honor still bound him to the half-truth, for all that the one who could be most damaged by the whole story had been in her grave these many years past. The full truth was known now only to himself and one other. But it was a fair question.

"It's a plain and unremarkable tale, but pride is a devilish thing, and I have more than my fair share. Ten years ago I was to be married. A woman your antithesis in every way. I had known her since childhood and it didn't occur to me to woo her. She was a sweet, meek soul who I assumed would make me a compliant and exemplary wife. Instead, she fell wildly in love with a fortune-hunting gamester, who most skillfully swept her off her feet. She cried off."

His voice was perfectly level, almost bland as he continued. "The role of jilted fiancé was a hard and humiliating one for me. I was rather young to face such public mortification with equanimity. I decided then that a man could live in perfect contentment without a wife."

"Did she marry the fortune hunter?"

What choice had she had . . . ? Poor little dupe. Marcus closed his eyes on the memory of Martha's battered face, closed his ears to the sound of her broken whimpers. An untamed lynx would never get herself into such a predicament. An unprincipled adventuress would arrange matters to suit herself. *Had she heard those voices on the stairs? Had she known who was in the taproom before she'd walked in, her clothes almost disheveled, the aura of a satisfied woman clinging to every curve and line of her body? Had she contrived this?* But even if she had, a man of honor had no choice.

"Yes, she married him," he said, "and died in child-bed nine months later, leaving him to game away her fortune." He shook his head in a dismissive gesture. "I don't wish to talk of Martha ever again. You and she are so different, one could almost believe you to be different species."

She wanted to ask him if he believed he could be happy married to her, but deep in her soul she knew the answer. His hand had been forced; he was making that clear with every word and intonation.

If it wasn't for Gracemere, it would be easy to let him off the hook. She'd be able to say that in her circles, reputation didn't matter, that she'd be perfectly happy to be his lover for as long as it suited them both. But she wasn't going to say any of those things. She was a game-ster and she'd been dealt a perfect hand.

She turned her head and met his cool gaze. "We have a bargain, then, my lord Carrington," she said simply. Marcus nodded in brief affirmation and returned his at-tention to the road.

Judith closed her eyes, listening to the roar of cannon growing ever closer. The road was thronged with col-umns of soldiers, horses and limbers, fleeing civilians mingling with the detritus of a retreating army. Suddenly all thought of passion and revenge seemed trivial in the midst of an event that would obliterate thousands of lives and shape the future of their world.

7

The village of Quatre Bras stood at a crossroads. To Judith's eyes it was a village out of Dante. The battle still raged and a heavy pall of gunsmoke hung over the shattered cottages and farmhouses along the road. The dead and the wounded lay anywhere a spare place could be found for them, and from the surgeons' field hospital, the sounds of agony rose, pitiable, on the evening air.

The main street of the village was clogged with men and horses; a wounded horse struggled in the traces of an overturned limber, screaming like a banshee as a group of soldiers fought to cut the traces and right the cannon.

"Dear God, you shouldn't be here," Marcus muttered to Judith. "What the devil am I going to do with you?"

"You don't have to do anything with me," Judith

declared. "I'm getting down here. There's work to be done."

Marcus glanced sideways at her, took in the resolute set of her white face, and drew rein. They were behind the front line but still close enough for danger. He laid a restraining hand on her arm as she prepared to jump from the cart. "Just a minute."

"We're wasting time," she said impatiently.

"It's not safe," he said.

"Nowhere's safe," she pointed out, gesturing to the chaos around them. "I'll be careful."

Marcus frowned, then shrugged in resignation. "Very well, then. Keep your head down and stay out of the open as much as possible. I'm going to Wellington's headquarters. Stay in the village and I'll find you when I know what's happening."

She nodded and jumped down. Gathering up her skirt, she ran across the narrow street to where a group of unattended wounded lay in the shade of a hedge.

For many hours, long after sunset brought an end to the day's fighting and the incessant bombardment of the cannon finally ceased, Judith fetched water for the parched, bandages from the field hospital to staunch the more accessible of wounds, and sat beside men as they died or drifted into a pain-filled world of merciful semi-consciousness. She heard dreams and terrors, confessions and deepest desires, and her heart filled with pity and horror for so much suffering, for such a waste of so many young lives.

Throughout the endless evening she was constantly on the watch for Sebastian, her ears pricked for the sound of his voice. He must surely be somewhere in this carnage. Unless he'd found his way to the battlefield, and some stray shot had . . . but she couldn't allow herself to think such a thought.

Marcus found her in the field hospital, holding the hand of a young ensign while a surgeon amputated his leg. The lad bit down on a leather strap and his fingers were bloodless as they clutched Judith's hand. Marcus watched from the shadows until the moment came when the patient entered the dark world beyond endurance and his hand fell inert to the table. Judith massaged her crushed fingers and looked around for where she might be most useful next.

She saw Marcus and gazed at him wearily as he came over to her. Her face was streaked with dust and soot from the gunfire, her skirt caked with blood, her eyes filmed with exhaustion. She brushed her hair away from her forehead, where it clung, lank with sweat, in the fetid heat of the hospital tent.

"What's happening?"

"The army's retreating to a new line at Mont St. Jean," Marcus said. "Wellington and his staff are still here, taking stock." He pulled out his handkerchief and mopped her forehead, then took her chin between finger and thumb and wiped a black streak off her cheek. His eyes were somber. "I'm trying to find some news of Charlie. The losses have been horrendous."

"I've been hoping to come across Sebastian." Judith glanced around the hospital. Lanterns now cast a blood-red glow over the scene, throwing huge shadows against the tent walls as the surgeons and their assistants moved between the tables laden with wounded. "What do we do now?"

"You're exhausted," Marcus said. "You need food and rest."

Judith's head drooped, as if her neck were no longer strong enough to support it. "There's still so much to do here."

"No more tonight. There'll be as much and more to

do tomorrow." He took her arm, easing her toward the tent opening. Her foot slipped in a pool of blood and she clutched at him desperately. His arms came strongly around her, holding her up, and for a moment she yielded to his strength, her lithe, tensile frame suddenly without sinew.

Marcus held her against him, feeling the formlessness of her body, like a small animal's. She smelled of blood and earth and sweat, and he was surprised by a wash of tenderness. It was not an emotion he was accustomed to, and certainly not with Judith, who aroused him, annoyed him, challenged him, amused him—often all at once—but hadn't sparked a protective instinct before. He dropped a kiss on her damp forehead and led her outside into the relatively cool night air.

"Before we do anything else," he said, "there's some business we have to attend to. I've arranged matters so that it'll be very discreet."

"What business?"

He took her left hand, which still bore his signet ring, and frowned down at her. "Your presence here with me has to be explained, and there is only one explanation. I intend to make it good without delay. There's a Belgian priest in the village who's prepared to perform the ceremony. It won't take long."

Judith realized that for some reason she'd expected the traditions to be observed when they formalized their relationship. Marcus was obviously interested only in expediency. It hurt, even though she told herself that her own motives were purely pragmatic. This was no love match. It was a simple bargain. But she couldn't help asking "Must it be now? In the midst of all this carnage?"

"It's a matter of honor," he replied curtly. "Mine . . . if not yours."

Judith detected his sardonic inflection and flushed

with annoyance. "The last time we discussed my honor, I had a pistol in my hand," she reminded him, squaring her shoulders despite her weariness.

Marcus's reply was cut off at birth by a loud hail.

"Judith . . . Ju—!" They both turned to see Sebastian in the shadow of a doorway.

"Sebastian!" Judith ran toward her brother, forgetting about Marcus and disputed honor. "I've been looking everywhere for you."

"What the devil are you doing here?" he demanded, hugging her. "I left you in Brussels."

"You didn't expect me to stay there, did you?" she retorted with a tired grin.

He shook his head ruefully. "Knowing you, I suppose I shouldn't have." He noticed Marcus for the first time, and his eyebrows lifted. "How d'ye do, Carrington."

"You haven't seen Charlie, have you?" Judith asked her brother abruptly before Marcus could respond to Sebastian's greeting. "Marcus has been trying to get news of him."

"Oh, I saw him a few hours ago," Sebastian replied. "He was with Neil Larson. Larson was wounded and Charlie carried him off the field. They were putting Larson into one of the wagons heading back to Brussels."

Judith felt the tension leave Marcus as if a black goblin had leaped from his shoulders. "Thank God for that," he murmured, the hardness gone from his eyes, the tautness from his mouth. His gaze suddenly focused on Sebastian. "Davenport, you're just in time to perform a very useful service."

"Oh?"

"Yes, you may give your sister away."

"I may *what?*"

"Marcus, would you mind if I talk with my brother privately for a few minutes?" Judith said quickly.

Marcus made a rather formal bow. "Of course not. The curé's house is beside the church, as you might expect. I'll meet you both there when you've done your explaining."

Judith watched him stroll off in the direction of the small roadside church, its steeple tumbled by a cannon ball earlier in the day.

"Tell," her brother demanded.

Judith explained as best she could. But it was awkward, for all her intimacy with her brother, to admit to the compulsion of that wild passion that had thrown her so far from their chosen track.

Sebastian was very still as he listened, his expression giving no indication of the turmoil of his emotions. He was astounded that his usually clear-headed sister could have lost her grip on reality so completely, yielding to a moment of madness that now bade fair to ruin everything they'd worked for. He tried to see Marcus Devlin as his sister's lover, to understand what it was about the man that could arouse such passion in Judith, but the image filled him with such a confusion of dismay and discomfort that he pushed it from him.

When he remained silent at the end of her story, Judith said tentatively, "Are you angry?"

"I don't know if that's the right word," he said slowly. "But, yes, I suppose I am." Angry and something else, he recognized. He was jealous of Marcus Devlin, who had broken into the tight exclusivity of their relationship. He didn't want to share his sister, Sebastian realized with a shock. He was ten months older than Judith and couldn't remember a time in his life when she had not been there, so close to him that sometimes it seemed as if they inhabited one skin. They shared everything: thoughts, dreams, desires, nightmares. They laughed at the same things and cried at the same things. And now Judith would have someone else to turn to . . . to share these things with.

"Do you *want* to marry him?" he asked abruptly. "Or are you doing this because you must?"

Judith bit her lip. "It doesn't really matter how I feel. I created this mess and I have to put it right. This is the only way we have open to us now to do what we must. And it'll be perfect, Sebastian. As Marchioness of Carrington, I'll be perfectly placed to befriend Gracemere, and as my brother, your position in Society will be assured. Nothing could be better, could it?"

"No, I suppose not." He stared, frowning into the darkness. Maybe if he could put it into the context of furthering their plan, it would hurt less. "What if Carrington ever discovers that you've used him?"

Judith shrugged. "Why should he?"

Sebastian ran his hands through his hair, clasping his temples with a distracted frown. "We'll have to make damn sure he doesn't, Ju. I don't know the man, but I'll lay odds he'd be a devilishly uncomfortable adversary."

Judith had formed a similar opinion, but she tried to make light of it. "Oh, the worst I know of him is that he's an autocrat. But I ought to be able to handle that. I'm sure he doesn't have any hideous vices or perversions." She laughed a little nervously. "I'm sure I'd sense something like that after . . . I mean, when . . ."

"Yes, I know what you mean," Sebastian interrupted dryly. "And if it's all the same to you, I prefer not to dwell on it."

"Sorry," she said. "I didn't mean to embarrass you."

"Oh, well, I'll get used to it," he said, suddenly all business. "And if you're sure about going through with it, we can certainly turn your position to good use. Besides, you have to get married sometime. I ought to be relieved to see you well established."

Judith was not wholly convinced by her brother's sudden briskness, but chose not to question it. "Let's go and do it, then," she said with matching determination.

Marcus was waiting for them in the little garden of the priest's house. He watched them come down the road, arm in arm, heads together, deep in conversation. What were they discussing—him? How easily he'd been manipulated?

He abruptly dismissed his suspicions. Judith and Sebastian understandably had a great deal to discuss. It was perfectly natural and didn't mean anything sinister. Judith was unconventional and unscrupulous, but that didn't mean she was a designing Delilah.

And despite everything, as he looked at her, at her luminous beauty barely dimmed by the blood and sweat of her day among the wounded, at the lithe frame, still graceful despite her bone-deep weariness, he wanted her now as powerfully as he had wanted her the night before. She would make him no ordinary wife, of that he was certain. She was too mercurial, had as many facets as a polished diamond, and he couldn't imagine tiring of her.

He stepped toward them as they turned into the garden, and held out his hand. "Well, Sebastian, I hope your sister has your permission. I suppose I should have asked for it formally myself."

Sebastian took the offered hand in a firm clasp. "Ju's never needed anyone's permission to do anything. And anyway," he said with a slight smile, "in the circumstances . . ."

Marcus found himself responding to the infectious, colluding smile, so like Judith's. "Quite so," he agreed. "Shall we go in? Oh, Judith, you'd better give me back the ring."

The curé seemed to consider this duty no more out of the way in the middle of a battle than ministering to the dying, as he'd been doing all day. He was as weary as the rest of them, took in Judith's blood-smeared, bedraggled state with a comprehending nod, summoned an ancient crone from the kitchen to act as the second witness, and escorted them into the ruined church. He mumbled through the service at high speed, his accent so local that even Judith, who had been speaking French from earliest childhood, had difficulty following.

But there amid fallen masonry, before an altar standing open to the sky, in the middle of a battlefield, surrounded by the hideousness of war, Judith Davenport married Marcus Devlin, Marquis of Carrington, in the eyes of the church. He placed his signet ring upon her finger, saying quietly, "We'll find something more suitable when we get to London." Following convention, he laid his lips lightly on hers.

"M'sieur . . . madame . . . s'il vous plaît . . ." The priest appeared from the vestry, carrying a leather-bound tome. "Le registre."

Judith and Marcus signed the book under the scrawled and mostly illegible marks of their predecessors.

"Eh, vous aussi, m'sieur." The priest nodded at Sebastian, who wrote his name beneath his sister's. The crone put a large X.

An awkward silence fell suddenly in the dark, ruined church. Judith cleared her throat just as Sebastian said with an unconvincing heartiness, "Well, that seems to be that. Congratulations." He kissed his sister and shook his brother-in-law's hand. "I've a bottle of cognac in my saddlebag. We should drink a toast."

Marcus nodded. "Why don't you two go outside while I settle up with the curé?"

Judith was staring down at the page on the register,

at the three signatures. A curious cold crept up the back of her neck, and her scalp crawled.

"Let's go outside," Sebastian said, taking her arm. Numbly she let him lead her out into the garden.

"It's not legal," she said in a shaky whisper.

He stared down at her. A fine crescent moon was just visible through the cloud and smoke pall. It gave her pallor a waxen hue. "Whatever do you mean?"

"The names," she whispered. "They're not our legal names."

"Sweet Jesus!" Sebastian whistled softly. "We haven't been known by our baptismal names since we were babies. I never even think about it."

"What should we do?"

"Nothing," he said. "No one will ever know. If we go back in there and try to put it right, Marcus will have to know everything."

Judith shivered. "This is absurd. I'm married but I'm not."

"Judith Davenport is married," Sebastian said firmly. "Charlotte Devereux hasn't existed since she was two years old."

"But what about children?" she said almost wildly. "They'll be illegitimate."

"No one knows except the two of us," her brother stated, gripping her hands in a hard clasp. "No one will ever know. We create our own facts . . . our own truths. . . . We always have."

"Yes," she said, taking herself in hand. "Yes, you're right. What's in a piece of paper?"

The door of the church banged shut, and in startled reflex they jumped guiltily apart. Frowning, Marcus came toward them, his suspicions flaring anew. "Am I intruding on family secrets?" His voice was stiff.

Desperately, Judith sought an answer that was not

wholly an untruth. Her smile was strained, but she made an effort to speak naturally. "We were talking about our father. He died last year in Vienna."

"He would have been happy to see Judith married." Sebastian stepped in smoothly. "He didn't have much happiness in his life."

"No," Judith agreed. "Our mother died when we were babies and he never recovered." She passed the back of her hand over her forehead. "If I don't sit down soon, I think I'm going to fall over."

"You need to eat," Marcus said immediately, the gnawing rat of mistrust for the moment appeased. "We'll go to the duke's headquarters."

Sebastian chose to return to his friends in the village tavern while Marcus hustled Judith into a stone farmhouse, one of the few buildings with its roof still intact, where they found Wellington's staff sitting around a table. The duke himself was chewing a hunk of barley bread as he fired off dispatches to a steady stream of runners.

Francis Tallent offered Judith a pewter cup of rough red wine, greeting her pleasantly and without surprise. Fleetingly, Judith wondered what he must have thought that morning when she'd drifted into the taproom with her shirt unbuttoned and her hair tumbling about her ears. It was best not to speculate, she decided, taking a seat at the table.

It didn't take long before she was completely at ease. The condition of her clothes, her exhaustion that matched their own, the part she'd played in the last hours, provided her pass into this group of battle-weary veterans. Even Wellington greeted her with an absent yet friendly acceptance, accused Marcus of being a secretive dog to keep his marriage plans under wraps, and suggested she try to wash the blood from her skirt with a mixture of salt and water.

Judith spent what was left of her wedding night wrapped up in a military greatcoat, asleep on a table at the end of the room, while the military conference went on around her. Marcus looked across at her and tried not to dwell on how they would have been spending this night in more traditional circumstances. He took off his coat, rolled it up into a pillow, and gently lifted her head, slipping it beneath her. Her eyelids fluttered, and she mumbled something inarticulate. He smiled, stroked her hair, its usual burnish faded, and returned to the table.

Judith was awakened just before dawn by an orderly, who touched her shoulder tentatively. "Ma'am . . . there's coffee, ma'am. We're on the move."

She opened her eyes and blinked up at him in bemusement. Slowly memory returned and she struggled into a sitting position, swinging her legs over the edge of the table. She took the steaming mug from the orderly with a grateful smile. Apart from the two of them, the room was empty.

"Where is everybody?"

"Outside, ready to move, ma'am," he said. "His lordship's waiting for you."

"Thank you." She slid off the table and made her way outside into the damp, gray light, her hands cupped around the comforting warmth of the mug.

Men and horses milled around the front door. Wellington was mounted on Copenhagen, his favorite charger, and the beast pranced impatiently, tossing his head, sniffing the wind. The village seemed quiet, after the frenzy of the previous evening, and a line of wagons moved away from the field hospital toward Brussels, transporting those the surgeons had managed to patch up. Burial parties were at work in a neighboring field, turning the sod with their shovels, wraithlike figures in the dawn mist.

Marcus, holding the bridle of a black stallion, stood talking with Francis Tallent. Judith hurried over to him. Colonel Tallent greeted her cheerfully, then made his excuses and went to join the duke.

Judith examined her husband. He looked tired but calm. "Are we to leave straightaway?"

Marcus gave her his own searching look. "As soon as you're ready. Are you rested at all? The table made a hard bed."

She laughed. "I've slept in many a hard place in my time, sir. Indeed, I'm very rested. I must have slept for three hours." She took an appreciative gulp of the coffee. "This is the elixir of the gods."

Marcus smiled. "A lifesaver I agree. You'll have to manage the cart today on your own, I'm afraid. Just keep up as best you can."

Judith looked at the stallion. "You're riding?"

"Yes, one of Francis's spares."

"I suppose he doesn't have one for me," she said disconsolately.

Marcus regarded her calmly. "It wouldn't matter if he did. After 'borrowing'—as you so charmingly put it— the cart and horse, it's your responsibility to look after it and make sure it's returned to its owner no worse for wear."

Judith pulled a face but couldn't dispute the justice of this. "I hadn't expected to keep it for so long."

A glimmer of amusement appeared in the ebony eyes. "No, I'm sure you hadn't. But then, rather a lot of unexpected things have happened in the last day or so."

"They have," agreed Judith with a tiny answering smile. "But I daresay the owner will be happy with a handsome compensation. I'm sure the tavern keeper will find him for me when we get back to Brussels."

"Conscience conveniently quietened?" he mocked.

Judith laughed. "My conscience was never uneasy. However, if I can't ride with you, then I'll stay here today. There's still work to be done at the hospital."

Marcus frowned, considering. She'd proved herself competent enough yesterday. "I suppose I could allow you to do that. I'll send someone for you later. When he comes, though, you're to go with him without delay. He'll have orders to bring you to me at once, because there's no knowing how long we'll be in any one place. If you delay, I may lose you. Is that clear?"

It had been a short moment of accord. "Yes, it's perfectly clear, and would have been equally so without your sounding so autocratic," she pointed out, reflecting that it was never too early to start her program of reform. "I'm not in the schoolroom."

"For heaven's sake, Judith, I don't have time to squabble with you in the middle of a war!"

"Oh, listen to you!" she exclaimed in a fierce undertone. "That's exactly what I mean."

Taking her shoulders, he pulled her toward him. "Maybe I am a trifle autocratic, but you're as bristly as a porcupine this morning." Despite the irritation in his voice, he couldn't control the flicker of desire in his eyes. Although her cheeks were flushed with indignation, dark currents of promise lurked below the surface of her eyes, and he could feel in memory the print of her soft mouth on his. "Porcupine or not, I want you," he murmured. "Somehow, I'll contrive something for later." He ran his finger over her mouth. "And we'll be a world away from any schoolroom, I can safely promise you that." His eyebrows rose and his eyes gleamed. "Will that guarantee your obedience, lynx?"

Judith grinned, her irritation vanished. "I'll come when I'm called, sir."

He caught her face and kissed her, a hard, assertive salute that left her lips tingling and heated her blood. "A further promise," he said, then turned, swung onto his horse, and rode off with a backward wave.

8

As the day wore on, passion became the last thing on Judith's mind. She was soon moving in a trance of fatigue, blindly putting one foot in front of the other, driven by the overpowering need and suffering around her. Wellington had lost five thousand men the previous day and they were still bringing in casualties from the battlefield, men who had lain outside all night. It began to seem as if the stream of wounded bodies would never cease.

The sky darkened toward the middle of the morning and within minutes was shot with jagged forks of lightning. The thunder was almost as violent as the gunfire of the preceding day, Judith thought, standing for a moment in the entrance of the hospital tent looking out at the sheeting rain.

All day the downpour was relentless. Judith was soon soaked to the skin, but was barely aware of it. Wagonloads of patched wounded continued throughout the day to bump along the road to the safety of Brussels, and toward evening Judith was trying to make some of the casualties more comfortable under a tarpaulin in one of the wagons when a hesitant voice called her.

"Charlie!" She looked up in glad surprise, water dripping from her hair. "Thank God, you're safe."

"Yes," he said, blushing crimson over his tunic as he stammered, "Um . . . Miss Daven . . . um . . . Jud . . . um . . . my cousin . . . my cousin sent me to fetch you. He's with the army at Waterloo. We're to go at once."

Judith climbed wearily down from the wagon. What had Marcus told Charlie? "Is it far?"

"No, a couple of miles. The army's in position across the Brussels road," Charlie said. "There's been no fighting today, because of the storm."

"I have to find my horse and cart."

"I have it," Charlie said. "Over by that farmhouse. Marcus told me where it would be." He stared into the middle distance, unable to meet her eye. "He said you . . . well, I gather congratulations are in order."

"Oh, Charlie, it's too difficult to explain at the moment," she said, taking his arm. "In fact, I don't know whether I *can* explain it. It happened very quickly."

"In Brussels, you weren't thinking of—"

"No," she interrupted, recognizing his mortifying suspicion that he'd been played for a fool by his elders, who'd had their own secret liaison all along. "No. It just happened very suddenly. I don't know how to ask you to understand it when I don't myself."

"Oh." Charlie still seemed unconvinced as he handed her up into the cart. "I'll tether my horse to the back and sit beside you. There's a tarpaulin we can put over us."

Judith took the reins. They both huddled beneath the tarpaulin, although they were already so wet it seemed rather pointless. After a minute Charlie said hotly, "My cousin never does surprising things. Why would he suddenly get married in the middle of a battle? I thought people only fell in love like that in Mrs. Radcliffe's romances."

Judith smiled and patted his hand. "You know what they say about truth being stranger than fiction." If that was the explanation he'd hit upon, then she'd leave him with it. He obviously wouldn't be able to handle the truth: violent passion, mutual seduction, inconvenient encounters, and a most scrupulous sense of honor . . . along with a quite unscrupulous seizing of an opportunity.

Wellington's army was drawn up outside the village of Waterloo, straddling the Brussels road behind the shelter of a small hill that would protect them from enemy observation and gunfire. It was a relatively strong position, and the duke was in cheerful mood when Judith, escorted by Charlie, walked into one of the string of farm buildings that protected both the army's flanks. A fire burned in the grate and the smell of gently steaming wet wool filled the air as the soaked inhabitants of the farmhouse jostled for position near the heat.

"We'll stand where we are, if Blücher promises us one corp in support," the duke was declaring, over a table laden with supper dishes. "Ah, Lady Carrington, you've been in the field hospital at Quatre Bras, your husband says." He waved a chop bone at her in greeting. "Come to the fire and dry off. Carrington's taking a look at the field. Boney's ensconced on the other hilltop."

Judith dropped onto a bench at the table, exhaustion

flooding her so she couldn't even summon up the energy to reach the fire. Charlie murmured his excuses and went off into the rain again to rejoin his regiment. Someone pushed a pewter mug of wine toward her, and she buried her nose in it with a grateful groan. As with last night, her presence was completely accepted. This didn't seem as surprising to her now that she'd met several women that day, laboring beside her in the hospital, all wives of soldiers, all accustomed to following the drum and enduring the same privations as the army while they waited behind the lines for their men. That Lord Carrington's wife chose to do the same was a little more remarkable, but then so was the marquis's position with Wellington's army as a civilian tactician.

Marcus came in a few minutes later, shaking water off his coat, tossing his soaked beaver hat onto a settle. "It's raining cats and dogs," he said. "The roads are enmired and the field's a mudbath." He saw his wife and came quickly to the table. "How are you?"

"Dripping," she said, smiling wearily. "But well enough. I'll be even better for another cup of wine."

"Take it easy," he cautioned, reaching for the bottle and refilling her cup. "Exhaustion and wine make the devil's own combination. Have you eaten?"

"Not yet," she said. "I think I'm too tired."

"You must eat. Then I'll show you to the chamber I've managed to lay claim to, and you can get out of those clothes."

Judith toyed with a cold mutton chop and listened to the conversation. Marcus sat beside her on the bench and, when her head drifted onto his shoulder, put an arm around her in support. Her clothes dried a little in the steamy warmth of the crowded room and she sipped wine sleepily, trying to make some sense of the discussion. Everything seemed to hang on the Prussians. Could they send a corps in support? If not, Wellington's army was alarmingly outnumbered by the French across the hill.

The tension in the room was too powerful for her to wish to go to bed, and she shook her head when Marcus suggested he show her to the bedchamber he'd found in a cottage across the yard. At three in the morning, a drenched runner tumbled through the door bearing the message they'd all been waiting for. At dawn, two corps of the Prussian army would move from Wavre against Napoleon's right flank.

"Twice as good as we'd hoped for!" Peter Welby exclaimed.

Marcus examined a map with a pair of compasses. "It's ten miles from Wavre to Waterloo and it'll be slow going during this terrible storm on muddy roads. I expect they'll be here midday."

"If the French attack before then, we'll have to hold the field until they get here," the duke said.

But there was renewed confidence in the low-ceilinged room and men rose from the table, intending to snatch what hours of rest they could before the attack opened.

"Come, Judith." Marcus shifted her head from his shoulder and stood up, pulling her with him. She obeyed readily, stumbling slightly as he led her out into the storm, across the swamped stableyard, and under the low lintel of a small cottage.

Men were asleep on the earth-packed floor and Judith trod delicately over them as Marcus hushed her with a finger on his lips. They climbed a rickety staircase and entered a tiny loft, smelling of apples and hay. A blanket-covered straw mattress lay on a roped bedframe. To Judith at that moment, nothing could have seemed more luxurious.

"Are the French expecting the Prussians?" she asked, sinking onto the mattress. There was another violent crash of thunder from outside.

"We're calculating that they won't be." Marcus bent to pull off her boots. "Napoleon's had Grouchy chasing a phantom Prussian retreat toward Liege, when in fact Blücher's been moving toward us. I think we've caught him unawares." He sat on the edge of the bed to pull off his own boots. "I *hope* we've caught him unawares. . . . You can't sleep in wet clothes."

"Neither can you," she responded, struggling upright again, fumbling with the buttons of her jacket. "My fingers are all thumbs."

"Let me do it." He pushed her hands away and unbuttoned her jacket. His hands brushed her breasts as he pushed the coat off her shoulders and her nipples instantly hardened, pressing darkly against the thin lawn of her shirt. Slowly he laid his hands over the soft mounds. Her tongue touched her lips as she stood immobile, her eyes locked with his. The rain beat against the closed shutters of the tiny window. Downstairs a soldier stirred and groaned in his sleep, the hilt of his sword scraping on the floor.

With abrupt urgency, and in total silence, Marcus stripped the clothes from her body. Her eyes were on fire but her skin was cold as he ran his hands over her nakedness. "Get under the blanket!" he rasped, pushing her to the bed.

Judith obeyed, huddling under the scratchy wool, watching as he threw off his own clothes. She held up the blanket for him as he slid beneath, pulling her against him, fitting her body to his. Soon there was warmth where her skin touched his and cool places where they were apart. His palm cupped the flare of her hip, flattened against her thigh, drew her leg across his own thighs, opening her body.

Judith shuddered, unfolding to the fervid, searching caress, the deep exploration of the heated furrow of her body. Her thighs slithered against the muscular hardness of his and her tongue dipped into the hollow of his shoulder, tasting the salt on his skin before her mouth locked with his. Their tongues warred, danced, plunged in a wild spiral of passion that excluded all but their partnered bodies and their frantic need.

"Love me," Judith whispered against his mouth. "Now, it must be now."

Marcus drew her beneath him. He parted her thighs, then paused for an instant on the threshold of her body. Her eyes were closed, her face lost in joy, but as he gazed down at her, the luxuriant fringe of her eyelashes swept up, showing him those great golden-brown lynx eyes awash with passion. "Love me," she whispered again.

With a little sigh he entered the moist tenderness of her core, and she closed around him. He eased deeper, feeling the suppleness of her body, and bent to brush her damp temples with his lips, to touch the corners of her eyes, trailing his tongue over the sensitive corner of her mouth. She smiled at the caress and reached down to touch him where his body was joined with hers. He drew breath as his pleasure surged. His hands closed over her buttocks, lifting her to meet him as he plunged to the very center of her being. The blossom of delight within her burst into full bloom, and she cried out against his mouth.

Marcus thrust once more, deep within her, feeling in his own flesh the pulsating throb of her climax. As he moved to withdraw from her, her arms tightened around him as if to hold him within, but he resisted the pressure, leaving her body the instant before his own core burst asunder.

They lay entwined as the fever abated, and Marcus felt Judith's heart slow as she slipped into sleep. He held her, wondering why he had withdrawn at the last. She was his wife now. She could carry his child. But the truth was that he hardly knew her, and had little reason to trust her.

He awoke slowly, wonderfully, to the awareness of his body coming alive beneath whispering caresses. He heard Judith's soft murmur of satisfaction as he rose beneath her ministering hands, and he reached down dreamily to twine his fingers into the curls resting on his belly as she concentrated on her task. In the aftermath of passion's extremity, she made love to him now with a languid pleasure, learning his body as she tasted every inch of him, exploring his planes and hollows, and he yielded to her orchestration before conducting his own symphony on her delicate, thrumming femininity.

Beyond the shuttered windows the rain-soaked sky lightened on the morning of Sunday, June 18, 1815. The storm had passed and a bird in the ivy began an insistent, stubborn song.

Judith stretched luxuriantly beneath the rough blanket, glorying in her body's satiation, its complete relaxation. She was warm and dry and thought life could hold no greater joy than to spend the day in this loft with Marcus, sharing and exploring their bodies. But her husband was already pushing aside the blanket.

"Must you?" she asked with a tenderly inviting smile.

"Yes, I must." He bent to kiss her. "But you stay here and sleep. I'll see what I can find in the way of breakfast." He stood up, shivering in the damp chill of early morning. He picked up his clothes and grimaced. "Everything's still wet. Stay under the blanket, and I'll take your clothes to dry by the fire."

"You can't hang up my clothes in front of all those men," Judith squeaked.

"This is neither the time nor the place for such niceties," he said, shuddering as he fastened his britches. "Now stay put and I'll be back soon."

"Yes, sir," Judith murmured, pulling the blanket over her head. "Without any clothes, I don't have much choice." His laugh hung in the air for a minute, then the door closed and she heard his booted feet on the staircase.

She fell asleep again for an hour and woke to the sound of a bugle and the tramp of feet. After struggling up on the bedframe, she pushed open the shutters and gazed down at the courtyard where men and horses were splashing purposefully through the puddles. The bugle sounded again, an urgent clarion call that stirred her blood with both fear and excitement.

The door banged closed below and Marcus's step sounded on the stairs. He came in with her clothes and a basket. "Good, you're awake," he said briskly. He looked distracted as he put the basket on the floor and dropped the bundle of clothes on the bed. "Your clothes are dry, at least. Other than that, there's not much I can say for them. There's coffee, bread, and jam in the basket. I'm going to have to leave you now."

"What's happening?" She sat on the bed, wrapping the blanket tightly around her.

"The French are advancing. We're—" A roll of cannon fire shattered the air, and for a second there was an eerie silence. Then it came again. "We've opened the attack," Marcus said, his mouth grim. "I don't know when I'll be back. You're to wait for me here."

"Where will you be?"

"With Wellington."

"On the field?" Her heart lurched. Somehow she hadn't thought of him under fire.

"Where else?" he said shortly. "Tactics change constantly as the position changes." Bending, he caught her shoulders and held her eyes with his. "I'll come back for you. *Be here.*"

"Don't go just yet." She put a hand on his arm.

His expression softened. "Don't be frightened."

"It's not that . . . not for me . . . but for you," she said hesitantly. "I want to be where you are."

"It's not possible, lynx. You know that." He brushed the line of her jaw with a gentle finger.

"Answer me a question." She didn't know why she was going to ask this question now; it was hardly an appropriate time or place for discussion of something so serious. But for some reason, after the passion of the night and in their present warm accord, she desperately needed to know his answer.

He waited.

"Why did you withdraw from me last night?" She regarded him steadily, waiting for his reply. When, last night, instinctively, she had tried to hold him within her and he had resisted, she had been drowning in the sensate glory of loving and had felt only the barest flicker of loss. In the cool clear light of day, she knew she was not ready for pregnancy herself; there was Gracemere to deal with before she could be ready for other responsibilities. And a husband to get to know before he could be the father of her child. Did Marcus feel the same way about her? About their situation? Or was it something else?

Marcus didn't immediately reply. He stood looking

down at her, his black eyes searching hers, almost as if he would look into her soul. Judith shivered, abruptly convinced that she was hovering on the edge of a chasm where something dark and repellent lurked.

Then Marcus turned and went to the door. He paused, his hand on the latch, and didn't turn to look at her as he said, "I'll answer that question with one of my own. Did you know who was in the taproom yesterday before you made such a dramatic entrance?"

The shocked silence stretched between them, and when she didn't answer him, he quietly opened the door and left.

He believed she had trapped him into marriage. Cold nausea lodged in her throat. Of course he wouldn't want children by a woman capable of such calculating deceit. How he must hate her. But it was a hatred and contempt that didn't extend to her body. As far as Marcus was concerned, she was his wife in name but his whore in body and soul.

Bitter bile rose into her mouth, and her head began to pound. Why hadn't she denied it? Why hadn't she poured out a torrent of violent denial, protestations of innocence, anger that he could think such a thing? But Judith knew why she had sat in silence. Because in essence he was right. He believed she had married him for his fortune and his position, and so she had. What did it matter that she hadn't known who was in the taproom when she'd strolled in. She'd still taken advantage of the situation . . . of Marcus's sense of honor. Why should he ever see her as anything other than a grasping, deceitful gold-digger?

Shivering and queasy, she dressed in her crumpled, stained riding habit. The ring on her finger caught a shaft of sunlight and the gold glowed dully. Once she and Sebastian had done what had to be done—once Sebastian was again in possession of his birthright, their father avenged, and Gracemere defeated—she would tell Marcus that no legal ties bound them. She would set him free. But until then, she must play out the masquerade. And what else was new? she thought with grim cynicism. Her whole life had been a masquerade.

Outside, she stood looking around, trying to decide where to go. The sounds of battle were loud and terrifying, the clash of steel, the boom of the cannon, the sharp volley of muskets. Men were running backward and forward, and wounded were beginning to trickle in.

Judith ran out of the yard and behind the group of farmhouses to a small hill. When she reached the top, she gazed in fascinated horror at the scene spread out before her. It was a field, bounded by hedgerows. Swaying backward and forward over those few acres were two massed armies, banners waving in the breeze, trumpets blaring. Wellington's infantry charged the squares of French soldiers. Cavalry rode over men and guns, lance and sword hacking and thrusting. Lines of infantry dropped to their knees, muskets aimed, there was a crashing boom, and the line of advancing French was decimated.

From the distance of her observation post, the scene looked like some kind of anarchical play, wrested from the twisted imagination of a demented playwright. What must it feel like to be in the middle of that hand-to-hand melee, men facing men with but one intention—to kill? Bodies carpeted the field, men and horses falling on all sides, and it was impossible to believe there was any direction, any coherent strategy to the killing on either side. And yet there had to be. Marcus was somewhere in that murderous scrimmage, presumably making some kind of sense of it.

She went back to the yard to work with the wounded but in the late afternoon climbed the hill again. The

Prussian advance on Napoleon's flank was beginning to have its effect now, although Judith didn't know that. But she could tell that the French seemed to be falling back, or at least that there seemed to be fewer of them. Peering into the melee, she distinguished a massive cannonade centered on a small rise, behind which a brigade of British Foot Guards sheltered. It seemed to Judith that the cannonade must split the earth with its violence. And then, abruptly, the firing ceased. There was an unearthly moment of silence. Then the smoke of the guns wafted away and she stared, transfixed, at the column of French Grenadiers, Napoleon's Imperial Guard, advancing toward the rise. A great cry of *"Vive l'Empereur"* seemed to reach the heavens as the column moved forward in deadly formation.

It was six o'clock in the evening.

Suddenly, from behind the little hill, the brigade of Foot Guards who had been sheltering from the cannonade rose seemingly out of the ground and fired round after round into the Imperial Guard. The effect was as if the fire itself was a battering ram, bodily forcing the front line of the French column backward. They began to fall like ninepins at a terrifying rate. The divisions at the rear began to fire over their comrades' head, the formation wavering as they milled in confusion. With an almost primeval scream that lifted the tiny hairs on her skin, the brigade of Foot Guards sprang forward, swords in hand. As Judith watched, the unthinkable happened. Napoleon's Imperial Guard, his last hope, his tool for certain victory, the veterans of ten years of war and innumerable triumphs, broke rank, turned, and ran, pursued by the bellowing brigade.

Slowly Judith turned and went back down the hill, unable to believe what she'd seen. But it seemed it was over. Wellington and Blücher had won the Battle of Waterloo. The atmosphere in the stableyard was one of exhausted jubilance as the sun set and the sound of firing became sporadic. The death toll was horrendous and the wounded were brought in in wagonloads; but Bonaparte had been defeated for the last time. The Prussians were pursuing the fleeing French army, leaving the depleted British to gather themselves together, recover their strength, and take stock of their losses.

Marcus rode into the stableyard toward midnight. He'd accompanied Wellington to his post-victory meeting with Blücher. The two men had kissed each other and Blücher had summed up the day's events in his sparse French. *"Quelle affaire!"*

Adequate words, it seemed to Marcus. Superlatives somehow wouldn't capture the sense of finality they all felt. The world as they knew it could now return to peace again.

He looked for his wife in the torch-lit stableyard. Finally, he saw her bending over a stretcher in the corner of the yard. As if she were aware of his arrival, she straightened, pushing her hair out of her eyes, turning toward him. His heart leaped at the sight of her. The bitterness of their parting, the sourness of suspicion, faded, and he wanted only to hold her.

"You're safe," she said, her voice shaky with relief as he dismounted beside her. There was a shadow of sorrow in her eyes as she met his gaze, a questioning apprehension that harked back to the wretchedness of the morning.

He was filled with an overpowering need to kiss the sadness from her eyes, the tremor from her soft mouth. Suddenly, nothing seemed to matter but that she was there for him. "Yes," he said, pulling her into his arms. He laid his lips against her eyelids, feeling their rapid flutter against his mouth. "Safe and sound, lynx."

Her arms went around him, and she reached her body against his, her head resting on his chest, the steady beat of his heart thudding against her ear. Her eyes closed and for this moment she lost herself in the security of his hold, the warmth of his presence, the promise of passion.

9

"That new butler of yours seemed inclined to deny me." Bernard Melville, third Earl of Gracemere, entered Lady Barret's boudoir without ceremony. "I trust it doesn't mean the gouty Sir Thomas is turning suspicious."

"No. He's at Brooks's, I believe. Snoring over his port, probably." Agnes stretched languidly on the striped chaise longue, where she had been taking a recuperative afternoon nap. "Hodgkins is overly scrupulous about his duties. He knew I was resting." She held out her hand. "I wasn't expecting you to return to town for another week."

He took her hand, carrying it to his lips. "I couldn't endure another day's separation, my love."

Agnes smiled. "Such pretty words, Bernard. And am I to believe them?"

"Oh, yes," he said, bending over her, catching her wrists and holding them down on either side of her head. "Oh, yes, my adorable Agnes, you are to believe them." His hard eyes, so pale their blueness was almost translucent, held hers, and she shivered, waiting for him to bring his mouth to hers, to underwrite his statement with the fierce possession of his body.

He laughed, reading her with the ease of long knowledge. "Oh, you are needy, aren't you, my love? It's amazing what an absence can do." Still he held himself above her, taunting her with promise.

"And you are cruel, Bernard," she stated softly. "Why does it please you to taunt me with my love?"

"Is it love? I don't think that's the right word," he murmured, bringing his face closer to hers but still not touching her. "Obsession, need, but not love. That's too tame an emotion for such a woman as you."

"And for you," she whispered.

"Obsession, need," he responded with a smile that did nothing to soften the cruel mouth. "We feed on each other."

"Kiss me," she begged, twitching her imprisoned hands in her need to touch him.

He let his weight fall onto her hands so that her wrists ached and very slowly brought his mouth to hers. She bit his lip, drawing blood, and he pulled back with a violent jerk of his head. "Bitch!"

"It's what you like," she said, with perfect truth.

He slapped her face lightly with his open palm and she gave an exultant crow of laughter, bringing her freed hand to his face, wiping the bead of blood from his lips with her fingertip and carrying it to her own mouth. Her tongue darted, licking the red smear, and her tawny eyes glittered. "Shall I come to you tonight, my lord?"

He caught her chin with hard fingers and kissed her, bruising her lips against her teeth in answer. A knock at the door brought him upright. He swung away from her, picking up a periodical from a drum table, idly flicking through the pages as a footman silently mended the fire.

"What's this I hear about Carrington taking a wife in Brussels?" Gracemere asked casually. "It's the talk of the town. Some nobody, I gather."

"Yes, I haven't met her yet. We came up to town ourselves only yesterday," Agnes said in the same tone. "Letitia Moreton says she's stunning and seems very much up to snuff. She's charmed the Society matrons at all events. Sally Jersey raves about her."

"Not another Martha, then?" He tossed the periodical onto the table again as the footman left, and he sat down, carefully smoothing out a crease in his buff pantaloons.

"Hardly," Agnes said. "No little brown mouse this, as I understand it. But no one knows anything about them . . . there's a brother too. Equally charming, according to Letitia."

"Plump in the pocket?" There was an arrested look in the pale eyes, a sudden predatory hunger.

Agnes shook her head. "That I don't know. But if he's Carrington's brother-in-law . . . why?"

Gracemere's manicured fingernails drummed on the carved arm of his chair. "I'm looking for another pigeon to pluck. Newcomers to town tend to provide the easiest pickings. I wonder if he plays."

"Who doesn't?" Agnes said. "I'll see what I can find out this evening at Cavendish House. But I have another idea for improving your financial situation, my love." She sat up, her tone suddenly brisk.

"Oh?" Gracemere raised his eyebrows. "I'm all ears, my dear."

"Letitia Moreton's daughter, Harriet," Agnes announced, and lay back again on the piled cushions with a complacent smile. "She has a fortune of thirty-thousand pounds. It should last you quite a while, I would have thought."

Gracemere frowned. "She must be barely out of the schoolroom."

"All the better," Agnes said. "She'll fall easily for the flattering attentions of a charming older man. You'll be able to sweep her off her feet before she has the chance to lay eyes on anyone else."

The earl tapped his teeth with a fingernail, considering. "What about Letitia and the girl's father? They'll be unlikely to look kindly on the suit of a fortune hunter."

"They don't know you're a fortune hunter," Agnes pointed out. "And you have the earldom. Letitia will jump at an earl for her daughter so long as you behave with circumspection. I've already become fast friends with the lady." She laughed unkindly. "Such a nincompoop she is, with die-away airs. She professes to be an invalid and can't chaperone her daughter as much as she should. So who do you think has offered to take her place?" Her eyebrows rose delicately, and Gracemere laughed.

"What a consummate plotter you are, my dear. So I can expect to meet the sweet child in your company."

"Frequently," Agnes agreed with another complacent smile.

"In the meantime, bring me your impressions of Carrington's brother-in-law. I might as well pluck a pigeon while I'm waiting for the heiress to ripen and fall," he said, rising. "I'm not invited to Cavendish House, since I'm still supposed to be in the country, so I'll rely on your acute senses, my love." He bent over her again, laying one hand on her breast, feeling the nipple rise in immediate response. "Adieu, until later."

Agnes shifted on the couch, one leg dropping to the floor. The earl moved his hand down, pressing the thin silk of her negligee against the opened cleft of her body, feeling her heat. "Until later," he repeated, and then left her.

Marcus tossed the reins to his tiger and alighted from his curricle in Berkeley Square.

"Take a good look at the leader's left hock when you get them to the mews, Henry. I sensed a slight imbalance as we took that last corner."

"Right you are, governor." The lad tugged a yellow forelock before going to the horses' heads.

Marcus strolled up the steps of the handsome double-fronted mansion. The front door opened just as he reached the head.

"Good afternoon, my lord. And it's a beautiful one, if I might be so bold." The butler's bow was as ponderous as his words.

"Afternoon, Gregson. Yes, you may be so bold." Marcus handed him his driving whip and curly-brimmed beaver hat. "Bring a bottle of the seventy-nine claret to my book room, will you?" He crossed the gleaming marble-tiled expanse of hallway and went down a narrow passage behind the staircase to a small, square room at the back of the house, where a young man was arranging papers on the massive cherrywood table that served as desk.

"Good afternoon, my lord." He greeted his employer's entrance with a bow.

"Afternoon, John. What are you going to entertain me with now?"

"Accounts, my lord," his secretary said. "And Lady Carrington's quarterly bills. You did say you wished to settle them yourself." His tone conveyed a degree of puzzlement, since in general he was responsible for settling on the marquis's account all the bills that came into the house.

"Yes, I did," Marcus said absently, picking up a neat pile of bills. "Are these they?"

"Yes, my lord. And there are some invitations you might want to look at."

"I can't think of anything I'd like to do less," Marcus said, leafing through the bills in his hand. "Give them to Lady Carrington."

"I did, my lord. But she said she didn't feel able to make up your mind for you." John blushed and he pulled awkwardly on his right ear, wishing he hadn't been put in the position of conveying Lady Carrington's forthright opinion to her husband. But his lordship merely shrugged.

"Very well. I'll discuss them with her." He dropped the bills to the table and picked up the pile of embossed cards, wrinkling his nose in distaste. The number of irksome invitations that came into the house of a married man far exceeded those he'd received as a bachelor. Everyone knew he didn't care for social events, and he couldn't understand why all these overzealous Society matrons now soliciting his company imagined that marriage would change the habits and interests of a lifetime.

"If that'll be all, my lord, I'll go and work on your speech to the House of Lords on the Corn Laws."

Marcus grimaced. "Can't you find something more interesting for me to talk on than the Corn Laws, John?"

His secretary looked startled. "But there is nothing more important at the moment, my lord."

"Nothing to do with the army or the navy . . . further reforms in the Admiralty, how about that?"

"I'll do some research, my lord." With a hurt look, John left the book room.

Marcus smiled. John's political interests were unfortunately not his employer's. He turned back to the papers on the desk, picking up the pile of bills again.

Gregson came in with the claret. "Is her ladyship in, Gregson?"

"Yes, my lord. I believe she's in the yellow drawing room." The butler drew the cork, examined it carefully, poured a small quantity of claret into a shallow taster, and sniffed and sipped with a critical frown.

"All right?"

"Yes, my lord. Very fine." He filled a crystal goblet and presented it to his employer. "Will that be all, sir?"

"For the moment. Thank you, Gregson."

Marcus took the scent of his wine before sipping appreciatively. He wandered over to the long narrow windows overlooking a small, walled garden. The leaves of a chestnut tree drifted thickly to the grass under the brisk autumnal wind. A gardener was gathering the richly burnished mass into a bonfire. Marcus was abruptly reminded of Judith's hair, glowing in the candlelight, spread over the white pillows . . . the silky matching triangle at the apex of those long, creamy thighs . . .

Abruptly he turned back to the desk and picked up the pile of bills again, tapping them against his palm. Judith certainly didn't count the cost when it came to her personal expenditures. *She was beautiful and passionate in bed and he paid her well for it.*

Why in God's name did he resent it? He was a generous man and always had been. Money had never concerned him—his fortune was too large for it ever to be an issue. And yet, as he looked through his wife's bills, saw what she'd spent on her wardrobe, he could think only of how different it must be for her now, after all those years of living from hand to mouth, of making over her gowns and wearing paste jewelry, of living in cheap lodgings . . . of pretending publicly that she had access to all the things she now had at her fingertips.

A house in Berkeley Square, a country estate in Berkshire, an unassailable social position . . . She must congratulate herself every moment of every day on how well her strategem had succeeded.

Marcus drained the claret in his glass and refilled it. Since Waterloo, they'd skimmed the surface of their relationship. There had been no further mention of the encounter in the taproom. And no reference in their lovemaking to his continued precautions against conception. Socially, they obeyed convention and went their separate ways. Except during the quiet, private hours of the night. Then the needs of their bodies transcended the bleak recognition of the true nature of their partnership, so that he would wake in the morning, filled with a warmth and contentment, only to have it destroyed immediately with the full return of memory.

She never talked of her past and he never asked. In all essentials they remained strangers, except in passion. Was that enough? Could it ever be enough? But it was all he was going to have, so he'd better learn to be satisfied.

He put his glass down and left the book room, still holding the sheaf of bills. The yellow drawing room was a small salon upstairs, at the back of the house. Judith had laid claim to it immediately, eschewing the heavy formality of the public rooms: the library, main drawing room, and dining room. He opened the door, to be greeted by a light trill of feminine laughter; it was abruptly cut off as the three women in the room saw who had entered, and for an instant he felt like an intruder in his own house.

"Why, Carrington, have you come to take a glass of ratafia with us?" Judith said, quirking her eyebrows with her habitual challenge.

"The day I find you drinking ratafia, ma'am, is the day I'll know I'm on my way to Bedlam," he observed, bowing. "I give you good afternoon, ladies. I don't wish to intrude, Judith, but I'd like to see you in my book room when you're at liberty."

Judith bristled visibly. She hadn't yet succeeded in moderating her husband's autocratic manner. "I have an appointment later this afternoon," she fibbed. "Maybe we could discuss whatever it is at some other time."

"Unfortunately not," he replied. "It's a matter of some urgency. I'll expect you in—" He glanced at the clock on the mantelpiece. "—within the hour, shall we say?"

Without waiting for her response, he bowed again to his wife's guests and left, closing the door gently behind him.

Judith seemed to have a natural talent for making friends, he reflected, and the door knocker was constantly banging, female trills and whispers filling the corners and crevices of his previously masculine-oriented house. Not only women either. There were men aplenty, anxious to play cicisbeo to the Marchioness of Carrington. Not that Judith had so far stepped out of line with her courtiers. Her flirtations were conducted, as far as he could see, with the light hand of an expert. But then that's only what he would expect from an expert.

As he reached the hallway, the door knocker sounded. He paused, waiting as the butler greeted the new arrival. "Good afternoon, Lady Devlin."

"Good afternoon, Gregson. Is her ladyship at home?" The visitor nervously adjusted the ostrich feather in her hat.

"In the yellow drawing room, my lady."

"Then I'll go straight up. There's no need to announce me. . . . Oh, Marcus . . . you startled me."

Marcus regarded his sister-in-law in some puzzlement. Sally's complexion was changing rapidly from pink to deathly white and back again. He knew she tended to be uncomfortable in his company, but this degree of discomposure was out of the ordinary.

"I beg your pardon, Sally." He bowed and stood aside to let her pass him on the stairs. "I trust all's well in Grosvenor Square." He waited with bored resignation to be told that one of his nephews had the toothache or come down with a chill.

To his surprise, Sally looked startled and, instead of launching into one of her minute descriptions of childish ailments, said, "Yes . . . yes, thank you, Marcus. So good of you to be concerned." Her gloved hand ran back and forth over the banister, for all the world as if she were polishing it. "I was hoping to see Judith."

"You'll find her in her drawing room."

Sally almost ran up the stairs, without a word of farewell. Marcus shook his head dismissively. He didn't object to Jack's wife, but she was a pretty widgeon with no conversation. Judith seemed to like her, though. Which was interesting, since he'd noticed that his wife didn't suffer fools gladly.

"Sally . . . why, whatever's the matter?" Judith jumped up at her sister-in-law's precipitate entrance.

"Oh, I have to talk to you." Sally grasped Judith's hands. "I don't know where to turn." Her eyes took in the other two women in the room. "Isobel, Cornelia . . . I'm at my wit's end."

"Good heavens, Sally." Isobel Henley examined a plate of sweet biscuits and took a macaroon. "Is it one of the children?"

"I wish it were as simple as that." Sally sat down on a sofa, gazing tragically around the room. Her usually merry blue eyes glittered with tears. She opened her reticule and dabbed at her eyes with a lacy scrap of handkerchief.

"Have some tea." Practically, Judith filled a teacup and passed it to her sister-in-law. Sally drank and struggled to pull herself together. She put the cup back on the table and took a deep breath.

"I've been racking my brains for three days until I think my head is about to explode. But I can't think what to do." The scrap of lace tore under her restless fingers.

"So tell us." Cornelia Forsythe leaned forward, patting Sally's hand reassuringly. Her lorgnette swung into her teacup, splashing her already slightly spotted gown. "Oh, dear." She dabbed ineffectually at the spots. "I was perfectly clean when I left the house."

Judith swallowed a smile. Cornelia was a large, untidy woman who never seemed in control of her dress, her possessions, her hair, the time, or her relationships. She was, however, possessed of a quick wit and an agile brain.

"I don't see how, unless you can put me in the way of acquiring four thousand pounds by tomorrow morning."

"Four thousand?" Judith whistled in the manner she'd picked up from Sebastian. "Whatever for?"

"Jeremy," Sally said. Her younger brother was an impoverished scapegrace. "I had to lend him four thousand pounds or he'd have been imprisoned for debt in the Fleet and now I have to get my money back. But what else could I have done?"

"Your husband?" Cornelia suggested.

Sally looked at Judith. "Jack might have helped him, but you know what Marcus thinks of Jeremy."

Judith nodded. Marcus had no tolerance for the dissipated excesses of young men with breeding and no fortune. He was inclined to declare that a career in the army was the answer for all such young fools. Either that, or politics. Judith didn't disagree with him. The reckless and undisciplined pursuit of pleasure was as alien to her as the man in the moon. However, saying so wouldn't help Sally at the moment.

"I suppose Marcus's advice to Jack is to let Jeremy suffer the consequences," Judith said.

Sally nodded. "And in truth, I can't really blame him. Jeremy's always going to be wanting more."

"So, how did you furnish him with four thousand pounds?" Isobel brought the conversation back to the point as she took another macaroon. She had an inveterate sweet tooth, but, much to Judith's amusement, even Isobel's lamentable fondness for ratafia couldn't sugar her tongue.

"I pawned the Devlin rubies," Sally said flatly.

Isobel dropped her macaroon to the carpet. "You did what?"

Judith closed her eyes for a minute, absorbing the full enormity of this.

Sally continued in a voice devoid of expression. "I didn't know what else to do. Jeremy was desperate. But Marcus has asked for them. Jack thinks they're being cleaned."

"Why has Marcus asked for them?" Judith asked.

Sally looked at her sister-in-law as if the answer were self-evident. "Because they're yours, Judith."

"Mine?"

"You're the Marchioness of Carrington. The Devlin jewels are rightfully yours. Marcus only loaned them to me . . . although no one expected him to marry, so I thought . . ." Her voice died.

A silence fell as her three companions contemplated the situation. "What a pickle," Cornelia said finally. "You should have had them copied."

"I did," Sally said. "But the copy won't fool Carrington."

"No," Judith agreed, thinking about her husband's sharpness of eye and intellect. "I suppose I could say I don't like rubies and I'm quite happy for you to keep them. . . . But no, that won't work. Marcus is still going to want to see them."

She stood up and walked around the room, thinking. There was one way to help Sally. It was risky. If Marcus found out, what little accord they had would be destroyed. But she could do it, and surely, if you had the means to help a friend, then you were honor bound to do so. At least, by her code of honor.

"When must you redeem them, Sally?"

"Jack said he wanted to return them to Marcus tomorrow." Sally wrung her hands. "Judith, I feel so terrible . . . as if I stole something that belonged to you."

"Oh, nonsense!" Judith dismissed this with a brisk gesture. "I don't give a tinker's damn for rubies. Your brother needed help and you gave it to him." This she understood as an absolute imperative. "I only wish you'd said something earlier. It'll be noticeable if I win such a sum in one evening. I would much prefer to have won it over several occasions. It looks rather singular to be spending the entire evening in the card room playing only for high stakes."

"What are you saying? I know you're fond of gaming, but—"

"Oh, it's a little more than that," Judith said. "I'm actually very skilled at cards."

"I had noticed." Cornelia surveyed Judith through her lorgnette. "You and your brother."

"Our father taught us," Judith said. Even in this company, she wasn't prepared to expand on her background. "We were both apt pupils and I enjoy it."

"But I don't fully understand . . ." Sally said hesitantly.

"If I went to Mrs. Dolby's card party this evening, I could probably win such a sum," Judith explained succinctly. "And it would draw no attention in such a place."

"But you can't play on Pickering Street, Judith." Isobel was shocked. The widow Dolby's card parties were notorious for their enormously high stakes and loose company.

"Why not? Many women do."

"Yes, but they're generally considered fast."

"Sebastian will escort me. If I go in my brother's company, there should be no gossip."

"What about Carrington?"

"There's no reason why he should discover it," Judith said. "It will serve very well. There's bound to be a table for macao." She smiled at Sally. "Cheer up. You will redeem the rubies in the morning."

"But how can you be so confident?"

"Practice," Judith said a touch wryly. "I have had a great deal of practice."

They left soon after, Sally looking a little more cheerful. Judith's confidence was infectious, although it was difficult to trust in such a promise of salvation.

Judith stood frowning in the empty salon. Since her

marriage, she'd played only socially, for moderate stakes. Serious gaming was something quite different. Was she out of practice? She closed her eyes, envisioning a macao table, seeing a hand of cards. The old, familiar prickle of excitement ran down her spine and she smiled to herself. No, she'd never lose the touch.

She'd have to have Sebastian's escort. He would probably have plans of his own for the evening and would need time to alter them. It didn't occur to her that her brother would fail her. She'd go to his lodgings right away . . . but, no. Marcus was waiting for her. Just what lay behind this brusque summons to his book room? For a minute, she toyed with the idea of ignoring the summons, then dismissed the urge. Matters were delicate enough between them as it was, without deliberately stirring things up.

Marcus opened the door himself at her brisk knock. "I was wondering how long your friends would keep you."

"They had the prior claim on my attention, sir," she said. "It would have been unpardonably rude to have asked them to leave prematurely . . . although you don't seem to share that opinion. You made it very clear they shouldn't prolong their visit."

Marcus glanced at the clock, observing wryly "I can't have been very persuasive. I've been waiting for you for well over an hour."

Judith put her head on one side, surveying him through narrowed eyes. "And what else did you expect, Carrington?"

That surprised a reluctant laugh from him. "Nothing else, lynx." A wispy strand of copper hair was escaping from a loosened pin in the knot on top of her head. It was irresistible, and without conscious decision, he pulled the pin out. Then it seemed silly to stop there and his fingers moved through the silken mass, finding and removing pins, demolishing the careful coiffure.

Judith made no protest. Whenever he put his hands on her, it was always the same. She became powerless to do anything but respond. As the hair tumbled around her face, he ran his hands through it, tugging at tangled ringlets with a rapt expression. Then he stood back and surveyed his handiwork.

"What did you do that for?" Judith asked.

"I don't know," he said with a puzzled headshake. "I couldn't seem to help myself." Cupping her face, he kissed her, a long, slow joining of their mouths that as always absorbed them totally.

Slightly breathless, Judith drew back from him when he let his hands fall from her face. "You do kiss remarkably well, husband," she observed with a tiny laugh.

"And you have, of course, vast experience from which to draw your comparisons."

"Now, that, sir, is for me to know and you to find out."

"I'm not sure this is the time or the place for such a discovery. I shall postpone the exercise until later."

"So what lies behind this urgent summons?" Judith asked, changing the subject in the hope that it would allow her heated blood to cool and put the stiffness back in her knees.

"Ah." Leaning against the desk, crossing his long legs in their fawn pantaloons at the ankles, he reached behind him for the pile of bills. "I've been examining your quarterly bills and I think . . . I really think you need to explain some of them."

"Explain them?" She looked at him in genuine confusion, arousal quenched as thoroughly as if she'd been dipped in an icy stream.

"Yes." He held out the bills and she took them, star-

ing down at the sheet on top bearing columns of John's
neat figures. The total was extravagant, certainly, but not
horrendous . . . at least not by the standards of London Society.

"So what do you want me to explain?" She leafed
through the bills. "They all seem quite straightforward."

"Do you usually spend four hundred guineas on a
gown?" he asked, taking the sheaf from her, riffling
through them until he found the offending document.
"Here."

"But that was my court dress," she said. "Magarethe
made it."

"And this . . . and this . . ." He held out two
more. "Fifty guineas for a pair of shoe buckles, Judith!"

Judith took a step back. "Let me understand what's
happening, Marcus. Are you questioning my expenditures?"

He pursed his lips. "That would be an accurate interpretation of this interview."

"And you're accusing me of extravagance?" There
was a faint buzzing in her ears as she grappled with the
humiliation of this: to be chastised like a child who's
overspent her pin money. No one, ever, had questioned
her expenditure. Since she had first put up her hair, she
had been managing her own finances as well as those of
their small household. She had juggled bills, paid rent,
ensured food of some kind appeared on the table; and in
the time since her father's death, she had managed the
growing fund that would underpin the plan for Gracemere's downfall.

"In a word, yes."

"Forgive me, but just how much would it be reasonable for me to spend in a quarter?" Her voice shook.
"You neglected to give me a limit."

"My error," he agreed. "I'll settle these bills and then

I'll instruct my bankers to make you a quarterly allowance. If you overspend, then I'll have to ask you to submit all bills to me for prior approval."

He stood up, tossing the bills on the desk as if to indicate the interview was over. "But I'm sure you'll remember how to put a rein on your spending, once you understand that marriage has not opened the gates to a limitless fund. I'm sorry if you didn't realize that earlier." He could hear the bite in his voice, could almost see the ugly twist to his mouth, and yet he couldn't help himself.

Afraid of what she would do or say if she stayed another minute in the same room with Marcus, Judith turned and left, closing the door with exaggerated care behind her. Her cheeks burned with humiliation. He was accusing her of taking advantage of her position to satisfy her own greed. What kind of person did he think she was? But she knew the answer: a conniving, unprincipled trickster who would stoop to anything to achieve her ambition.

But it wasn't true. Oh, on the surface, maybe. She wasn't dealing the cards of her marriage with total honesty. But she wasn't the despicable person he believed her to be.

And she wasn't going to submit to a meager allowance and a controlling hand on her purse strings. Her lips tightened with determination. What she could do for Sally, she could do for herself. She would simply return to the old days: Pay her own way at the tables. And Marcus Devlin and his quarterly allowance could go to the devil.

Half an hour later, footman in tow, she walked to her brother's lodgings on Albemarle Street. Sebastian was on his way out for a five o'clock ride in Hyde Park, but with customary good nature postponed the excursion and ushered his sister into his parlor.

"Sherry?"

"Please." She took the glass he handed her.

"So, what can I do for you, Ju?"

"Several things." She explained the matter of Sally and the four thousand pounds.

Sebastian frowned. "That's a devil of a haul in one night, Ju."

"I know, but what else is to be done? If Marcus ever discovered what she'd done, I can't think how he'd react. Jack might be a bit more understanding, but he'll follow Marcus's lead, he always does."

"He wields a lot of power, that husband of yours," Sebastian observed.

"Yes," Judith agreed shortly. "Jack's elder brother, Charlie's guardian . . . my husband," she added in an almost vicious undertone.

"What's happened?" Sebastian asked without preamble.

Judith told him, trying to keep her voice steady, but her anger surged anew as she recounted the mortifying interview. She paced Sebastian's parlor, the embroidered flounce of her walking dress swishing around her ankles. "It's intolerable," she finished with a sweep of her arm. "Marcus is intolerable and the situation is intolerable."

"What are you going to do about it?" Sebastian knew his sister well enough to know she would never submit meekly to her husband's edict.

"Provide for myself," she said. "At the tables. Just like before."

Sebastian whistled softly. "I suppose you couldn't just tell him that you didn't know who was in the taproom at Quatre Bras? Since that's what's causing the mischief."

Judith shook her head. "It wouldn't do any good. He's determined to believe the worst of me, and the truth's dubious enough, anyway." She looked helplessly at her brother. "Supposing I say: I didn't deliberately trap you into marriage, but it was too good an opportunity to pass up, for an adventuress in need of a good establishment in order to pursue her secret goal. And anyway, we're not really married, but I didn't want you to know that." She raised her eyebrows at her brother.

Sebastian pretended to consider this. "No, I'm afraid that wouldn't go over too well. At any rate, you know you can count on me. The deep play doesn't begin at Dolby's until the early hours. If you're going to Cavendish House, I'll escort you from there. Will that serve?"

"Perfectly. Marcus doesn't intend to put in an appearance at Cavendish House, and he'll not be surprised if I don't return home until near dawn. We always go our separate ways."

"You'd better dip into the 'Gracemere fund,'" Sebastian said. "You'll need decent stakes at the start, and clearly your husband isn't going to furnish them." He went into the next-door bedroom and returned with a pouch of rouleaux. "Eight hundred." He dropped it into her hand and grinned. "If you don't turn that into four thousand in one evening, I'll know you've lost your touch."

She smiled, weighing the pouch on the palm of her hand. "Never fear. Now, there's another matter in which I need your help." She put down her sherry glass. "Since I'm declaring war, I might as well do it properly. I wish you to acquire a high-perch phaeton and pair for me. Marcus has expressed himself very vigorously on the subject of loose women who drive themselves in sporting vehicles, so my driving one should nicely confirm his flattering opinion of me."

Sebastian scratched his nose and refilled his glass. Judith had lost her temper, and once she'd taken the high road, as he knew from a lifetime's experience, there was little he could do to turn her from the path. She'd pursue it until the momentum died. "Is it wise to be so blatantly provoking?" he asked, without much hope of success.

"I don't much care," his sister responded. "He thinks I'm a designing, conniving baggage, with no morals and no principles. And so I shall be."

Sebastian sighed. "How much do you want to spend for the pair?"

"Not above four hundred . . . unless it would be a crime to pass them up, of course."

"Grantham's in debt up to his neck . . . I could probably acquire his match-bays for around four hundred."

"Wonderful. Pay for them out of the 'fund,' and I'll replace it as soon as I've earned it."

She reached up and kissed him. "Now I'll leave you to Hyde Park."

"Ju?"

"Yes?" She stopped as she reached the door.

"Gracemere's in town."

"Ahhh. Have you seen him?"

"No, but Wellby was talking of him in Whites this morning."

"Ahhh," said Judith again, as a prickle of anticipation crept up her spine. "Then soon we begin, Sebastian."

"Yes," he agreed. "Soon we begin."

Judith stood on the pavement for a minute, gazing sightlessly down the narrow road. The footman waited patiently. A sudden gust of wind picked up a handful of fallen leaves from the gutter and sent them eddying around her. Absently she reached out and caught one. It was dry and crackly and crumbled to dust as her hand closed over it. Once the game with Gracemere was played out, there would be no need to continue the illegal charade of her marriage. Marcus would have his freedom from her. But not before she'd taught him a lesson.

10

Marcus could hear Judith's voice through the door connecting their bedchambers, talking with her maid as Millie dressed her for the evening. The afternoon's unpleasantness had left him with a sour taste in his mouth. He was perfectly entitled to keep a close hand on his wife's pursestrings, but he couldn't rid himself of the feeling that he wasn't behaving like himself. What difference did it make what she spent? It would take more than one lifetime of extravagance to run through his fortune. But disillusion had soured his customary generosity. This wasn't about Judith's spending habits. He wanted to punish her. It was as simple as that. And as disagreeable as that.

He inserted a diamond pin carefully into the snowy

folds of his cravat. "You needn't wait up for me, Cheveley."

"No, my lord." The valet turned from the armoire where he was rearranging his lordship's wardrobe with loving care. "If you say so, my lord," he said woodenly.

"I do," Marcus affirmed, a smile tugging at the corners of his mouth. Cheveley's sensitive dignity was always seriously affronted at the slightest hint that his employer could manage without him. "That cough of yours needs a hot toddy and an early bed, man."

Cheveley's thin cheeks pinkened and his stiffness vanished at this solicitude. His lordship was a considerate and just employer, quick to notice signs of discontent or ill health, and quick to act upon both. "That's too good of you, my lord. But I'll be right as a trivet in a day or so."

"Yes, I'm sure you will. But you don't want to take any chances with that weak chest. Leave that now, and take yourself off to bed."

He waited until the valet had left the bedchamber, then opened the door onto his wife's apartment. Judith was sitting at the dressing table, watching critically in the mirror as Millie threaded a gold velvet ribbon through her ringlets.

"Good evening, my lord." For form's sake, Judith offered him the semblance of a smile in the mirror, but didn't turn to greet him.

"Good evening, Judith." Marcus sat down in a velvet chair beside the crackling fire in the hearth. Millie turned her attention to the row of tiny buttons on the tight sleeves of the gown of pale-green crape. It was a color that suited his wife's vibrant coloring to perfection, Marcus reflected, and the thin silk cord circling her waist emphasized her slenderness.

"Did you wish to speak with me?" Judith asked after

a few minutes, wondering what could have brought him to her bedchamber in this conjugal fashion. They were hardly in charity with each other at the moment.

"Not about anything in particular," he said, observing without due consideration, "that's a delightful gown."

Judith's expression registered complete disbelief. She blinked and dismissed her maid. "Thank you, Millie, that will do very well. You may go."

The maid curtsied and left. Judith turned on her stool to survey her husband. He was impeccably dressed as always in black satin knee britches and white waistcoat, his only jewelry the diamond pin in his cravat and his heavy gold signet ring, now returned to him. His black hair was brushed *à la Brutus* and there was a distinct frown in the ebony eyes, but it didn't seem to be directed at her.

"Did I hear you aright?" she demanded, raising her eyebrows. "You approve of my gown, sir. Well, that's fortunate, since I daresay you'll be seeing it on many occasions over the next few years. I shall wear it until it falls off my back in shreds. That is what you intend, isn't it?"

"Don't be silly," Marcus said. He'd come in with the vague intention of making peace, but it looked like a forlorn hope. "You know perfectly well that was not what I meant this afternoon. Your allowance won't be ungenerous."

Judith swung back to the mirror. "Your kindness overwhelms me, my lord." She licked her finger and dampened the delicate arch of her eyebrows, struggling to calm herself. Losing her temper again would play havoc with her equilibrium and she needed a cool head tonight, if she was to win for Sally.

Marcus sighed and tried a new tack. "I thought I

would accompany you to Cavendish House this evening." Judith knew how he loathed such social engagements; she would surely understand the sacrifice as the peace offering it was meant to be.

He had expected her to be surprised. He had not expected to see a flash of shock in her eyes. It was replaced almost immediately by something that looked unnervingly like calculation.

"Such gallantry, my lord. But quite unnecessary." She laughed lightly, continuing to examine her reflection critically in the mirror. "It would be a sure way to ruin my evening . . . or perhaps that was your intention."

"My apologies, ma'am." He stood up, his lips thinned. "I wasn't intending to ruin your evening. Forgive me."

Judith relented slightly. She half turned on the stool again. "I only meant that I won't be able to enjoy myself because I'll know how bored you are."

She turned back to the dressing table and began tidying a pot of hairpins. "None of your friends will be there and mine won't amuse you."

She didn't want his company; it was as simple as that. Marcus bowed and said coldly, "As you wish. I'm sure you know best." He returned to his own bedchamber without a backward glance.

Oh, Lord, Judith thought miserably. Surely not even a forced marriage should be conducted in this sniping wasteland. She and Marcus were simply the wrong people to have chained themselves in this mutual bondage. The sooner she left him to his own devices the better.

It was after two o'clock when a hired hackney drew up outside Number 6, Pickering Street. Sebastian sprang down and assisted his sister to alight. Judith smoothed down her cloak of gold taffeta and adjusted the puffed muslin collar, looking up at the tall, narrow house. So this was London's equivalent of the more genteel gaming hells. She had frequented such places in most of the capitals of the Continent and was more than a little curious to see what London could produce.

A liveried footman admitted them, took their cloaks, and escorted them up the narrow staircase to a square hall at the head. Three brightly lit salons opened off the hall, all thronged with men and women in evening dress, flunkeys moving among them bearing trays of glasses. Above the relatively subdued level of conversation, the groom-porters could be heard calling the odds at the hazard table.

Judith glanced up at Sebastian and he grinned down at her in instant comprehension. They were home.

"Why, Mr. Davenport, I'm delighted you could honor us. And, Lady Carrington . . ." Amelia Dolby drifted toward them from the quinze table. She must be more than sixty, Judith thought, despite the heavy rouge, absurdly youthful hairstyle, and semitransparent gown. Harsh-featured, sharp-eyed, she offered Judith the piranha's smile of one welcoming a victim. Judith had received many such smiles in her life, and offered her own bland version. For the next few hours, her face would be a mask, revealing nothing.

"What's your game, Lady Carrington?" Amelia Dolby inquired. "Hazard, perhaps?"

Judith shook her head. She and Sebastian only ever played the dice for pleasure; there was no skill to counteract the element of chance. Only a fool would bet seriously on pure luck. "I'm not sure. What are you playing, Sebastian?"

"I've a mind to try the quinze table," he said carelessly, slipping black velvet ribands around his ruffled cuffs to keep them from flopping over his hands.

"Then I'll play macao." They never played at the same table; it would rather defeat the object of the exercise.

Amelia Dolby escorted her to the macao table, introducing her to the other players. Judith was slightly acquainted with several of them. They were all hardened gamesters and accepted Judith in their midst with the unquestioning assumption that she too was a slave to the cards and dice. She wouldn't be there if she wasn't in a position to play high, and that was all that interested any of them.

Three hours later she had won almost five thousand guineas. Enough to redeem the Devlin rubies and purchase her phaeton and pair. It was all very satisfactory and very exhilarating. She felt amazingly revivified and wondered why she'd taken so long to get back to serious play. Some pointless sense of obligation to Marcus, of course. She'd thought it might upset him. Laughable really, in the circumstances. Everything about her upset him anyway. Except in bed . . .

Swallowing that thought, Judith gathered up her winnings and excused herself from the macao table.

Sebastian was still heavily engaged at the quinze table, where silence reigned, and most of his fellow players wore masks to hide any emotional response to the fall of the cards. Recognizing that she couldn't expect him to leave yet, Judith strolled through the salons, relaxed now that her goal was achieved, and prepared to play purely for pleasure if a place opened up at one of the other tables.

"Lady Carrington . . ." A woman's voice hailed her from a faro table. "Do you care to join us?"

"If you've a place." Smiling, Judith went over to the

table. She didn't recall meeting the woman before. "You have the advantage of me, ma'am."

"Oh, permit me to perform introductions." Amelia was at her elbow. "Lady Barret . . . Lady Carrington."

"I only arrived in town the other day," Agnes Barret said. "My husband has been indisposed and it delayed our return from the country." She gestured to the chair beside her at the table. "Do, please. . . . I was hoping for an introduction at Cavendish House," she went on as Judith sat down. "But you were so surrounded by admirers, my dear, I couldn't come near you." She held out her hand with a laugh.

"You flatter me, ma'am," Judith demurred, taking the hand. As Lady Barret held her hand, she regarded Judith with an intensity that seemed to exclude the rest of the room. Judith's skin crawled and her scalp contracted. The buzz of voices, the calls of the groom-porters, faded into an indistinguishable hum; the brilliance of the massive chandeliers dimmed, became fuzzy.

It was as if she were held in thrall by some species of witchcraft. And then Lady Barret smiled and dropped her hand. "So you're a gamester, Lady Carrington. Does your brother share the passion?"

Judith forced herself to respond naturally, wondering what on earth was the matter with her. What kind of fanciful nonsense had gripped her? "He's at the quinze table," she said, laying her rouleaux around her selected cards.

Faro was essentially a game of chance and, in general, if her luck was out, she would move on to something else. But it was impossible to concentrate and she lost far more than she'd meant to risk before she realized it. Cross with herself, she made her excuses and rose from the table.

"Oh, your luck will turn, Lady Carrington, I'm

sure," her neighbor said, laying a restraining hand on her arm.

"Not when the devil's on my shoulder." Judith quoted her father's favorite excuse when the cards weren't falling right.

A flash shot through Lady Barret's tawny eyes and her color faded, highlighting the patches of rouge on her cheekbones. "I haven't heard that said in a long time."

Judith shrugged. "Is it unusual? I thought it was a common expression. . . . Oh, Sebastian." She turned to greet her brother with relief. "I don't believe you're acquainted with Lady Barret."

She watched her brother as he smiled and bowed over her ladyship's hand. Could he feel that strange, disturbing aura too? But Sebastian seemed quite untroubled by Agnes Barret. Indeed, he was exerting his customary powerful charm with smiling insouciance. The lady responded with an appreciative glint in her eye and a distinctly flirtatious little chuckle.

"It's late, Sebastian," Judith said abruptly. "If you'll forgive us, ma'am. . . ."

Her brother gave her a sharp glance, then made his own farewells rather more courteously. Once out of earshot, however, he observed, "That was a bit precipitate, Ju."

"My head's beginning to ache," she offered in excuse. All her previous exhilaration had dissipated, and she wanted only to leave the hot rooms, overpoweringly stuffy with the cloying scents of the women and the heat from the massive candlebra. "And my luck was out and I wasn't watching my losses."

This disconsolate confession earned her a disapproving frown. "You should have been concentrating," he reproved. "You know the rule."

"Yes, but I wasn't thinking clearly." She wondered

whether to tell him about her weird sensation with Lady Barret, then decided against it. To blame her clumsy play on a peculiar reaction to a fellow player would sound lunatic. "At least I've covered the rubies. And I've enough left for the horses."

She glanced over her shoulder. Lady Barret was standing talking to her hostess. She was a most arresting woman, tall and slender, strikingly dressed in an emerald-green gown of jaconet muslin with a deep décolletage and a broad flounce at the hem. In her youth, she would have been beautiful, Judith decided, with that massed auburn hair and the high cheekbones and chiseled mouth. The vivid color of her gown was one of Judith's own favorites. She made a mental note never to wear the color again, and then instantly chided herself for such childish fancies.

Dawn was breaking when the night porter let her in to Devlin House. She went light-footed upstairs to her own chamber. Knowing how late she'd be, she'd told Millie not to wait up for her, and the fire was almost out, the candles guttering. She threw off her clothes and stood for a minute at the window, watching the roseate bloom of the sky.

"Where the hell have you been?"

Judith spun round at the furious voice. Marcus lounged against the jamb of the connecting door, as naked as she, and his body seemed to thrum with the tension of a plucked violin string.

"To Cavendish House."

"I went to Cavendish House myself four hours ago, intending to escort you home. You were not there, madam wife." And for the last three hours, he had been lying awake listening for the sound of her return, imagin-

ing any number of scenarios, from footpads to an illicit
tryst. Everything he knew of her lent itself to the worst
possible construction, and within a short time, he had
ceased to be able to think of any sensible explanation.

Judith tried to think quickly, aware of her mental
fatigue after the hours at Pickering Street. She shrugged
and asked coldly, "Were you spying on me, sir?"

He had gone to Cavendish House with the best of
motives, determined to paper over their differences in the
only way he knew how: a lover's insistence on seduction.
But at the cold, sardonic question, all good intentions
vanished. "It seems I have cause. When my wife is not
where she's supposed to be and disappears God only
knows where for the greater part of the night, it's hardly
surprising I should feel a need to check up on you."

Abruptly Judith changed tactics. The last thing she
wanted was for Marcus to decide to dog her footsteps in
public. It would play merry hell with her gaming plans.
She offered him a conciliatory smile, and her voice was
quietly reasonable. "I was with Sebastian, Marcus. We
haven't had the opportunity for a comfortable talk for
some time."

Marcus knew how attached they were, how strong
the bond was between them. He looked at her closely,
frowning. It was distracting. The closer he looked, the
more he saw of Judith in her nakedness. He felt his body
stir, begin to harden. Judith's eyes flickered unerringly
downward and she came toward him, extending her
hands. "But since neither of us is asleep in the dawn, I
can think of any number of diversions."

He took her hands, holding them tightly, examining
her face, telling himself she had given him a perfectly
understandable explanation for her absence.

"So can I." He drew her to the bed and fell back,

pulling her with him. "Were you at your brother's lodgings?"

Judith froze beneath the stroking hand. "We had a great deal to talk about." Rolling over, she kissed his nipples, her tongue lifting the hard buds, her hand drifting down his body.

Marcus caught her hand in mid caress. "I don't think you've answered my question, Judith."

Hell and the devil. He was going to force her to lie. "Of course."

Was she lying? What reason had he for believing her? The perverse prod of disillusion drove him onward down this destructive path. "Why do I have the feeling you're being less than straightforward?" One hand still held hers, his other caressed her back in long, slow strokes.

"I can't imagine why." Her voice was muffled, buried in his skin. She still had the use of her lips and tongue, but that use didn't seem to be creating the hoped for distraction.

"If you're lying to me, my dear wife, you're going to discover that my patience and tolerance have certain limits. You are my wife, and as such the guardian of my honor. Honor and untruths make uneasy bedfellows."

"Damn you, Marcus!" Judith sat up, glaring at him. "Stop threatening me. Why would I lie?"

"I don't know," he said. "But by the same token, why wouldn't you?"

Judith closed her eyes on the hurt . . . a hurt she wasn't entitled to feel because she *was* lying. But whose fault was that?

Marcus hitched himself up against the pillows, regarding her through hooded eyes in the dim, gray light of dawn. He could feel her pain as he could feel his own, and he tried to find the words to put this mess into perspective, to salvage something out of the night.

"Judith, I can't have you running around in secret pursuits at all hours of the night, with or without your brother. It may be what you're used to doing, but your position is different now. The Marchioness of Carrington, my wife, has to be above reproach . . . whatever Judith Davenport may have done. You know that damn well."

"And why are you assuming that I was doing anything that was not above reproach?" she snapped. "I told you I was with my brother. Why isn't that enough?"

"You seem to forget I know what you and your brother get up to. Fleecing gulls with fan play . . ."

"Not anymore," she interrupted, flushing. "You can no longer have any justification for such an accusation."

"I trust not," he said. "Because let me tell you something, Judith." Reaching out, he caught her chin, his eyes and voice as hard as iron. "If I ever find that you and your brother have performed your little duet again, by the time I've finished with you, you will wish your parents had never met. Do I make myself clear?"

Judith jerked her head free of his grip, her voice frigid. "Such a statement would be impossible to misconstrue, sir."

"I had hoped to be perfectly lucid."

"You may rest assured you were."

But they were going to do it again, just once more.

And once it was over, she'd leave Marcus to find himself the kind of wife he wanted: a woman of honor and principle; meek and obedient; the epitome of virtue. And she'd wish him joy of her, she thought savagely.

"I don't think we can have anything further to discuss," she declared. "I bid you good night, my lord."

Marcus swung himself off the bed. "Good night, madam."

The door clicked shut. Judith huddled into bed,

swallowing the lump in her throat, tears pricking behind her eyes. She was miserable and she was disappointed. Her body ached for some other finale to the evening, for what had been promised and then so devastatingly denied. She stared, scratchy-eyed, into the pale light of early morning, her limbs aching, her mind as clear as a bell, her body throbbing for fulfillment.

Suddenly the door between their bedrooms flew open again and then slammed shut. Marcus stood at the end of the bed, and she could feel the force of his emotion as vitally as she could see the power in his aroused body.

"Damnation, Judith. I don't know what to do about you!" His voice was a contained whisper, but the fierce frustration was all the more potent for its containment. "I want you more than I have ever wanted another woman, and yet you madden me to such a degree sometimes, I can't distinguish between the need to love you and the need to subdue you."

He came round to the side of the bed and stood looking down at her.

Silently Judith kicked aside the cover, offering her body, opalescent in the pearly dawn. Marcus came down on the bed beside her. He gathered her against him, and his hand was hard on her body as he possessed the long length from waist to ankle, the indentations and the curves. Judith felt her skin come alive under the rough touch, her thighs dampen. His fingers probed with deep, intimate insistence, and his voice demanded that she tell him what pleased her, that she open herself to him fully, that she reveal to him the sites and touches that gave her greatest pleasure.

He branded her with tongue and hand, searing her with the mark of a lover who knew her in her vulnerability, in the wild passionate soaring of her need. And finally he knelt between her widespread thighs, his body etched against the light from the window. He drew her legs onto his shoulders, slipping his hands beneath her buttocks to lift her to meet the slow thrust of his entry that seemed to penetrate her core, to fill her with a sweet anguish that she could barely contain yet could not bear to relinquish.

Tears stood out in her eyes as she held his gaze. But they were tears of joy as the ravishment of her senses began anew, this time in shared glory, a tornado, a wild, escalating spiral that swept them into the void where the world has no sway and nothing mattered but the ability to be together in this way, to be a part of each other, she in him, he in her.

Afterward, he lay holding her, her head on his shoulder, her body soft against him as she slipped into sleep. And he was filled with a great tenderness, and a tiny spring crocus of hope pushed through the heavy soil of disillusion. Surely their passion counted for something. It couldn't be a complete lie. If only he could bring new eyes to bear . . . cut through the preconceptions . . . see another Judith.

11

Bernard Melville, third Earl of Gracemere. Judith gazed across the ballroom at the man who had ruined her father, the man who had driven George Devereux and his children out of England, the man who had ultimately driven George Davenport to his death. The slow burn of rage was followed by the same prickle of excitement she felt at the gaming tables, when she knew she had her fellow players on the run.

"Charlie, are you acquainted with the Earl of Gracemere?"

"Of course I am. Isn't everyone?" Her partner executed a smooth turn. "You dance wonderfully, Judith."

"A woman I fear is only as good as her partner," Judith observed, laughing. "Fortunately for me, you seem to have a natural talent."

Charlie blushed.

"It's a pity it doesn't run in the family," Judith said thoughtfully.

"What do you mean?"

"Well, your cousin isn't much for the dance floor."

"No, he never has been," Charlie said. "In fact, he's such a dull stick, I don't think he cares a fig for anything outside his history books and military politics." His voice was bitter.

"Are you and Marcus at outs?" Judith asked. Charlie's frequent visits to Devlin House had for some reason ceased in the last couple of weeks. She looked at him, noticing his rather drawn look, the constraint in his eye.

"He's so damn strict, Judith. He has such antiquated notions . . . he doesn't seem to understand that a man has to amuse himself somehow."

"That's not quite true," Judith demurred mildly. "He amuses himself a great deal with sporting pursuits and horses, and he has plenty of friends who don't seem to think him a dull stick."

"I'm sorry," Charlie said uncomfortably. "I spoke out of turn. He's your husband . . ."

"Yes, but I'm not blind to his faults," Judith said with a wry smile. "He's not overly tolerant of what he considers failings, I grant you. Have you angered him in some way?"

Charlie shook his head and tried to laugh. "Oh, it's nothing. It'll put itself right soon enough. . . . Have you had enough dancing? Shall I fetch you a glass of champagne?"

Judith let the subject drop since Charlie clearly didn't want to pursue it. "No, thank you," she said. "But I would like you to introduce me to Gracemere."

"Certainly, if you like. I'm not in his set, of course,

so I don't know him well, but I could effect an introduction."

Judith cast a rapid eye over the ballroom, looking for Sebastian. She spotted him dancing with Harriet Moreton. He was often dancing with Harriet Moreton, she realized with a start, though shy, soft-eyed, pretty, seventeen-year-olds weren't his usual style. She fixed her eye on her brother until he looked up from his partner. He knew she was going to engineer an introduction to the enemy tonight, one on which he would intrude quite naturally, and he was waiting for her signal.

"I swear, the country is a damnably tedious place at this time of year," the Earl of Gracemere was saying to the knot of people around him as Judith and Charlie approached. "Mud . . . nothing but mud as far as the eye can see."

"Can't think why you didn't come up to town sooner, Gracemere," one of the group observed.

"Oh, I had my reasons," the earl remarked with a little smile. His eye fell on Charlie and his companion and his smile broadened. "Ah, Fenwick, I trust you're going to introduce me to your charming companion. Lady Carrington, isn't it? I've been hoping for an introduction all evening." He bowed, raising her hand to his lips.

"My lord." Judith looked upon the man who had obsessed her thoughts, both sleeping and waking, for the better part of two years, from the moment she and her brother had read their father's deathbed letter and had finally understood that his disgrace and exile had not been the simple result of his own unbridled passion for gaming.

Bernard Melville had pale blue eyes—fish eyes, Judith thought with a surge of revulsion. They seemed to be looking into her soul.

She withdrew her hand from his, resisting the urge to wipe her palm on her skirt. She felt contaminated even through her satin gloves. He had a cruel mouth and a sharply pointed nose beneath the fish eyes. A dissolute countenance. How on earth was she to hide her loathing and revulsion sufficiently to charm him?

Of course she would. She was an expert at hiding her emotions . . . thanks to the Earl of Gracemere. She unfurled her fan and smiled at him over the top. "You've just returned from the country, sir. Whereabouts?"

"Oh, I have an estate in Yorkshire," he said. "A bleak place, but occasionally I feel a duty to inspect it."

Cranshaw. The estate he had won from her father. Sebastian's birthright. A hot, red surge of anger swept through her and she lowered her eyes abruptly. "I'm unfamiliar with Yorkshire, sir."

"I understand you've spent most of your life abroad, ma'am."

"I'm flattered you should know so much about me, sir." She laughed, the coquette's laugh that she'd perfected.

"My dear Lady Carrington, you must know that the news of your marriage enlivened an otherwise dull summer for us all."

"You pay me too high a compliment, Lord Gracemere. I had no idea my marriage could have competed with Waterloo as the summer's seminal event," she said smoothly. It was a mistake, but she hadn't been able to resist it.

An appreciative chuckle ran round the group and Gracemere's eyes flattened, a dull flush appearing on his cheeks. Then he laughed, too. "You're right, ma'am, to point out my foolishness. It was a facetious compliment. Forgive me, but your beauty has quite overtaken my wits."

"Now that, sir, is an irresistible compliment," she said, tapping his wrist lightly with her fan. "And an admirable recover."

He bowed again. "Is it too much to hope that you will honor me with this dance?"

"I had promised it to my brother, sir, but I don't imagine he'll insist on his prior claim." She turned to where Sebastian stood, having made his seemingly casual approach. "You'll release me, Sebastian?"

"A brother's claims are notoriously low, m'dear," he said cheerfully.

"Are you acquainted with my brother, Lord Gracemere?"

"I don't believe so," Gracemere said. "But the family resemblance is striking."

"Yes, so people say." Sebastian bowed. "Sebastian Davenport, at your service."

"Delighted." The earl returned the bow, his eyes calculating, as they scrutinized the young man, who maintained a rather fatuous smile. Agnes had seen him at Dolby's, so he must be a gamester. How good a one remained to be seen. "You must come to one of my card parties," he said with an air of condescension. "If you care for that sort of thing."

Sebastian assured him that he did and murmured something about being honored. Then Judith laid her hand on the earl's arm and Bernard Melville took her into the dance.

"So you didn't follow the world to Brussels for the great battle, my lord?"

"Alas, no. I have a shameful—or perhaps I mean shameless—lack of interest in military matters."

"Even when such matters involve Napoleon? That's indeed shameful." She laughed, peeping up at him through her eyelashes.

"I'm a lost cause, ma'am." He smiled at her. "Your husband, on the other hand, is known for his expertise on the subject."

An expertise that took him onto the battlefield, Judith reflected, remembering the agony of that day. It seemed so far away now, so far removed from this glittering round of pleasure. No wonder Marcus was often so scornful of Society's priorities. She inclined her head in silent acceptance of the earl's comment.

"Yes," he continued musingly, "your husband makes us all look like mere fribbles. It's well known that he looks down on our simple pleasures."

Judith sensed an underlying point to her partner's comments. It occurred to her that Bernard Melville didn't like Marcus Devlin. "Each to his own," she said neutrally.

The earl's glance sharpened. "But you I take it, ma'am, don't share Carrington's scorn for our idle amusements." He gestured expansively around the ballroom.

If you only knew, my Lord Gracemere, just how purposeful my idle amusements are, Judith thought. But she smiled and agreed, fluttering her eyelashes at him and watching with inward revulsion the shark of interest that swam under the flat surface of his pale eyes.

Marcus strolled up the staircase just as his hostess was about to abandon her post at its head, having decided the hour was now too advanced to expect further guests. Lady Gray greeted him with flattered surprise and the information that the last time she'd seen Lady Carrington, she'd been in the ballroom.

Marcus made his way to the ballroom. For a few

minutes he couldn't see her in the melee. And then he did.

His hands clenched involuntarily as he watched her turn gracefully in the circle of Bernard Melville's arm, her eyes laughing up at him, her hand resting on his arm.

What the devil was she doing with Gracemere? But it was a futile question. She was bound to have met him sometime. It would have been too much to hope that Gracemere would have remained in rustication throughout the Season. Presumably he needed to find another pigeon to repair his fortunes at the card tables.

The dance ended and he watched the earl escort his companion off the floor. Judith was smiling in a fashion that set her husband's teeth on edge. He had watched her accomplished flirtations in Brussels with amusement and not a little admiration, and hadn't been troubled by the lighthearted coquettry that made her so popular in London. But with Gracemere, it was a very different matter. Struggling with the old rage that had barely diminished over the years, he saw the earl lead Judith toward the open French doors.

Marcus threaded his way across the crowded ballroom, acknowledging greetings with the briefest of smiles, and stepped out onto the terrace. There was no reason why Judith and her partner should not have come outside. It was a warm evening and there were plenty of people on the terrace. But the age-old rage in his soul blazed pure and bright, and he had to fight to keep it from his face and voice as he made his way to where they stood against the parapet, apparently looking at the moon.

"Good evening, my dear."

"Marcus! What brings you here?" Judith turned at his soft greeting and for a moment he could have sworn there was a flash of pleasure in her eyes. But if it was ever there, it was gone in a trice, to be replaced with what looked like vexation, and then that too was gone and her countenance was as calm and untroubled as a doll's. Marcus knew that look. Both brother and sister wore it at the gaming tables. Prickles of unease ran up and down his spine.

"Lord Gracemere and I were just identifying the constellations," Judith said.

"Your wife appears to be an accomplished astronomer, Carrington."

"My wife has many accomplishments."

The tension in the air was as suffocating as a blanket. Judith instinctively moved to lift it. She laughed. "An odd assortment, though, I'm afraid. My formal schooling was lamentably neglected."

"Growing up on the Continent must have been an education in itself," Gracemere observed, offering his snuff box to Carrington, who refused with a flat, polite smile.

"I speak five languages," Judith said. "And my mathematics are quite sound . . . in some areas, at least." She shot Marcus an impishly conspiratorial look as she said this. "I count quite well, don't I, my lord?"

"Faultlessly," he agreed, unable to resist the invitation to collusion. Such invitations were all too rare, and he felt some of his tension dissipate, the slow burn of memory rage die down. Judith had nothing to do with the past, and at this moment she had eyes only for him, and there was no ambivalence now to cloud their brilliance. "I wonder if I can persuade you to dance with your husband, ma'am?"

Judith put her head on one side, considering. "Well, it's certainly unusual, and I wouldn't want it said that we lived in each other's pockets."

"Heaven forbid. If you think there's the slightest danger of that, I'll make myself scarce immediately."

It occurred to Gracemere, listening to this byplay, that they'd forgotten his presence completely. "You will excuse me," he said, bowing and walking away.

Marcus held out his hand. "A measure, madam wife."

"If you insist." She put her hand in his. "But I can't imagine why you'd wish to torture yourself in such fashion. We both know you find dancing a dead bore."

"That may be so," he said as they took their places in the set. "But I've yet to be bored in your company."

"No, just maddened," she said with an arch smile.

"And vastly amused and aroused and fulfilled," he responded with a bland smile quite at odds with his words and the sensual glitter in his eyes.

They moved down the set and were separated by the dance movements. When they came together again, he commented, "You, at all events, seem to have been enjoying yourself this evening."

"Is that a crime?" Her eyebrows lifted in a fine and distinctly challenging arch.

Marcus shook his head. "Put up your sword, lynx. I'm not going to quarrel with you this evening."

"No?" The word was weighted with disappointment. "But we quarrel so well together."

The dance took her from him again before he could come up with a response. When she was returned to him, she was suddenly preoccupied, her eyes fixed on something over his shoulder. "My poor efforts at conversation don't appear to be entertaining you, ma'am," he drawled, when she had failed to respond to his second observation in two minutes.

"I beg your pardon." But she continued to gaze over his shoulder, chewing her lip, and whenever he touched her, he could feel the tautness in the lithe, compact frame.

"What is it, Judith?"

She shook her head. "Nothing . . . only, do you know Lady Barret?"

"Agnes Barret, yes, of course. She's the wife of Sir Thomas Barret. She's been on the scene for many years . . . a widow of some Italian count, I believe, originally. Then she married Barret this last summer." He shrugged. "Barret's a gout-ridden old fogey, but quite well heeled, so I daresay he offered a port in a storm. Although she's a damnably attractive woman; I'm sure she could have done better for herself."

"Yes, she is," Judith agreed absently. Then she seemed to shake herself out of her reverie. "Did you come here to make sure I was where I was supposed to be, sir?"

"Don't be provoking, Judith."

"I don't mean to be provoking," she protested, all innocence. "But it's only natural, when you do something so out of character, I should look for a reason."

"I came to find you," he said.

"To check up on me," she declared with a triumphant nod.

"Don't put words into my mouth," he said. "I came to find you."

"But surely it comes to the same thing. You wanted to make sure I wasn't doing something I shouldn't be."

"Well, you'll certainly think twice another time if the urge to misbehave does hit you," he remarked. "Since you won't know whether I'm likely to turn up or not."

Judith was for a moment silenced, then suddenly she began to laugh. "I do believe we're quarreling," she observed with satisfaction. "I knew it couldn't be long."

"Hornet!" He led her out of the dance.

"Shall we go home?"

"An admirable idea." He steered her across the room, one flat palm in the small of her back.

"Good evening, Lady Carrington, Marcus . . . Permit me to offer my felicitations. I would have done so earlier, but Barret was kept in the country with a touch of the gout and we've only just returned to town."

Lady Barret materialized in their path, extending her hand to Judith as she smiled at Marcus. "This wretched war," she murmured. "It played havoc with one's social life. Everyone disappeared to Brussels."

"Hardly everyone," Marcus demurred, letting his hand fall from Judith's back and lifting Lady Barret's to his lips.

"Well, now that the ogre is safely put away on that island, it's to be hoped life can go back to normal." Lady Barret shuddered delicately.

"The war lasted fifteen years," Judith remarked into the air. "Peace is hardly the normal condition."

Agnes's smile froze and her eyes seemed to shrink to mere pinpricks in her suddenly sharpened face. She laughed, a harsh sound like breaking glass. "How true, my dear Lady Carrington. Such a sharp wit you have."

Judith felt that strange aura again and the unmistakable conviction that Agnes Barret was a dangerous woman to cross. She forced a smile to her lips. "I meant no discourtesy, ma'am. But the world has been at war throughout most of my life, so perhaps I see it from a different perspective."

Agnes's eyes narrowed at this reference to their differing ages. "I hope I may call upon you, Lady Carrington," she said coldly as Marcus eased his wife away.

"I should be honored," Judith said distantly.

At the door, Judith halted and looked over her shoulder. Agnes Barret was in close conversation with Bernard

Melville. They reminded her of a pair of hooded cobras, touching tongues. A shudder of revulsion ripped through her.

"What's troubling you, Judith?" Marcus asked softly. "You're wound as tight as a coiled spring. And you were unpardonably rude."

"I know. It's something about that woman." She shrugged. "Never mind. I'm just being fanciful." She moved to the staircase.

"Oh, Judith, are you leaving?" Charlie appeared from the shadows of a doorway on the landing, and Judith wondered why she felt he'd been lying in wait for them. He ducked his head at her and addressed his cousin, but without looking at him. "Marcus . . . could you spare me a few minutes tomorrow . . . . a matter of some urgency?"

"I'm always available for you, Charlie," Marcus said evenly. "Shall we say at around noon, if that will suit you?"

"Yes . . . yes, that'll be fine." Two bright spots of color burned on his cheekbones. "I'll see you then . . . uh . . . Judith, good night." With a jerky bob, he kissed her cheek and then turned and disappeared rapidly into the salon.

"Damn young fool," Marcus observed without heat.

"Why, what's happened?"

"He's in dun territory again. Up to his ears in gaming debts and he's going to want me to advance him the money to settle them. He doesn't know I know it, of course."

"And how do you know it?"

He looked down at her in some surprise. "Charlie's my ward, Judith. Not much happens in his life that I don't know about. He's my responsibility."

"And you take your responsibilities very seriously,"

she mused. Marcus might be a strict guardian, but he was a very caring one.

"Yes, I do," he said. "And don't you ever forget it, madam wife."

"Autocrat," she threw at him over her shoulder, but she was feeling too much in charity with him to take up the cudgels with any seriousness.

It was near dawn when Marcus went to his own bed, reflecting that if they continued to burn the candle at both ends in this fashion, they would need a repairing lease in the country before the Season was half done.

He awoke when Cheveley drew back the curtains on a brilliant sunny morning. Marcus flung aside the covers and stood up, stretching. "My dressing gown, Cheveley."

The valet held the brocade dressing gown for him. Tying the cord at his waist, Marcus strolled into his wife's apartment. "Good morning, lynx."

Judith was sitting up in bed, her copper hair tumbling against the piled white pillows. A tray of hot chocolate and sweet biscuits was on the bedside table, and her knees were lost beneath a cloud of prettily penned papers.

"Good morning, Marcus." She smiled at him over the rim of her cup of chocolate, thinking how pleasant it was to be at peace with her husband.

"You have a host of admirers, it seems." He bent to kiss the tip of her nose and picked up a handful of the billets-doux, letting them fall back to the bed in a shower. "And a nosegay." The little twist of violets in a chased silver holder lay beside the chocolate pot on the table. He glanced at the card and his face darkened.

"Gracemere. You must have made a significant impression on him last evening."

Judith inclined her head in vague acknowledgment. "He writes very pretty cards, at all events. And the violets are so delicate."

"I don't think it right for you to receive such gifts, Judith."

Judith sat back against her pillows, remembering for the first time that strange tension between the two men. "In general, or Gracemere in particular?"

He shrugged. "Does it matter?"

"I think it does, sir. It's perfectly normal for a woman to receive such little attentions."

Marcus said nothing, turning instead to walk over to the window, looking out at the square. A group of children under the eye of a nursemaid were playing ball in the railed garden in the center.

"You don't like Gracemere, do you?" It seemed to Judith that the matter had better be brought into the open quickly.

"No, Judith, I do not. And you must understand that I will not have the man under my roof under any circumstances."

"May I ask why?" Her fingers restlessly pleated the coverlet as she tried to see a way through this unexpected tangle.

"You may ask, but I can't give you an answer. The issue is perfectly simple: you may not count Gracemere among your friends." His voice was level, almost expressionless, as he remained looking down at the children in the square. But he wasn't seeing them. He was seeing Martha as she had been that morning ten years before. His fist clenched and he could almost feel again the cool silver handle of his horse whip nestling in his palm.

Judith frowned at her husband's back. "Oh, no, my lord, it's not that simple," she said in soft anger. "You cannot issue such a command without a reason."

Marcus turned from the window. "I can, Judith, and I have," he stated flatly. "And I expect you to comply." He gestured to the pile of correspondence on the bed and softened his tone. "You have so many friends . . . . one less can make little difference."

Judith thought rapidly. It was a damnably unexpected complication, but it was vital that Gracemere should not become a bone of contention between herself and Marcus. If she threw down the glove, Marcus would definitely pick it up, and there was no knowing to what length he would go to keep her away from her quarry. No . . . instead of defiance she must lull him into inattention. Gracemere would have to be cultivated out of eyesight and earshot of her husband.

"I have a suggestion to make," she said in a bland voice, as if the previous conversation had not taken place.

Marcus, on his guard at this sudden change of tone, raised his eyebrows slightly but said nothing.

"Supposing you asked me to do you a favor," Judith continued in a musing, conversational manner, playing idly with a copper ringlet on her shoulder. "Supposing you said *To please me, my dear wife, would you mind very much avoiding Gracemere like the plague?*" A delicately arched eyebrow rose in quizzical inquiry as she regarded her husband's set face, the taut line of his mouth.

Surprise jumped into his eyes, followed immediately by comprehension, and then his mouth curved in a slow smile. "Point taken, madam wife," he said softly. "But I think I can improve on your suggestion." He left her and went into his own apartment, returning after a minute with a bulky parcel.

He came up to the bed, to where she lay against the pillows, barely able to contain her curiosity. "What is it?"

"A present," he said with a smile, carefully placing

the parcel on the bed. "I've been waiting for a suitable moment to give it to you. Now seems like the moment."

"It's a bribe!" Judith said on a peal of laughter, eagerly pulling at the string. "Shameless! You would buy my compliance."

Marcus chuckled, entranced by her gleeful excitement—like a child on Christmas morning, he thought. It occurred to him that an impoverished, helter-skelter childhood wouldn't have included too many presents. The thought produced an unfamiliar tug of tenderness as he took deep pleasure in her delight.

"Oh, Marcus, it's beautiful," she breathed, tearing off the wrapping to reveal a massive slab of checkered marble. The black squares were almost indigo, the white a translucent ivory. Almost reverently she opened the box containing the chess pieces, heavy, beautifully sculptured marble figures. Her eyes shining, she held the board on her knees and set up the pieces.

"It's not a bribe," Marcus said softly, watching her. "It's a gift with no strings attached."

She looked up and smiled at him. "Thank you."

"And now," he said, bending over her, catching her chin with his forefinger. "Will you do me that favor?"

"You had only to *ask*," she responded with an air of mock dignity.

She fell back on the pillows under the press of his body, the chess pieces scattering in the folds of the coverlet as he brought his mouth to hers. As she fumbled with the tie of his robe, pushing her hands beneath the material to find his skin, she quieted her conscience with the thought that Marcus would ultimately benefit from her plan to best Gracemere.

12

"Well, what do you think, Judith? Could you do it?"

As Cornelia leaned forward eagerly, the spindle-legged chair tilted precariously beneath her. She grabbed at the side table, sending it rocking.

Judith automatically put out a hand to steady the table. "You're asking me to teach you to be gamesters?" There was a bubble of laughter in her voice as she contemplated this delicious prospect and glanced around the room at her three friends.

"It's a wonderful idea," Isobel said, sipping ratafia. "We all have difficulties about money. Sally because of Jeremy; and Cornelia has to supplement her mother's jointure out of her own allowance; and as for me . . ." Her mouth tightened and a shadow of distaste crossed her expression. "Henley doles out money to me as if he's doing me the most immense favor, and only after I've asked prettily at least three times. I put off asking for as long as possible because it's so humiliating."

"I could teach you some things," Judith reflected. "The techniques with the cards . . . strategies of wagering . . . things like that. But you have to have nerve, and some natural talent to be really successful."

"I can't believe I have less talent than Jeremy," Sally said with a resigned chuckle. "He only ever plays hazard, and how can you possibly win with the dice?"

"You can't," Judith said. "At least, you can't rely upon it. Macao, piquet, quinze, unlimited loo, and whist —although the stakes there are often not high enough to be really satisfying—are the only games to play for winning rather than pure entertainment."

"I don't think I'm brave enough to play in the hells," Sally went on thoughtfully. "If Jack found out . . ." She shuddered. "He'd pack me off to the country with the children indefinitely." She glanced at her sister-in-law over the rim of her sherry glass. "Marcus would decide it was the only sensible decision."

"And Jack always does as his elder brother suggests," Judith agreed dryly. "Marcus has that effect on his nearest and dearest."

"What happened when he gave you the rubies? I forgot to ask. I was so relieved when I handed them over to Jack, I didn't think I ever wanted to see them again."

Judith chuckled. "Oh, I expressed suitable astonishment and delight at such a magnificent heirloom, and then told Marcus that actually they would suit your coloring better than mine, so perhaps he should give them back to you."

"Judith, you didn't!" exclaimed Sally, her eyes widening as the others began to laugh.

"I did," Judith insisted, laughing too. "It seemed

such a delicious little twist. However," she added, "he wouldn't. It wasn't appropriate, or something." She shrugged.

"We don't *have* to play in gambling hells to make money, do we?" Isobel returned to the original subject.

"No," Judith agreed. "One can do quite well at the high-stakes tables at balls and soirees. I do think it's unfair that women can't go into White's or Watier's or Brooks's though," she grumbled. "Did you know the stakes at the Nonesuch almost always start at fifty guineas?" Her voice had a yearning note to it.

"So you'll teach us?" Cornelia asked.

"Oh, yes," Judith said. "With the greatest pleasure. We will have a school for gamesters." She refilled their glasses. "A toast, my friends: to women of independent means."

The door opened on their delighted laughter.

"Oh, Judith, I beg your pardon." Charlie hovered on the threshold. "I'm intruding."

Judith took in his hangdog expression, the white shade around his mouth, and immediately held out her hand in invitation. "No, of course you're not, Charlie. Come in. You know everyone, don't you?"

"How are you, Charlie?" Sally greeted him with a motherly smile, patting the sofa beside her.

He flung himself down and sighed, gazing morosely into the distance. Judith poured him a glass of sherry. "You've just come from Marcus's book room," she stated.

Charlie took the glass and drained its contents in one gulp. "I feel as if I've been flayed."

Sally winced and shot Judith another comprehending glance. Judith raised her eyebrows. "He told me yesterday he knew you were in debt."

"I had a sure thing at Newmarket—" Charlie began in aggrieved accents.

"Only of course it wasn't," Judith broke in. It was a familiar story.

Charlie shook his head. "The cursed screw came in last. I couldn't believe it, Judith."

"Horses are notoriously unreliable when one's counting upon them. I assume you were?" She leaned back in her deep armchair and sipped her sherry. She'd never been able to understand why anyone would bet tomorrow's dinner on a horse over which one had no control.

He nodded. "I put my shirt on it. I've had a run of bad luck at the tables, and I was convinced Merry Dancer would help me come about." He hunched over his knees, twisting his hands together, pulling at the fingers until the knuckles cracked.

Judith frowned. She knew Charlie would come into a princely inheritance when he came of age. "Surely Marcus didn't refuse to advance you enough to cover your debts of honor?" That was an inconceivable thought.

Charlie stared moodily at the carpet. "After he'd reduced me to the size of a worm, he said he would give me an advance on next quarter's allowance. And I'd have to manage on next to nothing next quarter, but at least I wouldn't find myself obliged to resign from my clubs." He laughed bitterly. "Some comfort that is. I can't possibly *eat* on what's left. But when I said that, he told me I could go into Berkshire and make myself useful on the estate, and that way I could manage with no expenses."

"It seems to me wives and wards have much in common," Judith observed, resting her chin on her elbow-propped palm on the arm of her chair.

"How's that?"

"Both live under someone else's thumb," she explained aridly.

"But for a male ward, at least there's an end to the sentence," Cornelia pointed out.

"I never know whether you're funning or not when you talk in such fashion," Charlie said, sighing.

Judith smiled. "Then you must guess."

Charlie jumped to his feet and began to pace the salon. "A man's got to play, for God's sake."

"Yes, but does he have to play as badly as you?" Judith asked with brutal frankness. "Perhaps you should join our school."

Chagrin warred with curiosity. The latter won. "What school?"

Judith explained, watching Charlie's face with ill-concealed merriment.

"Good God," he said. "You can't be serious. What a scandalous idea."

"Oh, but we are," Isobel declared, rising to her feet. "Very serious. We have every intention of earning ourselves a degree of financial independence." She drew on her lacy mittens. "I must go, Judith. It's been a most enlivening morning. Can I take you up as far as Mount Street, Cornelia?" She drifted to the door in a waft of filmy muslin.

"Thank you." Cornelia rose, tripped over her shawl, and sat down again with a thump. "Oh, dear."

Gregson announced the arrival of Sebastian just as Judith and Isobel bent to untangle Cornelia.

"Oh, Sebastian, I wasn't expecting you to call." Judith straightened as her brother entered.

"Well, I think you might have," he said, "since you're forever giving me commissions to execute for you."

"Now, what in the world do you mean?" Judith frowned.

Sebastian grinned. "I hope I haven't just bought Grantham's breakdowns for nothing. I could have sworn you asked—"

"Oh, Sebastian, you have them!" She kissed him soundly. "I didn't think you'd be able to do it so quickly."

"I have 'em right and tight." He was clearly very pleased with himself. "Only just did it, though. Steffington and Broughton were both after them."

"You're very clever, love," she said. "Where are they?"

"I put them up with my own for the moment, since I wasn't quite sure how or when you intended to spring 'em upon Carrington."

Judith pursed her lips. "Yes," she said. "I'll have to work that one out."

"What is this, Judith?" Sally refastened the ribbons of her chip-straw hat.

"Oh, I'm going to drive a perch phaeton and a pair of match-geldings," Judith announced. "Sebastian has procured them for me."

"That's very dashing," Cornelia said, steady on her feet again. "And I insist on being the first person to drive with you."

"The pleasure will be all mine." Judith kept to herself the alarming images of Cornelia combined with a high-axled perch phaeton. It didn't bear thinking about. She accompanied her friends down to the hall.

Sebastian poured himself a glass of sherry while a still slightly scandalized Charlie regaled him with the story of the gaming school. It occurred to him that his sister's philanthropic, educational zeal would have done them great disservice in the days when the more fools there were at the card tables, the better it suited them. But the edge of desperate need was blunted for both of them now. And once Bernard Melville, third Earl of Gracemere, had been constrained to return what he'd stolen, the need would be gone forever. His long fingers tightened around the delicate stem of his glass, then deliberately he loosened his grip, let the mental door drop over the turbulent emotions that would muddle cool thinking.

Judith, her head full of match geldings, bumped into her husband as she hurried back up the stairs.

"You seem a trifle distracted," he observed, taking hold of the banister. "What's on your mind?"

To her annoyance, Judith felt her cheeks warm with a guilty flush. "Oh, nothing," she said airily. "I'm in a hurry because I'm going to ride with Sebastian. It's such a beautiful day."

It had been rather gray and overcast when Marcus had last looked out the window. He raised his eyebrows. "The weather is, of course, very changeable at this time of year."

Judith chewed her lip, and her husband's eyes narrowed. "What mischief do you brew, lynx?"

"Mischief? Whatever can you mean?"

"I can read it in your eyes. You're up to something."

"Of course I'm not." She changed the subject abruptly and to good purpose. "Why must you be so horrid to Charlie? He does no more than most young men in his position."

Her husband's face closed. "As you, of course, know so well, ma'am. Such naiveté has its advantages."

Judith drew breath sharply at this well-placed dart as Marcus continued in clipped tones, "How I handle Charlie is my business and has nothing to do with you.

He's been my ward since he was little more than a baby, and in general we deal extremely well together."

"Yes, I know you do." Judith persisted, despite the snub. "And he's very fond of you and respects you. But he's young. . . ."

"If he were not, Judith, I would have no need to hold the reins, and we wouldn't be having this discussion." He drew his fob watch from the pocket of his waistcoat. "As I said, it is not your affair. I have an appointment. I must ask you to excuse me."

Discussion was hardly the word for it, Judith thought, standing aside as he moved past her on the stairs. She'd been most effectively put in her place when all she'd been trying to do was offer him a slant on Charlie's view of the situation. But then, Marcus Devlin had had no youth, so probably couldn't be expected to understand the ups and downs of that state. His father had died when he was a boy and his mother had been a semi-invalid ever since. Marcus had somehow jumped full-grown into adulthood, with the immense responsibility of an ancient title and an enormous estate. As far as she could tell, he'd assumed the whole without blinking an eye.

But then, she and Sebastian hadn't had much in the way of childhood either. Judith resolutely pushed aside her somber reflections as she returned to the drawing room.

13

The atmosphere in Sebastian's sitting room in his lodgings on Albemarle Street was relaxed and good-humored. The six men sitting around the card table were lounging back in their chairs, goblets of claret at their elbows, all exuding the well-fed complacence of satisfied dinner guests.

Sebastian was an attentive host, and none of his guests was aware that his single-minded concentration was on only one of their number—Bernard Melville, Earl of Gracemere.

Gracemere had accepted the invitation to dinner and macao with alacrity, and now that the initial approach had been made, Sebastian was confident that his strategy would keep such a hardened gamester on the hook.

It was not difficult to play to lose against him. The earl was a highly accomplished card player, and it was a simple matter for Sebastian to engineer a convincing loss. Gracemere held the bank. Occasionally, his eyes would flicker across the macao table to his host, who sprawled, relaxed and nonchalant, in an armed dining chair, apparently unconcerned that his losses were heavier than any at the table.

"Your luck is out tonight, Davenport," observed one of his guests.

Sebastian shrugged and raised his wineglass, drinking deeply. "It comes and goes, dear fellow. What do you think of the claret?"

"Excellent. Who's your wine merchant?"

"Harpers, Gracechurch Street." He pushed a rouleaux onto the table. "I'm calling." He laid his hand on the table and shook his head in resignation when the earl revealed twenty points to his own nineteen. Gracemere's tongue flickered over his lips as he noted the new loss on the paper at his side.

Rage and loathing twisted, venomous serpents in Sebastian's gut. How often had Gracemere looked like that while he was playing George Devereux for his heritage and fortune? At what point had he decided to resort to marked cards? Gracemere was a good player, but not as good as Sebastian's father had been. When had he decided he couldn't win in a fair game?

Many times Judith and Sebastian had gone over that last game, trying to picture it. The moment when their father lost the final hand, convinced Gracemere had been using marked cards. The moment when he was about to expose his opponent's cheating and thus retrieve his losses. And the dreadful moment when Gracemere had gathered up the cards and somehow "discovered" a marked card in Devereux's hand. What had happened then? Their father's last letter had not said. It had simply given them the complete explanation for the lives his children had led—an explanation that went beyond their previous knowledge of insuperable gambling debts that had forced their father's exile. This letter had been an exculpation of George Devereux, but it had not gone beyond the barest facts of Gracemere's accusation, the apparent overwhelming proof made so devastatingly public, his own innocence, and his knowledge that it was the earl who had cheated.

The ensuing scandal had sent George Devereux into exiled disgrace, disowned by his family, forced in his dishonor to relinquish the family name for himself and his children. It had driven his young wife, the mother of his children, to seek her own lonely death in an isolated convent in France. And, finally, its bitter legacy of disillusion and depression had driven George years later to follow in his wife's footsteps and take his own life.

And his children would be avenged.

The power of that conviction jolted Sebastian back to a recollection of the part he must play. Brooding in somber anger at his own table was not consonant with that part. "I think I've taken enough losses for one night," he said, yawning, pushing back his chair. "Gracemere, I'll have my revenge next time. . . ."

The earl gathered up his cards and smiled. "It'll be my pleasure, Davenport."

"Have you played often with Gracemere?" Viscount Middleton asked, standing in the narrow passage with Sebastian after the earl's departure. He looked a little uncomfortable.

"No, I understand he's only just come to town." Sebastian drew his friend back to the parlor with the inducement of a particularly fine cognac. "How about you, Harry? How well do you know his play?"

"Devil a bit." Harry squinted into his cognac. He was a handsome young man, slightly built, with a relentlessly cheerful nature that Sebastian decided had its roots in the security of an assured fortune and the confidence of an unshakeable social position. It didn't make him any the less likable.

"Don't want to speak out of turn, dear fellow," Harry continued. "But, well, fact is, it's said he can be a bad man to play with." He peered again into his goblet and swirled the golden liquid. Then he gave Sebastian a cock-eyed look meant to be shrewd.

"Fact is, Sebastian, you're new to town and—well, just a word, you understand—don't mean to interfere."

Sebastian shook his head. "You're warning me off, Harry?"

Harry swallowed his cognac. "Gracemere's a gamester with pockets to let. You wouldn't be the first pigeon—" He stopped and coughed awkwardly. It wasn't the thing to imply that one's friends could be taken in.

"Don't worry, Harry," Sebastian said. "I wasn't born yesterday."

"No . . . no, didn't mean to imply any such thing. Just thought, if you weren't aware . . . maybe you should, well, you know . . ."

"Yes, I know, and I appreciate the word." Sebastian flung a friendly arm around Harry's shoulder.

"So, you'll have a care?" Harry persisted, doggedly pursuing the path of friendship's duty. "A word to the wise."

"The wise has taken the word," Sebastian assured him with a smile. "I'm not such a gull as Gracemere might think me. Remember that, Harry."

Harry frowned, trying to absorb this, but it was too much for his befuddled brain and he soon took himself home.

Sebastian himself went to bed and allowed his mind to roam over pleasanter matters. A pair of shy blue eyes, a snub nose, a soft mouth, hovered in the air above his pillow as it did most nights these days—ever since he'd made the acquaintance of Harriet Moreton. He smiled to himself in the darkness. If he'd been asked before, he'd have said an ingenue in her first season wouldn't be able to hold his attention for five minutes. But Harriet was different. He didn't know why, she just was. She was soft and yielding and he wanted to keep her safe and untouched and . . .

Hell and the devil! He laughed softly at himself. What would Ju say if she could hear him? He must ask her to call on Harriet's mother. It would set a seal to his hitherto unmarked pursuit of Miss Moreton.

"Well, I've found my pigeon, ripe for the plucking," Gracemere declared, draining his port glass with a smile of satisfaction. "I won seven hundred guineas from him tonight." He pulled his cravat loose. "And he didn't seem in the least perturbed by it."

"I wonder where those two come from?" Agnes stretched out on the coverlet of the poster bed, greedily watching the earl disrobe, her eyes narrowed with anticipation. "No one seems to know, but of course where Marcus Devlin chooses to marry, who should question antecedents? A Carrington would hardly make a mismatch."

"Oh, you know what these hybrid continental families are like. They're always rich and studded with old baronies and such like." He threw off his shirt.

"So long as the gull will suit your purpose, that's all that matters." Agnes picked up a pair of scissors from the bedside table and absently pared a loose fingernail.

"*Our* purpose," the earl corrected gently. "But for my own purpose, I've a mind to cultivate Lady Carrington." He pushed off his knee britches and kicked them into a corner. "It will certainly annoy Marcus."

"Haven't you caused him sufficient annoyance?"

Bernard's laugh was as mirthless as his smile. "I still have a score to settle, my dear. One of these days I'll see his pride in the dust." His mouth took a vicious twist.

"Tell me what happened that morning when he ran you to earth in the inn with Martha?" She wondered if perhaps this time he would tell her, but as always the earl's face closed, all expression wiped clean away.

"That lies between Carrington and myself." He put one knee on the bed.

Agnes ran a hand over his thigh. She accepted that despite all that lay between them, all that they shared, and all the years in which they'd shared it, that morning at the inn was one incident Bernard would never discuss. He had disappeared from circulation for a month after it had happened, and when he'd returned to Society with his bride, he'd seemed to be his usual self, but she had detected a new twist to his darkness, one that he still carried deep in his soul.

"So you intend to amuse yourself with coquettish Judith?" Her fingers tiptoed into his groin. "You seemed to enjoy dancing with her the other evening."

The earl's mouth curved in the travesty of a smile as he brought his other knee onto the bed. "I am going to see Marcus Devlin's damnable pride humbled, trampled in the dust, my dear. And Judith is going to help me do it. If, of course, you've no objections?" he added with an ironic rise of an eyebrow.

Agnes laughed, touching his mouth with a fingertip. "Oh, are you going to seduce her, my love? I have no objections. On the contrary, I shall enjoy every minute of it." She laughed again, a low, husky throb of amusement and desire. "Come to me, love, I've been waiting this age for you."

For a moment he ignored the plea, looking down into her face, a glitter of cruelty in his eyes that matched the gleam in hers. He knew how aroused she became at the prospect of making serious mischief. It promised a long and exciting night. He came down on the bed, his mouth moving over hers.

"But you must be careful that dallying with Carrington's wife doesn't jeopardize your chances with the little Moreton chit," Lady Barret murmured against his lips, her hand stroking his back. "A fortune of thirty thousand pounds mustn't be sneezed away, my own."

"No," he agreed. "Particularly when we both have such expensive tastes." He ran his tongue over her lips. "Such very well-matched, expensive tastes, my sweet."

Judith picked up the delicate white marble pawn, caressing it for a second before moving it to queen four. She shot Marcus a mischievous grin, seeing his puzzlement. It was not a customary opening. She hugged her drawn-up knees, feeling the heat of the fire on her right cheek.

"What the devil does that mean?" Marcus demanded.

"If you make the same countermove, it becomes the queen's gambit," she said. "It's not very common, but it can make for an interesting game."

"And what if I don't?"

"Well, you have to, really. It's Black's only logical move. It's what happens next that starts the fun."

Marcus stretched his legs in front of him and leaned back against a footstool. They were both sitting on the floor, and Marcus wore only a shirt and britches; his coat, cravat, stockings, and shoes were scattered around the room.

"You're going to have my shirt and britches within the half hour," he prophesied with resignation.

Judith chuckled. "An enticing prospect."

"Since you've lost nothing but a hair ribbon and your shoes in the last two hours, I can't help feeling the stakes are somewhat uneven."

"Well, why don't I give you a knight handicap?" She took her queen's knight off the board.

"My pride!" He groaned. "You are a devil at this game, Judith."

"But the stakes are fun," she said with another grin.

"They would be if I were not the only one being stripped of my clothes." He moved his own pawn to queen four. "There, now what?"

"Let's play piquet instead. Maybe two hours of chess is enough." Again she picked up one of the pieces, holding it up to the light. The pale marble glowed, translucent and alive with hinted streaks of color in its depths. "They are exquisite. I don't know how to thank you."

"You could always start losing pieces and thus a few articles of clothing," he suggested.

"It's hard for me to lose at chess. Let's play piquet."

"Now, just a minute. Are you telling me you will deliberately lose hands to salvage my masculine pride?"

"If necessary." She gave him an impish smile.

"What is a man to do with such a wife!" Marcus leaned forward, grabbed her upper arms, and hauled her over the board and across his thighs.

"Play piquet with her." She traced his lips with her thumb. "Otherwise, I shall never get my clothes off."

He said nothing for a minute, gazing down at her upturned face, the smiling mouth, the banked fires in the gold-brown eyes.

"I'm not as good at piquet as I am at chess," she offered. "And you are skilled with the cards."

"Nevertheless, madam wife, I doubt I have your experience."

"Perhaps not," she said. "But necessity is the mother of experience." A shadow crossed her eyes.

"Tell me about your father." The request came without conscious decision just as the evening had developed.

Judith rarely spent an evening at home, but after dinner he'd found her in the library, examining the shelves for a book to read in bed. She'd said she was tired and hadn't felt like going to the Denholms' rout party, and matters had proceeded from there. Now there was something about the firelit intimacy of the evening, something about the sensual pleasure they were taking in and of each other that made it both natural and inevitable for him to probe into areas they ordinarily kept closed.

Judith remained leaning against his chest, idly twisting a ringlet on her shoulder between finger and thumb. "He was simply a gamester who lost everything, even his lands, the family estate . . . everything."

"Tell me about him . . . about you and Sebastian."

She hitched herself up on his thighs until she was sitting straight, staring across the chess board into the fire. "He took us with him when he left the country. Our mother hadn't been able to withstand the disgrace. She went to a convent in the Alps and died there. Father hinted that she took her own life. We were no more than babies when we left England. Sebastian was nearly three and I was just two. We traveled with a series of itinerant nursemaids until we were old enough to manage alone: Vienna, Rome, Prague, Paris, Brussels, and every city in between. Father gamed, we learned how to deal with landlords and bailiffs and merchants. Then we learned to play the tables ourselves. Father was often ill."

Judith paused, looking into the flames. Absently she reached for the black marble king. The blackness was of an obliterating depth. She caressed it.

"In what way was he ill?" Marcus asked softly, feeling the currents of memory in her body as she sat on his thighs.

"Black moods, dreadful gulfs of inexorable despair," she said. "When that happened, he would be unable to leave his bed. Sebastian and I had to fend for ourselves . . . and for him."

Marcus stroked her back, looking for adequate words, but suddenly she laughed. "It sounds horrendous, and often it was, but it was also exhilarating. We never went to school. We read what we pleased. No one ever told us what to do, what to eat, when to go to bed. We did exactly as we pleased within the constraints of necessity."

"An education of some richness," Marcus agreed, pulling her down against his chest again. "Unorthodox, but rich. An education Jean-Jacques Rousseau would have applauded."

"Yes, I daresay he would. We read *Émile* in Paris a few years ago." She stared into the fire for a minute. It was hardly an education Marcus would embrace for any child of his. But then, he was determined there would be no children of his . . . at least not conceived in *this* liaison.

"So," she said. "Piquet?"

"No," he said. "I am no longer prepared to play for

your nakedness. I have a much more efficient way in which to achieve it."

"Ah," said Judith, lying back. "Well, perhaps speed is becoming of the essence, my lord."

"Yes, I believe it is."

14

*L*ady Letitia Moreton fancied herself a semi-invalid and reclined on a chaise longue amid piled cushions, smelling salts and burned feathers at hand. She was a handsome woman, although her features were somewhat blurred by self-indulgence, and her voice was a plaintive thread, occasionally edged with shrillness.

"So, Lady Carrington, your brother has recently come from the Continent?"

"Yes, ma'am, from Brussels," Judith replied, performing her sisterly duty in Lady Moreton's drawing room. "After my marriage, he decided to set up in London."

Lady Moreton toyed with the silk fringe of her shawl, her eyes resting on Sebastian and Harriet. They were sitting on a sofa, Harriet's soft brown hair contrasting with Sebastian's copper head as they looked through a book of illustrations. "I'm unfamiliar with your family, Lady Carrington," she remarked.

In other words, what is your brother worth? Judith had no difficulty interpreting Lady Moreton's remark. Any woman with daughters of marriageable age would welcome young gentlemen of title and fortune to her drawing room as fervently as she would dismiss those lacking such assets. In this instance, since Harriet was an only child and a considerable heiress, her mother would also be on the watch for fortune hunters.

"My brother and I lived abroad with our father until his death," she said smoothly. "We spent much of our time in France."

"Ah, I see. A family chateau . . ." Lady Moreton's voice lifted delicately, investing the statement with questioning inflexion.

Judith smiled and inclined her head as if in agreement, repressing images of the endless series of grubby lodging houses that had comprised the family chateau.

There was more than a hint of calculation in Lady Moreton's responding smile, and the gaze she bent upon her daughter and Sebastian was tinged with complacence. Any family with which the Marquis of Carrington was willing to be allied had to be good enough for the Moretons.

"I hope you and your brother will honor us at dinner one evening," she said. "And Lord Carrington, of course, if something as ordinary as a family dinner could appeal to him."

"We should be delighted," Judith replied formally.

Their conversation was interrupted by the arrival of another caller. Agnes Barret swept into the drawing room, words of greeting on her lips, her hands extended to the room at large. She bent and kissed Lady Moreton with the familiarity of an intimate, embraced a blushing Harriet, shook Judith's hand with a degree of formality, and then turned a friendly smile on Sebastian, who kissed her hand, offering a twinkling compliment on her dress. Her green satin redingote with a tiny tulle ruff was set off by a dark-green silk hat with a bronze feather. The effect was certainly stunning. Judith was honest enough to recognize that if she hadn't felt perfectly satisfied with her own driving dress of severely cut turquoise broadcloth, trimmed with silver braiding, she might have experienced more than a hint of envy.

"Gracemere is following me up, Letitia. I knew you'd be pleased to receive him." Agnes took a low chair beside her friend's chaise longue. "He's so fond of Harriet and I couldn't convince him that she hadn't caught a chill the other afternoon when we walked in the park. The wind was particularly brisk, and he would have it that she was too lightly dressed for such weather. Of course, I explained that no self-respecting young lady would be seen in anything thicker than a wrap . . . the foolish vanity of the young!" Her laugh tinkled gently, and she patted Harriet's hand. "But such a pretty child."

"I'm sure Lord Gracemere is all condescension, Agnes," Letitia said, touching a burned feather to her nose.

"Lord Gracemere, my lady."

The earl stepped into the room before the butler had finished announcing him. "Lady Moreton . . . and Miss Moreton. I do hope you didn't contract a chill." He bowed. "I was sure you would scold me fiercely, my dear ma'am, for exposing your daughter to such a bitter wind."

"Harriet has taken no hurt, Lord Gracemere," her ladyship said. "But it's good of you to inquire."

"Oh, Gracemere has such a soft spot for Harriet," Agnes reiterated. She smiled at him and Judith recognized with a jolt the proprietorial quality to that smile. The earl's eyebrows lifted a fraction of an inch, conveying a whole world of private communication. Instantly Judith knew that Agnes Barret and Bernard Melville were lovers. But if that was so, why was Agnes promoting Gracemere's acquaintance with Harriet?

"Davenport, I see you've acquired Grantham's match-geldings." Gracemere's observation turned the conversation and Judith's contemplations. "Stolen a march on the rest of us, you lucky dog."

"Oh, they're my sister's," Sebastian said. "Although I had the charge of procuring 'em for her."

"Good God, Lady Carrington! You drive a high-perch phaeton?" The earl sounded genuinely surprised.

"As of this morning," Judith said. "The coachmaker delivered the phaeton just yesterday afternoon, so this morning is my first tryout."

"And how do you find it?"

"Splendid. The bays are beautiful goers."

"You'll be the envy of the Four Horse Club, ma'am," Gracemere said. "I know at least three men who've had their eyes on that pair since Grantham sprang 'em on the town."

"It's very dashing of you, Lady Carrington," Agnes said. "Although I confess I'm surprised Carrington countenances such an unusual conveyance. I've always thought him rather conventional."

Judith contented herself with a slight smile. Her conventional husband had not yet seen his wife on the driver's seat of her unconventional carriage. She wandered over to the window overlooking the street, where one of the Moreton's grooms was walking the horses to keep them from getting chilled. A small boy was crouching over the kennel, looking for scraps of anything that might be edible or useful. His elbows poked through the ragged sleeves of his filthy jacket as he sifted through the detritus of a rich man's street.

"I hope you'll take me up for a turn in the park," Gracemere said at her shoulder. "You must be an accomplished whip, ma'am."

"I was well taught, sir," she replied, forcing a warm smile as she looked up at him over her shoulder. "I should be delighted to demonstrate my skill."

"The pleasure will be all mine," he assured her, bowing with a smile. "I wonder, though, how Carrington would feel about your having such a passenger. He and I are—" he paused, as if searching for the right term. "Estranged, I think one could say." He regarded Judith with an air of resolute candor. "I don't know if your husband has mentioned anything." He waited for her response, his eyes grave, his expression concerned.

Judith was startled at the directness of this approach, but swiftly took the opportunity it offered.

"He's forbidden me to receive you," she said with a credible appearance of constraint, giving him a rather tremulous smile. "But since he won't tell me why, I'm not inclined to obey him." This last was said with a rush of bravado, and he smiled.

"It's a case of old wounds," he said. "Old resentments die hard, Lady Carrington . . . although, I must say, I would have thought in present circumstances that the past could be buried."

"You speak in riddles, sir." She fiddled nervously with the clasp of her reticule, hiding her acute attention to his words.

Gracemere shrugged. "A matter of love and jealousy," he said. "A matter for romantic literature and gothic melodrama." He smiled, a sad, wistful smile that Judith, if she hadn't known his true colors, would have believed in absolutely. "My wife . . . my late wife . . .

was engaged to Carrington before she gave me her heart. Your husband could never forgive me for taking her from him."

"*Martha,*" Judith whispered. What ever she'd been expecting, it hadn't been this.

"Just so. He's spoken of her?" The earl tried to hide his surprise.

Judith nodded. "Once. But your name wasn't mentioned."

"Perhaps not unexpected. I fear your husband's pride was badly lacerated, ma'am. Such a man as Carrington can accept almost anything but a wound to his pride."

Judith suspected that was the truth, although her spirit revolted against agreeing with Bernard Melville as he patronized her husband.

"You've been most enlightening, my lord," she said softly. "But I see no reason why we shouldn't still be friends." She forced herself to touch his hand in a conspiratorial gesture, and he put his hand over hers.

"I was hoping you'd say that."

Her skin crawled, but she gave him a radiant smile before turning back to the room. "I must make my farewells, Lady Moreton. I shouldn't keep my horses waiting above a half hour. Sebastian, do you accompany me?"

Sebastian was deep in conversation with Harriet and Lady Barret and looked up with both reluctance and surprise at this abrupt summons. Then he caught his sister's eye and rose immediately. "Of course. If you're going to take those beasts into the park for the first time, fresh as they are, you'd better have me beside you."

"I doubt they'll bolt with me," she said, her voice light. "I believe I have as much skill as you, my dear brother."

"Oh, surely not." This disclaimer surprisingly came

from Harriet, who blushed fiercely as she realized what she'd said.

Judith couldn't help laughing. "Don't confuse strength with skill, Harriet. My brother has more strength in his hands than I do, certainly, but control doesn't rest on strength."

"Indeed not, Lady Carrington," Agnes said. Then, with a sharp look, she added, "Just as skill with the cards won't compensate for the devil of bad luck on one's shoulder. Didn't you make some such observation the other evening?"

At Pickering Street, Judith remembered. She gave a careless shrug. "It was a common expression when we were growing up. Remember, Sebastian?"

"Of course." He turned to bid farewell to Harriet and missed the interested glimmer in Lady Barret's tawny eyes.

Gracemere took Judith's hand. "Until we meet again."

"I look forward to it, sir." Judith's smile was one of defiant invitation—a child preparing herself for a major act of rebellion—and Gracemere's lip curled. What a gullible little fool she was. There would soon be a seething brew abubbling in Berkeley Square.

Judith gained the cool, crisp morning air of the street with a sigh of relief.

"What's up, Ju?" Sebastian asked directly.

"I'll tell you in a minute." She felt through her reticule for a coin, drew out a sixpence, and went over to the child in the gutter. He looked up, his eyes scared, as she approached. His nose was running, and judging by his encrusted little face had been doing so for days. He cowered, raising a hand as if to ward off a blow.

"It's all right," she said gently. "I'm not going to hurt you. Here." She handed him the coin. He stared at

it as it lay winking in her palm. Then he grabbed at it
with a tiny clawlike hand and was off and running as if
pursued by every beadle who'd ever cried "Stop thief!"

"Poor little bugger," Sebastian said as she came back
to the carriage. "I wonder how far he'll get before some-
body bigger and stronger takes it from him." He handed
her up to the driving seat, perched precariously high
above the horses.

Judith shrugged sadly. "He'll probably steal a loaf of
bread one day, and they'll hang him at Newgate. We can
defeat Napoleon with great sound and fury at vast expense of money and lives. But we can't somehow ensure
that a tiny child gets enough to eat. Or even change a
penal system that hangs the same child for stealing the
bread that would keep him from starving. At least Bonaparte brought some species of enlightenment to the penal
codes in his empire."

Sebastian was accustomed to his sister's occasional
tirades against the world's injustices and offered no challenge. "Now what was going on with you and Gracemere?"

"It's the devil of a tangle." She took the reins and
told the groom to let go their heads. With a flick of the
whip, the bays started off down the street at a brisk trot.

She waited until she had turned through the Stanhope Gate into Hyde Park before telling her brother
what she'd learned from Gracemere. Sebastian heard her
out in silence, then shook his head in disbelief as he
realized the ramifications. "Carrington told you about
this broken engagement, then?"

"Yes, before we were married. But he didn't say who
the fortune hunter was, and I didn't ask. Sweet heaven,
why would it concern me?"

"Of all the damnable coincidences," Sebastian muttered. "It seems as if Gracemere is entwined in every strand of our lives."

"I would like to drive a knife between his ribs," Judith said in a savage undertone, forgetfully dropping her hands so that her horses, momentarily unchecked, plunged forward.

Sebastian watched critically while she brought them under control again. "Do try to restrain yourself," he said. "I'm sure we can bring this off without resorting to murder. Gracemere deserves a lot worse."

Judith smiled grimly. "Anyway, I've decided on my strategy. I'm going to draw him into a plot to defy Marcus. He thinks I'm a silly widgeon who doesn't like being dictated to by her husband, and I'm sure he relishes the idea of conducting a flirtation with the wife of the man he's bested over a woman once before."

"You're playing with fire, my girl," Sebastian observed.

"I'll be careful," she stated with quiet confidence, acknowledging the salute of a group of army officers standing beside the driveway. Her daring equipage and its driver were drawing a fair degree of notice, she thought with satisfaction.

Sebastian also noticed the attention. "I'll lay odds that within a week your phaeton will be all the rage," he said, amused. "Every woman who fancies herself a competent whip will have to have one."

"Marcus, of course, won't give a damn about that," she meditated.

"Well, I believe your moment for convincing him otherwise has arrived." Sebastian gestured toward the pathway, where Marcus stood talking with two friends.

"Ah," Judith said.

15

$\mathcal{P}$eter Wellby saw them first. "Damme, Carrington, isn't that Lady Carrington?"

"She certainly can handle the ribbons," Francis Tallent observed admiringly. "I don't believe I've seen a lady driving such a carriage. Driving 'em tandem, too."

Marcus watched as the vehicle approached at a fast trot, Judith very much at home on her precarious perch, her whip at an impeccable angle. Her brother seemed perfectly at his ease beside her, but what the hell did he think he was doing, permitting his sister to behave in such fashion in public? It was the height of vulgarity for a woman to drive a sporting vehicle. But then perhaps the Davenports didn't realize that, given their unschooled and unlicensed upbringing. Marcus struggled to give them the benefit of the doubt.

"She's driving Grantham's bays," Wellby said. "I had no idea he was selling up."

"Davenport obviously has an ear to the ground," Marcus replied casually.

He moved to the edge of the pathway as Judith drew rein. "You move quickly, Sebastian. Half London was waiting to hear Grantham was selling up."

Sebastian laughed. "Handsome, aren't they?"

"Very." He moved to the side of the phaeton and spoke quietly. "I don't know what you think you're doing, Judith. Give your brother back his reins and get down from there."

Brother and sister were smiling at him with a wicked glimmer in their matching eyes.

"They're not Sebastian's reins, Marcus; they're mine. He procured the carriage and horses for me," Judith said. "I'm taking him for a turn around the park."

For a moment Marcus was speechless. "Yield your place, Davenport," he demanded grimly, laying a hand on the step.

"By all means," Sebastian replied with an obliging smile. He jumped to the ground, laying a hand on his brother-in-law's arm in passing. Marcus turned to meet his eye. That mischievous glint was still there.

"Best not to go head to head with her," Sebastian murmured.

"When I want your advice, I'll ask for it," his brother-in-law declared in a savage undertone.

Sebastian, not in the least offended, merely inclined his head in acknowledgment.

Marcus swung himself up beside his wife. "Give me the reins."

"But I'm perfectly able to handle them myself, as you must have seen," Judith responded with an innocent smile.

"Give them to me."

Judith shrugged and passed them over, together with the whip. "If you wish to try their paces, be my guest."

Marcus ground his teeth, but was forced to mask his fury as best he could under the eyes of his friends, who still stood on the path beside the carriageway. He cracked the thong of the whip, and the leader sprang forward.

"It's unwise to drive a high-couraged pair when one's in a miff," Judith remarked in tones of earnest solicitude as Marcus took the phaeton through the park gates. "Don't you think you shaved the gate a trifle close?"

"Hold your tongue!"

Judith shrugged and sat back, surveying her husband's handling of the reins with a critical eye. Despite his fury, he was perfectly in control of the bays and she decided her jibe had been unnecessary.

The phaeton turned into Berkeley Square and drew up outside the house. "You'll have to alight unassisted," Marcus snapped.

Judith put her head on one side, narrowing her eyes. "If you mean to drive my horses in my absence, it would be only courteous to ask my permission."

Marcus inhaled sharply, his jaw clenched. He kept his eyes straight ahead and spoke almost without expression. "You will go into the house, go to my book room, and wait for me. I will join you there shortly."

Judith alighted from the awkward vehicle with creditable grace and mounted the steps to the house.

Marcus waited until she'd been admitted, then drove around to the mews at the back of the house to leave the carriage and horses. He understood that Judith was once again demonstrating to him that she lived by her own rules. But she was his wife, and if she didn't understand that her disreputable past and unknown lineage made it all the more imperative for her to behave impeccably, then he was going to have to demonstrate that fact once and for all.

In the hall, Judith paused. She had no intention of obediently going to Marcus's book room like a naughty schoolgirl.

"Gregson, I have a headache. I'm going to rest in my bedchamber. Would you send Millie to me . . . and I'd like a glass of Madeira."

"Yes, my lady." The butler bowed. "I'll have it sent up immediately."

"Thank you." Judith ran upstairs to her own apartment, where the morning sun poured brilliantly through the long windows, dimming the fire's glow. She went to the window and stared down at the square, tapping her teeth with a fingernail. She was rather looking forward to the next few minutes. It was high time Marcus learned a few things about the wife he had taken on.

Millie helped her out of her clothes and into a particularly fetching peignoir of jonquil silk, lavishly trimmed with lace. She poured Judith a glass of Madeira and hovered solicitously with a vinegar-soaked cloth and smelling salts for the supposed headache.

"No, I need nothing further, Millie. I'll rest quietly by the fire; it'll pass soon."

After Millie curtsied and left, Judith sat in a low chair in front of the chess board by the fire. Sipping her wine, she began to reconstruct a game she had played with Sebastian several days earlier. The concentration required in remembering the moves cleared her head of emotional turmoil, and kept her from watching the clock as she waited for her husband.

She knew the exact moment when he entered the house. Despite her conviction that he had neither right nor cause for complaint, her heart speeded and she tried to cool her palms, clutching the smooth marble of a pair of pawns. She heard his step in the passage outside and swiftly bent her head to the board, feigning complete absorption as the door opened behind her.

Marcus was inconveniently struck by how deliciously desirable she looked. The copper ringlets tumbled around her bent head, exposing the slender column of her neck. His eye traveled over her body, clad in the filmy peignoir that gave her an almost insubstantial air. One narrow, bare, white foot peeped from beneath the hem, and he knew with a jolt to his belly that she was naked beneath the delicate garment.

He stood for a second in the open door, waiting for her to acknowledge him. When she didn't, he closed the door with a snap.

Judith looked up. "Ah, there you are, my lord. How did you find my horses?" She returned her attention to the chess board.

Marcus, having been informed by Gregson that her ladyship had retired to her bedroom with a headache, had decided to ignore her disobedience over the book room rather than be sidetracked from the main issue. He had also intended to keep his temper, but at this blatant provocation all good resolutions flew out of the window. He strode to the fireplace. "I will not have my wife behaving like a vulgar hoyden!"

She looked up again, brushing a wisp of hair from her brow, where a slight, puzzled frown marred the smooth expanse. "There's nothing vulgar about driving oneself in the park, Marcus."

"Damn you, Judith! Don't play the innocent with me. You know quite well that driving a high-perch phaeton is as shameless and fast as Letty Lade. You're the Marchioness of Carrington, and it's time you learned to behave properly."

Judith shook her head, and her mouth took a distinctly stubborn turn. "You're so stuffy, Marcus. I know it's an unusual carriage for a woman, but unusual doesn't necessarily mean bad . . . vulgar . . . shameless . . . fast."

"Where you're concerned, it does," he snapped.

"Oh? Why so?"

"Because, my obtuse wife, someone of your dubious origins cannot get away with things that someone of impeccable family and background might. And as my wife you have a duty to uphold the honor of my family."

Judith paled. How had she thought this would be a simple confrontation, about a simple matter? "My family and my 'dubious' background have nothing to do with this. No one here knows anything about me, good or bad, and I'm perfectly capable of setting my own style without damaging your family's honor. I tell you straight, Carrington, that I will drive what I choose to drive." Breathless, she subsided to rearm.

"Madam, you've forgotten one essential fact." His voice was dangerously quiet. "You are my wife, and you owe me your obedience. You took a most solemn vow to that intent, as I recall."

And it wasn't worth a groat in a court of law. "I have a greater right to my own freedom. I can't be expected to obey unreasonable commands that trespass upon my right to make my own choices."

"You have no such right. Obviously you don't understand the nature of marriage," he said, white-faced, his voice cold and level. "You should have thought of its uncomfortable aspects before you decided to become my wife."

"But I didn't *decide* to become your wife," Judith objected.

"Didn't you?" Marcus's eyes drilled into her.

Judith's lips were dry and she wished with all her

heart that she'd never started this. "This isn't about our marriage," she said desperately. "Or not really. It's about something much more simple. I want you to trust me. My judgment has served me well all these years, and what I choose to drive is no concern of yours. I employed my brother as my agent—"

"I must remember to express my gratitude to him." The caustic interruption was delivered in the same cold, level tones. "As for you, ma'am. If your brother doesn't want those horses, then I'll send them to the block at Tattersalls first thing tomorrow." He turned away, as if the subject were closed.

"*No!* I won't tolerate such a thing."

"My dear wife, you have no choice."

"Oh, but I most certainly do. I shall simply keep the horses in my brother's stable and drive them whenever I please."

The gloves were well and truly off. Marcus, a white shade around his thinned mouth, advanced on her. "By God, ma'am, I am going to have to teach you that I mean what I say."

"You lay hands on me, Carrington, and so help me I'll shoot you!"

Judith sprang to her feet. Her knees caught the edge of the low table, sending it flying. Chess pieces tumbled and the massive marble board fell heavily across Marcus's feet. He yelled in pain, hopping from foot to foot.

"Oh, now look what you made me do," Judith said, anger forgotten in her consternation. "I didn't mean to hurt you!"

"No, you only meant to shoot me," Marcus muttered, standing on one leg as he bent to rub his left foot. "Make up your mind, woman."

"You know I wouldn't do such a thing," she said, wringing her hands. "Oh, dear, are you very hurt?"

"Abominably." He lowered his foot gingerly to the carpet and ministered to the right one.

"I am very sorry," Judith said wretchedly. "But you made me so very cross. I didn't do it deliberately."

"God only knows what pain you'd cause if you were trying." He lowered the right foot and straightened. His eyes narrowed abruptly. In her agitation, the silk wrapper had loosened at the neck, exposing the soft, creamy swell of her breast, lifting rapidly with the raging emotions of the last half hour. The golden eyes contained anxiety and the residue of her anger; her lips were parted in dismay.

"I think," Marcus stated deliberately, "that you will conduct the remainder of this heated discussion on your back. I'll feel safer that way." Reaching across the fallen table, he caught her under the arms and lifted her clear across the debris.

"What the devil are you doing?" Judith kicked her legs as he held her with relative ease.

"What do you think I'm doing?" He lowered her to the floor, his hands sliding to her waist, his eyes still narrowed, a predatory light in their ebony depths.

"No!" Judith turned her head aside just as he was about to lower his mouth to hers. "I will not permit you to make love to me when we're quarreling."

His lips, missing her mouth, found instead the soft spot behind her ear. His tongue darted suddenly, wickedly, and she squirmed as the hot lance probed her ear.

"I haven't asked your permission," he responded against her ear.

"Damn you, Marcus, no! You don't want to do this!" She pushed against him with her hands, turning and twisting in his hold.

"I'll be the judge of that." He bore her inexorably backward until she felt the edge of the bed behind her knees. Her arms flailing wildly, she fell back on the bed, twisting her body against him, pouring forth a string of expletives in every language she knew.

Marcus hooked a finger beneath the thin silk tie at her waist and pulled it loose. He caught her thrashing arms and pulled them above her head, gazing down into her flushed face, reading in her eyes the unbidden excitement that warred with her determination not to give in to him.

He looped the tie around her wrists. Judith craned her neck sideways, gasping with a mixture of anger and excitement as he fastened the tie to the carved cherrywood pillar behind her head.

"Now," he said cheerfully, "you may fight me with your tongue, my lynx, but nothing else. However, I'm willing to wager twenty guineas that I can defeat you handsomely with the same weapon."

Judith abruptly ceased her struggles. "Twenty guineas?"

For answer, he plucked the sides of her peignoir apart. Bending his head, he drew a tongue stroke down between her breasts and over her belly. "Unless you wish to make it fifty?" He parted her thighs, holding them wide with flat palms. His breath whispered cool yet warm over the secret sensitivity of her core.

Judith lost all interest in conflict. "I'm not fool enough to defy these odds," she managed to articulate, before coherent speech was denied her under the grazing mouth, the hot, sweet strokes of his tongue.

He should have listened to his brother-in-law, Marcus thought dreamily, as he fed upon the pleasure growing within her. Direct confrontation was a crude and exhausting tactic, doomed to failure. Defeating her with delight was an infinitely more subtle strategy for achieving mastery.

Her whimpers of pleasure were building to a crescendo, her thighs tautening as the spiral coiled ever tighter in her belly, until with a shuddering cry her body arced, taut as a bow string, and then she fell back on the bed, her breath swift and shallow.

Marcus moved up her body, dropping a light kiss on her mouth, brushing her closed eyelids with his lips, and she opened her eyes, giving him a dazed smile.

"You work miracles, sir."

"One of my minor talents," he said with a smug grin, holding himself over her on an elbow, while fumbling one-handed with the waistband of his britches, pushing them off his hips. Reaching above her, he pulled loose the silk tie that bound her wrists. "I think you're sufficiently tamed now to have your hands back. You might need them for the next stage."

"I might," Judith agreed. She brought her hands down, slipping them around him, grasping his buttocks, as he eased himself into her. "Ah, that feels wonderful."

Marcus sighed in agreement, moving with gentle rhythm within the smooth, warm quiver of her body. "Sometimes," he murmured, "I think you were made to hold me as I was made to fill you."

"You only think it sometimes?" She laughed up at him, an exultant spark in her eyes as she tightened around him, glorying in the feel of him, in the light in his eye, in the absolute knowledge of the pleasure they found in each other. She lifted her hips to meet him.

"Ah, Judith, don't move again unless you're ready to be with me."

"I'm ready," she said breathlessly.

She touched his lips fleetingly, then with wicked intent moved her hand to his belly. The muscles jumped against her flattened palm and he surged against her. Their cries mingled, redolent of a primitive exultation, and his body fell heavily upon hers, sweat-slick skin melding with sweat-slick skin.

They lay for long minutes in deep, satiated silence, before Judith stirred beneath Marcus. Her legs were still sprawled around him, her arms spread out as they had fallen in the aftermath of that climactic explosion.

"Was I crushing you?" Marcus murmured, rolling away from her. He propped himself on one elbow, looking down at her, smiling at the wanton sprawl of her body.

"Only pleasurably." Her eyes opened lazily.

"Now," he said, trailing a finger down between her breasts, "to return to the vexed question of perch phaetons . . ."

Judith pushed his hand away, sat cross-legged on the bed, and regarded him. "Now, listen to me," she said calmly. "You are an old stick-in-the-mud, Marcus Devlin. . . . No, don't interrupt. When, since we've been married, have I ever caused you the slightest embarrassment?"

"Never, to my knowledge," he conceded. "And you'd better not."

Judith patted his knee. "I'm not about to. I'm going to set a new trend. I'm not about to race at Epsom, or charge down the London-to-Brighton post road at full gallop. I'm simply going to do something different—a little daring, perhaps. But you just see. . . . In a week, I'll wager any odds that there'll be quite a few others driving perch phaetons. And," she added, "you'll see that none of them exhibits anything like my style and expertise."

"Conceited baggage," he said.

"Just wait and see," she responded stoutly.

Marcus didn't immediately answer, his thoughts having taken a new direction. "How did you learn to drive so well, Judith?"

"Oh," she said vaguely, "a friend taught me two years ago."

"A friend?"

"Yes, in Vienna. He drove a team of magnificent grays and was most obliging as to teach me."

"In exchange for what?"

"Why, for my company," she said, as if it were self-explanatory.

"One of your flirts, in other words."

"I suppose you could say that. He was a very respectable flirt, though. An Austrian count of some wealth."

"Of which you and your brother relieved him, I assume."

"A few thousand," she said with cheerful insouciance. "He could well afford it, and he enjoyed my company as compensation."

"And you wonder why I sometimes question your judgment."

Judith bit her lip hard. "This is different. Why do you always throw my past in my face?" She turned her head away, blinking back tears.

Why did he? He looked at her averted profile, saw the shimmer of a teardrop on her cheek. Perhaps he wasn't being fair to her. No matter how their marriage had come about, he couldn't help but take pride in his beautiful, elegant, intelligent wife. Maybe it was time to bury the past.

He leaned forward and smudged the tear on her cheek with his finger. "If you can satisfy me that you can handle in *every* contingency a spirited pair between the shafts of such a vehicle, then you may keep your perch phaeton."

She swallowed her tears and swung out of bed.

"We'll put the matter to the test immediately." Bending over, she playfully tugged at the coverlet. "Come along, lazy, get up. We'll drive to Richmond in your curricle with your grays and I'll show you how I can handle a four-in-hand. I promise you I'll prove to you that I can drive to an inch."

"Yes, I rather imagine you will." He stood up, then said consideringly, "By the way, I believe you owe me twenty guineas."

"Why, yes, sir, I believe I do," Judith replied in dulcet tones.

16

"*I* don't know what to do now." Charlie looked up from the cards in his hand, his expression baffled.

Sebastian, standing behind Charlie at the table, glanced down at the young man's hand of cards and grinned as he felt his sister's surging impatience. Judith was a good teacher, but she was short on forbearance. She looked up and caught Sebastian's eye. Taking a deep breath, she struggled for patience. "Do you think you want another card, Charlie?"

"I don't know exactly." He frowned. Judith was trying to explain how one could reduce the element of chance at macao. "I have eighteen points."

"Then you don't want anything higher than a three," she explained carefully. "That means there are twelve possible cards."

"Ten," Charlie said. "I already hold an ace and a two."

"You're getting there," Sebastian approved. He thrust his hands into the pockets of his buckskin britches, watching the lesson with amusement.

"All right," Judith said, gesturing to the dummy hands on the table. "We've had five rounds, two hands have folded, three are still left. What does that tell you about the three left?"

Charlie frowned. "That they have mostly low cards?"

"Exactly," she said. "Therefore, your chances of drawing one of the ten low cards that you don't have are . . . ?"

"Slim," he said with a grin of comprehension. "So I stay as I am."

"It's simple, isn't it?"

"I suppose so. What card would have been dealt me if I'd asked for one?"

Judith drew the top card from the depleted pack in front of her and slid it across to him. Charlie turned it over. It was a three.

"I never said it was an exact science." Judith smiled at his disconsolate expression.

"I always thought the fun with gaming *was* the risk."

"So it is, but doesn't it give you any satisfaction to overcome pure chance?"

Charlie looked puzzled. "Yes, it does, but it's not as thrilling as when luck smiles and I get a winning streak."

Sebastian gave a shout of laughter as his sister threw up her hands in frustration.

"Well, at least Marcus hasn't packed you off to Berkshire," she said, gathering up the cards.

"No," he agreed. "In fact, he's being deuced decent about things at the moment. I wanted to go to Repton with Giles Fotheringham for the hunting, and it was

Marcus who said I needed a second hunter. He accompanied me to Tattersalls and helped me pick out a magnificent animal." He grinned slightly. "Of course, he said if he hadn't advised me, I'd have been seduced by a showy hack with no bottom, but that's just Marcus."

Judith laughed at Charlie's accurate imitation of his cousin's invariable bluntness and began to deal the cards again.

"I must love you and leave you," Sebastian said, bending to kiss his sister. "Are you going to the rout at Hartley House this evening?"

"Yes, the rest of the gaming school are going to try their wings for the first time. Cornelia and Isobel are going to play macao, at separate tables of course, and Sally's all set to try her hand at quinze."

"How're they doing?"

Judith chuckled. "Pretty well, on the whole. Cornelia has the most difficulty. It's strange, because she's so clever in so many other areas. She plays the pianoforte beautifully and composes her own music, you know. And reads Latin and Greek."

"Very bookish," Sebastian agreed. "And completely cow-handed."

"Oh, that's unkind." But Judith couldn't help smiling. "Anyway, I'm looking forward to seeing how they do. They're all absolutely determined to succeed."

"Heaven preserve the husbands of London," Sebastian teased. "How will they ensure their wives' loyalty if they can't ensure their dependence?"

Judith grimaced. "That may be a quizzing observation, Sebastian, but it has an unpleasant ring of truth. If you could hear Isobel's description of the humiliating performance . . ." Remembering Charlie's presence, she stopped abruptly. Such details were not for his tender ears.

Sebastian nodded in instant comprehension. "I take it back . . . I must be off. I promised to escort Harriet and her mother to the Botanic Gardens." He pulled a comical face.

"Whatever for? I'm sure Harriet would prefer to visit the lions at the Exchange."

"And so would I, but her revered mama does not consider it edifying, so the Botanic Gardens it is."

"Well, make sure you have a plentiful supply of sal volatile, in case Lady Moreton becomes overcome with excitement among the orchids."

"You are a disrespectful wretch," Sebastian declared.

"Yes, I'd noticed that myself," came Carrington's voice from the doorway. "How do you do, Sebastian?" He tossed his riding whip onto the sofa and drew off his gloves.

"Well enough, thank you." Sebastian grinned at his brother-in-law and picked up his hat from the side table. "Perhaps you could cure m'sister's lamentable tongue."

"Oh, I've tried, Sebastian, I've tried. It's a lost cause."

"I suppose it is. Pity, though."

"Would you two stop talking about me as if I weren't here?" Judith demanded in half-laughing indignation.

"I'm away." Sebastian blew his sister a kiss and went to the door.

"Oh, there's something I need to discuss with you, Sebastian," Marcus said. "But I can see you're in a hurry."

"Orchids await him," Judith murmured as the door closed behind her brother.

"What?"

"Orchids. He's gone to dance attendance on Lady Moreton."

"Good God, why?"

"Because he intends her for his mother-in-law."

"Hell and the devil," Marcus said. "The daughter's a considerable heiress, of course."

"What has that to do with it?" Judith demanded, bristling.

"Why, only that all sane young men with barely a feather to fly with are on the lookout for heiresses," Marcus responded casually. "What are you playing, Charlie?" He strolled over to the card table.

Charlie didn't immediately reply. He could see Judith's face and he was wondering why Marcus hadn't noticed the reaction his words were causing.

Judith said stiffly, "You know nothing about Sebastian's circumstances."

"No, but I assume he supports himself at the tables. I doubt the Moretons will look kindly upon his suit." Marcus turned to pick up the sherry decanter from the pier table.

"Well, I trust you'll be in for a surprise."

"I'd be happy to believe it, but you must face facts, Judith." He poured sherry, blithely indifferent to the effect he was having on his wife. "People like the Moretons would look kindly on an impoverished suitor only if he brought a significant title."

"I see," Judith said icily, and firmly closed her lips. Rapidly, she finished dealing the cards.

"So what are you playing?" Marcus inquired again, casually sipping sherry.

"Macao," Charlie said, eager to change the subject. Judith was looking very dangerous, and he could detect the slightest tremor in the long white fingers. "You see, I'm not very good at gaming—" he began.

"No, you're abominable," Marcus agreed, interrupting. "A baby could beat you . . . which is why you're in the trouble you're in," he added. "I'd have thought you'd do better to find some other way of amusing yourself."

"But once I learn how to win, I won't have any debts," Charlie explained eagerly. "So Judith's teaching me."

"She's *what*?" Marcus exclaimed, his cheerful insouciance gone. Sebastian had been in the room too, and the memory of another macao table in a ballroom in Brussels filled his mind and chased away all rational thought. How could he ever have thought he could bury the past? "And just *how* is she teaching you to win?"

On top of the insult to Sebastian—insults Marcus didn't even seem aware of—this was too much. Judith knew quite well what he was implying, and the last shreds of control over her volcanic temper were severed.

"Well, there's a little trick I know," she declared, the lynx eyes ablaze. "It involves nicking the right-hand corner of the knaves . . . it's almost impossible to detect if one does it aright; and then there's—"

The goad found its mark. Marcus exploded, his expression livid. "That'll do!"

With an incoherent mumble Charlie leaped to his feet and hastily left the room, closing the door behind him.

"I will not have you interfering in my family concerns," Marcus stated. "I've already told you that Charlie is *my* business, and I will not have him influenced by your dubious ethics, your views, your practices—"

"How dare you!" Judith sprang up from the table in violent interruption. "How could you imagine I would teach Charlie to be a cardsharp?"

"From what I know of you, very easily," Marcus snapped. "You forget I know full well how you go about winning."

Judith was now as pale as she'd been flushed with anger a minute before. "You are unjust," she stated flatly. "First you accuse my brother of fortune hunting, and then you accuse me of the ultimate unscrupulousness. I wish to God we'd never met." The words were spoken before she had a chance to monitor them, and there they lay, like stones on the air between them.

For a moment Marcus was silent. The hiss and crackle of the fire in the hearth was the only sound in the room. Then he said, "Do you?" His eyes were fixed on her face with an almost aching intensity.

"Don't you?" Her voice was now flat, the fire had died in her eyes, and for some reason she was crying inside. But her face showed no emotion.

"Sometimes . . . when . . . sometimes," he said slowly. *When he found himself loving her and then he'd remember her trickery, the use to which she could put her beauty and her passion—that was when he wished they'd never met.* And that knowledge was never far from the surface, however hard he tried to bury it.

He went out of the room, closing the door quietly.

Judith stood in the middle of the room, the tears now coursing soundlessly down her cheeks. If they'd never met, she would have been spared this hurt. But if they'd never met, she would have missed . . .

She drew out her handkerchief and blew her nose. Soon enough she would be free to leave him. Soon enough he'd be free of his conniving trickster wife. Only why did such thoughts make her so miserable?

17

Bernard Melville was puzzled. He was losing to Sebastian Davenport and he couldn't work out how it was happening. His opponent was playing with his usual insouciance, lounging back in his chair, legs sprawled beneath the table, a goblet of cognac at his elbow. He laughed and joked with those who stopped beside the table to watch the play, often seemed careless of his discard, and yet the points were adding up with a remorseless momentum.

Bernard had lost the first hand, won the second by a hair, and was clearly about to lose the third. The cards seemed to be running evenly, although Davenport had laughingly congratulated himself when he'd looked at his hand, counted thirty points, and declared a repique. But the earl knew his own cards were certainly good enough to give him the edge even against a major hand when playing with someone less skilled than himself. And Sebastian Davenport was a careless, inexpert player . . . . wasn't he?

Sebastian watched his opponent. Gracemere was not aware of the observation, conducted as it was from beneath lazily drooping lids, but Sebastian was making a fairly accurate guess as to the earl's musings. He wondered whether to throw a guard that they would both know he should have kept. He would lose the hand, but he was ahead on points and could easily win the game with the next hand, after which he would rise the winner by a narrow margin. His fingers hovered over the cards, and a deep frown furrowed his brow. He reached for his cognac and drank.

Gracemere watched this performance of indecision with an inner smile. Despite his present success, the man was so transparent. When, with an almost defiant gesture of resolution, Sebastian threw down his only heart, the inner smile nearly broke to the surface. That was more like it. Careless, inexpert . . . positively bird-witted. Gracemere played to win the hand.

"Ah, I knew I should have retained the heart," Sebastian lamented. "I just couldn't remember what had gone before."

"I know how it is," Gracemere said with smooth reassurance, dealing the cards.

He lost the next hand so quickly, he could only put it down to the fall of the cards. "Your game, I believe, Davenport."

Sebastian smiled fuzzily as he began to count the points. "Not by much, but it makes a change, Gracemere."

"You must allow me my revenge." The earl gathered up the cards.

Sebastian yawned. "You'll have to excuse me tonight. Three games is as much as I can manage at one sitting . . . too much concentration." He laughed in cheerful self-deprecation. "Think I'll have a turn at hazard. See how the dice fall for me. I've a feeling my luck's in tonight."

"As you wish," Gracemere said, finding it hard to hide his contempt. "But I insist on a return game soon."

"By all means . . . by all means . . . wouldn't miss it for the world." Sebastian stood up, caught sight of a friend across the room, and strolled off. Gracemere watched him weave his way through the tables, an occasional unevenness in his step indication of the cognac he had been downing so liberally. He played with a wealthy man's improvidence.

Gracemere smiled. Fleecing such a careless fool would be easier than taking cake from a baby. And as for the sister . . . she'd fallen into his hand like a ripe plum with the tale of her husband's pride and jealousy. Really, such innocents shouldn't be let loose upon the world. However, his plans for her were going to prove highly entertaining for both himself and Agnes, who had declared herself a most eager partner. And he would humble Marcus Devlin at last.

For a moment, his surroundings faded into a mist and he no longer saw or heard the men at the tables, the soft slap of cards, the efficiently bustling waiters replacing bottles of burgundy, refilling the decanters of port and cognac. The flame on the branched candlestick that had lit the piquet table blurred in front of his eyes. Now he saw again the chamber above the stables on that long-ago dawn, and he saw again the pitiless ebony eyes. So vivid was the image that he could almost smell the terror he'd felt when he finally understood what Marcus Devlin was going to do to him.

Gracemere shook his head clear of the vision and slowly unclenched his fists, absently massaging his bloodless fingers. Judith would help him erase the memories and the burning wound of that unendurable humiliation.

Once out of the card room, Sebastian's step steadied, his eyes focused, his shoulders straightened. They were little adjustments, so discreetly made as to be almost unnoticeable by any not on the watch for them. Only Judith would have seen them.

"Still playing with Gracemere, I see," Viscount Middleton observed as Sebastian joined him in the hazard room.

"Yes, and my luck was in tonight," Sebastian said, watching the fall of the dice, listening to the groom porter intoning the odds, calculating how much he was prepared to lose to chance in the interests of appearances. He was supposed to be an addicted gamester, who was nevertheless unworried about his losses, and it would become quickly remarked if he chose only to play games of skill.

"Well, it's your business, I suppose," Harry observed in a tone that was not altogether approving. He tossed a rouleaux onto the baize table beneath the brilliant light of a massive candelabra. "But don't forget what I said."

"I haven't," Sebastian reassured him, making his own bet. "And if I tell you not to worry about me, Harry, I can assure you I mean it." He realized he would have liked to have said more, to repay his friend's kindness with a degree of confidence. Friendship was a dangerous thing. Until now, he'd only had one friend—his sister—and they'd both been content to have it so. But as their world had expanded, it had become harder to keep to themselves. And he'd be lying to himself if he said he didn't enjoy these new relationships.

Soon after, he left Watier's, making his way to the

soiree at Hartley House where he hoped he would find Harriet, although it was past midnight.

Judith was at the macao table when he entered the card room, having discovered that his beloved had been taken home by her mama an hour earlier. He strolled casually around the table to watch her play. Judith gave him a brief smile and returned all her attention to the cards. She knew her brother was watching with the eye of a critic. He would tell her afterward if he thought she'd made any errors, and he would be able to detail every one of them from an infallible memory for every hand played. It was a service they performed for each other, although Judith was the first to acknowledge that Sebastian was the better card player.

After a few minutes' observation, he gave her a short, unsmiling nod that told her she was playing well and wandered away, pausing beside the tables where Judith's pupils were playing. Sally looked up as he stood at her shoulder and gave him the smile of one amazed at her success. He saw that she had a substantial pile of rouleaux at her place. He watched her for a minute and, when she played a weak card, said quietly, "Stop soon. You're losing your concentration."

Sally flushed and looked put out. But then she bit her lower lip and nodded. A minute later she yielded her place to one of the spectators.

"Thank you, Sebastian."

He shook his head. "No need. It's as important a lesson as any other—stop the minute your play starts going bad."

There was little advice he could give Cornelia, whose play was wildly erratic. Sometimes it verged on the brilliant, but then she would forget everything and play like a rank amateur. Her winnings fluctuated as erratically as her play, and at no point could he advise her to stop because there was no certainty that she wouldn't win the next hand.

"How am I doing?" she asked in a loud whisper, dropping her fan.

He picked up the fan, saying quietly, "It's hard to say. How much do you want to win?"

"Two hundred guineas," she whispered at her original decibel level. The other players looked up from their cards, glaring at her, and she blushed, her arm jerked, knocking over a wineglass. A servant rushed forward to deal with the mess and in the confusion Sebastian said, "Let me take over your hand."

Cornelia stood up, apologizing vigorously for her clumsiness. "I do beg your pardon, but I seem to have wine on my gown. Oh, do take my place, Mr. Davenport. Thank you so much."

Sebastian winked at her and sat down. "If the table doesn't object."

There were no objections, and he increased Cornelia's winnings to the necessary sum within half an hour. Cornelia and Sally stood behind him, watching his play intently. He rose from the table and offered them both his arm with a little grin. "Did you learn anything, ladies?"

"Yes, you and Judith are the same when you play—you don't seem to notice anything that's going on around you," Sally said. "Your expressions are completely impassive, almost as if you've ceased to inhabit your faces." She laughed. "That sounds silly, doesn't it? But you know what I mean, Cornelia."

"Yes," Cornelia agreed. "And I suspect it's because Judith and Sebastian are not ordinary card players." She looked up at her escort. "You're true gamesters, aren't you?"

"And what's a true gamester, Mrs. Forsythe?" he

asked, laughing, hoping to deflect her. Cornelia Forsythe had too sharp a brain for comfort, even if she was cow-handed and inclined to erratic thought processes.

Cornelia looked at him for a minute, then she nodded her head. "You know what I mean. But it's none of my business. I'll not mention it again."

"What are you talking about?" Sally demanded.

Cornelia laughed, breaking the tension. "Nothing at all. I'm teasing Sebastian. Let's go and see how Isobel is doing."

Isobel was flushed with success. "Just look at what I've made," she said, opening her reticule to reveal the pile of shining rouleaux. "I'd have had to order Henley's favorite meals for a week, and sit on his knee and beg for hours to wrest this sum from him." Then she recollected Sebastian and blushed crimson. What one confided to one's women friends couldn't be shared with a man.

But Sebastian merely frowned and said, "How very unpleasant for you."

The three women exchanged a look of amazement. What kind of a man was Judith's brother?

"Let's see how Judith's doing," Sally said, to break the moment of startled silence.

"No," Sebastian said immediately. "She won't want to be disturbed. When she's won what she intended to win, she'll stop playing."

Cornelia smiled to herself and Sebastian caught the smile. Again, he reflected that friends could be hazardous when one had secrets to keep. He suggested they repair to the supper room while they waited for Judith.

She joined them there shortly. Her eyes were tired, Sebastian thought, and her face was drawn . . . much more than an evening's intense gaming would produce. In fact, it occurred to him that she'd been crying. He gave her a glass of champagne and sat quietly as she responded to her friends' eager accounts of their various successes.

"How much did you win?" Sally asked.

"A thousand," Judith said, as if it were nothing. "I don't owe 'the fund' anything for the horses, do I, Sebastian?"

"No, Pickering Street settled that, if you recall."

"Oh, yes, I remember."

"Fund?" Sally asked.

"Private language," Judith said, smiling with an effort.

"I'm going to escort you home," Sebastian said. "You look exhausted."

"I suppose I am a little." She stood up. "I'm glad the evening was a success."

"What about Charlie?" Sally asked. "Wasn't he going to play macao this evening?"

"Yes," Judith replied with a touch of constraint. "I hope he also profited from our sessions." She touched her brother's hand. "I don't need an escort, Sebastian. My chaise is waiting outside."

Sebastian knew she was telling him she wanted privacy, and he acceded without demur. He'd find out what was troubling her when she was ready to tell him. He escorted her to the waiting chaise with the Carrington arms emblazoned on the panels and kissed her good night.

Judith sat huddled in a corner of the carriage as the iron-wheeled vehicle bumped and rattled over the cobbles. She felt chilled, although there was a rug over her knees and a hot brick at her feet. Chilled and bone-weary, although she knew the weariness was of the spirit, not of the body. Intermittent moonlight flickered through the window, shedding a cold pale light on the dim interior . . . as cold and pale as her spirit, it seemed, in the fanciful reverie of her unhappiness.

Millie was waiting up for her, but the comforting warmth and soft lights of the firelit bedchamber did little to cheer Judith. "Help me with my dress, Millie, then you may go to bed. I can manage the rest myself."

The abigail unhooked the gown of emerald silk and the apple-green half slip embroidered with seed pearls. She hung them in the armoire and left, bidding her mistress good night.

Judith sat in her petticoat in front of the mirror, raising her hands to unfasten the emerald necklace and remove the matching drops in her ears. The connecting door opened with a shocking abruptness. Marcus stood in the doorway in his dressing gown, his eyes glowing like black coals.

"*No!*" he said.

Judith dropped an earring. It fell on the dresser with a clatter. "No what?"

"No, I do not wish we'd never met," he stated, striding into the room to where she sat on the dresser stool. Slowly she turned to face him.

His hands clasped her throat, his thumbs pushing up her chin. He could feel the slender fragility of that alabaster column warm and pulsing against his fingers. "No," he repeated softly. "Although you're an inflammable, brawling wildcat with a tongue so sharp I'm amazed you haven't cut yourself, I could never wish such a thing."

Judith found she couldn't say anything. His eyes burned into hers and the violent, jolting current of their sexuality ripped through her.

"And you?" he asked. "Do you wish such a thing, Judith? Tell me the truth."

She shook her head. Her throat was parched and she

could feel its pulse thrumming against the warm clasp of his hands. "No," she whispered finally. "No, I don't wish such a thing."

He bent his head and his mouth took hers as his hands still circled her throat. The power of the kiss blazed through her like a forest fire, laying waste the barriers of her soul, the thin defenses she might have put up to save herself from extinction in the power of his passion. She was lost in the kiss, his tongue possessing her mouth, becoming a part of her own body, and her skin where it touched his seemed no longer to belong to her.

Without moving his mouth from hers, he drew her to her feet with his hands around her throat. She obeyed blindly, inhaling the rich scents of his skin, tasting him in her mouth. He moved her backward until she felt the wall behind her, hard against her shoulderblades.

And then he lifted his mouth from hers, and she seemed to be drowning in the great black pools of his eyes, existing only in the tiny image of herself in the dark irises.

"Raise your petticoat."

It was the softest command, yet each word rang with the force and promise of fierce arousal. Slowly she drew the soft cambric up to her waist.

"Part your legs." His hands fell from her throat, opening his robe, revealing the erect shaft, poised for possession.

Obeying the jolting charge of lust, swept along on the turbulent current of passion, she moved her legs apart. Still holding her petticoat at her waist, she braced herself against the wall as, without preliminary, Marcus drove deep within her. His eyes held hers as he moved himself inside her, his hands resting lightly on his hips. Only their loins were touching, only their eyes spoke.

The black eyes seemed to swallow her as his body took control of hers. Judith felt herself losing herself, her identity, all will, joined to a power outside herself. A power that pleasured as it mastered. Her head fell back against the wall, her throat arching, white and vulnerable above the scalloped neck of her petticoat. Marcus took his hands from his hips for just long enough to pull the top of the flimsy garment down so that her breasts were bared. He nodded, a small nod of satisfaction, as he gazed down at the exposed creamy swell. He felt her submission, the yielding of her body to the power and will of his. A wave of triumph crashed over him, taking his breath away, and he surged within her as if he would make her a part of himself, indivisible, transcending her separateness, the secret parts of herself that she kept from him. For this moment, he had tamed his lynx . . . for this moment he had her bound in the chains of a delight that was in his hands to give or to withhold.

Slowly he withdrew to the edge of her body, holding himself there. Her eyes pleaded for his return but she remained mute, locked in the deep sensual silence of this world they were creating. He disengaged, and her little gasp of loss broke the silence, but he placed his hands on her hips and turned her to face the wall, fitting himself against the small of her back as she shifted to accommodate him, positioning herself so that he could slip easily within her again.

Her breasts were pressed to the wall, her cheek resting against the cool, cream paint. Denied eye contact, she was now totally possessed, submerged into his being. And Marcus gloried in an ownership that grew and fed upon the sensual purity of this union.

It was as if he had limitless resources that night. His powers of invention were unbounded, his drive and energy infinite. He commanded without words; only his hands indicated what he wanted of her, and she followed direction as blindly and willingly as if she were bewitched. There were times when she knew herself to be entranced in some fairy ring. Again and again he brought her to the outermost limit of pleasure, to the fine boundary where pleasure bordered upon pain, so intense was the delight. Again and again she surged beneath his body, his mouth, his hands, as he showed her an internal landscape she hadn't known existed; and in showing it to her, he entered the secret chambers of her soul.

There would be other nights . . . other times when Judith would take the initiative, would make her own demands and in their satisfaction satisfy in turn, but for this night, Marcus was both inventor and master of their pleasure. Through the hushed reaches of the night until dawn grayed the sky they moved silently around the room, from floor to bed, chair to couch. Sometimes she lay beneath him, sometimes over him. Her skin identified the slight roughness of the carpet, the nubby brocade of the chaise longue, the damask smoothness of the bed sheets.

Finally he laid her down on the polished, cold wood of a long rosewood table. The flat surface was hard against her shoulder blades, unyielding beneath her buttocks as he raised her legs, lifting them high onto his shoulders as he plunged for the last time deep into her body, in a fusion so complete that she could no longer tell where her own bodily limits ended and his began. The long silence of the night was at last broken when their elemental cries of a savage and primitive fulfillment mingled in the room.

Judith flung her arms high above her head, her hips arced, holding him inside her through the wild, pumping, climactic glory, then her body seemed to collapse, to go limp and weak as a newborn foal's, and she lay unseeing, unaware, a sacrifice to passion upon the cold flat altar of the table.

It was a long time before Marcus had sufficient strength to scoop her from the table and carry her to the bed. He didn't know whether she was asleep or unconscious, so deep and heavy was her breathing, so limp and relaxed her body. He fell down beside her, sinking into the mattress, as sleep rolled over him.

Judith swam upward from the dark depths of exhaustion about an hour later. She lay in the graying light, neither asleep nor awake, as memory returned to make sense of the night's excess of sensual joy. Vaguely she remembered that at the last, Marcus had not withdrawn from her body. Had he intended it that way, or was it simply that the night's loving had not admitted of such pragmatic, pedestrian concerns?

Sleep reclaimed her.

18

"How kind of you to call, Lady Carrington." Letitia Moreton smiled at her guest from the depths of her cushioned chaise longue. "Your brother isn't with you today?" Her complacent gaze rested on her daughter, sitting beside the window with her embroidery. Harriet was looking entrancingly pretty in a round gown of sprig muslin. Thoughts of weddings played most pleasurably in Letitia's head these days. Lady Carrington's brother had been making his preference for Harriet obvious, and with such a connection, Harriet would be assured of entree into the first circles.

"No, I haven't seen him today," Judith said, drawing off her gloves. "I was wondering if Harriet would care to drive with me this afternoon?"

Harriet gave her a quick, shy smile.

"Of course she would be delighted." Letitia spoke for her daughter. "Run and change your dress."

Harriet hesitated for a minute. "I understood Lady Barret was to call this afternoon, Mama. She promised to bring the topaz ribbons that we bought yesterday . . . the ones I left by accident in her barouche."

"Lady Barret will understand if you're not here. Now don't keep Lady Carrington waiting."

Harriet obeyed without further demur and Judith said reflectively, "Lady Barret's most attentive to Harriet. You must find it a great comfort to have such a friend, ma'am."

Letitia sighed. "It's such a trial to be so invalidish, Lady Carrington. And Agnes has been most kind in chaperoning Harriet."

"Perhaps you'll allow me to act as chaperone occasionally," Judith offered. "Maybe Harriet would like to accompany me to Almack's for the subscription ball next Thursday."

"Oh, you're too kind." Letitia dabbed her lips with a lace-edged handkerchief soaked in lavender water.

"Not at all. We'd be delighted if she'd join us for dinner beforehand. I'll send Sebastian with my carriage for her."

"Oh, you mustn't put yourself to such trouble."

"But I'm certain my brother will be only too happy to escort her," Judith said, offering a conspiratorial smile. It was returned with more than a hint of self-satisfaction.

"Ah, Harriet, that was quick." With relief, Judith greeted Harriet's return to the salon. "What a very dashing hat."

Harriet blushed. "Your brother was kind enough to compliment it."

Judith chuckled. "I can imagine. It's very much a

Sebastian kind of a hat." She rose from her chair. "If you're ready . . ."

Outside, Harriet regarded the high-axled vehicle with some trepidation. "It's quite safe, I assure you." Judith mounted easily and held her hand down. "I can safely promise that I won't overturn you."

"No, I'm not in the least afraid of that," Harriet declared, bravely taking the helping hand and climbing up to sit beside Judith. "But it's most dreadfully high up." She regarded the restless bays with the same trepidation. They were tossing their heads, bridles jingling in the crisp autumn air.

Judith felt their mouths with a sensitive movement of the reins. "They're very fresh," she said with a cheerful insouciance that Harriet couldn't begin to understand. "I didn't drive them yesterday so they're anxious to shake the fidgets from their legs." She told the boy holding them to let go their heads and the pair lunged forward the minute they were released. Harriet shuddered and suppressed a cry of alarm. Judith drew in the reins, controlling the plunge and bringing the animals to a sedate walk.

"That's better," she said as they swung around the corner into a busy thoroughfare. "I'll give them their heads when we reach the park."

Harriet made no response to this declaration of intent, but clutched her hands tightly in her lap as a curricle dashed past, narrowly shaving the wheel of the phaeton. A scraggy mongrel ran between the wheels, a dripping piece of meat in its mouth. It was pursued by a red-faced man in a blood-smeared apron, waving a cleaver. One of Judith's bays reared in the shaft as the dog dodged its hooves and the smell of blood from the meat hit the horse's nostrils. Harriet emitted a tiny scream, but Judith calmly steadied her horse, peering down into the street to see what had happened to the dog. "Oh, good," she said. "He managed to escape. I wouldn't fancy his chances with the butcher's cleaver, would you?" She laughed, glancing sideways at Harriet.

"Oh, dear, did that scare you?" she said, seeing the girl's white face. "I promise I can handle these horses in any situation. Marcus made me do all sorts of things, including driving a bolting team through a narrow gateway, before he was satisfied I was competent to drive this pair."

Harriet gave her a wan smile, and Judith took another tack. "Do you like to ride?"

"Oh, yes, and particularly the hunt." There was real enthusiasm in the girl's voice, and Judith heaved an internal sigh of relief. Sebastian was a bruising rider to hounds, and it was hard to imagine him with a soulmate who regarded the sport with the same apprehension she regarded perch phaetons.

They turned into the park, crowded with fashionable London. Judith watched with some amusement a young lady in a dashing driving dress struggling to control a pair of blacks between the shafts of a phaeton, while a visibly anxious groom sat beside her. Not every young woman who had rushed to emulate the daring Lady Carrington had her ladyship's skills. Those who did had formed an exclusive circle with Judith at its center. Judith raised her whip several times in greeting as one or other of these friends passed, and drew up several times to acknowledge other acquaintances, introducing Harriet where necessary. Harriet seemed to enjoy the attention and soon began to relax, chatting openly about her life, her family, her likes and dislikes. She had a ready sense of humor, Judith discovered, and it gave ample opportunity to hear her entrancing, musical laugh.

"I believe Lady Barret's waving to us," Harriet observed as they started their second circuit.

Agnes and Gracemere were standing on the path, smiling and waving. Judith drew rein beside them, saying pleasantly, "Good afternoon, Lady Barret . . . Lord Gracemere. As you see, Harriet and I are enjoying the air."

Gracemere raised heavy-lidded eyes to Judith's smiling countenance. That now-familiar shark of interest darted in his gaze as he offered her a conspiratorial smile. When she fluttered her eyelashes at him, his smile broadened.

"I was coming to call in Brook Street, Harriet," Agnes said. "To bring back your ribbons."

"Thank you, ma'am," Harriet murmured. "It was so careless of me to forget them."

"Oh, young people have other things on their minds, I'll wager," Gracemere declared with an avuncular chuckle that sounded to Judith more like the cackle of a hyena.

"Do you know, Lady Carrington, I really think I must ask you to take me up beside you." Lady Barret stepped up to the phaeton. "It's such a dashing conveyance. His lordship will be happy to bear Harriet company, I know, for one turn."

Judith felt Harriet tense beside her. Glancing down, she saw the girl's gloved hands tightly clasped in her lap. "There's nothing I'd like better, ma'am, but I most solemnly promised Lady Moreton that I'd return Harriet within the hour. On another occasion, I trust you'll do me the honor."

Harriet's hands relaxed. Lady Barret's smile stiffened, her eyes chilling with unmistakable annoyance. Judith's own expression remained blandly affable.

"I shall hold you to your promise, Lady Carrington.

Until later, Harriet." Agnes bowed and stepped back, laying her hand on Gracemere's arm. He, too, bowed, and Judith dropped her hands, setting the bays in motion.

"You don't care for Gracemere," she said without preamble.

Harriet shivered almost unconsciously. "I find him loathsome. I don't understand why a woman of Lady Barret's sensibility should make a friend of him."

And not just a friend. But that Judith kept to herself. "His manner's a trifle encroaching," she said.

"He's forever trying to walk and talk with me. I can't be uncivil, of course—especially as he and Lady Barret are such particular friends—so I don't know how to avoid him."

"Mmm." Judith said nothing further on the subject, but Gracemere's intentions were clearly worth exploring. If he and Sebastian were rivals for the heiress, it would add another knot to the tangle. Presumably, a rich wife needn't interfere with Gracemere's liaison with Agnes. If they deceived Sir Thomas, there was no reason why they'd scruple to deceive a young wife.

She encouraged the bays to a smart trot, weaving her way through the curricles, tilburys, and the more sedate laundelets and barouches thronging the carriageway. When she caught sight of Marcus approaching, driving his team of grays between the shafts of his curricle, she slowed her horses to a walk. An idea occurred to her that would nicely kill two birds with one stone.

"Harriet, I've just remembered an errand I must run immediately. I'm going to ask my husband to take you home."

"Oh, no . . . no, please, it's not necessary . . . I'll accompany you," Harriet stammered, utterly daunted by the prospect of enduring the Marquis of Carrington's exclusive company. What could she talk about with such an intimidatingly lofty member of the ton?

"You'll find it a dead bore," Judith stated. "And I know your mama will be pleased to see you escorted home in such irreproachable fashion."

Harriet looked up at her, startled, but then a glint of comprehension appeared in her eyes. "Yes, I'm certain she will," she said.

Judith smiled at her, well pleased. Harriet was quick on the uptake.

Marcus reined in his horses and the two carriages drew abreast of each other. "I give you good afternoon, madam wife." He greeted her with a narrow-eyed smile that spoke of many things before bowing to her companion. "Miss Moreton." Harriet blushed and returned the bow.

"Marcus, you're the very person I need," Judith said. "I've just remembered an errand I must run immediately. It'll be a great bore for Harriet, so you may escort her home for me."

Laughter sprang in the ebony eyes. Marcus, also, was quick on the uptake. "It'll be my pleasure." He tossed his reins to his tiger and sprang down from the curricle. "Miss Moreton, allow me to assist you."

Harriet's blush deepened when his lordship caught her around the waist and matter-of-factly lifted her to the ground before handing her into his own more easily managed vehicle.

Marcus stepped closer to the phaeton, resting one hand on the front axle. "Devious minx," he said. "Don't think I don't know what you're up to. You're more artful than a wagonload of monkeys."

Judith smiled demurely. "Since Sebastian has so little to offer as a suitor in his own right, he'd better make the most of his other family connections." Immediately she regretted the light, bantering words. They were too close to home, too close to the bitterness that had been so sweetly resolved.

But to her relief, Marcus chose to respond as if he had no memory of that confrontation. "You're a shameless baggage, but I've no objections to assisting Sebastian. However, I do have one crow to pluck with you."

"Oh?"

"Where is your groom?"

Judith pulled a face. "Grooms are the devil in an open carriage. They make it impossible to have a comfortable conversation."

"Nevertheless, they are indispensable."

Judith sighed. "The despot speaks again."

"And he will be obeyed."

It was a minor concession and a limited inconvenience. Matters were going so smoothly between them at the moment that she was not prepared to throw a wrench in the works over something so trivial. "Very well, if you insist, I'll not drive out again unaccompanied."

Marcus nodded. "You'd better take Henry with you for the moment."

"Oh, no!" Judith exclaimed. "That'll spoil everything. If you don't have your tiger, you won't be willing to leave your horses in order to call upon Lady Moreton when you return Harriet. The whole impact of the Marquis of Carrington's escort will be diminished."

Marcus couldn't help laughing. "I don't know why I should allow myself to be embroiled in your plots, but if you don't take Henry, then you must return home immediately."

Judith inclined her head in acknowledgment, waved gaily to Harriet, and started her horses. "Immediately" was a word open to interpretation, she decided, and she had given no verbal promise. Marcus would be safely occupied outside the park for at least forty-five minutes, and the opportunity to encourage the shark in Bernard Melville's eyes couldn't be missed.

She ran her quarry to earth near the Apsley House gate. He was engaged in conversation with a group of friends, but there was no sign of Lady Barret, which relieved Judith of the need to find a way of offering to take up Gracemere while excluding the lady.

"My lord, we meet again." She hailed him cheerfully. "Harriet has been returned home; may I offer to take you up for a turn?"

"I'm honored, Lady Carrington. I shall be the most envied man in the park."

"Fustian," she declared, laughing.

"Not in the least," he protested, swinging himself up beside her. "You're such a noted whip, ma'am. Did Carrington teach you?"

"No," Judith said, starting the horses as she prepared to water the seeds already sown. "In truth, my husband doesn't entirely approve of this turn-out." She gave her companion an up-from-under look as if to say: You know what I mean.

"But he doesn't exactly forbid it?" Gracemere asked.

"No, I don't take kindly to forbidding." She gave him an arch smile.

"I'm surprised Carrington is willing to yield. He's generally thought to have an unyielding temperament."

"He does," Judith said with a note of defiance. "But I don't see why I shouldn't amuse myself as I please."

"I see." Fancy Marcus of all men marrying a spoiled brat. It was a delicious thought and all the better for his purposes.

"However," Judith went on, her voice now low and confiding, "my husband remains adamant about refusing to receive you under his roof." She touched his knee fleetingly. "I think it a great piece of nonsense, myself, but he won't be moved." She gave him another arch smile. "So we'll have to pursue our friendship a little more . . . well, obliquely, if you see what I mean. As we're doing now."

"Yes, I see exactly what you mean." He could barely contain his amusement at having such a ripe plum fall into his lap. "But you're not afraid you might come across your husband in the park?"

Judith shook her head. "Not this afternoon. He's about some errand that will occupy him for at least an hour."

"I see you enjoy flirting with danger, Judith . . . I may call you Judith?"

"Yes, of course. It's not so much that I enjoy courting danger, sir; but I claim the right to make my friends where I choose. If Carrington can't accept that, then I'll circumvent his disapproval." She glanced sideways at him with a coquettish little pout. "Do I shock you, Bernard, with such unwifely sentiments?"

His eyes held hers for a long minute and the shark skimmed the surface of his gaze. "On the contrary, I've always appreciated an unvirtuous wife. My tastes have never run to the milksop, and if you wish to cultivate me in order to assert your independence, then, ma'am, I'm honored to be so cultivated."

Judith allowed a moment to pass while she continued to keep her eyes on his, then a small, inviting smile touched her mouth. "Then we're agreed, sir." She held out one hand to him, across her body. He took it, squeezing it firmly.

"We are agreed."

"But it's to be our secret."

"Of course," he said smoothly. "My lips are sealed.

We shall be merely civil in public and save our friendship for moments such as this."

"Just so, my lord." Judith contrived to produce a flirtatious little giggle that brought a complacent but condescending smirk to his lordship's lips.

"Miss Moreton's a very sweet-natured girl," Judith observed after a minute.

"Very," the earl concurred. "It's unfortunate her mother's ill health makes it difficult for her to be launched as she deserves."

"But Lady Barret seems willing to take a mother's place."

"Ah, yes, Agnes is all kindness," he said. "Harriet has reason to be grateful."

"I understand she's something of an heiress."

"Is she? I didn't know."

Thank you, my lord Gracemere. The disingenuous denial had told her everything she needed to know.

Shortly after, she set the earl down again at the Apsley House gate and turned her horses toward the Stanhope gate and home. It was later than she'd realized and she was now unlikely to be at home before Marcus. Sebastian, however, appeared fortuitously, just as she turned out of the gate. She drew rein.

"Sebastian, you must accompany me to Berkeley Square."

"Of course, if you like." Her brother acceded to this imperative declaration with customary good humor. "Any special reason?"

"I need to arrive home suitably escorted," she told him. "And besides, there's something we need to discuss."

"Carrington objects to your driving without a groom." There was no questioning inflexion to the remark.

Judith laughed. "How did you guess?"

"Because it's only natural he would. You're too care-less of convention, Ju."

"Goodness me! Since when have you become so straitlaced?"

"I haven't," Sebastian denied, startled. "At least, I don't believe I have."

"It's Harriet's influence, I'll lay odds."

"Well, what if it is?"

"Don't be so defensive. I think she's very sweet, and if you love her then so shall I. . . . But that brings me to what we have to discuss."

"Well?"

"I believe Gracemere is courting Harriet—or court-ing her fortune, at any rate."

Sebastian was very still beside her. When he spoke, his voice was almost neutral. "What makes you think so?"

Judith told him and he heard her out in silence. "After all, he's married one heiress . . . snatched her from under the nose of a most desirable suitor. It doesn't seem unlikely he'd try it again," she concluded. "And I can't think of any other reason why Agnes Barret should be so sedulously cultivating an innocent girl in her first Season. The situation's perfect: Harriet's mother can't— or won't—oversee her progress. Agnes steps in, wins their confidence, and what's more natural than that she should introduce Harriet to her own friends . . . or lover, as the case may be? The Moreton fortune will benefit both of them, presumably."

"Damn the man to hell!" Sebastian hissed with abrupt vehemence. "Everywhere we turn, he's there, twisting his black evil into every thread of our lives."

"You can defeat him on this," Judith said calmly.

"When you bring him down with the cards, you'll destroy every other plan he has."

Sebastian said nothing, but his jaw was tight as he stared rigidly ahead.

"Harriet loathes Gracemere."

"She told you?" Surprised, he turned to look at her.

"Yes. Although I'm sure she doesn't realize why he's so encroaching. But if she's not offering him any encouragement, he's going to have his work cut out to make any headway."

"If only this was over and done with!" Sebastian exclaimed in a vehement undertone.

Judith said nothing, knowing her brother would recover his equilibrium in his own way, and by the time they reached Berkeley Square, he was chatting quite easily again as if that impassioned wish had never been uttered.

Lacking a groom, she drove the horses to the mews herself. Marcus was standing in the cobbled yard, talking with the head stableman as his wife drove in. He strolled over to her. "One of these days, we must have a discussion on the concept of 'immediately,' Judith. It seems to be one of the increasingly long list of words we understand differently," he said in pleasant tones.

Judith scrutinized his countenance for indications of real annoyance. If there was any it was only slight. "But as you see," she pointed out, "I have an irreproachable escort."

Marcus nodded. "Do you ever object to being browbeaten and manipulated by your sister, Sebastian?"

"Not in general," Sebastian said. "I'm resigned. How about you?"

"Not yet resigned. I must persuade you to teach me how such a peaceful state can be attained."

"Oh, it's perfectly simple. The only drawback is that it takes a long time. Like rock erosion."

"I object to this habit you two have developed of talking about me as if I weren't here," Judith announced with offended dignity.

"I'm afraid you invite it, lynx. It's the only weapon we mere males have against your wiles. Let's have you down from there." Marcus reached up to grasp her waist, swinging her to the cobbles. "Do you come in, Sebastian? Or were you kidnapped en route to some other engagement?"

"The latter," he said. "I was engaged to meet some friends in the park. I daresay they've given me up now, so I may as well return home."

"If you think to make me feel guilty, brother, I can tell you you haven't succeeded." Marcus still held her by the waist and she took a step away from him. His hands tightened and she retraced the step, smiling slightly even as she wondered what the grooms and stablehands must be thinking.

"I never attempt lost causes," Sebastian said with a grin. "And I don't think you need me around at the moment, so I'll bid you farewell."

"We have some unfinished business," Marcus said, his bantering tone disappeared. Sebastian raised his eyebrows and his brother-in-law went on, "I've been trying to catch you these last five days. Will I find you at White's or Watier's later tonight?"

"White's," Sebastian said without hesitation. Gracemere had said he would be at the faro tables at White's that evening.

Marcus felt the stirring of the air between brother and sister as if it were palpable. He'd noticed before these strange, suspended instants of tension, when they both seemed to hear something different from the actual words spoken. "Then I'll find you there," he said.

"I'm intrigued," Judith said. "What unfinished business could you have with Sebastian?"

"None of your business, ma'am."

"Oh, is it not?" A flare ignited the golden eyes.

Sebastian, chuckling, left them to it and strolled out of the yard. Matters seemed to be going less bumpily between his sister and her husband these days.

"Inside," Marcus directed. "We're going to have that discussion on semantics."

"Oh, good," Judith said happily. "That's bound to be interesting."

"Yes, I believe it will be. Walk a little faster."

Meekly Judith obeyed the pressure in the small of her back. "How did you find Lady Moreton?"

"Invalidish, in a word. Toad-eating, in another. A dead bore, in three more. *Must we encourage this connection?*"

"Yes."

"I detect a note of finality."

"Admit that Harriet is charmingly pretty, has the sweetest manners, and will make Sebastian a splendid wife."

"I accept the first two, although she's shy as a church mouse, but for the third—it seems to me a veritable mismatch."

"Sebastian knows what he wants," Judith said with quiet confidence. "And what he wants, he gets."

"Not unlike his sister," Marcus observed, but Judith could hear no sting to the statement.

19

"I don't know why the silly chit should be so stand-offish." Gracemere paced the firelit salon, his mouth twisted with annoyance.

"She's shy, Bernard." Agnes poured tea. "And she's very young."

"So was Martha, but I didn't have such difficulty with her. I had her eating out of my hand in two weeks."

Agnes refrained from pointing out that the earl had been younger then. "Martha was ripe for the picking," she said. "Carrington's proprietorial indifference left her with so little self-esteem that she could be easily flattered into love."

"You do me such honor, ma'am," Gracemere said with chilly irony.

"Oh, don't fly into a pucker, Bernard. You know

perfectly well it's the truth. Harriet hasn't yet felt her wings. It's her first Season." She rose from the sofa, carrying his tea across to him. "However, have you noticed how Judith seems to have taken the child up? And Sebastian seems always to be at her side."

Gracemere gave a crack of derisive laughter. "That greenhorn! He's a ninny with more money than sense."

"So long as he's worth plucking." Agnes turned back to the tea tray.

"I only wish it could be more of a challenge," the earl said, sipping his tea.

Agnes looked up at him. "Count your blessings, my love. Why would you want to work harder than you must?"

He laughed, touching a finger to his lips in salutation. "I take your point. But to return to the Moreton chit. You must contrive to ensure she's more in my company."

"I'm not sure how much good it would do. If the child is doe-eyed for Sebastian, and Judith has decided to take up his cause, then we face some difficulties."

Gracemere's pale eyes hardened. "If the girl can't be persuaded, there are other methods."

Agnes pursed her lips. "Abduction, you mean?"

"If necessary. A night in that Hampstead inn is all that's required. It doesn't much matter if the girl spends it willingly or not. She'll be ruined either way."

"Society is so unjust," Agnes murmured with a smile. "A girl's innocence is wrested from her with an act of ravishment, and she's considered no longer fit for decent company." She glided toward Gracemere, a fluid, undulating walk, reminiscent of a serpent's slither.

"But an honorable marriage will conceal her shame," he replied, both lust and cruelty in his smile. Agnes went into his arms, her breathing swift, her lips parted, her eyes glittering with an almost feral excitement. He fastened on her mouth with a savage hunger, reflecting yet again that the planning of evil and the prospect of suffering were for Agnes the most potent aphrodisiacs. It was yet another link in the chain that bound them.

"An honorable marriage that will cost her family every penny of thirty thousand pounds," Agnes whispered against his mouth. "Poor child, I could almost pity her. Will you be kind to her?"

"I have kindness only for you, my own. The kindness that I know pleasures you." Gracemere smiled and bit down on her lower lip, his fingers closing fiercely over her right breast, pinching the rising nipple.

Agnes shuddered as the hurt blossomed and she moaned, pressing her loins against his, and the inevitable, blissful excitement surged in her blood.

The earl smiled to himself as he felt her response. Life was full of attractive propositions at the moment, with Carrington's wife begging like a fawning puppy for his help in taunting her husband and young Davenport offering himself as meekly as any sheep to the shearer.

"Judith, are you feeling quite well?" Sally looked anxiously at her sister-in-law, who seemed listless, lacking her usual burnished luster.

Judith had a headache and a dragging pain in the base of her belly. It had come on since she'd arrived at the Herons' soiree, and she didn't need a visit to the retiring room to confirm what she already knew. That wild and glorious night of lovemaking had had no fruitful consequences, and she didn't know whether she was glad or sorry.

"It's just the time of the month," she said. "And this party is so insipid." The soiree had so far featured a harpist of mediocre talent, a meager supper, and indifferent champagne. "Let's go into the card room," she suggested, putting aside her nearly untouched supper plate.

"There's a loo table in the small salon," Isobel said. "We could join that."

Judith's expression was not encouraging. "No, come and play basset instead. The stakes aren't too high, and I've explained how to make the best calculation on the card order, so at least you have some tool against pure chance."

"I don't feel clear-headed enough tonight," Sally said. "I don't think I can play properly if I haven't prepared myself beforehand."

"And all the preparation in the world doesn't necessarily help me," Cornelia declared. "I'm in favor of loo."

"But it's limited loo," Judith said disgustedly. "There's no challenge in that."

"The words of a true gamester, Lady Carrington." Agnes Barret's soft tones came from behind Judith, and it was only with the exercise of supreme self-control that she kept dislike and unease from her expression as she turned.

"Good evening, Lady Barret. Have you just arrived? I'm afraid you've missed the harpist." She offered a bland smile.

"I understand she performed magnificently."

"I fear I'm a poor judge," Judith said.

"But not of the cards. Anyone who plays at Amelia Dolby's must have both inclination and skill . . . or perhaps simply need?" she added, her eyes narrowing as she awaited Judith's reaction.

Judith bowed. "As you would know, ma'am."

Lady Barret smiled faintly. "Husbands can be so difficult about money, can't they?" Her tawny eyes held

Judith's for a long minute, then with a word of excuse, she moved away.

"Good heavens," Isobel said, taking a cream puff from a silver salver presented by a waiter. "Are you at war with Agnes Barret, Judith?"

"At war? What a strange idea. How should I be?"

"I don't know," Isobel said. "But the air was crackling. Wasn't it?" She appealed to her companions as she popped the creamy confection into her mouth with an unconsciously beatific smile.

Cornelia was frowning. "There's something about her, or is it about you, Judith? I can't put my finger on it, but when she was standing so close to you . . . Oh, I don't know what I'm talking about." She shook her head in exasperation. "I'm going to play loo. It may be poor-spirited of me, but I enjoy it, and I'm perfectly content to make pin money tonight."

"I am too," Isobel declared, beckoning to the footman with the pastries. "I find high-stakes playing exciting, but it makes me most dreadfully nervous . . . one of those, I think." She selected a strawberry tart. "These are quite delicious. Why don't you try one, Judith?"

"The chicken in aspic rather put me off," Judith said. "Besides, I haven't your sweet tooth."

"It's a great trial," Isobel said a touch dolefully. "I shall become very fat, I'm convinced."

Sally laughed. "You'll be magnificent, Isobel, a plump and indolent matron of unfailing generosity, dispensing hospitality from your sofa, and taking in every waif and stray who comes your way."

Judith smiled. It was a fairly safe prediction. Isobel had a heart to match her sweet tooth.

"Very well, we'll play loo," she agreed. "I've a belly-ache and a headache, so I might as well play schoolroom games." In fact, she would really prefer to be home in her bed with a book, drinking hot milk laced with brandy. And Marcus would come in later, and when he realized she didn't feel like making love, he'd make up the fire and bring his cognac and sit on her bed and talk to her. Would he be relieved that she hadn't conceived?

Judith dug up a smile and followed her friends into the salon where the loo table was set up.

The clock in the smoky room struck midnight when Marcus downed his mug of gin and water in the Daffy Club and stood up.

"Whither away?" Peter Wellby asked, watching the smoke from his clay pipe curl upward to the blackened timbers of the low ceiling.

"I have to track down my brother-in-law," Marcus told him. "He said I'd find him at White's this evening."

"Decent fellow, Davenport," Peter observed, rising with him. He extinguished his pipe and handed it to a waiting serving lad, who took it away to be hung up over the stained planking of the taproom counter until its owner came again. "Mind if I accompany you?" Peter picked up his cane. He glanced dispassionately into his empty tankard. "Had enough blue ruin for one evening."

"A glass of reasonable port won't come amiss," Marcus agreed.

Sebastian was at the faro table when his brother-in-law arrived. He was winning steadily but with such careless good humor that the growing pile of rouleaux and vowels in front of him seemed unremarkable.

Gracemere held the bank. He glanced up as Marcus strolled over to the table. For a moment, their eyes met and again Gracemere experienced the shiver of terror of that long-ago morning, when Carrington had found him with Martha.

Hatred flickered in the earl's pale eyes and was answered with a cold, mocking disdain before the marquis turned his black gaze on Sebastian.

"A word with you, Sebastian, when the table breaks up."

"Yes, of course." Sebastian carelessly arranged several rouleaux around his chosen cards. "I think I'll close after this hand, anyway . . . while I'm ahead."

Gracemere slid the top card off the pack in front of him, revealing the knave of hearts. He laid it to the right of the pack. "That's me done for the night," Viscount Middleton said with a sigh, pushing across his rouleaux that lay beside his own knave of hearts. "The play's getting too rich for my blood."

Gracemere turned up the second card: the king of spades. This one he laid to the left of the pack.

Sebastian had bet on its counterpart and chuckled amid a chorus of good-natured groans at his continuing luck. "Never mind, tomorrow it'll have deserted me completely. The lady's a fickle mistress."

Gracemere took up the rake and pushed three fifty-guinea rouleaux across to him. "You can't walk away just yet, Davenport. Not with the luck running so completely in your favor."

There was something in the earl's voice that made Sebastian instantly alert: an eagerness that Gracemere could barely conceal. Sebastian glanced across the table and saw a shimmer of anticipation in the pale eyes. *Gracemere expected to win the next cut.*

He shrugged acceptingly and sat back, watching as the earl dealt afresh. A new pack of cards was then put in front of him. "Stakes, gentlemen." He smiled around the table.

Sebastian placed two rouleaux against the seven of clubs. The others around the table made their own bets.

Gracemere turned up the first card in the pack and laid the seven of clubs to the right of the pack.

Sebastian pushed his stake across the table without a word. The earl smiled, his eyes meeting the other's cool gaze.

"Ill luck can't last. Try another," Gracemere suggested, his tongue running over his lips.

Sebastian shook his head. "Not tonight, my lord, my luck's turned. Carrington . . . at your service."

He followed Marcus to a chair by the fire. Gracemere had placed the seven of clubs. Sebastian had expected it, though he didn't know how it had been done. He knew most of the tricks of card sharping, but he'd missed that one, though he'd guessed that Gracemere was going to try something. The earl had been playing straight up to now, and a hundred guineas was no great sum, so why had he decided to win it in such risky fashion? Was it something he did occasionally to keep his hand in, as Judith and Sebastian did once in a while? Or could he really not endure to lose even once to a man he was determined to fleece?

Sebastian knew that his strategy had succeeded and Gracemere had picked him as his next victim. He had now to draw him in deep by offering alternate wins and losses, while Judith established her own place in the earl's sphere, so that he wouldn't think twice about her presence at his side in the card room. However, if he was going to have to pit his skill against devious play so soon, they would have to think again. Only trickery could defeat trickery, and they couldn't afford to play their double act prematurely. He might have to resign himself to more losses than they'd decided he could comfortably bear.

Having reached that decision, Sebastian dismissed Gracemere from his mind for the moment and smiled at his brother-in-law, reaching for the decanter of port on the table.

"So, what is this unfinished business, Marcus? I confess you have me intrigued."

"An outstanding debt," Marcus said, taking the glass he handed to him. "Thank you. How much did you pay for Judith's horses?"

"A fraction above four hundred," Sebastian said easily. "They were a bargain."

"I won't dispute that." Marcus sat down in the winged chair, crossing his long legs in olive pantaloons. "And the coach-builder?"

"Two-fifty, I believe." He sipped his port. "It's a capital turn-out. I'd not resent the outlay."

"Oh, no, I don't in the least." Marcus made haste to reassure him. "I'll give you a draft on my bank for six hundred and fifty guineas, if that'll suit you."

Sebastian choked on his port. "Whatever for?"

"You did act as your sister's agent in this matter?"

"Yes, of course I did, but . . . Oh." Comprehension dawned. "You think I was her banker . . . No, I assure you, Carrington, Judith paid every penny herself. I did nothing more than effect the purchase."

"*Judith.*" Marcus sat up abruptly. "Don't try to bamboozle me, Sebastian. I know full well your sister couldn't possibly have afforded such a sum. I know how much her quarterly allowance is, and I examine all her bills."

He put his glass on the table. "I've agreed to allow Judith to keep her carriage and horses, so you must understand that I can't permit you to assume an expense that is rightfully mine."

Sebastian frowned into his glass. A thorny thicket

seemed to have sprung up around him. It had slipped his mind that Marcus didn't know of Judith's financial independence. But even if it hadn't, he could hardly take Marcus's money on false pretenses. After a minute he said, "Evidently your arithmetic is at fault, Carrington. I assure you that my sister paid for that turn-out herself." He added with a bland smile, "She works miracles with the smallest amounts of money, Judith does."

"What possible source of—" The question died on his lips. How could he have been so naive? So blind? He'd placed a limit on her spending and she'd simply reverted to her old ways.

"I take it Judith continues to engage in high-stakes gaming as a source of income?" His voice was level, no hint of his seething fury.

Sebastian examined his brother-in-law's drawn countenance. The white shade around his mouth, the flint in the black depths of his eyes told their own tale.

"You couldn't expect Judith to accept a humiliating dependency," he said, giving up on trying to mislead Marcus. Clearly, it was useless. "When you limited her expenditure, she had no choice but to look after her own needs."

Marcus ignored this. His voice was still even. "Do you have any idea how much my wife manages to make in a week at the gaming tables?"

Sebastian sucked in his lower lip. "It would depend on where she played and whether she needed money. But on a good evening, playing high, she could probably come away with a thousand without it seeming too noticeable. Much more, of course, if she were playing at Pickering Street."

Marcus felt as if his head were about to explode. "So she frequents hells, does she? It must feel quite like old times."

Sebastian winced. "Ju's not like other women, Carrington. She has her pride . . . maybe more than most." He shook his head, feeling for words. "But if you try to impose your will on her, she'll fight back. She's never been financially dependent on anyone. If you'd simply trusted her to keep her expenditure within bounds, none of this would have happened."

"I'm indebted to you for pointing that out to me." Marcus stood up. "However, it just so happens that my fortune is not at the disposal of every adventuress who manages to lay some claim to it. Now, if you'll excuse me, I'm going to attend to your sister. So far, I've failed to impress her with the depth of my feelings on this score. I am now going to put that right."

Heavy-hearted, Sebastian watched Marcus stride from the room. The fragile edifice of his sister's marriage was about to be cracked wide open; that much he knew absolutely. Whether it could be repaired remained to be seen. But he had to be there for Judith. She would need him very soon.

He drank another glass of port and then went home to await developments.

20

Marcus strode up St. James's toward Curzon Street. It was a dark night but he'd have been unaware of his surroundings even in brightest moonlight. His mind was a seething witches' brew of anger, disappointment, and something that he vaguely recognized as sorrow. Sorrow for the savage, abrupt destruction of his budding belief that his marriage, founded on quicksand, could be reconstructed, grounded now in cement. He had begun to lay down the burden of mistrust, gradually to allow the warmth of his feelings for Judith to overcome the doubts, to be seduced by her in every respect as thoroughly as he'd been seduced simply by her body in Brussels. And now it was all gone, ashes on his tongue. She wanted what he could give her materially, and when he didn't satisfy those wants, she gave not a thought to his position, to her position, but simply took what she wanted, perpetrating her deceitful masquerade as shamelessly as ever. She had no interest in or intention of being his wife in the fullest sense, adapting her life-style to the obligations and duties of that position even as she enjoyed its advantages. She was using him, as she had used him from the start.

At the corner of Duke Street and Piccadilly, the sounds of uproar broke through his self-absorption. A group of young bloods of about Charlie's age were drunkenly weaving their way along the pavement, arm in arm, flourishing bottles of burgundy. One of them fired a flintlock pistol in the air, and their raucous hilarity brought an officer of the watch out of an alley, his lantern raised high, throwing a yellow circle of illumination over the disheveled band. It was an error. With a fox hunter's "view halloo," the group surged forward, surrounding the man, clearly intent on one of the favorite pastimes of inebriated, aristocratic youth: boxing the watch.

Marcus's anger, already in full flame, needed only this to create a conflagration. He strode into the middle of the group, wielding his cane to good purpose, until he reached the fallen watchman. One of the young men, his face red, his eyes bloodshot, swung an empty burgundy bottle at the cane-wielding spoiler of their fun. Slender fingers gripped his wrist and the pressure made the young man wince. The marquis stared at him in silence. His grip tightened and, with a sharply indrawn breath, the young man let the bottle crash to the pavement. He fell back under the piercing menace of those ebony eyes and his companions, infected by the unspoken threat embodied in this new arrival, melted away.

The officer of the watch scrambled up, retrieving his fallen lantern, straightening his coat, adjusting his wig that had slipped over one eye. He muttered about taking the young hooligans before the Justice, but the group had gone, and soon could be heard hooting and bellowing from the safety of a reasonable distance.

"Ruffians," Marcus stated disgustedly, kicking broken glass away from his gleaming Hessians. "Too much money and time and not enough to occupy them. Sometimes I think it would have been better if we hadn't beaten Bonaparte. A few years in the army would do them the world of good." The watchman agreed, but rather nervously. His rescuer seemed to be in as dangerous a mood as his assailants, judging by those intimidating eyes and the savage way his cane had thwacked across their shoulders. He ducked his head, mumbled his thanks, and took himself off on his rounds again, swinging his lantern.

The encounter had done nothing to quell the bright flame of rage as Marcus strode up the steps of the Herons' mansion on Curzon Street. Light poured from the windows, voices and the strains of dance music greeted him as he stepped into the hall. Instructing the butler curtly to summon Lady Carrington's chaise, Marcus strode up the stairs.

His hostess came fluttering over to him, all smiles, and Marcus forced himself to respond with due courtesy, but it was clear to Amanda Heron that the Most Honorable Marquis of Carrington's thoughts were elsewhere . . . and they weren't very pleasant thoughts, judging by the look in his eye. She was quite relieved when he excused himself and made straight for the card room, casting a quick glance into the drawing room, where the rug had been rolled up and a few couples still danced to the strains of a pianoforte.

Judith was not dancing. Neither was she in the main card room. Presumably the stakes at this insipid affair were not worthy of her skill, he thought savagely, turning aside to another, smaller salon.

He heard Judith's laughing voice as he stepped through the arched doorway. "For shame, Sally, you're looed. How could you have lost that trick?"

"Oh, it grows late," Sally protested. "And I haven't your powers of concentration, Judith."

The powers necessary to maintain a deceitful masquerade. Marcus stood for a minute in the shadow of a heavy curtain. Ten people sat in a cheerful circle around the loo table. They were playing limited loo, the penalty fixed at a shilling, but Judith had beside her a substantial pile of shillings, and as he watched, a man opposite pushed the pool across the table.

"Lady Carrington, you win again."

"How very surprising," Marcus murmured, crossing to the table.

Judith experienced a start of pleasure at the sound of his voice, and missed the tone at first. She turned, smiling, as he came up behind her shoulder. The smile faded as she saw his expression, a slowly creeping apprehension prickling between her shoulder blades. "Carrington, I wasn't expecting you."

"Isn't this rather tame sport for you, my dear?" he asked, gesturing to the cards and the mound of small coins. His voice was heavy with sarcasm, and the rage that he could barely contain flared in his eyes.

Two spots of color pricked her cheekbones and her scalp contracted as apprehension became absolute. She became aware of the uneasy shiftings around the table, the puzzled glances at Lord Carrington. "I've always liked party games," she offered, desperately trying to defuse whatever this was. "We've been enjoying ourselves famously." She appealed to the table at large.

"Oh, famously," Isobel agreed readily, gathering up

her cards, her eyes warm and encouraging as she smiled at Judith. "Won't you join us, Lord Carrington?"

He shook his head with brusque discourtesy. "I wait only for my wife to make her excuses."

Only immediate compliance would end this mortification. Judith's head pounded as she pushed back her chair, picking up her reticule.

"You've forgotten your winnings," her husband said pointedly.

"They can go back in the pool." Judith thrust the shiny mound of coins into the middle of the table. Bidding her companions good night, she tried to smile as if nothing out of the ordinary were happening, but she could feel the stiffness of her lips and read in every eye both discomfort and consternation.

"Such winnings are too insignificant to be worth keeping, I assume," Marcus muttered against her ear as he drew her arm through his. Judith stiffened and would have withdrawn her arm, except that he tightened his grip, squeezing the limb against his body, so that to pull free would look like a struggle.

She couldn't think of anything that could safely be said in public, so she painted the stiff smile on her lips as they progressed through the rooms, bowed, made her farewells like a marionette obeying the puppeteer, and allowed herself to be removed in short order from the Herons' mansion and handed into the chaise, waiting ready at the door.

"What is all this about, Marcus?" To her annoyance, her voice shook, and she tried to deny that it was as much fear that produced the quaver as her own anger at the embarrassment he'd caused her.

"We will not discuss it here," he declared with icy finality.

"But I demand—"

"You will demand nothing."

There was such ferocity, such purpose, investing the statement that Judith was silenced. She shrank into a corner of the carriage, trying desperately to marshall her forces, to look for some clue to whatever had happened . . . to whatever was about to happen. Something dreadful had occurred. But what?

The chaise drew up in Berkeley Square. The coachman let down the footstep. Marcus sprang down and assisted Judith to alight. In silence, they entered the house, and the night porter locked and bolted the door behind them, bidding them good night.

"We will deal with this in my book room." Marcus's hand closed over Judith's shoulder as she moved toward the staircase.

There would be no waiting servants there, she realized. No one to dismiss before he could unburden himself of whatever weight of rage lay on his shoulders. She moved away from his hand, in the first gesture of independence she had managed since this debacle had begun, and walked ahead of him down the passage to the square room at the back of the house.

"Now, perhaps you'll tell me what this is all about?" Her hands shook now as she drew off her long silk gloves, finger by finger, but her voice was once more steady.

The deep nighttime silence of the sleeping house enclosed them, and for a minute Marcus didn't reply. He tossed his cane and gloves onto the table and poured himself a glass of cognac, trying to master his fury. When he spoke, his voice was relatively calm and distant.

"I've been extraordinarily naive, I freely admit. For some inexplicable and doubtless foolish reason I had assumed that once you'd achieved your goal by this marriage, you'd see no need to pursue your career at the gaming tables."

So that was it. Her lips were bloodless as she said, "When you made it clear you resented paying my expenses, I saw no alternative to paying for them myself. I prefer to do that anyway. I don't care to be dependent on a whimsical generosity, my lord."

"At no point did I say I resented paying your expenses. I did however say that as your husband, I would control your expenditure. My fortune is not at your unlimited disposal, although I now understand that you'd expected it to be." Ice tipped every loaded, humiliating word.

Judith felt herself diminishing into a small, hot ball of shame under the power of his contempt, and she fought to hold on to herself, to the essence of her pride and her knowledge of how wrong he was. "I don't and never did expect unlimited access to your money," she denied in a low voice. "But as your wife, I assumed I would be granted the dignity of an appearance of freedom, instead of being reduced to the status of a poor relation, or a child in the schoolroom, begging for pin money."

"And so in retaliation you choose to take money from my friends, to supplement an allowance you consider meager?"

"I do not *take* money from your friends . . . I win it!" she cried. "And I win it because I have the greater skill."

"You win it because you're a gamester—an adventuress, and you'll never be anything else," he declared bitterly. "I thought . . . God help me . . . I thought we were finding some truth on which to stand. But there is only one truth, isn't there, Judith? You're a manipulator and you will manipulate whoever comes your way, if they can be used to your advantage."

"No," she whispered, the cramping ache in her belly intensifying as her muscles clenched against the hateful words. She pressed her hands to her cheeks. "No, it's not like that."

"Oh, really?" His eyebrows lifted, black question marks in his dark face. "When did you decide that I would be the most useful recipient of your inestimable virtue, Judith? When you first saw me? Or did you decide later . . . even as late as when we were on the way to Quatre Bras, perhaps?"

"What are you saying?" Her eyes, huge with distress, stared at the mask of his face. "I don't understand what you're saying."

"Oh, then let me explain, my perverse and obtuse wife." He swung away from her, his fists clenched at his sides as he fought for control. He wanted to hurt her as she had hurt him, and he knew the potential power of the violence in his soul if he ever let slip the leash of control.

"When a virtuous woman loses her maidenhead dishonorably to an honorable man, she has a claim on that man. How difficult it must have been for you, reining in that passionate nature of yours, my dear, until your most precious bargaining chip found the highest bidder. Only the bidder didn't know what he was bidding for, did he? The bidder was offered the masquerade of an experienced adventuress, and only when it was too late did he discover the virgin."

Judith felt sick. Her body was one tightly clenched muscle and the nausea rose in her throat. This had never occurred to her. All this time, he believed she had deliberately led him on, offering the wiles of a wanton, in order to trap him with her virtue.

"No," she said, her voice barely audible. "It's not true. I never thought of my virginity when I was with you. I thought only of you . . . you must remember how that was . . . how it is now," she said in passionate appeal to the passion they shared. "How could you believe I could *pretend* to feel for you in that way? I don't know *how* one would pretend it." Tears clogged her throat and she forced them down.

Marcus barely heard her. He moved a hand in harsh dismissal. "You are a consummate actress," he said. "And I've watched you perform once too often. And what an amazing piece of good fortune, it must have been, when Francis and the others turned up so opportunely. It set the seal on the trap perfectly, didn't it?"

"No," she whispered again. "No, it wasn't like that." But her heart was leaden, and she was filled with tears of pain and bewilderment, and suddenly the fight went out of her. She bowed her head in defeat.

"You will now listen to me very carefully," Marcus was continuing. He articulated each word with a slow emphasis that served as much to keep a rein on his rage as it did to increase the force of his speech. "Since, for better or worse, you *are* my wife, you will begin to behave like my wife. You're not to be trusted, so I shall take responsibility for correcting your faults myself. From this moment on, outside this house, you will play only whist and limited loo. From now on, I shall watch you: every move you make." He began to count off on his fingers. "You will accept no engagement without my express permission; and you will enter a card room only in my company; and if I ever find you seated at any table other than a loo table or a whist table, then I shall oblige you to leave immediately, regardless of the embarrassment this will cause you. Do you understand?"

"Oh, yes," Judith said softly. He was going to make a prison of their marriage with himself as her jailer.

"Furthermore," he continued coldly, "you will ask for my approval before you buy anything. I shall want to know what you wish to purchase, why it's necessary, and its cost. I'll then rule on whether you may do so or not. You'll not take advantage of me ever again, Judith." There was a bleakness in his voice now, and he turned away from her, going to the long French door and pulling aside the curtain, gazing out into the starless night.

He heard the door close quietly and knew that Judith had left the room. He could hear his voice, the harsh, punitive statements, the bleakness of betrayal beneath the cold fury. They faced a lifetime together . . . a lifetime of misery for both of them. And now he wished more than he had ever wished for anything that he'd never set eyes on her. Because knowing her from now on could only bring intensified pain. He had begun to love her, but he'd been loving a chimera.

He refilled his brandy goblet and tossed the mellow golden liquid down his throat in one swallow, then he went up to his own apartment. A sleepy Cheveley jumped up from a chair beside the fire. "I trust you had a pleasant evening, my lord."

"I don't remember passing a worse," Marcus replied, wearily. The valet closed his mouth and devoted his single-minded attention to the task of putting his lordship to bed.

Next door, Judith sat on the bed, waiting. She had sent Millie to bed as soon as she'd come up and had then locked the door behind the maid, before turning the key on the connecting door. Now she listened to the soft shufflings and footfalls from next door, waiting until she heard Cheveley bid his lordship good night and the door close on his departure.

She sat hunched over the woman's pain in her belly and the shank of despair driven deep into her soul. There was no future here. The life Marcus had just decreed couldn't be lived by either of them.

The line of yellow beneath the connecting door vanished as Marcus extinguished his bedside candle. Judith stood up, straightening her aching body with a low moan. She removed her evening dress and put on a riding habit, treading softly about the room, opening drawers and armoires with exaggerated care. Into a small valise, she packed her hairbrushes, nightclothes, tooth powder, and a change of clothes. It would do to be going on with, and anything else she needed, she would buy later.

She knew only that she could no longer stay under the same roof as Marcus. Leaving him so precipitately would ruin everything with Gracemere, but she could see no option. Sebastian would understand and they'd come up with an alternative plan.

But never had she felt so desolate, or so at a loss. She couldn't stay with him, but why then was leaving him as agonizing as peeling away a layer of skin?

Delicately she turned the key and let herself out of the room. In the corridor, where a dim light came from a single candle in a wall sconce, she paused, listening. The only sounds were the creaks and rustles of the sleeping house. She crept down the stairs, still hunched over the dragging pain in her belly, and turned down the passage leading to the book room. This was not an exit to be made through the front door.

She opened the French doors and stepped into the garden, closing them quietly at her back. The gate in the wall led into the mews. Horses whickered, hooves shuffled on straw as she moved in the shadows across the swept cobbles of the yard. The stablehands wouldn't start work for another hour and Judith had the sense of being the only human awake in the whole of London town. It occurred to her that it was perhaps foolhardy to walk the streets alone in the dark hour before dawn, and her hand closed over her pistol.

It was less than a ten-minute walk, however, to Albemarle Street, and she saw no one. Sebastian's rooms were on the ground floor, and she stood on tiptoe to tap at the window. If she had to use the knocker the landlord would answer the summons and it would be hard to explain herself at such an hour. She raised her hand to tap again, when the front door opened.

"Come in, Ju," Sebastian whispered.

"How did you know it was me?" She slipped past him into the dark passageway.

"Somehow I was expecting you," he replied, picking up her valise and gesturing to the sitting room.

"I didn't wake you, then."

"No, I was waiting for you." He set down her valise and examined her carefully. "You look the very devil. Brandy?"

"Please." She threw off her cloak and drew off her gloves. "Thank you." Cradling the glass in her hands, she went to the hearth, where the ashy glow of the embers of the dying fire put out a modicum of heat.

Her brother took kindling from the basket beside the grate and tossed it onto the embers. A reassuring hiss and spurt of flame resulted. He straightened, regarding his sister with sharp-eyed concern. She sipped her brandy, stroking her stomach in an unconscious gesture he recognized as the fiery spirit warmed her cramping muscles. "You're not feeling too well," he stated.

She gave him a wan smile of agreement. "To add insult to injury."

"So, what did he do?"

"How did you know . . . ? Oh, did you tell him?"

"He wanted to repay me for your turn-out. I told him you'd paid for it yourself. He made the correct deduction. Carrington's no fool, Ju."

"I never took him for one," she said. Bleakly she recounted the scene in the book room, leaving nothing out. Sebastian listened in grim silence. It occurred to him that his brother-in-law had shown about as much sensibility as a herd of rogue elephants.

"So where do you want to go?" he asked, when she'd fallen silent.

"Some small hotel, perhaps."

"In London?"

"Yes, but in an unfashionable part; somewhere where I won't run the risk of meeting anyone I know on the street."

"Kensington . . . Bloomsbury?"

"Either . . . look, I know this ruins everything, but—"

"Not necessarily," her brother said. "We'll work out something. But at the moment, you've got to sort yourself out. We'll find somewhere for you to stay first thing in the morning." He put down his glass. "You can have the bedroom, I'll sleep on the sofa."

"No, I don't mind sleeping in here."

"Oh, Ju, don't be a bore." He picked up her valise. "Apart from the fact that you've got the bellyache, there's no need to be so tiresomely independent with me. You'll sleep in the bed and I'll be perfectly happy on the sofa. We've both slept in many more uncomfortable places in our time."

Judith gave him a ruefully apologetic smile. "Sorry. I seem to have lost the power of cool thought tonight."

He smiled and kissed her cheek. "Hardly surprising."

Judith followed him into the bedroom. "I suppose it's possible Marcus might knock on your door at some point."

"Highly likely, I would have thought," her brother agreed with a dry smile. "He can hardly pretend you never existed."

"No, but I expect he wishes he could."

Sebastian shook his head. "I admit it looks bad at the moment, but things change with time and distance."

"I can't go back," she said, pulling back the coverlet.

"No," he said neutrally. "I suppose not." He took her hands. "You're worn to a frazzle, love. We'll work something out."

"Of course we will. We always do," she assented, with a conviction she didn't truly feel. She reached up to kiss him. "Thank you."

"Sleep well."

Judith crept into bed and, despite unhappiness and uncertainty, fell instantly into the deep sleep of total, emotional exhaustion.

21

$\mathcal{M}$arcus slept fitfully and woke leaden with depression. He lay in the big bed contemplating the bleak prospect of his marriage. After such a confrontation, after the things that had been said, he could see no possibility of anything other than a frigid, armed truce between them from now on. He knew that he would always be suspecting her of some ulterior motive, of employing some strategy to take advantage of him. He'd never again be able to trust in her responses or in her emotions . . . not even in bed. And he would watch her like a hawk. He would control every aspect of her life as it impinged upon him. And Judith's bitter resistance would fuel the vicious circle of mistrust.

He dragged himself out of bed in the cheerless dawn and padded softly to the connecting door. The handle turned but the door was locked. It didn't surprise him, but it angered him. He intended from now on that her life should be open to his inspection at all times, and he would not tolerate locked doors.

He went out into the passage to the outside door. This one opened, but the room when he stepped into it was empty. He stood in disbelief for a minute, trying to order his tumbling thoughts and a sudden morass of responses that couldn't yet be named. The bed had not been slept in, drawers stood open, their contents disturbed as if someone had gone through them in haste. The armoire was open. Judith's hairbrushes were no longer on the dressing table.

She had gone. At first, the stark recognition made no sense. His mind couldn't grasp the fact that Judith had left him. He caught and hung onto the simplest aspect: the public consequences of such an action. The response to this was equally simple: a surge of renewed anger. How dare she do such a thing? Put him in such a position? How could he possibly explain his wife's dead-of-night flight to the servants? How could he possibly explain her absence to the rest of the world? It was a piece of cowardly avoidance, something he would never have expected of Judith.

Furiously he unlocked the connecting door and stormed into his own apartment, pulling the bellrope for Cheveley.

"Her ladyship has gone into the country," he said curtly when his valet appeared. "She had news of a sick aunt and was obliged to leave immediately. Inform Millie of that fact, will you?"

"Yes, m'lord." Cheveley was far too good at keeping his feelings to himself to show the slightest surprise at this extraordinary information. He assisted his lordship into his clothes and stood patiently with a large supply of cravats in case the first attempts were unsuccessful. But the marquis seemed easily satisfied this morning and spent less than five minutes on the intricacies of cravat-tying.

He slipped a Sevres snuff box into his pocket and stalked downstairs to the breakfast parlor, throwing over his shoulder, "Gregson, have my curricle brought around."

Gregson bowed at the terse instruction.

The marquis marched into the breakfast parlor, closing the door with a controlled slam. He poured himself coffee, helped himself to a dish of eggs, fragrant with fresh herbs, and sat at the table. Slowly the conflicting emotions wrestling each other for precedence began to sort themselves out. He sipped coffee, staring sightlessly across the table, his eggs cooling in front of him. He had to find her and bring her back, of course. Whatever lay between them, whatever future they might have, she was still his wife, whether she liked it or not. Devious, scheming adventuress or not, she was his wife, whether he liked it or not. And by God, when he found her . . .

He pushed back his chair abruptly and went to the window. It was a bright morning, a hoar frost glittering on the grass. He was furious with her for putting him in this situation, but there was more to it than that. Yes, she had to come back. The scandal otherwise would be unthinkable. But he had felt more than anger when he'd stood in the doorway of her empty room . . . a room out of which all the spirit seemed to have been leached. Even the house felt different, as if it had lost some vital presence that gave it life. Slowly he forced himself to name what he had felt as he'd stood in the doorway. He had felt the terror of loss. He felt it now, pushing up through the anger. There was no other way of describing it.

He began to pace the parlor, trying to work out what this meant. Did it mean that her deceptions didn't matter? Did it mean he was willing to endure being used, if it was the price of her presence in his life? Or did it simply mean he was willing to rescind the punishment if Judith would offer her own compromises? Could they start afresh? What was he terrified of losing—the potential for love or the certainty of lust?

He heard her laugh—that wicked, sensual chuckle in his head—and the sound winded him. He felt her body under his hands, as if in some sensuously vivid dream. He could smell the delicate, lavender-scented freshness of her skin. The burnished copper head, the great golden-brown eyes, shimmered in his internal vision. But it wasn't just that, was it? It was Judith herself. Judith with her tempestuous spirit, her needle wit, her acerbic tongue, her delicious sense of humor. Judith of the lynx pride and ferocious independence. It was the woman who carried a pistol, who didn't buckle under adversity, who didn't think twice about slaving amid the gory detritus of a battlefield, who took responsibility for herself.

It was the woman he had thought he needed to lash into submission. The foolishness of such a misguided intention now brought a sardonic curve to his mouth. Whatever she was, whatever she had been, she belonged to him. And for some perverse reason, despite the scheming and the deceit, she seemed to be what he wanted. And if that was the case, then he'd have to try to modify the bad with rather more subtlety than he'd shown so far, and what he couldn't change he'd have to accept.

But first he had to retrieve her. The initial step was obvious. If it failed, the next was less obvious.

Gregson announced that his lordship's curricle was at the door. "Thank you. Lady Carrington has gone into the country to visit a sick aunt."

"Yes, my lord, so I understand from Cheveley. Do we know when her ladyship will return?"

"When the sick aunt is recovered, I assume," Marcus snapped, thrusting his arms into the many-caped driving coat held by Gregson.

He drove to Albemarle Street. It was eleven o'clock, hopefully too early for Sebastian to have left his lodgings. He was right, to a certain extent, in that his quarry was seated at breakfast, having returned to his lodgings after an early-morning journey to Kensington.

"Good morning, Marcus." Sebastian rose from the table as his servant announced his brother-in-law. "Breakfast?" He gestured to the laden table.

"No, I've already breakfasted. Where is she, Sebastian?"

"I thought that was probably the purpose of your call." Sebastian resumed his seat. "You don't mind if I continue . . . ?"

Marcus slapped at his Hessians with his driving whip. "I haven't got all day, Sebastian. *Where is she?*"

"Well, there's the difficulty," his host murmured, taking up a tankard of ale. "I can't say, you see."

"She came to you, of course?"

"Of course." He took a draft of ale.

Marcus glanced around the room. If Judith was anywhere in the vicinity, he would know it, would feel it in his bones and through his skin. She had that effect on him, and it was getting stronger the longer he lived with her. He knew she was no longer in her brother's lodgings.

"If you don't mind my saying so, you seem to have been rather unsubtle," Sebastian observed, spearing a deviled kidney.

"I'm willing to concede that," Marcus said. "But the provocation was overpowering."

Sebastian frowned. He'd been thinking things through for many hours now, ever since his sister had fallen asleep. He hadn't said anything to her, but he had come to the conclusion that a degree of interference might be in her best interests. Of course, putting Judith's marriage together again would be in his best interests also. He couldn't destroy Gracemere without her help, and until Gracemere was dealt with, he couldn't make a formal offer for Harriet. He'd had to wrestle with the issues for a long time before he satisfied himself that what he was going to do would be certainly as much for Judith as it would be for himself.

"If you hadn't jumped to conclusions in the first place, there'd have been no need for Ju to offer you provocation," he said deliberately.

"Perhaps you'd like to explain." Marcus sat down, flicking at his boot with his whip, his eyes resting on his brother-in-law with an arrested expression.

"Ju had no idea who was in the taproom at that inn, after you and she had . . ." Sebastian waved a hand in lieu of completing the sentence.

Marcus was suddenly very still. "But she said she did."

"Did she? You sure about that?" Sebastian buttered a piece of toast without looking at his visitor.

Marcus thought. He'd asked her in that little loft on the morning of Waterloo, and she'd said . . . but no, she hadn't said anything at all. He'd asked her and she hadn't denied it.

"If it wasn't true, why wouldn't she deny it?"

"Well, you'd have to understand Ju and her eccentric principles rather better than you do to see that," her brother declared. "She'd be so insulted that you could have suspected her of such an underhand trick that she wouldn't see any point defending herself."

"Are you telling me that all these months, she could have put my mind at rest with a single word and she deliberately chose not to?"

Sebastian nodded. It was a little more complicated than that, but he couldn't explain to Marcus that Judith had seen little difference between the accusation of manipulation and the truth of opportunism. The difference, however, struck her brother as crucial in the present turmoil. "You shouldn't have suspected such a thing of her," he said simply.

Marcus closed his eyes on a surge of exasperation that for the moment prevented his unhampered joy as he laid down the burden of mistrust. "It was not an unnatural suspicion, knowing how you and your sister were living," he pointed out after a minute.

"Oh, I beg to differ," Sebastian said. "You made a false deduction from the premise. You hardly knew her." He glanced across at Marcus. "The other matter, too," he said. "Rather delicate, but you had no grounds for—"

"All right," Marcus interrupted, a spot of color burning on his cheek. "There's no need to expand. I know what you're referring to. If your sister hadn't been ruled by that damnable lynx pride of hers, all of this could have been avoided." He slashed at his boot. "I'm not prepared to assume total responsibility for this, Sebastian."

"No," Sebastian agreed, taking up his tankard again. He drank deeply. "So what are you going to do when you find her?"

"Wring her neck and throw her body in the Serpentine," Marcus said promptly.

Sebastian chuckled and shook his head. "That might defeat the object of reconciliation."

Marcus stood up abruptly. "Damn it, Sebastian, where is she?"

Sebastian shook his head. "I'm afraid I can't help you, Marcus."

"You know where she is, though?"

Sebastian nodded. "But I'm sworn to secrecy."

Marcus regarded him through narrowed eyes, tapping the silver knob of his whip against the palm of one hand. "I daresay you'll be seeing her at some point today."

"Yes." There was cool comprehension in Sebastian's eyes.

Marcus inclined his head in acknowledgment and walked to the door. "Thank you, Sebastian."

The door closed on his visitor. Sebastian pushed his chair back from the table and stretched out his long legs. Judith would probably be annoyed at his interference, but he felt as if he'd just done some good work. He was fairly certain his sister's feelings for Marcus Devlin went deeper than she had so far been prepared to acknowledge. And Marcus, for all his autocratic temperament, felt a great deal more for Judith than he might have demonstrated.

Maybe it took a man in love to recognize the signs in others, Sebastian reflected complacently. He'd give Marcus time to set his spy in place before he went himself to see Judith.

Marcus drove his curricle round to the mews. "Where's Tom, Timkins?"

The head groom took the reins as they were tossed to him. "In the tack room, m'lord. Shall I fetch him?"

"Please."

A minute later a lad of about fourteen came hurrying across the cobbles, wiping his palms against his leather apron. "You wanted me, m'lord."

"Yes, I have a task for you." Marcus gave the boy his instructions. Tom received them in silence, nodding his head now and again to indicate comprehension. "Is that quite clear, Tom? I'm sure he'll be expecting someone on his tail and he won't try to throw you off, but I don't want you to make it obvious."

"Don't you worry, m'lord. Thinner than 'is shadow I'll be." The lad grinned cheerfully. "I could pick 'is pocket and the cove'd not know it."

"I'm sure you could," Marcus agreed. "But I beg you won't give in to the temptation."

Tom was an accomplished pickpocket, who two years earlier had had the great good fortune to pick the marquis's pocket in the crowd at a prize fight. Carrington hadn't realized his watch had gone, until an observant spectator had set up the cry of "pickpocket." The terror in the child's eyes as he'd been collared had had a powerful effect on Marcus, who'd suddenly seen the small body hanging from a scaffold in Newgate Yard. He'd taken him in charge over the protestations of the irate citizens, handed him over to his head groom with the instructions that he be taught the consequences of theft in no uncertain fashion, and then set to work. Tom had been his most devoted employee ever since, evincing a degree of intelligence that certainly qualified him for a task such as this.

The search put in motion, there was nothing to do but wait. He retreated to his book room, wondering how to apportion the blame for the misunderstanding that had caused so much grief. They both bore some responsibility, but when he turned the cold, clear eyes of honesty on the question, he was obliged to accept that he had thrown the first stone.

The barouche drew up outside a tall, well-maintained house in Cambridge Gardens, North Kensington, and three women descended, looking about them with the curiosity of those on unfamiliar territory. Kensington was a perfectly respectable place, of course, but unfashionable and definitely not frequented by the ton.

"What a strange place for Judith to choose," observed Isobel.

"What a strange thing for her to choose to do," Cornelia responded with more point, as she lifted the hem of her dress and shook ineffectually at some clinging substance. "How did that get there?" She directed a hostile stare at the material, as if it alone were responsible for its less than immaculate appearance.

Neither of her friends bothered to answer the clearly rhetorical question. "Walk the horses, we shall be about an hour," Sally instructed her coachman, before raising the knocker on the blue-painted door.

"It doesn't seem like a hotel." Isobel's experience of hotels was limited to establishments such as Brown's or Grillon's.

However, the door was promptly opened by a maidservant, who asserted that it was indeed Cunningham's Hotel, and Mrs. Cunningham would be with them directly.

Mrs. Cunningham was a respectable female in shiny bombazine, all affability as she welcomed three such clear members of the Quality to her establishment.

"We are visiting Lady—" Cornelia stopped as Sally trod on her toe.

"Mrs. Devlin," Sally put in swiftly. "We understand that Mrs. Devlin is staying here." Judith's note, delivered to Sally by Sebastian, had warned them she was staying at Cunningham's Hotel under Marcus's family name.

"Oh, yes." Mrs Cunningham's smile broadened. "She has the best suite at the back—nice and quiet it is, as she wanted, looking over the garden. Dora will take you up and I'll have some tea sent up."

They followed the maidservant upstairs and along a corridor to double doors at the rear of the house.

Judith was sitting in a chair by the window, in front of a chess board, when her friends entered. She sprang up with a glad cry. "Oh, how good of you all to come. I was feeling thoroughly sorry for myself and horribly lonely."

"But of course we would come," Sally said, looking around the sitting room. It was pleasant enough, but nothing to the yellow drawing room in Berkeley Square. "Whatever are you about, Judith? Your note didn't explain, and Sebastian wouldn't say anything."

"Thinking," Judith replied. "That's what I'm about, but so far I haven't come up with any sensible thoughts . . . or even comforting ones," she added.

"Well, what's happened?" Cornelia sat on the sofa. "Why are you in this place?"

"It's a perfectly pleasant place," Judith said. "I have a large bedroom as well as the sitting room, and the woman who owns it is very attentive—"

"Yes, but why are you here?" Isobel interrupted this irrelevant defense of the accommodations.

Judith sighed. "Marcus and I had a dreadful fight. I had to get away somewhere quiet to think."

"You left your husband?" Even Cornelia was shaken. "You just walked out and came here?"

"In a nutshell. Marcus has forbidden my gaming and intends to control every penny I spend." Judith fiddled with the chess pieces as she told as much of the story as she could without revealing Brussels. "So, since I can't possibly accept such edicts," she finished, "and Marcus is determined that I will obey him, what else could I do?"

Isobel shook her head, saying doubtfully, "It seems a

bit extreme. Husbands do demand obedience as a matter of course. One has to find a way around it."

The maidservant brought tea. "Mrs. Cunningham wants to know if you'd like some bread and butter, ma'am? Or cake?"

"Cake," Isobel said automatically, and Judith chuckled, feeling a little more cheerful. She'd been fighting waves of desolation all day . . . desolation and guilt, whenever she thought of how that moment of willful passion on the road to Quatre Bras had ruined all their carefully laid plans. And Sebastian had so far uttered not a word of reproach.

"But what are you going to do, Judith?" Sally asked, having sat in silence for some time, absorbing the situation.

"I don't know," Judith said truthfully.

"But you can't just disappear. How would Marcus explain that?" Sally persisted. "The family . . ." She stopped with a helpless shrug. The might and prestige of the Devlin family were perhaps more apparent to her than to Judith. She'd been married into it for five years. The thought of damaging that prestige, of inviting the wrath of that might, sent a fearful shudder down her spine.

"Maybe I'll just be conveniently dead," Judith said. For some reason, the thought of her mother came to her. Her mother had died quietly in a French convent, leaving barely a ripple on the surface of the world . . . if you didn't count two children.

"Judith!" Cornelia protested. "Don't talk like that."

"Oh, I don't mean *really* dead," she explained. "I'll disappear and Marcus can put it about that I've died of typhus, or a riding accident, or some such."

"You're mad," Sally pronounced. "If you believe for

one minute that the Devlin family will let you get away with that, you don't know anything about them."

Judith chewed her lip for a minute. She had a horrible feeling that Sally was probably right. "I'm not thinking clearly at the moment," she said finally. "I'll worry about the details later. Tell me some gossip. I feel so isolated at the moment."

"Oh, there's a famous story going around about Hester Stanning," Isobel said. "I had it from Godfrey Chauncet." She lowered her voice confidentially.

Judith listened to the on-dit with half an ear, her mind working on some way in which she could still play her part with Gracemere. Maybe, for the denouement, Sebastian could arrange a private card party and she could make an unexpected appearance . . .

"Don't you think that's funny, Judith?"

"Oh . . . yes . . . yes, very funny." She returned to the room with a jolt.

"You weren't listening," Isobel accused, eyeing the chocolate cake that Dora had brought in. "I wonder if I dare have another piece. It's really very good."

Judith cut another slice for her. "I was listening," she said.

"When you fight with Carrington, do you lose your temper?" Cornelia asked with the air of one who'd been pondering the question for some time.

The question brought such a wave of longing washing through her that Judith was for a moment silent, lost in the memories of the times when they'd fought tooth and nail and then made up with ferocious need. "Yes," she admitted. "I have a dreadful temper, and so does Marcus."

"Good heavens," Cornelia said. "I can't imagine Forsythe losing his temper. I wonder if I should try to provoke it. It might add a bit of excitement to life."

Judith couldn't help laughing. "You're too level-headed and even-tempered, Cornelia. You'd start arguing with yourself instead of your husband, because you'd immediately see the other point of view."

After her visitors had left, she sat in the gloom of late afternoon. Cornelia and Sally and Isobel really didn't understand. They'd stand by her, of course. They'd keep her company and keep her secret, but they couldn't begin to understand what would drive a woman to take such a desperate stance. Never having tasted freedom—the sometimes uncomfortable freedom of life outside Society—they couldn't imagine doing anything so drastic. Judith didn't blame them for it. On the contrary, she envied the simplicity and security of their lives.

It was getting dark, but she didn't ring for Dora to light the candles. The growing shadows suited her mood and she could feel herself sliding deeper and deeper into a pit of wretchedness. She hurt every time she remembered what Marcus had said to her, what he believed her to be, every time she recalled that, believing such things of her, he had still made love to her in the way he had, with such trust, such honesty, such absolute oneness with her in body and spirit. She had entrusted herself to him in those moments, as he had entrusted himself to her. And yet all the time . . .

A knock at the door shattered the grim cycle of her thoughts. Sebastian entered, and she blinked in the near darkness.

"Why are you sitting in the dark?" He struck flint against tinder and lit the branched candlestick on the table. He subjected his sister to a comprehending scrutiny, one that confirmed his suspicions and satisfied him that he'd done the right thing that morning.

"I thought you might like some company for dinner," he said, as if he didn't notice her pallor or the sheen of tears in her eyes. "Mrs. Cunningham informs me that she has a carp in parsley sauce and a boiled fowl with mushrooms. Sounds quite appetizing, I thought."

Judith managed to blink back her tears. "Thank you, Sebastian," she said with composure. "I was dreading a solitary dinner."

"I rather thought that might be the case." He bent to kiss her. "Blue-deviled?"

"An understatement," she said. "What are we going to do about Gracemere?"

"It's not important at the moment." He pulled the chess board over to the fire. "We'll work something out once you've recovered your equilibrium."

"But—"

"Which hand?" Sebastian interrupted, offering his clenched fists.

"I only want—"

"Which hand?" he repeated.

Judith pointed to his left. He opened it to reveal the black pawn.

"Oh, good, I have the advantage," he said cheerfully, sitting behind the white pieces. "Sit down, Ju, and stop looking like a week of wet Mondays."

She sat down and watched him move his pawn to king four. She moved her own in response. "Have you seen Marcus?" She tried to keep the quaver from her voice.

"He paid me a visit this morning." He moved up his queen's pawn.

She made the ritual responding move. "What did he say?"

Sebastian examined the neat center arrangement of four pawns. "He wanted to know where you were." He brought out his knight.

Judith moved her own knight and they exchanged pawns. "What did you say?"

"That I was sworn to secrecy." Sebastian sat back. The ritual opening moves made, the real play would begin.

"Was he angry?"

"Not pleased," her brother said, bringing his queen's bishop into play. "But then you wouldn't expect him to put his neck under your foot, would you?"

"I'd expect him to be more understanding," she snapped, hunching over the board. "He makes no effort to understand me."

"Oh, I wouldn't say that," Sebastian said judiciously, waiting for his sister to make her move. "I think on the whole he has a fairly good handle on you, Ju."

"How can you say that?" Judith's hand hovered over her knight.

"He knows damn well that if he allows you to ride roughshod over him, you'll have no relationship at all," Sebastian said. "Be honest, Ju. Do you want some nodcock for a husband, a man who couldn't stand up to you?"

"No," she said. "Of course not. But why do we have to stand up to each other, Sebastian? That's what I don't understand."

Her brother shrugged. "It's the kind of people you are. I don't think you're going to change that, quite frankly."

"Harriet won't stand up to you," she observed.

"She won't have to," he responded promptly. "I won't give her cause. I intend to become a country bumpkin—a squire, devoted to farming and hunting and my children."

"Yes, because when you and Harriet make your vows, you'll do it without deception," Judith said, bitterness lacing her words. "You'll be the person she believes you to be. She'll know nothing of father, of Gracemere . . . and she'll never have to know. All of that will be in the past forever. It won't come back to destroy your marriage before it's ever really begun." Her voice choked and she turned aside from the board. "I'm sorry."

Sebastian handed her his handkerchief. He had no doubts now that his interference had been justified. "Make your move, Ju," he said, indicating the board. "It's true that my marriage would be founded on something different from yours, but maybe you could move beyond that with Marcus. Once it's all over—"

"How could I possibly?" she exclaimed. "And how can you talk like this anyway? After what he believes, what he's said, what he intends to do . . . ?"

"I know," Sebastian said soothingly. "It's insupportable, I agree. I was thinking you might consider going to that little village in Bavaria, where the Helwigs are. They invited you to stay with them whenever you wished. It might tide you over an awkward few months."

"Yes," Judith agreed, wondering why Sebastian's company was so irritating. She couldn't remember ever before finding it so.

It was close to midnight when he left. Young Tom, shivering in a doorway opposite, heaved a sigh of relief.

Surveillance was a tedious business, he reckoned, setting off after the gentleman-cove in the beaver hat and long cloak. It involved hanging around for hours outside houses and clubs, going without his dinner in case the cove came out unexpectedly. However, he could take his lordship unerringly to every one of the places visited by his quarry.

Sebastian hailed a passing hackney and the jarvey pulled over immediately. If Sebastian was aware of the nonpaying passenger clinging to the back of the carriage as it swung through the quiet streets of nighttime London, he gave no sign.

Tom sprang off as the carriage turned into Albemarle Street. It seemed his quarry was going home for the night, which left his follower free to make his report to his lordship, and hopefully find some supper in the kitchen, before seeking his own bed above the stables.

Marcus had had no stomach for company that evening and had remained by his own fireside, trying to divert his thoughts with Caesar's *Gallic Wars*. The diversion was only minimally successful since he found contemplation of the war in his own back garden to be much more compelling.

The library door opened. "Young Tom is here to see you, my lord."

"Send him in, Gregson."

Tom came in on the words. "Take your cap off, lad," Gregson directed in an outraged whisper. Stableboys were not usual library visitors.

Tom snatched off his cap and stood awkwardly, twisting it between his hands. "The cove's gone 'ome to 'is bed, m'lord," he offered in explanation for his end of duty. "I thought as 'ow you'd like me report straightway."

"I would, indeed. Have you had your dinner?"

"No, m'lord. I didn't know as 'ow I could leave the doorway . . . although the cove stayed put all evening," he added, somewhat aggrieved.

"Gregson, make sure there's a good supper waiting for him in the kitchen," Marcus instructed.

The butler bowed himself out in silence, and if he felt discommoded by being instructed to see to the welfare of a stablehand he managed to keep it hidden.

"So, Tom, what have you to report?"

Tom faithfully detailed Sebastian's movements

throughout the day. Uninterestingly routine for the most part: Jackson's saloon, Watier's, Viscount Middleton's lodgings, a drive in the park. However, the gem came at the shank of the rigidly chronicled day.

"Kensington, you say?" Marcus looked into the deep ruby depths of his glass of port. It sounded promising . . . unless Sebastian kept a mistress there. But Sebastian was in love with Harriet Moreton, and Marcus didn't think his brother-in-law would deem a mistress compatible with courtship, despite his unorthodox lifestyle.

"I could take you there, m'lord."

"Tomorrow will be soon enough, Tom. Get to your dinner now. You've done well."

Beaming, Tom left the library, basking in his god's approval that made an empty belly and the long hours of shivering in doorways well worth while.

Marcus threw another log on the fire and refilled his glass. Tomorrow he would retrieve his wife, and he'd make damn sure he hung onto her from now on.

22

𝔐arcus was up early the next morning, and within minutes the household was scurrying under a barrage of orders. Gregson was informed that his lordship was going into the country for a couple of weeks. Cheveley and Millie were instructed to pack for their employers and then to travel immediately to Berkshire. The traveling chaise with two outriders was ordered to be at the door by ten o'clock.

Marcus then strode down to the breakfast parlor, a distinct spring in his step. He was addressing a platter of sirloin when Charlie precipitately entered the parlor.

Marcus looked up in surprise, a smile of greeting on his lips. It died as he recognized Charlie's air of somewhat defensive bellicosity. It was a look he'd worn as a child when he considered his guardian guilty of some injustice and had screwed up his courage for a confrontation.

"What's to do, Charlie?" Marcus asked, without preamble.

"Where's Judith?" his young cousin demanded. "Gregson says she's gone to look after a sick aunt, but she doesn't have an aunt . . . sick or otherwise—at least not in England."

"Oh, how do you know that?" Marcus inquired calmly, refilling his coffee cup.

"Because she told me," Charlie stated. He glared at Marcus. "So where is she?"

"Sit down," Marcus said, gesturing to a chair. "And stop glowering at me, Charlie."

"I don't want to sit down," Charlie said. "I want to know where Judith is. I saw her yesterday and she didn't say she was going anywhere."

"Does she give you a report on all her movements?" Marcus asked gently.

Charlie's neck reddened and his scowl deepened. "Of course not, but she wouldn't go off without telling me. I know it."

Marcus sighed. "So what are you suggesting? You're surely not accusing me of disposing of her in some way, are you?" His eyebrows lifted quizzically.

Charlie's flush deepened at the sardonic question. "No, of course not . . . only . . . only . . ."

"Yes?" Marcus prompted.

"Only maybe you upset her in some way," his cousin blurted out. "I know how deuced cutting you can be when you're displeased."

Marcus frowned. "Am I really that unpleasant in our dealings, Charlie? I intend only to stand your friend."

"Yes, I know." Charlie fiddled with a fork on the table, in evident embarrassment. "It's just that you're devilish strict in some things, and you've a rough tongue that can make a fellow feel like a worm."

Marcus winced at this plain speaking, but was obliged to acknowledge there was some justice in the complaint. He examined his cousin thoughtfully. This couldn't be easy for Charlie, who was never comfortable asserting himself. Judith certainly had the power to inspire loyalty and friendship. He wondered why he hadn't been struck before by the strength of the attachments she'd formed in the few short months since she'd been in London.

"I only want to ensure that you have a fortune to come into when you reach your majority," he said mildly.

"But where's Judith?" Charlie sat down abruptly and stabbed at a rasher of bacon with the fork. "She's not hurt, is she?"

Marcus shook his head. "Not as far as I know, Charlie. And certainly not at my hands, if that's what you're thinking."

Charlie chewed bacon and swallowed. "But where is she?"

Marcus sighed. "In Kensington. But we're going to Carrington Manor today for a couple of weeks."

"Kensington?" Charlie's amazement was as great as if his cousin had said Judith was on the moon. "Whatever for?"

"Now that I'm afraid is a secret I'm not prepared to divulge," Marcus said firmly. "I appreciate your concern, Charlie, but I have to tell you that it's a matter that lies between Judith and myself. I don't mean to snub you, or to be in the least harsh, but I'm afraid it's none of your business."

Charlie stabbed a grilled mushroom from the serving platter. "But she's all right?"

"Yes, Charlie. She's perfectly all right." Marcus smiled, watching with great amusement his cousin's careless, unconscious consumption of a considerable breakfast.

"Oh, well, that's all right then." Charlie heaved a sigh of relief. "I didn't mean to pry, but, well, you know how it is with Judith . . . a fellow can't help worrying about her."

Marcus nodded. "Yes, Charlie, I know just how it is. Now, if you'll excuse me, I have things to do, so I'll leave you to your breakfast."

"Oh, I don't want breakfast," Charlie said. "I breakfasted in my lodgings before I came."

"Really? I wonder how I could have thought otherwise." Laughing, Marcus flung an affectionate arm around his cousin and squeezed his shoulders.

A short while later, he emerged from the house and climbed into the waiting chaise with the Carrington crest emblazoned on the panels.

Tom scrambled onto the box beside the coachman and proceeded to direct him through the streets to Cambridge Gardens.

Marcus stepped out and stood for a minute looking around the quiet crescent, then up at Judith's hideaway: a discreet, modest accommodation patronized by solid burghers and their ladies, he decided, stepping up to the door.

Mrs. Cunningham gazed from her front room window at the magnificent emblazoned equipage, with its two outriders, drawing up at her doorstep. Its tall, elegant occupant in buckskins and top boots, a cloak thrown carelessly around his shoulders, jumped down and stood looking at the house for a minute before approaching the front door.

"Dora . . . Dora . . . the door, immediately!" she

called, smoothing down her skirt as she billowed into the hall to greet her visitor.

Dora flung open the door before Marcus could touch the door knocker. "Good morning, sir."

"Good morning," he said with a pleasant smile, seeing the ample figure of Mrs. Cunningham behind the maid. "I understand you have a lady residing—"

"Oh, yes, sir, Mrs. Devlin, sir," Mrs. Cunningham supplied helpfully. This gentleman could only be inquiring after *one* of her guests.

"Ah . . . Mrs. Devlin," Marcus murmured with another smile. He'd been fairly certain Judith wouldn't have registered under Lady Carrington and had been wondering if this would present him with any problem. But the eagerly helpful landlady had resolved his difficulty.

"And is she in?" he inquired, when the landlady seemed uncertain how to proceed.

"Oh, yes, sir. She has a lady with her, I believe."

Marcus frowned at this, wondering who could be visiting Judith here. "Perhaps you'll show me up."

"Yes . . . yes . . . of course, sir. Dora, escort the gentleman."

"Thank you." Marcus moved to the staircase, then paused, one hand on the newel post. "Lady Carrington will be leaving immediately. If you would have her account made up, I'll settle it directly."

Lady Carrington! Confusion and excitement played over Mrs. Cunningham's countenance. "But, sir, nothing was said by Mrs. Dev—I mean, Lady . . ."

Marcus held up a hand, halting the tangle of protestation. "Nevertheless, ma'am, Lady Carrington will be leaving directly. I am Lord Carrington, you should understand."

Mrs. Cunningham gulped, curtsied. "Yes, my lord
. . . I didn't know . . ."

"How should you?" he said gently, turning to follow
Dora's bouncing rear up the stairs. At Judith's door, she
raised her hand to knock with a flourish.

"No, I'll announce myself," he said swiftly. He
waited until the disappointed maid had retreated down
the stairs, then he opened the double doors.

Judith and Sally were sitting head to head on the
window seat, deep in intense conversation, and both
looked up as the door opened.

Judith stared at her husband, her color fluctuating
wildly. "Marcus?" she whispered, as if unsure whether he
was real or a vision.

"Just so," he agreed. "It seems I must be the only
person in London not invited to visit you in your self-
imposed seclusion." He heard the caustic note in his
voice as he frowned at his sister-in-law. He'd prepared for
this moment with great care, but Sally's presence threw
all plans into disarray.

Sally had jumped up and instinctively moved closer
to Judith, who managed to ask in a cracked voice "What
are you doing here, Marcus?"

"I've come to retrieve my wife," he replied, shrugging out of his cloak. "Sally, I must ask you to excuse
us." He held the door in wordless command.

Sally hesitated, then stepped even closer to Judith.
"I'm sorry, Marcus, but I'm here at Judith's invitation."
She met his astounded stare without flinching, her shoulders stiffening as she prepared to defend her friend
against all comers, including irate husbands.

First Charlie and now Sally, Marcus thought with
resignation. What on earth had got into his usually docile family these days? Silly question . . . Judith's influ-

ence, of course. He repeated calmly, "Nevertheless, I must ask you to excuse us."

"No," Sally said, closing her lips firmly.

Marcus began to laugh. "My dear Sally, what do you think I'm going to do?"

"I don't know," Sally replied. "But I'm not going to stand aside while you bully Judith."

Marcus's jaw dropped at this, and Judith recovered the power of speech. "It's all right, Sally. Why don't you wait downstairs for a few minutes?"

Sally looked between them as if assessing the risks, then she said doubtfully, "If you're sure . . ."

"Sally, I don't want to have to put you out," Marcus exclaimed in exasperation.

"That's exactly what I mean," Sally fired back. "Judith, do you really want me to leave?"

Judith had sunk back onto the window seat, covering her eyes, aware that she was on the verge of hysterical laughter. "Yes, really," she said in a stifled voice. "Marcus won't hurt me. Anyway, I've got my pistol."

"Well, if you're sure. I'll be downstairs, so just call if you need me." Sally marched to the door, shooting Marcus a darkling look as she passed him.

"Good God!" he said, closing the door behind her. "I always thought she was such a mouse."

"That's because you intimidate her," Judith said. "She's not like that at all. She's bright and funny, and a lot cleverer than either you or Jack could ever guess."

"Well, if she was intimidated just then, you could have fooled me," Marcus observed with a rueful chuckle. "I wish I knew why people imagine I'm going to do you some mischief. They've clearly never looked down the muzzle of your pistol." He took off his gloves, tossing them with his cloak onto the sofa.

Judith watched him in silence. He seemed in great

good humor but that was surely impossible. For herself, her emotions were in such turmoil she didn't know what she felt.

After regarding her for a minute, Marcus said, "You really are the most exasperating creature, lynx. What on earth do you mean by running off like that? How the hell was I supposed to explain it?"

"I'm not particularly interested in how you explain it," she declared. "I'm not coming back."

"Oh, but you are," he said.

"I am not coming back to live in that prison you would construct for me!" she said, her throat closing as the hurt resurfaced. "You care only for appearances. Well, I don't give a tinker's damn for appearances, Carrington. You'll think of something to salvage your precious pride and keep up appearances, I'm certain of it." She swung away from him toward the window. "Just leave me out of it."

"Come here," he commanded.

Judith didn't move from the window, where she stood staring out at the scudding clouds, the stark lines of the bare elm trees, a black crow sitting on the wall at the bottom of the garden.

"Come here, Judith," he repeated in the same level voice.

She turned slowly. He was perched on the scrolled arm of the sofa and his eyes were quiet as they looked at her, his mouth soft. He beckoned, and she found herself moving across to him as if in response to gravity's pull.

He stood up as she reached him and reached out one hand, catching her chin. "Why didn't you tell me the truth?"

"What truth?" Her eyes seemed locked with his and the warm grasp of his hand on her chin seemed imprinted on her skin.

"That you didn't know who was in the taproom."

Shock flashed in her eyes. "How do you know?"

"Sebastian told me."

She jerked her chin out of his hand. "He had no right . . ."

"Nevertheless, he told me," Marcus said, reaching for her again. "Keep still and listen to me. It was unforgivable of me to assume the worst of you. I only wish you'd lost that formidable temper at the outset and put me in my place at once."

He smiled, but there was a hunger and a yearning in his gaze. "It was unforgivable, lynx, but can you forgive me?"

Sebastian had betrayed her. He knew the real reason why she hadn't been able to deny Marcus's accusations, and he'd chosen to ignore them in order to patch things up. Because of Gracemere? Because of Harriet?

"Say something," Marcus begged, running a finger over her mouth. "Please, Judith, say something. I can't let you leave me, my love, but I don't know how else to apologize. It was torment believing you had taken advantage of me, that you were only using our passion to your own advantage. It drove me insane to think I was no more to you than a means to an end. Can you understand that at all?"

"Oh, yes," she said softly. "Yes, I can understand it." And yet even now as his words filled her with sweet joy, she knew that she continued to deceive him. He was still a means to an end, and yet he'd become so much more than that.

"Judith?" Marcus said, softly insistent. "I need more than understanding."

She grasped his wrist tightly. "It's over. We'll put it behind us."

Marcus brought his mouth to hers in a hard affirming kiss. Judith clung to him, desperate to grasp whatever happiness they could have in their remaining time together. Desperate to believe that there was a chance he'd never find out about Gracemere.

"How did you find me?" she asked, when finally he raised his mouth from hers.

"Through Sebastian." He smiled down at her, touching the line of her jaw with a lingering finger.

"He didn't tell you!"

"Not in so many words. I had him followed."

"Good heavens," Judith said. "How very theatrical of you."

Marcus shook his head in disclaimer. "When it comes to theatricals, my love, you're unsurpassed. That dead-of-night flight through a window was an outrageous piece of melodrama." He bundled her into his arms, kissing her again.

"Just one more thing . . ." Judith murmured against his mouth. "All that other business . . ."

"Ah." He released her reluctantly. "I've instructed my bankers that you're free to draw on the account. We're joint partners in this marriage and therefore in the fortune that maintains us both. I'll not question your expenditure again, any more than you question mine."

Hiding her bittersweet emotions at his trust in her, she gave him a brilliant smile. "Now that, sir, is an inventive and generous solution to an apparently intractable problem."

"But no more high-stakes gaming." He pinched her nose. "And if I see you within a hundred yards of a gaming hell, my love, I can't answer for the consequences. Understood?"

"Understood. I'll confine myself to social play from now on."

"Good. And now we're going into Berkshire for a

couple of weeks, so ring for the maidservant to pack your traps."

"Into Berkshire? Now?"

"This very minute."

"Why?"

"Because I say so," he declared cheerfully. "Now, I'd better go and reassure Sally that you're still in one piece." He shook his head in amazement. "I wonder if Jack knows what a spirited creature she is when roused."

"Probably not," Judith said, chuckling. "And it's clearly your fraternal duty to enlighten him."

In his sister's absence Sebastian devoted himself to courting Harriet. Lady Moreton watched with growing complacence, expecting each day to bring a formal offer for her daughter's hand. Sebastian fretted silently over his powerlessness to act, but until he was in possession of his birthright, he had nothing to offer a wife. Only Harriet was sunnily untroubled by the waiting, secure and trusting in the knowledge of Sebastian's love.

None of them was aware of the threat hanging over their happiness. The threat took concrete shape in a bedchamber in a tall house overlooking the River Thames. The mullioned casement rattled under the blustery winter wind from the river, and the fire in the grate spurted as needles of wind pierced tiny cracks between the panes.

Agnes drew a cashmere wrap tightly around her body as she slipped from the bed, her body languid with fulfillment despite the nip in the air. She went to the fire, bending to warm her hands.

"I swear the wretched chit sees and hears nothing that's not done or said by Sebastian," she said as if an interlude of passion hadn't broken their previous conversation. "How many times did you compliment her on her hat this afternoon before she seemed to hear you, let alone respond?"

"At least six," Gracemere responded, flipping open a delicate porcelain snuffbox. "Give me your wrist."

Smiling, Agnes straightened and held out her hand, wrist uppermost. The earl dropped a pinch of snuff exactly where her pulse throbbed and raised her wrist to his nose, breathing in the snuff. His lips lightly brushed her skin and then he dropped her hand and returned to the subject.

"Clearly Harriet's not to be wooed and won, therefore she must be taken."

"When?" Agnes moistened her lips. "You can't wait until Sebastian has declared himself."

"True enough. I will wait until I've bled Sebastian as white as it's possible—which should ruin his chances with Moreton anyway. And then we shall act." His lips tightened so that his mouth was a fleshy gash in his thin face.

"I don't doubt you, Bernard." Agnes touched his mouth with a fingertip. "Not for one minute."

He grasped her wrist again, sucking the finger into his mouth. His teeth bit down and his eyes stared down into hers, watching the pain develop, the excitement flare under the defiant challenge to endure. Agnes laughed, making no attempt to free her finger. She laughed, her head falling back, exposing the white column of her throat.

Gracemere released her wrist and circled her throat with his hands. "We *are* worthy of each other, my dear Agnes."

"Oh, yes," she whispered.

It was a long time before she spoke again. "With Judith and Carrington out of town, you must be missing a degree of entertainment."

Gracemere chuckled. "I have my plans well laid for her return. I may need you as message bearer, my dear."

"Messenger to whom?"

"Why, to Carrington, of course." A meager smile snaked over his lips. "There'd be no point compromising his wife if he's not to be aware of it."

"Oh, no," Agnes agreed. "None whatsoever. I'll convey the message of tarnished virtue with the utmost subtlety and the greatest pleasure."

"I thought the role might appeal to you, my love."

Judith clung to a shadowy corner of the conservatory. Her heart was beating swiftly with excitement and anticipation, her palms damp, moisture beading her brow from the exertion of the chase and the lush, hothouse atmosphere. The air was rich with the mingled, exotic scents of orchids, roses, and jasmine. The domed glass roof above her revealed the night sky, black infinity pricked with stars and the crescent sliver of the new moon offering the only light.

She had closed the drawing-room door that led into the conservatory, and the heavy velvet curtains had swung back, preventing the penetration of light from the house. Her ears strained to hear the sound of the door opening, the tap of a footstep on the smooth paving stones between the rows of shrubs and flowers. Would he guess where she was hiding? It was a relatively classic place for hide-and-seek. But then, it wasn't as if she didn't want to be found.

She stifled her laughter. Marcus had proved remarkably receptive to her penchant for nursery games. When she wasn't teasing him with outrageously provocative comments, which always produced the desired results, she was challenging him to horseraces through the meadow, making wagers on which raindrop would reach the bottom of the window first, throwing sticks from the bridge into the river and rushing to the other side to see which one was the first to emerge. They did nothing without laying odds, and the stakes were never for money. Indeed, they tried to outdo each other with the most imaginative and enticing wagers.

They'd spent the afternoon skating on the frozen horse pond, competing over who could make the most elaborate figures on the ice. Since Judith was no match for Marcus, who'd been skating on the pond every winter since early childhood, she'd spent a fair part of the afternoon on her backside. Marcus had made the most of the resulting bruises.

Hiding in her corner of the conservatory, ears stretched into the gloom for the slightest sound, Judith re-created the feel of his hands on her body, smoothing oil into the bruises he insisted he was discovering . . .

The door creaked, and there was a crack of light. It was extinguished so quickly, she could almost have imagined it. But she heard the faintest *click* as the door was closed again. There was silence, but she knew Marcus was in the conservatory. She could sense his presence just as she knew he could sense hers. Stepping backward on tiptoe, barely daring to breathe, she moved behind a potted orange tree, shrinking down into the deeper shadow, hugging herself as if she could thus make herself smaller. Her heart thudded in her ears as she waited to be discovered, as apprehensive as if she were truly being stalked by a predator.

Marcus stood by a bay tree, accustoming his eyes to the dimness, trying to sense where she was hiding. The conservatory was a wide, square building attached to the house, and he knew his quarry could evade him if he took off in the wrong direction. She could creep behind him to the door and be free and clear, with the rest of the vast house to offer for a further hiding place. But he was growing impatient with the game; he had another scenario in mind and was anxious to begin. The enticing curve of Judith's backside seemed imprinted on his palms, and his loins grew heavy at the thought of another anointing session, a more prolonged one—one that could continue until dawn if he chose.

He picked up a small scratching sound, tiny enough to have been a mouse. He stayed still, listening. It had come from the far corner and he stared into the gloom, straining his eyes to catch some movement in the shadows that wouldn't be a trick of the moonlight. The silence stretched, then a shower of gravel rolled across the paving from the same direction as the scratching. Marcus chuckled softly. Obviously Judith was also anxious to bring the game to a close.

Silently he removed his shoes, then trod on tiptoe toward the corner, hugging the shadows, hoping to surprise her, despite her clues. He thought he could detect a darker mass in the shadow of an orange tree, and with mischievous intent moved sideways, so that he could approach the tree from behind.

Judith crouched in her hiding place, listening for the sound of footfalls. Surely he'd picked up on her pointers. But she could hear nothing.

"Found you!"

Judith shrieked in genuine shock at the exultant statement from behind her. Marcus laughed. Bending, he caught her under the arms and hauled her to her feet.

"You lose, I believe."

Judith sank against him; her knees were quivering absurdly. "You frightened me!"

"I thought that was the point of the game. Hunter

and prey . . . quarry and predator." He stroked her hair where it rested against his chest.

"I know it is, but I didn't expect you to terrify me." She straightened, pushing against his chest, her smile a pearly glimmer in the dimness. "Sebastian never terrified me when we used to play as children. I always heard him coming."

"Perhaps maturity brings greater subtlety," he murmured, glancing down at his stockinged feet.

Judith followed his gaze and burst into a peal of laughter. "You took your shoes off!"

"Observant of you . . . but, since I found you, I believe you owe me a forfeit, ma'am."

Judith narrowed her eyes. "But would you have found me if I hadn't given you those clues?"

"That, I'm afraid, we'll never know."

She chewed her bottom lip in thought. "But I still wonder if the possibility doesn't alter the original terms of the agreement."

Marcus shook his head. "No, ma'am, it does not. I discovered you . . . most completely, I would have said."

"I suppose that's true."

"So, I claim my reward."

Judith smiled. "Very well, then. And you can pay your forfeit afterward."

"Since when have winners also paid a forfeit?" Marcus demanded.

"Since I decided to make the rules," she retorted. "This was not a winner-takes-all proposition."

A long time later, Judith lay sprawled in wanton abandonment under glowing candlelight, the thick pile of the library carpet against her back and shoulders. Marcus held her buttocks on the palms of his hands, lifting her for his own dewy caresses. One couldn't draw qualitative comparisons between the joys of the pleasure giver and the receiver, she decided, her hips arcing under the fierce and fiery strokes of his tongue, the delicate grazing of his mouth.

Around them, the house was silent, only the hiss and spurt of the fire disturbing the quiet. Its heat was on her bared thigh, matching the rising heat in her loins. The coil burst asunder, taking her by surprise, as sometimes it did. She laughed softly, feeling his breath warm on her heated core as he laughed with her, in his own pleasure at her surprised release.

When he rolled, bringing her with him, she lay along his length, feeling her own softnesses pressing into the muscled concavities of his body. He parted her thighs, slowly twisted his hips, and thrust upward within the still-pulsating entrance to her body. Judith tightened around him, pushing backward until she knelt astride him. She moved herself over and around him in languid circles, teasing them both. With the same languor, she turned her head toward the uncurtained French doors. The moonlit lawn stretched beyond the windows, the frosty grass sparkling. It occurred to her that she was truly, completely happy, for the first time in her life.

There had never been room for unalloyed happiness before. But at this moment, fused in passion, even revenge somehow had lost its spur . . . was somehow irrelevant. Soon enough, they'd return to London and she would have to go to work on Gracemere again, but she wasn't going to think of that now.

She brought her mouth to his.

23

"I hope you enjoyed your retreat, Judith." Bernard Melville guided his dance partner into a smooth turn.

Judith sighed. "No, it was extremely tedious. The country's so boring, and Carrington was closeted with his man of business the entire time."

"And he insisted you accompany him?" Gracemere shook his head and tutted. "How unkind of him. But then, as we know, Carrington has little interest in the preferences of others." His hand tightened on hers.

Judith controlled her shudder of revulsion and smiled up at him with a flutter of her eyelashes. "How true," she agreed. Her eyes darted swiftly around the crowded ballroom in a guilty check to assure herself that Marcus hadn't decided to abandon his own party and pay a surprise visit to the Sedgewicks' ball. Not that there was anything overtly wrong in dancing with the earl in public. Marcus himself was civil to Gracemere in company.

"My Lady Carrington was sorely missed," he assured her, a smile flickering on the fleshy lips.

"Nonsense, my lord. You know full well that redheads are not fashionable at the moment." Her laughing eyes flirtatiously invited his denial of this caveat.

He provided it without blinking an eye. "Red is not the description I would have chosen," he murmured, flicking at a copper ringlet with one finger. "And part of your charm, my dear Judith, is that you are not at all in the common way."

Judith gave him a coy look and changed the subject. "You're an accomplished card player, I understand."

"Oh, shameless evasion!" he exclaimed. "Is that your only response to my compliment?"

"Indeed, sir, a lady doesn't respond to compliments made her by stray dance partners." Her eyelashes fluttered as she gave him a mischievous smile.

"Stray dance partner! I must protest, ma'am, at such an unkind description."

"I must try to think of you in such terms, however, since I'm forbidden to consider you a friend," she responded archly.

Gracemere's pale eyes glittered. "But, as we're agreed, husbands need occasionally to be put in their places."

Judith's eyes gleamed with a conspiratorial thrill that brought a complacent smile to the earl's mouth—one that made her want to kick him hard in the shins. Fortunately, the waltz ended and he escorted her off the floor.

"My brother assures me that you're a most accomplished card player," she reiterated as they went into a small salon adjoining the ballroom.

"Your brother is a fair player himself." Gracemere offered the lie with a bland smile.

"But not as good as I am," Judith declared, closing her fan with a snap. "I challenge you to a game of piquet, my lord." She gestured to a small, unoccupied card table in the corner of the room.

"An enticing prospect," he said, with the same bland smile. "What stakes do you propose?"

Judith tapped her closed fan against her hand. "Ten guineas a point?"

Gracemere smiled at the proposal: the moderate stakes of a relatively confident gamester, who liked to think she played high. He'd seen her at the card tables and knew that Agnes had met her at Amelia Dolby's, so she couldn't be a complete novice. Presumably she played like her brother, with more enthusiasm than skill. "Stakes for a tea party, ma'am," he scoffed. "I propose something a little more enticing."

"What do you suggest, my lord?" Judith had expected him to accept her wager indulgently, and unease stirred beneath her expression of eager curiosity.

He stroked his chin, regarding her. "The honor of your company at a private dinner against . . . against . . . now, what could I offer you?" he mused.

Your head on a platter, Judith thought viciously. She had every intention of losing to him but no intention whatsoever of joining him in a tête-à-tête dinner. However, that bridge would have to be crossed when she reached it. "The chance to drive your blacks in Richmond Park," she suggested in dulcet accents. "I've envied you those horses since I first saw them."

"Then let us play, ma'am." He moved to the card table.

Judith had only one purpose behind the game: She wanted to know how he played, what habits he had, what techniques he favored. Then she and Sebastian would compare notes. As Gracemere had destroyed George Devereux playing piquet, so would Gracemere meet his own Waterloo at the hands of George's children.

She took her seat at the table with a fidgety eagerness, watching as he broke the pack. She didn't think he would bother to cheat with her; she'd been careful never to play at his table before, so he wouldn't know how well she played. He would probably assume she was a moderate player at best.

She gave him a middling performance, losing the first hand by a respectably small margin, winning the second by the appearance of a lucky retention, losing the third convincingly, but avoiding the Rubicon.

"You're certainly an accomplished player, Bernard," she said, smiling as he counted the points. "Perhaps one day you'd teach me some of your strategies." *What a delicious thought that was. . . . She knew now she was a fair match for Bernard Melville, in honest play or crooked.* She continued to smile, savoring the thought.

Bernard chuckled. "With pleasure, my dear. But first, I claim my winnings."

"But of course. However . . ." She glanced around the room. "We've already dined tonight, and this is hardly a private spot."

He chuckled again. "No, you must allow me to make the necessary arrangements, Judith. I'll inform you of the date, place, and time."

"I think, sir, that you must allow me to pick the date," she said carefully. "I'm not a free woman."

"No." Reaching for her hand, he carried it to his lips. "You are not. But are you a virtuous woman?" He smiled over her hand. "An improper question, forgive me, ma'am. . . . However, I firmly believe that you will find a tale to satisfy Carrington, when the need arises."

She would shoot him—no, that was too quick . . . a long and lingering death . . . "I daresay I could." She stood up. "But now I must return to the ballroom before anyone notices such a protracted absence."

Gracemere bowed and remained standing by the table, watching as she wafted back to the ballroom. Whatever tale she invented to put Carrington off the scent, the marquis would be apprised of his wife's intimate, clandestine rendezvous with his old enemy. The prospect of such a wonderfully apposite revenge was a heady one. But now, having played the sister, he would play her brother for rather more material stakes.

He made his way to the card room, where the serious play was taking place. Sebastian sat at the macao table and waved cheerfully at him. "Come and take a hand, Gracemere."

"Thank you." He sat down opposite Sebastian. "I just had a hand or two of piquet with your sister."

"Oh, did you win? Ju's not much of a player," Sebastian said, grinning, laying out his rouleaux.

"Calumny!" Judith's voice came from the doorway.

"But did you win?" her brother challenged, frowning over his cards before making his bet.

"No," she admitted, moving to stand behind the earl. "His lordship was more than my match, I fear."

Gracemere looked up. "The cards fell in my favor," he demurred. "I trust you're going to bring me luck now, Lady Carrington."

"Oh, I trust so," she murmured, smiling around the table. She had absorbed Gracemere's hand in a glance that barely skimmed his cards and now continued to look smilingly around the table, her fan moving lazily in front of her face.

Lord Sedgewick held the bank. His appreciative gaze rested on Lady Carrington. She was a devilishly attractive woman. Catching his eye, she smiled at him, and Sedgewick felt a distinct prickle of arousal. Marcus was a lucky dog, but then again such a woman would take a deal of handling. His lordship wondered slightly uneasily whether he himself would be up to such a task. He thought of his own wife, a matron of even temper with little interest in matters of the bedchamber beyond those necessary to ensure the succession. Lady Carrington, on the other hand, gave the distinct impression of one who might play rather nicely. . . .

Sedgewick forced his attention back to the cards. It was unseemly to think in such fashion of another man's wife. But she *was* devilishly attractive . . . and that wicked smile, when just the corners of her mouth lifted . . .

Sebastian glanced up now and again from his cards, joining in the lively conversation around the table. Judith was not the only woman standing at the table, observing the play; she was, however, the only one employing her fan. But then it was such an ordinary activity, only Sebastian truly took note.

Gracemere lost three hundred guineas to the bank in half an hour. It didn't strike him as remarkable that whenever he thought he had a winning count, Davenport played one better, declaring his hand before the earl was ready to declare his. Sebastian wasn't always the winner at the table, but Gracemere was always the loser. He put it down to ill luck.

Judith drifted out of the card room. She and Sebastian had only been practicing. They hadn't practiced in public since Brussels and both needed to see how they would handle Gracemere. The final act was fast approaching.

"Judith?"

Harriet's soft voice broke pleasantly into her musings.

"Harriet, I didn't see you here before." She drew the girl's arm through hers. "Let's go and sit by the window, it's so hot in here. You arrived late. Sebastian's been looking for you."

"Lady Barret was detained. She couldn't come for me until after eleven," Harriet confided. "And Mama is indisposed." A delicate flush mantled her cheek. "I haven't seen your brother. I thought perhaps he'd already left."

Judith chuckled. "He wouldn't leave if he was expecting to see you. He's in the card room."

Harriet received this information in silence. Her eyes were downcast while her fingers played with the silk fringe on her reticule. Gently, Judith asked if something was troubling her.

Without looking up, Harriet said, "I-I sometimes think that . . . I sometimes think that your brother plays too much," she finished in a rush.

Judith nibbled her lip. Harriet was a great deal more observant than she'd given her credit for. "He enjoys gaming," she said neutrally. "But I can safely promise you, Harriet, that he will never jeopardize your happiness, and therefore his own, with reckless play."

Harriet sighed with relief and looked up at Judith, her expression radiant, the clear eyes sparkling. "You believe that, Judith? I was so afraid he was a true gamester."

"Oh, yes," Judith said, placing her hand over Harriet's. "Not only do I believe it, Harriet, I *know* it. That doesn't mean he's not a gamester," she added judiciously. "But if he's away from the tables, he'll not miss them."

"Secrets . . . do you exchange secrets?" Agnes Barret's falsely cheery voice sounded from behind them.

"Good evening, Lady Barret," Judith said, unable to disguise the chill in her voice. "No, I don't believe Harriet and I share any secrets."

"No, indeed not," Harriet agreed, blushing and transparently flustered.

Lady Barret's gaze rested on her for a minute, a slightly contemptuous smile on her lips, before she turned back to Judith, who met the now cool and calculating scrutiny with one of her own. The animosity between them seemed to crackle and even Harriet was aware of it, her eyes darting between the two women.

"I understand you've recently returned from Berkshire, Lady Carrington." Agnes bowed.

"My husband had some estate business to attend to," Judith said, returning the bow.

Minimal courtesies satisfied, Agnes turned back to Harriet. "Harriet, my dear, should you object to remaining a little longer? I've promised to take up Lord Gracemere as far as his house when we leave, but he's engaged in the card room." A trilling laugh accompanied the explanation. "I don't think your mama will worry, since she knows you're with me."

Harriet mumbled something, but her eyes flickered toward Judith in a distinct plea.

"I'm about to order my own carriage," Judith suggested immediately. "If Harriet's fatigued, I'd be glad to take her home on my way. I'm sure Lady Moreton will find nothing to object to in such an arrangement."

"Oh, no," Harriet agreed hastily. "And, in truth, Lady Barret, I do find myself a little fatigued." She touched her temples and offered a wan smile. "I fear I'm getting the headache . . . it's so hot in here."

Judith read naked malevolence in the split-second glare Agnes directed at her. It chilled her, yet she met it with a slightly triumphant lift of her eyebrows. They *were* on a battleground . . . but what battleground and over what issue?

Routed, Agnes bowed, offered Harriet her sympathy, promised to call upon her and Letitia in the morning, and left them.

"Thank you," Harriet whispered.

Judith chuckled. "Don't thank me. Your performance was impeccable. I could almost believe in your headache myself. Let's go and drag Sebastian from the card room, and he will escort us home."

The suggestion found immediate favor with Harriet, and the two went in search of Sebastian. However, when they entered the card room, a strange expression crossed Sebastian's face. He cast in his hand immediately and came over to them.

"You shouldn't be in here," he said to Harriet almost brusquely, leading her back to the ballroom.

"We came to fetch you," Judith said, puzzled. "We thought you might escort us both home."

"With the greatest pleasure." He seemed to recollect himself, but his expression was still a little black. "I'll order your carriage immediately."

"What's the matter?" Judith whispered, as Harriet went off to fetch her cloak.

"I don't want Harriet in the card room," he stated with low-voiced vehemence. "It's no place for her."

"Oh." Judith followed Harriet to the retiring room, considering this. Sebastian wanted no taint of the gaming tables to touch his future wife. Interesting. For Sebastian, such places were associated with all that he intended to put behind him once Gracemere had paid his dues. They carried the taint of unscrupulous play, of desperation, of poverty and anger and injustice. But didn't they also carry the memories of the bond between himself and his sister? Of the years when all they'd had was each other?

The thought that she and Sebastian could be growing apart saddened her.

Marcus had just arrived home when the chaise deposited his wife at her own door. "I was about to come in search of you at the Sedgewicks'," he said as she came into the hall. "Did you have a pleasant evening?" He held open the door to the library.

Flirting with Gracemere and cheating at cards. An evening of deceit. She'd thought she'd be able to carry it off by reminding herself of the vital need for secrecy, of how much rode on maintaining that secrecy, but instead, at the sound of his voice, waves of panic broke over her. She could feel the color flooding her cheeks, sweat trickling beneath her arms, moistening her palms. How could Marcus possibly not sense her guilt? Her instinct was to plead fatigue and run upstairs without further conversation. Instead she forced herself to behave normally.

"Pleasant enough, thank you." She went past him into the library.

Now why the devil wouldn't she look at him properly? He could feel her jangling like an ill-hung bell.

"A glass of port before bed?" Marcus suggested, lifting a decanter from the salver on the pier table.

"I'd prefer Madeira, I think." She shrugged out of her evening cloak, dropping it on the couch, and went over to the window overlooking the square. She drew back the curtains, saying brightly, "It's a frosty night."

"Yes," he agreed, setting her glass of wine on a table, regarding her with puzzled amusement as she continued to stare out of the window. "What's so absorbing in the square at this time of night?"

She shrugged, laughed faintly, and turned back to the room. "Nothing, of course. For some reason I feel restless."

Marcus decided the insouciance lacked conviction.

"I wonder why you should feel restless." He sipped port, looking at her over the rim of his glass. "What have you been up to, lynx?"

"Up to? Whyever should I be up to anything?"

"You tell me." He continued to scrutinize her until her color deepened.

"It was a tedious crush," she said, taking an overlarge sip of her wine. "I daresay that's why I feel so restless."

"That would of course explain it," he observed gravely.

Judith shot him a suspicious glance. Her husband looked amused but far from satisfied. She yawned. "I'm tired. I think I'll go up to bed."

"But I thought you felt restless," he pointed out unhelpfully.

Judith nibbled a fingernail. "I do and I don't. It's a very peculiar feeling."

"Perhaps we should take a turn around the square," he suggested. "A little exercise in the night air might help you decide exactly which of the two you feel."

"Oh, stop teasing me, Marcus!" she exclaimed in frustration, wondering desperately how she could deflect the course of this inquiry. He *could* sense her guilt, although never in a blue moon would he be able to guess at how dire it was. However, that was no particular help.

"My apologies, ma'am." He came over to her and took the glass from her hand. "Let's go upstairs and I'll endeavor to wrest the truth from you by some other means of persuasion."

"There is no truth. I don't know what you're talking about."

"Don't you?" His eyebrows lifted. "Well, let me explain. I know that either you *have* been wading hip deep in trouble this evening, or that you're planning to do so."

"How can you know that . . . I mean, you can't

know it because there's nothing to know." Crossly she bit her lip at this inept denial.

Marcus shook his head. "If you'd not been up to mischief, lynx, you'd tell me what was bothering you. Since you're trying very hard to persuade me to drop the subject, I can only assume it's something I won't like."

This was dreadful. "You're talking to me as if I were a child, instead of a grown woman who's just come back from a tedious ball," she said, trying for an assumption of affronted dignity.

Marcus shook his head. "It won't do, Judith. Cut line, and tell me what mischief you've been brewing."

Desperately Judith cast around for something harmless to confess that would satisfy him. "I'm just being silly," she mumbled finally. "I don't want to talk about it." *Silly about what? Talk about what?* She had no idea, and crossed her fingers behind her back, hoping he would leave it at that. A vain hope.

"You're rather closing out my options," he observed, regarding her consideringly.

There was something about the look that put Judith instantly on her guard. The amusement was still there and there was a deeply sensual glimmer in the background, but these were not as reassuring as they might have been. There was a coiled purpose in the powerful frame, determination in the set of his mouth and the firmness of his jaw.

"You're making a mountain out of a molehill." She tried for a light touch again. "I'm out of sorts because I had a tedious evening and have the beginnings of a headache." It was feeble, and she wasn't much surprised that it didn't work.

"Fustian!" was Marcus's uncompromising response. "You're up to something, and it's been my invariable experience that when you decide to keep something from me, it develops into the most monumental bone of contention. I am not prepared to join battle with you yet again . . . either now, or at some point in the future when whatever it is is finally brought unassailably to my attention. So you will oblige me with chapter and verse, if you please."

If she hadn't had such a weight on her conscience, Judith could have responded to this provocation in the manner it deserved. But tonight she was too cowed by the truth to fight back. "Please," she said, pressing her temples. "I am truly too tired to be bullied."

"*Bullied!*" Marcus was momentarily thrown off balance. "I want to know what's troubling you, and I'm bullying you?"

"You don't want to know what's the matter," she cried, stung by this clear misrepresentation of the conversation so far. "You believe I've been up to something and I'm keeping it from you. That's not the same thing, I'll have you know."

"In my book, where you're concerned, Judith, it is." He shook his head with every appearance of reluctant resignation. "Oh, well, have it your own way. Don't say you weren't warned."

"*Marcus!*" Judith shrieked, as she found herself lifted onto a low table. His shoulder went into her stomach and the next instant, she was draped over his shoulder, staring at the carpet, her ringlets, falling loose from the ivory and pearl fillet, tumbling over her face.

"Yes, my dear?" he asked, all solicitude as he strode with her to the door.

"Put me down!" She pummeled his back with her fists and sneezed as her hair tickled her nose. The absurdity of her position struck her with full force as they reached the hall. Her gown of emerald taffeta was hardly suited to such rough handling, and the pearl drops in her ears dangled ludicrously against Marcus's back. She kicked her feet violently in their white satin slippers.

"When we get upstairs," he said calmly, placing a steadying hand on her upturned rear, but other than that ignoring her gyrations.

"But the servants." Judith gasped. "You can't possibly carry me through the house in this mortifying fashion."

"Can I not?" Laughter quivered in his voice. "You've had every opportunity to be cooperative, lynx."

Judith subsided with a groan, closed her eyes tightly and prayed that everyone had gone to bed . . . everyone, that is, except for Millie and Cheveley. She reared up against his shoulder at the thought. "Oh, God. Marcus, you have to let me walk into my room."

"Do I?"

"Please!"

He stopped, halfway up the stairs. "If you tell me straightway what I want to know, I'll allow you to enter your room on your own two feet."

"Oh, God," Judith muttered again. But inspiration came to her in the same instant. It must have something to do with all that blood rushing to her head. It wouldn't be a lie, either, just half the truth.

When she didn't immediately reply to his ultimatum, Marcus resumed climbing the stairs, carrying his burden seemingly with the greatest of ease.

"Please!" she yelped as they reached the head of the stairs. "Put me down and I'll tell you as soon as we're in my room. I will, I promise."

Marcus made no reply, merely continued down the corridor to Judith's chamber. At the door, however, mercifully, he stopped. "Word of a lynx?"

"Word of a Davenport," she said with a gasp. "I

couldn't bear to be carried in there like a sack of potatoes."

Laughing, he lowered her to the floor, holding her waist as her feet touched ground. "I did tell you I had various methods of persuasion to hand."

Judith brushed her hair out of her eyes and tried to smooth her much-abused gown. She glared up at him, her face pink with indignation and the results of her upside-down journey. "How could you?"

"Very easily." He opened the door for her, gesturing she should precede him, offering a gently mocking bow.

"Lawks-a-mercy, my lady!" Millie squawked, jumping up from her chair. "Look at your dress." She stared with some disbelief at Judith's rumpled gown and wildly tumbled ringlets.

"I feel as if I've been dragged through a hedge backward," Judith declared, shooting her husband a fulminating glare.

Marcus grinned. "You may have fifteen minutes to prepare yourself for bed, ma'am. Then you will fulfill your side of the bargain."

"Some bargain," Judith muttered as the connecting door closed on his departure. "Help me undress, Millie. Fifteen minutes is no great time."

"No, my lady. But whatever's happened?"

"It's his lordship's idea of a joke," Judith told her, peering at her image in the cheval glass. "What a mess!"

Millie helped Judith into her nightgown and brushed her hair, returning order to the copper cloud. "If that'll be all, I'll take this for sponging and pressing, m'lady." She picked up the much-abused gown on her way to the door.

"Yes, thank you, Millie. Good night."

Judith blew out all but one candle and hopped swiftly into bed, propping the pillows behind her head, pulling the sheet up to her chin, offering her husband a demure bedtime image when he came in to hear her explanation. Her guilty panic had vanished under the spur of action, and now she knew how to handle the situation, she was as calm as if she were playing for high stakes on Pickering Street.

"Well, madam wife?" Marcus closed the door behind him and trod to the darkened bed. "You may look as if butter wouldn't melt in your mouth, but I know better. Out with it!" He snapped his fingers.

Judith frowned and sat up straight against the pillows. "I told you it was silly and I was making a mountain out of a molehill, but since you insist, then I'll tell you. It's Agnes Barret." She sat back again, with the air of one who has discharged a difficult but possibly pointless duty.

"Agnes Barret?" Marcus sat on the end of the bed. "Explain."

"I don't know how to," she said, and the ring of truth was in the admission. "She upsets me dreadfully. I feel as if we're fighting some war to the death, but I don't know what the issue is or what the weapon is. Whenever I'm obliged to talk to her, I feel as if an entire regiment is tramping over my grave."

"Good God!" Marcus lifted the candle, holding it high so that her face was thrown into relief. He could read the truth in her eyes. "So what happened tonight?"

She shrugged. "We just had words . . . or, at least, not even that, but I prevented her from driving Harriet home and she was furious. We exchanged looks, I think you could say. For some reason, she's cultivating Harriet." She plucked at the coverlet. "I believe Agnes and Gracemere are lovers."

Marcus frowned. "It's not inconceivable, I suppose. I

gather they've known each other from childhood. Why should it concern you?"

"It makes things awkward," she said, catching a loose thread on the sheet and twisting it restlessly around her finger. "That's why I didn't want to talk about this. I think Gracemere is trying to court Harriet—only she won't have anything to do with him—and Agnes is constantly trying to throw them together."

"I see." It was a flat statement. Harriet wouldn't be the first heiress to receive Gracemere's attentions, Marcus mused. But if she was holding him at arm's length, she was no Martha. Presumably Sebastian was a more potent counterweight to Gracemere's courting than he had been.

"You're scowling," Judith said. "And I haven't said anything yet to annoy you."

He banished the scowl with the memories and smiled. "Oh, dear, lynx, are you about to?"

"I don't know whether it will or not," she said judiciously, still twisting the thread.

"Out with it!"

"Well, whenever I'm with Harriet and she's with Agnes, Gracemere is usually not too far away." She looked up at him, her dark eyebrows in a quizzical arch. "I didn't want to bring up a potentially contentious subject."

"My dear, Gracemere is not a contentious subject so long as you don't encourage him. You can't help but be in his company on occasion, and I won't shrivel and die at the mention of his name," he commented with a wry smile.

"I didn't want to run any risks," she said with perfect truth.

Marcus leaned over to catch a ringlet, twisting it

around his finger. "So that's what's been bothering you this evening?"

"Yes," she agreed. "But now that you've made me confess it, I feel as if I'm being fanciful about Agnes, so now I feel particularly silly."

Marcus laughed and threw off his brocade dressing gown. "Well, I'd better restore your self-esteem. Move over."

Judith obligingly did so, reflecting that she had pulled the chestnuts out of that particular fire without singeing herself too severely. She wondered how long her luck would hold.

24

"I can't understand how you can be so nonchalant about Gracemere's attentions to Harriet." Judith clasped her gloved hands tightly within her swansdown muff. It was a bitterly cold afternoon, not a comfortable one for walking at the fashionable hour in the park. However, Society's dictates always won out over comfort, and there were almost as many promenaders today as on the most clement afternoon.

Sebastian swished at the bare hedgerow with his cane. "Harriet detests him, you said as much yourself," he replied. "And she loves me," he added with a touch of complacence. "Why should I concern myself with Gracemere? If it were anyone else, I might even pity him on such a fruitless quest."

"Agnes Barret is his accomplice."

"Oh, Ju, don't be so melodramatic. Accomplice, indeed. What kind of conspiracy are you imagining?"

Judith shook her head. She didn't know, she just knew she sensed that Agnes and Bernard were pure evil. "They're lovers," she said.

Sebastian shrugged. "Maybe so. So what?"

Judith gave up and abruptly changed the subject. "You will come to Carrington Manor for Christmas?"

"Where else would I go?" He laughed down at her.

"You might prefer to spend it with Lord and Lady Moreton," Judith declared loftily. "I'm sure they'll make an exception for Christmas and put something other than gruel and weak tea on their table."

"Stuff!" her brother responded amiably, well aware that Judith intended to invite Harriet to Carrington Manor, while delicately excluding the parents.

Judith waved at a passing laundelet in response to the vigorous greetings of its passengers. "There's Isobel and Cornelia." The laundelet drew up beside the path.

"Judith, that is the most divine hat," Isobel said. "Good afternoon, Sebastian . . . I saw a hat just like that in Bridge's, Judith, but it didn't look like anything at all. I didn't even try it on. I thought it might make me look bald or something."

Sebastian noticed the hat in question for the first time: a tight helmet that completely enclosed his sister's head, hiding her hair, leaving the lines and planes of her face to look upon the world unadorned. It wouldn't suit everyone, he decided.

"Bone structure," Cornelia commented. "You've got to have bones in your face." Her nose was reddened with the cold and she dabbed at it with her handkerchief. "I do wish I hadn't let you persuade me into this, Isobel. It's freezing and I'd much rather be beside my fire with a book."

"Oh, it's good for you to get some fresh air," Isobel said. "You can't spend all day buried in some Latin text, can she, Judith? Sebastian, what's your opinion?"

Sebastian regarded the red-nosed and distinctly disconsolate Cornelia. "I think there's much to be said for firesides and books . . . although I can't say I'm a great one for the classics."

Cornelia sniffed and blew her nose. "As it happens, I wasn't reading Latin, I was reading *Guy Mannering.* Have you come across it, Judith?"

Judith nodded. "I have a copy, but I haven't yet read it. It's said to be by Walter Scott, isn't it?"

"Yes, it has the same touch as *Waverley* . . . although he won't admit to having written that either."

A gust of wind set the plume in Isobel's hat quivering, and the coachman coughed pointedly as the horses stamped on the roadway.

"Your horses are getting cold, Isobel," Sebastian said, stepping back onto the path. "It's no weather for standing around."

"It's no weather for walking either," Judith declared, huddling into her pelisse.

After waving the laundelet on its way, she turned back to her brother. "Sebastian, I think it's time to step up the play for Gracemere. We should aim to have the business over by Christmas."

Sebastian nodded. "We've got him exactly where we want him. I'll begin taking increasingly heavy losses to whet his appetite for the last night."

"I trust we still have the funds we need?"

He nodded. "Enough."

"Has he cheated again?"

"Twice. I lost carelessly, of course. He has no idea I know why I lost."

"The Duchess of Devonshire's ball is in three

weeks," Judith said thoughtfully. "A week before Christmas. It would be the perfect occasion for exposure— everyone will be there."

Sebastian thought for a minute, then nodded briskly. "I'll play mostly piquet with him from now on. Winning a little, losing a lot. The night before the ball, I'll lose so heavily he's bound to think I'm on the verge of ruin. On the night, he'll move in for the coup de grace."

"And on that night . . ." Judith shivered, but not with cold. On that night, together, they would destroy Bernard Melville, Earl of Gracemere.

With a resumption of briskness, she continued. "I'll become involved in the 'duel' you and he are engaged in —a playful thing, you understand. He'll think I'm wonderfully naive, to be seeing it as a game, not realizing that my brother is a fat pigeon that he's going to pluck clean."

"You'll have to make sure Marcus is somewhere else that night," Sebastian said matter-of-factly.

"Yes," Judith agreed. Then she said in a rush, "I don't know how much longer I can keep up this deceit, Sebastian. I feel such a traitor, so disloyal."

"Three more weeks," Sebastian said quietly. "That's all. I can't wait much longer either, Ju."

"No, I know that." She caught his hand, crushing his fingers in a convulsive grip. A minute later she spoke cheerfully, diminishing the intensity of the last few minutes. "Have you thought how you're going to manage Letitia?"

Sebastian groaned. "I'm hoping Yorkshire will prove too far for frequent visitations."

"Is Harriet able to stand up to her mother?"

Sebastian considered. "Yes, with support," he said finally. "She hasn't done so yet, of course, but I think, when we're married, she'll prefer to upset her mama than me."

Judith went into a peal of laughter. "Such a sweet, accommodating creature she is, Sebastian. It's fortunate she's fallen in love with someone who'll never injure her." That graveyard shiver ran across her scalp again and her laughter died as the twinned images of Agnes and Gracemere thrust themselves forward.

"I must go home," she said as they reached the Apsley gate. "Lord Castlereagh, Lord Liverpool, and the Duke of Wellington are dining with us."

"Such exalted circles you move in," Sebastian declared with a chuckle. "The prime minister and the foreign secretary no less."

"I suspect Marcus is turning his interests to politics, now that there aren't any wars being fought," Judith said. "And Wellington is certainly turning his attention that way. Marcus says it's because the duke has a very simple political philosophy: He's the servant of the Crown and obliged to do his duty by it in whatever way is necessary—on the battlefield or in Parliament. He's the most popular man in the country and he has such influence in the Lords, he can probably coordinate the Tories in a way that Liverpool can't." She frowned. "I wonder if Marcus is looking at a post in any ministry Wellington might set up. Funny, I only just thought of that."

"My sister a cabinet minister's wife," Sebastian said with mock awe. "You'd best hurry home and charm your husband's guests."

"Curiously, I don't find Wellington in the least intimidating," Judith said. "Maybe because I once spent the night sleeping on a table in his headquarters. And he's a shocking flirt," she added.

"Then I'm sure you and he get on like a house on fire," her brother teased.

Judith arrived home to find a note waiting for her. It was from the Earl of Gracemere, calling in her debt of honor with the request of the pleasure of her company the following night at a public ridotto at Ranelagh. Frowning, Judith took the note up to her bedchamber and rang for Millie. She thrust the invitation to the back of a drawer in her secretaire while she waited for her abigail.

Bernard had chosen a curious location for the payment of her debt. A public ridotto was a vulgar masquerade, one not in general frequented by members of the ton. But perhaps that was the point. Maybe he was considerately ensuring the secrecy of the rendezvous. And then again . . . What she knew of Gracemere didn't lend itself to consideration. He was much more likely to be making mischief.

She wasn't going to go, of course. But how to refuse the invitation without Gracemere's questioning her good faith in their friendship? If she put his back up this late in the game, she'd have little enough time to repair the damage before the Duchess of Devonshire's ball, and on that night she would have to stick closer to Gracemere than his shadow.

"My lady . . . which gown, my lady?"

"I beg your pardon, Millie?" Abstracted, she looked up. Millie was standing patiently beside the armoire.

"Which gown will you wear this evening, my lady?"

"Oh." Judith frowned, turning her attention to this all important question. "The straw-colored sarsenet, I think."

"With the sapphires," Marcus said from the connecting door. He lounged against the door jamb, fastening the buttons on his shirt cuffs, his black eyes twinkling. "They'll draw attention to the décolletage of that gown, which, as I recall is somewhat dramatic. The duke will appreciate it."

Judith chuckled. "And one must please one's guests, after all."

"It's the duty of a host," he agreed with gravity.

"And of a wife to further her husband's ambitions," she said in dulcet tones.

Marcus's smile was wry. "So you guessed?"

"What post appeals? Foreign secretary . . . home secretary, perhaps?"

He shrugged. "I don't know yet. It depends on what Peel and Canning want. Anyway, nothing's going to happen for a while. I'm just interested in preparing the ground."

"Well, I'll charm your guests," she said. "But Castlereagh's a dour individual. I'm sure he disapproves of flirtation."

Marcus laughed. "Never mind. It's with Wellington that my political future lies, my love."

Judith put her problem with Gracemere out of her head for the evening, devoting her single-minded attention to her husband's interests. It was a fascinating evening and she fell asleep in the early hours of the morning, thinking that she might well enjoy a role as political hostess.

It was bright sunshine when Marcus was awakened the next morning by the pretty chiming of the clock on the mantelshelf. It was nine o'clock, but Judith was still unstirring beside him. He hitched himself on one elbow to look down at her.

She lay on her back, her arms flung above her head, her lips slightly parted with the deep, even, trusting breath of a secure child. In sleep, without the usual vibrancy of expression, she appeared younger than her years and definitely more vulnerable. Her skin smelled

warm and soft, redolent of a curious, babylike innocence
—an innocence quite at odds with the charming, sophisticated hostess of the previous evening.

Perhaps he should have expected an upbringing
spent racketing around the Continent to produce such a
poised, well-informed, worldly cosmopolite. But he
didn't think she'd been mixing in the first circles on her
travels. And yet she never put a foot wrong; she behaved
with all the assurance of an aristocrat, all the confidence
of one who'd never gone without anything in her life.
And Sebastian was the same. George Davenport must
have been quite a character to have produced two such
children in such unfavorable circumstances. Not for the
first time, Marcus wondered about the Davenport antecedents. Judith always said she knew nothing about her
family origins. Their father had insisted they were irrelevant and as a family they had to create themselves. Marcus supposed he could see the reasoning.

He lay down beside Judith again, his thigh resting
against the warm, satiny length of her leg. It was impossible to resist the slow, gentle heat rising in his loins at the
feel and the scent of her. With a tiny sigh of contented
resignation, delicately, as if reluctant to wake her, he
turned her onto her side, facing away from him. She
murmured, but it was a wordless sound that came from
sleep. He fitted his body against hers, and in sleep she
nuzzled her bottom into his belly. He slipped his hand
between her thighs, feeling for the sleep-closed entrance
to her body with a tender, gossamery caress. He smiled as
he felt her body responding without any prompting from
her mind. She murmured again and drew her knees up,
pushing backward in wordless invitation.

He slipped inside her, his hands caressing her breasts,
his face buried in the fragrant burnished tumble of her
hair, and she tightened around him, the soft, sweet velvet

sheath enclosing him, so that he became a part of her. He felt her body come alive as she returned to full awareness, and it was as if his own body were a part of her waking process. He could feel the blood beginning to flow swiftly in her veins, vigor to fill the muscles and sinews of her body, the sharp clarity of a newly awakened brain. Fancifully he imagined he was giving birth to her, creating her for the new day.

"Good morning, lynx," he whispered into her hair as the ripples of pleasure filled her body.

She chuckled sleepily. "That was a very thoughtful way to wake someone up." Rolling onto her back again, she blinked up at him as he hung over her, his black eyes soft with his own pleasure. She touched his mouth with a fingertip. "Did you sleep well?"

"Beautifully." He swung himself out of bed, stretched and yawned. "What plans do you have for the day?"

Judith sat up against the pillows, enjoying the view. Marcus, naked, was a sight for sore eyes. However, the question brought the day's main issue to the forefront of her mind again. "Oh, I think I might ride with Sebastian this morning," she said vaguely. She would take the problem to her brother and between them they would come up with a solution.

Marcus blew her a kiss and left her, and Judith threw off the covers, pulling the bellrope for Millie.

In fact, the solution was remarkably simple. "Go to Ranelagh," Sebastian said. "And I'll ensure that I'm there with a large group of my own friends. We'll all be a trifle foxed, of course, very jolly and quite impossible to shake off. Gracemere will have your company, but you'll also be in the unexceptional company of your brother. You'll tell Marcus as soon as you get home, but you won't need to mention Gracemere, and I'll lay odds he'll think nothing of it. If he objects to your going to such a vulgar masquerade, you can put up with a scolding."

Judith pulled a rueful face. "Marcus's scoldings aren't much fun."

"In this case, it's a small price to pay."

Judith wasn't so sure, but she said no more.

25

Sebastian's plan worked like a charm. Marcus was engaged to dine with friends and was not in the house to see his wife leave, a cream domino and loo mask over one arm. Awaiting her in a hired chaise at the corner of the square was Gracemere.

Judith greeted him with a brilliant smile. "Such an adventure, my lord," she gushed with all the enthusiasm of a child being given a treat. "I've never been to a public ridotto before."

The earl bowed over her hand. "Then I'm honored to be the first to introduce you to its pleasures." He handed her into the chaise and climbed in after her. "I trust you'll be pleased with Ranelagh. It's said by some to be prettier than Vauxhall."

It was a relatively mild evening and Judith would

have been enchanted by her first sight of the gardens, brilliantly lit by myriad golden lanterns, if she hadn't had other things on her mind. She had to ensure that she and her companion met up with Sebastian's party before they all became lost in the anonymous throng parading along the gravel walks in dominoes and masks.

"I'd like to dance," she said. "May we go to the pavilion?"

"By all means." The earl bowed and took the loo mask from her. "Allow me."

She endured the feel of his fingers deftly tying the strings of the mask, struggling to hold herself away from him without giving him any indication of the depths of her revulsion. She left the cream domino hanging open from her shoulders, revealing her ball gown of sapphire taffeta. It was a startling color that set her hair on fire, and Sebastian would have little difficulty recognizing his sister in the crowd, despite the mask.

They had circled the ballroom only once, before Sebastian saw them. He was in a group of friends, lounging against the wall, ogling the dancers with the appearance of those who've escaped from the restraints of convention and are determined to enjoy themselves in whatever outrageous fashion presented itself. They held tankards of porter and blue ruin, and were imbibing freely as they exchanged indelicate observations on the company.

"Good God, it's m'sister," Sebastian declared, his voice slightly slurred, as Judith and Gracemere came within earshot.

Judith felt her partner's sudden rigidity. "Sebastian," she called, breaking free from the earl. "What are you doing here? Isn't it a famous adventure? I've never seen such people. Do you know, there were people chasing each other around the lily pond just now. They'd taken their masks off . . . Oh, my lord, I beg your pardon."

She turned with a radiant smile to the earl, whose expression was well hidden by his mask. "What a coincidence. My brother's here, too."

"So I see." Gracemere bowed. "Your sister had a great desire to sample the delights of a public ridotto, Davenport. I offered my services as escort."

"Why, Ju, you know I would have escorted you m'self," Sebastian said reproachfully. "But let me make you known to my friends."

A woman in a green domino moved out of the window embrasure as Judith took her brother's arm. There was no mischief to be wrought here, no tale of tarnished virtue to bear to the Most Honorable Marquis of Carrington. Agnes Barret went home.

From then on, the earl's carefully constructed scheme of seduction disintegrated. Sebastian, in the merry fuzziness engendered by gin and porter, remained convinced that Gracemere could only be as delighted as they all were at this serendipitous meeting, and nothing would satisfy him but that they should join together and have supper in one of the rotundas, where they could observe the cits and the ladies of the demimonde to their hearts' content. Several jesting references were made to the Marquis of Carrington's possible reactions to his wife's indulging herself in such vulgar fashion, and Judith seemed to become as tipsy as her brother and his companions as the evening wore on.

Gracemere could do nothing but sit amid the rowdy group, waiting impatiently for the evening to end. He felt like an elderly uncle who'd strayed into a party of exuberant youth. Judith's behavior was certainly inappropriate for the Marchioness of Carrington, but her identity was well concealed behind her mask, should any other members of the ton have also decided to pass such an unconventional evening. But in any event, she could be accused only of an excess of high spirits. There was nothing of which to make a public scandal, and no capital that the earl could make out of his escort. Instead of a private, intimate supper in a dimly lit box, they were supping very publicly under the full glare of a dozen candelabra in the company of Judith's brother. If it ever became known, Society's censure would be slight, tempered with indulgence. Instead of moving flirtation down the paths of overt seduction, he was obliged to watch his prey's disintegration into a giggling ingenue, leaning against her brother for the physical support she needed so vitally. He assumed Agnes had returned home.

At the end of the evening, he was forced to endure Sebastian's rollicking company in the chaise. He couldn't refuse his request for a ride home without it seeming most peculiar, so he sat in the corner of the chaise balefully listening to the brother and sister's drunken giggles and infelicitous observations.

When the chaise drew up in Berkeley Square, Sebastian lurched down the step. "I'll walk m'sister to her door," he said, hiccupping through the window at Gracemere. "My thanks for the ride. Famous evening . . . famous sport." He grinned crookedly, and put a finger to his lip. "Mustn't let it get about, though, must we?"

The earl sighed and agreed faintly, before taking Judith's hand and raising it to his lips. "You'll understand, I'm sure, my dear Judith, when I say that I don't consider your debt paid. The terms of the agreement have not been met by tonight's little entertainment."

Judith blinked at him, squinting as she tried to focus. She seemed to be struggling with an errant memory. "Debt, sir? How did it come about that we . . . Oh, yes." She smiled triumphantly. "I remember now. We must play piquet again, you know. Next time *I'll* win the wager and I'll drive your blacks in Richmond Park."

"Maybe so," he said with a dry smile. "But first we must settle the original debt. You'll not renege, I know."

"Oh, no . . . no . . . course not." Judith hiccupped, smiled fuzzily, and tripped down the step to the pavement, where she turned and waved merrily at him through the window. He knocked on the panel and the coachman set the horses in motion. Gracemere looked back through the window as they turned the corner of the square. Brother and sister were still giggling as they stumbled up the steps to the house.

Of all the wretched pieces of ill luck . . . and the gullible simpleton couldn't even hold her drink. He would contrive better next time.

"I think we pulled that one off rather neatly," Sebastian observed, reaching for the door knocker.

Judith shook her head. "So neatly that I fear he's going to call the payment null and void and demand a rerun."

"We'll find a way around it," her brother assured her.

Judith chuckled. "Yes, of course we will. But I'm sure he thinks you're even more of a nincompoop than ever."

They were still laughing when the night porter opened the door. "Good evening, my lady."

"Good evening, Norris. Is his lordship returned?"

"Yes, my lady. He's in the library, I believe."

A wicked idea occurred to Judith, borne on the ebullience of a successful masquerade. It was one of her more asinine ideas, she would subsequently admit. Wishing her brother a swift good night, she went into the house, making her way directly to the library as she retied her loo mask.

Marcus, ensconced beside the fire, awaiting his wife's return, looked up from his Tacitus as the door opened.

"I give you good night, my lord," Judith said, leaning against the door, smiling rather vaguely at him. "Did you pass a pleasant evening?" The question was punctuated with a discreet hiccup.

"Yes, thank you." Marcus closed the book over his finger, regarding his wife with some puzzlement. She seemed to be sagging against the door in a boneless kind of way, and her smile was rather unfocused. "How was your evening?"

"Oh, famous!" She said with another hiccup. "I beg your pardon . . ." She covered her mouth with one hand. "It just seems to happen . . . so silly . . ." A giggle escaped her.

Her loo mask was askew, Marcus noticed. "Judith, are you foxed?" It seemed an extraordinary explanation, but he was familiar enough with the condition to recognize it.

She shook her head vigorously. And then hiccupped again. "Course not . . . just a trifle bosky." She swayed and giggled again. "Oh, don't look so prim, Marcus. It's not kind when I feel so warm and woolly."

"Come here!" he commanded, putting his book aside.

Judith pushed herself off the door and weaved her way toward him, knocking against a spindle-legged drum table. "Oh, dear." She grabbed it and steadied it with great deliberation, swallowing another hiccup. "Careless of me. Didn't see it there."

"So how was your evening, truly?" She plopped onto his lap with a sigh of relief. "My legs are tired. I'll lay odds you were not as entertained as I was . . . oh, I beg your pardon." A spasm of hiccups overtook her for a minute, then she rested her head against his arm, smiling that skewed smile, her eyes heavy-lidded in the slits of the loo mask.

"Where the devil have you been?" he demanded, reaching behind her head to untie the mask, torn between amusement and disapproval.

"To Ranelagh," she said with a cozy smile. "A public ridotto. Very vulgar, but famous fun. Went with Sebastian and his friends." Her eyes closed but the smile remained.

Participating in a vulgar masquerade was one thing, coming back thoroughly under the hatches was another altogether. "What the hell have you been drinking?"

"Gin," she said.

"Gin!"

"Oh, and porter," she offered, as if in mitigation. "Blue ruin and porter." She snuggled into his shoulder, her body boneless in his lap. "You should have come."

"I don't recall receiving an invitation," he said drily. "But if I had done, you wouldn't have come home in this state, I can assure you."

Her eyelids fluttered coquettishly. "You're not going to be a prude and scold, are you?"

Marcus sighed. "There would be little point in your present condition. Anyway, the condition carries its own punishment. I wouldn't want your head in the morning."

"Stuff," she said on a renewed attack of hiccups.

"Just wait. Come on, I'll put you to bed." He stood up, lifting her in his arms. She flung one arm around his neck, burying her face in his neck.

"For God's sake, keep still. I don't want to drop you."

"Oh, no," she muttered. "Wouldn't want that. Think I told Millie not to wait up for me."

"With some foresight. I can't imagine what she'd think if she saw you like this."

"Oh, you are being a prude." She tweaked his nose.

"Stop it, Judith." Disapproval was gaining the upper hand over amusement.

In her bedchamber he dropped her onto the bed. She bounced and yawned, flinging her arms and legs wide. "I'll go to sleep now."

"You can't go to sleep in your clothes." He lifted her feet, pulling off her satin pumps and tossing them to the floor. Pushing up her skirt, he unfastened her garters and drew off her silk stockings. "Stand up." He hauled her to her feet and unhooked her gown, while she swayed, humming to herself, that beatific smile still on her lips.

The gown fell to the floor in a rich rustle of taffeta and Marcus was reminded of the first time he'd undressed her in the inn on the road to Quatre Bras. It was a memory that in any other circumstances would have aroused him. Not tonight. He pulled her petticoat over her head.

Judith chose that moment to fall back on the bed with a sigh. Marcus bent over her, his lips tightening as he unfastened the tapes of her pantalettes. "Lift up." Obligingly she raised her hips so he could pull the garment down.

Her eyes opened suddenly in sleepy, seductive invitation and she ran her hands over her body, naked except for the pearl collar she wore at her throat and the pearl drops in her ears. She offered him the same skewed but rather delightful smile.

"God in heaven," Marcus muttered. "Where's your nightgown?" He found it in the armoire and pulled her into a sitting position, dropping the fine lawn over her head. "Where are your arms?"

"Here," she mumbled from within the volumninous folds of material, flapping her arms helpfully.

"Dear God!" he muttered again, thrusting the unwieldy limbs into the long sleeves. "From now on, madam wife, outside these walls you drink nothing but orgeat and lemonade, is that clear?" He removed her jewelry before pulling back the covers and maneuvering her under the sheet. Then he stood looking down at her, shaking his head.

Suddenly her eyes shot open and she was laughing up at him, all traces of befuddlement gone from her expression, the curiously smudged lines of her face snapping back into their customary firm delineation. "I fooled you, and I really didn't think I'd be able to."

His jaw dropped. "Judith, you . . . you *devil*!" He stared at her, not trusting the evidence of his eyes. But it was absolutely clear that she was as sober as she'd ever been.

Judith hitched herself up on the pillows, chuckling. "You ought to know me well enough by now to know that I'd never really get foxed. It's just an act that Sebastian and I perfected. If you think I'm convincing on my own, you should see us together."

"I imagine it serves to disarm quite a few gulls," he said in a flat voice.

"Well, yes," Judith agreed. "On occasion it did. But it's perfectly harmless."

"Harmless? You are a baggage, and I cannot imagine how you've escaped being whipped at the cart's tail through every capital on the Continent." He turned from her, seething with fury. "How dare you play your tricks on me?"

Judith suddenly realized the magnitude of her error. In the exultant aftermath of foiling Gracemere, she'd allowed herself to get carried away. Of all the tactless, stupid ideas—to play Marcus for a fool with the tricks of her disreputable past!

"Oh, Marcus, it was just a little fun," she said, leaping out of bed. "I'm sorry if you don't like being teased." She put a hand on his arm but he snatched it away. "Oh, please," she said, putting her arms around his waist, laying her head between his shoulder blades. "*Please* don't be cross. I really didn't think you'd mind being teased, but I accept it was wrong and thoughtless of me."

"It isn't a matter of being teased," he said. "You played me for a fool, and I will *not* be treated like one of the simpletons you and your brother have been exploiting all your adult lives."

"I'm sorry," she said again. "It was a grave error of judgment, I understand that now, but I really didn't mean any harm by it. Please forgive me."

There was no mistaking the contrition in her voice. Marcus allowed his anger to subside, recognizing that it had two causes: his own feeling of foolishness at having fallen for such a trick, and his dislike of any reminders of her past life. He probably should have guessed the truth. Judith was too much in control of herself and her life to yield to intoxication . . . only the appearance of it as and when it suited her.

"Don't you *ever* treat me like that again."

"I won't, I promise." She squeezed his waist. "But you haven't said you forgive me."

"I forgive you."

"Penance?"

He pulled her arms free of his waist and hauled her around in front of him, placing his hands on her shoulders. "I'll think of something appropriate once you've told me just what you were doing at Ranelagh."

"But I have told you. I went to the ridotto with Sebastian and some of his friends."

"Why didn't you mention it before?"

"Because I knew you'd be stuffy about it." She gave him a roguish smile. "And you would have been, so don't deny it."

"I wasn't going to. A public ridotto is no place for the Marchioness of Carrington."

"I know, but no one recognized us . . . there was no one there to recognize us."

"Your brother's idea of evening entertainment leaves much to be desired. However, I assume he didn't escort his prospective fiancée?" he asked aridly.

"No, of course not," Judith said. "He doesn't even like it when Harriet goes into a card room. But it's different with me."

Marcus wondered how Harriet would feel once she came face to face with the exclusivity of her husband's relationship with his sister. "It would seem that Sebastian and I have similar attitudes to what's appropriate for a wife," he observed. "I could wish that occasionally he'd remember that as well as being his sister, you're also my wife."

"He doesn't forget that. But neither does he make decisions for me," Judith pointed out. "As it happens, going to Ranelagh was my idea." Not entirely true, but near enough.

"I would have escorted you if you'd asked." His hands slipped from her shoulders to clasp her arms. "Do you prefer Sebastian's company to mine, lynx?"

"No, how could you think such a thing?" She was genuinely distressed at such an interpretation, but the sticky threads of deceit were entangling her again. She couldn't tell the truth about the evening, but without the truth, it appeared that she had chosen her brother's company over her husband's—indeed, had deliberately excluded her husband.

"It's very easy to think such a thing," he said quietly.

"I didn't think it would have amused you," she improvised, with a touch of desperation. "London is still quite new to us and we're accustomed to thinking of different things to do in new places. We just fell into an old habit."

He let it go, although the ring of truth was somehow lacking despite the plausibility of the explanation. "Very well, let's leave it at that." His hands slipped from her arms.

It sounded rather grudging to Judith. She turned back to the bed, ebullience vanished in a fog of dejection.

"Just a minute."

Something in his voice banished melancholy. She paused, one knee on the bed, the other foot on the floor.

"There remains the small matter of penance."

Judith looked over her shoulder at him, her eyes now sparkling with anticipation. "Yes, my lord?" Eagerness laced the dulcet tones.

He trod over to the bed. "I think I'll let you choose your own . . . later. For the moment, kneel on the bed." Reaching across her, he pulled the pillows out, tucking them against her belly as he unfastened his britches.

Judith laughed softly, drawing her nightgown up to her waist, falling forward over the piled pillows. "A fitting end to a ribald evening, sir."

"Abominable woman," he said, one hand in the small of her back as he guided himself within her. "If I had a grain of common sense, I'd banish you to Berkshire, where you couldn't get up to any more mischief."

Judith had no immediate rejoinder and shortly was beyond any coherent verbal response, although her body spoke to him with perfect fluency.

26

"So what now?" Agnes said, looking up from the hot-house roses she was arranging in a wide crystal bowl. "Are you still set on revenge?"

"Certainly," Gracemere said. "It was annoying, meeting Davenport like that, although I wish you could have seen the pair of them. They couldn't see straight." He smiled contemptuously at the memory. "They're such simpletons, I almost wonder if they're worth the trouble I'm taking."

Agnes tossed a fading bloom into the basket at her feet. "One must never underestimate, Bernard."

"No," he agreed, taking snuff. "And I have every intention of holding Judith to her wager. She will pay her debt at a private dinner at a place of my choosing. And this time there'll be no possibility of unwanted company.

You will see her with me and you'll accidentally let the gossip fall within Carrington's earshot. Since his wife's an eager participant in this amusing liaison, he won't be able to challenge me over it, without exposing both of them to public ridicule, so he'll have to swallow it . . . and his pride."

"It'll ruin his marriage," Agnes commented with a cynical laugh.

Gracemere shrugged. "But of course. The main object of the exercise, really. I don't believe Judith cares a whit for him, anyway. She's all too eager to flout his authority." He smiled. "Where shall I arrange this intimate little dinner, my love? Somewhere rather more compromising than Ranelagh this time."

"A private parlor in a small hotel on Jermyn Street," Agnes suggested casually. "I'm sure you know such a one."

Gracemere gaped at her, then roared with laughter. "You never cease to amaze me, my dear. A brilliant idea. I'll entertain Carrington's wife in a whorehouse."

"It *is* an amusing idea," Agnes agreed. Her lip curled. "There's something about that little bitch . . . I don't know what it is, but whenever I'm in the same room with her, I feel she's trouble." She shook her head. "She never misses an opportunity to do or say something to annoy me. And I don't understand why I should allow myself to react to her insolence. But I can't help myself." She sucked a bead of blood off her finger where a rose thorn had pricked. "I shall really enjoy watching you humble her."

"Then you shall do so, my love," Gracemere said. "I shall entertain Carrington's wife in a house run by a lady of the night, and I'll lay odds his naive bride won't understand where she is."

"Therein lies the cream of the jest," Agnes assented.

"She'll flutter and feel it's all most improper, but she'll have no idea *how* grossly improper . . . how could she?"

"How indeed?" Gracemere went to the secretaire. "Come and help me compose my second invitation. It needs to be a little more inviting—or do I mean compelling—than the last, but still couched in terms of calling in a debt of honor. Whatever second thoughts she may have had, she'll not renege when it's put in those terms. She likes to think of herself as a true gamester, willing to play high and lose with panache." He laughed, shaking his head. "I wonder where the Davenports sprang from."

"Oh, as you said before, one of those hybrid foreign families." Agnes drew up a chair to the secretaire. "Now, let's compose this compelling missive."

Half an hour later the earl sanded the single sheet, folded it, and sealed it with his signet ring. "You struck just the right note, my love: a challenge to the chit's willingness to play high and take risks. She'll not be able to resist the temptation to prove herself daring and reckless, pursuing an amusing adventure to pique her husband."

Agnes smiled. "And once you've finished playing games with the Devlins, what do you intend with Harriet?"

"Simple abduction. She's always in your company. You'll bring her to me in a hired chaise. Perfectly straightforward, my love."

"You'll marry her out of hand." Agnes nodded. "One night is all it will take to persuade her to go before a preacher in the morning. And once she's married, then her parents will be able to do nothing. They'll want to put the best light upon it, for fear their precious reputation be ruined. We'll have our thirty thousand, my dear, and the story will be of a runaway love match—the exigencies of a powerful passion, et cetera, et cetera." Her cynical laugh hung in the air, and Gracemere recognized as always that when it came to cold-blooded assessments of human nature, his mistress matched him step for step.

The invitation arrived in conventional fashion with Judith's chocolate the following morning. The dinner was set for that very night, the arrangements crisply laid out. She would find an unmarked chaise awaiting her as before. The destination was a secret, but it was one the earl thought she would enjoy, appealing as it would to her sense of adventure and the gamester within her.

Judith crumpled the sheet with a soft exclamation. There was no way out of this one. She couldn't refuse without annoying Gracemere and, as before, she couldn't afford to annoy him, not this close to the endgame.

She dressed and went in search of Marcus. He was in his book room, closeted with John, but looked up, his eyes crinkling with pleasure at her entrance. "Good morning, my love. What can I do for you?"

Sweet heaven, how she hated lying to him. She smiled at John to take her mind off what she was saying. "I just wanted to tell you that I'm going to a very private dinner this evening."

"Oh," Marcus said, putting down his quill. "Am I not invited?"

"No, I'm afraid not." She turned her eyes to him, hoping she was now in control of her features. "It's all women, you see."

Marcus laughed. "Cornelia and the others?"

"Just so. I'm sure I won't be late, though."

John coughed apologetically. "Excuse me, your ladyship, but you and Lord Carrington are engaged to the Willoughbys this evening—the musicale," he said. "The harpist, if you recall?"

"Oh, I'd completely forgotten," Judith said. "And I

do so want to spend the evening with my friends. Marcus
. . . would you mind?"

He couldn't resist the appeal in those golden brown
eyes. "I must go alone, it would seem."

"You are a prince among husbands," she said, reaching across the desk to kiss him. John averted his eyes.

"I shall expect compensation," Marcus said.

"That goes without saying." She went to the door.
"And as I said, I won't be late."

In fact, if she managed matters aright, she wouldn't
be out of the house for much more than an hour. Bernard Melville, Earl of Gracemere, was not going to enjoy
the clandestine company of his enemy's wife . . . whatever he might think.

Thus resolved, Judith felt a little better about her lie.
Circumstances were working in her favor, since none of
her friends had been invited to the musicale. The Willoughbys were an elderly couple who didn't go about
much in Society, but were friends of Marcus's mother
and he had felt obliged to accept the invitation to a small
and select gathering of elderly music lovers. By the time
he came home, his wife would be virtuously abed, having
spent the greater part of the evening irreproachably by
her own fireside.

She dressed with care that evening, choosing a gown
with an unusually high neckline and arranging her hair
in a demure braided coronet. Her conduct tonight would
be the antithesis of flirtatious. Before leaving, she sent
Millie on an errand to the kitchen that greatly puzzled
the abigail. However, questions were not invited so she
fetched what was required and saved her curiosity for
later in the servants' hall, when her ladyship's strange
request could be discussed at length.

Judith dropped the small package into her reticule,
adjusted the shawl about her shoulders, and went down-

stairs. The Willoughbys kept early hours and Marcus had already left.

The unmarked chaise awaited her on the same corner as before, and as before the earl was inside to greet her.

"Good evening, Bernard," Judith said cheerfully. "I must say, sir, that you don't give much notice of your invitations."

"Adventures are supposed to take one by surprise," he said. "And you do like adventures, don't you, my dear Judith?"

Judith allowed a little giggle to escape her. "Life would be very dull without them, sir."

"Just so. And the so-staid husband . . . how was he disposed of for the evening?"

Judith gritted her teeth. "Marcus had his own engagement," she said. "Where do we go, Bernard?"

"Ah, that's a surprise," he told her. "I trust you'll be pleased."

"I'm sure I shall." She clapped her hands softly, her eyes glowing in the dim light of the chaise. "I like surprises as much as I like adventures."

"Splendid," he said, reaching across to take her hand. "I hope this one will be all that you expect."

"And I hope the evening will be all that you expect, Bernard," she said, smiling a little shyly.

He carried her hand to his lips.

The chaise drew up in front of a tall town house, its door lit by a lantern, light glowing from behind curtained windows. Judith stepped out and looked curiously up and down the street. "Where are we?"

"Jermyn Street," Gracemere said casually. "A small and very discreet hotel I frequent on occasion. Come, my dear." He escorted her to the door that was opened by an elderly butler in a powdered wig.

"My lord . . . madam." He bowed. "Madame is in the salon."

Judith allowed herself to be ushered into the salon. She looked around at the gilt moldings, the heavy satin draperies, the deep armchairs, and the women in their elegant gowns with just a little something out of place. The air was heavy with the fragrance of musk, a decadent, overblown scent, and Judith knew immediately what Gracemere had brought her to. She'd been in such places before: the luxurious bordello catering to the wealthy and whatever tastes they might have. There was nothing these women wouldn't do if the price was right.

She glanced sideways at her escort and saw the smile flickering on the cruel mouth as he greeted their ostensible hostess. He wouldn't think she knew what the place was, she realized. After all, what respectable lady of the ton would? He wasn't to know that her father had had many good friends who ran places like this one—friends who would provide free lodging on occasion to the impoverished gamester and his children . . . lodging and comfort to the lonely widower. Her father had never been short of female company, Judith remembered. Something about him appealed to women. She suspected he'd never paid for the comfort offered him in places such as this. Once his children had reached a certain age, however, George Davenport had stopped accepting this kind of hospitality, but Judith's memory was crystal clear.

Madame greeted her courteously, but her eyes were shrewdly assessing and she too seemed to share in the jest with Gracemere. They obviously knew each other well.

"Your private dining room is ready, my lord," she said. "Bernice will show you up." She beckoned to a young woman in crimson satin, who came over immediately. Her gown was rich, the fall of lace at the neck delicate, but the lace was slightly awry, and the neckline so low that it barely covered her nipples.

"This way, sir . . . madam." She barely acknowledged Judith but smiled at Gracemere, who chucked her beneath the chin with a lazy forefinger.

They went upstairs to a small parlor, as ostentatiously decorated as the one downstairs. A fire burned in the grate, and a round table was set for two. A richly cushioned divan was the only other furniture, apart from a worked screen in the corner. It would conceal the commode, Judith knew. Rooms such as this were equipped to cater in total privacy for all needs.

"Goodness me, Bernard," she said with an amazed little titter. "What a strange place. It's almost more like a bedchamber than a dining parlor."

"It's a very private hotel," he said, pouring wine into two glasses. "A toast, my dear Judith."

She took the glass. "And what shall we toast, sir?"

"Adventure and the confounding of dictatorial husbands." He raised his glass, laughing at her as he drank.

Judith took a sip, smiling, then, carrying her glass, she strolled over to the window and drew aside the curtain to look down on the street. Under cover of the curtain, she took the packet from her reticule and shook the contents in her wineglass.

"Are there many such hotels on this street, Bernard?" she asked in tones of innocent curiosity, turning back to him, giving him a wide-eyed smile as she drained the contents of her glass. "May I have some more wine?"

"Of course, my dear." He brought the decanter over to her. If she became foxed again, it would only add spice to the affair this time. She probably wouldn't remember what had happened, and he'd deposit her at her doorstep for her husband in a distinctly shop-soiled condition.

Judith raised the refilled glass, then gasped, slamming it back on the table. Her hand went to her throat and, under Gracemere's astonished, horrified gaze, she turned a delicate shade of green. With a sudden gasp, she flew behind the screen to the commode from whence came the most unromantic and unladylike sounds.

Marcus made his wife's excuses to the Willoughbys, offering a polite white lie. He did what was required of him, making the rounds of his fellow guests, most of whom he'd known since boyhood, ate an indifferent dinner, enjoyed good burgundy, and followed his fellow guests to the drawing room for the recital.

"My Lord Carrington, this is an unexpected encounter." Agnes Barret materialized on the arm of her elderly husband just as the harpist took her place. "We are come so late," she whispered, sitting beside the marquis. "We had another dinner engagement, but we couldn't offend the Willoughbys. Such old friends of my husband's." She fanned herself vigorously and looked around the room, nodding and smiling as she met recognition.

Marcus murmured something suitable, thinking that she was a most attractive woman, with those fine eyes and high cheekbones and that curiously familiar wicked curve to her mouth.

"Lady Carrington isn't with you?" Agnes turned her smile upon him.

"No, she had a previous engagement," he said.

"Ah." Agnes frowned as if in thought. "Not in Jermyn Street, of course."

Premonition shot up Marcus's spine like flame on a tarred stick. "I hardly think so, ma'am."

Agnes shook her head. "No, of course not. Silly of me, I had the unmistakable impression I'd seen her alighting from a chaise . . . it must have been a trick of the light. The lantern over the door was throwing strange shadows."

Marcus sat still, a smile fixed on his face, his eyes on the harpist as she began to pluck her instrument. He felt enwrapped in tendrils of malice, the evil mischief emanating from the woman beside him seeming to weave around him. Judith had been right. Agnes Barret was not harmless. Agnes Barret was dangerous. And if Agnes Barret was Gracemere's lover, then Judith was in danger. How or why, he couldn't guess. But he was as certain of it as he was of his own name. Martha's battered little face rose vividly in his memory, the despairing whimpers filling his ears anew.

He rose without excuse from his chair and left the room, while the harpist's gentle music continued behind him.

Agnes, startled, watched him stalk from the room. She'd done no more than sow the first little seed. She hadn't mentioned Bernard. That would come tomorrow or the next day, a whispered word to set the gossip on its way. What could possibly have driven the marquis to leave so precipitately?

Marcus left the house without making farewells and walked fast to Jermyn Street.

Gracemere listened for a minute in horrified impotence to the sounds of violent retching behind the screen. Then he strode to the door, flung it open, and bellowed for help. Madame came up the stairs, two of her girls on her heels.

"Whatever is it, my lord?"

He gestured to the room behind him. "Her ladyship appears to be unwell. Do something."

Madame listened for a minute, gave the earl a most

telling look, and hurried into the room, disappearing behind the screen.

Gracemere paced the corridor, unwilling to return to the scene of such a horribly intimate disintegration. He thumped a fist into the palm of his other hand, cursing all women. It couldn't have been the wine, she'd only had one glass and she'd been perfectly sober when they'd arrived.

Judith staggered out from behind the screen, supported by Madame and one of the women. She was waxen, a faint sheen of perspiration on her brow, her hair lackluster, her eyes watering.

"My lord, I don't know what . . ." She pressed her hand to her mouth. "Something I ate . . . so mortifying . . . I don't know how to apologize—"

"You must go home," he interrupted brusquely. "The chaise will take you."

She nodded feebly. "Yes, thank you. I have to lie down." Staggering, she fell onto the divan, lying back with her eyes closed.

Madame took her fan and began to ply it vigorously. "My lord, I can't have sick women in my house," she said, an edge to the refined accents. "It doesn't look good, and what my other guests would think, listening . . ."

"Yes, yes," Bernard interrupted. "Have her taken downstairs and put in the chaise. Tell the driver to take her back to Berkeley Square."

Somehow, a limp and groaning Judith was bundled down the stairs and into the waiting chaise. Bernard stood at the window, watching as the vehicle moved off down the street. Some devil was at work here, throwing all his carefully engineered schemes awry. He went to the table and flung himself into a chair, moodily refilling his glass. He might as well eat the dinner he'd ordered with such care.

Marcus turned onto Jermyn Street from St. James's. He was amazed at his own calm as he looked down the street. Three houses had lanterns outside their doors. Behind one of those doors he was certain he would find his wife in the company of Bernard Melville, Earl of Gracemere. He had no idea why she was there, why she would have allowed herself to be trapped by Gracemere, but the reasons didn't interest him at the moment. There would be time for that later. He had but one thought, to reach her before she was hurt.

The first door had no knowledge of the Earl of Gracemere. The butler in the powdered wig behind the second door bowed him within immediately. Madame emerged from the salon, all smiles, ready to greet a new customer.

"Where is Gracemere?"

The clipped question, the burning black eyes, the almost mask-like impassivity of expression impressed Madame as nothing else could have done. "I believe his lordship is abovestairs, sir. Is he expecting you?"

"If he's not, he should be," Marcus said. "Direct me to him, if you please."

Madame made a shrewd guess as to the business the new arrival might have with the earl. She gestured to Bernice. It was none of her business if Gracemere chose to invoke outraged husbands, and she wasn't prepared to have a scene in her hall. "Show this gentleman to Lord Gracemere's parlor."

Marcus strode up the stairs after the girl. At the door, he waved her away. He stood for a second listening. There was complete silence. After lifting the latch gently, he pushed the door open. The room had a single occupant.

Gracemere was sprawled in a chair at the table, a glass of claret in his hand, his eyes on the offensively cheerful glow in the grate. His head swiveled at the sound of the door opening.

"Ah, Gracemere," Marcus observed, deceptively pleasant. "There you are."

"I'm flattered you should seek me out, Carrington." Bernard sipped his wine. "To what do I owe this unlooked-for attention?"

"Oh, a simple matter." Marcus tossed his cane onto the divan and took the chair opposite the earl. He examined the place settings for a minute before returning his attention to the earl. "A simple matter," he repeated. "Where is my wife, Bernard?"

Gracemere gestured expansively around the room. "Why ask me, Marcus? I dine alone."

"It would appear so," Marcus agreed. "But you are clearly expecting a guest." He picked up the fork at his place, examining the tines with careful interest, before reaching for the second wineglass on the table. It was half full. "Has your guest made a temporary departure?"

The earl gave a crack of sardonic laughter. "I trust not temporary."

"Oh? You interest me greatly, Gracemere. Please explain." He turned the stem of the wineglass between finger and thumb, regarding the earl intently across the table.

"Your wife is not here," the earl said. "She has been here, but she is by now, I trust, safely tucked up in her own bed."

"I see." Marcus rose. "And the circumstances of her departure . . . ?"

Gracemere shuddered. "Quite innocent, I assure

you. Your wife's virtue remains untainted, Marcus. Now, perhaps you'd leave me to my dinner."

"By all means. But allow me to give you a piece of advice. If you should have any further plans involving the health and welfare of my wife, I suggest you drop them forthwith." He picked up his cane and tapped it thoughtfully into his palm. "I would hate to use a horse-whip on you again, but if it did become necessary, I can safely promise you that this time it will be no secret. It will be the most talked of on-dit of this or any other Season."

He bowed, mockery in every line of his body, but there was no concealing the menace in his eyes as they rested for a second on Gracemere's flushed face. "Don't underestimate me again, Bernard. And just remember that another time I'll not let pride conceal the truth. I'll face whatever I have to to expose you. That is all I have to say."

He walked out of the room, closing the door quietly behind him.

27

$\mathcal{M}$arcus walked back to Berkeley Square. Whatever reasons Judith had had for involving herself with Gracemere initially, she'd been perfectly capable of extricating herself from trouble. Judging by the half-full wineglass, she'd left in haste, and she must have made some considerable scene if her putative host hoped she wasn't going to return.

But why the hell had she been with Gracemere in the first place? Had she been defying her husband for principle's sake? But that didn't make sense—they'd resolved the issue amicably as far as he remembered. She'd agreed to do as he wished if he moderated his dictatorial manner. So why would she persist in cultivating such an acquaintanceship. No, it was much more than that. Acquaintances didn't dine tête-à-tête. So why?

The old serpents of mistrust began to wreathe and writhe in his gut, and he felt cold and sick. Did he know her at all? Had he ever known her? Had she colluded with Gracemere to wound him? But if that was so, why had she left her dinner companion against his will? Perhaps she hadn't expected seduction. His ingenuous wife had believed an invitation to a clandestine dinner to be completely innocent? Impossible. There was nothing ingenuous about Judith; she was far too worldly to fall for such a fabrication. But perhaps Gracemere had led her to believe the invitation was different—not a private party but one in company she knew. And when she'd discovered the truth . . . This explanation was more plausible, and he began to feel a little comforted. And then he remembered how she'd lied to him that morning—a party with her women friends. The serpents hissed and acid betrayal soured his mouth.

Judith was standing at her window, looking down on the square, when he came in sight of the house. She had been waiting for him, knowing what she had to do. She had known that Gracemere was capable of ruining a man with cheating and lies. She knew he was capable of running off with another man's fiancée. But this evening she had glimpsed the depths of maleficence that outdid anything that she already knew. A clandestine rendezvous was one thing, but to pick such a place for the kind of woman he believed Judith to be was evil beyond anything. Somehow Marcus was to have been injured by Gracemere's plotting and Marcus's wife had been just a tool. Judith was now convinced of it. Was Marcus to be somehow confronted with the information of his wife's rendezvous? Confronted and humiliated? Was it to be made public perhaps?

She stood at the window with her arms crossed over her breasts, still feeling weak and shaky after her violent vomiting but knowing that unless she could circumvent Gracemere's ulterior motive, she might just as well have yielded to seduction. If a public scandal was to be made, the simple fact of her willing presence in such a place with the earl would be sufficient cause.

She was going to have to tell Marcus the whole. If he heard it from her lips, he would be forewarned and forearmed. The thought of what she risked by such a course filled her with dread.

Marcus disappeared from view as he climbed the steps beneath her window.

She went out to the hall at the top of the stairs as Marcus was admitted to the house, then she sped lightly down the stairs toward him.

"Marcus, I need to talk with you."

He looked up, and despite the gall and wormwood of his suspicions, his eyes anxiously raked her face. She was pale and tense, but other than that, as far as he could tell seemed quite well.

"Did you enjoy your evening?" he asked, unsmiling as he handed his cloak and gloves to Gregson. Until he decided how to deal with the situation, he would pretend he knew nothing about it.

Judith shook her head dismissively. "Could we go into your book room? I have to talk to you."

Surely she wasn't going to tell him? A thrill of hope coursed through him. "It's a book-room matter?"

"I believe so." She was clasping her hands tightly, her expression one of painful intensity.

Marcus knew he wanted her confidence now more than he had ever wanted anything. Only her honesty would have the power to erase the suspicions, defang the serpents of mistrust. But just in case he was wrong, he continued the charade. "Oh, dear." He managed a faint smile of rueful comprehension at this choice of venue.

His book room seemed to have become the arena for discussion of all potentially explosive issues. "Could it wait until morning?"

"I don't think so."

"Very well. Let's get it over with, whatever it is."

Judith led the way. The candles were extinguished but the fire was still alight. She relit the candles while Marcus tossed a log onto the embers.

"Am I going to need fortification?" He gestured to the decanters on the sideboard.

"I imagine so. I'll have a glass of port also."

Marcus filled two glasses, watching as Judith bent to warm her hands at the fire, its light setting matching fires aglow in the burnished ringlets tumbling about her face.

"I have a confession to make," she said eventually, turning to face him, her pallor even more marked. "I'm afraid you're going to be very, very angry."

She was going to tell him. He kept the joy from his expression and said evenly, "I'm duly warned. Let me hear it."

"Very well." She put down her glass and squared her shoulders. "It's about Gracemere." She paused, but Marcus said nothing, although his eyes had narrowed. He sipped his port and waited.

Quietly she told him how she had played piquet with Gracemere, what the stakes were, and where he had taken her that evening. "I'm afraid he intends to create some scandal that would humiliate you," she finished. "I had to tell you . . . warn you. I couldn't bear you to hear it from anyone else."

She fell silent, twisting her hands against her skirt, her expression taut with anxiety as she waited for his response.

"You recognized the place for what it was?" His voice was level, and his eyes had not left her face.

She nodded. "As children we spent some time in similar establishments . . . but that's another story."

"You must tell me sometime," he commented calmly. "You didn't stay very long tonight, I gather."

"No, I put mustard in my wine and made myself very sick," she said. "It's a trick I've used before to get out of a ticklish situation." A gleam appeared in her eye, a hint of the customarily mischievous Judith. "I'm afraid the earl was rather put off by the results."

The Earl of Gracemere's disgruntlement was now explained. Against all the odds, laughter bubbled in Marcus's chest. "You vomited?"

She nodded. "Prodigiously . . . mustard has that effect. It's also very wearing," she added. "I still feel weak and shivery."

Marcus asked his most important question. "Am I to be told why you've been cultivating Gracemere despite our agreement that you would hold him at arm's length?"

Judith bit her lip. This was where it became tricky. "There is something I wasn't intending to tell you—"

"Dear God, Judith, you have more layers than an onion!" Marcus interrupted. "Every time I think I've peeled away the last skin and reached some core of truth and understanding, you reveal a dozen new layers."

"I'm sure you've never peeled an onion in your life," Judith said, momentarily diverted.

"That is beside the point."

Judith sighed. "I know that it was Gracemere who took Martha from you—" Marcus's sharply indrawn breath stopped her for a minute, but when he said nothing, she continued resolutely.

"Gracemere told me, as an explanation for why you held him in such enmity. I wanted—" She paused, casting a quick look up at him. His expression was impassive, neither encouraging nor threatening.

"I wanted to know something about Martha," she rushed on. "You wouldn't talk of her . . . except that once in the inn at Quatre Bras, and then you said you never wanted to talk about her again. You said she was my antithesis in every way, and I wanted to know what she was like—what that meant. It was almost an obsession," she finished, opening her hands in a gesture appealing for understanding.

Marcus stared, for the moment unable to respond. Feminine curiosity! Was that all it was? Judith simply wanted to know what her predecessor had been like? The simplicity of the answer confused him. It seemed too simple for someone as complex as Judith. And yet it was perfectly understandable. He had been adamant in his refusal to discuss that aspect of his past.

"I've never liked Gracemere, Marcus," Judith said when he remained silent. She was thinking fast now, and the distorted truth tripped convincingly off her tongue.

"I've never trusted him either, which is why I took the mustard. But I didn't think it would do any harm to cultivate him long enough to satisfy my curiosity. He was playing with me. I knew that. And I thought, so long as I knew it, I'd be able to play along without anything serious happening. I'd find out what I wanted and that would be that. I didn't intend to hurt you . . . I . . . oh, how can I convince you of that?"

He scrutinized her expression for a minute, then nodded slowly. "I believe you. Did he satisfy your curiosity?"

Judith shook her head. "There wasn't time. Once I realized what he was up to this evening, I had to move quickly."

Marcus turned to the fire and threw on another log. When he spoke, his voice was businesslike.

"It's true that Martha fell in love with Gracemere. It's true I think that had I been more attentive, she wouldn't have done so. I grew up with her. Her family's estates marched with my own, and it had always been assumed, from the cradle almost, that we would unite the two estates. I saw no reason to question the plan, but neither did I see any reason to pay Martha any particular attentions on that account."

A log slipped in a shower of sparks, and he kicked it back with a booted foot. "I amused myself in the manner of most young sprigs with too much money and not enough to occupy them. Martha was a meek dab of a girl, a little brown mouse."

He glanced across at Judith, who was all burnished radiance and luster despite the events of the evening. "You and she are chalk and cheese," he said. "Both physically and in temperament. Martha was meek and easily influenced. The perfect prey for someone like Gracemere, whose pockets were always to let and who spent his time dodging bailiffs and the Fleet prison. But he's of impeccable breeding, has considerable address and a honeyed tongue when it suits him. They eloped, putting me in the guise of a loathsome suitor forced upon an unwilling woman."

He turned his back to the room, leaning his arm along the mantelpiece, staring down into the rekindled fire as the memory of that time flooded his mind as vividly as if it were yesterday.

Martha's father had been a sick man, and she'd had no brothers. It had fallen to the hand of the jilted fiancé to go after the fugitives and bring Martha back before they joined hands over the anvil. He'd found them very quickly. Gracemere had had no intention of immediately taking Martha to Gretna Green.

She'd been a battered, gibbering wreck when he'd come up with them. Her lover, desperate to ensure there would be no possibility of annulment, had raped her within a few hours of their flight. Ruined, and possibly pregnant, Martha had had no option but to accept as husband the only man likely to offer for her.

"I backed out of the engagement with as much grace as I could muster," he said in the same level tones, giving no indication of the violent swirling of the age-old rage —a rage that had led him to thrash Bernard Melville to within an inch of his life.

"And nine months later Martha died giving birth to a stillborn child. Gracemere inherited her entire fortune except for the estate which her father left to a nephew. He was determined that Gracemere shouldn't take that . . . for which I can only be grateful, having been spared such a neighbor."

He looked up, his eyes unreadable. "Does that satisfy your curiosity, lynx?"

Judith nodded. But in truth the curiosity that had been a convenient fabrication was now reality. Marcus was leaving something out; she could hear the gaps in the story as if he'd underlined them. And she could feel the deep currents of emotion swirling behind his apparently bland expression. However, she had no choice under the circumstances but to accept what he'd said without question. The ease with which she'd managed to deceive him was somehow harder to endure than the deception itself. He now trusted her enough to believe her lies.

"I don't know why I needed to know so badly," she said. "It happened a long time ago, after all."

"Yes, when you were a little girl of twelve," Marcus responded with a dry half smile.

"Are you very angry?" Judith regarded him somberly. "You have the right, I freely admit it."

Marcus frowned, pulling at his chin. Her confession seemed to have made all the difference to his feelings. "No, I'm not angry. You put yourself in a highly dangerous and compromising situation, but you managed to extricate yourself neatly enough. However, I'm disappointed you didn't feel able to ask *me* your questions. I would have thought matters were running smoothly enough between us for that."

Oh, what a tangled web we weave, Judith thought, hearing the hurt in his voice. She couldn't possibly enter into any discussion about why she hadn't felt able to share her invented curiosity with him. She offered him a slightly helpless shrug of acceptance that he acknowledged with a resigned shake of his head.

"What are we going to do if Gracemere does decide to create a scandal?" She changed the subject.

Marcus's expression hardened. "He won't." It was a sharp, succinct statement.

"But how can you be so sure?"

"My dear Judith, don't you trust me to make sure of it?" he demanded in a voice like iron. "Believe me, I am a match for Gracemere."

Judith, looking at the set of his jaw, the uncompromising slash of his mouth, the eyes like black flint, didn't doubt for a minute that her husband was more than a match for Gracemere, or anyone else who might decide to meddle in his affairs.

And where did that leave his wife? His lying, conniving trickster of a wife. A shudder ripped up her spine, and she crossed her arms, hugging her breasts, staring up at him in silence.

His expression abruptly softened as he saw her shiver. "You need to be in bed," he said. "An evening spent hanging over the commode is enough to exhaust anyone." A smile tugged willy-nilly at the corners of his mouth as he imagined the scene. He could almost feel sorry for Gracemere. He picked up her discarded wineglass and handed it to her, saying lightly, "Be a good girl and finish your port, it'll warm you."

Judith's responding smile was somewhat tentative, but she obediently finished the wine and found it comforting in her sore and empty belly.

"Upstairs now." Marcus took the glass from her. "I'll come up later, when you're tucked in."

"I seem to need to be cuddled," Judith said in a voice that sounded small.

Marcus put his arms around her, holding her tightly against him, feeling her fragility. "I'll hold you all night," he promised into her fragrant hair. "I'll come as soon as Millie's helped you to bed."

He held her throughout the night, and she slept secure in his arms, but her dreams were filled with images of things cracked and broken under a tumultous reign of chaos.

28

A few days later, as he sat over the breakfast table, Marcus received an invitation from his old friend Colonel Morcby of the Seventh Hussars, requesting the pleasure of his company at a regimental dinner in the company of Arthur Wellesley, Duke of Wellington; Field Marshal Gebhard Leberecht von Blücher; and General Karl von Clausewitz, at eight o'clock in the evening of Wednesday, December 12 at regimental headquarters on Horseguard's Parade. December 12 was the night of the Duchess of Devonshire's ball.

Marcus drank his coffee, wondering how Judith would react if he cried off from the ball. It was the high point of the pre-Christmas festivities, and all fashionable London would be there. Would she feel neglected if she had to go alone? But her friends would be there, and her brother, he reasoned. It wasn't as if he'd see much of her all evening, even if he did escort her. Besides, Judith was not a woman to demand her husband's company when he'd received an invitation so vastly more appealing. He didn't doubt she'd understand the appeal of the invitation from Colonel Morcby.

He left the breakfast parlor and went upstairs to his wife's chamber. The atmosphere in the room was steamy and scented. The fire had been built as high as safety permitted and heat blasted the room, augmenting the steam wreathing from a copper hip bath drawn up before the hearth. Marcus blinked to clear his vision and then smiled.

Millie was pouring more water from a copper jug into the tub while Judith stood beside the bath, one toe delicately testing the temperature. Her hair was piled on top of her head and she hadn't a stitch of clothing on.

"Good morning, sir." She greeted him with a smile. "I think that'll do for the moment, Millie. But perhaps you should fetch up some more jugs from the kitchen for later. . . . I'm taking a bath, Marcus," she informed him somewhat unnecessarily.

"So I see." He stepped aside as Millie hurried past him through the doorway, carrying empty jugs.

"I intend to spend the entire morning luxuriating in hot water," she informed him, stepping into the tub. "It's a pity you can't join me."

"Who says I can't?"

"Well, no one." She let her head fall back against the rim, drawing her legs up so that her dimpled knees broke the surface of the water. "I simply assumed, since you're dressed for town, that you were not in the mood for beguilement."

"Sadly, I'm in the mood but unable to indulge," he said. "I'm on my way to Angelo's."

"Ah," said Judith, sitting up suddenly, slopping water over the edge of the bath onto the sheet spread beneath it. "I should like to learn to fence."

"You amaze me," Marcus said, shrugging out of his coat and rolling up his shirt sleeves. "I didn't think there was anything you didn't know how to do. Weren't you able to find an admirer to teach you?"

"Sadly, no," she said, sitting back again, regarding his preparations through narrowed eyes. "Perhaps you would like to take on the task."

"It'll be a pleasure." Marcus picked up the lavender-scented cake of soap from the dish beside the bath and moved behind her. "Lean forward and I'll do your back."

"You'll ruin your pantaloons, kneeling on the floor," she pointed out, remaining with her back against the tub.

"They are knitted, my dear, and mold themselves to my wishes," he observed. "Unlike my wife, it would seem." He slipped an arm around her, bending her forward so that he could soap the smooth plane of her back with firm circular movements, occasionally scribbling down her spine with a tantalizing fingernail.

Judith arched her back like a cat beneath the hard hands, bending her neck for the rough exploration of a fingertip creeping into her scalp.

"Oh, I was forgetting," Marcus murmured, sliding his hand down her back beneath the surface of the water on a more intimate laundering. "I've received an invitation to dine in Horseguard's Parade on Wednesday. Would you mind if I don't accompany you to the ball?" Gentle pressure bent her further over his encircling arm, and the sudden tension in her body, the ripple of her skin, he ascribed to its obvious cause.

"Who invited you?" She tried to sound casually interested, even though she knew the answer. Charlie had engineered the invitation from his own regimental colonel. Initially, he'd been puzzled by Judith's request that he do so, until she'd explained that she wanted it to be a surprise for Marcus, who would find the ball a dead bore and would much prefer to dine with his military friends.

Marcus was unable to hide his pleasure in the prospect of such an evening in such company as he told Judith what she already knew. It was slight balm to her guilty conscience.

Millie's reappearance with fresh jugs of hot water put an end to tantalizing play, and Marcus dropped the soap into the water, dried his hands, and stood up, rolling down his sleeves. "I'll leave you to your bath, lynx."

"Don't forget to tell John to accept the colonel's invitation before you go."

"I won't." Fleetingly he touched the topknot of copper ringlets as he went to the door. "An understanding wife is a pearl beyond price."

Oh, what a tangled web we weave. The desolate refrain seemed to have become a part of her bloodstream these days, thudding in time with the life blood in her veins.

Bernard Melville cast a covert glance at his opponent across the card table. Davenport was drinking heavily. His hair was tousled, flopping untidily over his broad forehead, and every now and again he would run his hands through it with a distracted air. He had been losing steadily for three hours and Bernard felt the gut-twisting excitement of the gamester who has his opponent on the run. He had ceased to keep count of his winnings, and knew from his own experience that Sebastian, in the grip of the same fever, would have no idea how much he'd lost. He had run out of rouleaux long since and now scribbled IOUs without apparent awareness; the pile of vowels mounted at Bernard's elbow.

Twice Bernard had used marked cards, when Sebastian had won the preceding hands and the earl, so addicted now to winning against him, hadn't been able to endure even the slightest possibility of further losses. He could smell blood, the taste of it was on his tongue. In another hour, he reckoned, Sebastian Davenport would be a ruined man.

"Sebastian, you've been at cards all evening." Harry Middleton strolled across to the table, trying to conceal his concern as he took in the vowels and rouleaux at Gracemere's elbow. "Leave it now, man, and come and be sociable."

Bernard was unable to conceal his fury at this interference and his breath hissed through his teeth. "Leave the man alone, Middleton, can't you see we're in the middle of play?"

Sebastian looked up and smiled in rather dazed fashion at his friend. "Devil take it, Harry, but I lost track of the time." His eyes focused again on his cards. "Last hand, Gracemere. I'm all rolled up for tonight." He laughed with an assumption of carelessness and discarded the knave of hearts.

Bernard had no choice but to accept the end of play when, at the end of the hand, Sebastian threw down his cards and yawned. "What's the damage, Gracemere?"

Bernard added up the points. "Ninety-eight."

"Rubiconed, by God!" Sebastian yawned again. "Tot up my vowels and I'll send you a draft on my bank in the morning."

The staggering sum handed to him had its effect. The earl examined him covertly, noting the sudden slight tremor of his hands, the tightening of his mouth. Then Sebastian looked up, raised his eyebrows in an assumption of carelessness, and whistled. "You'll give me a chance to come about, I trust, my lord?"

"But of course—tomorrow, at Devonshire House?" Bernard almost licked his fleshy lips in anticipation.

Sebastian nodded, tried to laugh, but it had a hollow ring. "Why not? It'll be a dull enough affair otherwise, I'll lay odds." Flinging a comradely arm around Harry's shoulder, he strolled off with his friend.

"It looked like you lost a fortune," Harry remarked, giving his friend an anxious stare.

Sebastian shrugged. "I'll get it back, Harry, tomorrow."

"I told you, Gracemere's a bad man to play with."

Sebastian looked down at his friend and Harry saw a different light in his eyes. He spoke softly. "So am I, Harry, as Gracemere is going to find out. You'll see."

Harry's scalp prickled. He had never seen Sebastian look like that, never heard that note in his voice. He suddenly saw Sebastian Davenport as a dangerous man, and he didn't know how or why he should have formed such an impression.

29

"Gregson, when my brother calls you may send him straight up to the yellow drawing room. But I'm not at home to anyone else." Judith crossed the hall to the stairs the following morning, pausing to rearrange a display of bronze chrysanthemums in a copper jug on a marble table.

"Very well, my lady."

"These are past their best," she said, giving up on the flowers. "Have them replaced, please."

"Yes, my lady." Gregson bowed. There was an unusual sharpness in her ladyship's voice this morning, a slight air of irritability about her.

Judith ran up to her own sanctum, where she sat down immediately in front of the chess board. The problem set out was sufficiently complex to occupy her mind for the next hour while she waited for her brother. They would spend the greater part of the day training for the evening's play, separating at the end of the afternoon with time enough to rest and compose themselves before the game began.

It was a pattern they had established long since, on their travels, but it had been many months since they'd used it. Despite her anxiety, the immense value of the stakes, Judith was aware of the old familiar prickle of excitement, the surge of exhilaration.

Sebastian arrived before midmorning. He greeted her briefly, then shrugged out of his coat and sat down in his shirt-sleeves, breaking the pack of cards on the table. "Let's go over the code for aces. The movement you make for the spade is very similar to the one for the heart. I want to see if we can sharpen the difference." Judith nodded and picked up her fan.

They worked steadily until noon, making minor adjustments to the code of signals, then they played a game of chess until Gregson announced nuncheon. Marcus walked into the dining room to find his wife and her brother eating scalloped oysters and cold chicken in absorbed silence.

"If I didn't know you both better, I'd think I was interrupting a quarrel," he observed, helping himself to oysters.

"No," Judith said, managing a smile. "We were just absorbed in our own thoughts. How was your morning?"

Marcus began to regale them with a tale he'd heard at Brooks's, and then realized that they weren't listening to him. He paused, waited for one of them to notice that he hadn't finished the story, and when neither of them did, shrugged and turned his attention to his plate.

"Are you dining at home this evening, Ju?" Sebastian asked abruptly.

"No, at the Henleys'," she answered. "Isobel's giving a dinner party before the ball."

"Oh, good." Marcus refilled his glass, smiling across the table at her. "I didn't like to think of you dining alone, lynx."

"Oh, I can usually avoid such a fate, if I wish to," she said with a lift of her eyebrows. "I'm not dependent upon my husband's company, my lord."

Ordinarily, the remark would have been bantering, but for some reason Marcus sensed a strain in the words, and her smile seemed effortful. Perhaps she *had* quarreled with Sebastian.

"Do you have something important to do this afternoon, Judith, or would you like to ride with me in Richmond Park? It's a beautiful afternoon," he asked at the end of the meal.

She shook her head. "Another day I'd come with pleasure, but this afternoon Sebastian and I have plans that can't be put off."

"Oh." He tossed his napkin on the table, concealing his hurt and puzzlement. "Then I'll leave you to them."

"Oh, dear," Judith whispered as the door closed softly behind him. "I didn't mean to sound so dismissive, but I couldn't think what other excuse to make."

"After tonight, you won't have to make excuses." Sebastian pushed back his chair. "Let's get back to work."

By five o'clock, they knew they had covered every eventuality, every combination of hands that skill and experience could come up with. They knew how Gracemere played when he played straight, and Sebastian knew what tricks he favored when he played crooked. They now had in place their own system that would defeat the earl's marked cards.

"We've done the best we can," Sebastian pronounced finally. "There's an element of chance, of course, but there always is."

"He's a gamester who's scented blood," Judith said. "We know what that madness is like. Once in the grip of it, he'll not stop until he's at *point non plus* . . . or you are."

"It will not be I," her brother said with quiet confidence.

"No." Judith held out her hand. They clasped hands in silent communion that held both promise and resolve. Then Sebastian bent and kissed her cheek and left. She listened to his feet receding on the stairs, before going up to her room to lie down with pads soaked in witch hazel on her eyes, and a swirling cloud of playing cards in her internal vision.

Gracemere escorted Agnes Barret to Devonshire House some time after ten o'clock. They were early, but not unfashionably so, and spent an hour circulating the salons. They danced twice and then Agnes was claimed by a bewhiskered acquaintance of her ailing husband's. "I shall enjoy watching you pluck your pigeon later," she said softly as they parted. Her lips curved in a smile of malicious anticipation, and her little white teeth glimmered for a minute. Gracemere bowed over her hand.

"Such an audience can only add spice to an already delicious prospect, madam."

"I trust you'll have another audience also," she murmured.

The earl's pale eyes narrowed vindictively. "The sister as well? Yes, ma'am. I trust so. It will add savor to the spice."

"It's to be hoped she doesn't vomit over you again." Agnes's soft laugh was as malicious as her earlier smile, and she went off on the arm of her partner.

Gracemere looked around the rapidly filling salon.

There was no sign as yet of Sebastian Davenport, but he saw Judith enter with Isobel Henley and her party and his lips tightened. Since the debacle at Jermyn Street, he had continued to cultivate her as assiduously as ever, although always out of sight of Marcus. His motive now was simple. A beloved sister would watch her brother's downfall. Judith would suffer in impotent horror as she witnessed her brother's destruction, and the earl would have some small satisfaction for the mortification she had caused him. Marcus's pride would be humbled at the public humiliation of his brother-in-law, and Gracemere and Agnes would have Harriet Moreton and her fortune.

The earl made his way over to Judith. "Magnificent," he murmured, raising her hand to his lips. His admiration was genuine. Emeralds blazed in her copper hair and around the white throat. Her gown of gold spider gauze over bronze satin was startlingly unusual, and a perfect foil for her hair.

"Flatterer," she declared, tapping his wrist with her fan. "But, indeed, my lord, I am not immune to flattery, so pray don't stop."

He laughed and escorted her to the dance floor. "Your husband doesn't accompany you?"

"Alas, no," she said with a mock sigh. "A regimental dinner claimed his attention."

"How fortunate." A smile touched his lips and Judith felt clammy. "I don't see your brother here either."

"Oh, I daresay he'll be along later," she said. "He was to dine with friends."

"We have an agreement to meet at the card table," the earl told her, still smiling. "We're engaged in battle."

"Oh, yes, Sebastian told me. A duel of piquet." She laughed. "Sebastian is determined to win tonight, Bernard, I should warn you. He says he lost out of hand last night and must recoup his losses if he's not to be completely rolled up." She laughed, as if at the absurdity of such an idea, and Gracemere allowed an answering chuckle to escape him.

"I'm most eager to give him his revenge. Dare I hope that his lovely sister will stand at my side?"

"Well, as to that, sir, it might seem disloyal in me to appear to favor my brother's adversary," she said archly. "But I shall maintain an impartial interest. I confess I derive much pleasure from watching two such accomplished players in combat." She leaned forward and said almost guiltily, "But I do believe, Bernard, that you have the edge."

"Now it's you who are guilty of flattery, ma'am," Gracemere said in barely concealed mockery. Fortunately, Judith appeared not to hear the mockery.

"But you did win last night," she pointed out very seriously. "However, perhaps the cards weren't running in Sebastian's favor. It does make a difference, after all."

"Oh, of course it does," he agreed. "All the difference in the world, my dear Judith. Let's hope luck smiles upon your brother tonight . . . just to even things up, you understand."

"Yes, of course." The music stopped and the earl was obliged to relinquish her to a new partner . . . but not without reminding her of her promise to be in the card room later. Judith agreed, all smiles, and then took her place in the set. *So far so good.*

When Sebastian arrived, he was all smiling good humor, greeting friends and acquaintances, obliging his hostess by dancing with several unfortunate ladies who were without partners, imbibing liberally of champagne, and generally behaving like any other young blood.

To his relief and Harriet's not-so-secret chagrin, Harriet had not received an invitation to the ball. It was her first Season and she was too young and unknown to move invariably in the first circles. Once Sebastian declared his suit and her engagement to the Marquis of Carrington's brother-in-law was known, that would change, as Letitia told her, but this was small comfort to Harriet, spending the evening in dutiful attendance upon her mama.

It was after midnight when Sebastian and Gracemere met in the card room. Judith was watching for the moment when they both disappeared from the dance floor. It had been agreed that she wouldn't make her own appearance at the table until after they'd been playing for a while, by which time Sebastian would have established a winning pattern and they assumed that Gracemere would be ready to resort to marked cards.

For nearly an hour she continued to dance, to smile, to talk. She ate supper, sipped champagne, and forced herself not to think of what was happening in the card room. If it was going according to plan, Bernard Melville would by now be wondering what was happening to him.

At one o'clock she made her way to the gaming room. Immediately it was clear that something unusual was happening. Although there were people playing at the hazard, faro, macao, and basset tables, there was a distracted air in the room. Eyes were flickering to a small table in an alcove, where two men played piquet.

Judith crossed the room. "I've come to keep my promise, my lord," she said gaily.

Gracemere looked up from his cards and she recognized the look in his eye. It was the haunted feverishness of a man in captivity to the cards. "Your brother's luck has turned, it would seem," he said, clearing his throat.

Judith saw the pile of rouleaux at her brother's elbow. The earl was not yet resorting to vowels, then. She took up her place, casually, behind the earl's chair.

Gracemere was confusedly aware that the man he was playing with was not the man he thought he knew. Davenport's face was utterly impassive, he was silent most of the time, and when he spoke it was with staccato precision. The only part of his body he seemed to move were his long white hands on the cards.

Initially, the earl put his losses down to an uneven fall of the cards. When first he thought there must be more to it than that, he dismissed the idea. He'd played often enough with Sebastian Davenport to know what quality of player he was. True, occasionally he had won, sometimes puzzlingly, but even poor gamesters had occasional successes. As Gracemere's losses mounted, the ridiculousness of it all struck him powerfully. He increased the stakes, knowing that everything would go back to normal in a minute—it always did. All he needed was to win one game when the stakes were really high, and he would recoup his losses in one fell swoop. With that knowledge in mind, he played his first marked card. His sleight-of-hand was so expert that Judith missed it the first time and he won heavily.

Sebastian was unmoved, merely pushing across a substantial pile of rouleaux. Judith gave an excited little cry, saying in an exaggerated whisper, "Oh, well done, sir."

Gracemere didn't seem to hear her. He increased the stakes yet again. By now people were drifting toward the table, attracted by the tension. It was warm and Judith opened her fan.

Gracemere began to have a dreadful sense of topsy-turvy familiarity. This scene had happened before but there was an essential difference. He was not winning. He played with a dogged concentration, writing vowels now much as his adversary had done the previous evening. He played his marked cards, and yet he still didn't win. At one point, he looked wildly across the small table at his opponent as he played a heart that would spoil a repique. But Davenport seemed prepared and played his own ten, keeping his point advantage. How could it be happening? There was no explanation, except that his adversary had changed from a conceited greenhorn to a card player of awesome skill. And not just skill—it would take a magician to withstand the earl's special cards.

He glanced up at the woman, gently fanning herself at his shoulder. She smiled reassuringly at him, as if she didn't understand what was happening to him . . . as if she simply thought her brother was having a run of good luck for once.

He was a gamester. He knew he needed only one win. If he staked everything he had left, then he could recoup everything and bring his opponent to the ground.

George Devereux had at the last wagered the family estates in Yorkshire. Bernard Melville drew another sheet of paper and wrote his stake, the estate he had won from George Devereux, pushing it across the table to his adversary. Sebastian glanced at it, then swept his own winnings, rouleaux and vowels, together with his own IOU to match his opponent's extraordinary stake, into a pile at the side of the table. He put his hand in his pocket and deliberately drew out an elaborately carved signet ring. This last game he played for his father. His eyes flicked upward to his sister, who nodded infinitesimally in acknowledgment, before he slipped the ring onto his finger, shook back the ruffles on his shirt-sleeves, and broke a new pack of cards, beginning to deal.

Agnes Barret stared at the ring on Sebastian Davenport's finger. Her world seemed to turn on its axis, a slow roll into a nightmare of disbelief. She wanted to scream some kind of a warning to Bernard, so powerful was her sense of the danger embodied in that ring, but no sound would emerge from her throat. Her eyes were riveted on it: the Devereux family ring. She tore her eyes from Sebastian's long slender fingers and gazed at his sister. For a second Judith's golden brown eyes met Agnes's gaze, and the shock of her own recognition stunned Agnes with its primitive, vital force. And she wondered with a horrified desperation why she hadn't known it before . . . why some instinctive maternal essence had failed to recognize the children she hadn't seen since their babyhood.

Marcus Devlin, Marquis of Carrington, stood in the open doorway of the card room. The buzz of the attentive crowd around the players was so low as to be almost subliminal. He could see across the throng. He could see his wife, the steady, purposeful movement of her fan. He knew what she was doing. She and her brother were defrauding the Earl of Gracemere under the eyes of fashionable London. He couldn't imagine why, he knew only that he could do nothing about it. Only by exposing them could he stop it.

Distantly, in abject cowardice, he wished his evening had not ended when it had, or that he had gone straight home from Horseguard's Parade instead of following temptation and coming to find his wife. Wretchedly he wished he could have been spared this knowledge, because it was a knowledge he didn't know what to do with. It was a knowledge that destroyed love . . . that made impossible any kind of trust and confidence on which love and marriage could be based.

The moment when the Devereux estate passed back into the hands of its rightful heir, Agnes Barret understood everything. Bernard Melville had been beaten at his own game by the children of the man he had destroyed twenty years earlier. She didn't know how they'd done it, but she knew both brother and sister were partners. The nincompoops, the greenhorns, the simpletons, had been working toward this moment from the day they'd set foot in London.

A sick, impotent rage filled her throat as she saw Bernard's blank incomprehension as he lost the final hand. Agnes's eyes rose again to the face of her daughter standing behind him. Judith's gaze met hers—met and read the wild fury, the depths of a vindictive rage. And Judith's eyes carried a cold triumph that met and matched that vindictive rage. Agnes dropped her wineglass. It fell from suddenly nerveless fingers to smash on the parquet at her feet, splattering ruby red drops.

The low buzz increased in volume. Desperately Gracemere struggled to control his disordered thoughts. There was one chance to salvage everything. Twenty years ago he had placed a marked card in the hand of his opponent. And George Devereux had been dishonored and destroyed. If he could do the same now, at this moment publicly expose his adversary, he would recoup his losses. A cheat would not be permitted to keep his dishonorable winnings.

Hope soared and his confusion died as his thoughts became icily clear. "Well played, Davenport," he said into the tense hush. Lightly he shook down his sleeve, palming a card.

Judith's fan snapped shut.

"You won't mind if I take a look at—"

Before he could finish the sentence, before his hand could reach to caress his opponent's cards on the table—to remove and substitute—Sebastian Davenport suddenly spoke, and the words sent a wave of nausea through the earl, bile filling his mouth.

"Permit me," George Devereux's son said, grasping his adversary's stretched wrist. "Permit me, my lord."

It was at this moment that Marcus moved. He pushed through the crowd, reaching his wife's side. He said nothing, but he grasped her elbow and the knuckles of his other hand punched into the small of her back, compelling her forward, away from the table.

She hadn't known he was there, and when she looked up at him, at the rigid set of his jaw, the fine line of his mouth, the black, adamantine eyes, she knew that he had seen it all. In that moment she fully understood what she was about to lose.

Marcus saw the dazed look in her eyes . . . the look of someone who has been inhabiting another world, a world of acute, single-minded concentration. He continued to compel her toward the door, oblivious of the scene still at the table.

"No . . ." Judith said, her voice thick. "Please, wait, just one minute. . . . It must be completed."

The intensity in the low voice caught him off balance, and he stopped. Sebastian's voice was cold and steady in the now totally hushed room.

"May I see the card in your hand, my lord."

Sebastian's long fingers were bloodless as they gripped Gracemere's wrist, forcing his hand over to reveal the card lying snug in the palm.

Marcus turned his head slowly, although he maintained his hold on Judith. He watched in amazement as his brother-in-law slid the card from the earl's now-slack grasp. He heard his brother-in-law say, "Such an interesting pip on the corner, Gracemere. I don't think I've seen its like before. Harry, do you care to look at this card?"

Judith sighed, her entire body seeming to lose its rigidity as Harry Middleton took the card from his friend. Marcus wondered if he would ever understand anything again. And then with cold ferocity he decided

that he would understand this if he had to put his wife
on the rack to do so.

"March!" he spat out, and the pressure of his knuckles in the small of her back increased.

Judith made no further protest. She had now to face
the one thing she'd feared more than anything.

They left Devonshire House without so much as a
polite farewell and journeyed home in a silence weighted
with dread. When the chaise drew up, Marcus sprang to
the pavement, lifted Judith down before she had a chance
to put a foot on the step, and swung her in front of him,
propelling her up the steps and into the hall with his
knuckles still pressed deeply into her back so she began
to imagine she would always bear their imprint.

Inside, she glanced bleakly up at him. "Book room?"

"Just so." But he still didn't allow her to make un-
hindered progress and drove her ahead of him down the
passage.

He pushed her into the room and flung the door
shut with similar roughness. Judith shivered, afraid not
so much of what he would do to her but of what she had
done to him. He let her go as the door slammed and
went to the fireplace, leaning his shoulders against the
mantelshelf, his expression black as he stared at her
standing silently in front of him.

"You are now going to tell me the truth," he said
flatly. "It's possible you have never told the whole truth
in your life before, but now you are going to do so.
Everything. You will dot every 'i' and cross every 't,'
because, so help me, if you leave anything out—if you
obfuscate in any way whatsoever—I will not answer for
the consequences. Now, begin."

It was the only chance to salvage anything out of the
ruins. But it was a desperate chance at best. Judith took a

deep breath and began at the beginning—twenty years earlier.

Marcus listened, unmoving, unspeaking, until she fell silent and the room seemed to close around them, the weight of her words a leaden pall to smother trust.

"I now understand why your brother was so anxious to make peace between us," he said, speaking slowly and carefully, articulating every word as if formulating the thought as he spoke. "Estranged from your husband, you wouldn't be much use to him, would you?"

"No," Judith agreed bleakly. What defense was there?

"So you were both looking for the perfect gull . . . that is the right word, isn't it? The perfect gull who would facilitate your long-planned vengeance."

Judith shook her head. "No, that's not true. I can see why you would think that, but it's not true. I didn't plot to marry you. Sebastian told the truth."

Marcus raised a skeptical eyebrow. "Deny if you can that I have been very useful to you."

"I can't deny that," she said miserably. "Any more than I can't fail to understand your anger and hurt. I ask only that you believe there was no deliberate intention to use you."

"But you didn't feel able to confide in me," he stated. "Even after matters were going smoothly between us. What have I done in these last weeks, Judith, that would deny me your trust?"

She shook her head again. "Nothing . . . nothing . . . but if I'd told you what we intended to do you would have prevented me, wouldn't you?"

"Oh, yes," he said savagely. "I would have locked you up and thrown away the key if it was the only way to prevent my wife from disgracing my honor in such despicable fashion."

Judith flushed and for the first time a note of vibrancy returned to her voice. "Gracemere got what he deserved. He's been robbing Sebastian blind for weeks now. Just as he defrauded our father . . . defrauded him and then accused *him* of cheating. Would you be so poor-spirited as to allow a man who did that to *your* father to go scot free? Can't you understand the need for vengeance, for justice, Marcus? The driving power that closes one's mind to all else but the need to avenge . . . to take back what has been stolen?"

Marcus didn't respond to this impassioned plea. Instead, he inquired in a tone of distant curiosity, "Tell me, was it pure coincidence that I received an invitation from Morcby for tonight?"

Judith's color deepened and the fight went out of her again as she saw the hopelessness of her position. "No," she confessed dismally. "Charlie—"

"Charlie? Are you telling me that you have involved my cousin in this deception . . . this betrayal?" His eyes were great black holes in his white face.

"Not exactly. . . . I mean, I did ask him to procure the invitation but I didn't tell him why." She stared at him, her hands pressed to her burning cheeks, devastated by what she had said, by what he was entitled to feel.

He drew a deep, shuddering breath. "Get out of my sight! I can't trust myself in the same room with you."

"Marcus, please—" She took a step toward him.

He flung out his hands as if to ward her off. "Go!"

"Please . . . please *try* to understand, to see it just a little through my eyes," she pleaded, unable to accept her dismissal, terrified that if she obeyed him, the vast gulf yawning between them would become infinite.

He took her by the upper arms and shook her until her head whipped back and forth and she felt sick. Then his hands fell from her as if she were a burning brand, or something disgusting that he couldn't endure to touch any longer. While she stood dazed in the middle of the room, rubbing her bruised arms, he stormed out, leaving the door swinging open.

Judith crept into a deep chair by the fire and huddled into it, curling in on herself, racked with deep shuddering spasms of devastation.

She didn't know how long she'd been crouching there like some small wounded animal in emeralds and spider gauze and satin before Marcus returned.

He stood over her and spoke with a distant politeness. "I'm sorry if I hurt you. I didn't intend to. Come upstairs now, you need your bed."

"I think I'd rather stay here, thank you." She heard her voice, as stiffly polite as his.

Marcus bent and scooped her out of the chair. He set her on her feet. "Must I carry you?"

She shook her head and started out of the room. Neither of them could endure such physical contact tonight—not with all the rich, sensual memories embedded in such a touching.

She walked ahead of him up the stairs and into her own room. Marcus turned aside through his own door.

30

Judith lay awake through the last remaining hours of darkness. She stared upward at the canopy over the bed, her eyelids peeled back as if they were held open with sticks, her eyeballs feeling shrunken and dried like shriveled peas. Despite a bone-deep bodily fatigue and total emotional exhaustion, she couldn't imagine sleeping. She lay straight-limbed in the bed, the sheet pulled up to her chin, her body perfectly aligned on the mattress, feeling the throbbing bruises on her arms where Marcus had held her and shaken her as the only truly alive parts of herself.

There ought to have been a sense of completion: The long dark road to vengeance had been traveled. Sebastian was in possession of his birthright and whatever depredations Gracemere's profligacy had worked upon the estate,

Sebastian would work to put right. George Devereux was avenged; his children had a place in the world he had been driven from.

There ought to have been a sense of completion, of satisfaction. But there was only emptiness. Where there should have been gain there was only the greatest loss. What price vengeance when set against the loss of love? She had tried to have both and what she'd won was ashes on the wind.

Except for Sebastian, she reminded herself. Sebastian could now have the love of his Harriet, now that he had something to offer her. Sebastian could retire to the country and fulfill his bucolic dreams. And for herself . . . ?

The only thing she could do for Marcus was to remove herself as gracefully as possible from his life. There was no legal impediment to such a disappearance. She would tell him so as soon as she could. On which melancholy decision, she managed to fall asleep just as the sun came up.

She awoke at midmorning, rang for Millie, rose and dressed in desultory silence. "Is his lordship in, do you know, Millie?"

"I believe he went out after breakfast, my lady." Millie brushed a speck of lint from the sleeve of a blue silk spencer before holding it out for her. "You're looking a trifle fatigued, my lady," she observed with concern. "A little rouge might help."

Judith examined herself in the glass. Her eyes were dull and heavy in a pallid complexion. She shook her head. "No, I think it would just make things worse." She fastened a string of coral around her throat and went downstairs to the yellow drawing room.

"Mr. Davenport left his card an hour ago, my lady." Gregson presented the silver salver.

"Thank you, Gregson. Could you bring me some coffee, please?"

Sebastian had scrawled a note on the back of the card: *Why aren't I jubilant? I feel as if we lost not won. Come to me when you can. I need to talk to you.*

Judith tossed the card into the fire. She would probably be feeling the same as her brother even without the catastrophe with Marcus. The intensity had been too great to leave one feeling anything but drained. And she needed Sebastian now as she'd never needed him before.

"Lady Barret, my lady," Gregson intoned, entering the room with a tray of coffee.

Judith saw Agnes's face as it had been last night, a mask of rage and hatred. Her heart jumped then seemed to drop into her stomach. She opened her mouth to tell Gregson to make her excuses, but Agnes walked in on the heels of the butler. Her face was almost as pale as Judith's.

"Lady Barret." Judith bowed, hearing how thin her voice sounded. "How kind of you to call. Another cup, Gregson."

"No, I don't wish for coffee, thank you," Agnes said. She didn't return Judith's bow but paced the room, waiting for Gregson to finish pouring Judith's coffee.

When the door closed on the butler, Agnes swung round on her daughter. Her eyes blazed in her face, where two spots of rouge burned in violent contrast to her pallor. "Let us take off the gloves, Judith. I don't know *how* you did it, but I know *what* you and your brother did last night."

"Oh?" Judith, struggling for calm, raised an ironic eyebrow. "And what was that?"

"Somehow, between you, you cheated Gracemere." Agnes's voice shook and her pallor had become even more pronounced. Her hands trembled and she clasped them tightly together. "You ruined him!" Her voice was a low hiss and she advanced on Judith, who stepped back, away from the force of this vengeful rage.

"He would have ruined my brother as he ruined our father," Judith said, a quaver in her voice. There was no point in denying the truth with this woman, who seemed somehow to know everything anyway. Unconsciously her hands passed through the air as if she could thus dispel the enveloping evil miasma.

Agnes laughed, a shocking crack of amusement. "Unlike you and your brother, your father was a weak fool. He had no idea how to stand up for himself . . . or to hold onto what he owned."

Judith stared at the woman. Even through her fear and outrage, she recognized the truth of what Agnes had said. But she had always assumed exile and poverty had destroyed George's stability and willpower. Agnes was implying that it had an earlier genesis. "What do you know of my father?" she demanded. "What could you possibly know of the life he led?"

Agnes laughed again and abruptly Judith turned from her. "Get out of my house, Lady Barret."

"I'll leave when I've said what I came here to say, Judith." Her voice dropped to barely a whisper, but each word had bell-like clarity in the still room. "You will pay for what you did . . . you and your brother."

"Oh, I am paying," Judith said softly, almost to herself. "You don't know how much." Then her voice strengthened. "But my brother will now enjoy his birthright. Sebastian will take his happiness with both hands now. *His* happiness and place in the world is assured."

"He will pay," Agnes reiterated with a cold certainty that sent renewed chills up Judith's spine.

She could think of nothing to say to combat the

menace in the room and, when Gregson opened the door, turned with blind relief toward the distraction.

"Lady Devlin, Lady Isobel Henley, and Mrs. Forsythe."

"Judith, it's the talk of the town," Isobel exclaimed, swirling into the room in a cloud of muslin. "Your brother exposed the Earl of Gracemere as a cheat!"

"I left before midnight," Cornelia put in. She tripped on the edge of the rug and caught herself just in time. "But Forsythe was full of it over the breakfast table. He says Gracemere will never be able to show his face in Society again . . . Oh, I beg your pardon, Lady Barret. I didn't see you standing there."

Under Judith's incredulous stare, a complete change came over Agnes. The ice left her eyes, a tinge of normal color returned to her cheeks. Her voice was as light and nonchalant as ever. "As Lady Isobel says, it's the talk of the town. I'm sure everyone will be beating a path to your door, Lady Carrington, to talk of your brother."

"I wonder how long the earl has been cheating," Sally commented, sitting down beside the fire. "It couldn't be that he only began last night, could it?"

"Unlikely," Judith said, trying to respond normally. If Agnes Barret could behave as if there were no history and the things that had been said in this room had never been spoken, then so could she. She drew on a lifetime's experience with a masquerade and showed her own mask of insouciance.

"But how did Sebastian know?"

"He's been playing with the earl for the last two months," Judith said, shrugging, averting her eyes from Agnes. "I imagine he realized something wasn't quite right before."

"Miss Moreton, my lady." The door again opened and an excited Harriet bounced in.

"Oh, Judith, I could barely contain myself . . . such extraordinary news. Is it true that Sebastian discovered the Earl of Gracemere cheating? Oh, how I wish I could have been there." Then Harriet saw Agnes and subsided, blushing furiously.

"You have, of course, never cared for Gracemere, have you, my dear?" Agnes remarked. "Nevertheless, one shouldn't gloat over another's misfortune."

"I find it hard to call it misfortune, ma'am," Isobel said, scrutinizing the plate of sweet biscuits on the coffee tray. "When a man deliberately sets out to injure another man and is unmasked, misfortune seems a misnomer." She selected a piece of shortbread.

Agnes bowed coldly and began to leaf through a periodical on a console table. Cornelia kicked Isobel's ankle with lamentable lack of delicacy and an uneasy silence fell for a minute. Then Sally spoke with customary good nature. "It's quite shocking news, of course. But one can only assume that the earl had a compelling reason to play in that manner. Debts of unmanageable magnitude . . . what other explanation could there be?"

"You're right," Cornelia said. "We shouldn't be the first to throw stones."

"No," Sally agreed, thinking of four thousand pounds' worth of pawned rubies.

In the next half hour, it seemed that half London was indeed beating a path to Judith's door, agog to learn any details that might not be generally known. Judith dispensed hospitality, asserted she had no inside snippets of gossip since she hadn't seen her brother since the previous evening, and all the while her head spun with conjecture. What possible revenge could Agnes and Gracemere have in mind? The speculation took her mind off her trouble with Marcus to some extent, but did nothing to restore her equilibrium. She waited impa-

tiently for her guests to take their leave, so that she could
go to Sebastian.

"Judith, I must go home, Annie has the croup."
Sally appeared at Judith's elbow. "Nurse is quite good
with her, but the poor little love frets if I'm away too
long."

"I'm sorry." Judith received this information with
less than her usual attention. "It's not serious, I hope."

"No . . . Judith, is something the matter?" Sally
regarded her friend closely. "You seem *distrait.*"

"It's hardly surprising," Judith said, trying to pass it
off, gesturing around the crowded room. "After last
night."

"I suppose not. What did Marcus have to say?" It
was a shrewd guess, but Sally was good at guessing games
when it came to Devlins.

Judith shook her head. "Not now, Sally."

Sally accepted this with a nod and a compassionate
kiss. "Oh, I was forgetting, Harriet had to leave . . .
some errand she has to run for her mother. You were
deep in conversation and she didn't want to interrupt, so
I said I'd say good-bye for her."

"Thanks. I expect Sebastian will be able to answer all
her questions later." Judith smiled, but the strain in the
smile was obvious. Sally pressed her hand briefly and left.

Judith looked around the room and realized that Agnes Barret had also made a discreet departure. But then
she wouldn't have expected her to make any farewells.

Judith walked to Albemarle Street as soon as the last
visitor had left. Sebastian had been watching for her from
his front window and came to open the door himself.
"I've been hiding," he confessed. "I saw Harry Middleton this morning, but I've had Broughton deny me to
everyone else."

"Wise of you," she said. "My drawing room's been

full since midmorning with people trying to pry some additional tidbit out of me." She unpinned her hat and drew off her gloves.

Sebastian poured sherry. "You look the very devil," he said frankly. "What happened to you last night? I looked up and you'd gone."

"Marcus took me away just as you were exposing Gracemere."

Sebastian whistled soundlessly. "He saw."

She nodded. "All of it."

"Bad?"

She nodded again. "Very. As bad as we knew it would be if he found out."

"I'm sorry, love." Sebastian took his sister in his arms and she wept quietly for a few moments while he stroked her hair. "When he's had time to calm down, to look at it clearly, he'll understand. He knows you love him. He'd have to be a blind man not to know it."

"I hoped he loved me," she said drearily. "But love is easily killed, it seems. He despises me." She heard again his voice telling her to go away . . . to get out of his sight. Such furious contempt.

"Stuff," her brother said. "Of course he doesn't despise you."

"Yes, he does. Anyway, let's not talk of it anymore now. Agnes Barret paid me a visit this morning."

She explained what Agnes had said and Sebastian listened attentively. "There's nothing she could do," he said at the end. "Neither of them has any redress, Ju. Gracemere will have to leave London. He's already been obliged to resign from his clubs, according to Harry. He can rusticate in the country or go abroad. But there's no place in Society for him now . . . or ever again."

"And Agnes?"

"She's untarnished. She can continue as before."

"But without her lover. And if her fortunes are tied with Gracemere's then his ruin is hers, one way or the other."

"Either she ends her relationship with Gracemere, or she abandons her place in Society and joins him in exile. Not comfortable choices. Now, what are we going to do about Marcus?"

Judith shook her head tiredly. "I don't believe there's anything to be done. I'll leave him as soon as I can decently do so without causing remark. We'll concoct some story to put me out of the way, and Marcus will be free to marry or to continue to live as he did before he met me."

Sebastian could think of nothing to say in the face of this dreary future. Any option he might offer would be just as wretched when compared with what might have been.

Judith reached for her hat and gloves. "I'd better go home. Maybe Marcus will be back by now."

She walked back to Berkeley Square and found Harriet's maid on the doorstep. "Beggin' your pardon, m'lady, but Lady Moreton sent me." The girl bobbed a curtsy. "She asks as 'ow could you send miss 'ome as soon as possible."

"Send her home?" Judith stared at the girl. "But she went home a long time ago." It was a mere ten minutes' walk from Berkeley Square to Brook Street. "Oh, but she said she had some errands to run for Lady Moreton. I expect that's where she is."

"Oh, no, m'lady," the girl corrected. "Miss already sent the footman home with her ladyship's tonic."

"You'd better come in," Judith said, and the girl followed her into the house.

"Gregson, did you see Miss Moreton leave earlier?"

"Oh, yes, my lady. She left with Lady Barret."

Judith felt the blood drain from her face. Harriet . . . with Agnes. She saw again those tawny eyes, glittering with maleficence, heard again the hissed threats.

She thought of Harriet, the perfect means of revenge upon Sebastian.

"Tell your mistress that Miss Moreton went with Lady Barret. I'm certain she'll be returning shortly," she instructed the maid. "Gregson, send someone to find his lordship." Her voice was crisp, offering no hint of the terror she felt. "In fact, send as many people as necessary. He may be at one of his clubs, or at Jackson's Saloon . . . at one of his friends' houses. But he must be found immediately."

"Is there a message, my lady?"

"Simply that he's needed at home immediately."

Judith went up to her drawing room. Once private, she paced the room in agitation, feeling completely helpless. What would they do with Harriet? Marcus had an inner knowledge of Gracemere, he'd have some idea of what he intended. She was far too agitated to worry about how she would face him after last night's hideous scene; neither did it occur to her that her husband would withhold his help, however deeply disgusted he was with his wife and her brother. Marcus was not vindictive. With the greatest difficulty, she resisted the urge to send a message to Sebastian. What could he do, except join her in impotent fear?

Marcus was in Gentleman Jackson's Saloon, when one of the six footmen ran him to earth. Stripped to the waist, pouring sweat, he was attempting to exorcise misery and disappointment in a violent bout with a punchball.

He had passed no better a night than Judith, but the sharpest spur of his hurt was becoming blunter and some elements of rationality beginning to offer a spark of light in his darkness. He could hear her voice clearly now demanding that he understand the driving power of vengeance. He knew that power. Once he'd obeyed its spur himself . . . and with Gracemere. There was a perfect appropriateness to the vengeance Judith and Sebastian had taken. But still he couldn't reconcile himself to the knowledge that he'd been used. If only she'd taken him into her confidence . . .

But how could she have done so? He would have stopped her. However sympathetic he might have been to her brother's situation, to her father's ruin, he would never have permitted Judith to do what she'd done. And the destruction of Bernard Melville, Earl of Gracemere, was central to Judith's view of the world. Until that had been accomplished, nothing else could take precedence . . . not even her husband. Had he the right to believe she should have dropped the most powerful imperative of her life—and her brother's life—simply because *he* had come on the scene? Her bond with her brother was too complex and too strong to be severed by the simple ties of passion . . . of lust and a burgeoning love.

He didn't countenance what she'd done, but he understood it. From understanding could come acceptance . . .

"My lord, one of your men has a message for you."

Marcus grabbed a towel, rubbing the sweat from his face. "Someone for me, Jackson?"

"Yes, my lord." Gentleman Jackson indicated the lad in Carrington livery, standing at the far side of the room, gazing wide-eyed at the sparring couples.

"What the devil can he want?" Marcus beckoned and the lad trotted across, his message spilling from his lips. "Her ladyship, my lord, wishes you to return home immediately."

"Her ladyship!" His heart lurched. Only the direst

necessity would send Judith in search of him in this fashion.

"Is her ladyship well?" he demanded, toweling his sweat-soaked head.

"Yes, my lord," the man said. "I believe so, my lord. Gregson said we was all to search London for you."

"All?"

"Yes, my lord. There's six of us."

"Go back to Berkeley Square and say I'm on my way," Marcus instructed tersely, his heart slowing as he went into the changing room. If Judith was well and unhurt, that was all that mattered. Surely she wouldn't have sent all over London for him just to tell him that she was leaving him . . . although, knowing his lynx, maybe he shouldn't be so sanguine. So far, he hadn't managed to keep a step ahead of her. Why should he assume he could do so now?

He dressed in haste and took a hackney home. Gregson had the door open as he ran up the steps. "Her ladyship . . . ?"

"In the yellow drawing room, my lord."

He took the stairs two at a time. "Judith, what is it?" The question was on his lips almost before he had the door open. Her white face and scared eyes stopped him on the threshold. "What is it?"

"Harriet," she said, moistening her lips. She wanted to run to him, but the memory of the previous night was too raw. "I believe Agnes and Gracemere have abducted her."

He closed his eyes for a minute. He didn't ever want to hear the name of Gracemere again. He had no interest in his old enemy and Agnes Barret. If he was to pick up the pieces of his shattered marriage, Bernard Melville, Earl of Gracemere, had to be consigned to the pits of hell. And then he saw Martha as she'd been that morning, ten years before, crouched in a corner of the room, her face bruised, her eyes sightless with tears, soft whimpers coming from her mouth as she'd rocked herself in her hurt. A man who raped once could do so again.

"Tell me what you know."

Judith explained, finding it possible to slow her thoughts and present facts rather than impressions under Marcus's calm attention. "I'm so frightened," she said at the end. "I've always felt the evil in both of them. What will they do to her, Marcus?"

Marcus thought swiftly. There was no point exacerbating her fears. Later, when it was over, he would tell her the truth about Gracemere and Martha. But for now he had to prevent the violation of another innocent. He had to get there in time. He had failed once; he wouldn't fail again.

He spoke suddenly with precision and clarity and Judith quailed at the fury and the purpose in his eyes.

"I will not permit any harm to come to Harriet. This lies between Gracemere and myself. You are to say nothing to anyone and you will stay here until I return. You and your brother will not involve yourselves in this. I'll brook no interference. Do you understand?"

"I understand," Judith said as he strode from the room.

But I don't accept it.

31

Judith ran upstairs, threw a cloak around her shoulders, thrust her pistol and a heavy purse into the pocket, and left the house through the French doors of the book room.

Marcus's curricle was being led from the mews as she crossed the cobbles. Drawing her hood over her head, she followed the curricle into the square and there hailed a passing hackney. "Wait on the corner, and then follow that curricle when its driver takes the reins," she instructed the jarvey, handing him a guinea. He touched a forelock.

"You don't want the cove to know 'e's bein' followed, lady?"

"Not if you can avoid it," she agreed, climbing inside. She peeped around the strip of leather shielding the window, watching as Marcus came out of the house and climbed into the curricle. She called softly up to the driver. "There's another two guineas in it if you don't lose him *and* he doesn't realize we're behind him."

"Gotcha!" The jarvey cracked a whip and the vehicle lurched forward. Judith sat back, taking shallow breaths of the fusty air. The last occupant of the vehicle must have been eating raw onions and smoking a particularly noxious tobacco.

Marcus never looked back. He drove fast through the city, taking the northern route out to Hampstead Heath. It was a journey he'd made once before in the same urgency, consumed with the same desperate fury. How long had Gracemere had with the girl? Four hours at the most. Was Agnes Barret with him? Having procured the girl, was she going to hold her for him? The nauseating images spun before his internal vision.

The Reading stage lumbered down the road toward him, the postboy blowing his horn. The postboy grabbed the side of the box and closed his eyes tightly as the curricle didn't slacken speed. The two vehicles passed with barely a centimeter to spare.

"Lord-a-mercy!" the jarvey yelled down to his passenger. "That's drivin' for you. Didn't even shave the varnish, I'll lay odds. He's in a powerful 'urry, your cove."

Judith clung onto the strap as the hackney swayed and swerved along the rutted road, trying to keep the curricle in sight. It occurred to her somewhat belatedly that she had no idea how far Marcus was going. He could be going anywhere—Reading, or Oxford. Somewhere well out of the ordinary reach of a hired London hackney. But how did he know where Gracemere had gone?

The road wound over the heath and she leaned out of the window. "Can you still see him?"

"Aye, he's just turned off at the crossroads. Reckon he's 'eaded for the Green Man," the jarvey called back. "It's the only place 'ereabouts. Folks don't much relish livin' too close to the gibbet."

"No, I don't suppose they do." Judith retreated into the fetid interior again, averting her eyes from the rotting corpse swinging on the gibbet as the carriage turned left at the crossroads.

Marcus drew up in the courtyard of a dark, shabby inn under the creaking sign of the Green Man. He jumped down, tossing the reins to a small lad picking his nose by the wall, and strode into the pitch-roofed building, ducking his head under the low lintel. He held his driving whip loosely in one hand.

Voices came from the taproom to the left of the hall, and the smell of boiling greens wafted from the kitchen at the rear, mingling with the reek of stale beer. The innkeeper came bustling out from the back regions, wiping his hands on a grimy apron. When he saw his visitor, his eyes widened as the years rolled back.

"Ah, Winkler, still in business I see," the marquis observed in a pleasant tone not matched by his expression. "I'm amazed the Bow Street Runners haven't caught up with you yet."

The innkeeper shuffled his feet and looked Marcus over with a calculating shiftiness that carried a degree of apprehension. "What can I do for you, my lord?"

"The same as before," Marcus said. "Nothing overly demanding, Winkler. Your . . . your *guests* are to be found above the stables as usual, I assume?"

The landlord licked his lips and glanced anxiously around, as if expecting to see a Bow Street Runner spring up out of the dust in the corners of the hallway. "If you say so, m'lord."

"I do," Marcus said aridly, turning on his heel. "Oh, and should you hear any undue disturbances, you will be sure to ignore them, won't you? I know how deaf you are, Winkler."

The landlord wiped his forehead with his apron. "Whatever you say, m'lord."

"Just so." Marcus smiled with the appearance of great affability and walked back outside. He crossed the yard at the back of the inn. The stable was a substantial red-brick building at the rear of the courtyard. Beneath its sloping roof were two connecting rooms available to those who knew of them and were able to pay substantially for their use. No questions were ever asked of the various, generally felonious, occupants, and what went on in those rooms was known only to the participants. So far, Winkler and his clients seemed to have escaped the attentions of the law.

Marcus glanced up at the latticed, tightly curtained windows overlooking the stableyard just before he entered the building. He saw no flicker of movement at the curtains and he could hear no sound of voices as he trod softly up the wooden stairs at the rear of the dim interior. He paused, listening at a door at the head of the stairs. His heart had started to thud and he realized he was listening for the sounds he'd heard once before at this door. The sounds that had sent him bursting into the room with his whip raised. But there were no whimpering cries this afternoon. A chair scraped on the wooden floor and then there was silence.

He lifted the latch, then kicked the door open with his booted foot.

Gracemere leaped to his feet, a foul oath on his lips. The chair clattered to the floor behind him. *"You!"*

"Surely you were expecting me, Gracemere," Marcus said. "You must know that I always keep my promises." He glanced around the room. The curtains were pulled tight over the windows blocking out the afternoon's sunlight. The room was lit by thick tallow candles and the bright glow of the fire.

Harriet huddled on a wooden settle beside the fire. At the sound of Marcus's voice, she sat up with a cry, staring wild-eyed at him as if he were an apparition. Her eyes were swollen with weeping, her hair in disarray, her expression distraught, but he could see no marks of brutality.

He crossed the room swiftly. "Are you hurt, child?"

She gulped, tried to shake her head, then burst into a torrent of weeping that mounted alarmingly toward hysteria.

Marcus wasted no time in soothing her. He turned back to the earl, who still stood as if stunned. "Foolish of you to return here, Gracemere, but then a rat usually goes back to its own dung heap," he observed, cracking the thong of his whip on the floor. His eyes went to the door in the middle of the wall; he knew of old that it connected this room with its partner. "Where is Lady Barret? I should like her to witness the next few minutes."

Gracemere's face was bloodless. He looked desperately around the room and then grabbed for a bread knife on the table. Marcus's whip snapped, catching him across the knuckles. He gave a cry of fury, of fear, of pain, snatching back his hand.

Marcus advanced on him, taking his time, his eyes never leaving his face, the whip curled loosely at his side. Suddenly the whip cracked again and his quarry jumped backward. Again the thong whistled and snapped, and again Gracemere jumped back. In this fashion, Marcus pursued his prey until the earl stood backed against a heavy armoire.

"Now," Marcus said softly. "Now, let us begin in earnest, sir."

"Let us indeed begin in earnest, my lord." Agnes Barret stood in the door connecting the two rooms. She held a serviceable-looking flintlock pistol in her hand, pointing directly at the marquis. "Give the whip to Gracemere. I think he might enjoy putting it to good use."

The earl chuckled and held out his hand.

"Don't think I won't shoot, Carrington," Agnes said with a tight smile. "Of course, I won't kill you. The consequences of your death might be a little difficult to avoid, but I will break your knees. We shall all three be long gone from here by the time you recover your senses sufficiently to drag yourself down the stairs."

Harriet screamed. Gracemere snatched the whip from Marcus.

Within the inn, the landlord was struggling for breath as the jarvey cheerfully tightened his boldly checkered scarf around his throat, inquiring for the second time, "Where'll we find the gennelman cove, friend?"

"Perhaps he can't speak," Judith suggested as the innkeeper flailed desperately in the jarvey's choke hold. "You are squeezing him rather tightly."

The jarvey slackened the material a trifle and Mr. Winkler gestured outside with a hoarse but informative, "stables." His expression clearly indicated that he no longer had the least interest in preserving anyone's privacy, and would willingly yield up whatever secrets of his house and its guests were demanded of him, and even those that weren't.

"Stay here and keep an eye on him," Judith instructed the jarvey, taking the pistol from her pocket. "If I need you, I'll call."

"Right you are, lady," the jarvey said. "'Andy with that popper, are you?"

"Handy enough," Judith said.

Gathering up her skirts, she ran to the stable building, having no idea what she would find. In the dark, manure-scented interior, she stopped and looked around. Then she heard Harriet's scream and the sickening hiss and crack of a whip.

She hurled herself at the stairs, stumbled, picked herself up, and flung open the door at the head. Her eyes, accustomed to simultaneous observation and assimilation of half a dozen hands of cards, instantly took in the tableau. Agnes Barret with her pistol raised, aimed at Marcus; the two men swaying, grappling for possession of a whip; Harriet, paralyzed with horror, her mouth open but now no sound issuing forth.

Judith didn't pause for reflection. She fired her pistol and the flintlock spun out of Agnes's grip. Agnes stared numbly at the hand that had held the gun. Blood welled from the torn flesh and dripped to the floor.

"Dear God in heaven!" Marcus breathed, wrenching the whip from Gracemere's abruptly slackened hold.

Judith sprang across the room to retrieve Agnes's pistol. She directed the flintlock at Gracemere and looked properly at Marcus for the first time.

"That's quite an aim you have," he observed. "But I can't imagine why that should surprise me."

No response seemed required and Judith glanced toward the settle where Harriet sat, now looking utterly bemused. "Harriet . . ."

"She's frightened but has taken no serious harm," Marcus said. "What interests me rather more is what the devil you think you're doing here." He pulled out his handkerchief and went over to where Agnes stood, still staring in disbelief at the blood welling from her hand.

"It seems fortunate I am here," Judith responded rather tartly. "You didn't really expect me to leave you to conduct this business alone?"

"I had thought I'd made it crystal clear that was exactly what I expected." Taking Agnes's hand, he wrapped the handkerchief over the wound.

"But I *love* you," Judith cried with an edge of exasperation. "I couldn't possibly stand by when you might be hurt."

Marcus looked up from his bandaging, and a smile touched his eyes, then spread slowly across his face. "No, I suppose you couldn't," he said. "Where you love, you love hard and long, don't you, lynx?"

"And you?" It was a tentative question and she seemed to be perched on a precipice with joy on one side, desolation on the other.

"I've never loved before," Marcus said, still smiling. "But it does seem to be a very powerful and exclusive emotion."

Despair, anxiety, tension drained slowly away, leaving her empty of all but bone-deep relief and a well of loving warmth. It was going to be all right. She hadn't lost Marcus and his love. "And forgiveness?" she asked. "Can love include that?"

"It seems to promote it," he said, tying a knot in the handkerchief. "Is that comfortable, Lady Barret?"

"Comfortable is hardly the word I would have used," Agnes stated. She looked across at Judith with a strange smile quirking her lips. "I have to say, Charlotte, that for two such mewling babes, you and Peter have certainly turned out unexpectedly. Whatever could George have done, I wonder, to have given you both so much strength of character?"

Gracemere flung himself on the settle beside a shrinking Harriet and began to laugh. It was an unsettling sound, totally without mirth.

Judith stared at Agnes. "What do you mean?" But she knew. She knew as she had always known. Only the knowledge had been in blood and bone and sinew, in the threads of a primitive instinct, not in absolute words speaking absolute truths.

"Can't you guess, my dear child?" Agnes said, a taunting note in her voice. "But yes, I see that you can. Curiously, I find you a worthy daughter. I hadn't expected George's children to have any red blood in their veins."

"I thought you were dead," Judith said, her voice hollow.

"Alice Devereux is dead," Agnes said. "She died a convenient death in a convent somewhere. And then she rose again, as you see." She passed her uninjured hand down her body in mocking explanation.

"Marcus . . . ?" Judith spoke his name hesitantly, her eyes searched for his, her free hand went out toward him in apprehensive plea.

"I'm here," he said softly, taking her hand, squeezing it tightly as her mother continued to talk.

"Your father was so blind. He never knew . . . never guessed that Gracemere and I had been lovers since we were little more than children. Since between us we hadn't a feather to fly with, one of us had to marry for money. But it didn't work out as it was supposed to. In the end, we had to get rid of George."

She was speaking quietly, cradling her bandaged hand, almost as if unaware of her audience. "He was in the way, always making demands . . . protestations of love. He wouldn't leave me alone. He made it impossible for me to be with Gracemere as I had to be. And there was Peter and then you, ten months apart, for heaven's sake. I had to get away from him."

Judith felt nauseated but she could no more move away or even interrupt than the fly stickily entwined in the web. She gazed at her mother, who continued her explanation with almost an assumption of shared comprehension.

"I couldn't simply leave your father, you must understand, because then I would have been as penniless as if I'd never married him. What were we to do?" It was a genuine question. "I could only leave your father if we had possession of his money. So Gracemere took it from him. We did what was necessary."

"Sebastian and I would have been in your way, of course," Judith heard herself say. "You'd hardly want to be saddled with a pair of brats when you started on your new life."

Agnes shook her head impatiently. "I never wanted children but George insisted. If he chose to take you with him when he left, why would it matter to me?"

"Why indeed?" Judith agreed distantly. "I quite see that." She shook her head as if to dispel the cobwebs of confusion. In some essential way, the story seemed to have nothing to do with her at all, but she couldn't quite clarify how or why that should be so.

"It seems that the affair has come full circle, ma'am," Marcus said into the silence, still holding Judith's hand. "Your children have ruined you and your lover as completely as you and your lover ruined their father. There's a nice symmetry to it, I'm sure you'll agree." And it did now seem to him that it was the only right thing to have happened. Listening to the evil in this woman, who for passion's sake had condemned her children to a life as outcasts, he felt only satisfaction for what Judith and her brother had achieved. Vengeance was an ancient and savage imperative.

"But my mother needn't be ruined. Perhaps she would prefer to remain with her present husband in London," Judith suggested with a razor-edged smile, her voice hard. "I'm sure Sebastian—or rather, Peter—and I would really enjoy getting to know her properly."

Agnes regarded her daughter with a glimmer of respect. "That could almost be an amusing prospect. However, my dear, you'll never see me again. You must make my farewells to your brother." She turned and went into the connecting room. Gracemere rose from the settle, offered a mocking bow to Judith, and followed his mistress.

Harriet whimpered. "I don't understand . . ."

"No, of course you don't," Judith said swiftly. "What a terrible time you must have had, love. There's a hackney downstairs. The jarvey is most reliable and he'll convey you back to Brook Street immediately. In fact, I'll accompany you—"

"No, you will not," Marcus interrupted. "I'm not letting you out of my sight again. Come, Harriet." He picked up the bewildered, tear-streaked girl, who lay limply in his arms. "I'm going to put you in the hackney and direct the jarvey to take you to Sebastian. I think you'll find greater strength there than in your mother's company, and he will know just how to explain matters to your parents so that they have no idea of the truth. Davenports are very good at that." He cast his wife a darkling look that nevertheless carried a hint of rueful amusement. "Stay here, Judith, until I come back."

"I'll be here," she said. She stood looking at the closed door to the other room. How much of her mother did she have in her? Was she infected with her mother's evil? But she knew she wasn't. The person she was had more to do with the circumstances of her childhood than to any blood, bone, and sinew she shared with Agnes Barret. Her mother's abandonment had been the greatest service she could have rendered her children. If she'd stayed in their lives, they would probably have learned to be as warped as she.

She went to the window, watching as Marcus carried Harriet across the yard. She felt curiously at peace, despite the dreadful revelations of the last minutes. It was as if something had been completed. The last piece of her past was fitted in place. She knew her mother, had avenged her father. Now she was free to be her own person.

"I can't imagine how Sebastian is going to adapt to life with a woman who collapses in the middle of adventures," Marcus observed, when he returned. "After a lifetime with you, my love, it seems impossible to imagine."

"I expect he'll find it a pleasant change," Judith said. "How did you know Gracemere would be here?"

"That's a story for later . . . much later."

Marcus came over to her, taking her hands in his. The black eyes gazed down at her intently. "How do you feel after all that?"

"I was shocked at first, but now it seems oddly irrelevant. She's nothing to me." She shrugged. "It's strange, but I really don't feel any connection with her at all. In fact, now I know *who* she is—*what* she is—it's a great weight off my mind. She's been disturbing me ever since I met her. It's a relief to know why."

Marcus nodded. "She is nothing to you. Now we can put all this behind us and start afresh."

Judith bit her lip. "Yes, well, there's just one thing more—"

"Oh, no." Marcus groaned, dropping her hands. "Not something else, Judith, *please.*"

"I wasn't going to tell you—"

"Judith, don't do this to me!"

"I have to," she wailed. "If you hadn't discovered about Gracemere and all this muddle, I would have kept quiet about it. Sebastian said it wasn't important because we create our own truths, but it *is* important, and since you know all the rest, you had better know this, too. In fact, it'll probably occur to you, anyway, at some point, when you have time to think."

Marcus closed his eyes briefly and said with heavy resignation, "Go on. What truth have you created now?" He moved away to the fireplace and stood waiting.

"Well, you see . . . you see, we aren't married," she blurted, wringing her hands.

"What!"

"Judith Davenport isn't a legal person; neither is Sebastian Davenport. I didn't think about it in the church, how should I have? It was only afterward, when I looked at the register. But we're Devereux . . . I don't ever remember being called Charlotte, but . . ." She saw comprehension in his eyes and fell silent, judging she'd said enough.

Marcus strode across the room. His fingers clamped one wrist, tightening around the fragile bones, as he dragged her to the door. She tripped over an uneven flagstone on the threshold but his pace didn't slacken as he hauled her after him, down the rickety stairs. She stumbled in his wake, her manacled wrist at full stretch, and they emerged in the sunlit stableyard. Judith blinked at the brightness of the light after the gloom above.

"Marcus, what are you doing? Where are we going?" she demanded breathlessly.

"I'll tell you where we're going," he replied in clipped accents. "We're going to find a bishop and a special license, and we're going to finalize this marriage beyond all possible doubt. After which I intend to exercise *all* my marital rights—including the one involving a rod no thicker than my finger. The only question is in which order I decide to exercise those rights." He caught her around the waist and tossed her unceremoniously into his curricle.

"Can't I have an opinion?" Judith asked, picking herself up and scrambling onto the seat.

"No, you may not!" He jumped up beside her. "If you have a grain of common sense, which I doubt, you'll sit very still and keep your mouth shut."

Judith sat back, smoothing down her skirt, catching her breath, as the thong of his whip flicked the leader's neck and the team plunged forward. They kept up a furious pace, pounding across the heath, and swung onto the deserted post road at the gibbet. Judith examined her companion's profile with a mischievous glint in her eye.

"Marcus, you're laughing," she stated.

"What the hell have I got to laugh about?" he demanded, keeping his eyes on the road ahead. "For the last seven months, I've been living in sin with a woman who took part in an illegal marriage ceremony, and if circumstances hadn't forced a confession from her, fully intended to leave me in ignorance for the rest of my mortal span!"

"Ignorance is supposed to be bliss," Judith offered, not a whit fooled by his ferocious tone. "Anyway, what's in a name?" A strange little sound came from him and his shoulders shook. "I *know* you're laughing," she insisted. "You once said it was very bad to repress laughter . . . I'm sure you said it would give one an apoplexy."

Marcus checked his horses and drove the curricle off the road into a stand of trees. There they stopped and he turned toward Judith. Her mischievous glint deepened as she saw the merriment in his eyes. "I knew you were laughing," she said with satisfaction.

He caught her chin. "Ever since I met you, I have taken leave of my senses. Why else would I permit a tempestuous, manipulative, unscrupulous wildcat to lead me the craziest dance a man has ever been led?"

"For a man who hates dancing, it does seem a little inconsistent," she agreed, smiling. "But, judging by my own experience, one doesn't choose where to love. Why else would I fall body and soul in lust and love with a tyrannical, stuffy despot, who insists on keeping me under his thumb, and is only happy when he's laying down the law to all and sundry?"

"But you do love him nevertheless?"

"Oh, yes," she said, reaching up to grasp his wrist. "As he loves a designing adventuress."

"Beyond reason," he said softly. "I love you beyond reason, you abominable lynx."

He brought his mouth to hers, his hand moving to palm her scalp as she reached against him, and his tongue plundered the sweetness of her mouth even as she drank greedily of the taste and scent of him, of the promise of an untrammeled future, where loyalties were simple and trust was absolute.

About the Author

Jane Feather is the *New York Times* bestselling, award-winning author of *Almost a Lady, Almost a Bride, The Accidental Bride, The Emerald Swan, The Silver Rose, The Diamond Slipper, Vanity, Violet,* and many other historical romances. She was born in Cairo, Egypt, and grew up in the New Forest, in the south of England. She began her writing career after she and her family moved to Washington, D.C., in 1981. She now has more than ten million copies of her books in print.